SELECTED ESSAYS, POEMS AND OTHER WRITINGS

Mary Ann (Marian) Evans was born in 1819 in Warwickshire. In 1828 she was sent to Miss Wallington's school in Nuneaton, where she met and was greatly influenced by the Rev. John Edmund Jones, an evangelical preacher who makes several appearances in her novels. In 1836 her mother died and Marian became her father's housekeeper, educating herself in her spare time. In 1841 she moved to Coventry, and met Charles and Caroline Bray, local progressive intellectuals. Through them she was commissioned to translate David Friedrich Strauss's *The Life of Jesus* and met the publisher John Chapman, who, when he purchased the *Westminster Review* in 1851, made her his managing editor. She moved to London and met Herbert Spencer (whom she nearly married, only he found her too 'morbidly intellectual') and the versatile man-of-letters George Henry Lewes. Lewes was separated from his wife, but with no possibility of divorce. In 1854 he and Marian decided to live together, and did so until Lewes's death in 1878. It was he who encouraged her to turn from philosophy to fiction, and during those years, under the name of George Eliot, she wrote *Scenes of Clerical Life, Adam Bede, The Mill on the Floss, Silas Marner, Romola, Felix Holt: the Radical, Middlemarch*, and *Daniel Deronda*, as well as numerous essays, articles and reviews. George Eliot died in 1880, only a few months after marrying J. W. Cross, an old friend and admirer, who became her first biographer. She was buried beside Lewes at Highgate. Eliot combined a formidable intelligence with imaginative sympathy and acute powers of observation, and became one of the greatest and most influential of English novelists. Her choice of material widened the horizons of the novel and her psychological insights radically influenced the novelist's approach to characterization. *Middlemarch*, considered by most to be her masterpiece, was said by Virginia Woolf to be 'one of the few English novels written for grown-up people'.

A. S. Byatt was born in 1936 and educated at York and Newnham College, Cambridge. She has taught at the Central School of Art and Design, and from 1972 to 1983 was a lecturer in English and American literature at University College, London, becoming a senior lecturer in 1981. She has broadcast regularly on the BBC and contributed to the *Independent*, *Encounter* and *The Times Literary Supplement*, as well as many other newspapers and weeklies. She has also written critical studies of Iris Murdoch and Wordsworth and Coleridge, and edited George Eliot's *The Mill on the Floss* for Penguin Classics. Her highly acclaimed novels include *Shadow of a Sun, The Game* (Penguin 1983), *The Virgin in the Garden* (Penguin 1981) and *Still Life* (Penguin 1986), winner of the Silver Pen Award. She has also published a collection of stories entitled *Sugar* (Penguin 1988) and her most recent novel is *Possession: A Romance* (1990). A. S. Byatt was awarded a CBE in 1989.

Nicholas Warren was born in Nottingham in 1955. He was educated at Kingston Polytechnic and at the Victorian Studies Centre of the University of Leicester. He has taught English in Mexico, worked as a door to door salesman and now lectures in English in London. He is presently working on a biography of Francis Newman.

GEORGE ELIOT

❧

SELECTED ESSAYS, POEMS AND OTHER WRITINGS

EDITED BY A. S. BYATT AND NICHOLAS WARREN
WITH AN INTRODUCTION BY A. S. BYATT

PENGUIN BOOKS

PENGUIN BOOKS

Published by the Penguin Group
Penguin Books Ltd, 27 Wrights Lane, London W8 5TZ, England
Viking Penguin, a division of Penguin Books USA Inc.
375 Hudson Street, New York, New York 10014, USA
Penguin Books Australia Ltd, Ringwood, Victoria, Australia
Penguin Books Canada Ltd, 2801 John Street, Markham, Ontario, Canada L3R 1B4
Penguin Books (NZ) Ltd, 182–190 Wairau Road, Auckland 10, New Zealand

Penguin Books Ltd, Registered Offices: Harmondsworth, Middlesex, England

This edition published in Penguin Classics 1990

1 3 5 7 9 10 8 6 4 2

This edition and Introduction copyright © A. S. Byatt, 1990
This edition copyright © Nicholas Warren, 1990

The moral right of the editors has been asserted

The Acknowledgements on p. vii constitute an extension of this copyright page.

Filmset in Baskerville (Monotype Lasercomp)

Printed in England by Clays Ltd, St Ives plc

Contents

Acknowledgements

WE ARE grateful to the staff of the London Library for their endless helpfulness and courtesy, and in particular to Richard Wilson for his generous assistance with the identification and translation of Eliot's references to Greek texts. We are also grateful to Professor Jean-Louis Chevalier, Marjorie Semple, Joan Stephenson, Dr Stanley Taylor and Margaret Whitehead for their assistance in the identification and translation of Eliot's foreign language quotations. Peter Caracciolo and Professor Kathleen Tillotson helped us to track down some particularly obscure allusions and, in the case of the latter, gave memorable guidance on bibliographical sources.

We are grateful to the Beinecke Rare Book and Manuscript Library at Yale University for permission to reproduce the extract from 'The Ilfracombe Journal' and the Eliot–Harrison correspondence from Gordon S. Haight's edition of *The George Eliot Letters*, and 'Notes on Form in Art'.

Introduction

IN 1885 William Hale White wrote a letter to the *Athenæum* in response to John Walter Cross's recently published *Life* of his dead wife, George Eliot.[1] It is worth quoting in full.

As I had the honour of living in the same house, 142, Strand, with George Eliot for about two years, between 1851 and 1854, I may perhaps be allowed to correct an impression which Mr Cross's book may possibly produce on its readers. To put it very briefly, I think he has made her too 'respectable'. She was really one of the most sceptical, unusual creatures I ever knew, and it was this side of her character which was to me the most attractive. She told me that it was worthwhile to undertake all the labour of learning French if it resulted in nothing more than reading one book – Rousseau's *Confessions*. That saying was perfectly symbolical of her, and reveals more completely what she was, at any rate in 1851–4, than page after page of attempt on my part at critical analysis. I can see her now, with her hair over her shoulders, the easy chair half sideways to the fire, her feet over the arms, and a proof in her hands, in that dark room at the back of No. 142, and I confess I hardly recognize her in the pages of Mr Cross's – on many accounts – most interesting volumes. I do hope that in some future edition, or in some future work, the salt and spice will be restored to the records of George Eliot's entirely unconventional life. As the matter now stands she has not had full justice done to her, and she has been removed from the class – the great and noble church, if I may so call it – of the Insurgents, to one more genteel, but certainly not so interesting.

It is this George Eliot – sceptical, unconventional, addicted to the daring, risqué, nakedly self-revelatory and subversive *Confessions* – whose presence can be sensed in the essays and reviews in this collection. She went to live in No. 142 Strand in 1851, when she was thirty-two, to lodge in the household of John Chapman, publisher and new owner of the *Westminster Review*. Chapman had already published her translation of David Friedrich Strauss's *The Life of Jesus* in 1846, and made her acquaintance in Coventry. Chapman was passionately addicted to women, and his family included his mistress, Elisabeth Tilley, as well as his wife, Susanna. Both women became very jealous of Miss Evans, and it is clear that there was good cause for this; her first visit to No. 142 lasted from January to March 1851, when a series of angry scenes and disputes culminated in her tearful departure. Chapman recorded in his diary, 'M. departed today. I accompanied her to the railway. She was very sad and hence made me feel so. She pressed me for some intimation of the state of my feelings. I told her that I felt great affection for her, but that I loved E. and S. also though each in a different way. At this avowal she burst into tears.'[2]

Chapman's offer for the *Westminster Review* was accepted in May 1851, and the deed of sale was signed in October of that year. He decided that the powerfully intelligent Marian Evans would be an ideal assistant; Susanna and Elisabeth were resolutely set against her return to No. 142 or indeed to London at all. For some months the two corresponded and Chapman negotiated with the other women. In September it was agreed that Marian Evans might return as a lodger; she lived there, apparently amicably, for the next two years.

She became, in effect, the secret editor of the *Westminster Review*. Chapman was known as chief editor; the letter sent out with the Prospectus referred to 'the Editors' and Marian Evans told Chapman, 'In regard to the secret of the Editorship, it will perhaps be the best plan for you to state, that for the present *you* are to be regarded as the responsible person, but that you employ an Editor in whose literary and general ability you confide.'[3]

Thomas Carlyle, who called himself 'clear for silence at present', wrote to Robert Browning, suggesting that Browning contribute, and said Chapman had 'an able Editor (name can't be given) and such an array of "talent" as was seldom gathered before'.[4] She edited ten numbers of the periodical; Gordon Haight tells us the *Westminster* reviewed about a hundred volumes in each of these ten.[5] The reviews were arranged at first under the heading of 'Contemporary Literature' of England, America, Germany and

France; later, at Herbert Spencer's suggestion, they were re-arranged under subject headings. The long articles were com-pilations of reviews by various authors: Marian Evans was responsible for running these together, editing and cutting. But it is not thought she wrote much herself, and some earlier attributions have been disproved. She did advise on the choice of authors and subjects, and was responsible for proofs and printing. She seems to have been paid nothing for all this work, but it transfigured her life. Chapman gave regular literary parties and took her to more; she met thinkers, poets and writers whose work she reviewed, such as R. W. Mackay and W. R. Greg, as well as Giuseppe Mazzini and Karl Marx. Her letters at the time are lively, incisive and busy. For a young woman from a merely respectable provincial family this was an immense increase of freedom and life. She mixed with others of her own kind – the Insurgents; like herself, they were not part of the established social and religious hierarchy, but were liberal, questioning, free-thinking, interested in reform.

The *Westminster Review* had a distinguished history. It was founded in 1824 by James Mill, with financial support from Jeremy Bentham. John Stuart Mill edited it from 1837–40, when it gained its highest reputation for intellectual excitement and radical thought. The Prospectus Chapman and Evans wrote for their first issue (January 1852) declared itself committed to advocating 'organic change' according to the Law of Progress, whilst respect-ing the 'variety of forms' in which 'the same fundamental truths are apprehended'.[6] It would not ignore 'the widespread doubts in relation to established creeds and systems' and would 'fearlessly examine' 'the elements of ecclesiastical authority and of dogma'; it would discuss 'without reservation, the results of the most advanced biblical criticism'. It advocated progress towards universal suffrage and reform of the judiciary, and a national system of education. There was to be an 'Independent Section' to provide freedom for the expression of views that opposed those of the editors, though this section was found to be impracticable and abandoned after the second number. The *Westminster*, under its anonymous editor, printed J. H. Froude on Tudor England, J. S. Mill on William Whewell's philosophy and Herbert Spencer's theory of evolution.

Herbert Spencer's *Psychology* included a footnote thanking

George Eliot for the happy phrase 'Things which have a constant relation to the same thing have a constant relation to each other.'[7] When he first met the 'translatress of Strauss', he described her as 'the most admirable woman, mentally, I have ever met'.[8] In 1852 they spent much time together, and were rumoured to be engaged. Her letters to him, kept secret until 1985, reveal a woman passionately and self-abasingly attached, begging for crumbs of attention, if not love. Spencer, who remained a bachelor, declined her affections and let it be known that this was because she was ugly. It says much for her generosity of spirit that she remained on good terms with him, even confiding in him that she was the 'George Eliot' who had written *Scenes of Clerical Life*, a confidence he unwisely betrayed to the garrulous Chapman.

By the turn of the year, however, she had shifted her affections to Spencer's friend, G. H. Lewes, whom at first she suspected of being flippant and lightweight. In 1850 Lewes was co-founder, with Thornton Leigh Hunt, of the *Leader*, a weekly newspaper, which, with the *Westminster*, published the bulk of George Eliot's reviews. Thornton Leigh Hunt was the father of the fifth son of Lewes's wife, Agnes (and subsequently of three more). Lewes was devoted to his own sons, and acknowledged this fifth one, thus rendering himself unable to seek a divorce, since he had condoned the adultery. But his marriage was over, and he was free, emotionally, to love Marian Evans. In September 1853 she moved from No. 142 Strand to lodgings in Cambridge Street. Her translation of Ludwig Feuerbach's *The Essence of Christianity* was written in the next few months and finally appeared in July 1854. It was in the same month that Marian Evans left for Germany with Lewes and embarked on the 'marriage' that was to last his lifetime and lead directly to the work of George Eliot. This step also led directly to the writing of the major essays printed in this collection, which were written between 1854 and 1857, and published in the *Westminster Review*. They were written for money, but they were also written with a new intellectual authority, freedom and sense of excitement. It is usual for critics of George Eliot to look for the weighty, the sibylline and the scrupulously just. But these essays are also at times savagely ironic, often very funny, and have a speed and sharpness that is less frequently remarked on.

It is possible to find in them hints of her private preoccupations at that time, and also thoughts about human nature, art and societies that will later form essential parts of the fiction of George Eliot. In the rest of this essay I shall discuss some of these and relate them to the development of her thought in the other non- fictional work in this collection – the translations, the poems, the correspondence with Frederic Harrison, and the 'Notes on Form in Art' (unpublished before Thomas Pinney's 1963 collection).

It is perhaps worth remarking at this stage, however, how much of her writing at this time drew its life from a kind of ferocious, witty and energetic rejection. The great essays on John Cumming and Edward Young are rejections of her own earlier religious and literary enthusiasms. 'Woman in France: Madame de Sablé' questions English conventional ideas about female virtues and the nature of marriage. 'Silly Novels by Lady Novelists' offers a radical rejection of the aims and moral vision of the novels currently being written by women, and ends with a statement of what women novelists *could* do, powered by anger as well as by hope. She was free, she was clearing the ground.

This is perhaps also the best point at which to discuss, at least briefly, the complex question of Eliot's attitude to 'the woman question'. At the height of her fame she was cautious, even ambivalent, in her support of Girton College and women's suffrage; she wrote, 'there is no subject on which I am more inclined to hold my peace and learn, than on the Woman Question. It seems to me to overhang abysses, of which even prostitution is not the worst . . . I have been made rather miserable lately by revelations about women, and have resolved to remain silent in my sense of helplessness.'[9] These inexplicit 'abysses' seem related in their anxiety to her earlier fear of becoming 'earthly sensual and devilish' at her father's death, and the removal of 'that purifying, restraining influence'.[10] She wrote brilliantly and passionately about the pain of thwarted intelligence, or artistic power, in women, but also insisted, throughout her life, on the importance of recognizing the differences between the sexes. The 'feminine' virtues of tenderness, sympathy and patience were to her real virtues, to be desired and respected *as feminine*. But at the same time she saw very clearly that to live only for personal affections was dangerously narrow: she wrote to a woman friend in 1870,

We women are always in danger of living too exclusively in the affections; and though our affections are perhaps the best gift we have, we ought also to have our share of the more independent life – some joy in things for their own sake. It is piteous to see the helplessness of sweet women when their affections are disappointed – because all their teaching has been, that they can only delight in study of any kind for the sake of a personal love. They have never contemplated an independent delight in ideas as an experience which they could confess without being laughed at. Yet surely women need this sort of defence against passionate affliction even more than men.[11]

Some feminists have criticized Eliot for accepting stereotyped ideas of 'feminine' characteristics. Others have criticized her for trying too hard to have what they think of as the 'male' patriarchal qualities of rationality and intellect (thus falling into the stereotyping trap themselves). She was a complex woman, at once freely independent and timidly clinging, powerfully intelligent and full of a compelled artistic ambition that sprang both from 'feeling' and the mind.

In the essay on Madame de Sablé (1854) she argued strongly both for the specificity of female talents and sensibilities and for 'unions formed in the maturity of thought and feeling, and grounded only on inherent fitness and mutual attraction', as opposed to the 'quiescence and security of the conjugal relation'. In 1855, reviewing Thomas Keightley's Life of Milton, she supported Milton's plea for divorce, and drew the analogy between Milton's plight and the campaign of Caroline Norton, which brought attention to the iniquities suffered by women, because of the divorce law. Milton's personal experience, she said, could be traced in his descriptions of the 'baleful muteness of a virgin' hiding 'all the unliveliness and natural sloth which is really unfit for conversation'.[12] Her own personal pleading can be traced in the essay on Madame de Sablé, which ends with the lines, 'Let the whole field of reality be laid open to woman as well as to man, and then that which is peculiar in her mental modification, instead of being, as it is now, a source of discord and repulsion between the sexes, will be found to be a necessary complement to the truth and beauty of life.'[13]

Eliot's sense of the 'discord and repulsion' caused by the deformations and distortions of the female self uneducated is as constant as her sense of the importance of the relations *between* the sexes. In an essay on Margaret Fuller and Mary Wollstonecraft she remarks that 'while men have a horror of such faculty or culture in the other sex as tends to place it on a level with their own, they are really in a state of subjection to ignorant and feeble-minded women'.[14] She goes on to quote Margaret Fuller's description of the 'petty power' of the 'ignorance and childish vanity' of uneducated women. Here is the hint of the beginning of both Rosamund Vincy in her complacent and destructive prettiness, and Gwendolen Harleth in the aimless power-mongering of her fatal coquetry. Eliot saw both Fuller and Wollstonecraft as mirrors for her sense of herself. She wrote in 1852, 'It is a help to read such a life as Margaret Fuller's. How inexpressibly touching that passage from her journal – "I shall always reign through the intellect, but the life, the life! O my god! shall that never be sweet?" I am thankful, as for myself, that it was sweet at last.'[15] And in 1871, writing to the Jewish scholar Emanuel Deutsch, who was ill and despairing, she used Mary Wollstonecraft as an example of hope, comparing her to her own painful, youthful, hopeless self. 'Remember, it has happened to many to be glad they did not commit suicide, though they once ran for the final leap, or as Mary Wollstonecraft did, wetted their garments well in the rain, hoping to sink the better when they plunged.'[16]

Out of this sympathetic feeling for the young Mary Wollstonecraft and the despairing Jew came the suicide attempt of Mirah, the woman artist in *Daniel Deronda* who lived to be happy, in contrast to the fiercely separate and ambitious Alchirisi, Daniel's mother, who sacrificed her affections to her art, and told her son, 'You can never imagine what it is to have a man's force of genius in you, and yet to suffer the slavery of being a girl.'[17] In *Daniel Deronda* the problems of Fuller, Wollstonecraft and the author of the essay on Madame de Sablé are studied with a novelist's fullness and sceptical passion in Gwendolen, Mirah, the Alchirisi and also Catherine Arrowpoint, an intelligent and gifted heiress

who gives up rich English philistinism for German-Jewish genius
and seriousness. In her poetic drama, *Armgart*, part of which is
reprinted in this collection, Eliot studied (in an earlier version) the
conflict between female genius and the domestic and affectionate
virtues; the singer rejects her suitor's definition of married love as
her highest fulfilment, only to lose her voice, and learn how much
egoism there was in her devotion to her talent. But the young
woman who wrote the essays of the 1850s was, for the first time,
happy as a woman, and full of new ambition as a writer. 'Silly
Novels by Lady Novelists' was written immediately before her
own first attempt at fiction, and its lightness of tone is partly a
result of her desire not to 'undertake an article that would give me
too much trouble'.[18] The story she was beginning was 'The Sad
Fortunes of the Rev. Amos Barton', and it is easy to see in it a
revision (in the Jamesian sense of re-vision, new looking at) the
works she characterized as the 'white neck-cloth' school of evangelical fiction. 'Why can we not have pictures of religious life
among the industrial classes in England, as interesting as Mrs
Stowe's pictures of religious life among the negroes?' she asked,
and went on, in 'Janet's Repentance' and *Silas Marner*, to provide
just such pictures. Gwendolen Harleth and Dorothea Brooke, with
their very real human limitations, can in one sense be seen as
corrective revisions of the beautiful, proficient, high-minded
mind-and-millinery heroine, who, despite being 'the ideal woman
in feelings, faculties and flounces', as often as not 'marries the
wrong person to begin with and suffers terribly from the plots and
intrigues of the vicious baronet'. Gwendolen, with hideous irony,
indeed resembles the type heroine, not an heiress, who 'has the
triumph of refusing many matches and securing the best, and she
wears some family jewels or other as a sort of crown of righteousness
at the end'. Gwendolen's jewels are a torturing crown of iniquity,
and she learns the Eliot lesson that resignation and suffering do *not*
produce 'compensation' and some divine reward for virtue. Eliot
began this essay out of a desire to review the novel *Compensation*,
and 'fire away at the doctrine of Compensation, which I detest'.[19]

The 'realism' of Eliot's fiction is partly a moral realism, rejecting
'compensation' and other consoling doctrines, and partly a related
technical realism, a desire for accuracy. At the end of 'Silly

Novels' Eliot observed, 'No educational restrictions can shut women out from the materials of fiction and there is no species of art which is so free from rigid requirements. Like crystalline masses it may take any form, and yet be beautiful; we have only to pour in the right elements – genuine observation, humour and passion.'

It is time to look at her ideas about the forms of art.

REALISM

Eliot's review of John Ruskin's *Modern Painters, Vol. III* was published in April 1856; in the summer of that year, at Tenby, 'The Sad Fortunes of the Rev. Amos Barton' was begun. In the essay on Ruskin, Eliot wrote, 'The truth of infinite value that he teaches is *realism* – the doctrine that all truth and beauty are to be attained by a humble and faithful study of nature, and not by substituting vague forms, bred by imagination on the mists of feeling, in place of definite, substantial reality.'[20]

In the journal she kept at Ilfracombe earlier the same summer (see pp. 214 ff.), she writes of her observation of the countryside in terms of both art and nature-study. It is 'a "Hunt" picture' and inspires in her a very clear linguistic ambition. 'I never before longed so much to know the names of things as during this visit to Ilfracombe. The desire is part of the tendency that is now constantly growing in me to escape from all vagueness and inaccuracy into the daylight of distinct, vivid ideas. The mere fact of naming an object tends to give definiteness to our conception of it – we have then a sign that at once calls up in our minds the distinctive qualities which mark out for us that particular object from all others.'

In the essays, particularly those on Cumming and Young, she comments again and again on inaccurate language. She says of Young that one of his most striking characteristics was

his *radical insincerity as a poetic artist* . . . The source of all grandiloquence is the want of taking for a criterion the true qualities of the object described, or the emotion expressed . . .

His hand the good man fixes on the skies,

> And bids earth roll, nor feels her idle whirl, –

may, perhaps, pass for sublime with some readers. But pause a moment to realize the image, and the monstrous absurdity of a man's grasping the skies, and hanging habitually suspended there, while he contemptuously bids the earth roll, warns you that no genuine feeling could have suggested so unnatural a conception . . . Examples of such vicious imagery, resulting from insincerity, may be found, perhaps, in almost every page of the *Night Thoughts*. But simple assertions or aspirations, undisguised by imagery, are often equally false. No writer whose rhetoric was checked by the slightest truthful intentions, could have said, –

> An eye of awe and wonder let me roll,
> And roll for ever.

Abstracting the more poetical associations with the eye, this is hardly less absurd than if he had wished to stand for ever with his mouth open.

In the essay on Cumming, she is even more uncompromising about the connection between accurate language and morality.

A distinct appreciation of the value of evidence – in other words, the intellectual perception of truth – is more closely allied to truthfulness of statement, or the moral quality of veracity, than is generally admitted. There is not a more pernicious fallacy afloat in common parlance, than the wide distinction made between intellect and morality. Amiable impulses without intellect, man may have in common with dogs and horses; but morality, which is specifically human, is dependent on the regulation of feeling by intellect.

Cumming, she says, is imprisoned, as an intellect, by the doctrine of verbal inspiration that deprives his mind of 'its proper function – the free search for truth'. Cumming's religious statements, as she wittily and devastatingly demonstrates, are a series of overblown untruths.

In Cumming's case it is the freedom of the intellect and philosophical truth that is at stake. In Lord Brougham's, whose style she also attacks, it is Art. (It is interesting in this context that she defines Dr Johnson's Wit, in the essay on Heinrich Heine, as 'reasoning raised to a higher power'. Wit, she says, has an affinity with ratiocination, and the higher the species of wit, the more it deals 'less with words and superficialities than with the essential qualities of things'.) She wrote to Charles Bray, defending her attack.

The article on Lord Brougham was written conscientiously, and you seem to have misunderstood its purpose, in taking it for mere word quibbling. I consider it criminal in a man to prostitute Literature for the purposes of his own vanity, and this is what Lord Brougham has done. A man who has something vitally important to mankind to say, may be excused for saying it in bad English. In such a case criticism of style is irrelevant. But Literature is fine art, and the man who writes mere literature with insolent slovenliness is as inexcusable as a man who gets up in a full drawing-room to sing Rossini's music in a cracked voice and out of tune. Because Lord Brougham has done some services to the public it does not follow that he is to be treated with anything else than justice when he is doing injury to the public, and I consider his *Lives, bad* and *injurious*.[21]

She was not herself afraid of clear distinct statements. There is a splendid letter from her to Chapman, criticizing his style, again on grounds of illogic and inaccuracy. 'I have a logical objection to the phrases "it *would* seem", "it *would* appear", "we *would* remark". Would – under what condition? The real meaning is – it *does* seem, it *does* appear, we *do* remark. These phrases are rarely found in good writers, and *ought* never to be found.'[22] As editor and essayist, she kept her own rules.

Also as novelist. Her early letters to her publisher about her fiction defend the precision of the detail in terms of accuracy. John Blackwood told her he would have liked to see, in her account of the confirmation in 'Janet's Repentance', 'some allusion to the solemn and affecting sight that a confirmation ought to be'.[23] Eliot replied,

My own impression on rereading very carefully the account of the confirmation is, that readers will perceive, what is the fact – that I am not in the least occupying myself with confirmation in general, or with Bishops in general, but with a particular confirmation and a particular Bishop.

Art must be either real and concrete, or ideal and eclectic. Both are good and true in their way, but my stories are of the former kind. I undertake to exhibit some things as they have been or are, seen through such a medium as my own nature gives me.

This clear statement also raises the problem of the relations between 'realist' art and the philosophical distinction between idealism and realism. This, in its turn, leads on to a consideration of the religious and scientific ideas (the two are inextricably inter-linked) in Eliot's writings.

DEVELOPMENT, POSITIVE SCIENCE AND INCARNATION

Eliot's first review for the *Westminster*, that of Mackay's *The Progress of the Intellect*, was published in 1851, before she became an editor. In it can be found clear statements of her own beliefs, which resonate throughout her work. The essay is also important as her first reference to the work of Auguste Comte. Comte's Positive Philosophy was uncompromisingly realist. He held that the age of scientific discovery had succeeded the earlier stages of human thought, the Theological and the Metaphysical, which explained the facts of the universe in terms of 'direct volitions of beings, real or imaginary, possessed of life and intelligence' (Theological) and of 'realized' abstractions, forces, or occult qualities such as Nature, or Vital Principles' (Metaphysical).[24] The age of Positive Science had understood that the world was governed by undeviating law – 'that invariability of sequence which is acknowledged to be the basis of physical science, but which is still perversely ignored in our social organization, our ethics and our religion'.[25] *Duty*, Eliot says here, is 'comprised in the earnest study of this law and patient obedience to its teaching'. In F. W. H. Myers's famous account of his conversation with the sibylline author in Trinity College garden, he quotes her discourse on God, immortality and duty, and her saying how 'inconceivable was the *first*, how unbelievable the *second*, and yet how peremptory and absolute the *third*'.[26] At the time of the *Westminster Review* essays Eliot was negotiating a book on the 'Idea of a Future Life' with Chapman (as well as her translation of Feuerbach) that might have addressed itself both to the untenable idea of 'Compensation' for suffering or virtuous self-denial, and to the requirement of obedience to duty for itself alone. Eliot shared the Comtean belief that scientific truth had superseded the truths of revelation or philosophical intuition, but she was sceptical of his later doctrinaire recipes for happiness. Comte saw the laws of evolution of human society as laws of the same nature, once established, as those of physics – which makes the Positivist precept of 'obedience' to these unavoidable laws a somewhat slurred and irrational idea.

Eliot quotes with approval Mackay's statements on faith.

Religion and science are inseparable. No object in nature, no subject of contemplation, is destitute of a religious tendency and meaning . . . Faith is to a great extent involuntary; it is a law or faculty of our nature, operating silently and intuitively to supply the imperfections of our knowledge. The boundary between faith and knowledge is indeed hard to distinguish . . . Faith as an inference from knowledge, should be consistently inferred from the whole of knowledge . . . Faith naturally arises out of the regular and the undeviating.

Eliot's own description of 'our civilization, and yet more our religion' in this essay is one of 'an anomalous blending of lifeless barbarisms, which have descended to us like so many petrifactions from distant ages, with living ideas, the offspring of a true process of development'. She calls Mackay's book 'perhaps the nearest approach in our language to a satisfactory natural history of religion'.

The idea of *natural history* is central, both to the thought of Eliot's time, and to her own work as a novelist. The phrase 'the natural history of religion' combines the ideas of objective science, the human past, the development of ideas and the study of morality conceived as a developing sequence of observations and 'living ideas'. The natural history of the earth included Charles Lyell's geology and Darwin's study of the *Origin of Species*. The 'natural history' of societies sought to supersede a history that concentrated on the isolated acts of great men, or decisions of rulers, to study the whole structure and interrelations of families and groups as though they were organisms. Nineteenth-century work on philology and mythology sought to study the thoughts and beliefs, and acts and agriculture, of men as they developed speech and tales to describe themselves to themselves. Eliot's essay on Wilhelm von Riehl ('The Natural History of German Life') makes clear her enthusiastic acceptance of these ideas. As with Mackay's 'natural history' of religion, Eliot stresses Riehl's interest in the life of the German people as *'incarnate history'*, and, as in the Mackay essay, she warns against any attempt to detach ahistorical precepts or descriptions from it.

[Riehl] sees in European society *incarnate history*, and any attempt to disengage it from its historical elements must, he believes, be simply destructive of social vitality. What has grown up historically can only die out historically, by the gradual operation of necessary laws. The external conditions which society has inherited from the past are but the manifestation of inherited internal conditions in the human beings who compose it; the internal conditions and the external are related to each other as the organism and its medium, and development can take place only by the gradual consentaneous development of both.

Here the 'inherited internal conditions' of men are presumably both biological and mental. Eliot goes on to say specifically 'The historical conditions of society may be compared with those of language' and to discuss the 'subtle shades of meaning and still subtler echoes of association' that 'make language an instrument which scarcely anything short of genius can wield with definiteness and certainty'. She contemplates a future universal language constructed on a rational basis, 'patent, deodorized and nonresonant', perfect and rapid as algebraic signs, a kind of prevision of computer language, made of ticks and dots. She uses a characteristic physiological analogy to reinforce her sense that the organism and its history must be respected.

The sensory and motor nerves that run in the same sheath, are scarcely bound together by a more necessary and delicate union than that which binds men's affection, imagination, wit and humour, with the subtle ramifications of historical language. Language must be left to grow in precision, completeness, and unity, as minds grow in clearness, comprehensiveness, and sympathy. And there is an analogous relation between the moral tendencies of men and the social conditions they have inherited.

This passage – and the succeeding paragraphs – are crucial to understanding Eliot's thought, and also the nature of her fictive world, which she sees as a developing organism, incarnate history, much as Riehl sees his world. She continues with an approving quote from Ruskin's *Modern Painters, Vol. IV* about the continuity between old ruins, the ancient world and more recent buildings: 'all is continuous; and the words "from generation to generation" understandable here'.[27] And then she expresses a conservative scepticism about the generalizations of Social Science, using the Comtean terms of progression 'from the general to the special, from the simple to the complex, analogous to that which is found in the series of the sciences, from Mathematics to Biology'. Social Science must study particular organisms. 'A wise social policy must be based, not simply on abstract social science, but on the Natural History of social bodies.' She approves Riehl's 'social-political-conservatism', as opposed to 'communistic theories which he regards as "the despair of the individual in his own manhood, reduced to a system"'. And in the Riehl essay her arguments for the specificity of Natural History are also used for artistic realism: there is a moral obligation to depict peasants as they are, not in a pastoral idealization. 'Art is the nearest thing to life; it is a mode of amplifying experience and extending our contact with our fellow-men beyond the bounds of our personal lot. All the more sacred is the task of the artist when he undertakes to paint the life of the People. Falsification here is far more pernicious than in the more artificial aspects of life.'

Images of natural history are intrinsic to her own art. One that foreshadows the natural-historical metaphors for the community of St Ogg's in *The Mill on the Floss* is to be found in the 'Ilfracombe Journal', where she describes Lantern Hill.

In hilly districts, where houses and clusters of houses look so tiny against the huge limbs of Mother Earth one cannot help thinking of man as a parasitic animal – an epizoon making his abode on the skin of the planetary organism. In a flat country a house or a town looks imposing – there is nothing to rival it in height, and we may imagine the earth a mere pedestal for us. But when one sees a house stuck on the side of a great hill, and still more a number of houses looking like a few barnacles clustered on the side of a great rock, we begin to think of the strong family likeness between ourselves and all other building, burrowing house-appropriating and shell-secreting animals. The difference between a man with his house and a mollusc with its shell lies in the number of steps or phenomena interposed between the fact of individual existence and the completion of the building.

Some such analogy as this underlies her description, in her 1855 review, of Lewes's *Life of Goethe* as such a '*natural history*' of his various productions as will show how they were the outgrowth of his mind at different stages of its culture'. And the same set of analogies and beliefs is at work in her review of *Wilhelm Meister*, where she describes Goethe himself, who 'quietly follows the stream of fact and of life; and waits patiently for the moral processes of nature as we all do for her material processes'.

The use of the word 'incarnation' in phrases such as 'incarnate history' calls up, of course, the whole problem of Christian theology and its partial, progressive and dubious abandonment. Many religious men and theologians clung to various forms of the idea of Christ as perfect or exemplary Man, or Ideal Man, even when they had conceded that the Bible as historical document was open to question, that the eyewitness evidence of the Miracles and the Resurrection were contradictory and unsupported, and that these were in conflict with the somehow more energetic and compelling universal and invariable laws of mind and matter. The young George Eliot was an evangelical Anglican; the growing George Eliot, compelled by Charles Hennell's *Inquiry into the Origins of Christianity*, by Strauss and by Feuerbach, was resolutely anti-Christian; the mature George Eliot saw Christian belief and morality as forms of human experience that must be studied and valued as part of our natural history. Nietzsche, in his only reference to Eliot (*Twilight of the Idols*, 1888), counted her among the English, who clung to the half-life of Christianity.

G. Eliot. – They have got rid of the Christian God, and now feel obliged to cling all the more firmly to Christian morality: that is *English* consistency, let us not blame it on little bluestockings à la Eliot. In England, in response to every little emancipation from theology, one has to reassert one's position in a fear-inspiring manner as a moral fanatic. That is the *penance* one pays there. – With us it is different. When one gives up Christian belief one thereby deprives oneself of the *right* to Christian morality.[28]

Nietzsche, according to his translator, R. J. Hollingdale, probably knew about Eliot only from hearsay. It is interesting to juxtapose the views he attributes to her with the letter she wrote to Chapman in 1852, in the days of her editorial work.

I feel that I am a wretched helpmate to you, almost out of the world, and incog. so far as I am in it. When you can afford to pay an Editor, if that time will ever come, you must get one. If you believe in Free Will, in the Theism that looks on manhood as a type of the godhead and on Jesus as the Ideal Man, get one belonging to the Martineau 'school of thought' and he will drill you a regiment of writers who will produce a Prospective on a larger scale, and so the Westminster may come to have 'dignity' in the eyes of Liverpool.

If not – if you believe as I do, that the thought which is to mould the Future has for its root a belief in necessity, that a nobler presentation of humanity has yet to be given in resignation to individual nothingness, than could ever be shown of a being who believes in the phantasmagoria of hope unsustained by reason – why then get a man of another calibre and let him write a fresh Prospectus, and if Liverpool theology and ethics are to be admitted, let them be put in the 'dangerous ward', *alias*, the Independent Section.

The only third course is the present one, that of Editorial compromise.[29]

INCARNATION

The long nineteenth-century debate about the precise meaning, or lack of meaning, of the Christian concept of the Incarnation, the meeting-point of the divine and the human, the infinite and the finite, is inextricably connected, consciously and unconsciously, to the development of the form of the novel. As the biblical narrative ceased to be privileged as unique truth, and became associated with partial histories of other kinds, or what Froude in *The Nemesis of Faith* calls 'Wonder Tales', so there arose, for certain kinds of speculative minds, an interest in the nature of the individuals and the values they represented, as portrayed in secular narrative. If Piers Plowman in a religious culture is a Type of Christ, what is Adam Bede, breaking bread and drinking wine before Hetty Sorrel's trial and condemnation in the fiction of a writer who explicitly rejected, in the letter I have just quoted, 'the Theism that looks on manhood as a type of the godhead, and on Jesus as the Ideal Man'? George Eliot's nature, like Dorothea Brooke's, was both ardent and theoretic, and, like Margaret Fuller's, intellectual and sensuous, both analytic and observant, both idealizing (theorizing) and realist.

She was also the translator of two of the most influential documents in the Higher Criticism and the demythologizing of Christianity: Strauss's *The Life of Jesus* and Feuerbach's *The Essence of Christianity*. The passages from these translations reprinted in this collection were chosen to illustrate their thinking on the meaning of the incarnation and its narrative, in the belief that, as well as being interesting in themselves, they illuminate the way in which Eliot thought about human nature and human stories.

The passages from Strauss are taken from the introduction and conclusion of his work. Strauss explains the biblical narrative as a series of 'mythi' analogous to those of other religions. He rejects the historical claims of the Bible on the ground that individual acts of divine intervention in human affairs are inconsistent with the modern conviction 'that all things are linked together by a chain of causes and effects which suffers no interruption'. He also tries to distinguish myths from lies and deceptions, by making an analogy with poetry and quoting the mythologist, Otfried Müller. 'How,' says Müller, 'shall we reconcile this combination of the true and the false, the real and the ideal, in mythi, with the fact of their being believed and received as truth? The ideal, it may be said, is nothing else than poetry and fiction clothed in the form of a narration.' Strauss then argues that this fiction cannot have *one* originator, but must be, in some now unimaginable way, the product of a common consciousness.

At the end of his book, Strauss discusses various ways in which philosophers have tried to preserve the meaning and importance of the concept of Incarnation, whilst acknowledging the fictiveness of a particular historical divine intervention. He examines the ideas of Spinoza and Kant, who believed that the ideal Christ, the eternal 'wisdom of god' or 'idea of moral perfection' could be believed; Strauss himself (see pp. 453-4) comes to a complicated definition of the union of idea and reality (infinite and finite) not in one historical individual but in *the species*.

This is indeed not the mode in which Idea realizes itself; it is not wont to lavish all its fullness on one exemplar, and be niggardly towards all others – to express itself perfectly in that one individual and imperfectly in all the rest: it rather loves to distribute its riches among a multiplicity of exemplars which reciprocally complete each other – in the alternate appearance and suppression of a series of individuals. And is this no true realization of the idea? is not the idea of the unity of the divine and human natures a real one in a far higher sense, when I regard the whole of mankind as its realization, than when I single out one man as such a realization?

The connection of this description of 'the alternate appearance and suppression of a series of individuals' – with the word 'suppression' universalizing and naturalizing the tragedy of the Passion – is a good description of the moral, even religious sense we have of Eliot's world. Lydgate and Dorothea, Maggie and Adam Bede, are invested, in their limited individuality, with the religious *value* that has been displaced from the incarnate Man to the succession of human beings. They are Types and individuals. Our sense of the way in which Eliot saw the relationship between their general humanity and their particular identity is made more subtle and precise by considering Feuerbach's idea of the Incarnation.

'With the principles of Feuerbach I everywhere agree,' Marian Evans wrote to Sarah Hennell, though she went on to add, 'but of course I should, of myself, alter his phraseology considerably.'[30] Feuerbach's book is still exciting to read, and her translation reads easily and urgently. The essential argument of *The Essence of Christianity* is that men invented religion – including the Persons of god, the sacraments and the Church – in order to be able to contemplate and worship their own nature. The book unravels the human needs that give rise to the particular beliefs it analyses, and passionately pleads for a recognition that mankind itself is the proper object of veneration and adoration. 'Not abstract beings – no! only sensuous living beings are merciful. Mercy is the *justice of sensuous life*,'[31] he argues, in her words, and with sentiments that are apparent throughout her works. It is also Feuerbach who proposes that we should celebrate real bread and real wine, not as symbols of flesh and blood, alienated from their true nature, but for themselves. 'Water is the purest, clearest of liquids; in virtue of this its natural character it is the image of the spotless nature of the Divine Spirit. In short, water has a significance in itself, as water.' 'But as religion alienates our own nature from us, and represents it as not ours, so the water of baptism is regarded as quite other than common water.' U. C. Knoepflmacher has argued that Adam Bede's meal is a Feuerbachian 'natural' sacrament in this sense.[32]

Both the passages from *The Essence of Christianity* included in this collection are concerned with the reinterpretation of the Incarnation. In the first, the chapter 'The Mystery of the Cosmogonical Principle in God', Feuerbach identifies the Son – 'i.e., God thought by himself, the original reflection of God' – with the principle of the *imagination*, the 'middle term' between the mind and the Other, the maker of images. God making the world is 'the mystic paraphrase of a psychological process', that is, human self-consciousness, the imagination of the self as an other.

The psychological truth and necessity which lies at the foundation of all these theogonies and cosmogonies, is the truth and necessity of the imagination as a middle term between the abstract and the concrete. And the task of philosophy, in investigating this subject, is to comprehend the relation of the imagination to the reason – the genesis of the image by means of which an object of thought becomes an object of sense, of feeling.

Thus if Christ is for Strauss the Idea present in the succession of particular individuals who make up the race, he is, at least as the Son of the Creator, for Feuerbach, related to the Romantic Imagination, the creative principle that 'bodies forth the forms of things unknown',[33] that makes concrete and particular images in order to know and understand itself. 'Consciousness of the world is consciousness of my limitation' Feuerbach goes on to say, a sentiment that is echoed in much of his translator's later commentary on human life. 'The consciousness of my limitation stands in contradiction with the impulse of my egoism towards unlimitedness.' She was the great analyst of egoism.

The other passage selected from Feuerbach echoes Strauss's belief that the Species is the true object of our moral and religious attention – but he adds to this the idea that the essence of the species is contained in the relation between the sexes, in the recognition of the Other, and in the sensuous passion of the flesh. 'Flesh and blood is nothing without the oxygen of sexual distinction. The distinction of sex is not superficial, or limited to certain parts of the body; it is an essential one: it penetrates bone and marrow.' (Here, perhaps, among other interesting thoughts, is one possible reason for George Eliot's conviction that the 'woman question' must not lose sight of the essential *difference* between the sexes.) 'Man is different in intercourse from what he is when alone. Love especially works wonders, and the love of the sexes most of all. Men and women are the complement of each other, and thus united they first present the species, the perfect man.' 'In love, the reality of the species, which otherwise is only a thing of reason, an object of mere thought, becomes a matter of feeling, a truth of feeling.' If the young George Eliot rejected Christ as ideal Man and believed in resignation to individual nothingness, she was at the same time involved in translating a work that substituted sexual love, the union of the sexes, as 'the perfect man'. And again, in love, *thought* becomes transmuted into *feeling*.

It is with these ideas in mind that we should look at the correspondence with Frederic Harrison that took place in 1866–8 (see pp. 237–57). It contains one of Eliot's best-known artistic statements of intent. What Harrison requires of her is to create a narrative that will embody 'the idealization of certain normal relations', which is 'the task of all art'. ('Normal' here must be read as closer to 'normative' than to usual or humdrum.) Harrison wants her to describe a society, and a political, religious and moral state of affairs that will show the 'Positivist relations' of its people. Eliot replied that he laid before her 'a tremendously difficult problem' of which he saw the difficulties,

though they can hardly press upon you as they do on me, who have gone through again and again the severe effort of trying to make certain ideas thoroughly incarnate, as if they had revealed themselves to me first in the flesh and not in the spirit. I think aesthetic teaching is the highest of all teaching because it deals with life in its highest complexity. But if it ceases to be purely aesthetic – if it lapses anywhere from the picture to the diagram – it becomes the most offensive of all teaching.

The language here, in terms of the Positivist beliefs, is clearly related (as the language of Positivism itself was) to the revalued Christian concepts discussed above. Eliot saw her work as making *incarnate certain ideas* that she apprehended in the flesh, i.e., sensuously, materially, through feeling. I want to come back to the way in which in *Middlemarch* she dealt with Harrison's proposals, but first I want to write briefly about a related set of ideas that arises in the correspondence and in 'Notes on form in Art', which was written about the same time.

The correspondence opens with Harrison praising *Felix Holt* for having 'the subtle finish of a poem' and being 'a romance constructed in the artistic spirit and aim of a poem'. Eliot went on to write *The Spanish Gypsy*, which was published in 1868, before returning to fiction with *Middlemarch*. Harrison welcomes *The Spanish Gypsy* as the statement he had been looking for. 'I need not say I am sure what pleasure it gives me to recognize the profound truths and sacred principles which [that which] we call the Faith of the Future is preparing, for the first time truly idealized.' But his distress at the characters of Zarca and Fedalma, in their idealism, reads comically in its honesty. They are *idealizations* of love of the Species, the Race, Humanity. Fedalma's sacrifice of her personal love in her devotion to her race is a precursor of Daniel Deronda's, and both have their roots in Eliot's sense of Duty, which we have discussed, as 'obedience' to the 'laws' of social organisms. Harrison's instincts are surely right. Zarca and Fedalma are strained, horrible and *unreal*. They, and the correspondence, tell us something about what happened to Eliot when she shifted too far from one pole of the debate between idealism and realism towards the other.

In 1862 and 1863 Edward Bulwer-Lytton wrote a series of articles in *Blackwood's* in which he opposed an aesthetic doctrine of idealism in art to the current realism. '*The artist never seeks to represent the positive truth, but the idealized image of a truth* [Bulwer's italics].'[34] As Hegel well observes, 'That which exists in nature is a something purely individual and particular. Art, on the contrary, is essentially destined to manifest the general.' Characters in novels, as Richard Stang points out, 'as embodiments of ideals created by the human imagination from the new facts of experience, are not individuals but types or symbols'.[35] Stang suggests that Bulwer-Lytton's 'general truths' seem 'dangerously near a kind of never-never-land to which he periodically escaped to forget all about unpleasant reality'. Gordon Haight thinks that Bulwer-Lytton's *Leila; or the Siege of Granada* (1838) is an unacknowledged source for *The Spanish Gypsy*.

Eliot's 'Notes on Form in Art', dated 1868, the year of *The Spanish Gypsy*, can be seen, in one light, as a continuation of her thought about the ideal and the real, the particular and the universal, and incarnation; indeed, she begins with a discussion of 'the philosophic use of the word "Form" in distinction from Matter'. Her idea of Form is intricately bound up with a series of images of organisms: she distinguishes between the 'accidental' form of a stone and the 'outline defining the wholeness of a human body' that is 'due to a consensus or constant interchange of effects among its parts'. It is part of the process of incarnation. Her definition of poetry is Feuerbachian. '*Poetry* begins when passion weds thought by finding expression in an image; but *poetic form* begins with a choice of elements, however meagre, as the accordant expression of emotional states.' Poetic form grows like 'the beautiful expanding curves of a bivalve shell', to go back to the imagery of Ilfracombe and Lewes's *Seaside Studies*. And earlier she writes a precise, clear sentence about the *range of poetry* that varies widely in the way it combines 'emotive force' with 'sequences that are not arbitrary and individual but true and universal'. Poetry combines the particular with the ideal, the 'true and universal' in its rhythms, its images, its sequences. Poetry, she says, has been defined to mean fiction, but fiction itself is only the expression of *predominant feeling* in 'an arrangement of events in feigned correspondences' – i.e., in constructed images, such as those by which Feuerbach's imagination recognized its limitations and the existence of the other. Form in its 'derivative meaning of outline' is 'the limit of that difference by which we discriminate one object from another'.

It could be argued that Eliot took to writing poetry because her interest shifted from the exactness and definiteness of her earlier realism to the system of correspondences, and general truths, and similarities and connections that make up the general reality. If her poem is a failure, her thoughts about poetic form surely affect the nature of the last two novels, *Middlemarch* and *Daniel Deronda*. The poetic web of metaphors in *Middlemarch* is unlike the forms of language in her earlier work. In the penultimate paragraph of 'Notes on Form in Art' she says, 'The old phrases should not give way to scientific explanation, for speech is to a great extent like sculpture, expressing observed phenomena, and remaining true in spite of Harvey and Bichat.'

The desire for the solid and *perceptually particular* language expressed here is reminiscent of her defence, in the essay on Riehl, of 'the subtle ramification of historical language'. In the Riehl essay she opposed this to a new universal scientific 'deodorized' code of scientific language. William Harvey and Marie François Bichat, the discoverers of the circulation of the blood and the hypothetical 'universal tissue' that made up all particular organs, can be seen as representing, in the incarnate organism, the kind of *informing* principle of life that takes on particular individual forms. (Something also like Noam Chomsky's 'deep structure' of language?) Bichat was one of Comte's heroes, and also the ideal of Lydgate, the Comtean scientist in *Middlemarch*. Bichat's universal tissue forms part of the recurring web of metaphors in *Middlemarch* that links and combines the diverse parts of the social organism in the novel. And that self-conscious web of metaphor itself is a conscious poetic strategy of universalization.

Which brings us back to what Eliot made of Harrison's prescription for an idealizing work of art. It has been pointed out, in subtle detail, just how far the plot of *Middlemarch* corresponds with Harrison's sketched plot.[36] We have the decayed and failing aristocracy and Church (Mr Brooke, Casaubon); we have the new 'positive' forces of scientist and capitalist (Lydgate and Bulstrode) combining to improve things (the hospital); we have in Dorothea the female influence Comte thought indispensable (which, according to him, must have *no other role* than maternity, no inheritance and no power that might corrupt its purity). If we look at Harrison's enthusiastic piety and the very dubious and bleak moral triumphs of *Middlemarch*, it seems clear that the novelist was actuated by something akin to the spirit of irony and contradiction that brought realism out of the genres described in 'Silly Novels' and truth out of the rejection of Cumming and Young. The moral and artistic triumphs of *Middlemarch* are ultimately more Feuerbachian than Comtean, and have to do with a moral sense of finite human limitations rather than with the March of Humanity. Dorothea has to learn the Feuerbachian lesson: the 'genesis of the image by means of which an object of thought becomes an object of sense, of feeling'.[37] Eliot's intelligence combined thought and feeling in a new form of poetic but ironic realist fiction.

The voice of the narrator of *Middlemarch* is more measured than that of the brilliant essayist; it speaks with a universalizing 'we' for the organic community, whereas the essayist (*vide* 'Madame de Sablé' or 'Heinrich Heine') often poses as a witty male. But the continuity is strong, and the essays and translations tell us vital things about the tone of the art.

We are all of us born in moral stupidity, taking the world as an udder to feed our supreme selves: Dorothea had early begun to emerge from that stupidity, but yet it had been easier to her to imagine how she would devote herself to Mr Casaubon, and become wise and strong in his strength and wisdom, than to conceive with that distinctness which is no longer reflection but feeling – an idea wrought back to the directness of sense, like the solidity of objects – that he had an equivalent centre of self, whence the lights and shadows must always fall with a certain difference.[38]

NOTES

1. *Athenæum*, 28 November 1885.
2. See Gordon S. Haight, *George Eliot and John Chapman* (1940 edition), p. 22.
3. *Letters, Vol. VIII*, p. 23.
4. Haight, *George Eliot and John Chapman*, pp. 41–2.
5. *Life*, p. 97.
6. See p. 5.
7. Herbert Spencer, *Principles of Psychology* (1855), p. 162.
8. Herbert Spencer, *Autobiography, Vol. I* (1904), pp. 394–5.
9. *Letters, Vol. V*, p. 58.
10. *Letters Vol. I*, p. 284.
11. *Letters, Vol. V*, p. 106.
12. Thomas Pinney, *Essays of George Eliot*, p. 157.
13. See below, p. 37.
14. See below, p. 333.
15. *Letters, Vol. II*, p. 15.
16. *Letters Vol. V*, pp. 160–61.
17. *Daniel Deronda*, Chapter 51.
18. *Journal*, 12 September 1856 (Pinney, p. 301).
19. *Letters, Vol. II*, p. 258.
20. See below, p. 368.
21. *Letters, Vol. II*, p. 210.

22. *Letters, Vol. II*, p. 205–7.

23. *Letters, Vol. II*, p. 362.

24. See J. S. Mill, *Auguste Comte and Positivism* (1865), pp. 9ff.

25. See p. 271.

26. *Life*, p. 464, citing *Century Magazine*, vol. 23 (November 1881), pp. 62–3.

27. *Modern Painters, Vol. IV*, Part 5, Chapter 1, Section 5.

28. Friedrich Nietzsche, *Twilight of the Idols* (1889), Penguin edition, p. 69.

29. *Letters, Vol. II*, pp. 48–9.

30. *Letters, Vol. II*, p. 153.

31. Ludwig Feuerbach, *The Essence of Christianity*, translator Marian Evans, end of Chapter 3. The phrase translated as 'the justice of sensuous life' is 'Das Rechtsgefuhl der Sinnlichkeit'.

32. U. C. Knoepflmacher, *Religious Humanism and the Victorian Novel* (1965), pp. 55ff.

33. Shakespeare, *A Midsummer Night's Dream*, Act V, Scene 1, lines 12–17.

34. Quoted in Richard Stang, *The Theory of the Novel in England 1850–70* (1959), p. 154.

35. ibid.

36. See James F. Scott, 'George Eliot, Positivism and the Social Vision of *Middlemarch*' in *Victorian Studies*, vol. 16 (September 1972), pp. 59–76, and Martha Vogeler, 'George Eliot and the Positivists' in *Nineteenth-Century Fiction*, vol. 36 (1980), pp. 406–31.

37. See p. 460.

38. *Middlemarch*, Chapter 21, Penguin edition, p. 243.

Suggested Further Reading

THERE ARE several useful introductory studies of George Eliot's work, although only Gillian Beer's *George Eliot* (Brighton, 1986) and Rosemary Ashton's *George Eliot* (Oxford, 1983) venture much beyond her work as a novelist. Jennifer Uglow's study, also called *George Eliot*, in the Virago Pioneers series, examines her feminist credentials, and discusses her critical and journalistic work in relation to her fiction.

The best sources of information about Eliot's life remain Gordon S. Haight's *George Eliot: A Biography* (Oxford and New York, 1968, cited as *Life* in the notes and elsewhere) and his edition of *The George Eliot Letters* (nine volumes, New Haven and London; Vols. I–VII, 1955; Vols. VIII–IX, 1978; cited as *Letters*). J. W. Cross's *George Eliot's Life as Related in Her Letters and Journals* (London, 1885; cited as *Cross*) is also worth consulting. Haight's *George Eliot and John Chapman* (London and New Haven, 1940, second edition 1969) is a good source of material about her career as an editor and critic. Readers wishing to know more about the reception of her work should consult Haight's *A Century of George Eliot Criticism* (London, 1966) and David Carroll's *George Eliot: The Critical Heritage* (London, 1971).

Other editions of Eliot's non-fictional work, apart from the *Essays* volume of the Cabinet Edition (London, 1884), are Thomas Pinney's *Essays of George Eliot* (London, 1963), to which we are heavily indebted, particularly for his very helpful bibliography of Eliot's reviews, and *George Eliot: A Writer's Notebook 1854–79 and Uncollected Writings*, ed. Joseph Wiesenfarth (Charlottesville, 1981). No modern scholar of the Victorian period can get very far without the assistance of the *Wellesley Index to Victorian Periodicals*

(London and Toronto, 1979 onwards), to which we are indebted for help in the attribution of certain reviews.

Critical studies of Eliot's non-fictional work are rare. Probably the best is William Myers's 'George Eliot's Essays and Reviews 1849–57' in *Prose Studies 1800–1900*, vol. 1 (1978), pp. 5–20. Less densely analytical is G. Robert Stange's 'The Voices of the Essayist' in *Nineteenth-Century Fiction*, vol. 35 (1980), pp. 312–30. Carol Martin's 'George Eliot: Feminist Critic' in *Victorian Newsletter*, vol. 65 (1984), pp. 22–5, along with the books by Beer and Uglow, is evidence of the growing interest of feminists in Eliot's career.

Eliot's poetry has also been neglected by critics. There is presently no modern edition available, although determined students might hunt out Cynthia Ann Secor's unpublished doctoral dissertation 'The Poems of George Eliot' (Cornell University, Ithaca, 1969). The journal *Victorian Poetry* has published a number of articles on her poetry in recent years, including Kathleen Blake's '*Armgart* – George Eliot on the Woman Artist', vol. 18 (1980), pp. 75–80; S. K. Marks's *The Spanish Gypsy*, vol. 21 (1983), pp. 184–90; and Bonnie Lisle's 'Art and Egoism in George Eliot's Poetry', vol. 22 (1984), pp. 263–78.

Readers wishing to understand the full context of the Eliot–Harrison correspondence in this volume and to assess the extent of Eliot's devotion to Positivism should consult Martha Vogeler's 'George Eliot and the Positivists' in *Nineteenth-Century Fiction*, vol. 35 (1980), pp. 406–31 and T. R. Wright's 'George Eliot and Positivism' in *Modern Language Review*, vol. 76 (1981), pp. 257–72.

Elinor Shaffer's '*Kubla Khan*' and '*The Fall of Jerusalem*': *The Mythological School in Biblical Criticism and Secular Literature 1770–1880* (Cambridge, 1975), especially Chapter 6 on *Daniel Deronda*, William Myers's *The Teaching of George Eliot* (Leicester, 1984) and Rosemary Ashton's *The German Idea: Four English Writers and the Reception of German Thought* (Cambridge, 1980) are helpful in placing her work in its intellectual and cultural context.

A Note on the Text

IN CHOOSING this selection of George Eliot's work, our guiding editorial principle has been to include items that, as well as being interesting in themselves, will be of value to anyone wishing to form a clearer understanding of the development of her thinking and of her work as a novelist. For this reason we have chosen pieces that help to illuminate her views about the nature and purpose of fiction, that illustrate the development of her thinking about religion, art and narrative form, and that record her formulation of the principles governing her own fictional work. Some items we have omitted (for example, the promisingly titled 'Pictures of Life in French Novels' in the *Saturday Review*, 17 May 1856) are little more than brief notices of the books under review. Others (such as her review of John Ruskin's *Modern Painters, Vol. IV* in the *Westminster Review*, July 1856, pp. 274–8) have been partially incorporated in the notes.

Eliot's essays and reviews were originally published in periodicals and are here reproduced from photocopies of the original publications. In this edition we have treated her essays as a discrete body of work in which she was, as A. S. Byatt remarks in her Introduction (pp. xii–xiii), 'clearing the ground' and have, therefore, separated them from her book reviews, which are, with rare exceptions, responses to individual works. Eliot's revision of some of her essays for publication in book form towards the end of her life (*Essays and Leaves from a Notebook*, 1884) indicates that she too regarded the essays as qualitatively distinct work. Significant variations are registered in the notes. Her quotations from the books she is reviewing are notoriously inaccurate, especially the foreign language texts. Again, we have chosen to reproduce the reviews as originally published, but have corrected spelling and have also noted substantive variations from the original. Obvious printers' errors (e.g., 'Bridgenorth' for 'Bridgworth') have been silently corrected. Because the copy texts come from a wide variety of printed sources, they were originally set in different house styles. Anomalies have been silently harmonized, although we have retained some of Eliot's consistent idiosyncracies (e.g., 'Shakspeare' for 'Shakespeare'). Her own annotations are reprinted as footnotes on the appropriate page; all other notes are to be found at the back of the volume, along with details about the circumstances of composition. Translations of passages in foreign languages are also printed in full in the notes.

The Eliot–Harrison correspondence, as well as extracts from letters referred to in the notes, and the extract from 'The Ilfracombe Journal' are taken from Gordon S. Haight's edition of *The George Eliot Letters*. The poems are reprinted from the first published edition, as are the extracts from her translations and the essay from *Impressions of Theophrastus Such*. The 1868 essay 'Notes on Form in Art' is reproduced from the manuscript at the Beinecke Rare Book and Manuscript Library, Yale University.

ESSAYS

❧

Prospectus of the
Westminster and Foreign Quarterly Review

(*Westminster Review*, January 1852)

According to the *Wellesley Index, Vol. III*, the Prospectus was written jointly by Eliot and John Chapman, though it is likely that Eliot was responsible for the bulk of it. The object was to seek support and potential contributors for the re-launched journal.

John Chapman had agreed to buy the *Westminster* from William Hickson on 1 May 1851, having previously been offered financial support from Edward Lombe, a philanthropic supporter of liberal causes. Realizing that he did not possess the requisite intellectual or editorial skills, Chapman turned to Eliot for assistance, visiting her in Coventry on 27 May. The following evening they cut short a visit to a concert in order to discuss plans for the new journal. He recorded in his diary on 29 May that he 'wrote the greater part of the Prospectus today, and then gave it to M. [i.e., Marian Evans] to finish' (Haight, *George Eliot and John Chapman*, 1969 edition, p. 30).

Eliot worked steadily on the revision, going without dinner in order to finish it. Charles Bray's printer set it in type, and it was quickly sent out to a dozen likely supporters. The reaction was not favourable. James Martineau wrote to Hickson that Chapman 'sent me a Prospectus in print, which I could not pretend to approve; for I thought it ill-written and poor in substance: and I fear I have offended by not praising it. If he assumes the Editor's office, the *Review* is conclusively ruined. He is an enterprising publisher and a clever man: but it is his misfortune that he does not know his limits, and is ambitious of a literary function, for which he is not qualified' (*Wellesley Index, Vol. III*, p. 546n). J. S. Mill was equally scathing, writing to Chapman that 'The Prospectus says that the *Review* is to be "distinctly characterized by certain definite but broad principles"; but instead of laying down any such principles it contains little else than details of the measures which the *Review* will advocate on the principal political questions just now discussed in the newspapers' (H. Elliott, ed., *Letters of John Stuart Mill, Vol. I*, 1910, pp. 162–4).

Eliot wrote to Chapman on 12 June 1851, 'I heartily wish the Prospectus had been longer delayed and thought over before it was sent out. . . . everything has been too hurried' (*Letters, Vol. I*, p. 351). The Prospectus was rewritten by her in August, and it is this second draft that was published in the first issue of the *Westminster* that she edited.

For a full account of the negotiations about her editorship (and their attendant emotional complications), see Haight's *George Eliot and John Chapman* (1969 edition), pp. 28–40.

THE NEWLY-appointed Editors will endeavour to confirm and extend the influence of the *Review* as an instrument for the development and guidance of earnest thought on Politics, Social Philosophy, Religion, and General Literature; and to this end they will seek to render it the organ of the most able and independent minds of the day.

The fundamental principle of the work will be the recognition of the Law of Progress. In conformity with this principle, and with the consequent conviction that attempts at reform – though modified by the experience of the past and the conditions of the present – should be directed and animated by an advancing ideal, the Editors will maintain a steady comparison of the actual with the possible, as the most powerful stimulus to improvement. Nevertheless, in the deliberate advocacy of organic changes, it will not be forgotten, that the institutions of man, no less than the products of nature, are strong and durable in proportion as they are the results of a gradual development, and that the most salutary and permanent reforms are those, which, while embodying the wisdom of the time, yet sustain such a relation to the moral and intellectual condition of the people, as to ensure their support.

In contradistinction to the practical infidelity and essentially destructive policy which would ignore the existence of wide-spread doubts in relation to established creeds and systems, and would stifle all inquiry dangerous to prescriptive claims, the *Review* will exhibit that untemporizing expression of opinion, and that fearlessness of investigation and criticism which are the results of a consistent faith in the ultimate prevalence of truth. Convinced that the same fundamental truths are apprehended under a variety of forms, and that, therefore, opposing systems may in the end prove complements of each other, the Editors will endeavour to institute such a radical and comprehensive treatment of those controverted questions which are practically momentous, as may aid in the conciliation of divergent views. In furtherance of this object, they have determined to render available a limited portion of the work, under the head of 'Independent Contributions', – for the reception of articles ably setting forth opinions which, though not discrepant with the general spirit of the *Review*, may be at variance with the particular ideas or measures it will advocate. The primary object of this department is to facilitate the expression of opinion by men of high mental power and culture, who, while they are zealous friends of freedom and progress, yet differ widely on special points of great practical concern, both from the Editors and from each other.

The *Review* will give especial attention to that wide range of topics which may be included under the term 'Social Philosophy'. It will endeavour to form a dispassionate estimate of the diverse theories on these subjects, to give a definite and intelligible form to the chaotic mass of thought now prevalent concerning them, and to ascertain both in what degree the popular efforts after a more perfect social state are countenanced by the teachings of politico-economical science, and how far they may be sustained and promoted by the actual character and culture of the people.

In the department of Politics careful consideration will be given to all the most vital questions, without regard to the distinctions of party; the only standard of consistency to which the Editors will adhere being the real, and not the accidental relations of measures

– their bearing, not on a ministry or a class, but on the public good. The work being designed as an exponent of growing thought, the Editors cannot fully indicate the course they will pursue, but their political tendencies may be inferred from their intention that the *Review* shall support the following Reforms:

A progressive Extension of the Suffrage, in proportion as the people become fitted for using it, with a view to its ultimate universality, as the only equitable system of representation.

Such an adjustment of the Central Government and the local liberties of the people as, while allowing full scope for the popular energies, will secure the effective execution of measures dictated by the highest intelligence of the nation.

The extension to all our Colonies of a Local Constitutional Government, adapted to their specific wants and capabilities, with the establishment of such relations between them and the mother country as shall best insure their permanent connection, and accord to them that influence in the Imperial Legislature to which they have a rightful claim, and which would tend to the consolidation and stability of the empire.

Free Trade in every department of Commerce.

A radical Reform in the Administration of Justice, especially in the Court of Chancery, including the simplification and expediting of all legal processes.

A thorough revisal of the Ecclesiastical Revenues, with a view to their national and equitable use in promoting the intellectual and spiritual advancement of the people.

National Education, under the combined management of locally-appointed officers and of Commissioners deriving their authority from Parliament; together with such a modification and extension of our University and Public School systems as may render them available irrespective of the distinctions of sect.

In the treatment of Religious Questions the *Review* will unite a spirit of reverential sympathy for the cherished associations of pure and elevated minds with an uncompromising pursuit of truth. The elements of ecclesiastical authority and of dogma will be fearlessly examined, and the results of the most advanced biblical criticism will be discussed without reservation, under the conviction that religion has its foundation in man's nature, and will only discard an old form to assume and vitalize one more expressive of its essence. While, however, the Editors will not shrink from the expression of what they believe to be sound negative views, they will bear in mind the pre-eminent importance of a constructive religious philosophy, as connected with the development and activity of the moral nature, and of those poetic and emotional elements, out of which proceed our noblest aspirations and the essential beauty of life.

In the department of General Literature the criticism will be animated by desire to elevate the standard of the public taste, in relation both to artistic perfection and moral purity; larger space will be afforded for articles intrinsically valuable by the omission of those minor and miscellaneous notices which are necessarily forestalled by newspapers and magazines, and equivalent information will be given in a series of Historical and Critical Sketches of Contemporary Literature, comprehending a notice of the most remarkable books, both English and foreign, that may appear during each successive quarter.

The *Review* will in future be published by JOHN CHAPMAN, 142 Strand, to whose care all communications for the Editors must be addressed.

Woman in France: Madame de Sablé

(Westminster Review, October 1854)

IN 1847, a certain Count Leopold Ferri died at Padua, leaving a library entirely composed of works written by women, in various languages, and this library amounted to nearly 32,000 volumes. We will not hazard any conjecture as to the proportion of these volumes which a severe judge, like the priest in Don Quixote,[1] would deliver to the flames, but for our own part, most of those we should care to rescue would be the works of French women. With a few remarkable exceptions, our own feminine literature is made up of books which could have been better written by men; books which have the same relation to literature in general, as academic prize poems have to poetry: when not a feeble imitation, they are usually an absurd exaggeration of the masculine style, like the swaggering gait of a bad actress in male attire. Few English women have written so much like a woman as Richardson's Lady C.[2] Now, we think it an immense mistake to maintain that there is no sex in literature. Science has no sex: the mere knowing and reasoning faculties, if they act correctly, must go through the same process, and arrive at the same result. But in art and literature, which imply the action of the entire being, in which every fibre of the nature is engaged, in which every peculiar modification of the individual makes itself felt, woman has something specific to contribute. Under every imaginable social condition, she will necessarily have a class of sensations and emotions – the maternal ones – which must remain unknown to man; and the fact of her comparative physical weakness, which, however it may have been exaggerated by a vicious civilization, can never be cancelled, introduces a distinctively feminine condition into the wondrous chemistry of the affections and sentiments, which inevitably gives rise to distinctive forms and combinations. A certain amount of psychological difference between man and woman necessarily arises out of the difference of sex, and instead of being destined to vanish before a complete development of woman's intellectual and moral nature, will be a permanent source of variety and beauty, as long as the tender light and dewy freshness of morning affect us differently from the strength and brilliancy of the mid-day sun. And those delightful women of France, who, from the beginning of the seventeenth to the close of the eighteenth century, formed some of the brightest threads in the web of political and literary history, wrote under circumstances which left the feminine character of their minds uncramped by timidity, and unstrained by mistaken effort. They were not trying to make a career for themselves; they thought little, in many cases not at all, of the public; they wrote letters to their lovers and friends, memoirs of their every-day lives, romances in which they gave portraits of their familiar acquaintances, and described the tragedy or comedy which was going on before their eyes. Always refined and graceful, often witty, sometimes judicious, they wrote what they saw, thought, and felt, in their habitual language, without proposing any model to themselves, without any intention to prove that women could write as well as men, without affecting manly views or suppressing womanly ones. One may say, at least with regard to the women of the seventeenth century, that their writings were but a charming accident of their more charming lives, like the petals which the wind shakes from the rose in its bloom. And it is but a twin fact with this, that in France alone woman has had a vital influence on the development of literature; in France alone the mind of woman has passed like an electric current through the language, making crisp and definite what is elsewhere heavy and blurred; in France alone, if the writings of women were swept away, a serious gap would be made in the national history.

Patriotic gallantry may perhaps contend that English women could, if they had liked, have written as well as their neighbours; but we will leave the consideration of that question to the reviewers of the literature that might have been. In the literature that actually is, we must turn to France for the highest examples of womanly achievement in almost every department. We confess ourselves unacquainted with the productions of those awful women of Italy, who held professional chairs, and were great in civil and canon law; we have made no researches into the catacombs of female literature, but we think we may safely conclude that they would yield no rivals to that which is still unburied; and here, we suppose, the question of pre-eminence can only lie between England and France. And to this day, Madame de Sévigné[3] remains the single instance of a woman who is supreme in a class of literature which has engaged the ambition of men; Madame Dacier[4] still reigns the queen of blue-stockings, though women have long studied Greek without shame;* Madame de Staël's[5] name still rises first to the lips when we are asked to mention a woman of great intellectual power; Madame Roland[6] is still the unrivalled type of the sagacious and sternly heroic, yet lovable woman; George Sand[7] is the unapproached artist who, to Jean Jacques'[8] eloquence and deep sense of external nature, unites the clear delineation of character and the tragic depth of passion. These great names, which mark different epochs, soar like tall pines amidst a forest of less conspicuous, but not less fascinating, female writers; and beneath these again are spread, like a thicket of hawthorns, eglantines, and honeysuckles, the women who are known rather by what they stimulated men to write, than by what they wrote themselves – the women whose tact, wit, and personal radiance, created the atmosphere of the *salon*, where literature, philosophy, and science, emancipated from the trammels of pedantry and technicality, entered on a brighter stage of existence.

What were the causes of this earlier development and more abundant manifestation of womanly intellect in France? The primary one, perhaps, lies in the physiological characteristics of the Gallic race: – the small brain and vivacious temperament which permit the fragile system of woman to sustain the superlative activity requisite for intellectual creativeness; while, on the other hand, the larger brain and slower temperament of the English and

---

* Queen Christina, when Madame Dacier (then Mademoiselle Le Fèvre) sent her a copy of her edition of *Callimachus*, wrote in reply; – 'Mais vous, de qui on m'assure que vous êtes une belle et agréable fille, n'avez vous pas honte de'être si savante?' [The sentence translates as 'But you, a handsome and pleasing maid, as I am told, are you not ashamed of being so learned?']

Germans are, in the womanly organization, generally dreamy and passive. The type of humanity in the latter may be grander, but it requires a larger sum of conditions to produce a perfect specimen. Throughout the animal world, the higher the organization, the more frequent is the departure from the normal form; we do not often see imperfectly-developed or ill-made insects, but we rarely see a perfectly-developed, well-made man. And thus the *physique* of a woman may suffice as the substratum for a superior Gallic mind, but is too thin a soil for a superior Teutonic one. Our theory is borne out by the fact, that among our own countrywomen, those who distinguish themselves by literary production, more frequently approach the Gallic than the Teutonic type; they are intense and rapid rather than comprehensive. The woman of large capacity can seldom rise beyond the absorption of ideas; her physical conditions refuse to support the energy required for spontaneous activity; the voltaic-pile is not strong enough to produce crystallizations; phantasms of great ideas float through her mind, but she has not the spell which will arrest them, and give them fixity. This, more than unfavourable external circumstances, is, we think, the reason why woman has not yet contributed any new form to art, any discovery in science, any deep-searching inquiry in philosophy. The necessary physiological conditions are not present in her. That under more favourable circumstances in the future, these conditions may prove compatible with the feminine organization, it would be rash to deny. For the present, we are only concerned with our theory so far as it presents a physiological basis for the intellectual effectiveness of French women.

A secondary cause was probably the laxity of opinion and practice with regard to the marriage-tie. Heaven forbid that we should enter on a defence of French morals, most of all in relation to marriage! But it is undeniable, that unions formed in the maturity of thought and feeling, and grounded only on inherent fitness and mutual attraction, tended to bring women into more intelligent sympathy with men, and to heighten and complicate their share in the political drama. The quiescence and security of the conjugal relation, are doubtless favourable to the manifestation of the highest qualities by persons who have already attained a high standard of culture, but rarely foster a passion sufficient to rouse all the faculties to aid in winning or retaining its beloved object – to convert indolence into activity, indifference into ardent partisanship, dullness into perspicuity. Gallantry and intrigue are sorry enough things in themselves, but they certainly serve better to arouse the dormant faculties of woman than embroidery and domestic drudgery, especially when, as in the high society of France in the seventeenth century, they are refined by the influence of Spanish chivalry, and controlled by the spirit of Italian causticity. The dreamy and fantastic girl was awakened to reality by the experience of wifehood and maternity, and became capable of loving, not a mere phantom of her own imagination, but a living man, struggling with the hatreds and rivalries of the political arena; she espoused his quarrels, she made herself, her fortune, and her influence, the stepping-stones of his ambition; and the languid beauty, who had formerly seemed ready to 'die of a rose', was seen to become the heroine of an insurrection. The vivid interest in affairs which was thus excited in woman, must obviously have tended to quicken her intellect, and give it a practical application; and the very sorrows – the heart-pangs and regrets which are inseparable from a life of passion – deepened her nature by the questioning of self and destiny which they occasioned, and by the energy demanded to surmount them and live on. No wise person, we imagine, wishes to restore the social condition of France in the seventeenth century, or considers the ideal programme of woman's life to be a *mariage de convenance* at fifteen, a career of gallantry from twenty to eight-and-thirty, and penitence and piety for the rest of her days. Nevertheless, that social condition had its good results, as much as the madly-superstitious Crusades had theirs.

But the most indisputable source of feminine culture and development in France was the influence of the *salons*; which, as all the world knows, were *réunions* of both sexes, where conversation ran along the whole gamut of subjects, from the frothiest *vers de société* to the philosophy of Descartes. Richelieu[9] had set the fashion of uniting a taste for letters with the habits of polite society and the pursuits of ambition; and in the first quarter of the seventeenth century, there were already several hôtels in Paris, varying in social position from the closest proximity of the Court to the debatable ground of the aristocracy and the bourgeoisie, which

served as a rendezvous for different circles of people, bent on
entertaining themselves either by showing talent or admiring it.
The most celebrated of these rendezvous was the Hôtel de Rambouillet, which was at the culmination of its glory in 1630, and did
not become quite extinct until 1648, when, the troubles of the
Fronde commencing, its *habitués* were dispersed or absorbed by
political interests. The presiding genius of this *salon*, the Marquise
de Rambouillet,[10] was the very model of the woman who can act
as an amalgam to the most incongruous elements; beautiful, but
not preoccupied by coquetry or passion; an enthusiastic admirer
of talent, but with no pretensions to talent on her own part;
exquisitely refined in language and manners, but warm and
generous withal; not given to entertain her guests with her own
compositions, or to paralyse them by her universal knowledge. She
had once *meant* to learn Latin, but had been prevented by an
illness; perhaps she was all the better acquainted with Italian
and Spanish productions, which, in default of a national literature, were then the intellectual pabulum of all cultivated persons
in France who were unable to read the classics. In her mild,
agreeable presence was accomplished that blending of the high-
toned chivalry of Spain with the caustic wit and refined irony of
Italy, which issued in the creation of a new standard of taste – the
combination of the utmost exaltation in sentiment with the utmost
simplicity of language. Women are peculiarly fitted to further
such a combination, – first, from their greater tendency to mingle
affection and imagination with passion, and thus subtilize it into
sentiment; and next, from that dread of what over-taxes their
intellectual energies, either by difficulty or monotony, which gives
them an instinctive fondness for lightness of treatment and airiness
of expression, thus making them cut short all prolixity and reject
all heaviness. When these womanly characteristics were brought
into conversational contact with the materials furnished by such
minds as those of Richelieu, Corneille, the Great Condé, Balzac,
and Bossuet, it is no wonder that the result was something piquant
and charming. Those famous *habitués* of the Hôtel de Rambouillet
did not, apparently, first lay themselves out to entertain the ladies
with grimacing 'small-talk', and then take each other by the sword-
knot to discuss matters of real interest in a corner; they rather

sought to present their best ideas in the guise most acceptable to intelligent and accomplished women. And the conversation was not of literature only; war, politics, religion, the lightest details of daily news – everything was admissible, if only it were treated with refinement and intelligence. The Hôtel de Rambouillet was no mere literary *réunion*; it included *hommes d'affaires* and soldiers as well as authors, and in such a circle, women would not become *bas bleus* or dreamy moralizers, ignorant of the world and of human nature, but intelligent observers of character and events. It is easy to understand, however, that with the herd of imitators who, in Paris and the provinces, aped the style of this famous *salon*, simplicity degenerated into affectation, and nobility of sentiment was replaced by an inflated effort to outstrip nature, so that the *genre précieux* drew down the satire, which reached its climax in the *Précieuses ridicules* and *Les Femmes savantes*,[11] the former of which appeared in 1660, and the latter in 1673. But Madelon and Cathos[12] are the lineal descendants of Mademoiselle Scudéry[13] and her satellites quite as much as of the Hôtel de Rambouillet. The society which assembled every Saturday in her *salon* was exclusively literary, and, although occasionally visited by a few persons of high birth, bourgeois in its tone, and enamoured of madrigals, sonnets, stanzas, and *bouts rimés*.[14] The affectation that decks trivial things in fine language, belongs essentially to a class which sees another above it, and is uneasy in the sense of its inferiority; and this affectation is precisely the opposite of the original *genre précieux*.

Another centre from which feminine influence radiated into the national literature was the Palais du Luxembourg, where Mademoiselle d'Orleans,[15] in disgrace at court on account of her share in the Fronde, held a little court of her own, and for want of anything else to employ her active spirit, busied herself with literature. One fine morning, it occurred to this princess to ask all the persons who frequented her court, among whom were Madame de Sévigné, Madame de la Fayette, and La Rochefoucauld,[16] to write their own portraits, and she at once set the example. It was understood that defects and virtues were to be spoken of with like candour. The idea was carried out; those who were not clever or not bold enough to write for themselves employing the pen of a friend.

'Such,' says M. Cousin, 'was the pastime of Mademoiselle and her friends during the years 1657 and 1658: from this pastime proceeded a complete literature. In 1659, Ségrais revised these portraits, added a considerable number in prose and even in verse, and published the whole in a handsome quarto volume, admirably printed, and now become very rare, under the title, *Divers Portraits*. Only thirty copies were printed, not for sale, but to be given as presents by Mademoiselle. The work had a prodigious success. That which had made the fortune of Mademoiselle de Scudéry's romances – the pleasure of seeing one's portrait a little flattered, curiosity to see that of others, the passion which the middle class always have had and will have for knowing what goes on in the aristocratic world (at that time not very easy of access), the names of the illustrious persons who were here for the first time described physically and morally with the utmost detail, great ladies transformed all at once into writers, and unconsciously inventing a new manner of writing, of which no book gave the slightest idea, and which was the ordinary manner of speaking of the aristocracy; this undefinable mixture of the natural, the easy, and at the same time of the agreeable, and supremely distinguished – all this charmed the court and the town, and very early in the year 1659 permission was asked of Mademoiselle to give a new edition of the privileged book for the use of the public in general.

The fashion thus set, portraits multiplied throughout France, until in 1688, La Bruyère[17] adopted the form in his *Characters*, and ennobled it by divesting it of personality. We shall presently see that a still greater work than La Bruyère's also owed its suggestion to a woman, whose *salon* was hardly a less fascinating resort than the Hôtel de Rambouillet itself.

In proportion as the literature of a country is enriched and culture becomes more generally diffused, personal influence is less effective in the formation of taste and in the furtherance of social advancement. It is no longer the coterie which acts on literature, but literature which acts on the coterie; the circle represented by the word *public*, is ever widening, and ambition, poising itself in order to hit a more distant mark, neglects the successes of the *salon*. What was once lavished prodigally in conversation, is reserved for the volume, or the 'article'; and the effort is not to betray originality rather than to communicate it. As the old coach-roads have sunk into disuse through the creation of railways, so journalism tends more and more to divert information from the channel of conversation into the channel of the Press: no one is satisfied with a more circumscribed audience than that very indeterminate abstraction 'the public', and men find a vent for their opinions not in talk, but in 'copy'. We read the *Athenæum* askance at the tea-table, and take notes from the *Philosophical Journal* at a soirée; we invite our friends that we may thrust a book into their hands, and presuppose an exclusive desire in the 'ladies' to discuss their own matters, 'that we may crackle the *Times*' at our ease. In fact, the evident tendency of things to contract personal communication within the narrowest limits makes us tremble lest some further development of the electric telegraph should reduce us to a society of mutes, or to a sort of insects, communicating by ingenious antennæ of our own invention. Things were far from having reached this pass in the last century; but even then, literature and society had outgrown the nursing of coteries, and although many *salons* of that period were worthy successors of the Hôtel de Rambouillet, they were simply a recreation, not an influence. Enviable evenings, no doubt, were passed in them; and if we could be carried back to any of them at will, we should hardly know whether to choose the Wednesday dinner at Madame Geoffrin's, with d'Alembert, Mademoiselle de l'Espinasse, Grimm, and the rest,[18] or the graver society which, thirty years later, gathered round Condorcet and his lovely young wife.[19] The *salon* retained its attractions, but its power was gone: the stream of life had become too broad and deep for such small rills to affect it.

A fair comparison between the Frenchwomen of the seventeenth century and those of the eighteenth would, perhaps, have a balanced result, though it is common to be a partisan on this subject. The former have more exaltation, perhaps more nobility of sentiment, and less consciousness in their intellectual activity – less of the *femme auteur*, which was Rousseau's horror in Madame d'Epinay;[20] but the latter have a richer fund of ideas – not more ingenuity, but the materials of an additional century for their ingenuity to work upon. The women of the seventeenth century, when love was on the wane, took to devotion, at first mildly and by halves, as English women take to caps, and finally without compromise; with the women of the eighteenth century, Bossuet and Massillon[21] had given way to Voltaire and Rousseau; and when youth and beauty failed, then they were thrown on their own moral strength.

M. Cousin is especially enamoured of the women of the seventeenth century, and relieves himself from his labours in philosophy by making researches into the original documents which throw light upon their lives. Last year he gave us some results of these researches, in a volume on the youth of the Duchesse de Longueville;[22] and he has just followed it up with a second volume, in which he further illustrates her career by tracing it in connexion with that of her friend, Madame de Sablé. The materials to which he has had recourse for this purpose, are chiefly two celebrated collections of manuscripts: that of Conrart,[23] the first secretary to the French Academy, one of those universally curious people who seem made for the annoyance of contemporaries and the benefit of posterity; and that of Valant, who was at once the physician, the secretary, and general steward of Madame de Sablé, and who, with or without her permission, possessed himself of the letters addressed to her by her numerous correspondents during the latter part of her life, and of various papers having some personal or literary interest attached to them. From these stores M. Cousin has selected many documents previously unedited; and though he often leaves us something to desire in the arrangement of his materials, this volume of his on Madame de Sablé is very acceptable to us, for she interests us quite enough to carry us through more than three hundred pages of rather scattered narrative, and through an appendix of correspondence in small type. M. Cousin justly appreciates her character as 'un heureux mélange de raison, d'esprit, d'agrément, et de bonté';[24] and perhaps there are few better specimens of the woman who is extreme in nothing, but sympathetic in all things; who affects us by no special quality, but by her entire being; whose nature has no *tons criards*, but is like those textures which, from their harmonious blending of all colours, give repose to the eye, and do not weary us though we see them every day. Madame de Sablé is also a striking example of the one order of influence which woman has exercised over literature in France; and on this ground, as well as intrinsically, she is worth studying. If the reader agrees with us he will perhaps be inclined, as we are, to dwell a little on the chief points in her life and character.

Madeline de Souvré, daughter of the Marquis of Courtenvaux, a nobleman distinguished enough to be chosen as governor of Louis XIII, was born in 1599, on the threshold of that seventeenth century, the brilliant genius of which is mildly reflected in her mind and history. Thus, when in 1635 her more celebrated friend, Mademoiselle de Bourbon,[25] afterwards the Duchesse de Longueville, made her appearance at the Hôtel de Rambouillet, Madame de Sablé had nearly crossed that table-land of maturity which precedes a woman's descent towards old age. She had been married, in 1614, to Philippe Emanuel de Laval-Montmorency, Seigneur de Bois-Dauphin, and Marquis de Sablé, of whom nothing further is known than that he died in 1640, leaving her the richer by four children, but with a fortune considerably embarrassed. With beauty and high rank added to the mental attractions of which we have abundant evidence, we may well believe that Madame de Sablé's youth was brilliant. For her beauty, we have the testimony of sober Madame de Motteville, who also speaks of her as having 'beaucoup de lumière et de sincérité';[26] and in the following passage very graphically indicates one phase of Madame de Sablé's character: –

The Marquise de Sablé was one of those whose beauty made the most noise when the Queen came into France. But if she was amiable, she was still more desirous of appearing so; this lady's self-love rendered her too sensitive to the regard which men exhibited towards her. There yet existed in France some remains of the politeness which Catherine de Médici had introduced from Italy, and the new dramas, with all the other works in prose and verse, which came from Madrid, were thought to have such great delicacy, that she (Madame de Sablé) had conceived a high idea of the gallantry which the Spaniards had learned from the Moors.

She was persuaded that men can, without crime, have tender sentiments for women – that the desire of pleasing them led men to the greatest and finest actions – roused their intelligence, and inspired them with liberality, and all sorts of virtues; but, on the other hand, women, who were the ornament of the world, and made to be served and adored, ought not to admit anything from them but their respectful attentions. As this lady supported her views with much talent and great beauty, she had given them authority in her time, and the number and consideration of those who continued to associate with her, have caused to subsist in our day what the Spaniards call *finezas*.

Here is the grand element of the original *femme précieuse*, and it appears further, in a detail also reported by Madame de Motteville, that Madame de Sablé had a passionate admirer in the accomplished Duc de Montmorency, and apparently reciprocated his regard; but discovering (at what period of their attachment is unknown) that he was raising a lover's eyes towards the Queen, she broke with him at once. 'I have heard her say,' tells Madame de Motteville, 'that her pride was such with regard to the Duc de Montmorency, that at the first demonstrations which he gave of his change, she refused to see him any more, being unable to receive with satisfaction attentions which she had to share with the greatest princess in the world.' There is no evidence, except the untrustworthy assertion of Tallemant de Réaux,[27] that Madame de Sablé had any other liaison than this; and the probability of the negative is increased by the ardour of her friendships. The strongest of these was formed early in life with Mademoiselle Dona d'Attichy, afterwards Comtesse de Maure; it survived the effervescence of youth and the closest intimacy of middle age, and was only terminated by the death of the latter in 1663. A little incident in this friendship is so characteristic in the transcendentalism which was then carried into all the affections, that it is worth relating at length. Mademoiselle d'Attichy, in her grief and indignation at Richelieu's treatment of her relative, quitted Paris, and was about to join her friend at Sablé, when she suddenly discovered that Madame de Sablé, in a letter to Madame de Rambouillet, had said, that her greatest happiness would be to pass her life with Julie de Rambouillet, afterwards Madame de Montausier. To Anne d'Attichy this appears nothing less than the crime of *lèse-amitié*.[28] No explanations will appease her: she refuses to accept the assurance that the offensive expression was used simply out of unreflecting conformity to the style of the Hôtel de Rambouillet – that it was mere '*galimatias*'.[29] She gives up her journey, and writes a letter, which is the only one Madame de Sablé chose to preserve, when, in her period of devotion, she sacrificed the records of her youth. Here it is: –

I have seen this letter in which you tell me there is so much *galimatias*, and I assure you that I have not found any at all. On the contrary, I find everything very plainly expressed, and among others, one which is too explicit for my satisfaction – namely, what you have said to Madame de Rambouillet, that if you tried to imagine a perfectly happy life for yourself, it would be to pass it all alone with Mademoiselle de Rambouillet. You know whether any one can be more persuaded than I am of her merit; but I confess to you that that has not prevented me from being surprised that you could entertain a thought which did so great an injury to our friendship. As to believing that you said this to one, and wrote it to the other, simply for the sake of paying them an agreeable compliment, I have too high an esteem for your courage to be able to imagine that complaisance would cause you thus to betray the sentiments of your heart, especially on a subject in which, as they were unfavourable to me, I think you would have the more reason for concealing them, the affection which I have for you being so well-known to every one, and especially to Mademoiselle de Rambouillet, so that I doubt whether she will not have been more sensible of the wrong you have done me, than of the advantage you have given her. The circumstance of this letter falling into my hands, has forcibly reminded me of these lines of Bertaut: –

> Malheureuse est l'ignorance.
> Et plus malheureux le savoir.[30]

Having through this lost a confidence which alone rendered life support-able to me, it is impossible for me to take the journey so much thought of. For would there be any propriety in travelling sixty miles in this season, in order to burthen you with a person so little suited to you, that after years of a passion without parallel, you cannot help thinking that the greatest pleasure of your life would be to pass it without her? I return, then, into my solitude, to examine the defects which cause me so much unhappiness, and unless I can correct them, I should have less joy than confusion in seeing you.

It speaks strongly for the charm of Madame de Sablé's nature that she was able to retain so susceptible a friend as Mademoiselle d'Attichy in spite of numerous other friendships, some of which, especially that with Madame de Longueville, were far from luke-warm – in spite too of a tendency in herself to distrust the affection of others towards her, and to wait for advances rather than to make them. We find many traces of this tendency in the affection-ate remonstrances addressed to her by Madame de Longueville, now for shutting herself up from her friends, now for doubting that her letters are acceptable. Here is a little passage from one of these remonstrances which indicates a trait of Madame de Sablé, and is in itself a bit of excellent sense, worthy the consideration of lovers and friends in general: –

I am very much afraid that if I leave to you the care of letting me know when I can see you, I shall be a long time without having that pleasure, and that nothing will incline you to procure it me, for I have always observed a certain lukewarmness in your friendship after our *explanations*, from which I have never seen you thoroughly recover; and that is why I dread explanations, for however good they may be in themselves, since they serve to reconcile people, it must always be admitted, to their shame, that they are at least the effect of a bad cause, and that if they remove it for a time they *sometimes leave a certain facility in getting angry again*, which, without diminishing friendship, renders its intercourse less agreeable. It seems to me that I find all this in your behaviour to me; so I am not wrong in sending to know if you wish to have me to-day.

It is clear that Madame de Sablé was far from having what Sainte-Beuve calls the one fault of Madame Necker – absolute perfection. A certain exquisiteness in her physical and moral nature was, as we shall see, the source of more than one weakness, but the perception of these weaknesses, which is indicated in Madame de Longueville's letters, heightens our idea of the attractive qualities which notwithstanding drew from her, at the sober age of forty, such expressions as these: – 'I assure you that you are the person in all the world whom it would be most agreeable to me to see, and there is no one whose intercourse is a ground of truer satisfaction to me. It is admirable that at all times, and amidst all changes, the taste for your society remains in me; and, *if one ought to thank God for the joys which do not tend to salvation*, I should thank him with all my heart for having preserved that to me at a time in which he has taken away from me all others.'

Since we have entered on the chapter of Madame de Sablé's weaknesses, this is the place to mention what was the subject of endless raillery from her friends – her elaborate precaution about her health, and her dread of infection, even from diseases the least communicable. Perhaps this anxiety was founded as much on æsthetic as on physical grounds, on disgust at the details of illness as much as on dread of suffering: with a cold in the head or a bilious complaint, the exquisite *précieuse* must have been considerably less conscious of being 'the ornament of the world', and 'made to be adored'. Even her friendship, strong as it was, was not strong enough to overcome her horror of contagion; for when Mademoiselle de Bourbon, recently become Madame de Longueville, was attacked by small-pox, Madame de Sablé for some time had not courage to visit her, or even to see Mademoiselle de Rambouillet, who was assiduous in her attendance on the patient. A little correspondence *à propos* of these circumstances so well exhibits the graceful badinage in which the great ladies of that day were adepts, that we are tempted to quote one short letter.

Mademoiselle de Rambouillet to the Marquise de Sablé

Mademoiselle de Chalais (*dame de compagnie* to the Marquise) will please to read this letter to Madame la Marquise, *out of* a draught.

Madame,
I do not think it possible to begin my treaty with you too early, for I am convinced that between the first proposition made to me that I should see you, and the conclusion, you will have so many reflections to make, so many physicians to consult, and so many fears to surmount, that I shall have full leisure to air myself. The conditions which I offer to fulfil for this purpose are, not to visit you until I have been three days absent from the Hôtel de Condé (where Madame de Longueville was ill), to choose a frosty day, not to approach you within four paces, not to sit down on more than one seat. You may also have a great fire in your room, burn juniper in the four corners, surround yourself with imperial vinegar, with rue and wormwood. If you can feel yourself safe under these conditions, without my cutting off my hair, I swear to you to execute them religiously; and if you want examples to fortify you, I can tell you that the Queen consented to see M. Chaudebonne, when he had come directly from Mademoiselle de Bourbon's room, and that Madame d'Aiguillon, who has good taste in such matters, and is free from reproach on these points, has just sent me word that if I did not go to see her, she would come to me.

Madame de Sablé betrays in her reply that she winces under this raillery, and thus provokes a rather severe though polite rejoinder, which, added to the fact that Madame de Longueville is convalescent, rouses her courage to the pitch of paying the formidable visit.

Mademoiselle de Rambouillet, made aware, through their mutual friend Voiture, that her sarcasm has cut rather too deep, winds up the matter by writing that very difficult production, a perfectly conciliatory yet dignified apology. Peculiarities like this always deepen with age, and accordingly, fifteen years later, we find Madame D'Orleans, in her *Princesse de Paphlagonia*[31] – a romance in which she describes her court, with the little quarrels and other affairs that agitated it – giving the following amusing picture, or rather caricature, of the extent to which Madame de Sablé carried her pathological mania, which seems to have been shared by her friend the Countess de Maure (Mademoiselle d'Attichy). In the romance, these two ladies appear under the names of the Princesse Parthénie and the Reine de Mionie.

There was not an hour in the day in which they did not confer together on the means of avoiding death, and on the art of rendering themselves immortal. Their conferences did not take place like those of other people; the fear of breathing an air which was too cold or too warm, the dread lest the wind should be too dry or too moist – in short, the imagination that the weather might not be as temperate as they thought necessary for the preservation of their health, caused them to write letters from one room to the other. It would be extremely fortunate if these notes could be found, and formed into a collection. I am convinced that they would contain rules for the regimen of life, precautions even as to the proper time for applying remedies, and also remedies which Hippocrates and Galen, with all their science, never heard of. Such a collection would be very useful to the public, and would be highly profitable to the faculties of Paris and Montpelier. If these letters were discovered, great advantages of all kinds might be derived from them, for they were princesses who had nothing mortal about them but the *knowledge* that they were mortal. In their writings might be learned all politeness in style, and the most delicate manner of speaking on all subjects. There is nothing with which they were not acquainted; they knew the affairs of all the States in the world, through the share they had in all the intrigues of its private members, either in matters of gallantry, as in other things on which their advice was necessary; either to adjust embroilments and quarrels, or to excite them, for the sake of the advantages which their friends could derive from them; – in a word, they were persons through whose hands the secrets of the whole world had to pass. The Princess Parthénie (Madame de Sablé) had a palate as delicate as her mind; nothing could equal the magnificence of the entertainments she gave; all the dishes were exquisite, and her cleanliness was beyond all that could be imagined. It was in their time that writing came into use; previously, nothing was written but marriage contracts, and letters were never heard of; thus it is to them that we owe a practice so convenient in intercourse.

Still later, in 1669, when the most uncompromising of the Port-Royalists[32] seemed to tax Madame de Sablé with lukewarmness that she did not join them at Port-Royal des Champs, we find her writing to the stern M. de Sévigny: 'En vérité, je crois que je ne pourrois mieux faire que de tout quitter et de m'en aller là. Mais que deviendroient ces frayeurs de n'avoir pas de médecins à choisir, ni de chirurgien pour me saigner?'[33]

Mademoiselle, as we have seen, hints at the love of delicate eating, which many of Madame de Sablé's friends numbered among her foibles, especially after her religious career had commenced. She had a genius in *friandise*,[34] and knew how to gratify the palate without offending the highest sense of refinement. Her sympathetic nature showed itself in this as in other things: she was always sending *bonnes bouches*[35] to her friends, and trying to communicate to them her science and taste in the affairs of the table. Madame de Longueville, who had not the luxurious tendencies of her friend, writes – 'Je vous demande au nom de Dieu, que vous ne me prépariez aucun ragoût. Surtout ne me donnez point de festin. Au nom de Dieu, qu'il n'y ait rien que ce qu'on peut manger, car vous savez que c'est inutile pour moi; de plus j'en ai scrupule.'[36] But other friends had more appreciation of her niceties. Voiture thanks her for her melons, and assures her that they are better than those of yesterday; Madame de Choisy hopes that her ridicule of Jansenism will not provoke Madame de Sablé to refuse her the receipt for salad; and La Rochefoucauld writes: 'You cannot do me a greater charity than to permit the bearer of this letter to enter into the mysteries of your marmalade and your genuine preserves, and I humbly entreat you to do everything you can in his favour. If I could hope for two dishes of those preserves, which I did not deserve to eat before, I should be indebted to you all my life.' For our own part, being as far as possible from fraternizing with those spiritual people who convert a deficiency into a principle, and pique themselves on an obtuse palate as a point of superiority, we are not inclined to number Madame de Sablé's *friandise* amongst her defects. M. Cousin, too, is apologetic on this point. He says:

It was only the excess of a delicacy which can be readily understood, and a sort of fidelity to the character of *précieuse*. As the *précieuse* did nothing according to common usage, she could not dine like another. We have cited a passage from Madame de Motteville, where Madame de Sablé is represented in her first youth at the Hôtel de Rambouillet, maintaining that woman is born to be an ornament to the world, and to receive the adoration of men. The woman worthy of the name, ought always to appear above material wants, and retain, even in the most vulgar details of life, something distinguished and purified. Eating is a very necessary operation, but one which is not agreeable to the eye. Madame de Sablé insisted on its being conducted with a peculiar cleanliness. According to her, it was not every woman who could with impunity be at table in the presence of a lover; the first distortion of the face, she said, would be enough to spoil all. Gross meals, made for the body merely, ought to be abandoned to *bourgeoises*, and the refined woman should appear to take a little nourishment merely to sustain her, and even to divert her, as one takes refreshments and ices. Wealth did not suffice for this; a particular talent was required. Madame de Sablé was a mistress in this art. She had transported the aristocratic spirit and the *genre précieux*, good breeding and good taste, even into cookery. Her dinners, without any opulence, were celebrated and sought after.

It is quite in accordance with all this, that Madame de Sablé should delight in fine scents, and we find that she did; for being threatened, in her Port-Royal days, when she was at an advanced age, with the loss of smell, and writing for sympathy and information to Mère Agnès, who had lost that sense early in life, she receives this admonition from the stern saint: 'You would gain by this loss, my very dear sister, if you made use of it as a satisfaction to God, for having had too much pleasure in delicious scents.' Scarron describes her as

La non pareille Bois-Dauphine,
Entre dames perle très fine,[37]

and the superlative delicacy implied by this epithet seems to have belonged equally to her personal habits, her affections, and her intellect.

Madame de Sablé's life, for anything we know, flowed on evenly enough until 1640, when the death of her husband threw upon her the care of an embarrassed fortune. She found a friend in Réné de Longueil, Seigneur de Maisons, of whom we are content to know no more than that he helped Madame de Sablé to arrange her affairs, though only by means of alienating from her family the estate of Sablé, that his house was her refuge during the blockade of Paris, in 1649, and that she was not unmindful of her obligations to him, when, subsequently, her credit could be serviceable to him at court. In the midst of these pecuniary troubles came a more terrible trial – the loss of her favourite son, the brave and handsome Guy de Laval, who, after a brilliant career in the campaigns of Condé, was killed at the siege of Dunkirk, in 1646, when scarcely four-and-twenty. The fine qualities of this young man had endeared him to the whole army, and especially to Condé, had won him the hand of the Chancellor Séguire's daughter, and had thus opened to him the prospect of the highest honours. His loss seems to have been the most real sorrow of Madame de Sablé's life. Soon after followed the commotions of the Fronde, which put a stop to social intercourse, and threw the closest friends into opposite ranks. According to Lenet, who relies on the authority of Gourville, Madame de Sablé was under strong obligations to the court, being in the receipt of a pension of 2,000 crowns; at all events, she adhered throughout to the Queen and Mazarin, but being as far as possible from a fierce partisan, and given both by disposition and judgement to hear both sides of a question, she acted as a conciliator, and retained her friends of both parties. The Countess de Maure, whose husband was the most obstinate of *frondeurs*,[38] remained throughout her most cherished friend, and she kept up a constant correspondence with the lovely and intrepid heroine of the Fronde, Madame de Longueville. Her activity was directed to the extinction of animosities, by bringing about marriages between the Montagues and Capulets of the Fronde – between the Prince de Condé, or his brother, and the niece of Mazarin, or between the three nieces of Mazarin and the sons of three noblemen who were distinguished leaders of the Fronde. Though her projects were not realized, her conciliatory position enabled her to preserve all her friendships intact, and when the political tempest was over,

she could assemble around her in her residence, in the Place
Royale, the same society as before. Madame de Sablé was now
approaching her twelfth lustrum, and though the charms of her
mind and character made her more sought after than most younger
women, it is not surprising that, sharing as she did in the religious
ideas of her time, the concerns of 'salvation' seemed to become
pressing. A religious retirement, which did not exclude the reception of literary friends, or the care for personal comforts, made the
most becoming frame for age and diminished fortune. Jansenism
was then to ordinary Catholicism what Puseyism is to ordinary
Church of Englandism in these days – it was a *recherché* form of
piety unshared by the vulgar; and one sees at once that it must
have special attractions for the *précieuse*. Madame de Sablé, then,
probably about 1655 or 1656, determined to retire to Port-Royal,
not because she was already devout, but because she hoped to
become so; as, however, she wished to retain the pleasure of
intercourse with friends who were still worldly, she built for herself
a set of apartments at once distinct from the monastery and
attached to it. Here, with a comfortable establishment, consisting
of her secretary, Dr Valant, Mademoiselle de Chalais, formerly
her *dame de compagnie*, and now become her friend; an excellent
cook; a few other servants, and for a considerable time a carriage
and coachman; with her best friends within a moderate distance,
she could, as M. Cousin says, be out of the noise of the world
without altogether forsaking it, preserve her dearest friendships,
and have before her eyes edifying examples – 'vaquer enfin à son
aise aux soins de son salut et à ceux de sa santé'.[39]

We have hitherto looked only at one phase of Madame de
Sablé's character and influence – that of the *précieuse*. But she was
much more than this: she was the valuable, trusted friend of noble
women and distinguished men; she was the animating spirit of a
society whence issued a new form of French literature: she was the
woman of large capacity and large heart, whom Pascal sought to
please, to whom Arnauld submitted the Discourse prefixed to his
Logic, and to whom La Rochefoucauld writes: 'Vous savez que je
ne crois que vous êtes sûr de certains chapitres, et surtout sur
les replis du cœur.'[40] The papers preserved by her secretary,
Valant, show that she maintained an extensive correspondence

with persons of various rank and character; that her pen was untiring in the interest of others; that men made her the depositary of their thoughts, women of their sorrows; that her friends were as impatient, when she secluded herself, as if they had been rival lovers and she a youthful beauty. It is into her ear that Madame de Longueville pours her troubles and difficulties, and that Madame de La Fayette communicates her little alarms, lest young Count de St Paul should have detected her intimacy with La Rochefoucauld.* The few of Madame de Sablé's letters which survive show that she excelled in that epistolary style which was the speciality of the Hôtel de Rambouillet; one to Madame de Montausier, in favour of M. Périer, the brother-in-law of Pascal, is a happy mixture of good taste and good sense; but amongst them all we prefer quoting one to the Duchesse de la Trimouille. It is light and pretty, and made out of almost nothing, like soap-bubbles.

Je crois qu'il n'y a que moi qui face si bien tout le contraire de ce que je veux faire, car il est vrai qu'il n'y a personne que j'honore plus que vous et j'ai si bien fait qu'il est quasi impossible que vous le puissiez croire. Ce n'estoit pas assez pour vous persuader que je suis indigne de vos bonnes grâces et de votre souvenir que d'avoir manqué fort longtemps à vous écrire; il falloit encore retarder quinze jours à me donner l'honneur de répondre à votre lettre. En vérité, madame, cela me fait parôitre si coupable, que vers tout autre que vous j'aimerois mieux l'etre en effet que d'entreprendre une chose si difficile qu'est celle de me justifier. Mais je me sens si innocente dans mon âme, et j'ai tant d'estime, de respect et d'affection pour vous, qu'il me semble que vous devez le connôitre à cent lieues de distance d'ici, encore que je ne vous dise pas un mot. C'est ce que me donne le courage de vous écrire à cette heure, mais non pas ce qui m'en a empêché si longtemps. J'ai commencé à faillir par force, ayant eu beaucoup de maux, et depuis je l'ai fait par honte, et je vous avoue que si

---

* The letter to which we allude has this charming little touch; – 'Je hais comme la mort que les gens de son age puissent croire que j'ai des galanteries. Il semble qu'on leur parait cent ans des qu'on est plus vieille qu' eux, et ils sont tout propre à s'étonner qu'il y ait encore question des gens.' [This translates as 'I hate like death the idea that people of his own age might believe me to have liaisons. To all appearances one is deemed to be a hundred years old the moment one is older than they – and they are all too prone to wonder at there still being men ['gens' may be translated in various ways] about one.' (Editors)].

je n'avois à cette heure la confiance que vous m 'avez donnée en me
rassurant, et celle que je tire de mes propres sentimens pour vous, je
n'oserois jamais entreprendre de vous faire souvenir de moi; mais je
m'assure que vous oublierez tout, sur la protestation que je vous fais de ne
me laisser plus endurceir en mes fautes et de demeurer inviolablement,
madame, votre, etc.[41]

Was not the woman, who could unite the ease and grace indicated by this letter, with an intellect that men thought worth
consulting on matters of reasoning and philosophy, with warm
affections, untiring activity for others, no ambition as an authoress,
and an insight into *confitures* and *ragoûts*, a rare combination? No
wonder that her *salon* at Port-Royal was the favourite resort of
such women as Madame de La Fayette, Madame de Montausier,
Madame de Longueville, and Madame de Hautefort; and of such
men as Pascal, La Rochefoucauld, Nicole, and Domat.[42] The
collections of Valant contain papers which show what were the
habitual subjects of conversation in this *salon*. Theology, of course,
was a chief topic; but physics and metaphysics had their turn, and
still more frequently morals, taken in their widest sense. There
were *Conferences on Calvinism*, of which an abstract is preserved.
When Rohault invented his glass tubes to serve for the baro-
metrical experiments, in which Pascal had roused a strong interest,
the Marquis de Sourdis entertained the society with a paper,
entitled *Why Water Mounts in a Glass Tube*.[43] Cartesianism was an
exciting topic here, as well as everywhere else in France; it had its
partisans and opponents; and papers were read, containing
Thoughts on the Opinions of M. Descartes. These lofty matters were
varied by discussions on love and friendship, on the drama, and on
most of the things in heaven and earth which the philosophy of
that day dreamt of. Morals – generalizations on human affections,
sentiments, and conduct – seem to have been the favourite theme;
and the aim was to reduce these generalizations to their briefest
form of expression, to give them the epigrammatic turn which
made them portable in the memory. This was the specialty of
Madame de Sablé's circle, and was, probably, due to her own
tendency. As the Hôtel de Rambouillet was the nursery of graceful
letter-writing, and the Luxembourg of 'portraits' and 'characters',
so Madame de Sablé's *salon* fostered that taste for the sententious

style, to which we owe, probably, some of the best *Pensées* of Pascal, and, certainly, the *Maximes* of La Rochefoucauld. Madame de Sablé herself wrote maxims, which were circulated among her friends; and, after her death, were published by the Abbé d'Ailly. They have the excellent sense and nobility of feeling which we should expect in everything of hers; but they have no stamp of genius or individual character: they are, to the *Maximes* of La Rochefoucauld, what the vase moulded in dull, heavy clay, is to the vase which the action of fire has made light, brittle, and transparent. She also wrote a treatise on Education, which is much praised by La Rochefoucauld and M. d'Andilly; but which seems no longer to be found: probably it was not much more elaborate than her so-called 'Treatise on Friendship', which is but a short string of maxims. Madame de Sablé's forte was evidently not to write herself, but to stimulate others to write; to show that sympathy and appreciation which are as genial and encouraging as the morning sunbeams. She seconded a man's wit with under-standing – one of the best offices which womanly intellect has rendered to the advancement of culture; and the absence of originality made her all the more receptive towards the originality of others.

The manuscripts of Pascal show that many of the *Pensées*, which are commonly supposed to be raw materials for a great work on religion, were remodelled again and again, in order to bring them to the highest degree of terseness and finish, which would hardly have been the case if they had only been part of a quarry for a greater production. Thoughts which are merely collected as ma-terials, as stones out of which a building is to be erected, are not cut into facets, and polished like amethysts or emeralds. Since Pascal was from the first in the habit of visiting Madame de Sablé at Port-Royal, with his sister, Madame Périer (who was one of Madame de Sablé's dearest friends), we may well suppose that he would throw some of his jewels among the large and small coin of maxims, which were a sort of subscription-money there. Many of them have an epigrammatic piquancy, which was just the thing to charm a circle of vivacious and intelligent women; they seem to come from a La Rochefoucauld, who has been dipped over again in philosophy and wit, and received a new layer. But whether or not Madame de Sablé's influence served to enrich the *Pensées* of Pascal, it is clear that but for her influence the *Maximes* of La Rochefoucauld would never have existed. Just as in some circles the effort is, who shall make the best puns (*horribile dictu!*), or the best charades, in the *salon* of Port-Royal the amusement was to fabricate maxims. La Rochefoucauld said, 'L'envie de faire des maximes se gagne comme le rhume.'[44] So far from claiming for himself the initiation of this form of writing, he accuses Jacques Esprit, another *habitué* of Madame de Sablé's *salon*, of having excited in him the taste for maxims, in order to trouble his repose. The said Esprit was an academician, and had been a frequenter of the Hôtel de Rambouillet. He had already published *Maximes en vers*, and he subsequently produced a book called *La Fausseté des vertus humaines*, which seems to consist of Rochefoucauldism become flat with an infusion of sour Calvinism. Nevertheless, La Rochefoucauld seems to have prized him, to have appealed to his judgement, and to have concocted maxims with him, which he afterwards begs him to submit to Madame de Sablé. He sends a little batch of maxims to her himself, and asks for an equivalent in the shape of good eatables: 'Voilà tout ce que j'ai de maximes; mais comme je ne donne rien pour rien, je vous demande un potage aux carottes, un ragoût de mouton,' etc.[45] The taste and the talent enhanced each other; until, at last, La Rochefoucauld began to be conscious of his pre-eminence in the circle of maxim-mongers, and thought of a wider audience. Thus grew up the famous *Maximes*, about which little need be said. Every one is now convinced, or professes to be convinced, that, as to form, they are perfect, and that as to matter, they are at once undeniably true and miserably false; true as applied to that condition of human nature in which the selfish instincts are still dominant, false if taken as a representation of all the elements and possibilities of human nature. We think La Rochefoucauld himself wavered as to their universality, and that this wavering is indicated in the qualified form of some of the maxims; it occasionally struck him that the shadow of virtue must have a substance, but he had never grasped that substance – it had never been present to his consciousness.

It is curious to see La Rochefoucauld's nervous anxiety about presenting himself before the public as an author; far from rushing into print, he stole into it, and felt his way by asking private opinions. Through Madame de Sablé he sent manuscript copies to various persons of taste and talent, both men and women, and many of the written opinions which she received in reply are still in existence. The women generally find the maxims distasteful, but the men write approvingly. These men, however, are for the most part ecclesiastics who decry human nature that they may exalt divine grace. The coincidence between Augustinianism or Calvinism, with its doctrine of human corruption, and the hard cynicism of the maxims, presents itself in quite a piquant form in some of the laudatory opinions of La Rochefoucauld. One writer says: – 'On ne pourroit faire une instruction plus propre à un catéchumène pour convertir à Dieu son esprit et sa volonté ... Quand il n'y auroit que cet escrit au monde et l'Evangile je voudrois être chrétien. L'un m'apprendroit à connoistre mes misères, et l'autre à implorer mon libérateur.'[46] Madame de Maintenon sends word to La Rochefoucauld, after the publication of his work, that the Book of Job and the *Maximes* are her only reading!

That Madame de Sablé herself had a tolerably just idea of La Rochefoucauld's character, as well as of his maxims, may be gathered not only from the fact that her own maxims are as full of the confidence in human goodness which La Rochefoucauld wants, as they are empty of the style which he possesses, but also from a letter in which she replies to the criticisms of Madame de Schomberg. 'The author,' she says, 'derived the maxim on indolence from his own disposition, for never was there so great an indolence as his, and I think that his heart, inert as it is, owes this defect as much to his idleness as his will. It has never permitted him to do the last action for others; and I think that, amidst all his great desires and great hopes, he is sometimes indolent even on his own behalf.' Still she must have felt a hearty interest in the *Maximes*, as in some degree her foster-child, and she must also have had considerable affection for the author, who was lovable enough to those who observed the rule of Helvetius, and expected nothing from him. She not only assisted him, as we have seen, in getting criticisms, and carrying out the improvements suggested by them, but when the book was actually published, she prepared a notice of it for the only journal then existing – the *Journal des savants*. This notice was originally a brief statement of the nature of the work, and the opinions which had been formed for and against it, with a moderate eulogy, in conclusion, on its good sense, wit, and insight into human nature. But when she submitted it to La Rochefoucauld he objected to the paragraph which stated the adverse opinion, and requested her to alter it. She, however, was either unable or unwilling to modify her notice, and returned it with the following note: –

Je vous envoie ce que j'ai pu tirer de ma teste pour mettre dans le *Journal des savants*. J'y ai mis cet endroit qui vous est le plus sensible, afin que cela vous fasse surmonter la mauvaise honte qui vous fit mettre la préface sans y rien retrancher, et je n'ai pas craint de le mettre, parce que je suis assurée que vous ne le ferez pas imprimer, quand même le reste vous plairoit. Je vous assure aussi que je vous serai plus obligée, si vous en usez comme d'une chose qui servit à vous pour le corriger ou pour le jeter au feu. Nous autres grands auteurs, nous sommes trop riches pour craindre de rien perdre de nos productions. Mandez-moi ce qu'il vous semble de ce dictum.[47]

La Rochefoucauld availed himself of this permission, and 'edited' the notice, touching up the style, and leaving out the blame. In this revised form it appeared in the *Journal des savants*. In some points, we see, the youth of journalism was not without promise of its future.

While Madame de Sablé was thus playing the literary confidante to La Rochefoucauld, and was the soul of a society whose chief interest was the *belles lettres*, she was equally active in graver matters. She was in constant intercourse or correspondence with the devout women of Port-Royal, and of the neighbouring convent of the Carmelites, many of whom had once been the ornaments of the court; and there is a proof that she was conscious of being highly valued by them in the fact that when the Princess Marie-Madeline, of the Carmelites, was dangerously ill, not being able or not daring to visit her, she sent her youthful portrait to be hung up in the sick-room, and received from the same Mère Agnès whose grave admonition we have quoted above, a charming note, describing the pleasure which the picture had given in the in-firmary of 'Notre bonne Mère'. She was interesting herself deeply in the translation of the New Testament, which was the work of Sacy, Arnauld, Nicole, Le Maître, and the Duc de Luynes con-jointly, Sacy having the principal share. We have mentioned that Arnauld asked her opinion on the Discourse prefixed to his *Logic*, and we may conclude from this that he had found her judgement valuable in many other cases. Moreover, the persecution of the Port-Royalists had commenced, and she was uniting with Madame de Longueville in aiding and protecting her pious friends. Mod-erate in her Jansenism,[48] as in everything else, she held that the famous formulary denouncing the Augustinian doctrine, and de-claring it to have been originated by Jansenius, should be signed without reserve, and, as usual, she had faith in conciliatory measures; but her moderation was no excuse for inaction. She was at one time herself threatened with the necessity of abandoning her residence at Port-Royal, and had thought of retiring to a religious house at Auteuil, a village near Paris. She did, in fact, pass some summers there, and she sometimes took refuge with her brother, the Commandeur de Souvré, with Madame de Mon-tausier, or Madame de Longueville. The last was much bolder in her partisanship than her friend, and her superior wealth and position enabled her to give the Port-Royalists more efficient aid. Arnauld and Nicole resided five years in her house; it was under her protection that the translation of the New Testament was carried on and completed, and it was chiefly through her efforts that, in 1669, the persecution was brought to an end. Madame de Sablé co-operated with all her talent and interest in the same direction; but here, as elsewhere, her influence was chiefly valuable in what she stimulated others to do, rather than in what she did herself. It was by her that Madame de Longueville was first won to the cause of Port-Royal; and we find this ardent brave woman constantly seeking the advice and sympathy of her more timid and self-indulgent, but sincere and judicious friend.

In 1669, when Madame de Sablé had at length rest from these anxieties, she was at the good old age of seventy, but she lived nine years longer – years, we may suppose, chiefly dedicated to her spiritual concerns. This gradual, calm decay allayed the fear of death which had tormented her more vigorous days; and she died with tranquillity and trust. It is a beautiful trait of these last moments, that she desired not to be buried with her family, or even at Port-Royal, among her saintly and noble companions, but in the cemetery of her parish, like one of the people, without pomp or ceremony.

It is worth while to notice, that with Madame de Sablé, as with some other remarkable Frenchwomen, the part of her life which is richest in interest and results, is that which is looked forward to by most of her sex with melancholy as the period of decline. When between fifty and sixty, she had philosophers, wits, beauties, and saints clustering around her; and one naturally cares to know what was the elixir which gave her this enduring and general attraction. We think it was, in a great degree, that well-balanced development of mental powers which gave her a comprehension of varied intellectual processes, and a tolerance for varied forms of character, which is still rarer in women than in men. Here was one point of distinction between her and Madame de Longueville; and an amusing passage, which Sainte-Beuve has disinterred from the writings of the Abbé St Pierre, so well serves to indicate, by contrast, what we regard as the great charm of Madame de Sablé's mind, that we shall not be wandering from our subject in quoting it.

I one day asked M. Nicole what was the character of Madame de Longueville's intellect; he told me it was very subtle and delicate in the penetration of character, but very small, very feeble; and that her comprehension was extremely narrow in matters of science and reasoning, and on all speculations that did not concern matters of sentiment. For example, he added, I one day said to her that I could wager and demonstrate that there were in Paris, at least two inhabitants who had the same number of hairs, although I could not point out who these two men were. She told me, I could never be sure of it until I had counted the hairs of these two men. Here is my demonstration, I said: – I take it for granted that the head which is most amply supplied with hairs has not more than 200,000 and the head which is least so has but one hair. Now, if you suppose that 200,000 heads have each a different number of hairs, it necessarily follows that they have each one of the numbers of hairs which form the series from 1 to 200,000; for if it were supposed that there were two among these 200,000 who had the same number of hairs, I should have gained my wager. Supposing, then, that these 200,000 inhabitants have all a different number of hairs, if I add a single inhabitant who has hairs, and who has not more than 200,000, it necessarily follows that this number of hairs, whatever it may be, will be contained in the series from 1 to 200,000, and consequently will be equal to the number of hairs on one of the previous 200,000 inhabitants. Now as, instead of one inhabitant more than 200,000, there are nearly 800,000 inhabitants in Paris, you see clearly that there must be many heads which have an equal number of hairs, though I have not counted them. Still Madame de Longueville could never comprehend that this equality of hairs could be demonstrated, and always maintained that the only way of proving it was to count them.[49]

Surely, the most ardent admirer of feminine shallowness must have felt some irritation when he found himself arrested by this dead wall of stupidity, and have turned with relief to the larger intelligence of Madame de Sablé, who was not the less graceful, delicate, and feminine, because she could follow a train of reasoning, or interest herself in a question of science. In this combination consisted her pre-eminent charm: she was not a genius, not a heroine, but a woman whom men could more than love – whom they could make their friend, confidante, and counsellor; the sharer, not of their joys and sorrows only, but of their ideas and aims.

Such was Madame de Sablé, whose name is, perhaps, new to some of our readers, so far does it lie from the surface of literature and history. We have seen, too, that she was only one amongst a crowd – one in a firmament of feminine stars which, when once the biographical telescope is turned upon them, appear scarcely less remarkable and interesting. Now, if the reader recollects what was the position and average intellectual character of women in the high society of England during the reigns of James I and the two Charleses – the period through which Madame de Sablé's career extends – we think he will admit our position as to the early superiority of womanly development in France: and this fact, with its causes, has not merely an historical interest, it has an important bearing on the culture of women in the present day. Women become superior in France by being admitted to a common fund of ideas, to common objects of interest with men; and this must

ever be the essential condition at once of true womanly culture
and of true social well-being. We have no faith in feminine con-
versazioni, where ladies are eloquent on Apollo and Mars; though
we sympathize with the yearning activity of faculties which,
deprived of their proper material, waste themselves in weaving
fabrics out of cobwebs. Let the whole field of reality be laid open
to woman as well as to man, and then that which is peculiar in her
mental modification, instead of being, as it is now, a source of
discord and repulsion between the sexes, will be found to be a
necessary complement to the truth and beauty of life. Then we
shall have that marriage of minds which alone can blend all the
hues of thought and feeling in one lovely rainbow of promise for
the harvest of human happiness.

Evangelical Teaching: Dr Cumming

(*Westminster Review*, October 1855)

GIVEN, a man with moderate intellect, a moral standard not higher than the average, some rhetorical affluence and great glibness of speech, what is the career in which, without the aid of birth or money, he may most easily attain power and reputation in English society? Where is that Goshen[1] of mediocrity in which a smattering of science and learning will pass for profound instruction, where platitudes will be accepted as wisdom, bigoted narrowness as holy zeal, unctuous egoism as God-given piety? Let such a man become an evangelical preacher; he will then find it possible to reconcile small ability with great ambition, superficial knowledge with the prestige of erudition, a middling morale with a high reputation for sanctity. Let him shun practical extremes and be ultra only in what is purely theoretic: let him be stringent on predestination, but latitudinarian on fasting; unflinching in insisting on the Eternity of punishment, but diffident of curtailing the substantial comforts of Time; ardent and imaginative on the pre-millennial Advent of Christ,[2] but cold and cautious towards every other infringement of the status quo. Let him fish for souls not with the bait of inconvenient singularity, but with the dragnet of comfortable conformity. Let him be hard and literal in his interpretation only when he wants to hurl texts at the heads of unbelievers and adversaries, but when the letter of the Scriptures presses too closely on the genteel Christianity of the nineteenth century, let him use his spiritualizing alembic and disperse it into impalpable ether. Let him preach less of Christ than of Antichrist; let him be less definite in showing what sin is than in showing who is the Man of Sin, less expansive on the blessedness of faith than on the accursedness of infidelity. Above all, let him set up as an interpreter of prophecy, and rival *Moore's Almanack*[3] in the prediction of political events, tickling the interest of hearers who are but moderately spiritual by showing how the Holy Spirit has dictated problems and charades for their benefit, and how, if they are ingenious enough to solve these, they may have their Christian graces nourished by learning precisely to whom they may point as the 'horn that had eyes', 'the lying prophet', and the 'unclean spirits'.[4] In this way he will draw men to him by the strong cords of their passions, made reason-proof by being baptized with the name of piety. In this way he may gain a metropolitan pulpit; the avenues to his church will be as crowded as the passages to the opera; he has but to print his prophetic sermons and bind them in lilac and gold, and they will adorn the drawing-room table of all evangelical ladies, who will regard as a sort of pious 'light reading' the demonstration that the prophecy of the locusts whose sting is in their tail, is fulfilled in the fact of the Turkish commander's having taken a horse's tail for his standard, and that the French are the very frogs predicted in the Revelations.

Pleasant to the clerical flesh under such circumstances is the arrival of Sunday! Somewhat at a disadvantage during the week, in the presence of working-day interests and lay splendours, on Sunday the preacher becomes the cynosure of a thousand eyes, and predominates at once over the Amphitryon[5] with whom he dines, and the most captious member of his church or vestry. He has an immense advantage over all other public speakers. The platform orator is subject to the criticism of hisses and groans. Counsel for the plaintiff expects the retort of counsel for the defendant. The honourable gentleman on one side of the House is liable to have his facts and figures shown up by his honourable friend on the opposite side. Even the scientific or literary lecturer, if he is dull or incompetent, may see the best part of his audience quietly slip out one by one. But the preacher is completely master of the situation: no one may hiss, no one may depart. Like the writer of imaginary conversations, he may put what imbecilities he pleases into the mouths of his antagonists, and swell with triumph when he has refuted them. He may riot in gratuitous assertions, confident that no man will contradict him; he may exercise perfect free-will in logic, and invent illustrative experience;

he may give an evangelical edition of history with the inconvenient
facts omitted: – all this he may do with impunity, certain that
those of his hearers who are not sympathizing are not listening.
For the Press has no band of critics who go the round of the
churches and chapels, and are on the watch for a slip or defect in
the preacher, to make a 'feature' in their article: the clergy are,
practically, the most irresponsible of all talkers. For this reason, at
least, it is well that they do not always allow their discourses to be
merely fugitive, but are often induced to fix them in that black
and white in which they are open to the criticism of any man who
has the courage and patience to treat them with thorough freedom
of speech and pen.

It is because we think this criticism of clerical teaching desirable
for the public good, that we devote some pages to Dr Cumming.
He is, as every one knows, a preacher of immense popularity, and
of the numerous publications in which he perpetuates his pulpit
labours, all circulate widely, and some, according to their title-
page, have reached the sixteenth thousand. Now our opinion of
these publications is the very opposite of that given by a newspaper
eulogist: we do *not* 'believe that the repeated issues of Dr Cumming's thoughts are having a beneficial effect on society', but the
reverse; and hence, little inclined as we are to dwell on his pages,
we think it worth while to do so, for the sake of pointing out in
them what we believe to be profoundly mistaken and pernicious.
Of Dr Cumming personally we know absolutely nothing: our
acquaintance with him is confined to a perusal of his works, our
judgement of him is founded solely on the manner in which he has
written himself down on his pages. We know neither how he looks
nor how he lives. We are ignorant whether, like St Paul, he has a
bodily presence that is weak and contemptible, or whether his
person is as florid and as prone to amplification as his style. For
aught we know, he may not only have the gift of prophecy, but
may bestow the profits of all his works to feed the poor, and be
ready to give his own body to be burned with as much alacrity as
he infers the everlasting burning of Roman-catholics and
Puseyites.[6] Out of the pulpit he may be a model of justice, truthfulness, and the love that thinketh no evil; but we are obliged to
judge of his charity by the spirit we find in his sermons, and shall

only be glad to learn that his practice is, in many respects, an amiable *non sequitur* from his teaching.

Dr Cumming's mind is evidently not of the pietistic order. There is not the slightest leaning towards mysticism in his Christianity – no indication of religious raptures, of delight in God, of spiritual communion with the Father. He is most at home in the forensic view of Justification, and dwells on salvation as a scheme rather than as an experience. He insists on good works as the sign of justifying faith, as labours to be achieved to the glory of God, but he rarely represents them as the spontaneous, necessary outflow of a soul filled with Divine love. He is at home in the external, the polemical, the historical, the circumstantial, and is only episodically devout and practical. The great majority of his published sermons are occupied with argument or philippic against Romanists and unbelievers, with 'vindications' of the Bible, with the political interpretation of prophecy, or the criticism of public events; and the devout aspiration, or the spiritual and practical exhortation, is tacked to them as a sort of fringe in a hurried sentence or two at the end. He revels in the demonstration that the Pope is the Man of Sin; he is copious on the downfall of the Ottoman empire; he appears to glow with satisfaction in turning a story which tends to show how he abashed an 'infidel'; it is a favourite exercise with him to form conjectures of the process by which the earth is to be burned up, and to picture Dr Chalmers and Mr Wilberforce[7] being caught up to meet Christ in the air, while Romanists, Puseyites, and infidels are given over to gnashing of teeth. But of really spiritual joys and sorrows, of the life and death of Christ as a manifestation of love that constrains the soul, of sympathy with that yearning over the lost and erring which made Jesus weep over Jerusalem, and prompted the sublime prayer, 'Father, forgive them', of the gentler fruits of the Spirit, and the peace of God which passeth understanding – of all this, we find little trace in Dr Cumming's discourses.

His style is in perfect correspondence with this habit of mind. Though diffuse, as that of all preachers must be, it has rapidity of movement, perfect clearness, and some aptness of illustration. He has much of that literary talent which makes a good journalist –

the power of beating out an idea over a large space, and of introducing far-fetched *à propos*. His writings have, indeed, no high merit: they have no originality or force of thought, no striking felicity of presentation, no depth of emotion. Throughout nine volumes we have alighted on no passage which impressed us as worth extracting, and placing among the 'beauties' of evangelical writers, such as Robert Hall, Foster the Essayist, or Isaac Taylor.[8] Everywhere there is commonplace cleverness, nowhere a spark of rare thought, of lofty sentiment, or pathetic tenderness. We feel ourselves in company with a voluble retail talker, whose language is exuberant but not exact, and to whom we should never think of referring for precise information, or for well-digested thought and experience. His argument continually slides into wholesale assertion and vague declamation, and in his love of ornament he frequently becomes tawdry. For example, he tells us (*Apocalyptic Sketches*, p. 265), that 'Botany weaves around the cross her amaranthine garlands; and Newton comes from his starry home – Linnæus from his flowery resting-place – and Werner and Hutton from their subterranean graves at the voice of Chalmers, to acknowledge that all they learned and elicited in their respective provinces, has only served to show more clearly that Jesus of Nazareth is enthroned on the riches of the universe': – and so prosaic an injunction to his hearers as that they should choose a residence within an easy distance of church, is magnificently draped by him as an exhortation to prefer a house 'that basks in the sunshine of the countenance of God'. Like all preachers of his class, he is more fertile in imaginative paraphrase than in close exposition, and in this way he gives us some remarkable fragments of what we may call the romance of Scripture, filling up the outline of the record with an elaborate colouring quite undreamed of by more literal minds. The serpent, he informs us, said to Eve, 'Can it be so? Surely you are mistaken, that God hath said you shall die, a creature so fair, so lovely, so beautiful. It is impossible. *The laws of nature and physical science tell you that my interpretation is correct;* you shall not die. I can tell you by my own experience as an angel that you shall be as gods, knowing good and evil' (*Apocalyptic Sketches*, p. 294). Again, according to Dr Cumming, Abel had so clear an idea of the Incarnation and Atonement, that when he offered his sacrifice 'he must have said, "I feel myself a guilty sinner, and that in myself I cannot meet thee alive; I lay on thine altar this victim, and I shed its blood as my testimony that mine should be shed; and I look for forgiveness and undeserved mercy through Him who is to bruise the serpent's head, and whose atonement this typifies"' (*Occasional Discourses, Vol. I,* p. 23). Indeed, his productions are essentially ephemeral; he is essentially a journalist, who writes sermons instead of leading articles, who, instead of venting diatribes against her Majesty's Ministers, directs his power of invective against Cardinal Wiseman and the Puseyites, – instead of declaiming on public spirit, perorates on the 'glory of God'. We fancy he is called, in the more refined evangelical circles, an 'intellectual preacher'; by the plainer sort of Christians, a 'flowery preacher'; and we are inclined to think that the more spiritually-minded class of believers, who look with greater anxiety for the kingdom of God within them than for the visible advent of Christ in 1864, will be likely to find Dr Cumming's declamatory flights and historico-prophetical exercitations as little better than 'clouts o' cauld parritch'.[9]

Such is our general impression from his writings after an attentive perusal. There are some particular characteristics which we shall consider more closely, but in doing so we must be understood as altogether declining any doctrinal discussion. We have no intention to consider the grounds of Dr Cumming's dogmatic system, to examine the principles of his prophetic exegesis, or to question his opinion concerning the little horn, the river Euphrates, or the seven vials.[10] We identify ourselves with no one of the bodies whom he regards it as his special mission to attack: we give our adhesion neither to Romanism, Puseyism, nor to that anomalous combination of opinions which he introduces to us under the name of Infidelity. It is simply as spectators that we criticize Dr Cumming's mode of warfare, and we concern ourselves less with what he holds to be Christian truth than with his manner of enforcing that truth, less with the doctrines he teaches than with the moral spirit and tendencies of his teaching.

One of the most striking characteristics of Dr Cumming's writings is *unscrupulosity of statement.* His motto apparently is, *Christianitatem, quocunque modo, Christianitatem;*[11] and the only system

he includes under the term Christianity is Calvinistic Protestantism. Experience has so long shown that the human brain is a
congenial nidus for inconsistent beliefs, that we do not pause to
inquire how Dr Cumming, who attributes the conversion of the
unbelieving to the Divine Spirit, can think it necessary to co-
operate with that Spirit by argumentative white lies. Nor do we
for a moment impugn the genuineness of his zeal for Christianity,
or the sincerity of his conviction that the doctrines he preaches are
necessary to salvation; on the contrary, we regard the flagrant
unveracity that we find on his pages as an indirect result of that
conviction – as a result, namely, of the intellectual and moral
distortion of view which is inevitably produced by assigning to
dogmas, based on a very complex structure of evidence, the place
and authority of first truths. A distinct appreciation of the value of
evidence – in other words, the intellectual perception of truth – is
more closely allied to truthfulness of statement, or the moral
quality of veracity, than is generally admitted. There is not a
more pernicious fallacy afloat in common parlance, than the wide
distinction made between intellect and morality. Amiable impulses
without intellect, man may have in common with dogs and horses;
but morality, which is specifically human, is dependent on the
regulation of feeling by intellect. All human beings who can be
said to be in any degree moral have their impulses guided, not
indeed always by their own intellect, but by the intellect of human
beings who have gone before them, and created traditions and
associations which have taken the rank of laws.[12] Now that highest
moral habit, the constant preference of truth both theoretically
and practically, pre-eminently demands the co-operation of the
intellect with the impulses; as is indicated by the fact that it is only
found in anything like completeness in the highest class of minds.
In accordance with this we think it is found that, in proportion as
religious sects exalt feeling above intellect, and believe themselves
to be guided by direct inspiration rather than by a spontaneous
exertion of their faculties – that is, in proportion as they are
removed from rationalism – their sense of truthfulness is misty
and confused. No one can have talked to the more enthusiastic
Methodists and listened to their stories of miracles without perceiving that they require no other passport to a statement than

that it accords with their wishes and their general conception of God's dealings; nay, they regard as a symptom of sinful scepticism an inquiry into the evidence for a story which they think unquestionably tends to the glory of God, and in retailing such stories, new particulars, further tending to his glory, are 'borne in' upon their minds. Now, Dr Cumming, as we have said, is no enthusiastic pietist: within a certain circle – within the mill of evangelical orthodoxy, his intellect is perpetually at work; but that principle of sophistication which our friends the Methodists derive from the predominance of their pietistic feelings, is involved for him in the doctrine of verbal inspiration; what is for them a state of emotion submerging the intellect, is with him a formula imprisoning the intellect, depriving it of its proper function – the free search for truth – and making it the mere servant-of-all-work to a foregone conclusion. Minds fettered by this doctrine no longer inquire concerning a proposition whether it is attested by sufficient evidence, but whether it accords with Scripture; they do not search for facts, as such, but for facts that will bear out their doctrine. They become accustomed to reject the more direct evidence in favour of the less direct, and where adverse evidence reaches demonstration they must resort to devices and expedients in order to explain away contradiction. It is easy to see that this mental habit blunts not only the perception of truth, but the sense of truthfulness, and that the man whose faith drives him into fallacies, treads close upon the precipice of falsehood.

We have entered into this digression for the sake of mitigating the inference that is likely to be drawn from that characteristic of Dr Cumming's works to which we have pointed. He is much in the same intellectual condition as that professor of Padua,[13] who, in order to disprove Galileo's discovery of Jupiter's satellites, urged that as there were only seven metals there could not be more than seven planets – a mental condition scarcely compatible with candour. And we may well suppose that if the Professor had held the belief in seven planets, and no more, to be a necessary condition of salvation, his mental vision would have been so dazed that even if he had consented to look through Galileo's telescope, his eyes would have reported in accordance with his inward alarms rather than with the external fact. So long as a belief in propositions is regarded as indispensable to salvation, the pursuit of truth *as such* is not possible, any more than it is possible for a man who is swimming for his life to make meteorological observations on the storm which threatens to overwhelm him. The sense of alarm and haste, the anxiety for personal safety, which Dr Cumming insists upon as the proper religious attitude, unmans the nature, and allows no thorough, calm-thinking, no truly noble, disinterested feeling. Hence, we by no means suspect that the unscrupulosity of statement with which we charge Dr Cumming, extends beyond the sphere of his theological prejudices; we do not doubt that, religion apart, he appreciates and practises veracity.

A grave general accusation must be supported by details, and in adducing these, we purposely select the most obvious cases of misrepresentation – such as require no argument to expose them, but can be perceived at a glance. Among Dr Cumming's numerous books, one of the most notable for unscrupulosity of statement is the *Manual of Christian Evidence*, written, as he tells us in his Preface, not to give the deepest solutions of the difficulties in question, but to furnish Scripture-readers, City Missionaries, and Sunday-school Teachers, with a 'ready reply' to sceptical arguments. This announcement that *readiness* was the chief quality sought for in the solutions here given, modifies our inference from the other qualities which those solutions present; and it is but fair to presume, that when the Christian disputant is not in a hurry, Dr Cumming would recommend replies less ready and more veracious. Here is an example of what in another place* he tells his readers is 'change in their pocket . . . a little ready argument which they can employ, and therewith answer a fool according to his folly'. From the nature of this argumentative small coin, we are inclined to think Dr Cumming understands answering a fool according to his folly to mean, giving him a foolish answer. We quote from the *Manual of Christian Evidence*, p. 62.

Some of the gods which the heathen worshipped were among the greatest monsters that ever walked the earth. Mercury was a thief; and because he was an expert thief, he was enrolled among the gods. Bacchus was a mere

* *Lectures on the Book of Daniel*, p. 6.

sensualist and drunkard; and therefore he was enrolled among the gods. Venus was a dissipated and abandoned courtesan; and therefore she was enrolled among the goddesses. Mars was a savage, that gloried in battle and in blood; and therefore he was deified and enrolled among the gods.

Does Dr Cumming believe the purport of these sentences? If so, this passage is worth handing down as his theory of the Greek myth – as a specimen of the astounding ignorance which was possible in a metropolitan preacher, AD 1854. And if he does not believe them ... The inference must then be, that he thinks delicate veracity about the ancient Greeks is not a Christian virtue, but only a 'splendid sin' of the unregenerate. This inference is rendered the more probable by our finding, a little further on, that he is not more scrupulous about the moderns, if they come under his definition of 'Infidels'. But the passage we are about to quote in proof of this has a worse quality than its discrepancy with fact. Who that has a spark of generous feeling, that rejoices in the presence of good in a fellow-being, has not dwelt with pleasure on the thought that Lord Byron's unhappy career was ennobled and purified towards its close by a high and sympathetic purpose, by honest and energetic efforts for his fellow-men? Who has not read with deep emotion those last pathetic lines, beautiful as the after-glow of sunset, in which love and resignation are mingled with something of a melancholy heroism? Who has not lingered with compassion over the dying scene at Missolonghi – the sufferer's inability to make his farewell messages of love intelligible, and the last long hours of silent pain? Yet for the sake of furnishing his disciples with a 'ready reply', Dr Cumming can prevail on himself to inoculate them with a bad-spirited falsity like the following:

We have one striking exhibition of *an infidel's brightest thoughts*, in some lines *written in his dying moments* by a man, gifted with great genius, capable of prodigious intellectual prowess, but of worthless principle and yet more worthless practices – I mean the celebrated Lord Byron. He says –

> Though gay companions o'er the bowl
>   Dispel awhile the sense of ill,
> Though pleasure fills the maddening soul,
>   The heart – *the heart* is lonely still.

Ay, but to die, and go, alas!
Where all have gone and all must go;
To be the *Nothing* that I was,
Ere born to life and living woe!

Count o'er the joys thine hours have seen,
Count o'er thy days from anguish free,
And know, whatever thou hast been,
'Tis *something better* not to be.

Nay, for myself, so dark my fate
Through every turn of life hath been,
Man and the *world* so much *I hate*,[14]
I care not when I quit the scene.

It is difficult to suppose that Dr Cumming can have been so grossly imposed upon – that he can be so ill-informed as really to believe that these lines were 'written' by Lord Byron in his dying moments; but, allowing him the full benefit of that possibility, how shall we explain his introduction of this feebly rabid doggerel as 'an infidel's brightest thoughts'?

In marshalling the evidences of Christianity, Dr Cumming directs most of his arguments against opinions that are either totally imaginary, or that belong to the past rather than to the present, while he entirely fails to meet the difficulties actually felt and urged by those who are unable to accept Revelation. There can hardly be a stronger proof of misconception as to the character of free-thinking in the present day, than the recommendation of Leland's[15] *Short and Easy Method with the Deists* – a method which is unquestionably short and easy for preachers disinclined to reconsider their stereotyped modes of thinking and arguing, but which has quite ceased to realize those epithets in the conversion of Deists. Yet Dr Cumming not only recommends this book, but takes the trouble himself to write a feebler version of its arguments. For example, on the question of the genuineness and authenticity of the New Testament writings, he says: – 'If, therefore, at a period long subsequent to the death of Christ, a number of men had appeared in the world, drawn up a book which they christened by the name of Holy Scripture, and recorded these things which appear in it as facts when they were only the fancies of their own imagination, surely the *Jews* would have instantly reclaimed that no such events transpired, that no such person as Jesus Christ appeared in their capital, and that *their* crucifixion of Him, and their alleged evil treatment of his apostles, were mere fictions.* It is scarcely necessary to say that, in such argument as this, Dr Cumming is beating the air. He is meeting a hypothesis which no one holds, and totally missing the real question. The only type of 'infidel' whose existence Dr Cumming recognizes is that fossil personage who 'calls the Bible a lie and a forgery'. He seems to be ignorant – or he chooses to ignore the fact – that there is a large body of eminently instructed and earnest men who regard the Hebrew and Christian Scriptures as a series of historical documents, to be dealt with according to the rules of historical criticism, and that an equally large number of men, who are not historical critics, find the dogmatic scheme built on the letter of the Scriptures opposed to their profoundest moral convictions. Dr Cumming's infidel is a man who, because his life is vicious, tries to convince himself that there is no God, and that Christianity is an imposture, but who is all the while secretly conscious that he is opposing the truth, and cannot help 'letting out' admissions 'that the Bible is the Book of God'. We are favoured with the following 'Creed of the Infidel': –

I believe that there is no God, but that matter is God, and God is matter; and that it is no matter whether there is any God or not. I believe also that the world was not made, but that the world made itself, or that it had no beginning, and that it will last for ever. I believe that man is a beast; that the soul is the body, and that the body is the soul; and that after death there is neither body nor soul. I believe that there is no religion, that *natural religion is the only religion, and all religion unnatural.* I believe not in Moses; I believe in the first philosophers. I believe not in the evangelists; I believe in Chubb, Collins, Toland, Tindal, and Hobbes. I believe in Lord Bolingbroke, and I believe not in Saint Paul. I believe not in revelation; *I believe in tradition: I believe in the Talmud: I believe in the Koran;* I believe not in the Bible. I believe in Socrates; I believe in Confucius; I believe in Mahomet; I believe not in Christ. And lastly, *I believe* in all unbelief.

* *Manual of Christian Evidence*, p. 81.

The intellectual and moral monster whose creed is this complex web of contradictions, is, moreover, according to Dr Cumming, a being who unites much simplicity and imbecility with his Satanic hardihood – much tenderness of conscience with his obdurate vice. Hear the 'proof': –

I once met with an acute and enlightened infidel, with whom I reasoned day after day, and for hours together; I submitted to him the internal, the external, and the experimental evidences, but made no impression on his scorn and unbelief. At length I entertained a suspicion that there was something morally, rather than intellectually wrong, and that the bias was not in the intellect, but in the heart; one day therefore I said to him – 'I must now state my conviction, and you may call me uncharitable, but duty compels me; you are living in some known and gross sin.' *The man's countenance became pale; he bowed and left me* (*Manual of Christian Evidence*, p. 254).

Here we have the remarkable psychological phenomenon of an 'acute and enlightened' man who, deliberately purposing to indulge in a favourite sin, and regarding the Gospel with scorn and unbelief, is, nevertheless, so much more scrupulous than the majority of Christians, that he cannot 'embrace sin and the Gospel simultaneously'; who is so alarmed at the Gospel in which he does not believe, that he cannot be easy without trying to crush it; whose acuteness and enlightenment suggest to him, as a means of crushing the Gospel, to argue from day to day with Dr Cumming; and who is withal so naïve that he is taken by surprise when Dr Cumming, failing in argument, resorts to accusation, and so tender in conscience that, at the mention of his sin, he turns pale and leaves the spot. If there be any human mind in existence capable of holding Dr Cumming's 'Creed of the Infidel', of at the same time believing in tradition and 'believing in all unbelief', it must be the mind of the infidel just described, for whose existence we have Dr Cumming's *ex officio* word as a theologian; and to theologians we may apply what Sancho Panza says of the bachelors of Salamanca,[16] that they never tell lies – except when it suits their purpose.

The total absence from Dr Cumming's theological mind of any demarcation between fact and rhetoric is exhibited in another passage, where he adopts the dramatic form: –

Ask the peasant on the hills – *and I have asked amid the mountains of Braemar and Dee-side*, – 'How do you know that this book is Divine, and that the religion you profess is true? You never read Paley?' 'No, I never heard of him.' – 'You have never read Butler?' 'No, I have never heard of him.' – 'Nor Chalmers?' 'No, I do not know him.' – 'You have never read any books on evidence?' 'No, I have read no such books.' – 'Then, how do you know this book is true?' 'Know it! Tell me that the Dee, the Clunie, and the Garrawalt, the streams at my feet, do not run; that the winds do not sigh amid the gorges of these blue hills; that the sun does not kindle the peaks of Loch-na-Gar; tell me my heart does not beat, and I will believe you; but do not tell me the Bible is not Divine. I have found its truth illuminating my footsteps; its consolations sustaining my heart. May my tongue cleave to my mouth's roof, and my right hand forget its cunning, if I ever deny what is my deepest inner experience, that this blessed book is the book of God' (*Church before the Flood*, p. 35).

Dr Cumming is so slippery and lax in his mode of presentation, that we find it impossible to gather whether he means to assert, that this is what a peasant on the mountains of Braemar *did* say, or that it is what such a peasant *would* say: in the one case, the passage may be taken as a measure of his truthfulness; in the other, of his judgement.

His own faith, apparently, has not been altogether intuitive, like that of his rhetorical peasant, for he tells us (*Apocalyptic Sketches*, p. 405), that he has himself experienced what it is to have religious doubts. 'I was tainted while at the University by this spirit of scepticism. I thought Christianity might not be true. The very possibility of its being true was the thought I felt I must meet and settle. Conscience could give me no peace till I had settled it. I read, and I have read from that day, for fourteen or fifteen years, till this, and now I am as convinced, upon the clearest evidence, that this book is the book of God as that I now address you.' This experience, however, instead of impressing on him the fact that doubt may be the stamp of a truth-loving mind – that *sunt quibus non credidisse honor est, et fidei futuræ pignus*[17] – seems to have produced precisely the contrary effect. It has not enabled him even to conceive the condition of a mind 'perplext in faith but pure in deeds',[18] craving light, yearning for a faith that will harmonize

and cherish its highest powers and aspirations, but unable to find
that faith in dogmatic Christianity. His own doubts apparently
were of a different kind. Nowhere in his pages have we found a
humble, candid, sympathetic attempt to meet the difficulties that
may be felt by an ingenuous mind. Everywhere he supposes that
the doubter is hardened, conceited, consciously shutting his eyes to
the light – a fool who is to be answered according to his folly – that
is, with ready replies made up of reckless assertions, of apocryphal
anecdotes, and, where other resources fail, of vituperative impu-
tations. As to the reading which he has prosecuted for fifteen years
– *either* it has left him totally ignorant of the relation which his own
religious creed bears to the criticism and philosophy of the nineteenth century, *or* he systematically blinks that criticism and that
philosophy; and instead of honestly and seriously endeavouring to
meet and solve what he knows to be the real difficulties, contents
himself with setting up popinjays to shoot at, for the sake of
confirming the ignorance and winning the cheap admiration of his
evangelical hearers and readers. Like the Catholic preacher who,
after throwing down his cap and apostrophizing it as Luther,
turned to his audience and said, 'You see this heretical fellow has
not a word to say for himself', Dr Cumming, having drawn his
ugly portrait of the infidel, and put arguments of a convenient
quality into his mouth, finds a 'short and easy method' of confounding this 'croaking frog'.

In his treatment of infidels, we imagine he is guided by a mental
process which may be expressed in the following syllogism: Whatever tends to the glory of God is true; it is for the glory of God that
infidels should be as bad as possible; therefore, whatever tends to
show that infidels are as bad as possible is true. All infidels, he tells
us, have been men of 'gross and licentious lives'. Is there not some
well-known unbeliever, David Hume,[19] for example, of whom even
Dr Cumming's readers may have heard as an exception? No
matter. Some one suspected that he was *not* an exception, and as
that suspicion tends to the glory of God, it is one for a Christian to
entertain (see *Manual of Christian Evidence*, p. 73). – If we were
unable to imagine this kind of self-sophistication, we should be
obliged to suppose that, relying on the ignorance of his evangelical
disciples, he fed them with direct and conscious falsehoods. 'Vol-

taire,' he informs them, 'declares there is no God'; he was 'an anti-
theist, that is, one who deliberately and avowedly opposed and
hated God; who swore in his blasphemy that he would dethrone
him'; and 'advocated the very depths of the lowest sensuality'.
With regard to many statements of a similar kind, equally at
variance with truth, in Dr Cumming's volumes, we presume that
he has been misled by hearsay or by the secondhand character of
his acquaintance with free-thinking literature. An evangelical
preacher is not obliged to be well-read. Here, however, is a case
which the extremest supposition of educated ignorance will not
reach. Even books of 'evidences' quote from Voltaire the line –

> Si Dieu n'existait pas, il faudrait l'inventer;[20]

even persons fed on the mere whey and buttermilk of literature,
must know that in philosophy Voltaire was nothing if not a theist
– must know that he wrote not against God, but against Jehovah,
the God of the Jews, whom he believed to be a false God – must
know that to say Voltaire was an atheist on this ground is as
absurd as to say that a Jacobite opposed hereditary monarchy,
because he declared the Brunswick family had no title to the
throne. That Dr Cumming should repeat the vulgar fables about
Voltaire's death,[21] is merely what we might expect from the
specimens we have seen of his illustrative stories. A man whose
accounts of his own experience are apocryphal, is not likely to put
borrowed narratives to any severe test.

The alliance between intellectual and moral perversion is strikingly typified by the way in which he alternates from the unver-
acious to the absurd, from misrepresentation to contradiction. Side
by side with the adduction of 'facts' such as those we have quoted,
we find him arguing on one page that the Trinity was too grand a
doctrine to have been conceived by man, and was *therefore* Divine;
and on another page, that the Incarnation *had* been preconceived
by man, and is *therefore* to be accepted as Divine. But we are less
concerned with the fallacy of his 'ready replies', than with their
falsity; and even of this we can only afford space for a very few
specimens. Here is one: 'There is a *thousand times* more proof that
the Gospel of John was written by him than there is that the
Αναβασις was written by Xenophon, or the *Ars Poetica* by Horace.'

If Dr Cumming had chosen Plato's *Epistles* or Anacreon's *Poems*, instead of the *Anabasis* or the *Ars Poetica*, he would have reduced the extent of the falsehood, and would have furnished a ready reply which would have been equally effective with his Sunday-school teachers and their disputants. Hence we conclude this prodigality of misstatement, this exuberance of mendacity, is an effervescence of zeal *in majorem gloriam Dei*.[22] Elsewhere he tells us that 'the idea of the author of the *Vestiges* is, that man is the development of a monkey, that the monkey is the embryo man, so that *if you keep a baboon long enough, it will develop itself into a man*'.[23] How well Dr Cumming has qualified himself to judge of the ideas in 'that very unphilosophical book', as he pronounces it, may be inferred from the fact that he implies the author of the *Vestiges* to have *originated* the nebular hypothesis.

In the volume from which the last extract is taken, even the hardihood of assertion is surpassed by the suicidal character of the argument. It is called *The Church before the Flood*, and is devoted chiefly to the adjustment of the question between the Bible and Geology. Keeping within the limits we have prescribed to ourselves, we do not enter into the matter of this discussion; we merely pause a little over the volume in order to point out Dr Cumming's mode of treating the question. He first tells us that 'the Bible has not a single scientific error in it'; that '*its slightest intimations of scientific principles or natural phenomena have in every instance been dem-*onstrated to be exactly and strictly true', and he asks: –

How is it that Moses, with no greater education than the Hindoo or the ancient philosopher, has written his book, touching science at a thousand points, so accurately, that scientific research has discovered no flaws in it; and yet in those investigations which have taken place in more recent centuries, it has not been shown that he has committed one single error, or made one solitary assertion which can be proved by the maturest science, or by the most eagle-eyed philosopher, to be incorrect, scientifically or historically?

According to this, the relation of the Bible to Science should be one of the strong points of apologists for Revelation: the scientific accuracy of Moses should stand at the head of their evidences; and they might urge with some cogency, that since Aristotle, who devoted himself to science, and lived many ages after Moses, does little else than err ingeniously, this fact, that the Jewish Lawgiver, though touching science at a thousand points, has written nothing that has not been 'demonstrated to be exactly and strictly true', is an irrefragable proof of his having derived his knowledge from a supernatural source. How does it happen, then, that Dr Cumming forsakes this strong position? How is it that we find him, some pages further on, engaged in reconciling Genesis with the discoveries of science, by means of imaginative hypotheses and feats of 'interpretation'? Surely, that which has been demonstrated to be exactly and strictly true does not require hypothesis and critical argument, in order to show that it may *possibly* agree with those very discoveries by means of which its exact and strict truth has been demonstrated. And why should Dr Cumming suppose, as we shall presently find him supposing, that men of science hesitate to accept the Bible, because it appears to contradict their discoveries? By his own statement, that appearance of contradiction does not exist; on the contrary, it has been demonstrated that the Bible precisely agrees with their discoveries. Perhaps, however, in saying of the Bible that its 'slightest intimations of scientific principles or natural phenomena have in every instance been demonstrated to be exactly and strictly true', Dr Cumming merely means to imply that theologians have found out a way of explaining the biblical text so that it no longer, in their opinion, appears to be in contradiction with the discoveries of science. One of two things, therefore: either, he uses language without the slightest appreciation of its real meaning; or, the assertions he makes on one page are directly contradicted by the arguments he urges on another.

Dr Cumming's principles – or, we should rather say, confused notions – of biblical interpretation, as exhibited in this volume, are particularly significant of his mental calibre. He says (*Church before the Flood*, p. 93):

Men of science, who are full of scientific investigation and enamoured of scientific discovery, will hesitate before they accept a book which, they think, contradicts the plainest and the most unequivocal disclosures they have made in the bowels of the earth, or among the stars of the sky. To all these we answer, as we have already indicated, there is not the least dissonance between God's written book and the most mature discoveries of geological science. One thing, however, there may be; *there may be a contradiction between the discoveries of geology and our preconceived interpretations of the Bible.* But this is not because the Bible is wrong, but because our interpretation is wrong. (The italics in all cases are our own.)

Elsewhere he says:

It seems to me plainly evident that the record of Genesis, when read fairly, and not in the light of our prejudices, – *and mind you, the essence of Popery is to read the Bible in the light of our opinions, instead of viewing our opinions in the light of the Bible, in its plain and obvious sense,* – falls in perfectly with the assertion of geologists.

On comparing these two passages, we gather that when Dr Cumming, under stress of geological discovery, assigns to the biblical text a meaning entirely different from that which, on his own showing, was universally ascribed to it for more than 3,000 years, he regards himself as 'viewing his opinions in the light of the Bible in its plain and obvious sense'! Now he is reduced to one of two alternatives: either, he must hold that the 'plain and obvious meaning' of the whole Bible differs from age to age, so that the criterion of its meaning[24] lies in the sum of knowledge possessed by each successive age – the Bible being an elastic garment for the growing thought of mankind; or, he must hold that some portions are amenable to this criterion, and others not so. In the former case, he accepts the principle of interpretation adopted by the early German rationalists; in the latter case, he has to show a further criterion by which we can judge what parts of the Bible are elastic and what rigid. If he says that the interpretation of the text is rigid wherever it treats of doctrines necessary to salvation, we answer, that for doctrines to be necessary to salvation they must first be true; and in order to be true, according to his own principle, they must be founded on a correct interpretation of the biblical text. Thus he makes the necessity of doctrines to salvation the criterion of infallible interpretation, and infallible interpretation the criterion of doctrines being necessary to salvation. He is whirled round in a circle, having, by admitting the principle of novelty in interpretation, completely deprived himself of a basis. That he should seize the very moment in which he is most palpably betraying that he has no test of biblical truth beyond his own opinion, as an appropriate occasion for flinging the rather novel reproach against Popery that its essence is to 'read the Bible in the light of our opinions', would be an almost pathetic self-exposure, if it were not disgusting. Imbecility that is not even meek, ceases to be pitiable and becomes simply odious.

Parenthetic lashes of this kind against Popery are very frequent with Dr Cumming, and occur even in his more devout passages, where their introduction must surely disturb the spiritual exercises of his hearers. Indeed, Roman-catholics fare worse with him even than infidels. Infidels are the small vermin – the mice to be bagged *en passant*. The main object of his chace – the rats which are to be nailed up as trophies – are the Roman-catholics. Romanism is the masterpiece of Satan; but reassure yourselves! Dr Cumming has been created. Anti-christ is enthroned in the Vatican; but he is stoutly withstood by the Boanerges[25] of Crown Court. The personality of Satan, as might be expected, is a very prominent tenet in Dr Cumming's discourses; those who doubt it are, he thinks, 'generally specimens of the victims of Satan as a triumphant seducer'; and it is through the medium of this doctrine that he habitually contemplates Roman-catholics. They are the puppets of which the devil holds the strings. It is only exceptionally that he speaks of them as fellow-men, acted on by the same desires, fears, and hopes as himself; his *rule* is to hold them up to his hearers as foredoomed instruments of Satan, and vessels of wrath. If he is obliged to admit that they are 'no shams', that they are 'thoroughly in earnest' – that is because they are inspired by hell, because they are under an 'infra-natural' influence. If their missionaries are found wherever Protestant missionaries go, this zeal in propagating their faith is not in them a consistent virtue, as it is in Protestants, but a 'melancholy fact', affording additional evidence that they are instigated and assisted by the devil. And Dr Cumming is inclined to think that they work miracles, because that is no more than might be expected from the known ability of Satan who inspires them.* He admits indeed, that 'there is a fragment of the Church of Christ in the very bosom of that awful apostasy',† and

---

* *Signs of the Times*, p. 38.
† *Apocalyptic Sketches*, p. 234.

that there are members of the Church of Rome in glory; but this admission is rare and episodical – is a declaration, *pro forma*, about as influential on the general disposition and habits as an aristocrat's profession of democracy.

This leads us to mention another conspicuous characteristic of Dr Cumming's teaching – the *absence of genuine charity*. It is true that he makes large profession of tolerance and liberality within a certain circle; he exhorts Christians to unity; he would have Churchmen fraternize with Dissenters, and exhorts these two branches of God's family to defer the settlement of their differences till the millennium. But the love thus taught is the love of the *clan*, which is the correlative of antagonism to the rest of mankind. It is not sympathy and helpfulness towards men as men, but towards men as Christians, and as Christians in the sense of a small minority. Dr Cumming's religion may demand a tribute of love, but it gives a charter to hatred; it may enjoin charity, but it fosters all uncharitableness. If I believe that God tells me to love my enemies, but at the same time hates His own enemies and requires me to have one will with Him, which has the larger scope, love or hatred? And we refer to those pages of Dr Cumming's in which he opposes Roman-catholics, Puseyites, and infidels – pages which form the larger proportion of what he has published – for proof that the idea of God which both the logic and spirit of his discourses keep present to his hearers, is that of a God who hates his enemies, a God who teaches love by fierce denunciations of wrath – a God who encourages obedience to his precepts by elaborately revealing to us that his own government is in precise opposition to those precepts. We know the usual evasions on this subject. We know Dr Cumming would say that even Roman-catholics are to be loved and succoured as men; that he would help even that 'unclean spirit', Cardinal Wiseman,[26] out of a ditch. But who that is in the slightest degree acquainted with the action of the human mind, will believe that any genuine and large charity can grow out of an exercise of love which is always to have an *arrière-pensée* of hatred? Of what quality would be the conjugal love of a husband who loved his spouse as a wife, but hated her as a woman? It is reserved for the regenerate mind, according to Dr Cumming's conception of it, to be 'wise, amazed, temperate and furious, loyal and neutral, in a moment'. Precepts of charity uttered with faint breath at the end of a sermon are perfectly futile, when all the force of the lungs has been spent in keeping the hearer's mind fixed on the conception of his fellow-men, not as fellow-sinners and fellow-sufferers, but as agents of hell, as automata through whom Satan plays his game upon earth, – not on objects which call forth their reverence, their love, their hope of good even in the most strayed and perverted, but on a minute identification of human things with such symbols as the scarlet whore, the beast out of the abyss, scorpions whose sting is in their tails, men who have the mark of the beast, and unclean spirits like frogs. You might as well attempt to educate a child's sense of beauty by hanging its nursery with the horrible and grotesque pictures in which the early painters represented the Last Judgement, as expect Christian graces to flourish on that prophetic interpretation which Dr Cumming offers as the principal nutriment of his flock. Quite apart from the critical basis of that interpretation, quite apart from the degree of truth there may be in Dr Cumming's prognostications – questions into which we do not choose to enter – his use of prophecy must be *a priori* condemned in the judgement of right-minded persons, by its results as testified in the net moral effect of his sermons. The best minds that accept Christianity as a divinely inspired system, believe that the great end of the Gospel is not merely the saving but the educating of men's souls, the creating within them of holy dispositions, the subduing of egotistical pretensions, and the perpetual enhancing of the desire that the will of God – a will synonymous with goodness and truth – may be done on earth. But what relation to all this has a system of interpretation which keeps the mind of the Christian in the position of a spectator at a gladiatorial show, of which Satan is the wild beast in the shape of the great red dragon, and two thirds of mankind the victims – the whole provided and got up by God for the edification of the saints? The demonstration that the Second Advent is at hand, if true, can have no really holy, spiritual effect; the highest state of mind inculcated by the Gospel is resignation to the disposal of God's providence – 'Whether we live we live unto the Lord; whether we die, we die unto the Lord'[27] – not an eagerness to see a temporal manifestation which shall confound the enemies of God and give exaltation to the saints; it is to dwell in Christ by spiritual communion with his nature, not to fix the date when He shall appear in the sky. Dr Cumming's delight in shadowing forth the downfall of the Man of Sin, in prognosticating the battle of Gog and Magog, and in advertising the pre-millennial Advent, is simply the transportation of political passions on to a so-called religious platform; it is the anticipation of the triumph of 'our party', accomplished by our principal men being 'sent for' into the clouds. Let us be understood to speak in all seriousness. If we were in search of amusement, we should not seek for it by examining Dr Cumming's works in order to ridicule them. We are simply discharging a disagreeable duty in delivering our opinion that, judged by the highest standard even of orthodox Christianity, they are little calculated to produce –

> A closer walk with God,
> A calm and heavenly frame;[28]

but are more likely to nourish egoistic complacency and pretension, a hard and condemnatory spirit towards one's fellow-men, and a busy occupation with the minutiæ of events, instead of a reverent contemplation of great facts and a wise application of great principles. It would be idle to consider Dr Cumming's theory of prophecy in any other light, – as a philosophy of history or a specimen of biblical interpretation; it bears about the same relation to the extension of genuine knowledge as the astrological 'house' in the heavens bears to the true structure and relations of the universe.

The slight degree in which Dr Cumming's faith is imbued with truly human sympathies, is exhibited in the way he treats the doctrine of Eternal Punishment. *Here* a little of that readiness to strain the letter of the Scriptures which he so often manifests when his object is to prove a point against Romanism, would have been an amiable frailty if it had been applied on the side of mercy. When he is bent on proving that the prophecy concerning the Man of Sin,[29] in the Second Epistle to the Thessalonians, refers to the Pope, he can extort from the innocent word καθισαι the meaning *cathedrize*, though why we are to translate 'He as God cathedrizes in the temple of God', any more than we are to translate 'cathedrize here, while I go and pray yonder',[30] it is for

Dr Cumming to show more clearly than he has yet done. But when rigorous literality will favour the conclusion that the greater proportion of the human race will be eternally miserable – *then* he is rigorously literal.

He says:

The Greek words, εἰς τοὺς αἰῶνας τῶν αἰώνων, here translated 'everlasting', signify literally 'unto the ages of ages'; αἰεὶ ὤν, 'always being', that is, everlasting, ceaseless existence. Plato uses the word in this sense when he says, 'The gods that live for ever.' *But I must also admit,* that this word is used several times in a limited extent, – as for instance, 'The everlasting hills'. Of course, this does not mean that there never will be a time when the hills will cease to stand; the expression here is evidently figurative, but it implies eternity. The hills shall remain as long as the earth lasts, and no hand has power to remove them but that Eternal One which first called them into being; *so the state of the soul* remains the same after death as long as the soul exists, and no one has power to alter it. The same word is often applied to denote the existence of God – 'the Eternal God'. Can we limit the word when applied to Him? Because occasionally used in a limited sense, we must not infer it is always so. 'Everlasting' plainly means in Scripture 'without end'; it is only to be explained figuratively when it is evident it cannot be interpreted in any other way.

We do not discuss whether Dr Cumming's interpretation accords with the meaning of the New Testament writers: we simply point to the fact that the text becomes elastic for him when he wants freer play for his prejudices, while he makes it an adamantine barrier against the admission that mercy will ultimately triumph, – that God, i.e., Love, will be all in all. He assures us that he does not 'delight to dwell on the misery of the lost': and we believe him. That misery does not seem to be a question of feeling with him, either one way or the other. He does not merely resign himself to the awful mystery of eternal punishment; he contends for it. Do we object, he asks,* to everlasting happiness? then why object to everlasting misery? – reasoning which is perhaps felt to be cogent by theologians who anticipate the everlasting happiness for themselves, and the everlasting misery for their neighbours.

The compassion of some Christians has been glad to take refuge

* *Manual of Christian Evidence,* p. 184.

in the opinion, that the Bible allows the supposition of annihilation for the impenitent: but the rigid sequence of Dr Cumming's reasoning will not admit of this idea. He sees that flax is made into linen, and linen into paper; that paper, when burnt, partly ascends as smoke and then again descends in rain, or in dust and carbon. 'Not one particle of the original flax is lost, although there may be not one particle that has not undergone an entire change: annihilation is not, but change of form is. *It will be thus with our bodies at the resurrection.* The death of the body means not annihilation. *Not one feature of the face* will be annihilated.' Having established the perpetuity of the body by this close and clear analogy, namely, that *as* there is a total change in the particles of flax in consequence of which they no longer appear as flax, *so* there will *not* be a total change in the particles of the human body, but they will reappear as the human body, he does not seem to consider that the perpetuity of the body involves the perpetuity of the soul, but requires separate evidence for this, and finds such evidence by begging the very question at issue; namely, by asserting that the text of the Scriptures implies 'the perpetuity of the punishment of the lost, and the consciousness of the punishment which they endure'. Yet it is drivelling like this which is listened to and lauded as eloquence by hundreds, and which a Doctor of Divinity can believe that he has his 'reward as a saint' for preaching and publishing!

One more characteristic of Dr Cumming's writings, and we have done. This is the *perverted moral judgement* that everywhere reigns in them. Not that this perversion is peculiar to Dr Cumming: it belongs to the dogmatic system which he shares with all evangelical believers. But the abstract tendencies of systems are represented in very different degrees, according to the different characters of those who embrace them; just as the same food tells differently on different constitutions: and there are certain qualities in Dr Cumming that cause the perversion of which we speak to exhibit itself with peculiar prominence in his teaching. A single extract will enable us to explain what we mean.

The 'thoughts' are evil. If it were possible for human eye to discern and to detect the thoughts that flutter round the heart of an unregenerate man – to mark their hue and their multitude, it would be found that they are indeed 'evil'. We speak not of the thief, and the murderer, and the adulterer, and such like, whose crimes draw down the cognizance of earthly tribunals, and whose unenviable character it is to take the lead in the paths of sin; but we refer to the men who are marked out by their practice of many of the seemliest moralities of life – by the exercise of the kindliest affections, and the interchange of the sweetest reciprocities – and of these men, if unrenewed and unchanged, we pronounce that their thoughts are evil. To ascertain this, we must refer to the object around which our thoughts ought continually to circulate. The Scriptures assert that this object is *the glory of God*; that for this we ought to think, to act, and to speak; and that in thus thinking, acting, and speaking, there is involved the purest and most endearing bliss. Now it will be found true of the most amiable men, that with all their good society and kindliness of heart, and all their strict and unbending integrity, they never or rarely think of the glory of God. The question never occurs to them – Will this redound to the glory of God? Will this make his name more known, his being more loved, his praise more sung? And just inasmuch as their every thought comes short of this lofty aim, in so much does it come short of good, and entitle itself to the character of evil. If the glory of God is not the absorbing and the influential aim of their thoughts, then they are evil; but God's glory never enters into their minds. They are amiable, because it chances to be one of the constitutional tendencies of their individual character, left uneffaced by the Fall; and *they are just and upright, because they have perhaps no occasion to be otherwise, or find it subservient to their interests to maintain such a character* (*Occasional Discourses, Vol. I*, p. 8).

Again we read (p. 236):

There are traits in the Christian character which the mere worldly man cannot understand. He can understand the outward morality, but he cannot understand the inner spring of it; he can understand Dorcas's liberality to the poor, but he cannot penetrate the ground of Dorcas's liberality. *Some men give to the poor because they are ostentatious, or because they think the poor will ultimately avenge their neglect; but the Christian gives to the poor, not only because he has sensibilities like other men,* but because inasmuch as ye did it to the least of these my brethren ye did it unto me.

Before entering on the more general question involved in these quotations, we must point to the clauses we have marked with italics, where Dr Cumming appears to express sentiments which, we are happy to think, are not shared by the majority of his brethren in the faith. Dr Cumming, it seems, is unable to conceive that the natural man can have any other motive for being just and upright than that it is useless to be otherwise, or that a character for honesty is profitable; according to his experience, between the feelings of ostentation and selfish alarm and the feeling of love to Christ, there lie no sensibilities which can lead a man to relieve want. Granting, as we should prefer to think, that it is Dr Cumming's exposition of his sentiments which is deficient rather than his sentiments themselves, still, the fact that the deficiency lies precisely here, and that he can overlook it not only in the haste of oral delivery but in the examination of proof-sheets, is strongly significant of his mental bias – of the faint degree in which he sympathizes with the disinterested elements of human feeling, and of the fact, which we are about to dwell upon, that those feelings are totally absent from his religious theory. Now, Dr Cumming invariably assumes that, in fulminating against those who differ from him, he is standing on a moral elevation to which they are compelled reluctantly to look up; that his theory of motives and conduct is in its loftiness and purity a perpetual rebuke to their low and vicious desires and practice. It is time he should be told that the reverse is the fact; that there are men who do not merely cast a superficial glance at his doctrine, and fail to see its beauty or justice, but who, after a close consideration of that doctrine, pronounce it to be subversive of true moral development, and therefore positively noxious. Dr Cumming is fond of showing up the teaching of Romanism, and accusing it of undermining true morality: it is time he should be told that there is a large body, both of thinkers and practical men, who hold precisely the same opinion of his own teaching – with this difference, that they do not regard it as the inspiration of Satan, but as the natural crop of a human mind where the soil is chiefly made up of egoistic passions and dogmatic beliefs.

Dr Cumming's theory, as we have seen, is that actions are good or evil according as they are prompted or not prompted by an exclusive reference to the 'glory of God'. God, then, in Dr Cumming's conception, is a being who has no pleasure in the exercise of love and truthfulness and justice, considered as effecting the well-being of his creatures; He has satisfaction in us only in so far as we exhaust our motives and dispositions of all relation to our fellow-beings, and replace sympathy with men by anxiety for the 'glory of God'. The deed of Grace Darling,[31] when she took a boat in the storm to rescue drowning men and women, was not good if it was only compassion that nerved her arm and impelled her to brave death for the chance of saving others; it was only good if she asked herself – Will this redound to the glory of God? The man who endures tortures rather than betray a trust, the man who spends years in toil in order to discharge an obligation from which the law declares him free, must be animated not by the spirit of fidelity to his fellow-man, but by a desire to make 'the name of God more known'. The sweet charities of domestic life – the ready hand and the soothing word in sickness, the forbearance towards frailties, the prompt helpfulness in all efforts and sympathy in all joys, are simply evil if they result from a 'constitutional tendency', or from dispositions disciplined by the experience of suffering and the perception of moral loveliness. A wife is not to devote herself to her husband out of love to him and a sense of the duties implied by a close relation – she is to be a faithful wife for the glory of God; if she feels her natural affections welling up too strongly, she is to repress them; it will not do to act from natural affection – she must think of the glory of God. A man is to guide his affairs with energy and discretion, not from an honest desire to fulfil his responsibilities as a member of society and a father, but – that 'God's praise may be sung'. Dr Cumming's Christian pays his debts for the glory of God; were it not for the coercion of that supreme motive, it would be evil to pay them. A man is not to be just from a feeling of justice; he is not to help his fellow-men out of good-will to his fellow-men: he is not to be a tender husband and father out of affection: all these natural muscles and fibres are to be torn away and replaced by a patent steel-spring – anxiety for the 'glory of God'.

Happily, the constitution of human nature forbids the complete prevalence of such a theory. Fatally powerful as religious systems have been, human nature is stronger and wider than religious systems, and though dogmas may hamper, they cannot absolutely repress its growth: build walls round the living tree as you will, the bricks and mortar have by and by to give way before the slow and sure operation of the sap. But next to that hatred of the enemies of

God which is the principle of persecution, there perhaps has been no perversion more obstructive of true moral development than this substitution of a reference to the glory of God for the direct promptings of the sympathetic feelings. Benevolence and justice are strong only in proportion as they are directly and inevitably called into activity by their proper objects: pity is strong only because we are strongly impressed by suffering; and only in proportion as it is compassion that speaks through the eyes when we soothe, and moves the arm when we succour, is a deed strictly benevolent. If the soothing or the succour be given because another being wishes or approves it, the deed ceases to be one of benevolence, and becomes one of defence, of obedience, of self-interest, or vanity. Accessory motives may aid in producing an *action*, but they presuppose the weakness of the direct motive; and conversely, when the direct motive is strong, the action of accessory motives will be excluded. If then, as Dr Cumming inculcates, the glory of God is to be 'the absorbing and the influential aim' in our thoughts and actions, this must tend to neutralize the human sympathies; the stream of feeling will be diverted from its natural current in order to feed an artificial canal. The idea of God is really moral in its influence – it really cherishes all that is best and loveliest in man – only when God is contemplated as sympathizing with the pure elements of human feeling, as possessing infinitely all those attributes which we recognize to be moral in humanity. In this light, the idea of God and the sense of His presence intensify all noble feeling, and encourage all noble effort, on the same principle that human sympathy is found a source of strength: the brave man feels braver when he knows that another stout heart is beating time with his; the devoted woman who is wearing out her years in patient effort to alleviate suffering or save vice from the last stages of degradation, finds aid in the pressure of a friendly hand which tells her that there is one who understands her deeds, and in her place would do the like. The idea of a God who not only sympathizes with all we feel and endure for our fellow-men, but who will pour new life into our too languid love, and give firmness to our vacillating purpose, is an extension and multiplication of the effects produced by human sympathy; and it has been intensified for the better spirits who have been under the influence of orthodox

Christianity, by the contemplation of Jesus as 'God manifest in the flesh'. But Dr Cumming's God is the very opposite of all this: he is a God who instead of sharing and aiding our human sympathies, is directly in collision with them; who instead of strengthening the bond between man and man, by encouraging the sense that they are both alike the objects of His love and care, thrusts himself between them and forbids them to feel for each other except as they have relation to Him. He is a God, who, instead of adding his solar force to swell the tide of those impulses that tend to give humanity a common life in which the good of one is the good of all, commands us to check those impulses, lest they should prevent us from thinking of His glory. It is in vain for Dr Cumming to say that we are to love man for God's sake: with the conception of God which his teaching presents, the love of man for God's sake involves, as his writings abundantly show, a strong principle of hatred. We can only love one being for the sake of another when there is an habitual delight in associating the idea of those two beings – that is, when the object of our indirect love is a source of joy and honour to the object of our direct love: but, according to Dr Cumming's theory, the majority of mankind – the majority of his neighbours – are in precisely the opposite relation to God. His soul has no pleasure in them, they belong more to Satan than to Him, and if they contribute to His glory, it is against their will. Dr Cumming then can only love *some* men for God's sake; the rest he must in consistency *hate* for God's sake.

There must be many, even in the circle of Dr Cumming's admirers, who would be revolted by the doctrine we have just exposed, if their natural good sense and healthy feeling were not early stifled by dogmatic beliefs, and their reverence misled by pious phrases. But as it is, many a rational question, many a generous instinct, is repelled as the suggestion of a supernatural enemy, or as the ebullition of human pride and corruption. This state of inward contradiction can be put an end to only by the conviction that the free and diligent exertion of the intellect, instead of being a sin, is a part of their responsibility – that Right and Reason are synonymous. The fundamental faith for man is faith in the result of a brave, honest, and steady use of all his faculties: –

Let knowledge grow from more to more
But more of reverence in us dwell;
That mind and soul according well
May make one music as before,
But vaster.[32]

Before taking leave of Dr Cumming, let us express a hope that we have in no case exaggerated the unfavourable character of the inferences to be drawn from his pages. His creed often obliges him to hope the worst of men, and to exert himself in proving that the worst is true; but thus far we are happier than he. We have no theory which requires us to attribute unworthy motives to Dr Cumming, no opinions, religious or irreligious, which can make it a gratification to us to detect him in delinquencies. On the contrary, the better we are able to think of him as a man, while we are obliged to disapprove him as a theologian, the stronger will be the evidence for our conviction, that the tendency towards good in human nature has a force which no creed can utterly counteract, and which ensures the ultimate triumph of that tendency over all dogmatic perversions.

German Wit: Heinrich Heine

(*Westminster Review*, January 1856)

'NOTHING,' SAYS Goethe, 'is more significant of men's character than what they find laughable.'[1] The truth of this observation would perhaps have been more apparent if he had said *culture* instead of character. The last thing in which the cultivated man can have community with the vulgar is their jocularity; and we can hardly exhibit more strikingly the wide gulf which separates him from them, than by comparing the object which shakes the diaphragm of a coal-heaver with the highly complex pleasure derived from a real witticism. That any high order of wit is exceedingly complex, and demands a ripe and strong mental development, has one evidence in the fact that we do not find it in boys at all in proportion to their manifestation of other powers. Clever boys generally aspire to the heroic and poetic rather than the comic, and the crudest of all their efforts are their jokes. Many a witty man will remember how in his school days a practical joke, more or less Rabelaisian, was for him the *ne plus ultra* of the ludicrous. It seems to have been the same with the boyhood of the human race. The history and literature of the ancient Hebrews gives the idea of a people who went about their business and their pleasure as gravely as a society of beavers; the smile and the laugh are often mentioned metaphorically, but the smile is one of complacency, the laugh is one of scorn. Nor can we imagine that the facetious element was very strong in the Egyptians; no laughter lurks in the wondering eyes and the broad calm lips of their statues. Still less can the Assyrians have had any genius for the comic: the round eyes and simpering satisfaction of their ideal faces belong to a type which is not witty, but the cause of wit in others.[2] The fun of these early races was, we fancy, of the after-dinner kind – loud-throated laughter over the wine-cup, taken too little account of in sober moments to enter as an element into their Art, and differing as much from the laughter of a Chamfort or a Sheridan[3] as the gastronomic enjoyment of an ancient Briton, whose dinner had no other 'removes' than from acorns to beechmast and back again to acorns, differed from the subtle pleasures of the palate experienced by his turtle-eating descendant. In fact they had to live seriously through the stages which to subsequent races[4] were to become comedy, as those amiable-looking pre-Adamite amphibia which Professor Owen has restored for us in effigy at Sydenham, took perfectly *au sérieux* the grotesque physiognomies of their kindred.[5] Heavy experience in their case as in every other, was the base from which the salt of future wit was to be made.

Humour is of earlier growth than Wit, and it is in accordance with this earlier growth that it has more affinity with the poetic tendencies, while Wit is more nearly allied to the ratiocinative intellect. Humour draws its materials from situations and characteristics; Wit seizes on unexpected and complex relations. Humour is chiefly representative and descriptive; it is diffuse, and flows along without any other law than its own fantastic will; or it flits about like a will-o'-the-wisp, amazing us by its whimsical transitions. Wit is brief and sudden, and sharply defined as a crystal; it does not make pictures, it is not fantastic; but it detects an unsuspected analogy or suggests a startling or confounding inference. Every one who has had the opportunity of making the comparison will remember that the effect produced on him by some witticisms is closely akin to the effect produced on him by subtle reasoning which lays open a fallacy or absurdity, and there are persons whose delight in such reasoning always manifests itself in laughter. This affinity of Wit with ratiocination is the more obvious in proportion as the species of wit is higher and deals less with words and with superficialities than with the essential qualities of things. Some of Johnson's most admirable witticisms consist in the suggestion of an analogy which immediately exposes the absurdity of an action or proposition; and it is only their ingenuity, condensation, and instantaneousness which lift them from reasoning into Wit – they are *reasoning raised to a higher power*. On the other hand,

Humour, in its higher forms, and in proportion as it associates itself with the sympathetic emotions, continually passes into poetry: nearly all great modern humorists may be called prose poets.

Some confusion as to the nature of humour has been created by the fact, that those who have written most eloquently on it have dwelt almost exclusively on its higher forms, and have defined humour in general as the *sympathetic* presentation of incongruous elements in human nature and life; a definition which only applies to its later development. A great deal of humour may co-exist with a great deal of barbarism, as we see in the Middle Ages; but the strongest flavour of the humour in such cases will come, not from sympathy, but more probably from triumphant egoism or intolerance; at best it will be the love of the ludicrous exhibiting itself in illustrations of successful cunning and of the *lex talionis*, as in *Reineke Fuchs*,[6] or shaking off in a holiday mood the yoke of a too exacting faith, as in the old Mysteries.[7] Again, it is impossible to deny a high degree of humour to many practical jokes, but no sympathetic nature can enjoy them. Strange as the genealogy may seem, the original parentage of that wonderful and delicious mixture of fun, fancy, philosophy, and feeling which constitutes modern humour, was probably the cruel mockery of a savage at the writhings of a suffering enemy – such is the tendency of things towards the good and beautiful on this earth.[8] Probably the reason why high culture demands more complete harmony with its moral sympathies in humour than in wit, is that humour is in its nature more prolix – that it has not the direct and irresistible force of wit. Wit is an electric shock, which takes us by violence, quite independently of our predominant mental disposition; but humour approaches us more deliberately and leaves us masters of ourselves. Hence it is, that while coarse and cruel humour has almost disappeared from contemporary literature, coarse and cruel wit abounds: even refined men cannot help laughing at a coarse *bon mot* or a lacerating personality, if the 'shock' of the witticism is a powerful one; while mere fun will have no power over them if it jar on their moral taste. Hence, too, it is, that while wit is perennial, humour is liable to become superannuated.

As is usual with definitions and classifications, however, this distinction between wit and humour does not exactly represent the actual fact. Like all other species, Wit and Humour overlap and blend with each other. There are *bons mots*, like many of Charles Lamb's[9] which are a sort of facetious hybrids, we hardly know whether to call them witty or humorous; there are rather lengthy descriptions or narratives, which, like Voltaire's *Micromégas*,[10] would be humorous if they were not so sparkling and antithetic, so pregnant with suggestion and satire, that we are obliged to call them witty. We rarely find wit untempered by humour, or humour without a spice of wit; and sometimes we find them both united in the highest degree in the same mind, as in Shakspeare and Molière. A happy conjunction this, for wit is apt to be cold, and thin-lipped, and Mephistophelean in men who have no relish for humour, whose lungs do never crow like Chanticleer[11] at fun and drollery; and broad-faced, rollicking humour needs the refining influence of wit. Indeed, it may be said that there is no really fine writing in which wit has not an implicit, if not an explicit action. The wit may never rise to the surface, it may never flame out into a witticism; but it helps to give brightness and transparency, it warns off from flights and exaggerations which verge on the ridiculous – in every *genre* of writing it preserves a man from sinking into the *genre ennuyeux*. And it is eminently needed for this office in humorous writing; for as humour has no limits imposed on it by its material, no law but its own exuberance, it is apt to become preposterous and wearisome unless checked by wit, which is the enemy of all monotony, of all lengthiness, of all exaggeration.

Perhaps the nearest approach Nature has given us to a complete analysis, in which wit is as thoroughly exhausted of humour as possible, and humour as bare as possible of wit, is in the typical Frenchman and the typical German. Voltaire, the intensest example of pure wit, fails in most of his fictions from his lack of humour. *Micromégas* is a perfect tale, because, as it deals chiefly with philosophic ideas and does not touch the marrow of human feeling and life, the writer's wit and wisdom were all-sufficient for his purpose. Not so with *Candide*. Here Voltaire had to give pictures of life as well as to convey philosophic truth and satire, and here we feel the want of humour. The sense of the ludicrous is continually defeated by disgust, and the scenes, instead of presenting us with an amusing or agreeable picture, are only the frame for a witticism. On the other hand, German humour generally shows no sense of measure, no instinctive tact; it is either floundering and clumsy as the antics of a leviathan, or laborious and interminable as a Lapland day, in which one loses all hope that the stars and quiet will ever come. For this reason, Jean Paul,[12] the greatest of German humorists, is unendurable to many readers, and frequently tiresome to all. Here, as elsewhere, the German shows the absence of that delicate perception, that sensibility to gradation, which is the essence of tact and taste, and the necessary concomitant of wit. All his subtlety is reserved for the region of metaphysics. For *Identität*[13] in the abstract, no one can have an acuter vision, but in the concrete he is satisfied with a very loose approximation. He has the finest nose for *Empirismus*[14] in philosophical doctrine, but the presence of more or less tobacco-smoke in the air he breathes is imperceptible to him. To the typical German – *Vetter Michel*[15] – it is indifferent whether his door-lock will catch, whether his tea-cup be more or less than an inch thick; whether or not his book have every other leaf unstitched; whether his neighbour's conversation be more or less of a shout; whether he pronounce *b* or *p*, *t* or *d*; whether or not his adored one's teeth be few and far between. He has the same sort of insensibility to gradations in time. A German comedy is like a German sentence: you see no reason in its structure why it should ever come to an end, and you accept the conclusion as an arrangement of Providence rather than of the author. We have heard Germans use the word *Langeweile*, the equivalent for ennui, and we have secretly wondered *what* it can be that produces ennui in a German. Not the longest of long tragedies, for we have known him to pronounce that *höchst fesselnd* (*so* enchaining!); not the heaviest of heavy books, for he delights in that as *gründlich* (deep, sir, deep!); not the slowest of journeys in a *Post-wagen*, for the slower the horses, the more cigars he can smoke before he reaches his journey's end. German ennui must be something as superlative as Barclay's treble X,[16] which, we suppose, implies an extremely unknown quantity of stupefaction.

It is easy to see that this national deficiency in nicety of perception must have its effect on the national appreciation and exhibi-

tion of humour. You find in Germany ardent admirers of Shakspeare, who tell you that what they think most admirable in him
is his *Wortspiel*, his verbal quibbles; and one of these, a man of
no slight culture and refinement, once cited to a friend of ours
Proteus's joke in *The Two Gentlemen of Verona* – 'Nod, I? why
that's Noddy,' as a transcendent specimen of Shakspearian wit.[17]
German facetiousness is seldom comic to foreigners, and an
Englishman with a swelled cheek might take up *Kladderadatsch*, the
German *Punch*, without any danger of agitating his facial muscles.
Indeed, it is a remarkable fact that, among the five great races
concerned in modern civilization, the German race is the only one
which, up to the present century, had contributed nothing classic
to the common stock of European wit and humour; for *Reineke
Fuchs* cannot be regarded as a peculiarly Teutonic product. Italy
was the birth-place of Pantomime and the immortal Pulcinello;
Spain had produced Cervantes; France had produced Rabelais
and Molière, and classic wits innumerable; England had yielded
Shakspeare and a host of humorists. But Germany had borne no
great comic dramatist, no great satirist, and she has not yet
repaired the omission; she had not even produced any humorist of
a high order. Among her great writers, Lessing[18] is the one who is
the most specifically witty. We feel the implicit influence of wit –
the 'flavour of mind' – throughout his writings; and it is often
concentrated into pungent satire, as every reader of the *Hamburgische Dramaturgie*[19] remembers. Still, Lessing's name has not become
European through his wit, and his charming comedy, *Minna von
Barnhelm*, has won no place on a foreign stage. Of course, we do
not pretend to an exhaustive acquaintance with German literature;
we not only admit – we are sure, that it includes much comic
writing of which we know nothing. We simply state the fact, that
no German production of that kind, before the present century,
ranked as European; a fact which does not, indeed, determine the
amount of the national facetiousness, but which is quite decisive as
to its *quality*. Whatever may be the stock of fun which Germany
yields for home consumption, she has provided little for the palate
of other lands. – All honour to her for the still greater things she
has done for us! She has fought the hardest fight for freedom of
thought, has produced the grandest inventions, has made magnifi

cent contributions to science, has given us some of the divinest poetry, and quite the divinest music, in the world. No one reveres and treasures the products of the German mind more than we do. To say that that mind is not fertile in wit, is only like saying that excellent wheat land is not rich pasture; to say that we do not enjoy German facetiousness, is no more than to say, that though the horse is the finest of quadrupeds, we do not like him to lay his hoof playfully on our shoulder. Still, as we have noticed that the pointless puns and stupid jocularity of the boy may ultimately be developed into the epigrammatic brilliancy and polished playfulness of the man; as we believe that racy wit and chastened delicate humour are inevitably the results of invigorated and refined mental activity; we can also believe that Germany will, one day, yield a crop of wits and humorists.

Perhaps there is already an earnest of that future crop in the existence of HEINRICH HEINE, a German born with the present century, who, to Teutonic imagination, sensibility, and humour, adds an amount of *esprit* that would make him brilliant among the most brilliant of Frenchmen. True, this unique German wit is half a Hebrew; but he and his ancestors spent their youth in German air, and were reared on *Wurst* and *Sauerkraut*, so that he is as much a German as a pheasant is an English bird, or a potato an Irish vegetable. But whatever else he may be, Heine is one of the most remarkable men of this age: no echo, but a real voice, and therefore, like all genuine things in this world, worth studying; a surpassing lyric poet, who has uttered our feelings for us in delicious song; a humorist, who touches leaden folly with the magic wand of his fancy, and transmutes it into the fine gold of art – who sheds his sunny smile on human tears, and makes them a beauteous rainbow on the cloudy background of life; a wit, who holds in his mighty hand the most scorching lightnings of satire; an artist in prose literature, who has shown even more completely than Goethe the possibilities of German prose; and – in spite of all charges against him, true as well as false – a lover of freedom, who has spoken wise and brave words on behalf of his fellow-men. He is, moreover, a suffering man, who, with all the highly-wrought sensibility of genius, has to endure terrible physical ills; and as such he calls forth more than an intellectual interest. It is true, alas! that there is a heavy weight in the other scale – that Heine's magnificent powers have often served only to give electric force to the expression of debased feeling, so that his works are no Phidian statue[20] of gold, and ivory, and gems, but have not a little brass, and iron, and miry clay mingled with the precious metal. The audacity of his occasional coarseness and personality is unparalleled in contemporary literature, and has hardly been exceeded by the licence of former days. Hence, before his volumes are put within the reach of immature minds, there is need of a friendly penknife to exercise a strict censorship. Yet, when all coarseness, all scurrility, all Mephistophelean contempt for the reverent feelings of other men, is removed, there will be a plenteous remainder of exquisite poetry, of wit, humour, and just thought. It is apparently too often a congenial task to write severe words about the transgressions committed by men of genius, especially when the censor has the advantage of being himself a man of *no* genius, so that those transgressions seem to him quite gratuitous; *he*, forsooth, never lacerated any one by his wit, or gave irresistible piquancy to a coarse allusion, and his indignation is not mitigated by any knowledge of the temptation that lies in transcendent power. We are also apt to measure what a gifted man has done by our arbitrary conception of what he might have done, rather than by a comparison of his actual doings with our own or those of other ordinary men. We make ourselves over-zealous agents of heaven, and demand that our brother should bring usurious interest for his five Talents, forgetting that it is less easy to manage five Talents than two.[21] Whatever benefit there may be in denouncing the evil, it is after all more edifying, and certainly more cheering, to appreciate the good. Hence, in endeavouring to give our readers some account of Heine and his works, we shall not dwell lengthily on his failings; we shall not hold the candle up to dusty, vermin-haunted corners, but let the light fall as much as possible on the nobler and more attractive details. Our sketch of Heine's life, which has been drawn from various sources, will be free from everything like intrusive gossip, and will derive its colouring chiefly from the autobiographical hints and descriptions scattered through his own writings. Those of our readers who happen to know nothing of Heine, will in this way be making their acquaintance with the writer while they are learning the outline of his career.

We have said that Heine was born with the present century; but this statement is not precise, for we learn that, according to his certificate of baptism, he was born 12 December 1799.[22] However, as he himself says, the important point is, that he was born, and born on the banks of the Rhine, at Düsseldorf, where his father was a merchant. In his *Reisebilder* he gives us some recollections, in his wild poetic way, of the dear old town where he spent his childhood, and of his schoolboy troubles there. We shall quote from these in butterfly fashion, sipping a little nectar here and there, without regard to any strict order: –

I first saw the light on the banks of that lovely stream, where Folly grows on the green hills, and in autumn is plucked, pressed, poured into casks, and sent into foreign lands. Believe me, I yesterday heard some one utter folly which, in anno 1811, lay in a bunch of grapes I then saw growing on the Johannisberg ... Mon Dieu! if I had only such faith in me that I could remove mountains, the Johannisberg would be the very mountain I should send for wherever I might be; but as my faith is not so strong, imagination must help me, and it transports me at once to the lovely Rhine ... I am again a child, and playing with other children on the Schlossplatz, at Düsseldorf on the Rhine. Yes, madam, there was I born; and I note this expressly, in case, after my death, seven cities – Schilda, Krähwinkel, Polkwitz, Bockum, Dülken, Göttingen, and Schöppenstädt – should contend for the honour of being my birth-place. Düsseldorf is a town on the Rhine; 16,000 men live there, and many hundred thousand men besides lie buried there ... Among them, many of whom my mother says, that it would be better if they were still living; for example, my grandfather and my uncle, the old Herr von Geldern and the young Herr von Geldern, both such celebrated doctors, who saved so many men from death, and yet must die themselves. And the pious Ursula, who carried me in her arms when I was a child, also lies buried there, and a rosebush grows on her grave; she loved the scent of roses so well in life, and her heart was pure rose-incense and goodness. The knowing old Canon, too, lies buried there. Heavens, what an object he looked when I last saw him! *He was made up of nothing but mind and plasters*, and nevertheless studied day and night, as if he were alarmed lest the worms should find an idea too little in his head. And the little William lies there, and for this I am to blame. We were school-fellows in the Franciscan monastery, and were playing on that side of it where the Düssel flows between stone walls, and I said – 'William, fetch out the kitten that has just fallen in' – and merrily he went down on to the plank which lay across the brook, snatched the kitten out of the water, but fell in himself, and was dragged out dripping and dead. *The kitten lived to a good old age* . . . Princes in that day were not the tormented race as they are now; the crown grew firmly on their heads, and at night they drew a nightcap over it, and slept peacefully, and peacefully slept the people at their feet; and when the people waked in the morning, they said – 'Good morning, father!' – and the princes answered – 'Good morning, dear children!' But it was suddenly quite otherwise; for when we awoke one morning at Düsseldorf, and were ready to say – 'Good morning, father!' – lo! the father was gone away; and in the whole town there was nothing but dumb sorrow, everywhere a sort of funeral disposition; and people glided along silently to the market, and read the long placard placed on the door of the Town Hall. It was dismal weather; yet the lean tailor, Kilian, stood in his nankeen jacket which he usually wore only in the house, and his blue worsted stockings hung down so that his naked legs peeped out mournfully, and his thin lips trembled while he muttered the announcement to himself. And an old soldier read rather louder, and at many a word a crystal tear trickled down to his brave old moustache. I stood near him and wept in company, and asked him – '*Why we wept*?' He answered – 'The Elector has abdicated.' And then he read again, and at the words, 'for the long-manifested fidelity of my subjects' and 'hereby set you free from your allegiance', he wept more than ever. It is strangely touching to see an old man like that, with faded uniform and scarred face, weep so bitterly all of a sudden. While we were reading, the electoral arms were taken down from the Town Hall; everything had such a desolate air, that it was as if an eclipse of the sun were expected . . . I went home and wept, and wailed out – 'The Elector has abdicated!' In vain my mother took a world of trouble to explain the thing to me. I knew what I knew; I was not to be persuaded, but went crying to bed, and in the night dreamed that the world was at an end.

The next morning, however, the sun rises as usual, and Joachim Murat is proclaimed Grand Duke, whereupon there is a holiday at the public school, and Heinrich (or Harry, for that was his baptismal name, which he afterwards had the good taste to change), perched on the bronze horse of the Electoral statue, sees quite a different scene from yesterday's: –

The next day the world was again all in order, and we had school as before, and things were got by heart as before – the Roman emperors, chronology, the nouns in *im*, the *verba irregularia*, Greek, Hebrew, geography, mental arithmetic! – heaven! my head is still dizzy with it – all must be learned by heart! And a great deal of this came in very conveniently for me in after life. For if I had not known the Roman kings by heart, it would subsequently have been quite indifferent to me whether Niebuhr had proved or had not proved that they never really existed . . . But oh! the trouble I had at school with the endless dates. And with arithmetic it was still worse. What I understood best was subtraction, for that has a very practical rule: 'Four can't be taken from three, therefore I must borrow one.' But I advise every one in such a case to borrow a few extra pence, for no one can tell what may happen . . . As for Latin, you have no idea, madam, what a complicated affair it is. The Romans would never have found time to conquer the world if they had first had to learn Latin. Luckily for them, they already knew in their cradles what nouns have their accusative in *im*. I, on the contrary, had to learn them by heart in the sweat of my brow; nevertheless, it is fortunate for me that I know them . . . and the fact that I have them at my finger-ends if I should ever happen to want them suddenly, affords me much inward repose and consolation in many troubled hours of life . . . Of Greek I will not say a word, I should get too much irritated. The monks in the middle ages were not so far wrong when they maintained that Greek was an invention of the devil. God knows the suffering I endured over it . . . With Hebrew it went somewhat better, for I had always a great liking for the Jews, though to this very hour they crucify my good name; but I could never get on so far in Hebrew as my watch, which had much familiar intercourse with pawnbrokers, and in this way contracted many Jewish habits – for example, it wouldn't go on Saturdays.

Heine's parents were apparently not wealthy, but his education was cared for by his uncle, Solomon Heine, a great banker in Hamburg, so that he had no early pecuniary disadvantages to struggle with. He seems to have been very happy in his mother, who was not of Hebrew, but of Teutonic blood; he often mentions her with reverence and affection, and in the *Buch der Lieder* there are two exquisite sonnets addressed to her, which tell how his proud spirit was subdued by the charm of her presence, and how her love was the home of his heart after restless weary wanderings: –

> Wie mächtig auch mein stolzer Muth sich blähe,
> In deiner selig süssen, trauten Nähe
> Ergreift mich oft ein demuthvolle Zagen.

*

Und immer irrte ich nach Liebe, immer
Nach Liebe, doch die Liebe fand ich nimmer,
Und kehrte um nach Hause, krank und trübe.
Doch da bist du entgegen mir gekommen,
Und ach! was da in deinem Aug' geschwommen,
Das war die süsse, langgesuchte Liebe.[23]

He was at first destined for a mercantile life, but Nature declared too strongly against this plan. 'God knows,' he has lately said in conversation with his brother, 'I would willingly have become a banker, but I could never bring myself to that pass. I very early discerned that bankers would one day be the rulers of the world.' So commerce was at length given up for law, the study of which he began in 1819 at the University of Bonn. He had already published some poems in the corner of a newspaper, and among them was one on Napoleon, the object of his youthful enthusiasm. This poem, he says in a letter to St René Taillandier, was written when he was only sixteen. It is still to be found in the *Buch der Lieder* under the title 'Die Grenadiere', and it proves that even in its earliest efforts his genius showed a strongly specific character.

It will be easily imagined that the germs of poetry sprouted too vigorously in Heine's brain for jurisprudence to find much room there. Lectures on history and literature, we are told, were more diligently attended than lectures on law. He had taken care, too, to furnish his trunk with abundant editions of the poets, and the poet he especially studied at that time was Byron. At a later period we find his taste taking another direction, for he writes, 'Of all authors, Byron is precisely the one who excites in me the most intolerable emotion; whereas Scott, in every one of his works, gladdens my heart, soothes, and invigorates me.' Another indication of his bent in these Bonn days, was a newspaper essay, in which he attacked the Romantic school; and here also he went through that chicken-pox of authorship – the production of a tragedy. Heine's tragedy – *Almansor* – is, as might be expected, better than the majority of these youthful mistakes. The tragic collision lies in the conflict between natural affection and the deadly hatred of religion and of race – in the sacrifice of youthful lovers to the strife between Moor and Spaniard, Moslem and Christian. Some of the situations are striking, and there are passages of considerable poetic merit; but the characters are little more than shadowy vehicles for the poetry, and there is a want of clearness and probability in the structure. It was published two years later, in company with another tragedy, in one act, called *William Ratcliffe*, in which there is rather a feeble use of the Scotch second-sight after the manner of the Fate in the Greek tragedy. We smile to find Heine saying of his tragedies, in a letter to a friend soon after their publication: 'I know they will be terribly cut up, but I will confess to you in confidence that they are very good, better than my collection of poems, which are not worth a shot.' Elsewhere he tells us, that when, after one of Paganini's concerts, he was passionately complimenting the great master on his violin-playing, Paganini interrupted him thus: 'But how were you pleased with my *bows*?'

In 1820 Heine left Bonn for Göttingen. He there pursued his omission of law studies; and at the end of three months he was rusticated for a breach of the laws against duelling. While there, he had attempted a negotiation with Brockhaus for the printing of a volume of poems, and had endured that first ordeal of lovers and poets – a refusal. It was not until a year after, that he found a Berlin publisher for his first volume of poems, subsequently transformed, with additions, into the *Buch der Lieder*. He remained between two and three years at Berlin, and the society he found there seems to have made these years an important epoch in his culture. He was one of the youngest members of a circle which assembled at the house of the poetess Elise von Hohenhausen, the translator of Byron – a circle which included Chamisso, Varnhagen, and Rahel (Varnhagen's wife).[24] For Rahel, Heine had a profound admiration and regard; he afterwards dedicated to her the poems included under the title *Heimkehr*, and he frequently refers to her or quotes her in a way that indicates how he valued her influence. According to his friend, F. von Hohenhausen, the opinions concerning Heine's talent were very various among his Berlin friends, and it was only a small minority that had any presentiment of his future fame. In this minority was Elise von Hohenhausen, who proclaimed Heine as the Byron of Germany; but her opinion was met with much head-shaking and opposition. We can imagine how precious was such a recognition as hers to the young poet, then only two or three and twenty, and with by no means an impressive personality for superficial eyes. Perhaps even the deep-sighted were far from detecting in that small, blond, pale young man, with quiet, gentle manners, the latent powers of ridicule and sarcasm – the terrible talons that were one day to be thrust out from the velvet paw of the young leopard.

It was apparently during this residence in Berlin that Heine united himself with the Lutheran Church. He would willingly, like many of his friends, he tells us, have remained free from all ecclesiastical ties if the authorities there had not forbidden residence in Prussia, and especially in Berlin, to every one who did not belong to one of the positive religions recognized by the State.

As Henri IV once laughingly said, 'Paris vaut bien une messe,' so I might with reason say, 'Berlin vaut bien une prêche';[25] and I could afterwards, as before, accommodate myself to the very enlightened Christianity, filtrated from all superstition, which could then be had in the churches of Berlin, and which was even free from the divinity of Christ, like turtle-soup without turtle.

At the same period, too, Heine became acquainted with Hegel. In his lately published *Geständnisse (Confessions)*, he throws on Hegel's influence over him the blue light of demoniacal wit, and confounds us by the most bewildering double-edged sarcasms; but that influence seems to have been at least more wholesome than the one which produced the mocking retractations of the *Geständnisse*. Through all his self-satire, we discern that in those days he had something like real earnestness and enthusiasm, which are certainly not apparent in his present theistic confession of faith.

On the whole, I never felt a strong enthusiasm for this philosophy, and conviction on the subject was out of the question. I never was an abstract thinker, and I accepted the synthesis of the Hegelian doctrine without demanding any proof, since its consequences flattered my vanity. I was young and proud, and it pleased my vainglory when I learned from Hegel that the true God was not, as my grandmother believed, the God who lives in heaven, but myself here upon earth. This foolish pride had not in the least a pernicious influence on my feelings, on the contrary, it heightened these to the pitch of heroism. I was at that time so lavish in generosity and self-sacrifice, that I must assuredly have eclipsed the most brilliant deeds of those good *bourgeois* of virtue who acted merely from a sense of duty, and simply obeyed the laws of morality.

His sketch of Hegel[26] is irresistibly amusing; but we must warn the reader that Heine's anecdotes are often mere devices of style by which he conveys his satire or opinions. The reader will see that he does not neglect an opportunity of giving a sarcastic lash or two, in passing, to Meyerbeer,[27] for whose music he has a great contempt. The sarcasm conveyed in the substitution of *reputation* for *music* and *journalists* for *musicians*, might perhaps escape any one unfamiliar with the sly and unexpected turns of Heine's ridicule.

To speak frankly, I seldom understood him, and only arrived at the meaning of his words by subsequent reflection. I believe he wished not to be understood; and hence his practice of sprinkling his discourse with modifying parentheses; hence, perhaps, his preference for persons of whom he knew that they did not understand him, and to whom he all the more willingly granted the honour of his familiar acquaintance. Thus every one in Berlin wondered at the intimate companionship of the profound Hegel with the late Heinrich Beer, a brother of Giacomo Meyerbeer, who is universally known by his reputation, and who has been celebrated by the cleverest journalists. This Beer, namely Heinrich, was a thoroughly stupid fellow, and indeed was afterwards actually declared imbecile by his family, and placed under guardianship, because instead of making a name for himself in art or in science by means of his great fortune, he squandered his money on childish trifles; and, for example, one day bought 6,000 thalers' worth of walking-sticks. This poor man, who had no wish to pass either for a great tragic dramatist, or for a great star-gazer, or for a laurel-crowned musical genius, a rival of Mozart and Rossini, and preferred giving his money for walking-sticks – this degenerate Beer enjoyed Hegel's most confidential society; he was the philosopher's bosom friend, his Pylades, and accompanied him everywhere like his shadow. The equally witty and gifted Felix Mendelssohn once sought to explain this phenomenon, by maintaining that Hegel did not understand Heinrich Beer. I now believe, however, that the real ground of that intimacy consisted in this – Hegel was convinced that no word of what he said was understood by Heinrich Beer; and he could therefore, in his presence, give himself up to all the intellectual outpourings of the moment. In general, Hegel's conversation was a sort of monologue, sighed forth by starts in a noiseless voice; the odd roughness of his expressions often struck me, and many of them have remained in my memory. One beautiful starlight evening we stood together at the window, and I, a young man of one-and-twenty, having just had a good dinner and finished my coffee, spoke with enthusiasm of the stars, and called them the habitations of the departed. But the master muttered to himself, 'The stars! hum! hum! The stars are only a brilliant leprosy on the face of the heavens.' 'For God's sake,' I cried, 'is there, then, no happy place above, where virtue is rewarded after death?' But he, staring at me with his pale eyes, said, cuttingly, 'So you want a bonus for having taken care of your sick mother, and refrained from poisoning your worthy brother?' At these words he looked anxiously round, but appeared immediately set at rest when he observed that it was only Heinrich Beer, who had approached to invite him to a game at whist.

In 1823, Heine returned to Göttingen to complete his career as a law student, and this time he gave evidence of advanced mental maturity, not only by producing many of the charming poems subsequently included in the *Reisebilder*, but also by prosecuting his professional studies diligently enough to leave Göttingen, in 1825, as *Doctor juris*. Hereupon he settled at Hamburg as an advocate, but his profession seems to have been the least pressing of his occupations. In those days, a small blond young man, with the brim of his hat drawn over his nose, his coat flying open, and his hands stuck in his trouser-pockets, might be seen stumbling along the streets of Hamburg, staring from side to side, and appearing to have small regard to the figure he made in the eyes of the good citizens. Occasionally an inhabitant, more literary than usual, would point out this young man to his companion as *Heinrich Heine*; but in general, the young poet had not to endure the inconveniences of being a lion. His poems were devoured, but he was not asked to devour flattery in return. Whether because the fair Hamburghers acted in the spirit of Johnson's advice to Hannah More[28] – to 'consider what her flattery was worth before she choked him with it' – or for some other reason, Heine, according to the testimony of August Lewald, to whom we owe these particulars of his Hamburgh life, was left free from the persecution of tea-parties. Not, however, from another persecution of genius – nervous headaches, which some persons, we are told, regarded as an improbable fiction, intended as a pretext for raising a delicate white hand to his forehead. It is probable that the sceptical persons alluded to were themselves untroubled with nervous head-ache, and that their hands were *not* delicate. Slight details these, but worth telling about a man of genius, because they help us to keep in mind that he is, after all, our brother, having to endure the petty every-day ills of life as we have; with this difference, that his heightened sensibility converts what are mere insect stings for us into scorpion stings for him.

It was, perhaps, in these Hamburgh days that Heine paid the visit to Goethe, of which he gives us this charming little picture: –

When I visited him in Weimar, and stood before him, I involuntarily glanced at his side to see whether the eagle was not there with the lightning in his beak. I was nearly speaking Greek to him; but, as I observed that he understood German, I stated to him in German, that the plums on the road between Jena and Weimar were very good. I had for so many long winter nights thought over what lofty and profound things I would say to Goethe, if ever I saw him. And when I saw him at last, I said to him, that the Saxon plums were very good! And Goethe smiled.

During the next few years, Heine produced the most popular of all his works – those which have won him his place as the greatest of living German poets and humorists. Between 1826 and 1829, appeared the four volumes of the *Reisebilder* (*Pictures of Travel*), and the *Buch der Lieder* (*Book of Songs*) – a volume of lyrics, of which it is hard to say whether their greatest charm is the lightness and finish of their style, their vivid and original imaginativeness, or their simple, pure sensibility. In his *Reisebilder*, Heine carries us with him to the Harz, to the isle of Norderney, to his native town Düsseldorf, to Italy, and to England, sketching scenery and charac-ter, now with the wildest, most fantastic humour, now with the finest idyllic sensibility, – letting his thoughts wander from poetry to politics, from criticism to dreamy reverie, and blending fun, imagination, reflection, and satire in a sort of exquisite, ever-varying shimmer, like the hues of the opal.

Heine's journey to England did not at all heighten his regard for the English. He calls our language the 'hiss of egoism' (*Zischlaute des Egoismus*); and his ridicule of English awkwardness is as merci-less as – English ridicule of German awkwardness. His antipathy towards us seems to have grown in intensity, like many of his other antipathies; and in his *Vermischte Schriften* he is more bitter than ever. Let us quote one of his philippics; since bitters are understood to be wholesome.

It is certainly a frightful injustice to pronounce sentence of condemnation on an entire people. But with regard to the English, momentary disgust might betray me into this injustice; and on looking at the mass, I easily forget the many brave and noble men who distinguished themselves by intellect and love of freedom. But these, especially the British poets, were always all the more glaringly in contrast with the rest of the nation; they were isolated martyrs to their national relations; and, besides, great geniuses do not belong to the particular land of their birth: they scarcely belong to this earth, the Golgotha of their sufferings. The mass – the English blockheads, God forgive me! – are hateful to me in my inmost soul; and I often regard them not at all as my fellow-men, but as miserable automata – machines, whose motive power is egoism. In these moods, it seems to me as if I heard the whizzing wheel-work by which they think, feel, reckon, digest, and pray: their praying, their mechanical Anglican church-going, with the gilt Prayer-book under their arms, their stupid, tiresome Sunday, their awkward piety, is most of all odious to me. I am firmly convinced that a blaspheming Frenchman is a more pleasing sight for the Divinity than a praying Englishman.

On his return from England, Heine was employed at Munich in editing the *Allgemeinen Politischen Annalen*, but in 1830 he was again in the north, and the news of the July Revolution surprised him on the island of Heligoland. He has given us a graphic picture of his democratic enthusiasm in those days in some letters, apparently written from Heligoland, which he has inserted in his book on Börne.[29] We quote some passages, not only for their biographic interest as showing a phase of Heine's mental history, but because they are a specimen of his power in that kind of dithyrambic writing which, in less masterly hands, easily becomes ridiculous: –

The thick packet of newspapers arrived from the Continent with these warm, glowing-hot tidings. They were sunbeams wrapped up in packing-paper, and they inflamed my soul till it burst into the wildest conflagration ... It is all like a dream to me; especially the name, Lafayette, sounds to me like a legend out of my earliest childhood. Does he really sit again on horseback, commanding the National Guard? I almost fear it may not be true, for it is in print. I will myself go to Paris, to be convinced of it with my bodily eyes . . . It must be splendid, when he rides through the streets, the citizen of two worlds, the god-like old man, with his silver locks streaming down his sacred shoulder . . . He greets, with his dear old eyes, the grandchildren of those who once fought with him for freedom and equality . . . It is now sixty years since he returned from America with the Declaration of Human Rights, the decalogue of the world's new creed, which was revealed to him amid the thunders and lightnings of cannon . . . And the tri-coloured flag waves again on the towers of Paris, and its streets resound with the Marseillaise! . . . It is all over with my yearning for repose. I now know again what I will do, what I ought to do, what I must do . . . I am the son of the Revolution, and seize again the hallowed weapons on which my mother pronounced her magic benediction . . . Flowers! flowers! I will crown my head for the death-fight. And the lyre too, reach me the lyre, that I may sing a battle-song . . . Words like flaming stars, that shoot down from the heavens, and burn up the palaces, and illuminate the huts . . . Words like bright javelins, that whirr up to the seventh heaven and strike the pious hypocrites who have skulked into the Holy of Holies . . . I am all joy and song, all sword and flame! Perhaps, too, all delirium . . . One of those sunbeams wrapped in brown paper has flown to my brain, and set my thoughts aglow. In vain I dip my head into the sea. No water extinguishes this Greek fire . . . Even the poor Heligolanders shout for joy, although they have only a sort of dim instinct of what has occurred. The fisherman who yesterday took me over to the little sand island, which is the bathing-place here, said to me smilingly, 'The poor people have won!' Yes; instinctively the people comprehend such events, perhaps better than we, with all our means of knowledge. Thus Frau von Varnhagen once told me that when the issue of the Battle of Leipzig was not yet known, the maid-servant suddenly rushed into the room with the sorrowful cry, 'The nobles have won!' . . . This morning another packet of newspapers is come. I devour them like manna. Child that I am, affecting details touch me yet more than the momentous whole. Oh, if I could but see the dog Medor . . . The dog Medor brought his master his gun and cartridge-box, and when his master fell, and was buried with his fellow-heroes in the Court of the Louvre, there stayed the poor dog like a monument of faithfulness, sitting motionless on the grave, day and night, eating but little of the food that was offered him – burying the greater part of it in the earth, perhaps as nourishment for his buried master!

The enthusiasm which was kept thus at boiling heat by imagination, cooled down rapidly when brought into contact with reality.

In the same book he indicates, in his caustic way, the commencement of that change in his political *temperature* – for it cannot be called a change in opinion – which has drawn down on him immense vituperation from some of the patriotic party, but which seems to have resulted simply from the essential antagonism between keen wit and fanaticism.

On the very first days of my arrival in Paris, I observed that things wore, in reality, quite different colours from those which had been shed on them, when in perspective, by the light of my enthusiasm. The silver locks which I saw fluttering so majestically on the shoulders of Lafayette, the hero of two worlds, were metamorphosed into a brown perruque, which made a pitiable covering for a narrow skull. And even the dog Medor, which I visited in the Court of the Louvre, and which, encamped under tri-coloured flags and trophies, very quietly allowed himself to be fed – he was not at all the right dog, but quite an ordinary brute, who assumed to himself merits not his own, as often happens with the French; and, like many others, he made a profit out of the glory of the Revolution ... He was pampered and patronized, perhaps promoted to the highest posts, while the true Medor, some days after the battle, modestly slunk out of sight, like the true people who created the Revolution.

That it was not merely interest in French politics which sent Heine to Paris in 1831, but also a perception that German air was not friendly to sympathizers in July revolutions, is humorously intimated in the *Geständnisse*.

I had done much and suffered much, and when the sun of the July Revolution arose in France, I had become very weary, and needed some recreation. Also, my native air was every day more unhealthy for me, and it was time I should seriously think of a change of climate. I had visions: the clouds terrified me, and made all sorts of ugly faces at me. It often seemed to me as if the sun were a Prussian cockade; at night I dreamed of a hideous black eagle, which gnawed my liver; and I was very melancholy. Add to this, I had become acquainted with an old Berlin Justizrath, who had spent many years in the fortress of Spandau, and he related to me how unpleasant it is when one is obliged to wear irons in winter. For myself I thought it very unchristian that the irons were not warmed a trifle. If the irons were warmed a little for us they would not make so unpleasant an impression, and even chilly natures might then bear them very well; it would be only proper consideration, too, if the fetters were perfumed with essence of roses and laurels, as is the case in this country (France). I asked my Justizrath whether he often got oysters to eat at Spandau? He said, No; Spandau was too far from the sea. Moreover, he said meat was very scarce there, and there was no kind of *volaille* except flies, which fell into one's soup . . . Now, as I really needed some recreation, and, as Spandau is too far from the sea for oysters to be got there, and the Spandau fly-soup did not seem very appetizing to me, as, besides all this, the Prussian chains are very cold in winter, and could not be conducive to my health, I resolved to visit Paris.

Since this time Paris has been Heine's home, and his best prose works have been written either to inform the Germans on French affairs or to inform the French on German philosophy and literature. He became a correspondent of the *Allgemeine Zeitung*, and his correspondence, which extends, with an interruption of several years, from 1831 to 1844, forms the volume entitled *Französische Zustände* (*French Affairs*), and the second and third volume of his *Vermischte Schriften*. It is a witty and often wise commentary on public men and public events: Louis Philippe, Casimir Périer, Thiers, Guizot, Rothschild, the Catholic party, the Socialist party, have their turn of satire and appreciation, for Heine deals out both with an impartiality which made his less favourable critics – Börne, for example – charge him with the rather incompatible sins of reckless caprice and venality. Literature and art alternate with politics: we have now a sketch of George Sand, or a description of one of Horace Vernet's pictures, – now a criticism of Victor Hugo, or of Liszt, – now an irresistible caricature of Spontini, or Kalkbrenner,[30] – and occasionally the predominant satire is relieved by a fine saying or a genial word of admiration. And all is done with that airy lightness, yet precision of touch, which distinguishes Heine beyond any living writer. The charge of venality was loudly made against Heine in Germany: first, it was said that he was paid to write; then, that he was paid to abstain from writing; and the accusations were supposed to have an irrefragable basis in the fact that he accepted a stipend from the French government. He has never attempted to conceal the reception of that stipend, and we think his statement (in the *Vermischte Schriften*) of the circumstances under which it was offered and received, is a sufficient vindication of himself and M. Guizot from any dishonour in the matter.

It may be readily imagined that Heine, with so large a share of the Gallic element as he has in his composition, was soon at his ease in Parisian society, and the years here were bright with intellectual activity and social enjoyment. 'His wit,' wrote August Lewald, 'is a perpetual gushing fountain; he throws off the most delicious descriptions with amazing facility, and sketches the most comic characters in conversation.' Such a man could not be neglected in Paris, and Heine was sought on all sides – as a guest in distinguished salons, as a possible proselyte in the circle of the Saint Simonians. His literary productiveness seems to have been furthered by this congenial life, which, however, was soon to some extent embittered by the sense of exile; for since 1835 both his works and his person have been the object of denunciation by the German governments. Between 1833 and 1845 appeared the four volumes of the *Salon*, *Die Romantische Schule* (both written, in the first instance, in French), the book on Börne, *Atta Troll*, a romantic poem, *Deutschland*, an exquisitely humorous poem, describing his last visit to Germany, and containing some grand passages of serious writing; and the *Neue Gedichte*, a collection of lyrical poems. Among the most interesting of his prose works are the second volume of the *Salon*, which contains a survey of religion and philosophy in Germany, and the *Romantische Schule*, a delightful introduction to that phase of German literature known as the Romantic school. The book on Börne, which appeared in 1840, two or three years after the death of that writer, excited great indignation in Germany, as a wreaking of vengeance on the dead, an insult to the memory of a man who had worked and suffered in the cause of freedom – a cause which was Heine's own. Börne, we may observe parenthetically for the information of those who are not familiar with recent German literature, was a remarkable political writer of the ultra-liberal party in Germany, who resided in Paris at the same time with Heine: a man of stern, uncompromising partisanship and bitter humour. Without justifying Heine's production of this book, we see excuses for him which should temper the condemnation passed on it. There was a radical opposition of nature between him and Börne; to use his own distinction, Heine is a Hellene – sensuous, realistic, exquisitely alive to the beautiful; while Börne was a Nazarene – ascetic, spiritualistic, despising the pure artist as destitute of earnestness. Heine has too keen a perception of practical absurdities and damaging exaggerations ever to become a thorough-going partisan; and with a love of freedom, a faith in the ultimate triumph of democratic principles, of which we see no just reason to doubt the genuineness and consistency, he has been unable to satisfy more zealous and one-sided liberals by giving his adhesion to their views and measures, or by adopting a denunciatory tone against those in the opposite ranks. Börne could not forgive what he regarded as Heine's epicurean indifference and artistic dalliance, and he at length gave vent to his antipathy in savage attacks on him through the press, accusing him of utterly lacking character and principle, and even of writing under the influence of venal motives. To these attacks Heine remained absolutely mute – from contempt according to his own account; but the retort, which he resolutely refrained from making during Börne's life, comes in this volume published after his death with the concentrated force of long-gathering thunder. The utterly inexcusable part of the book is the caricature of Börne's friend, Madame Wohl, and the scurrilous insinuations concerning Börne's domestic life. It is said, we know not with how much truth, that Heine had to answer for these in a duel with Madame Wohl's husband, and that, after receiving a serious wound, he promised to withdraw the offensive matter from a future edition. That edition, however, has not been called for. Whatever else we may think of the book, it is impossible to deny its transcendent talent – the dramatic vigour with which Börne is made present to us, the critical acumen with which he is characterized, and the wonderful play of wit, pathos, and thought which runs through the whole. But we will let Heine speak for himself, and first we will give part of his graphic description of the way in which Börne's mind and manners grated on his taste: –

To the disgust which, in intercourse with Börne, I was in danger of feeling towards those who surrounded him, was added the annoyance I felt from his perpetual talk about politics. Nothing but political argument, and again political argument, even at table, where he managed to hunt me out. At dinner, when I so gladly forget all the vexations of the world, he spoiled the best dishes for me by his patriotic gall, which he poured as a bitter sauce over everything. Calf's feet, *à la maître d'hôtel*, then my innocent *bonne bouche*, he completely spoiled for me by Job's tidings from Germany, which he scraped together out of the most unreliable newspapers. And then his accursed remarks, which spoiled one's appetite! . . . This was a sort of table-talk which did not greatly exhilarate me, and I avenged myself by affecting an excessive, almost impassioned indifference for the objects of Börne's enthusiasm. For example, Börne was indignant that immediately on my arrival in Paris, I had nothing better to do than to write for German papers a long account of the Exhibition of Pictures. I omit all discussion as to whether that interest in Art which induced me to undertake this work was so utterly irreconcilable with the revolutionary interests of the day: but Börne saw in it a proof of my indifference towards the sacred cause of humanity, and I could in my turn spoil the taste of his patriotic *Sauerkraut* for him by talking all dinner-time of nothing but pictures, of Robert's *Reapers*, Horace Vernet's *Judith*, and Scheffer's *Faust* . . . That I never thought it worth while to discuss my political principles with him it is needless to say; and once when he declared that he had found a contradiction in my writings, I satisfied myself with the ironical answer, 'You are mistaken, *mon cher*; such contradictions never occur in my works, for always before I begin to write, I read over the statement of my political principles in my previous writings, that I may not contradict myself, and that no one may be able to reproach me with apostacy from my liberal principles.'

And here is his own account of the spirit in which the book was written: –

I was never Börne's friend, nor was I ever his enemy. The displeasure which he could often excite in me was never very important, and he atoned for it sufficiently by the cold silence which I opposed to all his accusations and raillery. While he lived I wrote not a line against him, I never thought about him, I ignored him completely; and that enraged him beyond measure. If I now speak of him, I do so neither out of enthusiasm nor out of uneasiness; I am conscious of the coolest impartiality. I write here neither an apology nor a critique, and as in painting the man I go on my own observation, the image I present of him ought perhaps to be regarded as a real portrait. And such a monument is due to him – to the greater wrestler who, in the arena of our political games, wrestled so courageously, and earned, if not the laurel, certainly the crown of oak leaves. I give an image with his true features, without idealization – the more like him the more honourable for his memory. He was neither a genius nor a hero; he was no Olympian god. He was a man, a denizen of this earth; he was a good writer and a great patriot . . . Beautiful delicious peace, which I feel at this moment in the depths of my soul! Thou rewardest me sufficiently for everything I have done and for everything I have despised ... I shall defend myself neither from the reproach of indifference nor from the suspicion of venality. I have for years, during the life of the insinuator, held such self-justification unworthy of me; now even decency demands silence. That would be a frightful spectacle! – polemics between Death and Exile! Dost thou stretch out to me a beseeching hand from the grave? Without rancour I reach mine towards thee ... See how noble it is and pure! It was never soiled by pressing the hands of the mob, any more than by the impure gold of the people's enemy. In reality thou hast never injured me ... In all thy insinuations there is not a *louis-d'or*'s worth of truth.

In one of these years Heine was married, and, in deference to the sentiments of his wife, married according to the rites of the Catholic Church. On this fact busy rumour afterwards founded the story of his conversion to Catholicism, and could of course name the day and the spot on which he abjured Protestantism. In his *Geständnisse* Heine publishes a denial of this rumour; less, he says, for the sake of depriving the Catholics of the solace they may derive from their belief in a new convert, than in order to cut off from another party the more spiteful satisfaction of bewailing his instability: –

That statement of time and place was entirely correct. I was actually on the specified day in the specified church, which was, moreover, a Jesuit church, namely Saint Sulpice; and I then went through a religious act. But this act was no odious abjuration, but a very innocent conjugation; that is to say, my marriage, already performed according to the civil law, there received the ecclesiastical consecration, because my wife, whose family are staunch Catholics, would not have thought her marriage sacred enough without such a ceremony. And I would on no account cause this beloved being any uneasiness or disturbance in her religious views.

For sixteen years – from 1831 to 1847 – Heine lived that rapid concentrated life which is known only in Paris; but then, alas! stole on the 'days of darkness', and they were to be many. In 1847 he felt the approach of the terrible spinal disease which has for seven years chained him to his bed in acute suffering. The last time he went out of doors, he tells us, was in May 1848: –

With difficulty I dragged myself to the Louvre, and I almost sank down as I entered the magnificent hall where the ever-blessed goddess of beauty, our beloved Lady of Milo, stands on her pedestal. At her feet I lay long, and wept so bitterly that a stone must have pitied me. The goddess looked compassionately on me, but at the same time disconsolately, as if she would say: Dost thou not see, then, that I have no arms, and thus cannot help thee?

Since 1848, then, this poet, whom the lovely objects of Nature have always 'haunted like a passion', has not descended from the second storey of a Parisian house; this man of hungry intellect has been shut out from all direct observation of life, all contact with society, except such as is derived from visitors to his sick-room. The terrible nervous disease has affected his eyes; the sight of one is utterly gone, and he can only raise the lid of the other by lifting it with his finger. Opium alone is the beneficent genius that stills his pain. We hardly know whether to call it an alleviation or an intensification of the torture that Heine retains his mental vigour, his poetic imagination, and his incisive wit; for if this intellectual activity fills up a blank, it widens the sphere of suffering. His brother described him in 1851 as still, in moments when the hand of pain was not too heavy on him, the same Heinrich Heine, poet and satirist by turns. In such moments, he would narrate the strangest things in the gravest manner. But when he came to an end, he would roguishly lift up the lid of his right eye with his finger to see the impression he had produced; and if his audience had been listening with a serious face, he would break into Homeric laughter. We have other proof than personal testimony that Heine's disease allows his genius to retain much of its energy, in the *Romanzero*, a volume of poems published in 1851, and written chiefly during the first three years of his illness; and in the first volume of the *Vermischte Schriften*, also the product of recent years. Very plaintive is the poet's own description of his condition, in the epilogue to the *Romanzero*: –

Do I really exist? My body is so shrunken that I am hardly anything but a voice; and my bed reminds me of the singing grave of the magician Merlin, which lies in the forest of Brozeliand, in Brittany, under tall oaks whose tops soar like green flames towards heaven. Aha! I envy thee those trees and the fresh breeze that moves their branches, brother Merlin, for no green leaf rustles about my mattress-grave in Paris, where early and late I hear nothing but the rolling of vehicles, hammering, quarrelling, and piano-strumming. A grave without repose, death without the privileges of the dead, who have no debts to pay, and need write neither letters nor books – that is a piteous condition. Long ago the measure has been taken for my coffin and for my necrology, but I die so slowly, that the process is tedious for me as well as my friends. But patience; everything has an end. You will one day find the booth closed where the puppet-show of my humour has so often delighted you.

As early as 1850, it was rumoured that since Heine's illness a change had taken place in his religious views; and as rumour seldom stops short of extremes, it was soon said that he had become a thorough pietist, Catholics and Protestants by turns claiming him as a convert. Such a change in so uncompromising an iconoclast, in a man who had been so zealous in his negations as Heine, naturally excited considerable sensation in the camp he was supposed to have quitted, as well as in that he was supposed to have joined. In the second volume of the *Salon*, and in the *Romantische Schule*, written in 1834 and 1835, the doctrine of Pantheism is dwelt on with a fervour and unmixed seriousness which show that Pantheism was then an animating faith to Heine, and he attacks what he considers the false spiritualism and asceticism of Christianity as the enemy of true beauty in Art, and of social well-being. Now, however, it was said that Heine had recanted all his heresies; but from the fact that visitors to his sick-room brought away very various impressions as to his actual religious views, it seemed probable that his love of mystification had found a tempting opportunity for exercise on this subject, and that, as one of his friends said, he was not inclined to pour out unmixed wine to those who asked for a sample out of mere curiosity. At length, in the epilogue to the *Romanzero*, dated 1851, there appeared, amidst much mystifying banter, a declaration that he had embraced Theism and the belief in a future life, and what chiefly lent an air of seriousness and reliability to this affirmation, was the fact that he took care to accompany it with certain negations: –

As concerns myself, I can boast of no particular progress in politics; I adhered (after 1848) to the same democratic principles which had the homage of my youth, and for which I have ever since glowed with increasing fervour. In theology, on the contrary, I must accuse myself of retrogression, since, as I have already confessed, I returned to the old superstition – to a personal God. This fact is, once for all, not to be stifled, as many enlightened and well-meaning friends would fain have had it. But I must expressly contradict the report that my retrograde movement has carried me as far as to the threshold of a Church, and that I have even been received into her lap. No: my religious convictions and views have remained free from any tincture of ecclesiasticism; no chiming of bells has allured me, no altar-candles have dazzled me. I have dallied with no dogmas, and have not utterly renounced my reason.

This sounds like a serious statement. But what shall we say to a convert who plays with his newly-acquired belief in a future life, as Heine does in the very next page? He says to his reader: –

Console thyself; we shall meet again in a better world, where I also mean to write thee better books. I take for granted that my health will there be improved, and that Swedenborg has not deceived me. He relates, namely, with great confidence, that we shall peacefully carry on our old occupations in the other world, just as we have done in this; that we shall there preserve our individuality unaltered, and that death will produce no particular change in our organic development. Swedenborg is a thoroughly honourable fellow, and quite worthy of credit in what he tells us about the other world, where he saw with his own eyes the persons who had played a great part on our earth. Most of them, he says, remained unchanged, and busied themselves with the same things as formerly; they remained stationary, were old-fashioned, *rococo* – which now and then produced a ludicrous effect. For example, our dear Dr Martin Luther kept fast by his doctrine of Grace, about which he had for 300 years daily written down the same mouldy arguments – just in the same way as the late Baron Ekstein, who during twenty years printed in the *Allgemeine Zeitung* one and the same article, perpetually chewing over again the old cud of jesuitical doctrine. But, as we have said, all persons who once figured here below were not found by Swedenborg in such a state of fossil immutability: many had considerably developed their character, both for good and evil, in the other world; and this gave rise to some singular results. Some who had been heroes and saints on earth had *there* sunk into scamps and good-for-nothings; and there were examples, too, of a contrary transformation. For instance, the fumes of self-conceit mounted to Saint Anthony's head when he learned what immense veneration and adoration had been paid to him by all Christendom; and he who here below withstood the most terrible temptations, was now quite an impertinent rascal and dissolute gallows-bird, who vied with his pig in rolling himself in the mud. The chaste Susanna, from having been excessively vain of her virtue, which she thought indomitable, came to a shameful fall, and she who once so gloriously resisted the two old men, was a victim to the seductions of the young Absalom, the son of David. On the contrary, Lot's daughters had in the lapse of time become very virtuous, and passed in the other world for models of propriety: the old man, alas! had stuck to the wine-flask.

In his *Geständnisse*, the retractation of former opinions and profession of Theism are renewed, but in a strain of irony that repels our sympathy and baffles our psychology. Yet what strange, deep pathos is mingled with the audacity of the following passage! –

What avails it me, that enthusiastic youths and maidens crown my marble bust with laurel, when the withered hands of an aged nurse are pressing Spanish flies behind my ears? What avails it me, that all the roses of Shiraz glow and waft incense for me? Alas! Shiraz is 2,000 miles from the Rue d'Amsterdam, where, in the wearisome loneliness of my sick-room, I get no scent except it be, perhaps, the perfume of warmed towels. Alas! God's satire weighs heavily on me. The great Author of the universe, the Aristophanes of Heaven, was bent on demonstrating, with crushing force, to me, the little, earthly, German Aristophanes, how my wittiest sarcasms are only pitiful attempts at jesting in comparison with His, and how miserably I am beneath Him in humour, in colossal mockery.

For our own part, we regard the paradoxical irreverence with which Heine professes his theoretical reverence as pathological, as the diseased exhibition of a predominant tendency urged into anomalous action by the pressure of pain and mental privation – as the delirium of wit starved of its proper nourishment. It is not for us to condemn, who have never had the same burthen laid on us; it is not for pygmies at their ease to criticize the writhings of the Titan chained to the rock.

On one other point we must touch before quitting Heine's personal history. There is a standing accusation against him in some quarters of wanting political principle, of wishing to denationalize himself, and of indulging in insults against his native country. Whatever ground may exist for these accusations, that ground is not, so far as we see, to be found in his writings. He may not have much faith in German revolutions and revolutionists;

experience, in his case as in that of others, may have thrown his millennial anticipations into more distant perspective; but we see no evidence that he has ever swerved from his attachment to the principles of freedom, or written anything which to a philosophic mind is incompatible with true patriotism. He has expressly denied the report that he wished to become naturalized in France; and his yearning towards his native land and the accents of his native language is expressed with a pathos the more reliable from the fact that he is sparing in such effusions. We do not see why Heine's satire of the blunders and foibles of his fellow-countrymen should be denounced as the crime of *lèse-patrie*, any more than the political caricatures of any other satirist. The real offences of Heine are his occasional coarseness and his unscrupulous personalities, which are reprehensible, not because they are directed against his fellow-countrymen, but because they are *personalities*. That these offences have their precedents in men whose memory the world delights to honour does not remove their turpitude, but it is a fact which should modify our condemnation in a particular case; unless, indeed, we are to deliver our judgements on a principle of compensation – making up for our indulgence in one direction by our severity in another. On this ground of coarseness and personality, a true bill may be found against Heine; *not*, we think, on the ground that he has laughed at what is laughable in his compatriots. Here is a specimen of the satire under which we suppose German patriots wince: –

Rhenish Bavaria was to be the starting-point of the German revolution. Zweibrücken was the Bethlehem in which the infant Saviour – Freedom – lay in the cradle, and gave whimpering promise of redeeming the world. Near his cradle bellowed many an ox, who afterwards, when his horns were reckoned on, showed himself a very harmless brute. It was confidently believed that the German revolution would begin in Zweibrücken, and everything was there ripe for an outbreak. But, as has been hinted, the tender-heartedness of some persons frustrated that illegal undertaking. For example, among the Bipontine conspirators there was a tremendous braggart, who was always loudest in his rage, who boiled over with the hatred of tyranny, and this man was fixed on to strike the first blow, by cutting down a sentinel who kept an important post . . . 'What!' cried the man, when this order was given him – 'What! – me! Can you expect so horrible, so bloodthirsty an act of me? I – *I*, kill an innocent sentinel? I, who am father of a family! And this sentinel is perhaps also father of a family. One father of a family kill another father of a family? Yes! Kill – murder!'

In political matters, Heine, like all men whose intellect and taste predominate too far over their impulses to allow of their becoming partisans, is offensive alike to the aristocrat and the democrat. By the one he is denounced as a man who holds incendiary principles, by the other as a half-hearted 'trimmer'. He has no sympathy, as he says, with 'that vague, barren pathos, that useless effervescence of enthusiasm, which plunges, with the spirit of a martyr, into an ocean of generalities, and which always reminds me of the American sailor, who had so fervent an enthusiasm for General Jackson, that he at last sprang from the top of a mast into the sea, crying, *I die for General Jackson!*'

But thou liest, Brutus, thou liest, Cassius, and thou, too, liest, Asinius, in maintaining that my ridicule attacks those ideas which are the precious acquisition of Humanity, and for which I myself have so striven and suffered. No! for the very reason that those ideas constantly hover before the poet in glorious splendour and majesty, he is the more irresistibly overcome by laughter when he sees how rudely, awkwardly, and clumsily those ideas are seized and mirrored in the contracted minds of contemporaries ... There are mirrors which have so rough a surface that even an Apollo reflected in them becomes a caricature, and excites our laughter. *But we laugh then only at the caricature, not at the god.*

For the rest, why should we demand of Heine that he should be a hero, a patriot, a solemn prophet, any more than we should demand of a gazelle that it should draw well in harness? Nature has not made him of her sterner stuff – not of iron and adamant, but of pollen of flowers, the juice of the grape, and Puck's mischievous brain, plenteously mixing also the dews of kindly affection and the gold-dust of noble thoughts. It is, after all, a *tribute* which his enemies pay him when they utter their bitterest dictum, namely, that he is '*nur Dichter*' – only a poet. Let us accept this point of view for the present, and, leaving all consideration of him as a man, look at him simply as a poet and literary artist.

Heine is essentially a lyric poet. The finest products of his genius are

> Short swallow flights of song that dip
> Their wings in tears, and skim away;[31]

and they are so emphatically songs that, in reading them, we feel as if each must have a twin melody born in the same moment and by the same inspiration. Heine is too impressible and mercurial for any sustained production; even in his short lyrics his tears sometimes pass into laughter and his laughter into tears; and his longer poems, *Atta Troll* and *Deutschland*, are full of Ariosto-like transitions. His song has a wide compass of notes: he can take us to the shores of the Northern Sea and thrill us by the sombre sublimity of his pictures and dreamy fancies; he can draw forth our tears by the voice he gives to our own sorrows, or to the sorrows of 'Poor Peter'; he can throw a cold shudder over us by a mysterious legend, a ghost story, or a still more ghastly rendering of hard reality; he can charm us by a quiet idyll, shake us with laughter at his overflowing fun, or give us a piquant sensation of surprise by the ingenuity of his transitions from the lofty to the ludicrous. This last power is not, indeed, essentially poetical; but only a poet can use it with the same success as Heine, for only a poet can poise our emotion and expectation at such a height as to give effect to the sudden fall. Heine's greatest power as a poet lies in his simple pathos, in the ever varied but always natural expression he has given to the tender emotions. We may perhaps indicate this phase of his genius by referring to Wordsworth's beautiful little poem, 'She Dwelt among the Untrodden Ways'; the conclusion –

> She dwelt alone, and few could know
> When Lucy ceased to be;
> But she is in her grave, and, oh!
> The difference to me –[32]

is entirely in Heine's manner; and so is Tennyson's poem of a dozen lines, called 'Circumstance'. Both these poems have Heine's pregnant simplicity. But, lest this comparison should mislead, we must say that there is no general resemblance between either Wordsworth, or Tennyson, and Heine. Their greatest qualities lie quite away from the light, delicate lucidity, the easy, rippling music, of Heine's style. The distinctive charm of his lyrics may best be seen by comparing them with Goethe's. Both have the same masterly, finished simplicity and rhythmic grace; but there is more thought mingled with Goethe's feeling – his lyrical genius is a vessel that draws more water than Heine's, and, though it seems to glide along with equal ease, we have a sense of greater weight and force accompanying the grace of its movement. But, for this very reason, Heine touches our hearts more strongly; his songs are all music and feeling – they are like birds that not only enchant us with their delicious notes, but nestle against us with their soft breasts, and make us feel the agitated beating of their hearts. He indicates a whole sad history in a single quatrain: there is not an image in it, not a thought; but it is beautiful, simple, and perfect as a 'big round tear' – it is pure feeling breathed in pure music: –

> Anfangs wollt' ich fast verzagen
> Und ich glaubt' ich trug es nie,
> Und ich hab' es doch getragen, –
> Aber fragt mich nur nicht, wie.*

He excels equally in the more imaginative expression of feeling: he represents it by a brief image, like a finely-cut cameo; he expands it into a mysterious dream, or dramatizes it in a little story, half ballad, half idyll; and in all these forms his art is so perfect, that we never have a sense of artificiality or of unsuccessful effort; but all seems to have developed itself by the same beautiful necessity that brings forth vine-leaves and grapes and the natural curls of child-hood. Of Heine's humorous poetry, *Deutschland* is the most charm-ing specimen – charming, especially, because its wit and humour grow out of a rich loam of thought. *Atta Troll* is more original, more various, more fantastic; but it is too great a strain on the imagination to be a general favourite. We have said, that feeling is the element in which Heine's poetic genius habitually floats; but he can occasionally soar to a higher region, and impart deep significance to picturesque symbolism; he can flash a sublime thought over the past and into the future; he can pour forth a lofty strain of hope or indignation. Few could forget, after once hearing them, the stanzas at the close of *Deutschland*, in which he warns the

---

* At first I was almost in despair, and I thought I could never bear it, and yet I have borne it – only do not ask me *how*?

King of Prussia not to incur the irredeemable hell which the injured poet can create for him – the *singing flames* of a Dante's *terza rima*!

> Kennst du die Hölle des Dante nicht,
> Die schrecklichen Terzetten?
> Wen da der Dichter hineingesperrt
> Den kann kein Gott mehr retten.
>
> Kein Gott, kein Heiland, erlöst ihn je
> Aus diesen singenden flammen!
> Nimm dich in Acht, das wir dich nicht
> Zu solcher Hölle verdammen.[33]

As a prosaist, Heine is, in one point of view, even more distinguished than as a poet. The German language easily lends itself to all the purposes of poetry; like the ladies of the Middle Ages, it is gracious and compliant to the Troubadours. But as these same ladies were often crusty and repulsive to their unmusical mates, so the German language generally appears awkward and unmanageable in the hands of prose writers. Indeed, the number of really fine German prosaists before Heine, would hardly have exceeded the numerating powers of a New Hollander, who can count three and no more. Persons the most familiar with German prose testify that there is an extra fatigue in reading it, just as we feel an extra fatigue from our walk when it takes us over ploughed clay. But in Heine's hands German prose, usually so heavy, so clumsy, so dull, becomes, like clay in the hands of the chemist, compact, metallic, brilliant; it is German in an *allotropic* condition. No dreary, labyrinthine sentences in which you find 'no end in wandering mazes lost'; no chains of adjectives in linked harshness long drawn out; no digressions thrown in as parentheses; but crystalline definiteness and clearness, fine and varied rhythm, and all that delicate precision, all those felicities of word and cadence, which belong to the highest order of prose. And Heine has proved – what Madame de Staël seems to have doubted – that it is possible to be witty in German; indeed, in reading him, you might imagine that German was pre-eminently the language of wit, so flexible, so subtle, so piquant does it become under his management. He is far more an artist in prose than Goethe. He has not the breadth and repose, and the calm development which belong to Goethe's style, for they are foreign to his mental character; but he excels Goethe in susceptibility to the manifold qualities of prose, and in mastery over its effects. Heine is full of variety, of light and shadow: he alternates between epigrammatic pith, imaginative grace, sly allusion, and daring piquancy; and athwart all these there runs a vein of sadness, tenderness, and grandeur which reveals the poet. He continually throws out those finely-chiselled sayings which stamp themselves on the memory, and become familiar by quotation. For example: 'The People have time enough, they are immortal; kings only are mortal.' – 'Wherever a great soul utters its thoughts, there is Golgotha.' – 'Nature wanted to see how she looked, and she created Goethe.' – 'Only the man who has known bodily suffering is truly a *man*; his limbs have their Passion-history, they are spiritualized.' He calls Rubens 'this Flemish Titan, the wings of whose genius were so strong that he soared as high as the sun, in spite of the hundred weight of Dutch cheeses that hung on his legs.' Speaking of Börne's dislike to the calm creations of the true artist, he says, 'He was like a child which, insensible to the glowing significance of a Greek statue, only touches the marble and complains of cold.'

The most poetic and specifically humorous of Heine's prose writings are the *Reisebilder*. The comparison with Sterne is inevitable here; but Heine does not suffer from it, for if he falls below Sterne in raciness of humour, he is far above him in poetic sensibility and in reach and variety of thought. Heine's humour is never persistent, it never flows on long in easy gaiety and drollery; where it is not swelled by the tide of poetic feeling, it is continually dashing down the precipice of a witticism. It is not broad and unctuous; it is aërial and sprite-like, a momentary meeting-place between his poetry and his wit. In the *Reisebilder* he runs through the whole gamut of his powers, and gives us every hue of thought, from the wildly droll and fantastic to the sombre and the terrible. Here is a passage almost Dantesque in conception: –

Alas! one ought in truth to write against no one in this world. Each of us is sick enough in this great lazaretto, and many a polemical writing reminds me involuntarily of a revolting quarrel, in a little hospital at Cracow, of which I chanced to be a witness, and where it was horrible to hear how the patients mockingly reproached each other with their infirmities: how one who was wasted by consumption jeered at another who was bloated by dropsy; how one laughed at another's cancer in the nose, and this one again at his neighbour's locked-jaw or squint, until at last the delirious fever-patient sprang out of bed and tore away the coverings from the wounded bodies of his companions, and nothing was to be seen but hideous misery and mutilation.

And how fine is the transition in the very next chapter, where, after quoting the Homeric description of the feasting gods, he says: –

Then suddenly approached, panting, a pale Jew, with drops of blood on his brow, with a crown of thorns on his head, and a great cross laid on his shoulders; and he threw the cross on the high table of the gods, so that the golden cups tottered, and the gods became dumb and pale, and grew ever paler, till they at last melted away into vapour.

The richest specimens of Heine's wit are perhaps to be found in the works which have appeared since the *Reisebilder*. The years, if they have intensified his satirical bitterness, have also given his wit a finer edge and polish. His sarcasms are so subtly prepared and so slily allusive, that they may often escape readers whose sense of wit is not very acute; but for those who delight in the subtle and delicate flavours of style, there can hardly be any wit more irresistible than Heine's. We may measure its force by the degree in which it has subdued the German language to its purposes, and made that language brilliant in spite of a long hereditary transmission of dullness. As one of the most harmless examples of his satire, take this on a man who has certainly had his share of adulation: –

Assuredly it is far from my purpose to depreciate M. Victor Cousin. The titles of this celebrated philosopher even lay me under an obligation to praise him. He belongs to that living pantheon of France, which we call the peerage, and his intelligent legs rest on the velvet benches of the Luxembourg. I must indeed sternly repress all private feelings which might seduce me into an excessive enthusiasm. Otherwise I might be suspected of servility; for M. Cousin is very influential in the State by means of his position and his tongue. This consideration might even move me to speak of his faults as frankly as of his virtues. Will he himself disapprove of this? Assuredly not. I know that we cannot do higher honour to great minds than when we throw as strong a light on their demerits as on their merits. When we sing the praises of a Hercules, we must also mention that he once laid aside the lion's skin and sat down to the distaff: what then? he remains notwithstanding a Hercules! So when we relate similar circumstances concerning M. Cousin, we must nevertheless add, with discriminating eulogy: *M. Cousin, if he has sometimes sat twaddling at the distaff, has never laid aside the lion's skin* ... It is true that, having been suspected of demagogy, he spent some time in a German prison, just as Lafayette and Richard Cœur de Lion. But that M. Cousin there in his leisure hours studied Kant's *Critique of Pure Reason* is to be doubted on three grounds. First, this book is written in German. Secondly, in order to read this book, a man must understand German. Thirdly, M. Cousin does not understand German ... I fear I am passing unawares from the sweet waters of praise into the bitter ocean of blame. Yes, on one account I cannot refrain from bitterly blaming M. Cousin; namely, that he who loves truth far more than he loves Plato and Tenneman, is unjust to himself when he wants to persuade us that he has borrowed something from the philosophy of Schelling and Hegel. Against this self-accusation, I must take M. Cousin under my protection. On my word and conscience! this honourable man has not stolen a jot from Schelling and Hegel, and if he brought home anything of theirs, it was merely their friendship. That does honour to his heart. But there are many instances of such false self-accusation in psychology. I knew a man who declared that he had stolen silver spoons at the king's table; and yet we all knew that the poor devil had never been presented at court, and accused himself of stealing these spoons to make us believe that he had been a guest at the palace. No! In German philosophy M. Cousin has always kept the sixth commandment; here he has never pocketed a single idea, not so much as a salt-spoon of an idea. All witnesses agree in attesting that in this respect M. Cousin is honour itself ... I prophesy to you that the renown of M. Cousin, like the French Revolution, will go round the world! I hear some one wickedly add: Undeniably the renown of M. Cousin is going round the world, and *it has already taken its departure from France.*

The following 'symbolical myth' about Louis Philippe is very characteristic of Heine's manner: –

I remember very well that immediately on my arrival (in Paris) I hastened to the Palais-Royal to see Louis Philippe. The friend who conducted me told me that the king now appeared on the terrace only at stated hours, but that formerly he was to be seen at any time for five francs. 'For five-francs!' I cried, with amazement; 'does he then show himself for money?' 'No; but he is shown for money, and it happens in this way: — There is a society of *claqueurs, marchands de contremarques*, and such riff-raff, who offered every foreigner to show him the king for five francs: if he would give ten francs, he might see the king raise his eyes to heaven, and lay his hand protestingly on his heart; if he would give twenty francs, the king would sing the Marseillaise. If the foreigner gave five francs, they raised a loud cheering under the king's windows, and his Majesty appeared on the terrace, bowed and retired. If ten francs, they shouted still louder, and gesticulated as if they had been possessed, when the king appeared, who then, as a sign of silent emotion, raised his eyes to heaven, and laid his hand on his heart. English visitors, however, would sometimes spend as much as twenty francs, and then the enthusiasms mounted to the highest pitch: no sooner did the king appear on the terrace, then the Marseillaise was struck up and roared out frightfully, until Louis Philippe, perhaps only for the sake of putting an end to the singing, bowed, laid his hand on his heart, and joined in the Marseillaise. Whether, as is asserted, he beat time with his foot, I cannot say.'

One more quotation, and it must be our last: —

O the women! We must forgive them much, for they love much — and many. Their hate is properly only love turned inside out. Sometimes they attribute some delinquency to us, because they think they can in this way gratify another man. When they write, they have always one eye on the paper and the other on a man; and this is true of all authoresses, except the Countess Hahn-Hahn, who has only one eye.[34]

The Natural History of German Life

(Westminster Review, July 1856)

IT IS an interesting branch of psychological observation to note the images that are habitually associated with abstract or collective terms – what may be called the picture-writing of the mind, which it carries on concurrently with the more subtle symbolism of language. Perhaps the fixity or variety of these associated images would furnish a tolerably fair test of the amount of concrete knowledge and experience which a given word represents, in the minds of two persons who use it with equal familiarity. The word *railways*, for example, will probably call up, in the mind of a man who is not highly locomotive, the image either of a 'Bradshaw',[1] or of the station with which he is most familiar, or of an indefinite length of tram-road; he will alternate between these three images, which represent his stock of concrete acquaintance with railways. But suppose a man to have had successively the experience of a 'navvy', an engineer, a traveller, a railway director and share-holder, and a landed proprietor in treaty with a railway company, and it is probable that the range of images which would by turns present themselves to his mind at the mention of the *word* 'railways', would include all the essential facts in the existence and relations of the *thing*. Now it is possible for the first-mentioned personage to entertain very expanded views as to the multiplication of railways in the abstract, and their ultimate function in civilization. He may talk of a vast network of railways stretching over the globe, of future 'lines' in Madagascar, and elegant refreshment-rooms in the Sandwich Islands, with none the less glibness because his distinct conceptions on the subject do not extend beyond his one station and his indefinite length of tram-road. But it is evident that if we want a railway to be made, or its affairs to be managed, this man of wide views and narrow observation will not serve our purpose.

Probably, if we could ascertain the images called up by the terms 'the people', 'the masses', the proletariat', 'the peasantry', by many who theorize on those bodies with eloquence, or who legislate for them without eloquence, we should find that they indicate almost as small an amount of concrete knowledge – that they are as far from completely representing the complex facts summed up in the collective term, as the railway images of our non-locomotive gentleman. How little the real characteristics of the working classes are known to those who are outside them, how little their natural history has been studied, is sufficiently disclosed by our Art as well as by our political and social theories. Where, in our picture exhibitions, shall we find a group of true peasantry? What English artist even attempts to rival in truthfulness such studies of popular life as the pictures of Teniers or the ragged boys of Murillo?[2] Even one of the greatest painters of the pre-eminently realistic school, while, in his picture of 'The Hireling Shepherd', he gave us a landscape of marvellous truthfulness, placed a pair of peasants in the foreground who were not much more real than the idyllic swains and damsels of our chimney ornaments.[3] Only a total absence of acquaintance and sympathy with our peasantry, could give a moment's popularity to such a picture as 'Cross Purposes', where we have a peasant girl who looks as if she knew L. E. L.'s[4] poems by heart, and English rustics, whose costume seems to indicate that they are meant for ploughmen, with exotic features that remind us of a handsome *primo tenore*. Rather than such cockney sentimentality as this, as an education for the taste and sympathies, we prefer the most crapulous group of boors that Teniers ever painted. But even those among our painters who aim at giving the rustic type of features, who are far above the effeminate feebleness of the 'Keepsake' style, treat their subjects under the influence of traditions and prepossessions rather than of direct observation. The notion that peasants are joyous, that the typical moment to represent a man in a smock-frock is when he is cracking a joke and showing a row of sound teeth, that cottage matrons are usually buxom, and village children necessarily rosy and merry, are prejudices difficult to dislodge from the artistic mind, which looks for its subjects into literature instead of life. The painter is still under the influence of idyllic literature, which has always expressed the imagination of the cultivated and town-bred, rather than the truth of rustic life. Idyllic ploughmen are jocund when they drive their team afield; idyllic shepherds make bashful love under hawthorn bushes; idyllic villagers dance in the chequered shade and refresh themselves, not immoderately, with spicy nut-brown ale. But no one who has seen much of actual ploughmen thinks them jocund; no one who is well acquainted with the English peasantry can pronounce them merry. The slow gaze, in which no sense of beauty beams, no humour twinkles, – the slow utterance, and the heavy slouching walk, remind one rather of that melancholy animal the camel, than of the sturdy countryman, with striped stockings, red waistcoat, and hat aside, who represents the traditional English peasant. Observe a company of haymakers. When you see them at a distance, tossing up the forkfuls of hay in the golden light, while the wagon creeps slowly with its increasing burthen over the meadow, and the bright green space which tells of work done gets larger and larger, you pronounce the scene 'smiling', and you think these companions in labour must be as bright and cheerful as the picture to which they give animation. Approach nearer, and you will certainly find that haymaking time is a time for joking, especially if there are women among the labourers; but the coarse laugh that bursts out every now and then, and expresses the triumphant taunt, is as far as possible from your conception of idyllic merriment. That delicious effervescence of the mind which we call fun, has no equivalent for the northern peasant, except tipsy revelry; the only realm of fancy and imagin-ation for the English clown exists at the bottom of the third quart pot.

The conventional countryman of the stage, who picks up pocket-books and never looks into them, and who is too simple even to know that honesty has its opposite, represents the still lingering mistake, that an unintelligible dialect is a guarantee for ingenu-ousness, and that slouching shoulders indicate an upright dispo-sition. It is quite true that a thresher is likely to be innocent of any adroit arithmetical cheating, but he is not the less likely to carry home his master's corn in his shoes and pocket; a reaper is not given to writing begging-letters, but he is quite capable of cajoling the dairymaid into filling his small-beer bottle with ale. The selfish instincts are not subdued by the sight of buttercups, nor is integrity in the least established by that classic rural occupation, sheep-washing. To make men moral, something more is requisite than to turn them out to grass.

Opera peasants, whose unreality excites Mr Ruskin's indignation,[5] are surely too frank an idealization to be misleading; and since popular chorus is one of the most effective elements of the opera, we can hardly object to lyric rustics in elegant laced bodices and picturesque motley, unless we are prepared to advocate a chorus of colliers in their pit costume, or a ballet of char-women and stocking-weavers. But our social novels profess to represent the people as they are, and the unreality of their representations is a grave evil. The greatest benefit we owe to the artist, whether painter, poet, or novelist, is the extension of our sympathies. Appeals founded on generalizations and statistics require a sympathy ready-made, a moral sentiment already in activity; but a picture of human life such as a great artist can give, surprises even the trivial and the selfish into that attention to what is apart from themselves, which may be called the raw material of moral sentiment. When Scott takes us into Luckie Mucklebackit's cottage,[6] or tells the story of 'The Two Drovers', – when Wordsworth sings to us the reverie of 'Poor Susan', – when Kingsley shows us Alton Locke gazing yearningly over the gate which leads from the highway into the first wood he ever saw,[7] – when Hornung[8] paints a group of chimney-sweepers, – more is done towards linking the higher classes with the lower, towards obliterating the vulgarity of exclusiveness, than by hundreds of sermons and philosophical dissertations. Art is the nearest thing to life; it is a mode of amplifying experience and extending our contact with our fellow-men beyond the bounds of our personal lot. All the more sacred is the task of the artist when he undertakes to paint the life of the People. Falsification here is far more pernicious than in the more artificial aspects of life. It is not so very serious that we should have false ideas about evanescent fashions – about the manners and conversation of beaux and duchesses; but it *is* serious that our sympathy with the perennial joys and struggles, the toil, the tragedy, and the humour in the life of our more heavily-laden fellow-men, should be perverted, and turned towards a false object instead of the true one.

This perversion is not the less fatal because the misrepresentation which gives rise to it has what the artist considers a moral end. The thing for mankind to know is, not what are the motives and influences which the moralist thinks *ought* to act on the labourer or the artisan, but what are the motives and influences which *do* act on him. We want to be taught to feel, not for the heroic artisan or the sentimental peasant, but for the peasant in all his coarse apathy, and the artisan in all his suspicious selfishness.

We have one great novelist who is gifted with the utmost power of rendering the external traits of our town population; and if he could give us their psychological character – their conceptions of life, and their emotions – with the same truth as their idiom and manners, his books would be the greatest contribution Art has ever made to the awakening of social sympathies. But while he can copy Mrs Plornish's colloquial style[9] with the delicate accuracy of a sun-picture, while there is the same startling inspiration in his description of the gestures and phrases of 'Boots',[10] as in the speeches of Shakspeare's mobs or numskulls, he scarcely ever passes from the humorous and external to the emotional and tragic, without becoming as transcendent in his unreality as he was a moment before in his artistic truthfulness. But for the precious salt of his humour, which compels him to reproduce external traits that serve, in some degree, as a corrective to his frequently false psychology, his preternaturally virtuous poor children and artisans, his melodramatic boatmen and courtesans, would be as noxious as Eugène Sue's idealized proletaires[11] in encouraging the miserable fallacy that high morality and refined sentiment can grow out of harsh social relations, ignorance, and want; or that the working classes are in a condition to enter at once into a millennial state of *altruism*,[12] wherein everyone is caring for everyone else, and no one for himself.

If we need a true conception of the popular character to guide our sympathies rightly, we need it equally to check our theories, and direct us in their application. The tendency created by the splendid conquests of modern generalization, to believe that all social questions are merged in economical science, and that the relations of men to their neighbours may be settled by algebraic equations, – the dream that the uncultured classes are prepared for a condition which appeals principally to their moral sensibilities, – the aristocratic dilettantism which attempts to restore the 'good old times' by a sort of idyllic masquerading, and to grow feudal fidelity and veneration as we grow prize turnips, by an artificial system of culture,[13] – none of these diverging mistakes can co-exist with a real knowledge of the People, with a thorough study of their habits, their ideas, their motives. The landholder, the clergyman, the mill-owner, the mining-agent, have each an opportunity for making precious observations on different sections of the working classes, but unfortunately their experience is too often not registered at all, or its results are too scattered to be available as a source of information and stimulus to the public mind generally. If any man of sufficient moral and intellectual breadth, whose observations would not be vitiated by a foregone conclusion, or by a professional point of view, would devote himself to studying the natural history of our social classes, especially of the small shopkeepers, artisans, and peasantry, – the degree in which they are influenced by local conditions, their maxims and habits, the points of view from which they regard their religious teachers, and the degree in which they are influenced by religious doctrines, the interaction of the various classes on each other, and what are the tendencies in their position towards disintegration or towards development, – and if, after all this study, he would give us the result of his observations in a book well-nourished with specific facts, his work would be a valuable aid to the social and political reformer.

What we are desiring for ourselves has been in some degree done for the Germans by Riehl, the author of the very remarkable books the titles of which are placed at the head of this article; and we wish to make these books known to our readers, not only for the sake of the interesting matter they contain and the important reflections they suggest, but also as a model for some future or actual student of our own people. By way of introducing Riehl to those who are unacquainted with his writings, we will give a rapid sketch from his picture of the German Peasantry, and perhaps this indication of the mode in which he treats a particular branch of his subject may prepare them to follow us with more interest when we enter on the general purpose and contents of his works.

In England, at present, when we speak of the peasantry, we mean scarcely more than the class of farm-servants and farm-labourers; and it is only in the most primitive districts, as in Wales, for example, that farmers are included under the term. In order to appreciate what Riehl says of the German peasantry, we must remember what the tenant-farmers and small proprietors were in England half a century ago, when the master helped to milk his own cows, and the daughters got up at one o'clock in the morning to brew, – when the family dined in the kitchen with the servants, and sat with them round the kitchen fire in the evening. In those days, the quarried parlour was innocent of a carpet, and its only specimens of art were a framed sampler and the best tea-board; the daughters even of substantial farmers had often no greater accomplishment in writing and spelling than they could procure at a dame-school; and, instead of carrying on sentimental correspondence, they were spinning their future table-linen, and looking after every saving in butter and eggs that might enable them to add to the little stock of plate and china which they were laying in against their marriage. In our own day, setting aside the superior order of farmers, whose style of living and mental culture are often equal to that of the professional class in provincial towns, we can hardly enter the least imposing farm-house without finding a bad piano in the 'drawing-room', and some old annuals, disposed with a symmetrical imitation of negligence, on the table; though the daughters may still drop their *h*'s, their vowels are studiously narrow; and it is only in very primitive regions that they will consent to sit in a covered vehicle without springs, which was once thought an advance in luxury on the pillion.

The condition of the tenant-farmers and small proprietors in Germany is, we imagine, about on a par, not, certainly, in material prosperity, but in mental culture and habits, with that of the English farmers who were beginning to be thought old-fashioned nearly fifty years ago, and if we add to these the farm servants and labourers, we shall have a class approximating in its characteristics to the *Bauernthum*, or peasantry, described by Riehl.

In Germany, perhaps more than in any other country, it is among the peasantry that we must look for the historical type of the national *physique*. In the towns this type has become so modified to express the personality of the individual, that even 'family likeness' is often but faintly marked. But the peasants may still be distinguished into groups by their physical peculiarities. In one part of the country we find a longer-legged, in another a broader-shouldered race, which has inherited these peculiarities for centuries. For example, in certain districts of Hesse are seen long faces, with high foreheads, long, straight noses, and small eyes with arched eyebrows and large eyelids. On comparing these physiognomies with the sculptures in the church of Saint Elizabeth, at Marburg, executed in the thirteenth century, it will be found that the same old Hessian type of face has subsisted unchanged, with this distinction only, that the sculptures represent princes and nobles, whose features then bore the stamp of their race, while that stamp is now to be found only among the peasants. A painter who wants to draw mediæval characters with historic truth, must seek his models among the peasantry. This explains why the old German painters gave the heads of their subjects a greater uniformity of type than the painters of our day: the race had not attained to a high degree of individualization in features and expression. It indicates, too, that the cultured man acts more as an individual; the peasant, more as one of a group. Hans drives the plough, lives, and thinks just as Kunz does; and it is this fact, that many thousands of men are as like each other in thoughts and habits as so many sheep or oysters, which constitutes the weight of the peasantry in the social and political scale.

In the cultivated world each individual has his style of speaking and writing. But among the peasantry it is the race, the district, the province, that has its style; namely, its dialect, its phraseology, its proverbs and its songs, which belong alike to the entire body of the people. This provincial style of the peasant is again, like his *physique*, a remnant of history to which he clings with the utmost tenacity. In certain parts of Hungary, there are still descendants of German colonists of the twelfth and thirteenth centuries, who go about the country as reapers, retaining their old Saxon songs and manners, while the more cultivated German emigrants in a very short time forget their own language, and speak Hungarian. Another remarkable case of the same kind is that of the Wends, a Slavonic race settled in Lusatia,[14] whose numbers amount to 200,000, living either scattered among the German population or in separate parishes. They have their own schools and churches, and are taught in the Slavonic tongue. The Catholics among them are rigid adherents of the Pope; the Protestants not less rigid adherents of Luther, or *Doctor* Luther, as they are particular in calling him – a custom which, a hundred years ago, was universal in Protestant Germany. The Wend clings tenaciously to the usages of his Church, and perhaps this may contribute not a little to the purity in which he maintains the specific characteristics of his race. German education, German law and government, service in the standing army, and many other agencies, are in antagonism to his national exclusiveness; but the *wives* and *mothers* here, as elsewhere, are a conservative influence, and the habits temporarily laid aside in the outer world are recovered by the fireside. The Wends form several stout regiments in the Saxon army; they are sought far and wide, as diligent and honest servants; and many a weakly Dresden or Leipzig child becomes thriving under the care of a Wendish nurse. In their villages they have the air and habits of genuine, sturdy peasants, and all their customs indicate that they have been, from the first, an agricultural people. For example, they have traditional modes of treating their domestic animals. Each cow has its own name, generally chosen carefully, so as to express the special qualities of the animal; and all important family events are narrated to the *bees* – a custom which is found also in Westphalia. Whether by the help of the bees or not, the Wend farming is especially prosperous; and when a poor Bohemian peasant has a son born to him, he binds him to the end of a long pole and turns his face towards Lusatia, that he may be as lucky as the Wends who live there.

The peculiarity of the peasant's language consists chiefly in his retention of historical peculiarities, which gradually disappear under the friction of cultivated circles. He prefers any proper name that may be given to a day in the calendar, rather than the abstract date, by which he very rarely reckons. In the baptismal names of his children he is guided by the old custom of the country, not at all by whim and fancy. Many old baptismal names, formerly common in Germany, would have become extinct but for their preservation among the peasantry, especially in North Germany; and so firmly have they adhered to local tradition in this matter, that it would be possible to give a sort of topographical statistics of proper names, and distinguish a district by its rustic names as we do by its Flora and Fauna. The continuous inheritance of certain favourite proper names in a family, in some districts, forces the peasant to adopt the princely custom of attaching a numeral to the name, and saying, when three generations are living at once, Hans I, II, and III; or – in the more antique fashion – Hans the elder, the middle, and the younger. In some of our English counties there is a similar adherence to a narrow range of proper names, and as a mode of distinguishing collateral branches in the same family, you will hear of Jonathan's Bess, Thomas's Bess, and Samuel's Bess – the three Bessies being cousins.

The peasant's adherence to the traditional has much greater inconvenience than that entailed by a paucity of proper names. In the Black Forest and in Hüttenberg you will see him in the dog-days wearing a thick fur cap, because it is an historical fur cap – a cap worn by his grandfather. In the Wetterau, that peasant girl is considered the handsomest who wears the most petticoats. To go to field-labour in seven petticoats can be anything but convenient or agreeable, but it is the traditionally correct thing, and a German peasant girl would think herself as unfavourably conspicuous in an untraditional costume, as an English servant-girl would now think herself in a 'linsey-woolsey' apron or a thick muslin cap. In many districts no medical advice would induce the rustic to renounce the tight leather belt with which he injures his digestive functions; you could more easily persuade him to smile on a new communal system than on the unhistorical invention of braces. In the eighteenth century, in spite of the philanthropic preachers of potatoes, the peasant for years threw his potatoes to the pigs and the dogs, before he could be persuaded to put them on his own table. However, the unwillingness of the peasant to adopt innovations has a not unreasonable foundation in the fact, that for him experiments are practical, not theoretical, and must be made with expense of money instead of brains – a fact that is not, perhaps, sufficiently taken into account by agricultural theorists, who complain of the farmer's obstinacy. The peasant has the smallest possible faith in theoretic knowledge; he thinks it rather dangerous than otherwise, as is well indicated by a Lower Rhenish proverb – 'One is never too old to learn, said an old woman; so she learned to be a witch.'

Between many villages an historical feud, once perhaps the occasion of much bloodshed, is still kept up under the milder form of an occasional round of cudgelling, and the launching of traditional nicknames. An historical feud of this kind still exists, for example, among many villages on the Rhine and more inland places in the neighbourhood. *Rheinschnacke* (of which the equivalent is perhaps 'water-snake') is the standing term of ignomy for the inhabitant of the Rhine village, who repays it in kind by the epithet *karst* (mattock) or *kukuk* (cuckoo), according as the object of his hereditary hatred belongs to the field or the forest. If any Romeo among the 'mattocks' were to marry a Juliet among the 'water-snakes', there would be no lack of Tybalts and Mercutios to carry the conflict from words to blows, though neither side knows a reason for the enmity.

A droll instance of peasant conservatism is told of a village on the Taunus, whose inhabitants, from time immemorial, had been famous for impromptu cudgelling. For this historical offence the magistrates of the district had always inflicted the equally historical punishment of shutting up the most incorrigible offenders, not in prison, but in their own pig-sty. In recent times, however, the government, wishing to correct the rudeness of these peasants, appointed an 'enlightened' man as magistrate, who at once abolished the original penalty above-mentioned. But this relaxation of punishment was so far from being welcome to the villagers, that they presented a petition praying that a more energetic man might be given them as a magistrate, who would have the courage to punish according to law and justice, 'as had been beforetime'. And the magistrate who abolished incarceration in the pig-sty could never obtain the respect of the neighbourhood. This happened no longer ago than the beginning of the present century.

But it must not be supposed that the historical piety of the German peasant extends to anything not immediately connected with himself. He has the warmest piety towards the old tumble-down house which his grandfather built, and which nothing will induce him to improve, but towards the venerable ruins of the old castle that overlooks his village he has no piety at all, and carries off its stones to make a fence for his garden, or tears down the gothic carving of the old monastic church, which is 'nothing to him', to mark off a foot-path through his field. It is the same with historical traditions. The peasant has them fresh in his memory, so far as they relate to himself. In districts where the peasantry are unadulterated, you discern the remnants of the feudal relations in innumerable customs and phrases, but you will ask in vain for historical traditions concerning the empire, or even concerning the particular princely house to which the peasant is subject. He can tell you what 'half people and whole people' mean; in Hesse you will still hear of 'four horses making a whole peasant', or of 'four-day and three-day peasants'; but you will ask in vain about Charlemagne and Frederic Barbarossa.

Riehl well observes that the feudal system, which made the peasant the bondman of his lord, was an immense benefit in a country, the greater part of which had still to be colonized, – rescued the peasant from vagabondage, and laid the foundation of persistency and endurance in future generations. If a free German peasantry belongs only to modern times, it is to his ancestor who was a serf, and even, in the earliest times, a slave, that the peasant owes the foundation of his independence, namely, his capability of a settled existence, – nay, his unreasoning persistency, which has its important function in the development of the race.

Perhaps the very worst result of that unreasoning persistency is the peasant's inveterate habit of litigation. Every one remembers the immortal description of Dandie Dinmont's importunate application to Lawyer Pleydell to manage his 'bit lawsuit', till at length Pleydell consents to help him ruin himself, on the ground that Dandie may fall into worse hands.[15] It seems, this is a scene which has many parallels in Germany. The farmer's lawsuit is his point of honour; and he will carry it through, though he knows from the very first day that he shall get nothing by it. The litigious peasant piques himself, like Mr Saddletree,[16] on his knowledge of the law, and this vanity is the chief impulse to many a lawsuit. To the mind of the peasant, law presents itself as the 'custom of the country', and it is his pride to be versed in all customs. *Custom with him holds the place of sentiment, of theory, and in many cases of affection.* Riehl justly urges the importance of simplifying law proceedings, so as to cut off this vanity at its source, and also of encouraging, by every possible means, the practice of arbitration.

The peasant never begins his lawsuit in summer, for the same reason that he does not make love and marry in summer, – because he has no time for that sort of thing. Anything is easier to him than to move out of his habitual course, and he is attached even to his privations. Some years ago, a peasant youth, out of the poorest and remotest region of the Westerwald, was enlisted as a recruit, at Weilburg in Nassau. The lad, having never in his life slept in a bed, when he had to get into one for the first time began to cry like a child; and he deserted twice because he could not reconcile himself to sleeping in a bed, and to the 'fine' life of the barracks: he was homesick at the thought of his accustomed poverty and his thatched hut. A strong contrast, this, with the feeling of the poor in towns, who would be far enough from deserting because their condition was too much improved! The genuine peasant is never ashamed of his rank and calling; he is rather inclined to look down on every one who does not wear a smock-frock, and thinks a man who has the manners of the gentry is likely to be rather windy and unsubstantial. In some places, even in French districts, this feeling is strongly symbolized by the practice of the peasantry, on certain festival days, to dress the images of the saints in peasant's clothing. History tells us of all kinds of peasant insurrections, the object of which was to obtain relief for the peasants from some of their many oppressions; but of an effort on their part to step out of their hereditary rank and calling, to become gentry, to leave the plough and carry on the easier business of capitalists or government-functionaries, there is no example.

The German novelists who undertake to give pictures of peasant-life, fall into the same mistake as our English novelists; they transfer their own feelings to ploughmen and woodcutters, and give them both joys and sorrows of which they know nothing. The peasant never questions the obligation of family-ties – he questions *no custom*, – but tender affection, as it exists amongst the refined part of mankind, is almost as foreign to him as white hands and filbert-shaped nails. That the aged father who has given up his property to his children on condition of their maintaining him for the remainder of his life, is very far from meeting with delicate attentions, is indicated by the proverb current among the peasantry – 'Don't take your clothes off before you go to bed.' Among rustic moral tales and parables, not one is more universal than the story of the ungrateful children, who made their grey-headed father, dependent on them for a maintenance, eat at a wooden trough, because he shook the food out of his trembling hands. Then these same ungrateful children observed one day that their own little boy was making a tiny wooden trough; and when they asked him what it was for, he answered – that his father and mother might eat out of it, when he was a man and had to keep them.

Marriage is a very prudential affair, especially among the peasants who have the largest share of property. Politic marriages are as common among them as among princes; and when a peasant-heiress in Westphalia marries, her husband adopts her name, and places his own after it with the prefix *geborner* (*née*). The girls marry young, and the rapidity with which they get old and ugly is one among the many proofs that the early years of marriage are fuller of hardships than of conjugal tenderness. 'When our writers of village stories,' says Riehl, 'transferred their own emotional life to the peasant, they obliterated what is precisely his most predominant characteristic, namely, that with him general custom holds the place of individual feeling.'

We pay for greater emotional susceptibility too often by nervous diseases of which the peasant knows nothing. To him headache is the least of physical evils, because he thinks headwork the easiest and least indispensable of all labour. Happily, many of the younger sons in peasant families, by going to seek their living in the towns, carry their hardy nervous system to amalgamate with the overwrought nerves of our town population, and refresh them with a little rude vigour. And a return to the habits of peasant life is the best remedy for many moral as well as physical diseases induced by perverted civilization. Riehl points to colonization as presenting the true field for this regenerative process. On the other side of the ocean, a man will have the courage to begin life again as a peasant, while at home, perhaps, opportunity as well as courage will fail him. *Apropos* of this subject of emigration, he remarks the striking fact, that the native shrewdness and mother-wit of the German peasant seem to forsake him entirely when he has to apply them under new circumstances, and on relations foreign to his experience. Hence it is that the German peasant who emigrates, so constantly falls a victim to unprincipled adventurers in the preliminaries to emigration; but if once he gets his foot on the American soil, he exhibits all the first-rate qualities of an agricultural colonist; and among all German emigrants, the peasant class are the most successful.

But many disintegrating forces have been at work on the peasant character, and degeneration is unhappily going on at a greater pace than development. In the wine districts especially, the inability of the small proprietors to bear up under the vicissitudes of the market, or to ensure a high quality of wine by running the risks of a late vintage, and the competition of beer and cider with the inferior wines, have tended to produce that uncertainty of gain which, with the peasant, is the inevitable cause of demoralization. The small peasant proprietors are not a new class in Germany, but many of the evils of their position are new. They are more dependent on ready money than formerly; thus, where a peasant used to get his wood for building and firing from the common forest, he has now to pay for it with hard cash; he used to thatch his own house, with the help perhaps of a neighbour, but now he pays a man to do it for him; he used to pay taxes in kind, he now pays them in money. The chances of the market have to be discounted, and the peasant falls into the hands of money-lenders. Here is one of the cases in which social policy clashes with a purely economical policy.

Political vicissitudes have added their influence to that of economical changes in disturbing that dim instinct, that reverence for traditional custom, which is the peasant's principle of action. He is in the midst of novelties for which he knows no reason – changes in

political geography, changes of the government to which he owes
fealty, changes in bureaucratic management and police regulations. He finds himself in a new element before an apparatus for
breathing in it is developed in him. His only knowledge of modern
history is in some of its results – for instance, that he has to pay
heavier taxes from year to year. His chief idea of a government is
of a power that raises his taxes, opposes his harmless customs, and
torments him with new formalities. The source of all this is the
false system of 'enlightening' the peasant which has been adopted
by the bureaucratic governments. A system which disregards the
traditions and hereditary attachments of the peasant, and appeals
only to a logical understanding which is not yet developed in him,
is simply disintegrating and ruinous to the peasant character. The
interference with the communal regulations has been of this fatal
character. Instead of endeavouring to promote to the utmost the
healthy life of the Commune, as an organism the conditions of
which are bound up with the historical characteristics of the
peasant, the bureaucratic plan of government is bent on improvement by its patent machinery of state-appointed functionaries and
off-hand regulations in accordance with modern enlightenment.
The spirit of communal exclusiveness – the resistance to the indis-
criminate establishment of strangers, is an intense traditional
feeling in the peasant. 'This gallows is for us and our children',
is the typical motto of this spirit. But such exclusiveness is
highly irrational and repugnant to modern liberalism; therefore a
bureaucratic government at once opposes it, and encourages to
the utmost the introduction of new inhabitants in the provincial
communes. Instead of allowing the peasants to manage their
own affairs, and, if they happen to believe that five and four
make eleven, to unlearn the prejudice by their own experience
in calculation, so that they may gradually understand processes,
and not merely see results, bureaucracy comes with its 'Ready
Reckoner' and works all the peasant's sums for him – the surest
way of maintaining him in his stupidity, however it may shake
his prejudice.

Another questionable plan for elevating the peasant, is the
supposed elevation of the clerical character by preventing the
clergyman from cultivating more than a trifling part of the land

attached to his benefice; that he may be as much as possible of a scientific theologian, and as little as possible of a peasant. In this, Riehl observes, lies one great source of weakness to the Protestant Church as compared with the Catholic, which finds the great majority of its priests among the lower orders; and we have had the opportunity of making an analogous comparison in England, where many of us can remember country districts in which the great mass of the people were christianized by illiterate Methodist and Independent ministers, while the influence of the parish clergyman among the poor did not extend much beyond a few old women in scarlet cloaks, and a few exceptional church-going labourers.

Bearing in mind the general characteristics of the German peasant, it is easy to understand his relation to the revolutionary ideas and revolutionary movements of modern times. The peasant, in Germany as elsewhere, is a born grumbler. He has always plenty of grievances in his pocket, but he does not generalize those grievances; he does not complain of 'government' or 'society', probably because he has good reason to complain of the burgomaster. When a few sparks from the first French Revolution fell among the German peasantry, and in certain villages of Saxony the country people assembled together to write down their demands, there was no glimpse in their petition of the 'universal rights of man', but simply of their own particular affairs as Saxon peasants. Again, after the July revolution of 1830, there were many insignificant peasant insurrections; but the object of almost all was the removal of local grievances. Toll-houses were pulled down; stamped paper was destroyed; in some places there was a persecution of wild boars, in others, of that plentiful tame animal, the German *Rath*, or councillor who is never called into council. But in 1848, it seemed as if the movements of the peasants had taken a new character; in the small western states of Germany, it seemed as if the whole class of peasantry was in insurrection. But in fact, the peasant did not know the meaning of the part he was playing. He had heard that everything was being set right in the towns, and that wonderful things were happening there, so he tied up his bundle and set off. Without any distinct object or resolution, the country people presented themselves on the scene

of commotion, and were warmly received by the party leaders.
But, seen from the windows of ducal palaces and ministerial
hotels, these swarms of peasants had quite another aspect, and it
was imagined that they had a common plan of co-operation. This,
however, the peasants have never had. Systematic co-operation
implies general conceptions, and a provisional subordination of
egoism, to which even the artisans of towns have rarely shown
themselves equal, and which are as foreign to the mind of the
peasant as logarithms or the doctrine of chemical proportions.
And the revolutionary fervour of the peasant was soon cooled. The
old mistrust of the towns was reawakened on the spot. The Tyrolese
peasants saw no great good in the freedom of the press and the
constitution, because these changes 'seemed to please the gentry so
much'. Peasants who had given their voices stormily for a German
parliament, asked afterwards, with a doubtful look, whether it
were to consist of infantry or cavalry. When royal domains were
declared the property of the State, the peasants in some small
principalities rejoiced over this, because they interpreted it to
mean that every one would have his share in them, after the
manner of the old common and forest rights.

The very practical views of the peasants, with regard to the
demands of the people, were in amusing contrast with the abstract
theorizing of the educated townsmen. The peasant continually
withheld all State payments until he saw how matters would turn
out, and was disposed to reckon up the solid benefit, in the form of
land or money, that might come to him from the changes obtained.
While the townsman was heating his brains about representation
on the broadest basis, the peasant asked if the relation between
tenant and landlord would continue as before, and whether the
removal of the 'feudal obligations' meant that the farmer should
become owner of the land?

It is in the same naïve way that Communism is interpreted by
the Germany peasantry. The wide spread among them of communistic doctrines, the eagerness with which they listened to a
plan for the partition of property, seemed to countenance the
notion, that it was a delusion to suppose the peasant would be
secured from this intoxication by his love of secure possession
and peaceful earnings. But, in fact, the peasant contemplated

'partition' by the light of an historical reminiscence rather than of novel theory. The golden age, in the imagination of the peasant, was the time when every member of the commune had a right to as much wood from the forest as would enable him to sell some, after using what he wanted in firing, – in which the communal possessions were so profitable that, instead of his having to pay rates at the end of the year, each member of the commune was something in pocket. Hence the peasants in general understood by 'partition', that the State lands, especially the forests, would be divided among the communes, and that, by some political legerdemain or other, everybody would have free fire-wood, free grazing for his cattle, and over and above that, a piece of gold without working for it. That he should give up a single clod of his own to further the general 'partition', had never entered the mind of the peasant Communist; and the perception that this was an essential preliminary to 'partition', was often a sufficient cure for his Communism.

In villages lying in the neighbourhood of large towns, however, where the circumstances of the peasantry are very different, quite another interpretation of Communism is prevalent. Here the peasant is generally sunk to the position of the proletaire, living from hand to mouth; he has nothing to lose, but everything to gain by 'partition'. The coarse nature of the peasant has here been corrupted into bestiality by the disturbance of his instincts, while he is as yet incapable of principles; and in this type of the degenerate peasant is seen the worst example of ignorance intoxicated by theory.

A significant hint as to the interpretation the peasants put on revolutionary theories, may be drawn from the way they employed the few weeks in which their movements were unchecked. They felled the forest trees and shot the game; they withheld taxes; they shook off the imaginary or real burdens imposed on them by their mediatized princes, by presenting their 'demands' in a very rough way before the ducal or princely *Schloss*; they set their faces against the bureaucratic management of the communes, deposed the government functionaries who had been placed over them as burgomasters and magistrates, and abolished the whole bureaucratic system of procedure, simply by taking no notice of its regulations, and recurring to some tradition – some old order or disorder of things. In all this it is clear that they were animated not in the least by the spirit of modern revolution, but by a purely narrow and personal impulse towards reaction.

The idea of constitutional government lies quite beyond the range of the German peasant's conceptions. His only notion of representation is that of a representation of ranks – of classes; his only notion of a deputy is of one who takes care, not of the national welfare, but of the interests of his own order. Herein lay the great mistake of the democratic party, in common with the bureaucratic governments, that they entirely omitted the peculiar character of the peasant from their political calculations. They talked of the 'people', and forgot that the peasants were included in the term. Only a baseless misconception of the peasant's character could induce the supposition that he would feel the slightest enthusiasm about the principles involved in the reconstitution of the Empire, or even about that reconstitution itself. He has no zeal for a written law, as such, but only so far as it takes the form of a living law – a tradition. It was the external authority which the revolutionary party had won in Baden that attracted the peasants into a participation in the struggle.

Such, Riehl tells us, are the general characteristics of the German peasantry – characteristics which subsist amidst a wide variety of circumstances. In Mecklenburg, Pomerania, and Brandenburg, the peasant lives on extensive estates; in Westphalia he lives in large isolated homesteads; in the Westerwald and in Sauerland, in little groups of villages and hamlets; on the Rhine, land is for the most part parcelled out among small proprietors, who live together in large villages. Then, of course, the diversified physical geography of Germany gives rise to equally diversified methods of land-culture; and out of these various circumstances grow numerous specific differences in manner and character. But the generic character of the German peasant is everywhere the same: in the clean mountain hamlet and in the dirty fishing village on the coast; in the plains of North Germany and in the backwoods of America. 'Everywhere he has the same historical character – everywhere custom is his supreme law. Where religion and patriotism are still a naïve instinct – are still a sacred *custom*, there begins the class of the German Peasantry.'

Our readers will perhaps already have gathered from the foregoing portrait of the German peasant, that Riehl is not a man who looks at objects through the spectacles either of the doctrinaire or the dreamer; and they will be ready to believe what he tells us in his Preface, namely, that years ago he began his wanderings over the hills and plains of Germany for the sake of obtaining, in immediate intercourse with the people, that completion of his historical, political, and economical studies which he was unable to find in books. He began his investigations with no party prepossessions, and his present views were evolved entirely from his own gradually amassed observations. He was, first of all, a pedestrian, and only in the second place a political author. The views at which he has arrived by this inductive process, he sums up in the term – *social-political- conservatism*; but his conservatism is, we conceive, of a thoroughly philosophical kind. He sees in European society *incarnate history*, and any attempt to disengage it from its historical elements must, he believes, be simply destructive of social vitality.* What has grown up historically can only die out historically, by the gradual operation of necessary laws. The external conditions which society has inherited from the past are but the manifestation of inherited internal conditions in the human beings who compose it; the internal conditions and the external are related to each other as the organism and its medium, and development can take place only by the gradual consentaneous development of both. Take the familiar example of attempts to abolish titles, which have been about as effective as the process of cutting off poppy-heads in a corn-field. 'Jedem Menschen,' says Riehl, 'ist sein Zopf angeboren, warum soll denn der sociale Sprachgebrauch nicht auch seinen Zopf haben?' – which we may render – 'As long as snobbism runs in the blood, why should it not run in our speech?' As a necessary preliminary to a purely rational society, you must obtain purely rational men, free from the sweet and bitter prejudices of hereditary affection and antipathy; which is as easy as to get running streams without springs, or the leafy shade of the forest without the secular growth of trunk and branch.

* Throughout this article, in our statement of Riehl's opinions, we must be understood not as quoting Riehl, but as interpreting and illustrating him.

The historical conditions of society may be compared with those of language. It must be admitted that the language of cultivated nations is in anything but a rational state; the great sections of the civilized world are only approximatively intelligible to each other, and even that, only at the cost of long study; one word stands for many things, and many words for one thing; the subtle shades of meaning, and still subtler echoes of association, make language an instrument which scarcely anything short of genius can wield with definiteness and certainty. Suppose, then, that the effort which has been again and again made to construct a universal language on a rational basis has at length succeeded, and that you have a language which has no uncertainty, no whims of idiom, no cumbrous forms, no fitful shimmer of many-hued significance, no hoary archaisms 'familiar with forgotten years' – a patent deodorized and nonresonant language, which effects the purpose of communication as perfectly and rapidly as algebraic signs. Your language may be a perfect medium of expression to science, but will never express *life*, which is a great deal more than science. With the anomalies and inconveniences of historical language, you will have parted with its music and its passion, with its vital qualities as an expression of individual character, with its subtle capabilities of wit, with everything that gives it power over the imagination; and the next step in simplification will be the invention of a talking watch, which will achieve the utmost facility and dispatch in the communication of ideas by a graduated adjustment of ticks, to be represented in writing by a corresponding arrangement of dots. A melancholy 'language of the future'! The sensory and motor nerves that run in the same sheath, are scarcely bound together by a more necessary and delicate union than that which binds men's affections, imagination, wit, and humour, with the subtle ramifications of historical language. Language must be left to grow in precision, completeness, and unity, as minds grow in clearness, comprehensiveness, and sympathy. And there is an analogous relation between the moral tendencies of men and the social conditions they have inherited. The nature of European men has its roots intertwined with the past, and can only be developed by allowing those roots to remain undisturbed while the process of development is going on, until that perfect ripeness of the seed which carries with it a life independent of the root. This vital connexion with the past is much more vividly felt on the Continent than in England, where we have to recall it by an effort of memory and reflection; for though our English life is in its core intensely traditional, Protestantism and commerce have modernized the face of the land and the aspects of society in a far greater degree than in any continental country: –

'Abroad,' says Ruskin, 'a building of the eighth or tenth century stands ruinous in the open street; the children play round it, the peasants heap their corn in it, the buildings of yesterday nestle about it, and fit their new stones in its rents, and tremble in sympathy as it trembles. No one wonders at it, or thinks of it as separate, and of another time; we feel the ancient world to be a real thing, and one with the new; antiquity is no dream; it is rather the children playing about the old stones that are the dream. But all is continuous; and the words "from generation to generation" understandable here.'

This conception of European society as incarnate history, is the fundamental idea of Riehl's books. After the notable failure of revolutionary attempts conducted from the point of view of abstract democratic and socialistic theories, after the practical demonstration of the evils resulting from a bureaucratic system which governs by an undiscriminating, dead mechanism, Riehl wishes to urge on the consideration of his countrymen, a social policy founded on the special study of the people as they are – on the natural history of the various social ranks. He thinks it wise to pause a little from theorizing, and see what is the material actually present for theory to work upon. It is the glory of the Socialists – in contrast with the democratic doctrinaires who have been too much occupied with the general idea of 'the people' to inquire particularly into the actual life of the people – that they have thrown themselves with enthusiastic zeal into the study at least of one social group, namely, the factory operatives; and here lies the secret of their partial success. But unfortunately, they have made this special study of a single fragment of society the basis of a theory which quietly substitutes for the small group of Parisian proletaires or English factory-workers, the society of all Europe – nay, of the whole world. And in this way they have lost the best fruit of their investigations. For, says Riehl, the more deeply we penetrate into the knowledge of society in its details, the more thoroughly we shall be convinced that *a universal social policy has no validity except on paper*, and can never be carried into successful practice. The conditions of German society are altogether different from those of French, of English, or of Italian society; and to apply the same social theory to these nations indiscriminately, is about as wise a procedure as Triptolemus Yellowley's application of the agricultural directions in Virgil's *Georgics* to his farm in the Shetland Isles.[17]

It is the clear and strong light in which Riehl places this important position, that in our opinion constitutes the suggestive value of his books for foreign as well as German readers. It has not been sufficiently insisted on, that in the various branches of Social Science there is an advance from the general to the special, from the simple to the complex, analogous with that which is found in the series of the sciences, from Mathematics to Biology. To the laws of quantity comprised in Mathematics and Physics are super-added, in Chemistry, laws of quality; to these again are added, in Biology, laws of life; and lastly, the conditions of life in general, branch out into its special conditions, or Natural History, on the one hand, and into its abnormal conditions, or Pathology, on the other. And in this series or ramification of the sciences, the more general science will not suffice to solve the problems of the more special. Chemistry embraces phenomena which are not explicable by Physics; Biology embraces phenomena which are not explicable by Chemistry; and no biological generalization will enable us to predict the infinite specialities produced by the complexity of vital conditions. So Social Science, while it has departments which in their fundamental generality correspond to mathematics and physics, namely, those grand and simple generalizations which trace out the inevitable march of the human race as a whole, and, as a ramification of these, the laws of economical science, has also, in the departments of government and jurisprudence, which embrace the conditions of social life in all their complexity, what may be called its Biology, carrying us on to innumerable special phenomena which outlie the sphere of science, and belong to Natural History. And just as the most thorough acquaintance with physics, or chemistry, or general physiology will not enable you at once to establish the balance of life in your private vivarium, so that your particular society of zoophytes, molluscs, and echinoderms may feel themselves, as the Germans say, at ease in their skin; so the most complete equipment of theory will not enable a statesman or a political and social reformer to adjust his measures wisely, in the absence of a special acquaintance with the section of society for which he legislates, with the peculiar characteristics of the nation, the province, the class whose well-being he has to consult. In other words, a wise social policy must be based not simply on abstract social science, but on the Natural History of social bodies.

Riehl's books are not dedicated merely to the argumentative maintenance of this or of any other position; they are intended chiefly as a contribution to that knowledge of the German people on the importance of which he insists. He is less occupied with urging his own conclusions than with impressing on his readers the facts which have led him to those conclusions. In the volume entitled *Land und Leute*, which, though published last, is properly an introduction to the volume entitled *Die Bürgerliche Gesellschaft*, he considers the German people in their physical-geographical relations; he compares the natural divisions of the race, as determined by land and climate, and social traditions, with the artificial divisions which are based on diplomacy; and he traces the genesis and influences of what we may call the ecclesiastical geography of Germany – its partition between Catholicism and Protestantism. He shows that the ordinary antithesis of North and South Germany represents no real ethnographical distinction, and that the natural divisions of Germany, founded on its physical geography, are threefold; namely, the low plains, the middle mountain region, and the high mountain region, or Lower, Middle, and Upper Germany; and on this primary natural division all the other broad ethnographical distinctions of Germany will be found to rest. The plains of North or Lower Germany include all the seaboard the nation possesses; and this, together with the fact that they are traversed to the depth of 600 miles by navigable rivers, makes them the natural seat of a trading race. Quite different is the geographical character of Middle Germany. While the northern plains are marked off into great divisions, by such rivers as the

Lower Rhine, the Weser, and the Oder, running almost in parallel lines, this central region is cut up like a mosaic by the capricious lines of valleys and rivers. Here is the region in which you find those famous roofs from which the rain-water runs towards two different seas, and the mountain-tops from which you may look into eight or ten German States. The abundance of water-power and the presence of extensive coal-mines allow of a very diversified industrial development in Middle Germany. In Upper Germany, or the high mountain region, we find the same symmetry in the lines of the rivers as in the north; almost all the great Alpine streams flow parallel with the Danube. But the majority of these rivers are neither navigable nor available for industrial objects, and instead of serving for communication, they shut off one great tract from another. The slow development, the simple peasant life of many districts is here determined by the mountain and the river. In the south-east, however, industrial activity spreads through Bohemia towards Austria, and forms a sort of balance to the industrial districts of the Lower Rhine. Of course, the boundaries of these three regions cannot be very strictly defined; but an approximation to the limits of Middle Germany may be obtained by regarding it as a triangle, of which one angle lies in Silesia, another in Aix-la-Chapelle, and a third at Lake Constance.

This triple division corresponds with the broad distinctions of climate. In the northern plains the atmosphere is damp and heavy; in the southern mountain region it is dry and rare, and there are abrupt changes of temperature, sharp contrasts between the seasons, and devastating storms; but in both these zones men are hardened by conflict with the roughnesses of the climate. In Middle Germany, on the contrary, there is little of this struggle; the seasons are more equable, and the mild, soft air of the valleys tends to make the inhabitants luxurious and sensitive to hardships. It is only in exceptional mountain districts that one is here reminded of the rough, bracing air on the heights of Southern Germany. It is a curious fact that, as the air becomes gradually lighter and rarer from the North German coast towards Upper Germany, the average of suicides regularly decreases. Mecklenburg has the highest number, then Prussia, while the fewest suicides occur in Bavaria and Austria.

Both the northern and southern regions have still a large extent of waste lands, downs, morasses, and heaths; and to these are added, in the south, abundance of snow-fields and naked rock; while in Middle Germany culture has almost overspread the face of the land, and there are no large tracts of waste. There is the same proportion in the distribution of forests. Again, in the north we see a monotonous continuity of wheat-fields, potato-grounds, meadow lands, and vast heaths, and there is the same uniformity of culture over large surfaces in the southern table-lands and the Alpine pastures. In Middle Germany, on the contrary, there is a perpetual variety of crops within a short space; the diversity of land surface and the corresponding variety in the species of plants are an invitation to the splitting up of estates, and this again encourages to the utmost the motley character of the cultivation.

According to this threefold division, it appears that there are certain features common to North and South Germany in which they differ from Central Germany, and the nature of this difference Riehl indicates by distinguishing the former as *Centralized Land* and the latter as *Individualized Land*; a distinction which is well symbolized by the fact that North and South Germany possess the great lines of railway which are the medium for the traffic of the world, while Middle Germany is far richer in lines for local communication, and possesses the greatest length of railway within the smallest space. Disregarding superficialities, the East Frieslanders, the Schleswig-Holsteiners, the Mecklenburghers, and the Pomeranians are much more nearly allied to the old Bavarians, the Tyrolese, and the Styrians, than any of these are allied to the Saxons, the Thuringians, or the Rhinelanders. Both in North and South Germany original races are still found in large masses, and popular dialects are spoken; you still find there thoroughly peasant districts, thorough villages, and also, at great intervals, thorough cities; you still find there a sense of rank. In Middle Germany, on the contrary, the original races are fused together or sprinkled hither and thither; the peculiarities of the popular dialects are worn down or confused; there is no very strict line of demarcation between the country and the town population, hundreds of small towns and large villages being hardly distinguishable in their characteristics; and the sense of rank, as part of the organic structure of society, is almost extinguished. Again, both in the north and south there is still a strong ecclesiastical spirit in the people, and the Pomeranian sees Anti-christ in the Pope as clearly as the Tyrolese sees him in Doctor Luther; while in Middle Germany the confessions are mingled, they exist peaceably side by side in very narrow space, and tolerance or indifference has spread itself widely even in the popular mind. And the analogy, or rather the causal relation, between the physical geography of the three regions and the development of the population goes still further:

'For,' observes Riehl, 'the striking connexion which has been pointed out between the local geological formations in Germany and the revolutionary disposition of the people has more than a metaphorical significance. Where the primæval physical revolutions of the globe have been the wildest in their effects, and the most multiform strata have been tossed together or thrown one upon the other, it is a very intelligible consequence that on a land surface thus broken up, the population should sooner develop itself into small communities, and that the more intense life generated in these smaller communities, should become the most favourable nidus for the reception of modern culture, and with this a susceptibility for its revolutionary ideas; while a people settled in a region where its groups are spread over a large space will persist much more obstinately in the retention of its original character. The people of Middle Germany have none of that exclusive one-sidedness which determines the peculiar genius of great national groups, just as this one-sidedness or uniformity is wanting to the geological and geographical character of their land.'

This ethnographical outline Riehl fills up with special and typical descriptions, and then makes it the starting-point for a criticism of the actual political condition of Germany. The volume is full of vivid pictures, as well as penetrating glances into the maladies and tendencies of modern society. It would be fascinating as literature, if it were not important for its facts and philosophy. But we can only commend it to our readers, and pass on to the volume entitled *Die Bürgerliche Gesellschaft*, from which we have drawn our sketch of the German peasantry. Here Riehl gives us a series of studies in that natural history of the people, which he regards as the proper basis of social policy. He holds that, in European society, there are *three natural ranks* or *estates*: the hereditary landed aristocracy, the citizens or commercial class, and the peasantry or agricultural class. By *natural ranks* he means ranks which have their roots deep in the historical structure of society, and are still, in the present, showing vitality above ground; he means those great social groups which are not only distinguished externally by their vocation, but essentially by their mental character, their habits, their mode of life, – by the principle they represent in the historical development of society. In his conception of the 'Fourth Estate' he differs from the usual interpretation, according to which it is simply equivalent to the proletariat, or those who are dependent on daily wages, whose only capital is their skill or bodily strength – factory-operatives, artisans, agricultural labourers, to whom might be added, especially in Germany, the day-labourers with the quill, the literary proletariat. This, Riehl observes, is a valid basis of economical classification, but not of social classification. In his view, the Fourth Estate is a stratum produced by the perpetual abrasion of the other great social groups; it is the sign and result of the decomposition which is commencing in the organic consti-tution of society. Its elements are derived alike from the aristocracy, the bourgeoisie, and the peasantry. It assembles under its banner the deserters of historical society, and forms them into a terrible army, which is only just awaking to the consciousness of its corpor-ate power. The tendency of this Fourth Estate, by the very process of its formation, is to do away with the distinctive historical character of the other estates, and to resolve their peculiar rank and vocation into a uniform social relation founded on an abstract conception of society. According to Riehl's classification, the day-labourers, whom the political economist designates as the Fourth Estate, belong partly to the peasantry or agricultural class, and party to the citizens or commercial class.

Riehl considers, in the first place, the peasantry and aristocracy as the 'forces of social persistence', and, in the second, the bour-geoisie and the 'Fourth Estate' as the 'forces of social movement'.

The aristocracy, he observes, is the only one among these four groups which is denied by others besides Socialists to have any natural basis as a separate rank. It is admitted that there was once an aristocracy which had an intrinsic ground of existence, but now, it is alleged, this is an historical fossil, an antiquarian relic, venerable because grey with age. In what, it is asked, can consist the peculiar vocation of the aristocracy, since it has no longer the monopoly of the land, of the higher military functions, and of government offices, and since the service of the court has no longer any political importance? To this Riehl replies that in great revolutionary crises, the 'men of progress' have more than once 'abolished' the aristocracy. But remarkably enough, the aristocracy has always reappeared. This measure of abolition showed that the nobility were no longer regarded as a real class, for to abolish a real class would be an absurdity. It is quite possible to contemplate a voluntary breaking up of the peasant or citizen class in the socialistic sense, but no man in his senses would think of straightway 'abolishing' citizens and peasants. The aristocracy, then, was regarded as a sort of cancer, or excrescence of society. Nevertheless, not only has it been found impossible to annihilate an hereditary nobility by decree; but also, the aristocracy of the eighteenth century outlived even the self-destructive acts of its own perversity. A life which was entirely without object, entirely destitute of functions, would not, says Riehl, be so persistent. He has an acute criticism of those who conduct a polemic against the idea of an hereditary aristocracy while they are proposing an 'aristocracy of talent', which after all is based on the principle of inheritance. The Socialists are, therefore, only consistent in declaring against an aristocracy of talent. 'But when they have turned the world into a great Foundling Hospital, they will still be unable to eradicate the "privileges of birth".' We must not follow him in his criticism, however; nor can we afford to do more than mention hastily his interesting sketch of the mediæval aristocracy, and his admonition to the Germany aristocracy of the present day, that the vitality of their class is not to be sustained by romantic attempts to revive mediæval forms and sentiments, but only by the exercise of functions as real and salutary for actual society as those of the mediæval aristocracy were for the feudal age. 'In modern society the divisions of rank indicate *division of labour*, according to that distribution of functions in the social organism which the historical constitution of society has determined. In this way the principle of differentiation and the principle of unity are identical.'

The elaborate study of the German bourgeoisie, which forms

the next division of the volume, must be passed over, but we may pause a moment to note Riehl's definition of the social *Philister* (Philistine), an epithet for which we have no equivalent, not at all, however, for want of the object it represents. Most people, who read a little German, know that the epithet *Philister* originated in the *Burschen-leben*, or Student-life, of Germany, and that the anti-thesis of *Bursch* and *Philister* was equivalent to the antithesis of 'gown' and 'town'; but since the word has passed into ordinary language, it has assumed several shades of significance which have not yet been merged in a single, absolute meaning; and one of the questions which an English visitor in Germany will probably take an opportunity of asking is, 'What is the strict meaning of the word *Philister*?' Riehl's answer is, that the *Philister* is one who is indifferent to all social interests, all public life, as distinguished from selfish and private interests; he has no sympathy with political and social events except as they affect his own comfort and pros-perity, as they offer him material for amusement or opportunity for gratifying his vanity. He has no social or political creed, but is always of the opinion which is most convenient for the moment. He is always in the majority, and is the main element of unreason and stupidity in the judgement of a 'discerning public'. It seems presumptuous in us to dispute Riehl's interpretation of a German word, but we must think that, in literature, the epithet *Philister* has usually a wider meaning than this – includes his definition and something more. We imagine the *Philister* is the personification of the spirit which judges everything from a lower point of view than the subject demands – which judges the affairs of the parish from the egotistic or purely personal point of view – which judges the affairs of the nation from the parochial point of view, and does not hesitate to measure the merits of the universe from the human point of view. At least, this must surely be the spirit to which Goethe alludes in a passage cited by Riehl himself, where he says that the Germans need not be ashamed of erecting a monument to him as well as to Blucher; for if Blucher had freed them from the French, he (Goethe) had freed them from the nets of the *Philister*: –

> Ihr mögt mir immer ungescheut
> Gleich Blüchern Denkmal setzen!

Von Franzosen hat er euch befreit,
Ich von Philister-netzen.[18]

Goethe could hardly claim to be the apostle of public spirit; but he is eminently the man who helps us to rise to a lofty point of observation, so that we may see things in their relative proportions.

The most interesting chapters in the description of the Fourth Estate, which concludes the volume, are those on the 'Aristocratic Proletariat' and the 'Intellectual Proletariat'. The Fourth Estate in Germany, says Riehl, has its centre of gravity not, as in England and France, in the day-labourers and factory-operatives, and still less in the degenerate peasantry. In Germany, the *educated* proletariat is the leaven that sets the mass in fermentation; the dangerous classes there go about, not in blouses, but in frock-coats; they begin with the impoverished prince and end in the hungriest *littérateur*. The custom that all the sons of a nobleman shall inherit their father's title, necessarily goes on multiplying that class of aristocrats who are not only without function but without adequate provision, and who shrink from entering the ranks of the citizens by adopting some honest calling. The younger son of a prince, says Riehl, is usually obliged to remain without any vocation; and however zealously he may study music, painting, literature, or science, he can never be a regular musician, painter, or man of science; his pursuit will be called a 'passion', not a 'calling', and to the end of his days he remains a dilettante. 'But the ardent pursuit of a fixed practical calling can alone satisfy the active man.' Direct legislation cannot remedy this evil. The inheritance of titles by younger sons is the universal custom, and custom is stronger than law. But if all government preference for the 'aristocratic proletariat' were withdrawn, the sensible men among them would prefer emigration, or the pursuit of some profession, to the hungry distinction of a title without rents.

The intellectual proletaires Riehl calls the 'church militant' of the Fourth Estate in Germany. In no other country are they so numerous; in no other country is the trade in material and industrial capital so far exceeded by the wholesale and retail trade, the traffic and the usury, in the intellectual capital of the nation. *Germany yields more intellectual produce than it can use and pay for.*

This over-production, which is not transient but permanent, nay, is constantly on the increase, evidences a diseased state of the national industry, a perverted application of industrial powers, and is a far more pungent satire on the national condition than all the poverty of operatives and peasants . . . Other nations need not envy us the preponderance of the intellectual proletariat over the proletaires of manual labour. For man more easily becomes diseased from over-study than from the labour of the hands; and it is precisely in the intellectual proletariat that there are the most dangerous seeds of disease. This is the group in which the opposition between earnings and wants, between the ideal social position and the real, is the most hopelessly irreconcilable.

We must unwillingly leave our readers to make acquaintance for themselves with the graphic details with which Riehl follows up this general statement; but before quitting these admirable volumes, let us say, lest our inevitable omissions should have left room for a different conclusion, that Riehl's conservatism is not in the least tinged with the partisanship of a class, with a poetic fanaticism for the past, or with the prejudice of a mind incapable of discerning the grander evolution of things to which all social forms are but temporarily subservient. It is the conservatism of a clear-eyed, practical, but withal large-minded man – a little caustic, perhaps, now and then in his epigrams on democratic doctrinaires who have their nostrum for all political and social diseases, and on communistic theories which he regards as 'the despair of the individual in his own manhood, reduced to a system', but nevertheless able and willing to do justice to the elements of fact and reason in every shade of opinion and every form of effort. He is as far as possible from the folly of supposing that the sun will go backward on the dial, because we put the hands of our clock backward; he only contends against the opposite folly of decreeing that it shall be mid-day, while in fact the sun is only just touching the mountain-tops, and all along the valley men are stumbling in the twilight.

Silly Novels by Lady Novelists

(*Westminster Review*, October 1856)

SILLY NOVELS by Lady Novelists are a genus with many species, determined by the particular quality of silliness that predominates in them – the frothy, the prosy, the pious, or the pedantic. But it is a mixture of all these – a composite order of feminine fatuity, that produces the largest class of such novels, which we shall distinguish as the *mind-and-millinery* species. The heroine is usually an heiress, probably a peeress in her own right, with perhaps a vicious baronet, an amiable duke, and an irresistible younger son of a marquis as lovers in the foreground, a clergyman and a poet sighing for her in the middle distance, and a crowd of undefined adorers dimly indicated beyond. Her eyes and her wit are both dazzling; her nose and her morals are alike free from any tendency to irregularity; she has a superb *contralto* and a superb intellect; she is perfectly well-dressed and perfectly religious; she dances like a sylph, and reads the Bible in the original tongues. Or it may be that the heroine is not an heiress – that rank and wealth are the only things in which she is deficient; but she infallibly gets into high society, she has the triumph of refusing many matches and securing the best, and she wears some family jewels or other as a sort of crown of righteousness at the end. Rakish men either bite their lips in impotent confusion at her repartees, or are touched to penitence by her reproofs, which, on appropriate occasions, rise to a lofty strain of rhetoric; indeed, there is a general propensity in her to make speeches, and to rhapsodize at some length when she retires to her bedroom. In her recorded conversations she is amazingly eloquent, and in her unrecorded conversations, amazingly witty. She is understood to have a depth of insight that looks through and through the

shallow theories of philosophers, and her superior instincts are a
sort of dial by which men have only to set their clocks and
watches, and all will go well. The men play a very subordinate
part by her side. You are consoled now and then by a hint that
they have affairs, which keeps you in mind that the working-day
business of the world is somehow being carried on, but ostensibly
the final cause of their existence is that they may accompany the
heroine on her 'starring' expedition through life. They see her at a
ball, and are dazzled; at a flower-show, and they are fascinated;
on a riding excursion, and they are witched by her noble horse-
manship; at church, and they are awed by the sweet solemnity of
her demeanour. She is the ideal woman in feelings, faculties, and
flounces. For all this, she as often as not marries the wrong person
to begin with, and she suffers terribly from the plots and intrigues
of the vicious baronet; but even death has a soft place in his heart
for such a paragon, and remedies all mistakes for her just at the
right moment. The vicious baronet is sure to be killed in a duel,
and the tedious husband dies in his bed, requesting his wife, as a
particular favour to him, to marry the man she loves best, and
having already dispatched a note to the lover informing him of the
comfortable arrangement. Before matters arrive at this desirable
issue our feelings are tried by seeing the noble, lovely, and gifted
heroine pass through many *mauvais moments*, but we have the
satisfaction of knowing that her sorrows are wept into embroidered
pocket-handkerchiefs, that her fainting form reclines on the very
best upholstery, and that whatever vicissitudes she may undergo,
from being dashed out of her carriage to having her head shaved
in a fever, she comes out of them all with a complexion more
blooming and locks more redundant than ever.

We may remark, by the way, that we have been relieved from a
serious scruple by discovering that silly novels by lady novelists
rarely introduce us into any other than very lofty and fashionable
society. We had imagined that destitute women turned novelists,
as they turned governesses, because they had no other 'lady-like'
means of getting their bread. On this supposition, vacillating
syntax and improbable incident had a certain pathos for us, like
the extremely supererogatory pincushions and ill-devised night-
caps that are offered for sale by a blind man. We felt the commodity

to be a nuisance, but we were glad to think that the money went to relieve the necessitous, and we pictured to ourselves lonely women struggling for a maintenance, or wives and daughters devoting themselves to the production of 'copy' out of pure heroism, – perhaps to pay their husband's debts, or to purchase luxuries for a sick father. Under these impressions we shrank from criticizing a lady's novel: her English might be faulty, but, we said to ourselves, her motives are irreproachable; her imagination may be uninventive, but her patience is untiring. Empty writing was excused by an empty stomach, and twaddle was consecrated by tears. But no! This theory of ours, like many other pretty theories, has had to give way before observation. Women's silly novels, we are now convinced, are written under totally different circumstances. The fair writers have evidently never talked to a tradesman except from a carriage window; they have no notion of the working classes except as 'dependants'; they think £500 a year a miserable pittance; Belgravia and 'baronial halls' are their primary truths; and they have no idea of feeling interest in any man who is not at least a great landed proprietor, if not a prime minister. It is clear that they write in elegant boudoirs, with violet-coloured ink and a ruby pen; that they must be entirely indifferent to publishers' accounts, and inexperienced in every form of poverty except poverty of brains. It is true that we are constantly struck with the want of verisimilitude in their representations of the high society in which they seem to live; but then they betray no closer acquaintance with any other form of life. If their peers and peeresses are improbable, their literary men, tradespeople, and cottagers are impossible; and their intellect seems to have the peculiar impartiality of reproducing both what they *have* seen and heard, and what they have *not* seen and heard, with equal unfaithfulness.

There are few women, we suppose, who have not seen something of children under five years of age, yet in *Compensation*,[1] a recent novel of the mind-and-millinery species, which calls itself a 'story of real life', we have a child of four and a half years old talking in this Ossianic[2] fashion –

'Oh, I am so happy, dear gran'mamma; – I have seen, – I have seen such a delightful person: he is like everything beautiful, – like the smell of sweet flowers, and the view from Ben Lomond; – or no, *better than that* – he is like what I think of and see when I am very, very happy; and he is really like mamma, too, when she sings; and his forehead is like *that distant sea*,' she continued, pointing to the blue Mediterranean; 'there seems no end – no end; or like the clusters of stars I like best to look at on a warm fine night ... Don't look so ... your forehead is like Loch Lomond, when the wind is blowing and the sun is gone in; I like the sunshine best when the lake is smooth ... So now – I like it better than ever ... it is more beautiful still from the dark cloud that has gone over it, *when the sun suddenly lights up all the colours of the forests and shining purple rocks, and it is all reflected in the waters below.*'

We are not surprised to learn that the mother of this infant phenomenon, who exhibits symptoms so alarmingly like those of adolescence repressed by gin, is herself a phœnix. We are assured, again and again, that she had a remarkably original mind, that she was a genius, and 'conscious of her originality', and she was fortunate enough to have a lover who was also a genius, and a man of 'most original mind'.

This lover, we read, though 'wonderfully similar' to her 'in powers and capacity', was 'infinitely superior to her in faith and development', and she saw in him the '"Agape"'[3] – so rare to find – of which she had read and admired the meaning in her Greek Testament; having, *from her great facility in learning languages*, read the Scriptures in their original *tongues*.' Of course! Greek and Hebrew are mere play to a heroine; Sanscrit is no more than *a b c* to her; and she can talk with perfect correctness in any language except English. She is a polking polyglot, a Creuzer[4] in crinoline. Poor men! There are so few of you who know even Hebrew; you think it something to boast of if, like Bolingbroke, you only 'understand that sort of learning, and what is writ about it'; and you are perhaps adoring women who can think slightingly of you in all the Semitic languages successively. But, then, as we are almost invariably told, that a heroine has a 'beautifully small head', and as her intellect has probably been early invigorated by an attention to costume and deportment, we may conclude that she can pick up the Oriental tongues, to say nothing of their dialects, with the same aërial facility that the butterfly sips nectar. Besides, there can be no difficulty in conceiving the depth of the heroine's erudition, when that of the authoress is so evident.

In *Laura Gay*,[5] another novel of the same school, the heroine seems less at home in Greek and Hebrew, but she makes up for the deficiency by a quite playful familiarity with the Latin classics – with the 'dear old Virgil', 'the graceful Horace, the humane Cicero, and the pleasant Livy'; indeed, it is such a matter of course with her to quote Latin, that she does it at a picnic in a very mixed company of ladies and gentlemen, having, we are told, 'no conception that the nobler sex were capable of jealousy on this subject. And if, indeed,' continues the biographer of Laura Gay, 'the wisest and noblest portion of that sex were in the majority, no such sentiment would exist; but while Miss Wyndhams and Mr Redfords abound,[6] great sacrifices must be made to their existence.' Such sacrifices, we presume, as abstaining from Latin quotations, of extremely moderate interest and applicability, which the wise and noble minority of the other sex would be quite as willing to dispense with as the foolish and ignoble majority. It is as little the custom of well-bred men as of well-bred women to quote Latin in mixed parties; they can contain their familiarity with 'the humane Cicero' without allowing it to boil over in ordinary conversation, and even references to 'the pleasant Livy' are not absolutely irrepressible. But Ciceronian Latin is the mildest form of Miss Gay's conversational power. Being on the Palatine with a party of sightseers, she falls into the following vein of well-rounded remark: –

Truth can only be pure objectively, for even in the creeds where it predominates, being subjective, and parcelled out into portions, each of these necessarily receives a hue of idiosyncrasy, that is, a taint of superstition more or less strong; while in such creeds as the Roman Catholic, ignorance, interest, the bias of ancient idolatries, and the force of authority, have gradually accumulated on the pure truth, and transformed it, at last, into a mass of superstition for the majority of its votaries; and how few are there, alas! whose zeal, courage, and intellectual energy are equal to the analysis of this accumulation, and to the discovery of the pearl of great price which lies hidden beneath this heap of rubbish.

We have often met with women much more novel and profound in their observations than Laura Gay, but rarely with any so inopportunely long-winded. A clerical lord, who is half in love with her, is alarmed by the daring remarks just quoted, and begins to suspect that she is inclined to free-thinking. But he is mistaken; when in a moment of sorrow he delicately begs leave to 'recall to her memory, a *dépôt* of strength and consolation under affliction, which, until we are hard pressed by the trials of life, we are too apt to forget', we learn that she really has 'recurrence to that sacred *dépôt*', together with the tea-pot. There is a certain flavour of orthodoxy mixed with the parade of fortunes and fine carriages in *Laura Gay*, but it is an orthodoxy mitigated by study of 'the humane Cicero', and by an 'intellectual disposition to analyse'.

Compensation is much more heavily dosed with doctrine, but then it has a treble amount of snobbish worldliness and absurd incident to tickle the palate of pious frivolity. Linda, the heroine, is still more speculative and spiritual than Laura Gay, but she has been 'presented', and has more, and far grander, lovers; very wicked and fascinating women are introduced – even a French *lionne*; and no expense is spared to get up as exciting a story as you will find in the most immoral novels. In fact, it is a wonderful *pot pourri* of Almack's, Scotch second-sight, Mr Rogers's breakfasts,[7] Italian brigands, death-bed conversions, superior authoresses, Italian mistresses, and attempts at poisoning old ladies, the whole served up with a garnish of talk about 'faith and development', and 'most original minds'. Even Miss Susan Barton, the superior authoress, whose pen moves in a 'quick decided manner when she is composing', declines the finest opportunities of marriage; and though old enough to be Linda's mother (since we are told that she refused Linda's father), has her hand sought by a young earl, the heroine's rejected lover. Of course, genius and morality must be backed by eligible offers, or they would seem rather a dull affair; and piety, like other things, in order to be *comme il faut*, must be in 'society', and have admittance to the best circles.

Rank and Beauty[8] is a more frothy and less religious variety of the mind-and-millinery species. The heroine, we are told, 'if she inherited her father's pride of birth and her mother's beauty of person, had in herself a tone of enthusiastic feeling that perhaps belongs to her age even in the lowly born, but which is refined into the high spirit of wild romance only in the far descended, who feel that it is their best inheritance'. This enthusiastic young lady, by dint of reading the newspaper to her father, falls in love with the *prime minister*, who, through the medium of leading articles and 'the *resumé* of the debates', shines upon her imagination as a bright particular star, which has no parallax for her, living in the country as simple Miss Wyndham. But she forthwith becomes Baroness Umfraville in her own right, astonishes the world with her beauty and accomplishments when she bursts upon it from her mansion in Spring Gardens, and, as you foresee, will presently come into contact with the unseen *objet aimé*. Perhaps the words 'prime minister' suggest to you a wrinkled or obese sexagenarian; but pray dismiss the image. Lord Rupert Conway has been 'called while still almost a youth to the first situation which a subject can hold in the *universe*', and even leading articles and a *resumé* of the debates have not conjured up a dream that surpasses the fact.

The door opened again, and Lord Rupert Conway entered. Evelyn gave one glance. It was enough; she was not disappointed. It seemed as if a picture on which she had long gazed was suddenly instinct with life, and had stepped from its frame before her. His tall figure, the distinguished simplicity of his air – it was a living Vandyke, a cavalier, one of his noble cavalier ancestors, or one to whom her fancy had always likened him, who long of yore had, with an Umfraville, fought the Paynim far beyond sea. Was this reality?

Very little like it, certainly.

By and by, it becomes evident that the ministerial heart is touched. Lady Umfraville is on a visit to the Queen at Windsor, and, –

The last evening of her stay, when they returned from riding, Mr Wyndham took her and a large party to the top of the Keep, to see the view. She was leaning on the battlements, gazing from that 'stately height' at the prospect beneath her, when Lord Rupert was by her side. 'What an unrivalled view!' exclaimed she.

'Yes, it would have been wrong to go without having been up here. You are pleased with your visit?'

'Enchanted! "A Queen to live and die under"', to live and die for!'

'Ha!' cried he, with sudden emotion, and with a *eureka* expression of countenance, as if he had *indeed found a heart in unison with his own*.

The '*eureka* expression of countenance', you see at once to be prophetic of marriage at the end of the third volume; but before that desirable consummation, there are very complicated mis-understandings, arising chiefly from the vindictive plotting of Sir Luttrell Wycherley, who is a genius, a poet, and in every way a most remarkable character indeed. He is not only a romantic poet, but a hardened rake and a cynical wit; yet his deep passion for Lady Umfraville has so impoverished his epigrammatic talent, that he cuts an extremely poor figure in conversation. When she rejects him, he rushes into the shrubbery, and rolls himself in the dirt; and on recovering, devotes himself to the most diabolical and laborious schemes of vengeance, in the course of which he disguises himself as a quack physician, and enters into general practice, foreseeing that Evelyn will fall ill, and that he shall be called in to attend her. At last, when all his schemes are frustrated, he takes leave of her in a long letter, written, as you will perceive from the following passage, entirely in the style of an eminent literary man: –

Oh, lady, nursed in pomp and pleasure, will you ever cast one thought upon the miserable being who addresses you? Will you ever, as your gilded galley is floating down the unruffled stream of prosperity, will you ever, while lulled by the sweetest music – thine own praises, – hear the far-off sigh from that world to which I am going?

On the whole, however, frothy as it is, we rather prefer *Rank and Beauty* to the two other novels we have mentioned. The dialogue is more natural and spirited; there is some frank ignorance, and no pedantry; and you are allowed to take the heroine's astounding intellect upon trust, without being called on to read her conversational refutations of sceptics and philosophers, or her rhetorical solutions of the mysteries of the universe.

Writers of the mind-and-millinery school are remarkably unanimous in their choice of diction. In their novels, there is usually a lady or gentleman who is more or less of a upas tree: the lover has a manly breast; minds are redolent of various things; hearts are hollow; events are utilized; friends are consigned to the tomb; infancy is an engaging period; the sun is a luminary that goes to his western couch, or gathers the rain-drops into his refulgent bosom; life is a melancholy boon; Albion and Scotia are conversational epithets. There is a striking resemblance, too, in the character of their moral comments, such, for instance, as that 'It is a fact, no less true than melancholy, that all people, more or less, richer or poorer, are swayed by bad example'; that 'Books, however trivial, contain some subjects from which useful information may be drawn'; that 'Vice can too often borrow the language of virtue'; that 'Merit and nobility of nature must exist, to be accepted, for clamour and pretension cannot impose upon those too well read in human nature to be easily deceived'; and that, 'In order to forgive, we must have been injured'. There is, doubtless, a class of readers to whom these remarks appear peculiarly pointed and pungent; for we often find them doubly and trebly scored with the pencil, and delicate hands giving in their determined adhesion to these hardy novelties by a distinct *très vrai*, emphasized by many notes of exclamation. The colloquial style of these novels is often marked by much ingenious inversion, and a careful avoidance of such cheap phraseology as can be heard every day. Angry young gentlemen exclaim – ''Tis ever thus, methinks'; and in the half hour before dinner a young lady informs her next neighbour that the first day she read Shakspeare she 'stole away into the park, and beneath the shadow of the greenwood tree, devoured with rapture the inspired page of the great magician'. But the most remarkable efforts of the mind-and-millinery writers lie in their philosophic reflections. The authoress of *Laura Gay*, for example, having married her hero and heroine, improves the event by observing that 'if those sceptics, whose eyes have so long gazed on matter that they can no longer see aught else in man, could once enter with heart and soul into such bliss as this, they would come to say that the soul of man and the polypus are not of common origin, or of the same texture'. Lady novelists, it appears, can see something else besides matter; they are not limited to phenomena, but can relieve their eyesight by occasional glimpses of the *noumenon*, and are, therefore, naturally better able than any one else to confound sceptics, even of that remarkable, but to us unknown school, which maintains that the soul of man is of the same texture as the polypus.

The most pitiable of all silly novels by lady novelists are what we may call the *oracular* species – novels intended to expound the writer's religious, philosophical, or moral theories. There seems to be a notion abroad among women, rather akin to the superstition that the speech and actions of idiots are inspired, and that the human being most entirely exhausted of common sense is the fittest vehicle of revelation. To judge from their writings, there are certain ladies who think that an amazing ignorance, both of science and of life, is the best possible qualification for forming an opinion on the knottiest moral and speculative questions. Apparently, their recipe for solving all such difficulties is something like this: – Take a woman's head, stuff it with a smattering of philosophy and literature chopped small, and with false notions of society baked hard, let it hang over a desk a few hours every day, and serve up hot in feeble English, when not required. You will rarely meet with a lady novelist of the oracular class who is diffident of her ability to decide on theological questions, – who has any suspicion that she is not capable of discriminating with the nicest accuracy between the good and evil in all church parties, – who does not see precisely how it is that men have gone wrong hitherto, – and pity philosophers in general that they have not had the opportunity of consulting her. Great writers, who have modestly contented themselves with putting their experience into fiction, and have thought it quite a sufficient task to exhibit men and things as they are, she sighs over as deplorably deficient in the application of their powers. 'They have solved no great questions' – and she is ready to remedy their omission by setting before you a complete theory of life and manual of divinity, in a love story, where ladies and gentlemen of good family go through genteel vicissitudes, to the utter confusion of Deists, Puseyites,[9] and ultra-Protestants, and to the perfect establishment of that particular view of Christianity which either condenses itself into a sentence of small caps, or explodes into a cluster of stars on the three hundred and thirtieth page. It is true, the ladies and gentlemen will probably seem to you remarkably little like any you have had the fortune or misfortune to meet with, for, as a general rule, the ability of a lady novelist to describe actual life and her fellow-men, is in inverse proportion to her confident eloquence about God and the other world, and the means by which she usually chooses to conduct you to true ideas of the invisible is a totally false picture of the visible.

As typical a novel of the oracular kind as we can hope to meet

with, is *The Enigma: A Leaf from the Chronicles of Wolchorley House.*[10]
The 'enigma' which this novel is to solve, is certainly one that
demands powers no less gigantic than those of a lady novelist,
being neither more nor less than the existence of evil. The problem
is stated, and the answer dimly foreshadowed on the very first
page. The spirited young lady, with raven hair, says, 'All life is an
inextricable confusion'; and the meek young lady, with auburn
hair, looks at the picture of the Madonna which she is copying,
and – '*There* seemed the solution of that mighty enigma.' The style
of this novel is quite as lofty as its purpose; indeed, some passages
on which we have spent much patient study are quite beyond our
reach, in spite of the illustrative aid of italics and small caps; and
we must await further 'development' in order to understand them.
Of Ernest, the model young clergyman, who sets every one right
on all occasions, we read, that 'he held not of marriage in the
marketable kind, after a social desecration'; that, on one eventful
night, 'sleep had not visited his divided heart, where tumultuated,
in varied type and combination, the aggregate feelings of grief and
joy'; and that, 'for the *marketable* human article he had no toleration, be it of what sort, or set for what value it might, whether for
worship or class, his upright soul abhorred it, whose ultimatum,
the self-deceiver, was to him THE *great spiritual lie*, "living in a vain
show, deceiving and being deceived"; since he did not suppose the
phylactery and enlarged border on the garment to be *merely* a
social trick.' (The italics and small caps are the author's, and we
hope they assist the reader's comprehension.) Of Sir Lionel, the
model old gentleman, we are told that 'the simple ideal of the
middle age, apart from its anarchy and decadence, in him most
truly seemed to live again, when the ties which knit men together
were of heroic cast. The first-born colours of pristine faith and
truth engraven on the common soul of man, and blent into the
wide arch of brotherhood, where the primæval law of *order* grew
and multiplied, each perfect after his kind, and mutually interdependent.' You see clearly, of course, how colours are first engraven on a soul, and then blent into a wide arch, on which arch
of colours – apparently a rainbow – the law of order grew and
multiplied, each – apparently the arch and the law – perfect after
his kind? If, after this, you can possibly want any further aid

towards knowing what Sir Lionel was, we can tell you, that in his soul 'the scientific combinations of thought could educe no fuller harmonies of the good and the true, than lay in the primæval pulses which floated as an atmosphere around it!' and that, when he was sealing a letter, 'Lo! the responsive throb in that good man's bosom echoed back in simple truth the honest witness of a heart that condemned him not, as his eye, bedewed with love, rested, too, with something of ancestral pride, on the undimmed motto of the family – LOIAUTÉ.'

The slightest matters have their vulgarity fumigated out of them by the same elevated style. Commonplace people would say that a copy of Shakspeare lay on a drawing-room table; but the authoress of The Enigma, bent on edifying periphrasis, tells you that there lay on the table, 'that fund of human thought and feeling, which teaches the heart through the little name, "Shakspeare"'. A watchman sees a light burning in an upper window rather longer than usual, and thinks that people are foolish to sit up late when they have an opportunity of going to bed; but, lest this fact should seem too low and common, it is presented to us in the following striking and metaphysical manner: 'He marvelled – as man will think for others in a necessarily separate personality, consequently (though disallowing it) in false mental premise, – how differently he should act, how gladly he should prize the rest so lightly held of within.' A footman – an ordinary Jeames, with large calves and aspirated vowels – answers the door-bell, and the opportunity is seized to tell you that he was a 'type of the large class of pampered menials, who follow the curse of Cain – "vagabonds" on the face of the earth, and whose estimate of the human class varies in the graduated scale of money and expenditure . . . These, and such as these, O England, be the false lights of thy morbid civilization!' We have heard of various 'false lights', from Dr Cumming to Robert Owen, from Dr Pusey to the Spirit-rappers,[11] but we never before heard of the false light that emanates from plush and powder.

In the same way very ordinary events of civilized life are exalted into the most awful crises, and ladies in full skirts and manches à la chinoise, conduct themselves not unlike the heroines of sanguinary melodramas. Mrs Percy, a shallow woman of the world, wishes her son Horace to marry the auburn-haired Grace, she being an heiress; but he, after the manner of sons, falls in love with the raven-haired Kate, the heiress's portionless cousin; and, moreover, Grace herself shows every symptom of perfect indifference to Horace. In such cases, sons are often sulky or fiery, mothers are alternately manœuvring and waspish, and the portionless young lady often lies awake at night and cries a good deal. We are getting used to these things now, just as we are used to eclipses of the moon, which no longer set us howling and beating tin kettles. We never heard of a lady in a fashionable 'front' behaving like Mrs Percy under these circumstances. Happening one day to see Horace talking to Grace at a window, without in the least knowing what they are talking about, or having the least reason to believe that Grace, who is mistress of the house and a person of dignity, would accept her son if he were to offer himself, she suddenly rushes up to them and clasps them both, saying, 'with a flushed countenance and in an excited manner' – 'This is indeed happiness; for, may I not call you so, Grace? – my Grace – my Horace's Grace! – my dear children!' Her son tells her she is mistaken, and that he is engaged to Kate, whereupon we have the following scene and tableau: –

Gathering herself up to an unprecedented height,(!) her eyes lightning forth the fire of her anger: –

'Wretched boy!' she said, hoarsely and scornfully, and clenching her hand. 'Take then the doom of your own choice! Bow down your miserable head and let a mother's –'

'Curse not!' spake a deep low voice from behind, and Mrs Percy started, scared, as though she had seen a heavenly visitant appear, to break upon her in the midst of her sin.

Meantime, Horace had fallen on his knees at her feet, and hid his face in his hands.

Who, then, is she – who! Truly his 'guardian spirit' hath stepped between him and the fearful words, which, however unmerited, must have hung as a pall over his future existence; – a spell which could not be unbound – which could not be unsaid.

Of an earthly paleness, but calm with the still, iron-bound calmness of death – the only calm one there, – Katherine stood; and her words smote on the ear in tones whose appallingly slow and separate intonation rung on the heart like the chill, isolated tolling of some fatal knell.

'He would have plighted me his faith, but I did not accept it; you cannot, therefore – you *dare* not curse him. And here,' she continued, raising her hand to heaven, whither her large dark eyes also rose with a chastened glow, which, for the first time, *suffering* had lighted in those passionate orbs, – 'here I promise, come weal, come woe, that Horace Wolchorley and I do never interchange vows without his mother's sanction – without his mother's blessing!'

Here, and throughout the story, we see that confusion of purpose which is so characteristic of silly novels written by women. It is a story of quite modern drawing-room society – a society in which polkas are played and Puseyism discussed; yet we have characters, and incidents, and traits of manner introduced, which are mere shreds from the most heterogeneous romances. We have a blind Irish harper 'relic of the picturesque bards of yore', startling us at a Sunday-school festival of tea and cake in an English village; we have a crazy gypsy, in a scarlet cloak, singing snatches of romantic song, and revealing a secret on her death-bed which, with the testimony of a dwarfish miserly merchant, who salutes strangers with a curse and a devilish laugh, goes to prove that Ernest, the model young clergyman, is Kate's brother; and we have an ultra-virtuous Irish Barney, discovering that a document is forged, by comparing the date of the paper with the date of the alleged signature, although the same document has passed through a court of law, and occasioned a fatal decision. The 'Hall' in which Sir Lionel lives is the venerable country-seat of an old family, and this, we suppose, sets the imagination of the authoress flying to donjons and battlements, where 'lo! the warder blows his horn'; for, as the inhabitants are in their bedrooms on a night certainly within the recollection of Pleaceman X.,[12] and a breeze springs up, which we are at first told was faint, and then that it made the old cedars bow their branches to the greensward, she falls into this mediæval vein of description (the italics are ours): 'The banner *unfurled it* at the sound, and shook its guardian wing above, while the startled owl *flapped her* in the ivy; the firmament looking down through her "argus eyes" –

Ministers of heaven's mute melodies.

And lo! two strokes tolled from out the warder tower, and "Two o'clock" re-echoed its interpreter below.'

Such stories as this of *The Enigma* remind us of the pictures clever children sometimes draw 'out of their own head', where you will see a modern villa on the right, two knights in helmets fighting in the foreground, and a tiger grinning in a jungle on the left, the several objects being brought together because the artist thinks each pretty, and perhaps still more because he remembers seeing them in other pictures.

But we like the authoress much better on her mediæval stilts than on her oracular ones, – when she talks of the *Ich* and of 'subjective' and 'objective', and lays down the exact line of Christian verity, between 'right-hand excesses and left-hand declensions'. Persons who deviate from this line are introduced with a patronizing air of charity. Of a certain Miss Inshquine she informs us, with all the lucidity of italics and small caps, that '*function*, not *form*, AS THE INEVITABLE OUTER EXPRESSION OF THE SPIRIT IN THIS TABERNACLED AGE, weakly engrossed her'. And *à propos* of Miss Mayjar, an evangelical lady who is a little too apt to talk of her visits to sick women and the state of their souls, we are told that the model clergyman is 'not one to disallow, through the *super* crust, the undercurrent towards good in the *subject*, or the positive benefits, nevertheless, to the *object*'. We imagine the double-refined accent and protrusion of chin which are feebly represented by the italics in this lady's sentences. We abstain from quoting any of her oracular doctrinal passages, because they refer to matters too serious for our pages just now.

The epithet 'silly' may seem impertinent, applied to a novel which indicates so much reading and intellectual activity as *The Enigma*; but we use this epithet advisedly. If, as the world has long agreed, a very great amount of instruction will not make a wise man, still less will a very mediocre amount of instruction make a wise woman. And the most mischievous form of feminine silliness is the literary form, because it tends to confirm the popular prejudice against the more solid education of women. When men see girls wasting their time in consultations about bonnets and ball dresses, and in giggling or sentimental love-confidences, or middle-aged women mismanaging their children, and solacing themselves with acrid gossip, they can hardly help saying, 'For Heaven's sake, let girls be better educated; let them have some better objects of thought – some more solid occupations.' But after a few hours' conversation with an oracular literary woman, or a few hours' reading of her books, they are likely enough to say, 'After all, when a woman gets some knowledge, see what use she makes of it! Her knowledge remains acquisition, instead of passing into culture; instead of being subdued into modesty and simplicity by a larger acquaintance with thought and fact, she has a feverish consciousness of her attainments; she keeps a sort of mental pocket-mirror, and is continually looking in it at her own 'intellectuality'; she spoils the taste of one's muffin by questions of metaphysics; 'puts down' men at a dinner-table with her superior information; and seizes the opportunity of a *soirée* to catechize us on the vital question of the relation between mind and matter. And then, look at her writings! She mistakes vagueness for depth, bombast for eloquence, and affectation for originality; she struts on one page, rolls her eyes on another, grimaces in a third, and is hysterical in a fourth. She may have read many writings of great men, and a few writings of great women; but she is as unable to discern the difference between her own style and theirs as a Yorkshireman is to discern the difference between his own English and a Londoner's: rhodomontade is the native accent of her intellect. No – the average nature of women is too shallow and feeble a soil to bear much tillage; it is only fit for the very lightest crops.'

It is true that the men who come to such a decision on such very superficial and imperfect observation may not be among the wisest in the world; but we have not now to contest their opinion – we are only pointing out how it is unconsciously encouraged by many women who have volunteered themselves as representatives of the feminine intellect. We do not believe that a man was ever strengthened in such an opinion by associating with a woman of true culture, whose mind had absorbed her knowledge instead of being absorbed by it. A really cultured woman, like a really cultured man, is all the simpler and the less obtrusive for her knowledge; it has made her see herself and her opinions in something like just proportions; she does not make it a pedestal from which she flatters herself that she commands a complete view of men and things, but makes it a point of observation from which to form a right estimate of herself. She neither spouts poetry nor quotes Cicero on slight provocation; not because she thinks that a sacrifice must be made to the prejudices of men, but because that mode of exhibiting her memory and Latinity does not present itself to her as edifying or graceful. She does not write books to confound philosophers, perhaps because she is able to write books that delight them. In conversation she is the least formidable of women, because she understands you, without wanting to make you aware that you *can't* understand her. She does not give you information, which is the raw material of culture, – she gives you sympathy, which is its subtlest essence.

A more numerous class of silly novels than the oracular, (which are generally inspired by some form of High Church, or transcendental Christianity,) is what we may call the *white neck-cloth* species, which represent the tone of thought and feeling in the Evangelical party. This species is a kind of genteel tract on a large scale, intended as a sort of medicinal sweetmeat for Low Church young ladies; an Evangelical substitute for the fashionable novel, as the May Meetings[13] are a substitute for the Opera. Even Quaker children, one would think, can hardly have been denied the indulgence of a doll; but it must be a doll dressed in a drab gown and a coal-scuttle bonnet – not a worldly doll, in gauze and spangles. And there are no young ladies, we imagine, – unless they belong to the Church of the United Brethren,[14] in which people are married without any love-making – who can dispense with love stories. Thus, for Evangelical young ladies there are Evangelical love stories, in which the vicissitudes of the tender passion are sanctified by saving views of Regeneration and the Atonement. These novels differ from the oracular ones, as a Low Churchwoman often differs from a High Churchwoman: they are a little less supercilious, and a great deal more ignorant, a little less correct in their syntax, and a great deal more vulgar.

The Orlando[15] of Evangelical literature is the young curate, looked at from the point of view of the middle class, where cambric bands are understood to have as thrilling an effect on the hearts of young ladies as epaulettes have in the classes above and below it. In the ordinary type of these novels, the hero is almost sure to be a young curate, frowned upon, perhaps, by worldly mammas, but carrying captive the hearts of their daughters, who can 'never forget *that* sermon'; tender glances are seized from the pulpit stairs instead of the opera-box; *tête-à-têtes* are seasoned with quotations from Scripture, instead of quotations from the poets; and questions as to the state of the heroine's affections are mingled with anxieties as to the state of her soul. The young curate always has a background of well-dressed and wealthy, if not fashionable society; – for Evangelical silliness is as snobbish as any other kind of silliness; and the Evangelical lady novelist, while she explains to you the type of the scapegoat on one page, is ambitious on another to represent the manners and conversation of aristocratic people. Her pictures of fashionable society are often curious studies considered as efforts of the Evangelical imagination; but in one particular the novels of the White Neck-cloth School are meritoriously realistic, – their favourite hero, the Evangelical young curate, is always rather an insipid personage.

The most recent novel of this species that we happen to have before us, is *The Old Grey Church*.[16] It is utterly tame and feeble; there is no one set of objects on which the writer seems to have a stronger grasp than on any other; and we should be entirely at a loss to conjecture among what phases of life her experience has been gained, but for certain vulgarisms of style which sufficiently indicate that she has had the advantage, though she has been unable to use it, of mingling chiefly with men and women whose manners and characters have not had all their bosses and angles rubbed down by refined conventionalism. It is less excusable in an Evangelical novelist, than in any other, gratuitously to seek her subjects among titles and carriages. The real drama of Evangelicalism – and it has abundance of fine drama for any one who has genius enough to discern and reproduce it – lies among the middle and lower classes; and are not Evangelical opinions understood to give an especial interest in the weak things of the earth, rather than in the mighty? Why then, cannot our Evangelical lady novelists show us the operation of their religious views among people (there really are many such in the world) who keep no carriage, 'not so much as a brass-bound gig', who even manage to eat their dinner without a silver fork, and in whose mouths the authoress's questionable English would be strictly consistent? Why can we not have pictures of religious life among the industrial classes in England, as interesting as Mrs Stowe's pictures of religious life among the negroes?[17] Instead of this, pious ladies nauseate us with novels which remind us of what we sometimes see in a worldly woman recently 'converted'; – she is as fond of a fine dinner table as before, but she invites clergymen instead of beaux; she thinks as much of her dress as before, but she adopts a more sober choice of colours and patterns; her conversation is as trivial as before, but the triviality is flavoured with Gospel instead of gossip. In *The Old Grey Church*, we have the same sort of Evangelical travesty of the fashionable novel, and of course the vicious, intriguing baronet is not wanting. It is worth while to give a sample of the style of conversation attributed to this high-born rake – a style that in its profuse italics and palpable innuendoes, is worthy of Miss Squeers. In an evening visit to the ruins of the Colosseum, Eustace, the young clergyman, has been withdrawing the heroine, Miss Lushington, from the rest of the party, for the sake of a *tête-à-tête*. The baronet is jealous, and vents his pique in this way: –

There they are, and Miss Lushington, no doubt, quite safe; for she is under the holy guidance of Pope Eustace the First, who has, of course, been delivering to her an edifying homily on the wickedness of the heathens of yore, who, as tradition tells us, in this very place let loose the wild *beasties* on poor Saint Paul! – Oh, no! by the bye, I believe I am wrong, and betraying my want of clergy, and that it was not at all Saint Paul, nor was it here. But no matter, it would equally serve as a text to preach from, and from which to diverge to the degenerate *heathen* Christians of the present day, and all their naughty practices, and so end with an exhortation to 'come out from among them, and be separate'; – and I am sure, Miss Lushington, you have most scrupulously conformed to that injunction this evening, for we have seen nothing of you since our arrival. But every one seems agreed it has been a *charming party of pleasure*, and I am sure we all feel *much indebted* to Mr Grey for having *suggested* it; and as he seems so capital a cicerone, I hope he will think of something else equally agreeable to *all*.

This drivelling kind of dialogue, and equally drivelling narrative, which, like a bad drawing, represents nothing, and barely indicates what is meant to be represented, runs through the book; and we have no doubt is considered by the amiable authoress to constitute an improving novel, which Christian mothers will do well to put into the hands of their daughters. But everything is relative; we have met with American vegetarians whose normal diet was dry meal, and who, when their appetite wanted stimulating, tickled it with *wet* meal; and so, we can imagine that there are Evangelical circles in which *The Old Grey Church* is devoured as a powerful and interesting fiction.

But, perhaps, the least readable of silly women's novels, are the *modern-antique* species, which unfold to us the domestic life of Jannes and Jambres, the private love affairs of Sennacherib, or the mental struggles and ultimate conversion of Demetrius the silversmith.[18] From most silly novels we can at least extract a laugh; but those of the modern-antique school have a ponderous, a leaden kind of fatuity, under which we groan. What can be more demonstrative of the inability of literary women to measure their own powers, than their frequent assumption of a task which can only be justified by the rarest concurrence of acquirement with genius? The finest effort to reanimate the past is of course only approximative – is always more or less an infusion of the modern spirit into the ancient form, –

> Was ihr den Geist der Zeiten heisst,
> Das ist im Grund der Herren eigner Geist,
> In dem die Zeiten sich bespiegeln.[19]

Admitting that genius which has familiarized itself with all the relics of an ancient period can sometimes, by the force of its sympathetic divination, restore the missing notes in the 'music of humanity', and reconstruct the fragments into a whole which will really bring the remote past nearer to us, and interpret it to our duller apprehension, – this form of imaginative power must always be among the very rarest, because it demands as much accurate and minute knowledge as creative vigour. Yet we find ladies constantly choosing to make their mental mediocrity more conspicuous, by clothing it in a masquerade of ancient names; by putting their feeble sentimentality into the mouths of Roman vestals or Egyptian princesses, and attributing their rhetorical arguments to Jewish high-priests and Greek philosophers. A recent example of this heavy imbecility is *Adonijah, a Tale of the Jewish Dispersion*,[20] which forms part of a series, 'uniting,' we are told, 'taste, humour, and sound principles'. *Adonijah*, we presume, exemplifies the tale of 'sound principles'; the taste and humour are to be found in other members of the series. We are told on the cover, that the incidents of this tale are 'fraught with unusual interest', and the preface winds up thus: 'To those who feel interested in the dispersed of Israel and Judea, these pages may afford, perhaps, information on an important subject, as well as amusement'. Since the 'important subject' on which this book is to afford information is not specified, it may possibly lie in some esoteric meaning to which we have no key; but if it has relation to the dispersed of Israel and Judea at any period of their history, we believe a tolerably well-informed school-girl already knows much more of it than she will find in this 'Tale of the Jewish Dispersion'. *Adonijah* is simply the feeblest kind of love story, supposed to be instructive, we presume, because the hero is a Jewish captive, and the heroine a Roman vestal; because they and their friends are converted to Christianity after the shortest and easiest method approved by the 'Society for Promoting the Conversion of the Jews'; and because, instead of being written in plain language, it is adorned with that peculiar style of grandiloquence which is held by some lady novelists to give an antique colouring; and which we recognize at once in such phrases as these: – 'the splendid regnal talents undoubtedly possessed by the Emperor Nero' – 'the expiring scion of a lofty stem' – 'the virtuous partner of his couch' – 'ah, by Vesta!' – and 'I tell thee, Roman'. Among the quotations which serve at once for instruction and ornament on the cover of this volume, there is one from Miss Sinclair,[21] which informs us that 'Works of imagination are *avowedly* read by men of science, wisdom, and piety'; from which we suppose the reader is to gather the cheering inference that Dr Daubeny, Mr Mill, or Mr Maurice,[22] may openly indulge himself with the perusal of *Adonijah*, without being obliged to secrete it among the sofa cushions, or read it by snatches under the dinner-table.

'Be not a baker if your head be made of butter,' says a homely proverb, which, being interpreted, may mean, let no woman rush into print who is not prepared for the consequences. We are aware that our remarks are in a very different tone from that of the reviewers who, with a perennial recurrence of precisely similar emotions, only paralleled, we imagine, in the experience of monthly nurses, tell one lady novelist after another that they 'hail' her productions 'with delight'. We are aware that the ladies at whom our criticism is pointed are accustomed to be told, in the choicest phraseology of puffery, that their pictures of life are brilliant, their characters well-drawn, their style fascinating, and their sentiments lofty. But if they are inclined to resent our plainness of speech, we ask them to reflect for a moment on the chary praise, and often captious blame, which their panegyrists give to writers whose works are on the way to become classics. No sooner does a woman show that she has genius or effective talent, than she receives the tribute of being moderately praised and severely criticized. By a peculiar thermometric adjustment, when a woman's talent is at zero, journalistic approbation is at the boiling pitch; when she attains mediocrity, it is already at no more than summer heat; and if ever she reaches excellence, critical enthusiasm drops to the freezing point. Harriet Martineau, Currer Bell, and Mrs Gaskell[23] have been treated as cavalierly as if they had been men. And every critic who forms a high estimate of the share women may ultimately take in literature, will, on principle, abstain from any exceptional indulgence towards the productions of literary women. For it must be plain to every one who looks impartially and extensively into feminine literature, that its greatest deficiencies are due hardly more to the want of intellectual power than to the want of those moral qualities that contribute to literary excellence – patient diligence, a sense of the responsibility involved in publication, and an appreciation of the sacredness of the writer's art. In the majority of women's books you see that kind of facility which springs from the absence of any high standard; that fertility in imbecile combination or feeble imitation which a little self-criticism would check and reduce to barrenness; just as with a total want of musical ear people will sing out of tune, while a degree more melodic sensibility would suffice to render them silent. The foolish vanity of wishing to appear in print, instead of being counterbalanced by any consciousness of the intellectual or moral derogation implied in futile authorship, seems to be encouraged by the extremely false impression that to write *at all* is a proof of superiority in a woman. On this ground, we believe that the average intellect of women is unfairly represented by the mass of feminine literature, and that while the few women who write well are very far above the ordinary intellectual level of their sex, the many women who write ill are very far below it. So that, after all, the severer critics are fulfilling a chivalrous duty in depriving the mere fact of feminine authorship of any false prestige which may give it a delusive attraction, and in recommending women of mediocre faculties – as at least a negative service they can render their sex – to abstain from writing.

The standing apology for women who become writers without any special qualification is, that society shuts them out from other spheres of occupation. Society is a very culpable entity, and has to answer for the manufacture of many unwholesome commodities, from bad pickles to bad poetry. But society, like 'matter', and Her Majesty's Government, and other lofty abstractions, has its share of excessive blame as well as excessive praise. Where there is one woman who writes from necessity, we believe there are three women who write from vanity; and, besides, there is something so antiseptic in the mere healthy fact of working for one's bread, that the most trashy and rotten kind of feminine literature is not likely to have been produced under such circumstances. 'In all labour there is profit'; but ladies' silly novels, we imagine, are less the result of labour than of busy idleness.

Happily, we are not dependent on argument to prove that Fiction is a department of literature in which women can, after their kind, fully equal men. A cluster of great names, both living and dead, rush to our memories in evidence that women can produce novels not only fine, but among the very finest; – novels, too, that have a precious speciality, lying quite apart from masculine aptitudes and experience. No educational restrictions can shut women out from the materials of fiction, and there is no species of art which is so free from rigid requirements. Like crystalline masses, it may take any form, and yet be beautiful; we have only to pour in the right elements – genuine observation, humour, and passion. But it is precisely this absence of rigid requirement which constitutes the fatal seduction of novel-writing to incompetent women. Ladies are not wont to be very grossly deceived as to their power of playing on the piano; here certain positive difficulties of execution have to be conquered, and incompetence inevitably breaks down. Every art which has its absolute *technique* is, to a certain extent, guarded from the intrusions of mere left-handed imbecility. But in novel-writing there are no barriers for incapacity to stumble against, no external criteria to prevent a writer from mistaking foolish facility for mastery. And so we have again and again the old story of La Fontaine's ass,[24] who puts his nose to the flute, and, finding that he elicits some sound, exclaims, 'Moi, aussi, je joue de la flute'; – a fable which we commend, at parting, to the consideration of any feminine reader who is in danger of adding to the number of 'silly novels by lady novelists'.

Worldliness and Other-Worldliness: The Poet Young

(Westminster Review, January 1857)

THE STUDY of men, as they have appeared in different ages, and under various social conditions, may be considered as the natural history of the race. Let us, then, for a moment imagine ourselves, as students of this natural history, 'dredging' the first half of the eighteenth century in search of specimens. About the year 1730, we have hauled up a remarkable individual of the species *divine* – a surprising name, considering the nature of the animal before us, but we are used to unsuitable names in natural history. Let us examine this individual at our leisure. He is on the verge of fifty, and has recently undergone his metamorphosis into the clerical form. Rather a paradoxical specimen, if you observe him narrowly: a sort of cross between à sycophant and a psalmist; a poet whose imagination is alternately fired by the 'Last Day' and by a creation of peers,[1] who fluctuates between rhapsodic applause of King George and rhapsodic applause of Jehovah. After spending 'a foolish youth, the sport of peers and poets', after being a hanger-on of the profligate Duke of Wharton,[2] after aiming in vain at a parliamentary career, and angling for pensions and preferment with fulsome dedications and fustian odes, he is a little disgusted with his imperfect success, and has determined to retire from the general mendicancy business to a particular branch; in other words, he has determined on that renunciation of the world implied in 'taking orders', with the prospect of a good living and an advantageous matrimonial connexion. And no man can be better fitted for an Established Church. He personifies completely her nice balance of temporalities and spiritualities.[3] He is equally impressed with the momentousness of death and of burial fees; he languishes at once for immortal life and for 'livings'; he has a fervid attachment to patrons in general, but on the whole prefers the Almighty. He will teach, with something more than official conviction, the nothingness of earthly things; and he will feel something more than private disgust if his meritorious efforts in directing men's attention to another world are not rewarded by substantial preferment in this. His secular man believes in cambric bands and silk stockings as characteristic attire for 'an ornament of religion and virtue';[4] hopes courtiers will never forget to copy Sir Robert Walpole; and writes begging-letters to the King's mistress. His spiritual man recognizes no motives more familiar than Golgotha and 'the skies'; it walks in graveyards, or it soars among the stars. His religion exhausts itself in ejaculations and rebukes, and knows no medium between the ecstatic and the sententious. If it were not for the prospect of immortality, he considers, it would be wise and agreeable to be indecent, or to murder one's father; and, heaven apart, it would be extremely irrational in any man not to be a knave. Man, he thinks, is a compound of the angel and the brute: the brute is to be humbled by being reminded of its 'relation to the stalls', and frightened into moderation by the contemplation of death-beds and skulls; the angel is to be developed by vituperating this world and exalting the next; and by this double process you get the Christian – 'the highest style of man'. With all this, our new-made divine is an unmistakable poet. To a clay compounded chiefly of the worldling and the rhetorician, there is added a real spark of Promethean fire. He will one day clothe his apostrophes and objurgations, his astronomical religion and his charnel-house morality, in lasting verse, which will stand, like a Juggernaut made of gold and jewels, at once magnificent and repulsive: for this divine is Edward Young, the future author of the *Night Thoughts*.

It would be extremely ill-bred in us to suppose that our readers are not acquainted with the facts of Young's life; they are amongst the things that 'every one knows'; but we have observed that, with regard to these universally-known matters, the majority of readers like to be treated after the plan suggested by M. Jourdain. When that distinguished bourgeois was asked if he knew Latin, he replied, 'Oui, mais faîtes comme si je ne le savais pas.'[5] Assuming, then, as a polite writer should, that our readers know everything about

Young, it will be a direct *sequitur* from that assumption that we should proceed as if they knew nothing, and recall the incidents of his biography with as much particularity as we may, without trenching on the space we shall need for our main purpose – the reconsideration of his character as a moral and religious poet.

Judging from Young's works, one might imagine that the preacher had been organized in him by hereditary transmission through a long line of clerical forefathers, – that the diamonds of the *Night Thoughts* had been slowly condensed from the charcoal of ancestral sermons. Yet it was not so. His grandfather, apparently, wrote himself *gentleman*, not *clerk*; and there is no evidence that preaching had run in the family blood before it took that turn in the person of the poet's father, who was quadruply clerical, being at once rector, prebendary, court chaplain, and dean. Young was born at his father's rectory of Upham, in 1681.[6] We may confidently assume that even the author of the *Night Thoughts* came into the world without a wig, but, apart from Dr Doran's authority, we should not have ventured to state that the excellent rector 'kissed, *with dignified emotion*, his only son and intended namesake'.[7] Dr Doran doubtless knows this, from his intimate acquaintance with clerical physiology and psychology. He has ascertained that the paternal emotions of prebendaries have a sacerdotal quality, and that the very chyme and chyle[8] of a rector are conscious of the gown and band.

In due time the boy went to Winchester College, and subsequently, though not till he was twenty-two, to Oxford, where, for his father's sake, he was befriended by the wardens of two colleges, and in 1708, three years after his father's death, nominated by Archbishop Tenison to a law fellowship at All Souls. Of Young's life at Oxford in these years, hardly anything is known. His biographer, Croft, has nothing to tell us but the vague report that, when 'Young found himself independent and his own master at All Souls, he was not the ornament to religion and morality that he afterwards became', and the perhaps apocryphal anecdote, that Tindal, the atheist,[9] confessed himself embarrassed by the originality of Young's arguments. Both the report and the anecdote, however, are borne out by indirect evidence. As to the latter, Young has left us sufficient proof that he was fond of arguing on the theological side, and that he had his own way of treating old subjects. As to the former, we learn that Pope, after saying other things which we know to be true of Young, added, that he passed 'a foolish youth, the sport of peers and poets';[10] and, from all the indications we possess of his career till he was nearly fifty, we are inclined to think that Pope's statement only errs by defect, and that he should rather have said, 'a foolish youth and *middle age*'. It is not likely that Young was a very hard student, for he impressed Johnson, who saw him in his old age, as 'not a great scholar', and as surprisingly ignorant of what Johnson thought 'quite common maxims' in literature; and there is no evidence that he filled either his leisure or his purse by taking pupils. His career as an author did not commence till he was nearly thirty, even dating from the publication of a portion of the *Last Day*, in the *Tatler*; so that he could hardly have been absorbed in composition. But where the fully developed insect is parasitic, we believe the larva is usually parasitic also, and we shall probably not be far wrong in supposing that Young at Oxford, as elsewhere, spent a good deal of his time in hanging about possible and actual patrons, and accommodating himself to their habits with considerable flexibility of conscience and of tongue; being none the less ready, upon occasion, to present himself as the champion of theology, and to rhapsodize at convenient moments in the company of the skies or of skulls. That brilliant profligate, the Duke of Wharton, to whom Young afterwards clung as his chief patron, was at this time a mere boy; and, though it is probable that their intimacy had commenced, since the Duke's father and mother were friends of the old Dean, that intimacy ought not to aggravate any unfavourable inference as to Young's Oxford life. It is less likely that he fell into any exceptional vice, than that he differed from the men around him chiefly in his episodes of theological advocacy and rhapsodic solemnity. He probably sowed his wild oats after the coarse fashion of his times, for he has left us sufficient evidence that his moral sense was not delicate; but his companions, who were occupied in sowing their own oats, perhaps took it as a matter of course that he should be a rake, and were only struck with the exceptional circumstance that he was a pious and moralizing rake.

There is some irony in the fact that the two first poetical

productions of Young, published in the same year, were his 'Epistle to Lord Lansdowne', celebrating the recent creation of peers – Lord Lansdowne's creation in particular; and the *Last Day*. Other poets, besides Young, found the device for obtaining a Tory majority by turning twelve insignificant commoners into insignificant lords, an irresistible stimulus to verse; but no other poet showed so versatile an enthusiasm – so nearly equal an ardour for the honour of the new baron and the honour of the Deity. But the twofold nature of the sycophant and the psalmist is not more strikingly shown in the contrasted themes of the two poems, than in the transitions from bombast about monarchs, to bombast about the resurrection, in the *Last Day* itself. The dedication of this poem to Queen Anne, Young afterwards suppressed, for he was always ashamed of having flattered a dead patron. In this dedication, Croft tells us, 'he gives her Majesty praise indeed for her victories, but says that the author is more pleased to see her rise from this lower world, soaring above the clouds, passing the first and second heavens, and leaving the fixed stars behind her; nor will he lose her there, he says, but keep her still in view through the boundless spaces on the other side of creation, in her journey towards eternal bliss, till he behold the heaven of heavens open, and angels receiving and conveying her still onward from the stretch of his imagination, which tires in her pursuit, and falls back again to earth'.[11]

The self-criticism which prompted the suppression of the dedication, did not, however, lead him to improve either the rhyme or the reason of the unfortunate couplet –

> When other Bourbons reign in other lands,
> And, if men's sins forbid not, other Annes.[12]

In the 'Epistle to Lord Lansdowne', Young indicates his taste for the drama; and there is evidence that his tragedy of *Busiris* was 'in the theatre' as early as this very year, 1713, though it was not brought on the stage till nearly six years later; so that Young was now very decidedly bent on authorship, for which his degree of BCL,[13] taken in this year, was doubtless a magical equipment. Another poem, 'The Force of Religion; or, Vanquished Love', founded on the execution of Lady Jane Grey and her husband, quickly followed, showing fertility in feeble and tasteless verse; and on the Queen's death, in 1714, Young lost no time in making a poetical lament for a departed patron a vehicle for extravagant laudation of the new monarch. No further literary production of his appeared until 1716, when a Latin oration which he delivered on the foundation of the Codrington Library at All Souls, gave him a new opportunity for displaying his alacrity in inflated panegyric.

In 1717 it is probable that Young accompanied the Duke of Wharton to Ireland, though so slender are the materials for his biography, that the chief basis for this supposition is a passage in his 'Conjectures on Original Composition', written when he was nearly eighty, in which he intimates that he had once been in that country. But there are many facts surviving to indicate that for the next eight or nine years, Young was a sort of *attaché* of Wharton's. In 1719, according to legal records, the Duke granted him an annuity, in consideration of his having relinquished the office of tutor to Lord Burleigh, with a life annuity of £100 a year, on his Grace's assurances that he would provide for him in a much more ample manner. And again, from the same evidence, it appears that in 1721 Young received from Wharton a bond for £600, in compensation of expenses incurred in standing for Parliament at the Duke's desire, and as an earnest of greater services which his Grace had promised him on his refraining from the spiritual and temporal advantages of taking orders, with a certainty of two livings in the gift of his college. It is clear, therefore, that lay advancement, as long as there was any chance of it, had more attractions for Young than clerical preferment; and that at this time he accepted the Duke of Wharton as the pilot of his career.

A more creditable relation of Young's was his friendship with Tickell, with whom he was in the habit of interchanging criticisms, and to whom in 1719 – the same year, let us note, in which he took his doctor's degree – he addressed his 'Lines on the Death of Addison'. Close upon these followed his 'Paraphrase of Part of the Book of Job', with a dedication to Parker, recently made Lord Chancellor, showing that the possession of Wharton's patronage did not prevent Young from fishing in other waters. He knew nothing of Parker, but that did not prevent him from magnifying the new Chancellor's merits; on the other hand, he *did* know Wharton, but this again did not prevent him from prefixing to his tragedy, *The Revenge*, which appeared in 1721, a dedication attributing to the Duke all virtues,[14] as well as all accomplishments. In the concluding sentence of this dedication, Young naïvely indicates that a considerable ingredient in his gratitude was a lively sense of anticipated favours. 'My present fortune is his bounty, and my future his care; which I will venture to say will always be remembered to his honour; since he, I know, intended his generosity as an encouragement to merit, though, through his very pardonable partiality to one who bears him so sincere a duty and respect, I happen to receive the benefit of it.' Young was economical with his ideas and images; he was rarely satisfied with using a clever thing once, and this bit of ingenious humility was afterwards made to do duty in the 'Instalment', a poem addressed to Walpole: –

> Be this thy partial smile, from censure free,
> 'Twas meant for merit, though it fell on me.

It was probably *The Revenge*, that Young was writing when, as we learn from Spence's anecdotes, the Duke of Wharton gave him a skull with a candle fixed in it, as the most appropriate lamp by which to write tragedy. According to Young's dedication, the Duke was 'accessory' to the scenes of this tragedy in a more important way, 'not only by suggesting the most beautiful incident in them, but by making all possible provision for the success of the whole'. A statement which is credible, not indeed on the ground of Young's dedicatory assertion, but from the known ability of the Duke, who, as Pope tells us, possessed

> each gift of Nature and of Art,
> And wanted nothing but an honest heart.[15]

The year 1722 seems to have been the period of a visit to Mr Dodington, at Eastbury, in Dorsetshire – the 'pure Dorsetian downs', celebrated by Thomson, – in which Young made the acquaintance of Voltaire; for in the subsequent dedication of his 'Sea Piece' to 'Mr Voltaire', he recalls their meeting on 'Dorset Downs'; and it was in this year that Christopher Pitt,[16] a gentleman-poet of those days, addressed on 'Epistle to Dr Edward Young, at Eastbury, in Dorsetshire', which has at least the merit of this biographical couplet –

> While with your Dodington retired you sit,
> Charm'd with his flowing Burgundy and wit.

Dodington, apparently, was charmed in his turn, for he told Dr Warton that Young was 'far superior to the French poet in the variety and novelty of his *bons mots* and repartees'.[17] Unfortunately, the only specimen of Young's wit on this occasion that has been preserved to us, is the epigram represented as an extempore retort (spoken aside, surely) to Voltaire's criticism of Milton's episode of Sin and Death: –

> Thou art so witty, profligate, and thin,
> At once we think thee Milton, Death, and Sin; –

an epigram which, in the absence of 'flowing Burgundy', does not strike us as remarkably brilliant. Let us give Young the benefit of the doubt thrown on the genuineness of this epigram by his own poetical dedication, in which he represents himself as having 'soothed' Voltaire's 'rage' against Milton 'with gentle rhymes'; though in other respects that dedication is anything but favourable to a high estimate of Young's wit. Other evidence apart, we should not be eager for the after-dinner conversation of the man who wrote, –

> Thine is the Drama, how renown'd!
> Thine Epic's loftier trump to sound; –
> *But let Arion's sea-strung harp be mine:*
> *But where's his dolphin? Know'st thou where?*
> *May that be found in thee, Voltaire!*

The *Satires* appeared in 1725 and 1726,[18] each, of course, with its laudatory dedication and its compliments insinuated amongst the rhymes. The seventh and last is dedicated to Sir Robert Walpole, is very short, and contains nothing in particular except lunatic flattery of George I and his prime minister, attributing that royal hog's[19] late escape from a storm at sea to the miraculous influence of his grand and virtuous soul – for George, he says, rivals the angels: –

> George, who in foes can soft affections raise,
> And charm envenom'd satire into praise.

> Nor human rage alone his pow'r perceives,
> But the mad winds and the tumultuous waves.
> Ev'n storms (Death's fiercest ministers!) forbear,
> And in their own wild empire learn to spare.
> Thus, Nature's self, supporting Man's decree,
> Styles Britain's sovereign, sovereign of the sea.

As for Walpole, what *he* felt at this tremendous crisis

> No powers of language, but his own, can tell, –
> His own, which Nature and the Graces form,
> At will, to raise, or hush, the civil storm.

It is a coincidence worth noticing, that this Seventh Satire was published in 1726, and that the warrant of George I, granting Young a pension of £200 a year from Lady Day, 1725, is dated 3 May 1726. The gratitude exhibited in this satire may have been chiefly prospective, but the 'Instalment', a poem inspired by the thrilling event of Walpole's installation as Knight of the Garter, was clearly written with the double ardour of a man who has got a pension, and hopes for something more. His emotion about Walpole is precisely at the same pitch as his subsequent emotion about the Second Advent. In the 'Instalment' he says, –

> With invocations some their hearts inflame;
> *I need no muse, a Walpole is my theme.*

And of God coming to judgement, he says, in the *Night Thoughts*: –

> I find my inspiration is my theme;
> *The grandeur of my subject is my muse.*

Nothing can be feebler than this 'Instalment', except in the strength of impudence with which the writer professes to scorn the prostitution of fair fame, the 'profanation of celestial fire'.

Herbert Croft tells us that Young made more than £3,000 by his *Satires*, – a surprising statement, taken in connexion with the reasonable doubt he throws on the story related in *Spence's Anecdotes*, that the Duke of Wharton gave Young £2,000 for this work. Young, however, seems to have been tolerably fortunate in the pecuniary results of his publications; and with his literary profits, his annuity from Wharton, his fellowship, and his pension, not to mention other bounties which may be inferred from the high merits he discovers in many men of wealth and position, we may fairly suppose that he now laid the foundation of the considerable fortune he left at his death.

It is probable that the Duke of Wharton's final departure for the Continent and disgrace at Court in 1726, and the consequent cessation of Young's reliance on his patronage, tended not only to heighten the temperature of his poetical enthusiasm for Sir Robert Walpole, but also to turn his thoughts towards the Church again, as the second-best means of rising in the world. On the accession of George II, Young found the same transcendent merits in him as in his predecessor, and celebrated them in a style of poetry previously unattempted by him – the Pindaric ode, a poetic form which helped him to surpass himself in furious bombast. 'Ocean, an Ode: Concluding with a Wish', was the title of this piece. He afterwards pruned it, and cut off, amongst other things, the concluding Wish, expressing the yearning for humble retirement, which, of course, had prompted him to the effusion; but we may judge of the rejected stanzas by the quality of those he has allowed to remain. For example, calling on Britain's dead mariners to rise and meet their 'country's full-blown glory' in the person of the new King, he says, –

> What powerful charm
> Can Death disarm?
> Your long, your iron slumbers break?
> *By Jove, by Fame,*
> *By George's name*
> Awake! awake! awake! awake!

Soon after this notable production, which was written with the ripe folly of forty-seven, Young took orders, and was presently appointed chaplain to the King. *The Brothers*, his third and last tragedy, which was already in rehearsal, he now withdrew from the stage, and sought reputation in a way more accordant with the decorum of his new profession, by turning prose writer. But after publishing *A True Estimate of Human Life*, with a dedication to the Queen, as one of the 'most shining representatives' of God on earth, and a sermon, entitled 'An Apology for Princes; or, the Reverence Due to Government', preached before the House of

Commons, his Pindaric ambition again seized him, and he matched his former ode by another, called 'Imperium Pelagi; a Naval Lyric, Written in Imitation of Pindar's Spirit, Occasioned by his Majesty's Return from Hanover, 1729, and the Succeeding Peace'. Since he afterwards suppressed this second ode, we must suppose that it was rather worse than the first. Next came his two 'Epistles to Pope, Concerning the Authors of the Age', remarkable for nothing but the audacity of affectation with which the most servile of poets professes to despise servility.

In 1730 Young was presented by his college with the rectory of Welwyn, in Hertfordshire, and, in the following year, when he was just fifty, he married Lady Elizabeth Lee, a widow with two children, who seems to have been in favour with Queen Caroline, and who probably had an income – two attractions which doubtless enhanced the power of her other charms. Pastoral duties and domesticity probably cured Young of some bad habits; but, unhappily, they did not cure him either of flattery or of fustian. Three more odes followed, quite as bad as those of his bachelorhood, except that in the third he announced the wise resolution of never writing another. It must have been about this time, since Young was now 'turned of fifty', that he wrote the letter to Mrs Howard (afterwards Lady Suffolk), George II's mistress, which proves that he used other engines, besides Pindaric ones, in 'besieging Court favour'. The letter is too characteristic to be omitted: –

MONDAY MORNING.

MADAM, – I know his majesty's goodness to his servants, and his love of justice in general, so well, that I am confident, if his Majesty knew my case, I should not have any cause to despair of his gracious favour to me.

Abilities	Want	
Good Manners	Sufferings	} for his
Service	and	
Age	Zeal	} majesty.

These, madam, are the proper points of consideration in the person that humbly hopes his majesty's favour.

As to *Abilities*, all I can presume to say is, I have done the best I could to improve them.

As to *Good manners*, I desire no favour, if any just objection lies against them.

As for *Service*, I have been near seven years in his majesty's, and never omitted any duty in it, which few can say.

As for *Age*, I am turned of fifty.

As for *Want*, I have no manner of preferment.

As for *Sufferings*, I have lost £300 per annum by being in his majesty's service; as I have shown in a *Representation* which his majesty has been so good as to read and consider.

As for *Zeal*, I have written nothing without showing my duty to their majesties, and some pieces are dedicated to them.

This, madam, is the short and true state of my case. They that make their court to the ministers, and not their majesties, succeed better. If my case deserves some consideration, and you can serve me in it, I humbly hope and believe you will: I shall, therefore, trouble you no farther; but beg leave to subscribe myself, with truest respect and gratitude,

Yours, &c.,

EDWARD YOUNG.

P.S. I have some hope that my Lord Townshend is my friend; if therefore soon, and before he leaves the court, you had an opportunity of mentioning me, with that favour you have been so good to show, I think it would not fail of success; and, if not, I shall owe you more than any (*Suffolk Letters, Vol. I*, p. 285[20]).

Young's wife died in 1741, leaving him one son, born in 1733. That he had attached himself strongly to her two daughters by her former marriage, there is better evidence in the report, mentioned by Mrs Montagu, of his practical kindness and liberality to the younger, than in his lamentations over the elder as the 'Narcissa' of the *Night Thoughts*. 'Narcissa' had died in 1735, shortly after marriage to Mr Temple, the son of Lord Palmerston; and Mr Temple himself, after a second marriage, died in 1740, a year before Lady Elizabeth Young. These, then, are the three deaths supposed to have inspired 'The Complaint', which forms the three first books of the *Night Thoughts*: —

> Insatiate archer, could not one suffice?
> Thy shaft flew thrice; and thrice my peace was slain;
> And thrice, ere thrice yon moon had fill'd her horn.

Since we find Young departing from the truth of dates, in order to heighten the effect of his calamity, or at least of his climax, we need not be surprised that he allowed his imagination great freedom in other matters besides chronology, and that the character of 'Philander' can, by no process, be made to fit Mr Temple. The supposition that the much-lectured 'Lorenzo' of the *Night Thoughts* was Young's own son, is hardly rendered more absurd by the fact that the poem was written when that son was a boy, than by the obvious artificiality of the characters Young introduces as targets for his arguments and rebukes. Among all the trivial efforts of conjectural criticism, there can hardly be one more futile than the attempt to discover the original of those pitiable lay-figures, the 'Lorenzos' and 'Altamonts' of Young's didactic prose and poetry. His muse never stood face to face with a genuine, living human being; she would have been as much startled by such an encounter as a necromancer whose incantations and blue fire had actually conjured up a demon.

The *Night Thoughts* appeared between 1741 and 1745.[21] Although he declares in them that he has chosen God for his 'patron' henceforth, this is not at all to the prejudice of some half-dozen lords, duchesses, and right honourables, who have the privilege of sharing finely-turned compliments with their co-patron. The line which closed the Second Night in the earlier editions, –

Wits spare not Heaven, O Wilmington! – nor thee –

is an intense specimen of that perilous juxtaposition of ideas by which Young, in his incessant search after point and novelty, unconsciously converts his compliments into sarcasms; and his apostrophe to the moon as more likely to be favourable to his song if he calls her 'fair Portland of the skies', is worthy even of his Pindaric ravings. His ostentatious renunciation of worldly schemes, and especially of his twenty-years' siege of Court favour, is in the tone of one who retains some hope, in the midst of his querulousness.

He descended from the astronomical rhapsodies of his Ninth Night, published in 1745, to more terrestrial strains in his 'Reflections on the Public Situation of the Kingdom', dedicated to the Duke of Newcastle; but in this critical year we get a glimpse of him through a more prosaic and less refracting medium. He spent a part of the year at Tunbridge Wells; and Mrs Montagu, who was there too, gives a very lively picture of the 'divine Doctor' in her letters to the Duchess of Portland, on whom Young had bestowed the superlative bombast to which we have recently alluded. We shall borrow the quotations from Dr Doran, in spite of their length, because, to our mind, they present the most agreeable portrait we possess of Young: –

'I have great joy in Dr Young, whom I disturbed in a reverie. At first he started, then bowed, then fell back into a surprise; then began a speech, relapsed into his astonishment two or three times, forgot what he had been saying; began a new subject, and so went on. I told him your grace desired he would write longer letters; to which he cried "Ha!" most emphatically, and I leave you to interpret what it meant. He has made a friendship with one person here, whom I believe you would not imagine to have been made for his bosom friend. You would, perhaps, suppose it was a bishop or dean, a prebend, a pious preacher, a clergyman of exemplary life, or, if a layman, of most virtuous conversation, one that had paraphrased Saint Matthew, or wrote comments of Saint Paul . . . You would not guess that this associate of the doctor's was – old Cibber! Certainly, in their religious, moral, and civil character, there is no relation; but in their dramatic capacity there is some.' – Mrs Montagu was not aware that Cibber, whom Young had named not disparagingly in his *Satires*, was the brother of his old school-fellow; but to return to our hero. 'The waters,' says Mrs Montagu, 'have raised his spirits to a fine pitch, as your grace will imagine, when I tell you how sublime an answer he made to a very vulgar question. I asked him how long he stayed at the Wells: he said, As long as my rival stayed;– as long as the sun did.' Among the visitors at the Wells were Lady Sunderland, (wife of Sir Robert Sutton,) and her sister, Mrs Tichborne. 'He did an admirable thing to Lady Sunderland: on her mentioning Sir Robert Sutton, he asked her where Sir Robert's lady was; on which we all laughed very heartily, and I brought him off, half ashamed, to my lodgings, where, during breakfast, he assured me he had asked after Lady Sunderland, because he had a great honour for her; and that, having a respect for her sister, he designed to have inquired after her, if we had not put it out of his head by laughing at him. You must know, Mrs Mrs Tichborne sat next to Lady Sunderland. It would have been admirable to have had him finish his compliment in that manner . . . His expressions all bear the stamp of novelty, and his thoughts of sterling sense. He practises a kind of philosophical abstinence . . . He carried Mrs Rolt and myself to Tunbridge, five miles from hence, where we were to see some fine old ruins . . . First rode the doctor on a tall steed, decently caparisoned in dark grey; next, ambled Mrs Rolt on a hackney horse; . . . then followed your humble servant on a milk-white palfrey. I rode on in safety, and at leisure to observe the company, especially the two figures that brought up the rear. The first was my servant, valiantly armed with two uncharged pistols; the last was the doctor's man, whose uncombed hair so resembled the mane of the horse he rode, one could not help imagining they were of kin, and wishing, for the honour of the family, that they had had one comb betwixt them. On his head was a velvet cap, much resembling a black saucepan, and on his side hung a little basket. – At last we arrived at the King's Head, where the loyalty of the doctor induced him to alight; and then, knight-errant-like, he took his damsels from off their palfreys, and courteously handed us into the inn ... The party returned to the Wells; and 'the silver Cynthia held up her lamp in the heavens' the while. 'The night silenced all but our divine doctor, who sometimes uttered things fit to be spoken in a season when all nature seems to be hushed and hearkening. I followed, gathering wisdom as I went, till I found, by my horse's stumbling, that I was in a bad road, and that the blind was leading the blind. So I placed my servant between the doctor and myself; which he not perceiving, went on in a most philoso-phical strain, to the great admiration of my poor clown of a servant, who, not being wrought up to any pitch of enthusiasm, nor making any answer to all the fine things he heard, the doctor, wondering I was dumb, and grieving I was so stupid, looked round and declared his surprise.'[22]

Young's oddity and absence of mind are gathered from other sources besides these stories of Mrs Montagu's, and gave rise to the report that he was the original of Fielding's 'Parson Adams'; but this Croft denies, and mentions another Young, who really sat for the portrait, and who, we imagine, had both more Greek and more genuine simplicity than the poet. His love of chatting with Colley Cibber[23] was an indication that the old predilection for the stage survived, in spite of his emphatic contempt for 'all joys but joys that never can expire'; and the production of *The Brothers*, at Drury Lane in 1753, after a suppression of fifteen years, was perhaps not entirely due to the expressed desire to give the proceeds to the Society for the Propagation of the Gospel. The author's profits were not more than £400 – in those days a disappointing sum; and Young, as we learn from his friend Richardson, did not make this the limit of his donation, but gave a thousand guineas to the Society. 'I had some talk with him,' says Richardson, in one of his letters, 'about this great action. "I always," said he, "intended to do something handsome for the Society. Had I deferred it to my demise, I should have given away my son's money. All the world are inclined to pleasure; could I have given myself a greater by disposing of the sum to a different use, I should have done it." '24 Surely he took his old friend Richardson for 'Lorenzo'!

His next work was *The Centaur Not Fabulous; in Six Letters to a Friend, on the Life in Vogue*, which reads very much like the most objurgatory parts of the *Night Thoughts* reduced to prose. It is preceded by a preface which, though addressed to a lady, is in its denunciations of vice as grossly indecent and almost as flippant as the epilogues written by 'friends', which he allowed to be reprinted after his tragedies in the latest edition of his works. We like much better than *The Centaur*, *Conjectures on Original Composition*, written in 1759, for the sake, he says, of communicating to the world the well-known anecdote about Addison's death-bed, and, with the exception of his poem on Resignation, the last thing he ever published.

The estrangement from his son, which must have embittered the later years of his life, appears to have begun not many years after the mother's death. On the marriage of her second daughter, who had previously presided over Young's household, a Mrs Hallows, understood to be a woman of discreet age, and the daughter (or widow) of a clergyman who was an old friend of Young's, became housekeeper at Welwyn. Opinions about ladies are apt to differ. 'Mrs Hallows was a woman of piety, improved by reading,' says one witness.25 'She was a very coarse woman,' says Dr Johnson;26 and we shall presently find some indirect evidence that her temper was perhaps not quite so much improved as her piety. Servants, it seems, were not fond of remaining long in the house with her; a satirical curate, named Kidgell, hints at 'drops of juniper' taken as a cordial (but perhaps he was spiteful, and a teetotaller); and Young's son is said to have told his father that 'an old man should not resign himself to the management of anybody'. The result was, that the son was banished from home for the rest of his father's lifetime, though Young seems never to have thought of disinheriting him.

Our latest glimpses of the aged poet are derived from certain letters of Mr Jones, his curate, – letters preserved in the British

Museum, and, happily, made accessible to common mortals in
Nichols's *Anecdotes*.[27] Mr Jones was a man of some literary activity
and ambition,– a collector of interesting documents, and one of
those concerned in the *Free and Candid Disquisitions*, the design of
which was 'to point out such things in our ecclesiastical establishment as want to be reviewed and amended'. On these and kindred
subjects he corresponded with Dr Birch,[28] occasionally troubling
him with queries and manuscripts. We have a respect for Mr
Jones. Unlike any person who ever troubled *us* with queries or
manuscripts, he mitigates the infliction by such gifts as 'a fat
pullet', wishing he 'had anything better to send; but this de-
pauperizing vicarage (of Alconbury) too often checks the freedom
and forwardness of my mind'. Another day comes a 'pound canister
of tea', another, a 'young fatted goose'. Clearly, Mr Jones was
entirely unlike your literary correspondents of the present day; he
forwarded manuscripts, but he had 'bowels', and forwarded
poultry too.[29] His first letter from Welwyn is dated June 1759, not
quite six years before Young's death. In June 1762, he expresses a
wish to go to London 'this summer'. But, he continues, –

My time and pains are almost continually taken up here, and . . . I have
been (I now find) a considerable loser, upon the whole, by continuing
here so long. The consideration of this, and the incoveniences I sustained,
and do still experience, from my late illness, obliged me at last to acquaint
the Doctor (Young) with my case, and to assure him that I plainly
perceived the duty and confinement here to be too much for me; for
which reason I must (I said) beg to be at liberty to resign my charge at
Michaelmas. I began to give him these notices in February, when I was
very ill: and now I perceive, by what he told me the other day, that he is
in some difficulty: for which reason he is at last (he says) resolved to
advertise, *and even (which is much wondered at) to raise the salary considerably
higher*. (What he allowed my predecessors was £20 per annum; and now
he proposes £50, as he tells me.) I never asked him to raise it for me,
though I well knew it was not equal to the duty; nor did I say a word
about myself when he lately suggested to me his intentions upon this
subject.

In a postscript to this letter he says, –

I may mention to you farther, as a friend that may be trusted, that, in all
likelihood, the poor old gentleman will not find it a very easy matter,

unless by dint of money, *and force upon himself*, to procure a man that he can like for his next curate, *nor one that will stay with him so long as I have done*. Then, his great age will recur to people's thoughts; and if he has any foibles, either in temper or conduct, they will be sure not to be forgotten on this occasion by those who know him; and those who do not, will probably be on their guard. On these and the like considerations, it is by no means an eligible office to be seeking out for a curate for him, as he has several times wished me to do; and would, if he knew that I am now writing to you, wish your assistance also. But my best friends here, *who well foresee the probable consequences*, and wish me well, earnestly dissuade me from complying; and I will decline the office with as much decency as I can: but high salary will, I suppose, fetch in somebody or other, soon.

In the following July, he writes, –

The old gentleman here (I may venture to tell you freely) seems to me to be in a pretty odd way of late, – moping, dejected, self-willed, and as if surrounded with some perplexing circumstances. Though I visit him pretty frequently for short intervals, I say very little to his affairs, not choosing to be a party concerned, especially in cases of so critical and tender a nature. There is much mystery in almost all his temporal affairs, as well as in many of his speculative theories. Whoever lives in this neighbourhood to see his exit, will probably see and hear some very strange things. Time will show; – I am afraid, not greatly to his credit. There is thought to be *an irremovable obstruction to his happiness within his walls, as well as another without them*; but the former is the more powerful, and like to continue so. He has this day been trying anew to engage me to stay with him. No lucrative views can tempt me to sacrifice my liberty or my health, to such measures as are proposed here. *Nor do I like to have to do with persons whose word and honour cannot be depended on*. So much for this very odd and unhappy topic.

In August, Mr Jones's tone is slightly modified. Earnest entreaties, not lucrative considerations, have induced him to cheer the Doctor's dejected heart by remaining at Welwyn some time longer. The Doctor is, 'in various respects, a very unhappy man', and few know so much of these respects as Mr Jones. In September, he recurs to the subject: –

My ancient gentleman here is still full of trouble: which moves my concern, though it moves only the secret laughter of many, and some untoward surmises in disfavour of him and his household. The loss of a very large sum of money (about £200) is talked of; whereof this vill and neighbourhood is full. Some disbelieve; others say, '*It is no wonder, where about eighteen or more servants are sometimes taken and dismissed in the course of a year.*' The gentleman himself is allowed by all to be far more harmless and easy in his family than some one else who hath too much the lead in it. This, among others, was one reason for my late motion to quit.

No other mention of Young's affairs occurs until 2 April 1765, when he says that Dr Young is very ill, attended by two physicians.

Having mentioned this young gentleman (Dr Young's son), I would acquaint you next, that he came hither this morning, having been sent for, as I am told, by the direction of Mrs Hallows. Indeed, she intimated to me as much herself. And if this be so, I must say, that it is one of the most prudent acts she ever did, or could have done in such a case as this; as it may prove a means of preventing much confusion after the death of the Doctor. I have had some little discourse with the son: he seems much affected, and I believe really is so. He earnestly wishes his father might be pleased to ask after him; for you must know he has not yet done this, nor is, in my opinion, like to do it. And it has been said farther, that upon a late application made to him on the behalf of his son, he desired that no more might be said to him about it. How true this may be, I cannot as yet be certain; all I shall say is, it seems not improbable . . . I heartily wish the antient man's heart may prove tender towards his son; *though, knowing him so well, I can scarce hope to hear such desirable news.*

Eleven days later, he writes, –

I have now the pleasure to acquaint you, that the late Dr Young, though he had for many years kept his son at a distance from him, yet has now at last left him all his possessions, after the payment of certain legacies; so that the young gentleman (who bears a fair character, and behaves well, as far as I can hear or see) will, I hope, soon enjoy and make a prudent use of a handsome fortune. The father, on his death-bed, and since my return from London, was applied to in the tenderest manner, by one of his physicians, and by another person, to admit the son into his presence, to make submission, intreat forgiveness, and obtain his blessing. As to an interview with his son, he intimated that he chose to decline it, as his spirits were then low, and his nerves weak. With regard to the next particular, he said, '*I heartily forgive him;*' and upon mention of this last, he gently lifted up his hand, and letting it gently fall, pronounced these words, '*God bless him!*' . . . I know it will give you pleasure to be farther informed, that he was pleased to make respectful mention of me in his will; expressing his satisfaction in my care of his parish, *bequeathing to me a handsome legacy*, and appointing me to be one of his executors.

So far Mr Jones, in his confidential correspondence with a 'friend who may be trusted'. In a letter communicated apparently by him to the *Gentleman's Magazine*, seven years later, namely, in 1782,[30] on the appearance of Croft's biography of Young, we find him speaking of 'the ancient gentleman' in a tone of reverential eulogy, quite at variance with the free comments we have just quoted. But the Rev. John Jones was probably of opinion, with Mrs Montagu, whose contemporary and retrospective letters are also set in a different key, that 'the interests of religion were connected with the character of a man so distinguished for piety as Dr Young'.[31] At all events, a subsequent quasi-official statement weighs nothing as evidence against contemporary, spontaneous, and confidential hints.

To Mrs Hallows, Young left a legacy of £1,000, with the request that she would destroy all his manuscripts. This final request, from some unknown cause, was not complied with, and among the papers he left behind him, was the following letter from Archbishop Secker, which probably marks the date of his latest effort after preferment.

Deanery of St Paul's, 8 July 1758.

Good Dr Young, – I have long wondered that more suitable notice of your great merit hath not been taken by persons in power. But how to remedy the omission I see not. No encouragement hath ever been given me to mention things of this nature to his Majesty. And therefore, in all likelihood, the only consequence of doing it would be weakening the little influence which else I may possibly have on some other occasions. *Your fortune and your reputation set you above the need of advancement; and your sentiments above that concern for it, on your own account*, which, on that of the public, is sincerely felt by

Your loving Brother,
THO. CANT.[32]

The loving brother's irony is severe!

Perhaps the least questionable testimony to the better side of Young's character, is that of Bishop Hildesley, who, as the vicar of a parish near Welwyn, had been Young's neighbour for upwards of twenty years. The affection of the clergy for each other, we have observed, is, like that of the fair sex, not at all of a blind and infatuated kind; and we may therefore the rather believe them when they give each other any extra-official praise. Bishop Hildesley, then, writing of Young to Richardson, says, –

The impertinence of my frequent visits to him was amply rewarded; forasmuch as, I can truly say, he never received me but with agreeable open complacency; and I never left him but with profitable pleasure and improvement. He was one or other, the most modest, the most patient of contradiction, and the most informing and entertaining I ever conversed with – at least, of any man who had so just pretensions to pertinacity and reserve.[33]

Mr Langton, however, who was also a frequent visitor of Young's, informed Boswell –

That there was an air of benevolence in his manner; but that he could obtain from him less information than he had hoped to receive from one who had lived so much in intercourse with the brightest men of what had been called the Augustan age of England; and that he showed a degree of eager curiosity concerning the common occurrences that were then passing, which appeared somewhat remarkable in a man of such intellectual stores, of such an advanced age, and who had retired from life with declared disappointment in his expectations.[34]

The same substance, we know, will exhibit different qualities under different tests; and, after all, imperfect reports of individual impressions, whether immediate or traditional, are a very frail basis on which to build our opinion of a man. One's character may be very indifferently mirrored in the mind of the most intimate neighbour; it all depends on the quality of that gentleman's reflecting surface.

But, discarding any inferences from such uncertain evidence, the outline of Young's character is too distinctly traceable in the well-attested facts of his life, and yet more in the self-betrayal that runs through all his works, for us to fear that our general estimate of him may be false. For, while no poet seems less easy and spontaneous than Young, no poet discloses himself more completely. Men's minds have no hiding-place out of themselves – their affectations do but betray another phase of their nature. And if, in the present view of Young, we seem to be more intent on laying bare unfavourable facts than on shrouding them in 'charitable speeches', it is not because we have any irreverential pleasure in turning men's characters 'the seamy side without', but because we see no great advantage in considering a man as he was *not*. Young's biographers and critics have usually set out from the position that he was a great religious teacher, and that his poetry is morally sublime; and they have toned down his failings into harmony with their conception of the divine and the poet. For our own part, we set out from precisely the opposite conviction – namely, that the religious and moral spirit of Young's poetry is low and false; and we think it of some importance to show that the *Night Thoughts* are the reflex of a mind in which the higher human sympathies were inactive. This judgement is entirely opposed to our youthful predilections and enthusiasm. The sweet garden-breath of early enjoyment lingers about many a page of the *Night Thoughts*, and even of the *Last Day*, giving an extrinsic charm to passages of stilted rhetoric and false sentiment; but the sober and repeated reading of maturer years has convinced us that it would hardly be possible to find a more typical instance than Young's poetry, of the mistake which substitutes interested obedience for sympathetic emotion, and baptizes egoism as religion.

Pope said of Young, that he had 'much of a sublime genius without common sense'.[35] The deficiency Pope meant to indicate was, we imagine, moral rather than intellectual: it was the want of that fine sense of what is fitting in speech and action, which is often eminently possessed by men and women whose intellect is of a very common order, but who have the sincerity and dignity which can never co-exist with the selfish preoccupations of vanity or interest. This was the 'common sense' in which Young was conspicuously deficient; and it was partly owing to this deficiency that his genius, waiting to be determined by the highest prizes, fluttered uncertainly from effort to effort, until, when he was more than sixty, it suddenly spread its broad wing, and soared so as to arrest the gaze of other generations besides his own. For he had no versatility of faculty to mislead him. The *Night Thoughts* only differ from his previous works in the degree and not in the kind of power they manifest. Whether he writes prose or poetry, rhyme or blank verse, dramas, satires, odes, or meditations, we see everywhere the same Young – the same narrow circle of thoughts, the same love of abstractions, the same telescopic view of human things, the same appetency towards antithetic apothegm and rhapsodic climax. The passages that arrest us in his tragedies are those in which he anticipates some fine passage in the *Night Thoughts*, and where his characters are only transparent shadows through which we see the bewigged *embonpoint*[36] of the didactic poet, excogitating epigrams or ecstatic soliloquies by the light of a candle fixed in a skull. Thus, in *The Revenge*, 'Alonzo', in the conflict of jealousy and love that at once urges and forbids him to murder his wife, says, –

> This vast and solid earth, that blazing sun,
> Those skies, through which it rolls, must all have end.
> What then is man? The smallest part of nothing.
> Day buries day; month, month; and year the year!
> Our life is but a chain of many deaths.
> Can then Death's self be feared? Our life much rather:
> *Life is the desert, life the solitude;*
> Death joins us to the great majority:
> 'Tis to be born to Plato and to Cæsar;
> 'Tis to be great for ever;
> 'Tis pleasure, 'tis ambition, then, to die.

His prose writings all read like the *Night Thoughts*, either diluted into prose, or not yet crystallized into poetry. For example, in his *Thoughts for Age*, he says, –

Though we stand on its awful brink, such our leaden bias to the world, we turn our faces the wrong way; we are still looking on our old acquaintance, *Time*; though now so wasted and reduced, that we can see little more of him than his wings and his scythe: our age enlarges his wings to our imagination; and our fear of death, his scythe; as Time himself grows less. His consumption is deep; his annihilation is at hand.

This is a dilution of the magnificent image: –

> Time in advance behind him hides his wings,
> And seems to creep decrepit with his age.
> Behold him when past by! What then is seen
> But his proud pinions, swifter than the winds?

Again: –

A requesting Omnipotence? What can stun and confound thy reason more? What more can ravish and exalt thy heart? It cannot but ravish and exalt; it cannot but gloriously disturb and perplex thee, to take in all *that* thought suggests. Thou child of the dust! Thou speck of misery and sin! How abject thy weakness! how great is thy power! Thou crawler on earth, and possible (I was about to say) controuller of the skies! Weigh, and weigh well, the wondrous truths I have in view: which cannot be weighed too much; which the more they are weighed, amaze the more; which to have supposed, before they were revealed, would have been as great madness, and to have presumed on as great sin, as, it is now madness and sin not to believe.

Even in his Pindaric odes, in which he made the most violent effort against nature, he is still neither more nor less than the Young of the *Last Day*, emptied and swept of his genius, and possessed by seven demons of fustian and bad rhyme. Even here, his 'Ercles' vein' alternates with his moral platitudes, and we have the perpetual text of the *Night Thoughts*: —

Gold pleasure buys;
But pleasure dies,
For soon the gross fruition
  cloys;
Though raptures court,
The sense is short;
But virtue kindles living joys; —

Joys felt alone!
Joys asked of none!
Which Time's and Fortune's
  arrows miss;
Joys that subsist,
Though fates resist,
An unprecarious, endless bliss!

Unhappy they!
And falsely gay!
Who bask for ever in success;
A constant feast
Quite palls the taste,
And long enjoyment is distress.

In the *Last Day*, again, which is the earliest thing he wrote, we have an anticipation of all his greatest faults and merits. Conspicuous among the faults is that attempt to exalt our conceptions of Deity by vulgar images and comparisons, which is so offensive in the later *Night Thoughts*. In a burst of prayer and homage to God, called forth by the contemplation of Christ coming to judgement, he asks, Who brings the change of the seasons? and answers —

> Not the great Ottoman, or greater Czar;
> Not Europe's arbitress of peace and war!

Conceive the soul in its most solemn moments, assuring God that it doesn't place his power below that of Louis Napoleon or Queen Victoria!

But in the midst of uneasy rhymes, inappropriate imagery, vaulting sublimity that o'erleaps itself, and vulgar emotions, we have in this poem an occasional flash of genius, a touch of simple grandeur, which promises as much as Young ever achieved. Describing the on-coming of the dissolution of all things, he says, –

> No sun in radiant glory shines on high;
> *No light but from the terrors of the sky.*

And again, speaking of great armies, –

> Whose rear lay wrapt in night, while breaking dawn,
> Rous'd the broad front, and call'd the battle on.

And this wail of the lost souls is fine: –

> And this for sin?
> Could I offend if I had never been?
> But still increas'd the senseless, happy mass,
> Flow'd in the stream, *or shiver'd in the grass?*
> Father of mercies! Why from silent earth
> Didst thou awake and curse me into birth?
> Tear me from quiet, ravish me from night,
> And make a thankless present of thy light?
> Push into being a reverse of Thee,
> And *animate a clod with misery?*

But it is seldom in Young's rhymed poems that the effect of a felicitous thought or image is not counteracted by our sense of the constraint he suffered from the necessities of rhyme, – that 'Gothic demon', as he afterwards called it, 'which modern poetry tasting, became mortal'. In relation to his own power, no one will question the truth of his dictum, that 'blank verse is verse unfallen, uncurst; verse reclaimed, reinthroned in the true language of the gods; who never thundered nor suffered their Homer to thunder in rhyme'.[37] His want of mastery in rhyme is especially a drawback on the effect of his *Satires*; for epigrams and witticisms are peculiarly susceptible to the intrusion of a superfluous word, or to an inversion which implies constraint. Here, even more than elsewhere, the art that conceals art is an absolute requisite, and to have a witticism presented to us in limping or cumbrous rhythm is as counteractive to any electrifying effect, as to see the tentative grimaces by which a comedian prepares a grotesque countenance. We discern the process, instead of being startled by the result.

This is one reason why the *Satires*, read *seriatim*, have a flatness to us, which, when we afterwards read picked passages, we are inclined to disbelieve in, and to attribute to some deficiency in our own mood. But there are deeper reasons for that dissatisfaction. Young is not a satirist of a high order. His satire has neither the terrible vigour, the lacerating energy of genuine indignation, nor the humour which owns loving fellowship with the poor human nature it laughs at; nor yet the personal bitterness which, as in Pope's characters of Sporus and Atticus,[38] ensures those living touches by virtue of which the individual and particular in Art becomes the universal and immortal. Young could never describe a real complex human being; but what he *could* do with eminent success, was to describe with neat and finished point, obvious *types*, of manners rather than of character, – to write cold and clever epigrams on personified vices and absurdities. There is no more emotion in his satire than if he were turning witty verses on a waxen image of Cupid, or a lady's glove. He has none of those felicitous epithets, none of those pregnant lines, by which Pope's satires have enriched the ordinary speech of educated men. Young's wit will be found in almost every instance to consist in that antithetic combination of ideas which, of all the forms of wit, is most within reach of clever effort. In his gravest arguments, as well as in his lightest satire, one might imagine that he had set himself to work out the problem, how much antithesis might be got out of a given subject. And there he completely succeeds. His neatest portraits are all wrought on this plan. 'Narcissus', for example, who –

> Omits no duty; nor can Envy say
> He miss'd, these many years, the Church or Play:

He makes no noise in Parliament, 'tis true;
But pays his debts, and visit when 'tis due;
His character and gloves are ever clean,
And then he can out-bow the bowing Dean;
A smile eternal on his lip he wears,
Which equally the wise and worthless shares.
In gay fatigues, this most undaunted chief,
Patient of idleness beyond belief,
Most charitably lends the town his face
For ornament in every public place;
As sure as cards he to th' assembly comes,
And is the furniture of drawing-rooms:
When Ombre calls, his hand and heart are free,
And, joined to two, he fails not – to make three:
Narcissus is the glory of his race;
For who does nothing with a better grace?
To deck my list by nature were designed
Such shining expletives of human kind,
Who want, while through blank life they dream along,
Sense to be right and passion to be wrong.

It is but seldom that we find a touch of that easy slyness which
gives an additional zest to surprise; but here is an instance: –

See Tityrus, with merriment possest,
Is burst with laughter ere he hears the jest.
What need he stay? for when the joke is o'er,
His *teeth* will be no whiter than before.

Like Pope, whom he imitated, he sets out with a psychological
mistake as the basis of his satire, attributing all forms of folly to
one passion – the love of fame, or vanity, – a much grosser
mistake, indeed, than Pope's exaggeration of the extent to which
the 'ruling passion' determines conduct in the individual. Not that
Young is consistent in his mistake. He sometimes implies no more
than what is the truth – that the love of fame is the cause, not of all
follies, but of many.

Young's satires on women are superior to Pope's, which is only
saying that they are superior to Pope's greatest failure. We can
more frequently pick out a couplet as successful than an entire
sketch. Of the too emphatic 'Syrena', he says: –

> Her judgement just, her sentence is too strong;
> Because she's right, she's ever in the wrong.

Of the diplomatic 'Julia': –

> For her own breakfast she'll project a scheme,
> Nor take her tea without a stratagem.

Of 'Lyce', the old painted coquette: –

> In vain the cock has summoned sprites away;
> She walks at noon, and blasts the bloom of day.

Of the nymph who, 'gratis, clears religious mysteries': –

> 'Tis hard, too, she who makes no use but chat
> Of her religion, should be barr'd in that.

The description of the literary *belle*, 'Daphne', well prefaces that of
'Stella', admired by Johnson: –

> With legs toss'd high, on her sophee she sits,
> Vouchsafing audience to contending wits:
> Of each performance she's the final test;
> One act read o'er, she prophesies the rest;
> And then, pronouncing with decisive air,
> Fully convinces all the town – *she's fair*.
> Had lonely Daphne Hecatessa's face,
> How would her elegance of taste decrease!
> Some ladies' judgement in their features lies,
> And all their genius sparkles in their eyes.
> But hold, she cries, lampooner! have a care:
> Must I want common sense because I'm fair?
> O no; see Stella: her eyes shine as bright
> As if her tongue was never in the right;
> And yet what real learning, judgement, fire!
> She seems inspir'd, and can herself inspire.
> How then (if malice ruled not all the fair)
> *Could Daphne publish, and could she forbear?*

After all, when we have gone through Young's seven *Satires*, we
seem to have made but an indifferent meal. They are a sort of
fricassee, with little solid meat in them, and yet the flavour is not
always piquant. It is curious to find him, when he pauses a
moment from his satiric sketching, recurring to his old platitudes: –

> Can gold calm passion, or make reason shine?
> Can we dig peace or wisdom from the mine?
> Wisdom to gold prefer; –

platitudes which he seems inevitably to fall into, for the same reason that some men are constantly asserting their contempt for criticism – because he felt the opposite so keenly.

The outburst of genius in the earlier books of the *Night Thoughts* is the more remarkable, that in the interval between them and the *Satires*, he had produced nothing but his Pindaric odes, in which he fell far below the level of his previous works. Two sources of this sudden strength were the freedom of blank verse and the presence of a genuine emotion. Most persons, in speaking of the *Night Thoughts*, have in their minds only the two or three first Nights, the majority of readers rarely getting beyond these, unless, as Wilson says, they 'have but few books, are poor, and live in the country'.[39] And in these earlier Nights there is enough genuine sublimity and genuine sadness to bribe us into too favourable a judgement of them as a whole. Young had only a very few things to say or sing – such as that life is vain, that death is imminent, that man is immortal, that virtue is wisdom, that friendship is sweet, and that the source of virtue is the contemplation of death and immortality, – and even in his two first Nights he had said almost all he had to say in his finest manner. Through these first outpourings of 'complaint' we feel that the poet is really sad, that the bird is singing over a rifled nest; and we bear with his morbid picture of the world and of life, as the Job-like lament of a man whom 'the hand of God hath touched'.[40] Death has carried away his best-beloved, and that 'silent land' whither they are gone has more reality for the desolate one than this world which is empty of their love: –

> This is the desert, this the solitude;
> How populous, how vital is the grave!

Joy died with the loved one: –

> The disenchanted earth
> Lost all her lustre. Where her glitt'ring towers?
> Her golden mountains, where? All darken'd down
> To naked waste; a dreary vale of tears:

The great magician's dead!

Under the pang of parting, it seems to the bereaved man as if love were only a nerve to suffer with, and he sickens at the thought of every joy of which he must one day say – '*it was*'. In its unreasoning anguish, the soul rushes to the idea of perpetuity as the one element of bliss: –

> O ye blest scenes of permanent delight! –
> Could ye, so rich in rapture, fear an end, –
> That ghastly thought would drink up all your joy,
> And quite unparadise the realms of light.

In a man under the immediate pressure of a great sorrow, we tolerate morbid exaggerations; we are prepared to see him turn away a weary eye from sunlight and flowers and sweet human faces, as if this rich and glorious life had no significance but as a preliminary of death; we do not criticize his views, we compassionate his feelings. And so it is with Young in these earlier Nights. There is already some artificiality even in his grief, and feeling often slides into rhetoric, but through it all we are thrilled with the unmistakable cry of pain, which makes us tolerant of egoism and hyperbole: –

> In every varied posture, place, and hour,
> How widow'd ev'ry thought of ev'ry joy!
> Thought, busy thought! too busy for my peace!
> Through the dark postern of time long elapsed
> Led softly, by the stillness of the night, –
> Led like a murderer (and such it proves!)
> Strays (wretched rover!) o'er the pleasing past, –
> In quest of wretchedness, perversely strays;
> And finds all desert now; and meets the ghosts
> Of my departed joys.

But when he becomes didactic, rather than complaining, – when he ceases to sing his sorrows, and begins to insist on his opinions, – when that distaste for life which we pity as a transient feeling, is thrust upon us as a theory, we become perfectly cool and critical, and are not in the least inclined to be indulgent to false views and selfish sentiments.

Seeing that we are about to be severe on Young's failings and failures, we ought, if a reviewer's space were elastic, to dwell also on his merits, – on the startling vigour of his imagery, – on the occasional grandeur of his thought, – on the piquant force of that grave satire into which his meditations continually run. But, since our 'limits' are rigorous, we must content ourselves with the less agreeable half of the critic's duty; and we may the rather do so, because it would be difficult to say anything new of Young, in the way of admiration, while we think there are many salutary lessons remaining to be drawn from his faults.

One of the most striking characteristics of Young is his *radical insincerity as a poetic artist*. This, added to the thin and artificial texture of his wit, is the true explanation of the paradox – that a poet who is often inopportunely witty has the opposite vice of bombastic absurdity. The source of all grandiloquence is the want of taking for a criterion the true qualities of the object described, or the emotion expressed. The grandiloquent man is never bent on saying what he feels or what he sees, but on producing a certain effect on his audience; hence he may float away into utter inanity without meeting any criterion to arrest him. Here lies the distinction between grandiloquence and genuine fancy or bold imaginativeness. The fantastic or the boldly imaginative poet may be as sincere as the most realistic: he is true to his own sensibilities or inward vision, and in his wildest flights he never breaks loose from his criterion – the truth of his own mental state. Now, this disruption of language from genuine thought and feeling is what we are constantly detecting in Young; and his insincerity is the more likely to betray him into absurdity, because he habitually treats of abstractions, and not of concrete objects or specific emotions. He descants perpetually on virtue, religion, 'the good man', life, death, immortality, eternity – subjects which are apt to give a factitious grandeur to empty wordiness. When a poet floats in the empyrean, and only takes a bird's-eye view of the earth, some people accept the mere fact of his soaring for sublimity, and mistake his dim vision of earth for proximity to heaven. Thus: –

> His hand the good man fixes on the skies,
> And bids earth roll, nor feels her idle whirl, –

may, perhaps, pass for sublime with some readers. But pause a moment to realize the image, and the monstrous absurdity of a man's grasping the skies, and hanging habitually suspended there, while he contemptuously bids the earth roll, warns you that no genuine feeling could have suggested so unnatural a conception.

Again, –

> See the man immortal: him, I mean,
> Who lives as such; whose heart full bent on heaven,
> Leans all that way, his bias to the stars.

This is worse than the previous example; for you can at least form some imperfect conception of a man hanging from the skies, though the position strikes you as uncomfortable, and of no particular use; but you are utterly unable to imagine how his heart can lean towards the stars.[41] Examples of such vicious imagery, resulting from insincerity, may be found, perhaps, in almost every page of the *Night Thoughts*. But simple assertions or aspirations, undisguised by imagery, are often equally false. No writer whose rhetoric was checked by the slightest truthful intentions, could have said, –

> An eye of awe and wonder let me roll,
> And roll for ever.

Abstracting the more poetical associations with the eye, this is hardly less absurd than if he had wished to stand for ever with his mouth open.

Again: –

> Far beneath
> A soul immortal is a mortal joy.

Happily for human nature, we are sure no man really believes that. Which of us has the impiety not to feel that our souls are only too narrow for the joy of looking into the trusting eyes of our children, of reposing on the love of a husband or wife, – nay, of listening to the divine voice of music, or watching the calm brightness of autumn afternoons? But Young could utter this falsity without detecting it, because, when he spoke of 'mortal joys', he rarely had in his mind any object to which he could attach sacredness. He was thinking of bishoprics and benefices, of smiling monarchs, patronizing prime ministers, and a 'much indebted muse'. Of anything between these and eternal bliss, he was but rarely and moderately conscious. Often, indeed, he sinks very much below even the bishopric, and seems to have no notion of earthly pleasure, but such as breathes gaslight and the fumes of wine. His picture of life is precisely such as you would expect from a man who has risen from his bed at two o'clock in the afternoon with a headache, and a dim remembrance that he has added to his 'debts of honour': –

> What wretched repetition cloys us here!
> What periodic potions for the sick,
> Distemper'd bodies, and distemper'd minds!

And then he flies off to his usual antithesis: –

> In an eternity what scenes shall strike!
> Adventures thicken, novelties surprise!

'Earth' means lords and levees, duchesses and Dalilahs, South Sea dreams and illegal percentage; and the only things distinctly preferable to these are, eternity and the stars. Deprive Young of this antithesis, and more than half his eloquence would be shrivelled up. Place him on a breezy common, where the furze is in its golden bloom, where children are playing, and horses are standing in the sunshine with fondling necks, and he would have nothing to say. Here are neither depths of guilt, nor heights of glory; and we doubt whether in such a scene he would be able to pay his usual compliment to the Creator: –

> Where'er I turn, what claim on all applause!

It is true that he sometimes – not often – speaks of virtue as capable of sweetening life, as well as of taking the sting from death and winning heaven; and, lest we should be guilty of any unfairness to him, we will quote the two passages which convey this sentiment the most explicitly. In the one, he gives 'Lorenzo' this excellent recipe for obtaining cheerfulness: –

> Go, fix some weighty truth;
> Chain down some passion; do some generous good;

Teach Ignorance to see, or Grief to smile;
Correct thy friend; befriend thy greatest foe;
Or, with warm heart, and confidence divine,
Spring up, and lay strong hold on Him who made thee.

The other passage is vague, but beautiful, and its music has murmured in our minds for many years: –

The cuckoo seasons sing
The same dull note to such as nothing prize
But what those seasons from the teeming earth
To doting sense indulge. But nobler minds,
Which relish fruit unripen'd by the sun,
Make their days various; various as the dyes
On the dove's neck, which wanton in his rays.
On minds of dove-like innocence possess'd,
On lighten'd minds that bask in Virtue's beams,
Nothing hangs tedious, nothing old revolves
In that for which they long, for which they live.
Their glorious efforts, wing'd with heavenly hopes,
Each rising morning sees still higher rise;
Each bounteous dawn its novelty presents
To worth maturing, new strength, lustre, fame;
While Nature's circle, like a chariot wheel,
Rolling beneath their elevated aims,
Makes their fair prospect fairer every hour;
Advancing virtue in a line to bliss.

Even here, where he is in his most amiable mood, you see at what a telescopic distance he stands from mother Earth and simple human joys – 'Nature's circle rolls beneath'. Indeed, we remember no mind in poetic literature that seems to have absorbed less of the beauty and the healthy breath of the common landscape than Young's. His images, often grand and finely presented – witness that sublimely sudden leap of thought,

Embryos we must be till we burst the shell,
Yon ambient azure shell, and spring to life –

lie almost entirely within that circle of observation which would be familiar to a man who lived in town, hung about the theatres, read the newspaper, and went home often by moon and star light.

There is no natural object nearer than the moon that seems to have any strong attraction for him, and even to the moon he chiefly appeals for patronage, and 'pays his court' to her. It is reckoned among the many deficiencies of 'Lorenzo', that he 'never asked the moon one question' – an omission which Young thinks eminently unbecoming a rational being. He describes nothing so well as a comet, and is tempted to linger with fond detail over nothing more familiar than the day of judgement and an imaginary journey among the stars. Once on Saturn's ring, he feels at home, and his language becomes quite easy: –

> What behold I now?
> A wilderness of wonders burning round,
> Where larger suns inhabit higher spheres;
> Perhaps *the villas of descending gods!*

It is like a sudden relief from a strained posture when, in the *Night Thoughts*, we come on any allusion that carries us to the lanes, woods, or fields. Such allusions are amazingly rare, and we could almost count them on a single hand. That we may do him no injustice, we will quote the three best: –

> Like *blossom'd trees o'erturned by vernal storm*,
> Lovely in death the beauteous ruin lay.
>
> *
>
> In the same brook none ever bathed him twice:
> To the same life none ever twice awoke.
> We call the brook the same – the same we think
> Our life, though still more rapid in its flow;
> Nor mark the much irrevocably lapsed,
> And mingled with the sea.
>
> *
>
> The crown of manhood is a winter joy;
> An evergreen that stands the northern blast,
> And blossoms in the rigour of our fate.

The adherence to abstractions, or to the personification of abstractions, is closely allied in Young to the *want of genuine emotion*. He sees Virtue sitting on a mount serene, far above the mists and storms of earth: he sees Religion coming down from the skies, with this world in her left hand and the other world in her right: but we never find him dwelling on virtue or religion as it really exists – in the emotions of a man dressed in an ordinary coat, and seated by his fire-side of an evening, with his hand resting on the head of his little daughter; in courageous effort for unselfish ends, in the internal triumph of justice and pity over personal resentment, in all the sublime self-renunciation and sweet charities which are found in the details of ordinary life. Now, emotion links itself with particulars, and only in a faint and secondary manner with abstractions. An orator may discourse very eloquently on injustice in general, and leave his audience cold; but let him state a special case of oppression, and every heart will throb. The most untheoretic persons are aware of this relation between true emotion and particular facts, as opposed to general terms, and implicitly recognize it in the repulsion they feel towards any one who professes strong feeling about abstractions, – in the interjectional 'humbug!' which immediately rises to their lips. Wherever abstractions appear to excite strong emotion, this occurs in men of active intellect and imagination, in whom the abstract term rapidly and vividly calls up the particulars it represents, these particulars being the true source of the emotion; and such men, if they wished to express their feeling, would be infallibly prompted to the presentation of details. Strong emotion can no more be directed to generalities apart from particulars, than skill in figures can be directed to arithmetic apart from numbers. Generalities are the refuge at once of deficient intellectual activity and deficient feeling.[42]

If we except the passages in 'Philander', 'Narcissa', and 'Lucia', there is hardly a trace of human sympathy, of self-forgetfulness in the joy or sorrow of a fellow-being, throughout this long poem, which professes to treat the various phases of man's destiny. And even in the 'Narcissa' Night, Young repels us by the low moral tone of his exaggerated lament. This married step-daughter died at Lyons, and, being a Protestant, was denied burial, so that her friends had to bury her in secret – one of the many miserable results of superstition, but not a fact to throw an educated, still less a Christian man, into a fury of hatred and vengeance, in contemplating it after the lapse of five years. Young, however, takes great pains to simulate a bad feeling: –

> Of grief
> And indignation rival bursts I pour'd,
> Half execration mingled with my pray'r;
> Kindled at man, while I his God ador'd;
> Sore grudg'd the savage land her sacred dust;
> Stamp'd the cursed soil; *and with humanity*
> (*Denied Narcissa*) *wish'd them all a grave.*

The odiously bad taste of this last clause makes us hope that it is
simply a platitude, and not intended as a witticism, until he
removes the possibility of this favourable doubt by immediately
asking, 'Flows my resentment into guilt?'

When, by an afterthought, he attempts something like sympathy, he only betrays more clearly his want of it. Thus, in the first
Night, when he turns from his private griefs to depict earth as a
hideous abode of misery for all mankind, and asks, –

> What then am I, who sorrow for myself?

he falls at once into calculating the benefit of sorrowing for
others: –

> More generous sorrow, while it sinks, exalts;
> *And conscious virtue mitigates the pang.*
> Nor virtue, more than prudence, bids me give
> Swollen thought a second channel.

This remarkable negation of sympathy is in perfect consistency
with Young's theory of ethics: –

> Virtue is a crime,
> A crime to reason, if it costs us pain
> Unpaid . . .

If there is no immortality for man, –

> Sense! take the rein; blind Passion, drive us on;
> And Ignorance! befriend us on our way . . .
> Yes; give the pulse full empire; live the Brute,
> Since as the brute we die. The sum of man,
> Of godlike man, to revel and to rot.

*

> If this life's gain invites him to the deed,
> Why not his country sold, his father slain?

*

> Ambition, avarice, by the wise disdain'd,
> Is perfect wisdom, while mankind are fools,
> And think a turf or tombstone covers all.
>
> *
>
> Die for thy country, thou romantic fool!
> Seize, seize the plank thyself, and let her sink.
>
> *
>
> As in the dying parent dies the child,
> Virtue with Immortality expires.
> Who tells me he denies his soul immortal,
> *Whate'er his boast, has told me he's a knave.*
> *His duty 'tis to love himself alone,*
> *Nor care though mankind perish, if he smiles.*

We can imagine the man who 'denies his soul immortal', replying, 'It is quite possible that *you* would be a knave, and love yourself alone, if it were not for your belief in immortality; but you are not to force upon me what would result from your own utter want of moral emotion. I am just and honest, not because I expect to live in another world, but because, having felt the pain of injustice and dishonesty towards myself, I have a fellow-feeling with other men, who would suffer the same pain if I were unjust or dishonest towards them. Why should I give my neighbour short weight in this world, because there is not another world in which I should have nothing to weigh out to him? I am honest, because I don't like to inflict evil on others in this life, not because I'm afraid of evil to myself in another. The fact is, I do *not* love myself alone, whatever logical necessity there may be for that in your mind. I have a tender love for my wife, and children, and friends, and through that love I sympathize with like affections in other men. It is a pang to me to witness the suffering of a fellow-being, and I feel his suffering the more acutely because he is *mortal* – because his life is so short, and I would have it, if possible, filled with happiness and not misery. Through my union and fellowship with the men and women I *have* seen, I feel a like, though a fainter, sympathy with those I have *not* seen; and I am able so to live in imagination with the generations to come, that their good is not alien to me, and is a stimulus to me to labour for ends which may not benefit myself, but will benefit them. It is possible that you might prefer to "live the brute", to sell your country, or to slay your father, if you were not afraid of some disagreeable consequences from the criminal laws of another world; but even if I could conceive no motive but by my own worldly interest or the gratification of my animal desires, I have not observed that beastliness, treachery, and parricide, are the direct way to happiness and comfort on earth. And I should say, that if you feel no motive to common morality but your fear of a criminal bar in heaven, you are decidedly a man for the police on earth to keep their eye upon, since it is matter of world-old experience that fear of distant consequences is a very insufficient barrier against the rush of immediate desire. Fear of consequences is only one form of egoism, which will hardly stand against half-a-dozen other forms of egoism bearing down upon it. And in opposition to your theory that a belief in immortality is the only source of virtue, I maintain that, so far as moral action is dependent on that belief, so far the emotion which prompts it is not truly moral – is still in the stage of egoism, and has not yet attained the higher development of sympathy. In proportion as a man would care less for the rights and the welfare of his fellow, if he did not believe in a future life, in that proportion is he wanting in the genuine feelings of justice and benevolence; as the musician who would care less to play a sonata of Beethoven's finely in solitude than in public, where he was to be paid for it, is wanting in genuine enthusiasm for music.'[43]

Thus far might answer the man who 'denies himself immortal'; and, allowing for that deficient recognition of the finer and more indirect influences exercised by the idea of immortality which might be expected from one who took up a dogmatic position on such a subject, we think he would have given a sufficient reply to Young and other theological advocates who, like him, pique themselves on the loftiness of their doctrine when they maintain that 'virtue with immortality expires'.[44] We may admit, indeed, that if the better part of virtue consists, as Young appears to think, in contempt for mortal joys, in 'meditation of our own decease', and in 'applause' of God in the style of a congratulatory address to Her Majesty – all which has small relation to the well-being of mankind on this earth – the motive to it must be gathered from something that lies quite outside the sphere of human sympathy.

But, for certain other elements of virtue, which are of more obvious importance to untheological minds, – a delicate sense of our neighbour's rights, an active participation in the joys and sorrows of our fellow-men, a magnanimous acceptance of privation or suffering for ourselves when it is the condition of good to others, in a word, the extension and intensification of our sympathetic nature, – we think it of some importance to contend, that they have no more direct relation to the belief in a future state than the interchange of gases in the lungs has to the plurality of worlds.[45] Nay, to us it is conceivable that in some minds the deep pathos lying in the thought of human mortality – that we are here for a little while and then vanish away, that this earthly life is all that is given to our loved ones and to our many suffering fellow-men – lies nearer the fountains of moral emotion than the conception of extended existence. And surely it ought to be a welcome fact, if the thought of *mortality*, as well as of immortality, be favourable to virtue. Do writers of sermons and religious novels prefer that men should be vicious in order that there may be a more evident political and social necessity for printed sermons and clerical fictions? Because learned gentlemen are theological, are we to have no more simple honesty and good-will?[46] We can imagine that the proprietors of a patent water-supply have a dread of common springs; but, for our own part, we think there cannot be too great a security against a lack of fresh water or of pure morality. To us it is matter of unmixed rejoicing that this latter necessary of healthful life is independent of theological ink, and that its evolution is ensured[47] in the interaction of human souls as certainly as the evolution of science or of art, with which, indeed, it is but a twin ray, melting into them with undefinable limits.

To return to Young. We can often detect a man's deficiencies in what he admires more clearly than in what he condemns, – in the sentiments he presents as laudable rather than in those he decries. And in Young's notion of what is lofty he casts a shadow by which we can measure him without further trouble. For example, in arguing for human immortality, he says –

> First, what is *true ambition*? The pursuit
> Of glory *nothing less than man can share*.

> The Visible and Present are for brutes,
> A slender portion, and a narrow bound!
> These Reason, with an energy divine
> O'erleaps, and claims the Future and Unseen;
> The vast Unseen, the Future fathomless!
> When the great soul buoys up to this high point,
> Leaving gross Nature's sediments below,
> Then, and then only, Adam's offspring quits
> The sage and hero of the fields and woods,
> Asserts his rank, and rises into man.

So, then, if it were certified that, as some benevolent minds have tried to infer, our dumb fellow-creatures would share a future existence, in which it is to be hoped we should neither beat, starve, nor maim them, our ambition for a future life would cease to be 'lofty'! This is a notion of loftiness which may pair off with Dr Whewell's[48] celebrated observation, that Bentham's moral theory is low, because it includes justice and mercy to brutes.

But, for a reflection of Young's moral personality on a colossal scale, we must turn to those passages where his rhetoric is at its utmost stretch of inflation – where he addresses the Deity, discourses of the Divine operations, or describes the last judgement. As a compound of vulgar pomp, crawling adulation, and hard selfishness, presented under the guise of piety, there are few things in literature to surpass the Ninth Night, entitled 'Consolation', especially in the pages where he describes the last judgement – a subject to which, with naïve self-betrayal, he applies phraseology favoured by the exuberant penny-a-liner. Thus, when God descends, and the groans of hell are opposed by 'shouts of joy', much as cheers and groans contend at a public meeting where the resolutions are *not* passed unanimously, the poet completes his climax in this way: –

> Hence, in one peal of loud, eternal praise,
> The *charmed spectators* thunder their applause.

In the same taste, he sings –

> Eternity, the various sentence past,
> Assigns the sever'd throng distinct abodes,
> *Sulphureous or ambrosial*.

Exquisite delicacy of indication! He is too nice to be specific as to the interior of the 'sulphureous' abode; but when once half the human race are shut up there, hear how he enjoys turning the key on them!

> What ensues?
> The deed predominant, the deed of deeds!
> Which makes a hell of hell, a *heaven of heaven*!
> The goddess, with determin'd aspect, turns
> Her adamantine key's enormous size
> Through Destiny's inextricable wards,
> *Deep driving every bolt* on both their fates.
> Then, from the crystal battlements of heaven,
> Down, down she hurls it through the dark profound,
> Ten thousand, thousand fathom; there to rust
> And ne'er unlock her resolution more.
> The deep resounds; and Hell, through all her glooms,
> Returns, in groans, the melancholy roar.

This is one of the blessings for which Dr Young thanks God most: –

> For all I bless thee, most, for the severe;
> Her death – my own at hand – *the fiery gulf,*
> *That flaming bound of wrath omnipotent!*
> *It thunders; – but it thunders to preserve;*
> ... its wholesome dread
> Averts the dreaded pain; *its hideous groans*
> *Join Heaven's sweet Hallelujahs in Thy praise,*
> Great Source of good alone! How kind in all!
> In vengeance kind! Pain, Death, Gehenna, *save* ...

i.e., save *me*, Dr Young, who, in return for that favour, promise to give my divine patron the monopoly of that exuberance in laudatory epithet, of which specimens may be seen at any moment in a large number of dedications and odes to kings, queens, prime ministers, and other persons of distinction. *That*, in Young's conception, is what God delights in. His crowning aim in the 'drama' of the ages, is to vindicate his own renown. The God of the *Night Thoughts* is simply Young himself, 'writ large' – a didactic poet, who 'lectures' mankind in the antithetic hyperbole of mortal and immortal joys, earth and the stars, hell and heaven; and expects the tribute of inexhaustible 'applause'. Young has no conception of religion as anything else than egoism turned heavenward; and he does not merely imply this, he insists on it. Religion, he tells us, in argumentative passages too long to quote, is 'ambition, pleasure, and the love of gain', directed towards the joys of the future life instead of the present. And his ethics correspond to his religion. He vacillates, indeed, in his ethical theory, and shifts his position in order to suit his immediate purpose in argument; but he never changes his level so as to see beyond the horizon of mere selfishness. Sometimes he insists, as we have seen, that the belief in a future life is the only basis of morality; but elsewhere he tells us —

> In self applause is virtue's golden prize.

Virtue, with Young, must always squint — must never look straight towards the immediate object of its emotion and effort. Thus, if a man risks perishing in the snow himself, rather than forsake a weaker comrade, he must either do this because his hopes and fears are directed to another world, or because he desires to applaud himself afterwards! Young, if we may believe him, would despise the action as folly unless it had these motives. Let us hope he was not so bad as he pretended to be! The tides of the divine life in man move under the thickest ice of theory.

Another indication of Young's deficiency in moral, i.e., in sympathetic emotion, is his unintermitting habit of pedagogic moralizing. On its theoretic and preceptive side, morality touches Science; on its emotional side, Art. Now, the products of Art are great in proportion as they result from that immediate prompting of innate power which we call Genius, and not from laboured obedience to a theory or rule; and the presence of genius or innate prompting is directly opposed to the perpetual consciousness of a rule. The action of faculty is imperious, and excludes[49] the reflection *why* it should act. In the same way, in proportion as morality is emotional, i.e., has affinity with Art,[50] it will exhibit itself in direct sympathetic feeling and action, and not as the recognition of a rule. Love does not say, 'I ought to love' — it loves. Pity does not say, 'It is right to be pitiful' — it pities. Justice does not say, 'I am bound to be just' — it feels justly. It is only where moral emotion is comparatively weak that the contemplation of a rule or theory habitually mingles with its action; and in accordance with this, we think experience, both in literature and life, has shown that the minds which are pre-eminently didactic[51] – which insist on a 'lesson', and despise everything that will not convey a moral, are deficient in sympathetic emotion. A certain poet is recorded to have said, that he 'wished everything of his burnt that did not impress some moral; even in love-verses, it might be flung in by the way'. What poet was it who took this medicinal view of poetry? Dr Watts, or James Montgomery,[52] or some other singer of spotless life and ardent piety? Not at all. It was *Waller*.[53] A significant fact in relation to our position, that the predominant didactic tendency proceeds rather from the poet's perception that it is good for other men to be moral, than from any overflow of moral feeling in himself. A man who is perpetually thinking in apophthegms, who has an unintermittent flux of admonition, can have little energy left for simple emotion. And this is the case with Young. In his highest flights of contemplation, and his most wailing soliloquies, he interrupts himself to fling an admonitory parenthesis at 'Lorenzo', or to hint that 'folly's creed' is the reverse of his own. Before his thoughts can flow, he must fix his eye on an imaginary miscreant, who gives unlimited scope for lecturing, and recriminates just enough to keep the spring of admonition and argument going to the extent of nine books. It is curious to see how this pedagogic habit of mind runs through Young's contemplation of Nature. As the tendency to see our own sadness reflected in the external world has been called by Mr Ruskin the 'pathetic fallacy',[54] so we may call Young's disposition to see a rebuke or a warning in every natural object, the 'pedagogic fallacy'. To his mind, the heavens are 'for ever *scolding* as they shine'; and the great function of the stars is to be a 'lecture to mankind'. The conception of the Deity as a didactic author is not merely an implicit point of view with him; he works it out in elaborate imagery, and at length makes it the occasion of his most extraordinary achievement in the 'art of sinking', by exclaiming, *à propos*, we need hardly say, of the nocturnal heavens,

> Divine Instructor! Thy first volume this
> For man's perusal! all in CAPITALS!

It is this pedagogic tendency, this sermonizing attitude of Young's mind, which produces the wearisome monotony of his pauses. After the first two or three Nights, he is rarely singing, rarely pouring forth any continuous melody inspired by the spontaneous flow of thought or feeling. He is rather occupied with argumentative insistence, with hammering in the proofs of his propositions by disconnected verses, which he puts down at intervals. The perpetual recurrence of the pause at the end of the line throughout long passages, makes them as fatiguing to the ear as a monotonous chant, which consists of the endless repetition of one short musical phrase. For example –

> Past hours,
> If not by guilt, yet wound us by their flight,
> If folly bound our prospect by the grave,
> All feeling of futurity be numb'd,
> All godlike passion for eternals quench'd,
> All relish of realities expired;
> Renounced all correspondence with the skies;
> Our freedom chain'd; quite wingless our desire;
> In sense dark-prison'd all that ought to soar;
> Prone to the centre; crawling in the dust;
> Dismounted every great and glorious aim;
> Enthralled every faculty divine,
> Heart-buried in the rubbish of the world.

How different from the easy, graceful melody of Cowper's blank verse![55] Indeed, it is hardly possible to criticize Young, without being reminded at every step of the contrast presented to him by Cowper. And this contrast urges itself upon us the more from the fact that there is, to a certain extent, a parallelism between the *Night Thoughts* and *The Task*. In both poems, the author achieves his greatest in virtue of the new freedom conferred by blank verse; both poems are professedly didactic, and mingle much satire with their graver meditations; both poems are the productions of men whose estimate of this life was formed by the light of a belief in immortality, and who were intensely attached to Christianity. On some grounds, we might have anticipated a more morbid view of things from Cowper than from Young. Cowper's religion was dogmatically the more gloomy, for he was a Calvinist; while

Young was a 'low' Arminian, believing that Christ died for all, and that the only obstacle to any man's salvation lay in his will, which he could change if he chose. There was real and deep sadness involved in Cowper's personal lot; while Young, apart from his ambitious and greedy discontent, seems to have had no great sorrow.

Yet, see how a lovely, sympathetic nature manifests itself in spite of creed and circumstance! Where is the poem that surpasses *The Task* in the genuine love it breathes, at once towards inanimate and animate existence – in truthfulness of perception and sincerity of presentation – in the calm gladness that springs from a delight in objects for their own sake, without self-reference – in divine sympathy with the lowliest pleasures, with the most short-lived capacity for pain? Here is no railing at the earth's 'melancholy map', but the happiest lingering over her simplest scenes with all the fond minuteness of attention that belongs to love; no pompous rhetoric about the inferiority of the 'brutes', but a warm plea on their behalf against man's inconsiderateness and cruelty, and a sense of enlarged happiness from their companionship in enjoyment; no vague rant about human misery and human virtue, but that close and vivid presentation of particular sorrows and privations, of particular deeds and misdeeds, which is the direct road to the emotions. How Cowper's exquisite mind falls with the mild warmth of morning sunlight on the commonest objects, at once disclosing every detail and investing every detail with beauty! No object is too small to prompt his song – not the sooty film on the bars, or the spoutless tea-pot holding a bit of mignonette that serves to cheer the dingy town-lodging with a 'hint that Nature lives'; and yet his song is never trivial, for he is alive to small objects, not because his mind is narrow, but because his glance is clear and his heart is large. Instead of trying to edify us by supercilious allusions to the 'brutes' and the 'stalls', he interests us in that tragedy of the hen-roost when the thief has wrenched the door,

Where Chanticleer amidst his harem sleeps
In unsuspecting pomp;

in the patient cattle, that on the winter's morning

> Mourn in corners where the fence
> Screens them, and seem half petrified to sleep
> *In unrecumbent sadness*;

in the little squirrel, that, surprised by him in his woodland walk,

> At once, swift as a bird,
> Ascends the neighbouring beech; there whisks his brush,
> And perks his ears, and stamps, and cries aloud,
> With all the prettiness of feign'd alarm
> And anger insignificantly fierce.

And then he passes into reflection, not with curt apophthegm and snappish reproof, but with that melodious flow of utterance which belongs to thought when it is carried along in a stream of feeling: –

> The heart is hard in nature, and unfit
> For human fellowship, as being void
> Of sympathy, and therefore dead alike
> To love and friendship both, that is not pleased
> With sight of animals enjoying life,
> Nor feels their happiness augment his own.

His large and tender heart embraces the most every-day forms of human life – the carter driving his team through the wintry storm; the cottager's wife who, painfully nursing the embers on her hearth, while her infants 'sit cowering o'er the sparks',

> Retires, content to quake, so they be warm'd;

or the villager, with her little ones, going out to pick

> A cheap but wholesome salad from the brook;

and he compels our colder natures to follow his in its manifold sympathies, not by exhortations, not by telling us to meditate at midnight, to 'indulge' the thought of death, or to ask ourselves how we shall 'weather an eternal night', *but by presenting to us the object of his compassion truthfully and lovingly.* And when he handles greater themes, when he takes a wider survey, and considers the men or the deeds which have a direct influence on the welfare of communities and nations, there is the same unselfish warmth of feeling, the same scrupulous truthfulness. He is never vague in his remonstrance or his satire; but puts his finger on some particular vice or folly, which excites his indignation or 'dissolves his heart in pity', because of some specific injury it does to his fellow-man or to a sacred cause. And when he is asked why he interests himself about the sorrows and wrongs of others, hear what is the reason he gives. Not, like Young, that the movements of the planets show a mutual dependence, and that

> Thus man his sovereign duty learns in this
> Material picture of benevolence –

or that, –

> More generous sorrow while it sinks, exalts,
> And conscious virtue mitigates the pang.

What is Cowper's answer, when he imagines some 'sage erudite, profound', asking him 'What's the world to you?' –

> Much. *I was born of woman, and drew milk*
> *As sweet as charity from human breasts.*
> I think, articulate, I laugh and weep,
> And exercise all functions of a man.
> How then should I and any man that lives
> Be strangers to each other?

Young is astonished that men can make war on each other – that any one can 'seize his brother's throat', while

> The Planets cry, 'Forbear.'

Cowper weeps because –

> There is no flesh in man's obdurate heart:
> *It does not feel for man.*

Young applauds God as a monarch with an empire and a court quite superior to the English, or as an author who produces 'volumes for man's perusal'. Cowper sees his Father's love in all the gentle pleasures of the home fire-side, in the charms even of the wintry landscape, and thinks –

> Happy who walks with him! whom what he finds
> Of flavour or of scent in fruit or flower,
> Or what he views of beautiful or grand
> In nature, from the broad, majestic oak
> To the green blade that twinkles in the sun
> *Prompts with remembrance of a present God.*

To conclude – for we must arrest ourselves in a contrast that would lead us beyond our bounds: Young flies for his utmost consolation to the day of judgement, when

> Final Ruin fiercely drives
> Her ploughshare o'er Creation;

when earth, stars, and suns are swept aside,

> And now, all dross removed, Heaven's own pure day
> Full on the confines of our ether, flames:
> While (dreadful contrast!) far (how far!) beneath,
> Hell, bursting, belches forth her blazing seas,
> And storms sulphureous; her voracious jaws
> Expanding wide, and roaring for her prey, –

Dr Young, and similar 'ornaments of religion and virtue', passing, of course, with grateful 'applause' into the upper region. Cowper finds his highest inspiration in the Millennium – in the restoration of this our beloved home of earth to perfect holiness and bliss, when the Supreme

> Shall visit earth in mercy; shall descend
> Propitious in his chariot paved with love;
> And what his storms have blasted and defaced
> For man's revolt, shall with a smile repair.

And into what delicious melody his song flows at the thought of that blessedness to be enjoyed by future generations on earth! –

> The dwellers in the vales and on the rocks
> Shout to each other, and the mountain tops
> From distant mountains catch the flying joy;
> Till, nation after nation taught the strain,
> Earth rolls the rapturous Hosanna round!

The sum of our comparison is this: – In Young we have the type of that deficient human sympathy, that impiety towards the present and the visible, which flies for its motives, its sanctities, and its religion, to the remote, the vague, and the unknown: in Cowper we have the type of that genuine love which cherishes things in proportion to their nearness, and feels its reverence grow in proportion to the intimacy of its knowledge.

The Ilfracombe Journal

(8 May–26 June 1856)

Eliot and Lewes set off for a holiday in Ilfracombe on 8 May 1856. One reason for the trip was Lewes's persistent ill-health, 'that terrible singing in the ears which has never left him since the commencement of his illness two years ago' (*Letters, Vol. II*, p. 253). But Lewes was perhaps more concerned to observe specimens of marine life at first hand, thus disproving T. H. Huxley's criticism that he was merely a 'book-scientist' (*Life*, pp. 195–7). According to Haight, he wanted, through 'the observation and dissection of marine animals, to try to discover some of the "complex facts of life"'.

For Lewes, the fruit of the visit was his *Seaside Studies* (1858). For Eliot, it afforded an opportunity to work on articles for the *Westminster* (including 'The Natural History of German Life') and the *Leader*. More importantly, she had time to consider John Ruskin's ideas about 'realism', which she had recently encountered in his *Modern Painters, Vol. III*, and which permeate her account of the visit. As she wrote, 'I never before longed so much to know the names of things as during this visit to Ilfracombe. The desire is part of the tendency that is now constantly growing in me to escape from all vagueness and inaccuracy into the daylight of distinct, vivid ideas.'

RECOLLECTIONS OF ILFRACOMBE, 1856

It was a cold unfriendly day – the eighth of May on which we set out for Ilfracombe, with our hamper of tall glass jars, which we meant for our sea-side Vivarium. We had to get down at Windsor, and were not sorry that the interval was long enough to let us walk round the Castle, which I had never seen before, except from a distance. The famous 'slopes', the avenues in the Park and the distant landscape looked very lovely in the fresh and delicate greens of Spring, and the Castle is surely the most delightful royal residence in the world. We took our places from Windsor all the way to Exeter, having bravely made up our minds to do the greatest part of our journey in one day. At Bristol, where we had to wait three hours, the misery of my terrible headache was mitigated by the interest we felt in seeing the grand old church of St Mary Redcliffe, for ever associated with the memory of Chatterton –

> It stands the maestrie of a human hand
> The pride of Bristowe and the western land.[1]

For the rest, Bristol looked dismal enough to us: a compound of dingy streets, bad smells, and dreary waiting at a dirty Railway Station.

At last the time came for the train to set off and after a short journey we reached Exeter Station where we were delighted to find that we could get beds, and so save the drive into the town. The next morning before the hour of starting for Barnstaple, we had time for a stroll in the sunshine as far as the town. The country round looked lovely. A fine hilly road bordered by tall trees led us towards the higher part of the town, which commenced, like a cathedral town, with a row of gothic almshouses on one side and park-like grounds, probably belonging to the episcopal residence, on the other. Our object was to get to the Cathedral; and after inquiring our way for a little while along clean, cheerful-looking streets, we found a narrow, flagged side-street which led us into the pleasant square, shaded by tall trees and surrounded by quaintish houses, where stands the fine old temple with its two great square towers. The façade is extremely elaborate and the arch of the doorway especially beautiful; but the rest of the exterior is heavy, and even the façade is spoiled by the gable being so low as to hide part of the rosace window and give the whole roof the appearance of having been cut down from below. However, the two towers, though rather heavy in shape, are very exquisite in the grace and *moderation* of their ornamental detail. As we passed the door it was ajar and we peeped in across the locked gate which shut out free entrance. The interior seemed very fine, but our glimpse was interrupted by the approach of the hard, dry-looking woman that alternates as key-keeper with the oily sexton in English cathedrals. 'Can we see the Cathedral?' I said. 'Yes, I can *show* you the Cathedral.' We declined to be 'shown' and walked on, taking a few more glances at the pleasant streets. One interesting object we passed on our way was a very old bit of building, apparently Saxon, which appeared to be used as a Police Station. Back again to the Railway in the sunshine, with the birds singing about the hedges. The journey to Barnstaple lay through a charming country; – gently sloping hills, roads winding by the side of hanging woods, little streams, and here and there patches of grey houses.

At Barnstaple we said good bye to the Railway and took to the good old-fashioned stage coach. A great fuss, of course, in getting all the luggage on the top, and all the people settled inside and out. I foolishly chose to go inside, being headachy, and had for my companions, a pale, thin, affected lady, and a reddish, stout, affected lady. G. had a pleasanter journey outside, and won golden opinions from the thin lady's husband and daughter, whose name turned out to be Webster. I was not sorry when our coach rattled and swung up the hilly street of Ilfracombe and stopped at the door of the 'Clarence Hotel'.

Our next task was to find lodgings, and we went forthwith to look for Mrs Williams of Northfield, whom Gosse recommends in his *Devonshire Coast*.[2] The reasons for his recommendation were not very patent to us when we saw the shabby ill-furnished parlour and bedroom, so we determined to go a little farther and fare better, if possible. At this spot, called Northfield, the beauty of Ilfracombe burst upon us, though we had as yet no glimpse of the sea and no idea – at least *I* had none – in which direction it lay.

On our left were gracefully sloping green hills, on our right the clustering houses, and beyond, hills with bold, rocky sides. Walking on a few yards to the right, we came to a pretty house with a veranda, surrounded by a nice garden, with a carriage road up to the door. A notice at the gate told us it was Runnymede Villa and moreover that it was 'to let', but we thought it was far too smart and expensive a dwelling for us. However there could be no harm in asking, so we knocked at the door, and were shown by a pleasant-looking young woman into a drawing-room, where we remained to admire and long while she went to ask her mother the rent. The mother came, and we found to our great satisfaction that we could have this large double drawing-room for a guinea a week during May and a guinea and a half in June. Before we had decided, another knock came at the door – it was our travelling companion Mr Webster, who had also been attracted by the pretty outside of the house. The end was, that we took the drawing-room with the bedroom and dressing room above, and the Websters – that is, the wife and daughter, for the husband was to be always away on business except on short fly away visits – took the dining-room on the other side. Having deposited our luggage,[3] and ordered our *thé dinatoire*, we set out in search of the sea, and were directed to the 'Tunnels' – three long passages cut in the rock. At the end of the first we turned down. We passed through them all and came upon the most striking bit of coast I had ever beheld – steep, precipitous rocks behind and on each side of us, and before us sharply-cut fragments of dark rock jutting out of the sea for some distance beyond the land, for the tide was now approaching its height. We were in raptures with this first look, but could only stay long enough to pick up a few bits of coralline, which, novices as we were, we supposed to be polyps.

It was cheering the next morning to get up with a head rather less aching, and to walk up and down the little garden after breakfast in the bright sunshine. I had a great deal of work before me – the writing of an article on Riehl's books,[4] which I had not half read, as well as the article on *belles lettres* – but my head was still dizzy and it seemed impossible to sit down to writing at once in these new scenes, so we determined to spend the day in explorations.

There can hardly be an uglier town – an uglier cluster of human
nests lying in the midst of beautiful hills, than Ilfracombe. The
colour of the houses is the palest dingiest grey, and the lines are all
rectangular and mean. Overtopping the whole town in ugliness as
well as height are two 'Terraces', which make two factory-like
lines of building on the slope of the green hill. From our windows
we had a view of the higher part of the town, and generally it
looked uninteresting enough; but what is it that light cannot
transfigure into beauty? One evening, after a shower, as the sun
was setting over the sea behind us, some peculiar arrangement of
clouds threw a delicious evening light on the irregular cluster of
houses and merged the ugliness of their forms in an exquisite flood
of colour – as a stupid person is made glorious by a noble deed. A
perfect rainbow arched over the picture.

Walking on from our gate towards Wildersmouth – a little
opening in the hills which allows one to wet one's feet in the sea
without descending a precipice or groping through a tunnel – we
got a view of the lower part of the town, and turning up a pleasant
foot-path to our right we were led on past a dissenting chapel,
and then past a new church which is being built, into the streets
that lead immediately to the quay, where we see the physical-
geographical reason why Ilfracombe was built here and nowhere
else. Returning from the quay, we entered the promenade round
the Capstone, which has been made at great expense since Ilfracombe became a place for visitors. From this end of the Capstone
we have an admirable bit for a picture. In the background rises
old Hillsborough jutting out far into the sea – rugged and rocky as
it fronts the waves, green and accessible landward; in front of this
stands Lantern Hill, a picturesque mass of green and grey surmounted by an old bit of building that looks as if it were the
habitation of some mollusc that had secreted its shell from the
material of the rock; and quite in the foreground, contrasting
finely in colour with the rest are some lower perpendicular rocks,
of dark brown tints patched here and there with vivid green. In
hilly districts, where houses and clusters of houses look so tiny
against the huge limbs of Mother Earth one cannot help thinking
of man as a parasitic animal – an epizoon making his abode on the
skin of the planetary organism. In a flat country a house or a town

looks imposing – there is nothing to rival it in height, and we may imagine the earth a mere pedestal for us. But when one sees a house stuck on the side of a great hill, and still more a number of houses looking like a few barnacles clustered on the side of a great rock, we begin to think of the strong family likeness between ourselves and all other building, burrowing house-appropriating and shell-secreting animals. The difference between a man with his house and a mollusc with its shell lies in the number of steps or phenomena interposed between the fact of individual existence and the completion of the building. Whatever other advantages we may have over molluscs and insects in our habitations, it is clear that their architecture has the advantage of ours in beauty – at least considered as the architecture of the species. Look at man in the light of a shellfish and it must be admitted that his shell is generally ugly, and it is only after a great many more 'steps or phenomena' that he secretes here and there a wonderful shell in the shape of a temple or a palace.

But it is time to walk on round the Capstone and return home by Wildersmouth. On clear days, I could see the Welsh Coast with the smoke of its towns very distinctly, and a good way southward the outline of Lundy Island. Mounting the Capstone, we had the best view of the whole town – the Quay, the High Street, and the old Church standing high up on the hill and looking very handsome with its three-gabled end. Our narrow path from Wildersmouth to Runnymede Villa led us by the side of a miniature river, the Wilder, which of course empties itself at Wildersmouth into the sea. It was always a fresh pleasure to me to look at this clear little stream, fringed with Veronica and Stellaria.

About five o'clock, the tide being then low, we went out on our first zoophyte hunt. The littoral zone at Ilfracombe is nothing but huge boulders and jutting rocks of granwacke or clay slate, which when not made slippery by sea-weed are not very difficult to scramble over. It is characteristic enough of the wide difference there is between having eyes and seeing, that in this region of sea-anemones, where the Mesembryanthemum especially is as 'plenty as blackberries', we climbed about for two hours without seeing one anemone, and went in again with scarcely anything but a few stones and weeds to put into our deep well-like jars, which we had taken the trouble to carry in a hamper from London, and which we had afterwards the satisfaction of discovering to be quite unfit for our purpose. On our next hunt, however, after we had been out some time, G. exclaimed, 'I see an anemone!' and we were immensely excited by the discovery of this little red Mesembry-anthemum, which we afterwards disdained to gather as much as if it had been a nettle. It was a crescendo of delight when we found a 'Strawberry', and a *fortissimo* when I for the first time saw the pale fawn-coloured tentacles of an *Anthea cereus* viciously waving like little serpents, in a low tide pool. But not a polyp for a long, long while could even G. detect after all his reading; so necessary is it for the eye to be educated by objects as well as ideas. When we put our anemones into our glass wells, they floated topsy-turvy in the water and looked utterly uncomfortable; and I was constantly called upon to turn up my sleeve and plunge in my arm up to the elbow to set things right. But after a few days, G. adventurously made a call on the Curate Mr Tugwell,[5] of whom we had heard as a collector of anemones and he returned to me not only with the announcement that Mr Tugwell was a very 'nice little fellow', and with three treasures – an *Eolis pellucida*, a *Doris billomellata*, and an Aplysia, the first of each genus I had ever seen – but also with new light as to glass jars. So we determined to dismiss our deep wells, and buy some moderately-sized jars with shoulders to them. We had before this found out that yellow pie-dishes were the best artificial habitat for Actiniæ.

It was a considerable stretch to my knowledge of animal forms to pay a visit to Hele's shop, which lies in a quiet pleasant little nook at the back of the dissenting chapel opposite Wildersmouth. Hele gets his bread now by collecting marine animals and sending them to Lloyd[6] in London, and he has a sweet-faced intelligent daughter who goes out with him collecting and manages the stock on hand. The first time we went there, they had a fine show of the *Actinia crassicornis* and a Gemacea, some Holothuriæ (the first I had ever seen) and the green *Anthea cereus*, which was new to me. But I had a still greater addition to my knowledge when G. went to Mort Stone with Mr Tugwell and Mr Broderie and brought home several varieties of polyps, which I had gathered a very imperfect conception of from books – Tubularian, Plumularian and Sertularian – exquisite little Eolides, and some compound

Ascidians. Indeed, every day I gleaned some little bit of naturalistic experience, either through G.'s calling on me to look through the microscope or from hunting on the rocks; and thus in spite of my preoccupation with my article, which I worked at considerably à contre-cœur, despairing of its ever being worth anything.

When at last, by the seventeenth of June both my articles were dispatched, I felt delightfully at liberty and determined to pay some attention to sea-weeds which I had never seen in such beauty as at Ilfracombe. For hitherto I had been chiefly on chalky and sandy shores where there were no rock-pools to show off the lovely colours and forms of the Algæ. There are tide-pools to be seen almost at every other step on the littoral zone at Ilfracombe, and I shall never forget their appearance when we first arrived there. The *Corallina officinalis* was then in its greatest perfection, and with its purple pink fronds threw into relief the dark olive fronds of the Laminariæ on one side and the vivid green of the Ulva and Entero-morpha on the other. After we had been there a few weeks the Corallina was faded and I noticed the *Mesogloia vermicularis* and the *M. virescens*, which look very lovely in the water from the white cilia which make the most delicate fringe to their yellow-brown whip like fronds, and some of the commoner Polysiphoniæ. But I had not yet learned to look for the rarer Rhodospermiæ under the olive and green weeds at the surface. These tide-pools made one quite in love with sea-weeds, in spite of the disagreeable importunity with which they are made to ask us from shop-windows – 'Call us not weeds', so I took up Landsborough's book[7] and tried to get a little more light on their structure and history.

Our zoological expeditions alternated with delicious inland walks. I think the country looked its best when we arrived. It was just that moment in Spring when the trees are in full leaf, but still keep their delicate varieties of colouring and that *transparency* which belongs only to this season. And the furze was in all its golden glory! I never saw it in such abundance as here; over some hills the air is laden with its scent, and the gorgeous masses of blossom perpetually invited me to gather them as the largest possible specimens. It was almost like the fading away of the evening red when the furze blossoms died off from the hills, and the only contrast left was that of the marly soil with the green crops and woods. The primroses were the contemporaries of the furze and sprinkled the sides of the hills with their pale stars almost as plentifully as daisies or buttercups elsewhere. Perhaps the most enchanting of all our walks was that to Lee, because we had the double beauties of rocky coast and wooded inland hill. Lee is a tiny hamlet which has lodged itself, like a little colony of *Aurora actiniæ*, in the nick between two ranges of hills, where the sea runs in and makes a miniature bay. From the hills we have to pass over in reaching it, there is an exquisite view on looking back towards Ilfracombe: first the green slopes forming the inland aspect of the Tors, which always reminded me of some noble animal that has reared itself on its fore-legs to look at something, powerfully arresting its attention – as if the land had lifted itself up in amazed contemplation of the glorious sea; then Ilfracombe, at the meeting of many hills, with the graceful green Capstone Hill, surmounted by its Flag staff, and beyond it Hillsborough with its crag of rich, violet-veiled brown, standing like a rugged grand old warrior being played with by that capricious beauty the sea; while in the farther distance the sombre *Hangman* lifts its round, blackened shoulder, softened too with a violet veil, but of a different tone from that of Hillsborough. Another picture of a smaller kind was a single crag sloping in a very obtuse angle towards the sea and sheltering a little sandy bay where the gulls are fond of resting. We saw it once in the bright *Sunday* evening light, when there was a nice platform of sand for the gulls, and the colour of the cliff was a *blue* violet.

Turning again towards Lee and pursuing our walk, we come at last in sight of the dip or valley in which the hamlet lies. The wooded hills that slope down towards it on the farther side were not yet of a monotonous summer green when we first saw them, and their sister hills were glowing with furze blossoms. Down and down we go until we get into the narrow road or lane that winds through the valley. Here we see an ornamental cottage or two as well as genuine cottages, and close by the side of the road a tiny gothic chapel where our nice Mr Tugwell preaches every Sunday. But the great charm of this road, as of all Devonshire lanes, is the springs that you detect gushing in shady recesses covered with liverwort, with here and there waving tufts of fern and other broad leaved plants that love obscurity and moisture. Springs are sacred places still for those who love and reverence Nature. The first time we went to Lee we thought of varying our walk by returning through Slade, but we somehow lost our way and found ourselves after a long journey at a parting of the road where we were in utter uncertainty which way to turn for Ilfracombe. There was no fingerpost, no men near enough to shout to, so we could only adopt Corporal Nym's philosophy[8] – say 'Things must be as they may', and prove the existence of free will by making a choice without a motive. At last we came in sight of a lone farm-house, and I waited at the gate while G. went to inquire. After considerable knocking, a woman put her head reluctantly out of an upper window and after some parleying conveyed the half-comforting, half-distracting information that we were on the right way for Ilfracombe, but were still *tu mile* away from it. It requires some desperate courage to make these interrogatory visits to lone farmhouses, for you are likely to get a prompt but not categorical answer to your questions from a great dog who protects the premises in the absence of the males.

Our next long walk was to Chambercombe – a name apparently belonging to some woods and a solitary farmhouse, for we could see nothing else except fields. G. found out this walk one day and then took me there one lovely, sunshiny day. The chief beauties of the walk began when we arrived at a gate leading into a farmyard which forms a sort of ganglion to two lanes branching from it. Close to this gate there is a spring which is a perfect miniature of some Swiss 'Falls'. It spreads itself like a crystal fan on successive ledges of the hedge-bank until it reaches a much broader ledge where it forms a little lake on a bed of brown pebbles; then down it goes again till it reaches the level of the road and runs along as a tiny river. What a picture this farm-yard remains in my memory! The cows staring at us with formidable timidity, such as I have sometimes seen in a human being who frightens others while he is frightened himself; and the cow-man who pointed out our way to us through the next gate. Just beyond this gate there was a little widening in the lane – several gateways occurring together and here the wild verdure and flowers of the hedgerow and the roadside seemed to take the opportunity of becoming more luxuriant than usual. A few rough trunks lying against the tufts of fern and a

quiet donkey made the bit perfect as a foreground, and close
behind it rose a steep hill half orchard and half grass. The first
time we took this walk the primroses were still abundant, but they
were beginning to be eclipsed by the other flowers of the hedgerow.
As we advanced along this lane chatting happily and gathering
flowers we could see before us the overlapping hills covered by the
Chambercombe woods. At length we came to a spot where a
brook runs across the lane and a little wooden bridge is provided
for foot-passengers. A rough hurdle is fixed up where the brook
gushes from the field into the lane over brown stones that the
water polishes into agate; against the little bridge there is a tree,
and all round its roots by the side of the brook there are tufts of
varied leafage. Over the bridge and through a little gate and you
approach another farm-yard – if it is large enough for so dignified
a name. There is a small shabby house, with broken windows
mended with rags, called the Haunted House, and from the yard
there suddenly rises a rough hill clothed with trees and brushwood.
A great awkward puppy which came flopping after us was always
an incident at this yard as we passed it. On and on, looking at the
fields and woods, until we came to a shady spot which tempted us
to sit down. G. smoked a cigar and we looked at the sunlight living
like a spirit among the branches of the hanging woods – looked too
at a caterpillar which happened to be spending its transitional life,
happily knowing nothing of transitions, on the bush beside us.
Then we walked on towards the wood and threaded our way
under its low branches, listening to the birds and the dash and
ripple of water, until we came to the water itself – a streamlet
running between the hills, and winding its way among the trees
while the sunlight made its way between the leaves and flashed on
the braided ripples. Here and everywhere about Ilfracombe the
base of the trees and the banks of the lanes are made peculiarly
lovely by a delicate trefoil. As we came home again the sea,
stretching beyond the massive hills towards the horizon, looked all
the finer to us because we had been turning our backs upon it,
and contemplating another sort of beauty.

Of other walks by and by, when I have said something of our
evenings, and other Ilfracombe experience. We seemed to make
less of our evenings here than we have ever done elsewhere. We

used often to be tired with our hunting or walking and we were reading books which did not make us take them up very eagerly – Gosse's *Rambles on the Devonshire Coast*,[9] for example; Trench's Calderon;[10] and other volumes taken up in a desultory way. One bit of reading we had there, however, which interested me deeply. It was Masson's *Life of Chatterton*, which happily linked itself with the impressions I had received from the sight of the old church at Bristol. An hour of the evening light used often to slip away in attention to our animals. This helped to make our reading time scanty; and another *distraction* was an occasional visit to Mrs and Miss Webster – a visit always made agreeable by music. I enjoyed playing to them, because G. seemed to like it as well as they.

On the twenty-ninth of May, of course, Ilfracombe set itself to work to rejoice by royal command, at the ratification of the Peace,[11] and we expected to be considerably amused by the spectacle of the Ilfracombe festivities. Pretty, bright little Mrs Ashwell, our hostess's daughter, helped her brother to make a grand maypole of coloured streamers floating among boughs of laburnum, which was hoisted on the roof of the house, and at 4 o'clock, she told us, she was to go and help make tea which was to be given in the High Street to the working people. So at 4 o'clock, we walked to the High Street, which seemed a chaos of people and tables. Here and there tea was really going on: pretty children were seated with their mug in one hand and their piece of cake in the other, and near them we saw Mrs Ashwell looking red hot in a primrose-coloured bonnet. Passing along the High Street, we met a cavalcade mounting the hill, which, I suppose, was intended to symbolize the Allied Armies – four or five men in miscellaneous uniforms mounted on Rosinantes.[12] After a turn or two on the Capstone we came back again to the High Street to see the festivities in a more advanced stage. The melancholy foot-races of the boys suggested the idea that they were conducted on the principle of the donkey races – the slowest boy winning. At all events at Ilfracombe 'the race is not to the swift'.[13] In the evening there were some feeble fire-works on the Capstone, and, what was better, bonfires on Hillsborough and the highest of the Tors. It was fine to see these bonfires flashing upwards and then gradually dying out, and made one think of the times when such fires were lighted as signals to arm – the symbol of a common cause and a common feeling.

Another bit of primitive provincial life which used to amuse us were the announcements of the Town crier. On one occasion, for example, he came to inform us, with supererogatory aspirates, that 'Hironsides, the American Wonder' would start from the London Inn, and walk so many miles in so many minutes, carrying tremendous weights during the last mile. A graver announcement was the fact of two burglaries having been committed, and we never heard that the offenders had been discovered during our stay.

Mr Tugwell's acquaintance was a real acquisition to us, not only because he was a companion and helper in zoological pursuits, but because to know him was to know of another sweet nature in the world. It is always good to know, if only in passing, a charming human being – it refreshes one like flowers, and woods and clear brooks. One Sunday evening we walked up to his pretty house to carry back some proofs of his, and he induced us to go in and have coffee with him. He played on his Harmonium and we chatted pleasantly. The last evening of our stay at Ilfracombe he came to see us in Mrs Webster's drawing-room, and we had music until nearly 11 o'clock. A pleasant recollection!

We only twice took the walk beyond Watermouth towards Berry Narbor. The road lies through what are called the 'Meadows', which look like a magnificent park. A stream fringed with wild flowers and willows runs along the valley, two or three yards from the side of the road. This stream is clear as crystal, and about every twenty yards it falls over a little artificial precipice of stones. The long grass was waving in all the glory of June before the mower has come to make it suffer a 'love-change' from beauties into sweet odours; and the slopes on each side of us were crowned or clothed with fine trees. Little Gyp, Mrs Webster's dog, whom we had made our pet, was our companion in this walk, exciting, as usual, a sensation among the sheep and lambs with his small person, and giving us strong hints to move on when we rested a little too long for his taste. The last time we went through these meadows was on our last day at Ilfracombe. Such sunlight and such deep peace on the hills and by the stream! Coming back we rested on a gate under the trees, and a blind man came up to rest also. He told us in his slow way what a fine 'healthy spot' this was – yes a very healthy spot – a healthy spot. And then we went on our way and saw his face no more.

More frequently we walked only as far as Watermouth – and this was a grand walk – over the edges of tall cliffs, revealing to us one inlet after another, each differing in its shades of colour. The limit of our walk was usually somewhere near a handsome castel-lated house belonging to Mr Basset, and standing near the little arm of the sea which I suppose is properly 'Watermouth', so that he has two very different kinds of beauty from his windows – the sea and the bold rocks, and the charming valley of Meadows, with their rippling stream.

One more favourite walk I must record. It was along the Braunton Road for a little way; then we turned up a lane which led us by the cemetery and here just where a clear brook (where is there *not* a clear brook in Devonshire?) the lane brought us to a gateway leading into a wood. And now we could either take a steep road leading up the hill among the trees until we came out where this same road formed a belt below the furze covered summit of the hill; or we could go right on along the lane that skirted the wood until we came to another gateway leading into another wood, which clothed another hill. Skirting this second wood, we had a ravine below us on our right hand, and could hear the music of the brook at the bottom. The sides of this ravine were feathered with the light, graceful boughs of the ash occasionally thrown into relief by the darker oak. On and on, till we came to a turn on our left, and mounted a very steep road where the wood ceases and we had on one side a wall starred with the delicate pink flowers of a lovely rock plant and on the other some picturesque broken ground. From the breezy field at the top we had a fine view, and G. took advantage of the freedom from the criticism of neighbouring ears to have a lusty shout.

One day we carried out our project of approaching the ravine from the Braunton road, and attempting to walk along it close by the stream. Just about the spot where this ravine begins there is a cottage which seems to be a tributary to a rather important looking farm-house standing near. As we approached this cottage, we were descried by a black pig, probably of an amiable and sociable disposition. But as unfortunately our initiation in porcine physiognomy was not deep enough to allow any decisive inferences, we felt it an equivocal pleasure to perceive that piggie had made up his mind to join us in our walk without the formality of an introduction. So G. put himself in my rear and made intimations to piggie that his society was not desired, and though very slow to take a hint, he at last turned back and we entered the path by the stream among the brushwood, not without some anxiety on my part lest our self-elected companion should return. Presently a grunt assured us that he was on our traces; G. resorted in vain to hishes, and, at last, instigated as he says by me, threw a stone and hit piggie on the chop. This was final. He trotted away, squealing, as fast as his legs would carry him; but my imagination had become so fully possessed with fierce pigs and the malignity of their bite, that I had no more peace of mind until we were fairly outside the gate that took us out of piggie's haunts. G.'s peace of mind was disturbed for another reason: he was remorseful that he had bruised the cheek of a probably affectionate beast, and the sense of this crime hung about him for several days. I satisfied my conscience by thinking of the addition to the pig's *savoir-vivre* that might be expected from the blow; he would in future wait to be introduced.

I have talked of the Ilfracombe lanes without describing them, for to describe them one ought to know the names of all the lovely wild flowers that cluster on their banks. Almost every yard of these banks is a 'Hunt'[14] picture – a delicious crowding of mosses and delicate trefoil, and wild strawberries, and ferns great and small. But the crowning beauty of the lanes is the springs, that gush out in little recesses by the side of the road – recesses glossy with liverwort and feathery with fern. Sometimes you have the spring when it has grown into a brook, either rushing down a miniature cataract by the lane side, or flowing gently, as a 'braided streamlet' across your path. I never before longed so much to know the names of things as during this visit to Ilfracombe. The desire is part of the tendency that is now constantly growing in me to escape from all vagueness and inaccuracy into the daylight of distinct, vivid ideas. The mere fact of naming an object tends to give definiteness to our conception of it – we have then a sign that at once calls up in our minds the distinctive qualities which mark out for us that particular object from all others.

We ascended the Tors only twice; for a tax of 3d. per head was demanded on this luxury, and we could not afford a sixpenny walk very frequently. On both occasions Mr Webster was with us – on the second, Mr Tugwell and Alice Webster, so that I associate the walk rather with conversation than with scenery. Yet the view from the Tors is perhaps the very finest to be had at Ilfracombe. Bay behind bay fringed with foam, and promontory behind promontory each with its peculiar shades of purple light – the sweep of the Welsh Coast faintly visible in the distance, and the endless expanse of sea flecked with ships stretching on our left.

One evening we went down to the shore through the Tunnels to see the sunset. Standing in the 'Ladies' Cove' we had before us the sharp fragments of rock jutting out of the waves and standing black against the orange and crimson sky. How lovely to look into that brilliant distance and see the ship on the horizon seeming to sail away from the cold and dim world behind it right into the golden glory! I have always that sort of feeling when I look at sunset; it always seems to me that there, in the west, lies a land of light and warmth and love.

On the twenty-sixth of June it was that we said good bye to Ilfracombe and started by the steamer at 9 o'clock for Swansea, where we had to wait three hours before going on by railway to Narberth Road, on our way to Tenby. Swansea looked dismal and smelt detestably, but we had one sight there quite worth the annoyance of waiting. It was the sight of two 'cockle women', who would make a fine subject for a painter. One of them was the grandest woman I ever saw – six feet high, carrying herself like a Greek Warrior, and treading the earth with unconscious majesty. They wore large woollen shawls of a rich brown, doubled lengthwise, with the end thrown back again over the left shoulder so as to fall behind in graceful folds. The grander of the two carried a great pitcher in her hand, and wore a quaint little bonnet set upright on her head. Her face was weather beaten and wizened, but her eyes were bright and piercing and the lines of her face, with its high cheek-bones, strong and characteristic. The other carried her pitcher on her head, and was also a fine old woman, but less majestic in her port than her companion. The guard at the railway told us that one of the porters had been insolent the other day to a cockle woman, and that she immediately pitched him off the platform into the road below!

Tenby, 22 July 1856.

Notes on Form in Art

(1868)

This essay, from a notebook now in the possession of Yale University Library, was first published in 1963 by Thomas Pinney (who refers us to an article describing this notebook by Bernard J. Paris, 'George Eliot's Unpublished Poetry', *Studies in Philology*, vol. 56, July 1959, pp. 593–658). Although written in 1868, at the time of *The Spanish Gypsy*, its formal preoccupations extend beyond poetry (see Introduction, pp. xxx–xxxi).

ABSTRACT WORDS and phrases which have an excellent genealogy are apt to live a little too much on their reputation and even to sink into dangerous impostors that should be made to show how they get their living. For this reason it is often good to consider an old subject as if nothing had yet been said about it; to suspend one's attention even to revered authorities and simply ask what in the present state of our knowledge are the facts which can with any congruity be tied together and labelled by a given abstraction.

For example, to any but those who are under the dire necessity of using the word and cannot afford to wait for a meaning, it must be more fruitful to ask, what relations of things can be properly included under the word 'Form' as applied to artistic composition, than to decide without any such previous inquiry that a particular work is wanting in form, or to take it for granted that the works of any one period or people are the examples of all that is admissible in artistic form.

Plain people, though indisposed to metaphysical subtleties, can

231

yet understand that Form, as an element of human experience, must begin with the perception of separateness, derived principally from touch of which the other senses are modifications; and that things must be recognized as separate wholes before they can be recognized as wholes composed of parts, or before these wholes again can be regarded as relatively parts of a larger whole.

Form, then, as distinguished from merely massive impression, must first depend on the discrimination of wholes and then on the discrimination of parts. Fundamentally, form is unlikeness, as is seen in the philosophic use of the word 'Form' in distinction from 'Matter'; and in consistency with this fundamental meaning, every difference is Form. Thus, sweetness is a form of sensibility, rage is a form of passion, green is a form both of light and of sensibility. But with this fundamental discrimination is born in necessary antithesis the sense of wholeness or unbroken connexion in space and time: a flash of light is a whole compared with the darkness which precedes and follows it; the taste of sourness is a whole and includes parts or degrees as it subsides. And as knowledge continues to grow by its alternating processes of distinction and combination, seeing smaller and smaller unlikenesses and grouping or associating these under a common likeness, it arrives at the conception of wholes composed of parts more and more multiplied and highly differenced, yet more and more absolutely bound together by various conditions of common likeness or mutual dependence. And the fullest example of such a whole is the highest example of Form: in other words, the relation of multiplex interdependent parts to a whole which is itself in the most varied and therefore the fullest relation to other wholes. Thus, the human organism comprises things as diverse as the finger-nails and tooth-ache, as the nervous stimulus of muscle manifested in a shout, and the discernment of a red spot on a field of snow; but all its different elements or parts of experience are bound together in a more necessary wholeness or more inseparable group of common conditions than can be found in any other existence known to us. The highest Form, then, is the highest organism, that is to say, the most varied group of relations bound together in a wholeness which again has the most varied relations with all other phenomena.

It is only in this fundamental sense that the word 'Form' can be applied to Art in general. Boundary or outline and visual appearance are modes of Form which in music and poetry can only have a metaphorical presence. Even in the plastic arts Form obviously, in its general application, means something else than mere imitation of outline, more or less correctness of drawing or modelling – just as, with reference to descriptive poetry, it means something more than the bare delineation of landscape or figures. Even those who use the phrase with a very dim understanding, always have a sense that it refers to structure or composition, that is, to the impression from a work considered as a whole. And what is a structure but a set of relations selected and combined in accordance with the sequence of mental states in the constructor, or with the preconception of a whole which he has inwardly evolved? Artistic form, as distinguished from mere imitation, begins in sculpture and painting with composition or the selection of attitudes and the formation of groups, let the objects be of what order they may. In music it begins with the adjustment of tones and rhythm to a climax, apart from any direct imitation. But my concern is here chiefly with poetry which I take in its wider sense as including all literary production of which it is the prerogative and not the reproach that the choice and sequence of images and ideas – that is, of relations and groups of relations – are more or less not only determined by emotion but intended to express it. I say more or less; for even the ravings of madness include multitudinous groups and sequences which are parts of common experience; and in the range of poetry we see wide distances of degree in the combination of emotive force with sequences that are not arbitrary and individual but true and universal, just as the guiding emotion varies from an idiosyncrasy only short of madness to a profoundly human passion which is or must come to be the heritage of all mankind. Sometimes the wider signification of poetry is taken to be fiction or invention as opposed to ascertained external fact or discovery. But what is fiction other than an arrangement of events or feigned correspondences according to predominant feeling? We find what destiny pleases; we make what pleases us – or what we think will please others.

Even taken in its derivative meaning of outline, what is Form but the limit of that difference by which we discriminate one object from another? – a limit determined partly by the intrinsic relations or composition of the object, and partly by the extrinsic action of other bodies upon it. This is true whether the object is a rock or a man; but in the case of the inorganic body, outline is the result of a nearly equal struggle between inner constitution and the outer play of forces; while in the human organism the outline is mainly determined by the intrinsic relation of its parts, and what is called fitness, beauty, or harmony in its outline and movements is dependent on the inward balance. The muscular strength which hurls, the muscular grace which gives a rhythmic movement to half a dozen balls, show a moving outline of which the chief factors are relations within the body; but the line with which a rock cuts the sky, or the shape of a boulder, may be more due to outer forces than to inner constitution. In ordinary language, the form of a stone is accidental. But the true expression of the difference is, that the wholeness of the stone depends simply on likeness of crystalliz- ation and is merely a wholeness of mass which may be broken up into other wholes; whereas the outline defining the wholeness of the human body is due to a consensus or constant interchange of effects among its parts. It is wholeness not merely of mass but of strict and manifold dependence. The word 'consensus' expresses that fact in a complex organism by which no part can suffer increase or diminution without a participation of all other parts in the effect produced and a consequent modification of the organism as a whole.

By this light, forms of art can be called higher or lower only on the same principle as that on which we apply these words to organisms; viz. in proportion to the complexity of the parts bound up into an indissoluble whole. In Poetry – which has this superior- ity over all the other arts, that its medium, language, is the least imitative, and is in the most complex relation with what it expresses – Form begins in the choice of rhythms and images as signs of a mental state, for this is a process of grouping or association of a less spontaneous and more conscious order than the grouping or association which constitutes the very growth and natural history of mind. *Poetry* begins when passion weds thought by finding expression in an image; but *Poetic Form* begins with a choice of elements, however meagre, as the accordant expression of emotional states. The most monotonous burthen chanted by an Arab boatman on the Nile is still a beginning of poetic form.

Poetic Form was not begotten by thinking it out or framing it as a shell which should hold emotional expression, any more than the shell of an animal arises before the living creature; but emotion, by its tendency to repetition, i.e., rhythmic persistence in proportion as diversifying thought is absent, creates a form by the recurrence of its elements in adjustment with certain given conditions of sound, language, action, or environment. Just as the beautiful expanding curves of a bivalve shell are not first made for the reception of the unstable inhabitant, but grow and are limited by the simple rhythmic conditions of its growing life.

It is a stale observation that the earliest poetic forms arose in the same spontaneous unreflecting way — that the rhythmic shouts with clash of metal accompanying the huntsman's or conqueror's course were probably the nucleus of the ballad epic; that the funeral or marriage sing-song, wailing or glad, with more or less violent muscular movement and resonance of wood or metal made the rude beginnings of lyric poetry. But it is still worth emphasis that this spontaneous origin is the most completely demonstrated in relation to a form of art which ultimately came to be treated more reflectively than any other — the tragic and comic drama.

A Form being once started must by and by cease to be purely spontaneous: the form itself becomes the object and material of emotion, and is sought after, amplified and elaborated by discrimination of its elements till at last by the abuse of its refinement it preoccupies the room of emotional thinking; and poetry, from being the fullest expression of the human soul, is starved into an ingenious pattern-work, in which tricks with vocables take the place of living words fed with the blood of relevant meaning, and made musical by the continual intercommunication of sensibility and thought.

The old phrases should not give way to scientific explanation, for speech is to a great extent like sculpture, expressing observed phenomena and remaining true in spite of Harvey and Bichat.[1]

In the later development of poetic fable the ἀναγνώρισις tends to consist in the discernment of a previously unrecognized *character*, and this may also form the περιπέτεια,[2] according to Aristotle's notion that in the highest form the two coincide.

THE GEORGE ELIOT – FREDERIC
HARRISON
CORRESPONDENCE

ELIOT FIRST met Frederic Harrison (1831–1923) in 1860 at the house of Richard Congreve (1818–99), a leading figure in the Positivist movement. Congreve had been his tutor at Oxford. For Harrison, Positivism, defined as the 'reorganization of life, at once intellectual, moral, and social, by faith in our common humanity' (*DNB*), was almost a religion. According to Auguste Comte, the founder of Positivism, human thought passes through three stages: Theological, Metaphysical and Positive. In the positive stage the universe is viewed as an ordered organism governed by necessary laws. This entails the abandonment of theistic religion in favour of an organized religion of humanity, complete with a priesthood and rituals, famously defined by T. H. Huxley as 'Catholicism minus Christianity'. Eliot's poem 'O May I Join the Choir Invisible' was adopted as one of its hymns.

Although a barrister by profession, Harrison's principal interest lay in social reform, and he was a lifelong supporter of many liberal causes. He contributed articles on trade unions to the *Fortnightly Review*, which was edited by Lewes, and was the person to whom Eliot turned when she required detailed legal advice during the writing of *Felix Holt*. He read parts of the manuscript for her, as well as the proofs, and provided much invaluable assistance.

It was on the basis of this acquaintance that he wrote to her in 1866, suggesting the outline of a story that would illustrate, in its completeness, what 'a Positive system of life would be'. The ensuing correspondence is interesting for both the quality and content of Eliot's response: her tactful scepticism about Positivism and, more importantly, her very clear statement of some of her central aesthetic principles. For a detailed account of her (ironized) assimilation of Harrison's suggestions, see James F. Scott's 'George Eliot, Positivism and the Social Vision of *Middlemarch*' in *Victorian Studies*, vol. 16 (September 1972), pp. 59–76.

In May 1868 Eliot wrote to Harrison to tell him that she had made arrangements for a copy of *The Spanish Gypsy* to be sent to him during her absence in Germany 'to express my value for the help and sympathy you gave me two years ago'. Undoubtedly the poem, described by Congreve as 'a mass of Positivism', fell far short of Harrison's expectations. He had hoped that she would use her art to promote the ideal of 'healthy moral control over societies' (*Letters, Vol. IV*, p. 289). His disappointment found a further outlet in his review of J. W. Cross's *George Eliot's Life as Related in Her Letters and Journals*, where he wrote that although she possessed 'mental equipment of the first order, her principal instrument was art. And so she played a double part – as the most philosophical artist, or the most artistic philosopher in recent literature . . . But the question comes in, and it must be answered, "Could she play the double part perfectly?"' The answer, of course, was no. 'It is given only to the one or two of the greatest to interpret the profoundest thought, to embody the ripest knowledge, in the inimitable mystery of art' ('The Life of George Eliot' in *Choice of Books*, 1887, pp. 215–16).

In later life Harrison noted, more charitably, his further reflections on Eliot's attitude to Positivism as she expressed it in this correspondence. 'George Eliot,' he wrote, 'had been a careful student of all his [Comte's] works for many years, and through the Congreves she was familiar with every phase of the Positivist ideal, with the general idea of which she had entire sympathy.' As far as her response to his suggestion for a tale set in 'a beautiful part of Northern France' was concerned, he wrote, 'She was no doubt quite right. She shrank from any Utopia in which there was a danger that "the picture might lapse into the diagram"' (*Memories and Thoughts*, 1906, pp. 146–7).

Harrison to Eliot, 19 July 1866

7 New Square, Lincoln's Inn, 19 July.

My dear Mrs Lewes,

KNOWING THAT you were gone to take a complete rest abroad, I have waited to thank you for the most welcome and most unexpected copy of *Felix Holt* which I received through your kindness on the morning of publication. I read it all through again just as if it was new to me altogether and I have read it over four or five times again. I find myself taking it up as I take up Tennyson or Shelley or Browning and thinking out the sequences of thought suggested by the undertones of the thought and the harmony of the lines. Can it be right to put the subtle finish of a poem into the language of a prose narrative? It is not a waste of toil? And yet whilst so many readers must miss all that, most of them even not consciously observing the fact, that they have a really new species of literature before them (a romance constructed in the artistic spirit and aim of a poem) yet it is not all lost. I know whole families where the three volumes have been read chapter by chapter and line by line and reread and recited as are the stanzas of *In Memoriam*. Of course the really worthy readers have taken their feast well and rightly. Indeed I observe that just those whose opinion one most wishes to have have taken the most pains to form it truly and have quite seized the task before them and the standard of thought upon which they have been called. The right people have I think read it in the right way so far as they could.

You will not need me to tell you and will not care to know about the general public or the library world or that sort of thing or what they think or say. The public (poor beast) as you know is greatly delighted and consumes the good thing largely with dim conscious reason to himself why he wags his tail over it. The critics have been too much abashed to commit much folly and some of them have risen into real sense and life. But you know a great deal more of that than you care to know already, I am sure. Enough if I say that public, critics, and people of sense have come to agree (as I ventured to say at first they would) that this is the most complete delightful and abiding thing they have yet had and each party and school are determined to see their own side in it – the religious people, the non-religious people, the various sections of religious people, the educated, the simple, the radicals, the Tories, the socialists, the intellectual reformers, the domestic circle, the critics, the metaphysicians, the artists, the Positivists, the squires, are all quite convinced that it has been conceived from their own point of view.

Not all – I have met a dissentient. At a big house at a big dinner of big people where for my many sins the Devil entrapped me a very beautiful and most stony young lady of fashion – a girl with brains who understood the good and with an ossified heart which just beat strong enough to hate it declared to me with much decision and discrimination that she disliked it all exceedingly. She hated to have such people brought before her or before the world. There might be such people as Felix Holt but they should be put down. It was wrong to encourage their vagaries. It might be natural but not a subject for art. Felix and Esther might have lived and perhaps do but their wrong-headed ways are simply tiresome and disagreeable to men and women of the world. Low rough unregulated natures must be dealt with by schoolmasters parsons and constables, kept out of the way of art and society and beauty – a girl like a block of ice, clear hard and beautiful – a female Lord Cranbourne[1] only beautiful.

Are you sure that your destiny is not to produce a poem – not a poem in prose but in measure – a drama? Is it possible that there is not one yet existing or does it lie like the statue in the marble block? I am no fortune-teller but I believe it is in the Stars.

I am no fortune-teller but if I were and found ground enough to prophesy I should say that your destiny might take this turn to achieve such a picture as this. Positivism is a conception of society with all the old elements reknit and recast. In it society and men exist under the old relations reharmonized. Its dogma is vast, abstract, unpopular. The social and human form is eminently sympathetic, capable of idealization, and popular. Comte designed to close his life by the work of moulding the normal state into an ideal in a great comprehensive poem – a task which he would never have accomplished and did not begin. But some one will some day. In the meantime the idealization of certain normal relations is eminently the task of all art. I believe, we believe, probably with no more reason than the Tories, metaphysicians and others I mentioned above that this is being done. But we are fanatics, we are people of one idea (a big idea it is true), we want more. To us it seems that the great elements of society and human life can even now be treated with completeness in their normal forms with conscious relation to the complete ideal of Comte. There is not any one, there never has been any one but yourself to whom we could look for this.

It is presumptuous and foolish for me to say this knowing so little of your plans, your interest in Comte, and the rest. But as I have ventured to unfold an old fancy of mine will you bear with me whilst I make it clear what I mean. I certainly do not mean anything which would directly put forth doctrines or notions of Comte or even imply that the reader had ever heard of him or his ideas. I presume that art must use the 'milieu' before it, and not, except for some special purposes, create a new world fill it and people it with new beings. I suppose an ideal tale relating to [the] state of society which should have subjectively and objectively realized in its completeness a Positive system of life would be, even if an artistic marvel, valuable and intelligible exclusively (like Bekker's *Charicles*[2]) to the actual student of Comte; as one might suppose a romance of society in Mars and Venus, with habits and customs of the Martial and Aphrodisian natives might be to an astronomer. I presume no true art is directly didactic or dogmatic. But I can conceive – and forgive me for wearying you with a dream – an ever present dream of mine that the grand features of Comte's world might be sketched in fiction in their normal relations though under the forms of our familiar life. There is nothing in Positive existence which is not in the depths of human nature and civilized society. There is no social force which it uses which is not now in germ or in disuse present around us – no human passion which it supposes absent or which it will not set itself to govern. Now I have imagined the temporal and the spiritual power outlined so in their main functions – the home, the school, the temple, the workroom, the teacher, the ruler, the capitalist, the labourer, the wife, the mother, the child, of the future might be drawn so as to do no violence to our familiar ideas yet consciously standing in their normal place. Types of these all exist about us. All I conceive is a state of society sufficiently favourable for them to develop themselves freely, and hold their natural relations, a surrounding adequate for them to perform normally where for instance the moral and practical forces are sufficiently elevated to control without arousing too strong resistance, and where the good forces are sufficiently strong to show their value by practical results.

But I must try and make my meaning still somewhat plainer. I just add a practical example. Let us conceive somewhere in a corner remote from disturbance say of Normandy or French Canada where something of the social tone of Catholicism lingers (a social tone I should suppose almost indispensable as a background for the Positivist relations) yet where the Revolution and Progress has deeply penetrated so far as to destroy all strictly dogmatic religion – leaving a thorough and conscious doctrinal blank with a residuum of the Catholic *social* spirit – say for instance a secluded manufacturing village near Rouen in which the Revolution and Industrial Progress had uprooted the doctrines and rights both of Catholicism and Feudalism but had left the sentiment of both, sufficiently near to the centres of modern life to be thoroughly abreast of the results of Progress of thought labour and Society yet not shaken or poisoned by the ceaseless action of the negative solvent. In such a society one could conceive the manufacturer roughly fulfilling the conditions of the normal capitalist sufficiently master of the situation to be independent of the different tone and conduct of the actual capitalist – supplemented it might be by a rural capitalist – a transformed French noble with just the best sentiments of Feudalism surviving and none of its vices. Then the actual Church and curé receding into the background the spiritual power would be represented by the local physician for instance – a man of the new world with complete scientific and moral cultivation who should gradually acquire a free spontaneous and entirely moral ascendancy over both capitalist and labourer – who should found and superintend schools free in every sense, dogmatically and materially one who without coming into conflict with the Church or its representatives might practically succeed to the whole influence and spiritual duties of the Catholic priest and from the conscience of the powerful capitalist or capitalists and the grateful confidence of the people whom he taught and healed might have gained the requisite basis to exercise moral control of the best kind. Once given such a spiritual and such a temporal power as this under conditions favourable enough to permit them full scope and there would be little difficulty in supposing a sufficient number of families enjoying physical intellectual and moral advantages to make the tone of the place a fair representation of a new society, without supposing anything but a French village of the nineteenth century – and some one or two of these families might easily throw up normal types of the domestic forces and relations. If the conditions were such as to make possible one normal proletariate family, one normal capitalist family, one normal school, the conception of society in its main features would be complete. In France it would not be impossible to have at once the revolutionized social system with the Catholic traditions and sentiments.

Of course I do not mean a state of things in which evil was extinct – *couleur de rose* – too impassive to sustain any keen interests and too much removed from real life to be life-like. In such a state of things it would be right to imagine all the passions and most of the evils which afflict men and societies now. Only they must not be dominant or sufficient to shake the controlling forces to pieces. Every conflict possible in the breast of man or between classes might be there and yet the humanizing powers which govern them sufficiently vigorous and disciplined. There are such forces now in every society even in the worst, but in the best they are hardly enough concerted and harmonious to show their action very clearly. All that would be necessary to invent would be the conditions which would give an organic unity to the good elements. They now fight like untrained heroes without a chief. Conceive conditions in which they become disciplined veterans under a scientific leader. A strike for instance in such a society would bring out all the grave dangers of industrial existence and many of the darker passions both of workman and capitalist but if it yielded before the habitual principles common to both sides and the active intervention of a trusted teacher it would easily illustrate the superiority of the new to the old life. So too a domestic tragedy would be curbed within the narrowest limits by more systematic intervention of the feminine influences and the priest teacher adviser or friend. What the world yet wants to be shown is the possibility in real life of healthy moral control over societies – and the infinite scope and power of wealth used morally. They are the two great elements of the future civilization on which men are blindly sceptical. And nothing I think but a miracle or a great work of art can flash it into their souls. That this miracle may be furnished to them I do not despair when I see the finest artistic mastery devoted to the solution of the greatest problems and the highest purposes. Believe me to be

Most sincerely yours
Frederic Harrison.

Eliot to Harrison, 4 August 1866

The Priory, 21 North Bank, Regents Park. 4 August 66.

My dear Mr Harrison

WE RETURNED from our health-seeking journey on Thursday evening, and your letter was the most delightful thing that awaited me at home. Be sure it will be much read and meditated, and may I not take it as an earnest that your help which has already done so much for me, will be continued? I mean, that you will help me by your thoughts and your sympathy, not that you will be teased with my proofs.

I meant to write you a long letter about the æsthetic problem, but Mr Lewes, who is still tormented with headachy effects from our rough passage, comes and asks me to walk to Hampstead with him. I do not like to leave your letter longer without acknowledgement, so I send these hasty lines. Come and see us soon.

Always yours sincerely

M. E. Lewes

Eliot to Harrison, 15 August 1866

21 North Bank, 15 August.

My dear Mr Harrison

I HAVE read several times your letter of the nineteenth which I found awaiting me on my return, and I shall read it many times again. Pray do not ever say, or inwardly suspect, that anything you take the trouble to write to me will not be valued. On the contrary, please to imagine as well as you can the experience of a mind morbidly desponding, of a consciousness tending more and more to consist in memories of error and imperfection rather than in a strengthening sense of achievement — and then consider how such a mind must need the support of sympathy and approval from those who are capable of understanding its aims. I assure you your letter is an evidence of a fuller understanding than I have ever had expressed to me before. And if I needed to give emphasis to this simple statement, I should suggest to you all the miseries one's obstinate egoism endures from the fact of being a writer of novels — books which the dullest and silliest reader thinks himself competent to deliver an opinion on. But I despise myself for feeling any annoyance at these trivial things.

That is a tremendously difficult problem which you have laid before me, and I think you see its difficulties, though they can hardly press upon you as they do on me, who have gone through again and again the severe effort of trying to make certain ideas thoroughly incarnate, as if they had revealed themselves to me first in the flesh and not in the spirit. I think æsthetic teaching is the highest of all teaching because it deals with life in its highest complexity. But if it ceases to be purely æsthetic — if it lapses anywhere from the picture to the diagram — it becomes the most offensive of all teaching. Avowed Utopias are not offensive, because they are understood to have a scientific and expository character: they do not pretend to work on the emotions, or couldn't do it if they did pretend. I am sure, from your own statement, that you see this quite clearly. Well, then, consider the sort of agonizing labour to an English-fed imagination to make art a sufficiently real background, for the desired picture, to get breathing, individual forms, and group them in the needful relations, so that the presentation will lay hold on the emotions as human experience – will, as you say, 'flash' conviction on the world by means of aroused sympathy.

I took unspeakable pains in preparing to write *Romola* – neglecting nothing I could find that would help me to what I may call the 'Idiom' of Florence, in the largest sense one could stretch the word to. And there I was only trying to give *some* out of the normal relations. I felt that the necessary idealization could only be attained by adopting the clothing of the past. And again, it is my way (rather too much so perhaps) to urge the human sanctities through tragedy – through pity and terror as well as admiration and delights.

I only say all this to show the tenfold arduousness of such a work as the one your problem demands. On the other hand, my whole soul goes with your desire that it should be done, and I shall at least keep the great possibility (or impossibility) perpetually in my mind, as something towards which I must strive, though it may be that I can do so only in a fragmentary way.

At present I am going to take up again a work which I laid down before writing *Felix*.[3] It is – *but please let this be a secret between ourselves* – an attempt at a drama, which I put aside at Mr Lewes's request, after writing four acts, precisely because it was in that stage of Creation, or *Werden*, in which the idea of the characters predominates over the incarnation. Now I read it again, I find it impossible to abandon it: the conceptions move me deeply, and they have never been wrought out before. There is not a thought or symbol that I do not long to use: but the whole requires recasting, and as I never recast anything before, I think of the issue very doubtfully. When one has to work out the dramatic action for one's self under the inspiration of an idea, instead of having a grand myth or an Italian novel ready to one's hand, one feels anything but omnipotent. Not that I should have done any better if I had had the myth or the novel, for I am not a good user of opportunities. I think I have the right locus and historic conditions, but much else is wanting.

I have almost read through the *International Essays*.[4] I hope they are selling enough to serve as leaven. We shall be very glad if you can spare us a sight of you before you go away. I have not, of course, said half what I want to say, but I hope opportunities of exchanging thoughts will not be wanting between us.

Always yours sincerely
M. E. Lewes

Harrison to Eliot, 25 May 1868

Dear Mrs Lewes

I AM very grateful for this great mark of kindness. I have been of course expecting this new book with the greatest interest, and had told them to get me the earliest copy procurable. When you return I shall ask you to write the name in the fly-leaf, and it will be a thing to be kept for ever.

But I hope this kind recollection of me will not be associated with the remembrance of my once having given you a great deal of trouble a long time ago.

I had been intending to write to you for some time, but I knew how busy you were, and talking is impossible in your Sunday *conversazione*. Perhaps in your leisure abroad you will let me write about it. It is just this. I do not know if you remember a long time ago I took heart to suggest as a subject worthy of you, the idealization of the Positive vision of society as a whole, especially to typify the great institutions and social functions of the future. How far this accorded with ideas already present to you, how you judged it I do not exactly know. I think you considered it too abstract and wide for real art. Perhaps you may remember that I drew out a sketch of the form in which it presented itself to my mind. Since then that same sketch has been taking shape and growing on me and I feel a sort of craving to realize or see it realized in words. Now I want to ask you how far you think it possible. Perhaps you will not think I trouble you too much if during your holiday I write to put this into shape to you.

With many grateful thanks, I am,

Yours sincerely
F. Harrison.

Harrison to Eliot, 11 November 1868

7 New Square, Lincoln's Inn, 11 November.

My dear Mrs Lewes,

I THINK you know how it comes that all these months I have never seen you or written to you though having so much to say. The gift of your poem, and your letter to me when you left, have not indeed been thought lightly of. But they have imposed a task on me that I have never yet been able and am not yet ready to fulfil. I want very much to tell you fully all that I feel able; but I cannot gather up my ideas. Nor do I yet know very clearly what they are. And I have been in no condition of repose to make this very easy. I have indeed read your poem many many times to myself and to others, and thought over it and talked of it constantly. But I am little nearer the telling you how I feel when I rise from it than I was, yet it seems somewhat unnatural to write to you and say nothing. But this I must do even now. Nothing that is but this – That I read it still and see better continually what is required of one who would do it justice, and who desires to learn how to rise up to the level on which it stands.

During your tour abroad I was often about to write to you. And still the consciousness of the crude state of my own mind held me back. Since July I have been quite immersed in my Trades-Union work. I felt it essential to make up and put forth my ideas. Accordingly I went down into the country, where I shut myself out from professional, literary, political, and all other distractions, and seeing no one and never coming into London I thought of nothing but my 20,000 questions in the Evidence. It has been the most continuous kind of effort I have ever had to make, but I think I now am well saturated with the 20,000 answers (!), understand the law and am ready for the trumpet to sound. 'J'ai dit mon dernier mot' – which 'mot' unluckily consists of fifty pages of a bluebook, and finally left the printer only yesterday.[5]

I tell you all this, to show you how much my mind has been absorbed in work, except for a few weeks when I went to the Alps, and very nearly managed to get drowned.

After this interval I am returned to my work here. I shall read *The Spanish Gypsy* again, which I am conscious that I have not half mastered. I need not say I am sure what pleasure it gives me to recognize the profound truths and sacred principles which [that which] we call the Faith of the Future is preparing, for the first time truly idealized. I see in it the first fruits of the movement to the development of which we hope everything.

But as I say I have all this to learn and to understand. The purpose, the ἦθος,[6] the very form of the work holds out to us something that we are invited to learn from. I have my lesson yet to study, and I am trying to do so rightly. I know no worse instance of the monkey-like criticism of the day, than the way in which the hedge-sparrows of the reviews (forgive this 'happy family' of metaphors) chirrup out their blame or praise on Saturday of a book which left the printer on Monday. I wonder if sprightly contributors dashed off a notice of the first performance of *King Lear* between the closing of the Theatre that night and the appearance of the Daily Papers next morning.

Well I am neither a hedge-sparrow critic, nor a critic at all. And will not let myself stray into anything which looks like criticism at all. There can be little need for me to tell you that I *do* recognize how deeply planned are the foundations and lines of the structure which we have contemplated, how subtly one must seek who desires to see into the thoughts beneath and behind, how untiring and self-restrained is the art and the work. But I shall say no more of this; for I know that you will give me credit, when I say that I am honestly studying a great work, of doing my best to study it aright.

This is far too serious a matter, and one which involves social interests so far higher than any personal, for me to say anything which does not fairly represent the state of my mind. And I should be doing wrong if I were to let you think that I was of any clear and resolved mind about it. On the contrary, I am not. I am far from clear that I at all apprehend, or even that I do not misconceive what are the real human traits of character in the principal personages, nor at all clear what is the sum or moral of the whole; nor am I at all sure that even if I knew these aright that the same view would force itself on my convictions. For instance I hesitate, and the more I think the more I hesitate, how Zarca and Fedalma stand in a true ethical judgement. I am not sure that I like the problem. I am not sure that there is any definite problem to be solved. I am not sure that either are real types of human nature. I am not sure if the conduct of both of them, or of one of them is not treason to human life. Nor am I at all clearly resolved whether the new poetic resource which mingles narrative and drama gains more than it sacrifices. Nor can I feel quite sure that the form equals the conception and does it full justice; in a word whether equally great ends might not be realized in prose rather than in verse.

I honestly and literally mean that my mind is not clear on these questions – not that it is made up in an adverse sense. No! these are the things which I am meditating. I wish simply to tell you the problems before my mind. For I cannot bear to leave you to suppose that they are not there. There they are: and I pass through revulsions of mind like a man in a religious crisis of scepticism and faith. For the most part I believe I shall solve them in the sense in which you would yourself – (except by the way the union of drama with epos). I am ashamed of my own paralytic state of mind. Everyone with whom I would most trust my judgement, is clear and triumphant. I stand like Thomas fingering the very nail-prints and yet striving to believe. Yet Thomas did not afterwards lack zeal.

However, of one thing I do not doubt – that I have before me to make the most of something profound, noble, and beautiful which must speak to every worthy intellect and every pure heart. Nor do I doubt that the same kindness with which you wrote to me when you went away last will be shown to this letter, this weak exhibition of a weak mind.

I am still living in the country, and now am very busy. But I shall return to London in a week or ten days and then I hope to come and see you. Believe me to be

Your sincerely
Frederic Harrison.

Eliot to Harrison, 15 January 1870

21 North Bank, 15 January 1870.

My dear Mr Harrison

I AM moved to write to you rather by the inclination to remind
you of me, than by the sense of having anything to say. On
reading 'The Positivist Problem'[7] a second time, I gained a
stronger impression of its general value, and I also felt less jarred
by the more personal part at the close. Mr Lewes would tell
you that I have an unreasonable aversion to personal statements,
and when I come to like them it is usually by a hard process of
*con*version. But – to tell you all just for the sake of telling, and
not because the matter can have any weight – my second reading gave me a new and very strong sense that the last two or
three pages have an air of an appendix added at some distance
of time from the original writing of the article. Some more thoroughly explanatory account of your non-adhesion seems requisite
as a nexus – since the statement of your non-adhesion had to be
mentioned after an argument for the system against the outer
Gentile world. However, it is more important for me to say that
I felt the thorough justice of your words, when in conversation
with me, you said, 'I don't see why there should be any mystification: having come to a resolution after much inward debate, it
is better to state the resolution.' Something like that you said
and I give a hearty 'Amen', praying that I may not be too apt
myself to prefer the haze to the clearness. But the fact is, I
shrink from decided 'deliverances' on momentous subjects, from
the dread of coming to swear by my own 'deliverances' and
sinking into an insistent echo of myself. That is a horrible destiny
– and one cannot help seeing that many of the most powerful
men fall into it.

I should have scribbled this nothing-in-particular before now, but that bodily infirmities have hindered me.

Always yours most sincerely
M. E. Lewes.

REVIEWS

Brothers in Opinion:
Edgar Quinet and Jules Michelet

(Coventry Herald and Observer, 30 October 1846)

THESE PUBLICATIONS are three of a series of translations from contemporary French authors, which, on the whole, form a not unwelcome addition to our rapidly increasing stock of cheap literature. It is true that a translation can never be more than a second-best vehicle for an author's thoughts, and the more abundant his excellencies, the more does he suffer from this method of presentation, – the finer the nectar, the greater the risk of transferring it from one vessel to another. But an acquaintance with foreign modes of thought, especially on the grander questions which occupy the human mind, is too important an element in the true enlightenment of a nation, to be dispensed with until all English readers shall have faculties or leisure to become linguists. These remarks apply very forcibly to the works before us. The authors suffer perhaps more than in the average degree from the translating process; but notwithstanding this disadvantage, it is well that ordinary readers should have the means of knowing what writers so influential in their own country have to say on subjects of universal interest. Still, though we can thus approve the introduction of these works to the English public, they are far from obtaining our unqualified admiration. While they exhibit much fervid eloquence, expansiveness of view, and ardour for human liberty and human progress, they are too vague and allusive to be very rich in instruction to persons less informed than their authors, and they have the fault, perhaps inevitable to the works of an antagonistic character, of putting statements too broadly, and painting facts in too strong lights and shadows. Moreover, all the philosophy of the writers has not delivered them from an almost ridiculous excess of *amour de la patrie*, which leads them to represent the French people as a sort of second chosen race, who alone have the mission to propagate, by pen and sword, the truth which is to regenerate the nations. But national egotism is the last foible on which we English must allow ourselves to be severe.

Whatever may be the reception of the above works amongst us, the friends of Jesuitism have done them the honour of showing the most vehement indignation and alarm at their tendency, while, on the other hand, their authors have been warmly supported by those who think that France and Christendom in general have reason to regret the revival of the Society of Jesus in 1814. MM. Michelet and Quinet are, as they are fond of telling their readers, brothers not only in office, but in opinion, sharing the same views so intimately and completely, that whenever the one speaks or writes, he knows himself to be expressing the mind of the other: and one of the works before us, *The Jesuits*, is a visible sign of this unity, being the joint production of the two friends. It consists of two series of lectures, – the first, by M. Michelet, too declamatory and general to be suited for anything but a *viva voce* delivery, to an audience who shared in the excitement that produced 'long inter- ruption' of the speaker, by 'applause, murmurs, and violent lan- guage'. The second course, by M. Quinet, is of more intrinsic value, containing a rapid and well-marked sketch of the origin and fortunes of the Society of Jesus, the nature of its discipline and constitution, its missions, political agency, and relation to theology and philosophy. With a candid acknowledgement of the true genius and enthusiasm which gave birth to the idea of the Society in the mind of its founder, of the pure earnestness and simple faith which carried a Xavier from India to Japan, and from thence to the shores of China, compelling from the inhabitants of those strange lands the tribute of veneration for him as a holy man, – M. Quinet shows that the system of Loyola[1] runs counter to the grand law which God has impressed on all nature, – the production and development of life; that wherever it presides there must be moral, social, and intellectual death; its first aim being to annihilate in its agents, and consequently in those on whom they act, all spon- taneity, all will. Let man become as a corpse, *ut cadaver*, were the death-bed words of Loyola – let him be as a staff in the hand of an old man, *senis baculus*,[2] which is taken up and cast away again at pleasure: and one of the rules in his Spiritual Exercises is equally startling: '*If authority declares that what seems to you white is black, affirm it to be black.*'

Michelet's *Priests, Women, and Families* is more special in its object, and much more likely to be extensively read. The author selects from history and biography samples of the effects of religious direction, by which he means a spiritual superintendence over individuals of a closer and more rigid character than that of the confessor. He gives some melancholy proofs of the too undeniable fact, that women have ever been the victims and the instruments of priestly despotism, and in the latter part of the work he dilates especially on the baneful influence of the director on the peace of domestic life. There is certainly much truth very cogently stated in the form both of facts and principles in this work of Michelet's, but we confess that to us, loving, as we do, to dwell in the serene atmosphere of admiration for mankind, its perusal has been exquisitely painful, and with all deferences to the author's experience and judgement, we advise his readers to bear in mind, that there is a large amount of truth to be urged in vindication of the defendant, which Michelet, as counsel for the other party, is not to be expected to state. We have not space for many quotations, but we give the following as rather a happy illustration of the power of habit: –

I read once in an old story what is really affecting, and very significant. It was about a woman, a wandering princess, who, after many sufferings, found for her asylum a deserted palace, in the midst of a forest. She felt happy in reposing there, and remaining some time: she went to and fro from one large empty room to another, without meeting with any obstacle: she thought herself alone and free. All the doors were open; only at the hall-door, no one having passed through since herself, the spider had woven his web in the sun, a thin, light, and almost invisible network; a feeble obstacle, which the princess, who wishes at last to go out, thinks she can remove without difficulty. She raises the web; but there is another behind it, which she also raises without trouble. The second conceals a third; that she must also raise, – strange! there are four; no, five! or rather six, – and more beyond. Alas! how will she get rid of so many? She is already tired. No matter! she perseveres; by taking breath a little she may continue. But the web continues too, and is ever renewed with a malicious obstinacy. What is she to do? She is overcome with fatigue and perspiration, her arms fall by her sides. At last, exhausted as she is, she sits down on the ground, on that insurmountable threshold: she looks mournfully at the serial obstacle fluttering in the wind, lightly and triumphantly. Poor princess! poor fly! now you are caught! But why did you stay in that fairy dwelling, and give the spider time to spin his web?[3]

Too much credit cannot be given to Messrs Longmans & Co., for the style in which these publications are got up. As regards paper, type, and form, we think them superior to any cheap issue of popular literature that has hitherto appeared, and we trust that the spirited publishers will follow up their praiseworthy commencement in this department of the public service.

J. A. Froude's *The Nemesis of Faith*

(Coventry Herald and Observer, 16 March 1849)

ON CERTAIN red-letter days of our existence, it happens to us to discover among the *spawn* of the press, a book which, as we read, seems to undergo a sort of transfiguration before us. We no longer hold heavily in our hands an octavo of some hundred pages, over which the eye laboriously travels, hardly able to drag along with it the restive mind: but we seem to be in companionship with a spirit, who is transfusing himself into our souls, and is vitalizing them by his superior energy, that life, both outward and inward, presents itself to us for higher relief, in colours brightened and deepened – we seem to have been bathing in a pool of Siloam, and to have come forth reeling. The books which carry this magic in them are the true products of genius, and their influence, whether for good or evil, is to the influence of all the respectable results of mere talent and industry, as the mighty Nile to the dykes which receive and distribute its heaven-fed waters. Such a book is *The Nemesis of Faith*. We are sure that its author is a bright particular star,[1] though he sometimes leaves us in doubt whether he be not a fallen 'son of the morning'.[2] Much there is in the work of a questionable character: yet more which hardly falls within the scope of a newspaper editor's notice: but its trenchant remarks on some of our English conventions, its striking sketches of the dubious aspect which many chartered respectabilities are beginning to wear under the light of this nineteenth century, its suggestive hints as to the necessity of recasting the currency of our religion and virtue, that it may carry fresh and bright the stamp of the age's highest and best idea – these have a practical bearing, which may well excite the grave, perhaps the alarmed attention of some important classes among us. We will resign the work into the hands of judges of more ability, and more unquestioned credentials, only quoting one or two passages as a slight sample for our readers. Surely there is work for our augurs when a Clergyman writes thus of his co-ordinates: –

I cannot understand why, as a body, the Clergy are so fatally uninteresting: they who through all their waking hours ought to have for their one thought, the deepest and most absorbing interests of humanity. It is the curse of making it a profession – a road to get on upon, to succeed in life upon. The base stain is apparent in their very language, too, and an index of what they are. Their '*duty*' – what is it? To patter through the two Sunday's services. For a little money one of them will take the other's *duty* for him. And what do they all aim at? Getting livings! – not cures of souls, but *livings*: something which will keep their wretched bodies living in the comforts they have found indispensable. What business have they, any one of them, with a thought of what becomes of their poor wretched selves at all? To hear them preaching, to hear the words they use in these same duties of theirs, one would suppose they really believed that getting on, and getting rich, and getting comfortable, were quite the last things a Christian should propose to himself. They certainly say so. Alas! with the mass of them, the pulpit keeps its old meaning, and is but a stage. Off the stage there is the old plate of the old world stories, the patronage of this rich man and that, the vacant benefice or Cathedral stall. So and so, lucky fellow, has married a Bishop's daughter, and the Bishop himself has the best-dressed wife, and the best equipage in London: and oh, bitterest satire of all! the very pulpit eloquence with which they can paint the better life, the beauty of Christianity, is valued only as a means of advancing them into what they condemn ... Oh, what a Clergyman might do! To have them all [the poor] for an hour at least each week, collected to be taught by him, really wishing to listen, if he will but take the trouble to understand them, and to learn what they require to be told. How sick one is of all sermons, such as they are! Why will men go on thrashing over and again the old withered straw that was thrashed out centuries ago, when every field is waving with fresh, and quit other crops craving for their hand ...

But there are many other things besides what are in the Bible, which he (the Clergyman) ought to learn if he would assist the people to do what he tells them to do, if he would really give them rest from the painful vacancy of mind, which life spent in routine of never-ending work entails upon them; he should study their work, and the natural laws that are working in it: he should make another version of the Bible for them in what is for ever before their eyes, in the corn-field, in the meadow, in the workshop, at the weaver's loom, in the market-places and in the ware-houses ... Let every flower have a second image to their eyes; let him bring in for witness to the love of the great Creator, every bird, every beast, every poorest insect; let the teeming earth tell of Him as in her unwearied labour-pangs she fashions up the material elements into the great rolling flood of life which ebbs and flows around them. They might do something, these Clergy, if they would go to work over this ground; labouring in good earnest would they be for the souls of mankind.[3]

The following passage is at least as forcible: –

The men that write books, Carlyle says, are now the world's priests, the spiritual directors of mankind. No doubt they are; and it shows the folly and madness of trying still to enforce texts, that you do but silence a man in the pulpit, to send his voice along the press into every corner of the land. God abolished texts for all purposes, except of mischief and vexation, when he gave mankind the printing-press. What is the result of sustaining them, but that we are all at the mercy now of some clever self-assumer? and while our nominal teachers answer no end for us, except the hour's sleep on Sunday, the minds of all of us, from highest Lords to enlightened operatives, are formed in reading-rooms, in lecture-rooms, at the bar of public-houses, by all the shrewdest, and often the most worthless, novel writers or paper editors. Yet even this is better than nothing, better than that people should be left to their pulpit teachers, such as they are.[4]

R. W. Mackay's *The Progress of the Intellect*

(*Westminster Review*, January 1851)

THERE ARE many, and those not the least powerful thinkers and efficient workers amongst us, who are prone to underrate critical research into ancient modes of life and forms of thought, alleging that what it behoves us chiefly to ascertain is the truth which comes home to men's business and bosoms in these our days, and not by-gone speculations and beliefs which we can never fully comprehend, and with which we can only yet more imperfectly sympathize. Holding, with Auguste Comte,[1] that theological and metaphysical speculation have reached their limit, and that the only hope of extending man's sources of knowledge and happiness is to be found in positive science, and in the universal application of its principles; they urge that the thinkers who are in the van of human progress should devote their energies to the actual rather than to the retrospective.

There is, undeniably, truth in this view. It is better to discover and apply improved methods of draining our own towns, than to be able to quote Aristophanes in proof that the streets of Athens were in a state of unmacadamized muddiness − better to reason justly on some point of immediate concern, than to know the fallacies of the ancient sophists − better to look with 'awful eye'[2] at the starry heavens, and, under the teaching of Newton and Herschel, feel the immensity, the order, the sublimity of the universe, and of the forces by which it subsists, than to pore over the grotesque symbols, whereby the Assyrian or Egyptian shadowed forth his own more vague impression of the same great facts. But it would be a very serious mistake to suppose that the study of the past and the labours of criticism have no important practical bearing on the present. Our civilization, and, yet more, our religion, are an anomalous blending of lifeless barbarisms, which have descended to us like so many petrifactions from distant ages, with living ideas, the offspring of a true process of development. We are in bondage to terms and conceptions which, having had their root in conditions of thought no longer existing, have ceased to possess any vitality, and are for us as spells which have lost their virtue. The endeavour to spread enlightened ideas is perpetually counteracted by these *idola theatri*,[3] which have allied themselves, on the one hand with men's better sentiments, and on the other with institutions in whose defence are arrayed the passions and the interests of dominant classes. Now, though the teaching of positive truth is the grand means of expelling error, the process will be very much quickened if the negative argument serve as its pioneer; if, by a survey of the past, it can be shown how each age and each race has had a faith and a symbolism suited to its need and its stage of development, and that for succeeding ages to dream of retaining the spirit along with the forms of the past, is as futile as the embalming of the dead body in the hope that it may one day be resumed by the living soul.

But apart from this objective utility of critical research, it has certain highly advantageous influences on the mind which pursues it. There is so far justice in the common sarcasms against men of erudition *par excellence*, that they have rarely been distinguished for warmth of moral sympathy, or for fertility and grandeur of conception; but your eminently practical thinker is often beset by a narrowness of another kind. It may be doubted, whether a mind which has no susceptibility to the pleasure of changing its point of view, of mastering a remote form of thought, of perceiving identity of nature under variety of manifestation – a perception which resembles an expansion of one's own being, a pre-existence in the past – can possess the flexibility, the ready sympathy, or the tolerance, which characterizes a truly philosophic culture. Now and then, however, we meet with a nature which combines the faculty for amassing minute erudition with the largeness of view necessary to give it a practical bearing; a high appreciation of the genius of antiquity, with a profound belief in the progressive character of human development – in the eternal freshness of the founts of inspiration, a wonderful intuition of the mental conditions of past ages with an ardent participation in the most advanced ideas and most hopeful efforts of the present; a nature like some mighty river, which, in its long windings through unfrequented regions, gathers mineral and earthy treasures only more effectually to enrich and fertilize the cultivated valleys and busy cities which form the habitation of man.

Of such a nature, with valuable qualities thus 'antithetically mixt', we have evidence in the work before us. It exhibits an industry in research which reminds us of Cudworth,[4] and for which, in recent literature, we must seek a parallel in Germany rather than in England, while its philosophy and its aims are at once lofty and practical. Scattered through its more abstruse disquisitions we find passages of pre-eminent beauty – gems into which are absorbed the finest rays of intelligence and feeling. We believe Mr Mackay's work is unique in its kind. England has been slow to use or to emulate the immense labours of Germany in the departments of mythology and biblical criticism; but when once she does so, the greater solidity and directness of the English mind ensure a superiority of treatment.

The series of subjects which Mr Mackay has chosen as waymarks in tracing the *Progress of the Intellect*, is – after an introductory chapter on Intellectual Religion – Ancient Cosmogony; the Metaphysical Idea of God; the Moral Notion of God; the Theory of Mediation; the Hebrew Theory of Retribution and Immortality; the Messianic Theory; Christian Forms and Reforms; and Speculative Christianity. In the introductory dissertation on Intellectual Religion, he develops his view concerning the true basis and character of religion and morals, and the relation between ancient and modern ideas on these subjects, and it is perhaps here that he presents himself to the greatest advantage; this preliminary chapter is a sort of lofty, airy vestibule, in which we gather breath and courage to descend with the author into the crypts of citation and conjecture, into which he is about to introduce us. It is Mr Mackay's faith that divine revelation is not contained exclusively or pre-eminently in the facts and inspirations of any one age or nation, but is co-extensive with the history of human development, and is perpetually unfolding itself to our widened experience and investigation, as firmament upon firmament becomes visible to us in proportion to the power and range of our exploring instruments. The master key to this revelation, is the recognition of the presence of undeviating law in the material and moral world – of that invariability of sequence which is acknowledged to be the basis of physical science, but which is still perversely ignored in our social organization, our ethics and our religion. It is this invariability of sequence which can alone give value to experience and render education in the true sense possible. The divine yea and nay, the seal of prohibition and of sanction, are effectually impressed on human deeds and aspirations, not by means of Greek and Hebrew, but by that inexorable law of consequences, whose evidence is confirmed instead of weakened as the ages advance; and human duty is comprised in the earnest study of this law and patient obedience to its teaching. While this belief sheds a bright beam of promise on the future career of our race, it lights up what once seemed the dreariest region of history with new interest; every past phase of human development is part of that education of the race in which we are sharing; every mistake, every absurdity into which poor human nature has fallen, may be looked on as an experiment of which we may reap the benefit. A correct generaliz-ation gives significance to the smallest detail, just as the great inductions of geology demonstrate in every pebble the working of laws by which the earth has become adapted for the habitation of man. In this view, religion and philosophy are not merely concili-ated, they are identical; or rather, religion is the crown and consummation of philosophy – the delicate corolla, which can only spread out its petals in all their symmetry and brilliance to the sun, when root and branch exhibit the conditions of a healthy and vigorous life. Mr Mackay's preliminary chapter has an in-dependent value, and would be read with interest by many who might not care to follow him in his subsequent inquiry. The dilemma of sensuousness and sentimentalism is thus excellently put: –

Religion often appears to be a mere sentiment, because the reason by which it should be disciplined requires long cultivation, and can only gradually assume its proper prominence and dignity. The faculties are seldom combined in its avowed service; and from its consequent misdirection has been inferred the impossibility of finding within the limits of the mind an effectual religious guide. It has even been said that religion has properly nothing to do with the head, but is exclusively an exercise of the heart and feelings; that all the teaching or education which can properly be called 'religious', consists 'in the formation of the temper and behaviour, the infusing of devotional feeling, and the implanting of Christian principles'. In other words, the highest faculty of the mind is not required in the service of him who bestowed it. Through this narrow view the sentiments are over-excited; the judgement becomes proportionately languid and incapable, the connexion between the theory of practice and duty[5] is unobserved, and dogmas are blindly learned without regard to their origin or meaning. Superficial religion has everywhere the same result; it fluctuates between the extremes of sensibility[6] and superstition, and exhibits in this respect a curious parallel to the analogous catastrophe of natural[7] philosophy. The uneducated feeling has only the alternative of unquestioning credulity, or of sacrificing and abrogating itself. This is the universal dilemma of artificial creeds; their votaries divide into formalists and sceptics, Pharisees and Sadducees; Calvinism, in our own days, has swung back to rationalism, and the symbolical forms of ancient religion are pronounced by a competent observer to have generally led to these extremes.* The passage is easy from one to the other. The devotional feeling of a Catholic of the middle age might have been destroyed, if the doctrines of Copernicus or Galileo had induced him to mistrust the infallibility of the Pope; and in the days of Sir Thomas Browne, it may have been correct to say that a disbelief in witchcraft implied 'a sort of atheism'. Horace was startled out of his irreligious philosophy by a clap of thunder; but if a heathen who saw an angry Hecate in the eclipsed moon could have understood a modern almanack, he might at once have fallen into the impiety from which Horace was a convert (Sec. 3, p. 9).

Admirable again is the section on Faith, from which we cannot resist giving a long extract: –

Religion and science are inseparable. No object in nature, no subject of contemplation is destitute of a religious tendency and meaning. If religion be made to consist only in traditional and legendary forms, it is of course as distinguishable from science as the Mosaic cosmogony from geology; but if it be the *ascensio mentis in Deum per scalas creatarum rerum*,[8] the evolving the grounds of hope, faith, and duty from the known laws of our being

*Plutarch, *Isis and Osiris*, Chapter 67.

and the constitution of the universe; a religion may be said to include science as its minister, and antiquity, which beheld a divinity in all things, erred only in mistaking its intelligible character, and in making it a mere matter of mystic speculation. In a more limited sense, religion may be contrasted with science, as something beyond and above it; as beginning where science ends, and as a guide through the realms of the unknown. But the known and the unknown are intimately connected and correlative. A superstructure of faith can be securely built only on the foundations of the known. Philosophy and religion have one common aim; they are but different forms of answer to the same great question – that of man and his destination ... Faith is, to a great extent, involuntary; it is a law or faculty of our nature, operating silently and intuitively to supply the imperfections of our knowledge. The boundary between faith and knowledge is, indeed, hard to distinguish. We are said to know our own impressions; to believe in their reality, or in the existence of an external[9] cause of them. It follows that the immediate as well as the more remote inferences from phenomena, are the blended fruit of faith and knowledge; and that though faith, properly speaking, is not knowledge, but the admission of certain inferences beyond knowledge, yet it is almost impossible, in tracing back the operations of the mind, to find any, even the most elementary inference, which is not in some degree a compound of both, and which may not ultimately be resolved into a consistent belief in the results of experience. Faith being thus the inseparable companion and offspring of knowledge, is, like it, liable to modification and correction; that which we call our knowledge of the ultimate purpose of existence being, in fact, only a belief or inference from experience, which would lose its rational value if it were supposed to be so complete and infallible as to exempt us from the necessity of further reflection. All human knowledge must partake of the imperfection of the faculties through which it is derived; and the limited and unsatisfactory character of what we know leaves a wide and most important void to be filled up by our belief. But the more imperfect our knowledge, the more necessary it becomes to examine with suspicion the foundations of the faith so closely connected with it. Faith, as opposed to credulity, and to that blind submission to inexplicable power which usurped its name in the ancient East, is an allegiance of the reason; and as the 'evidence of things unseen', stands on the verge of mysticism, its value must depend on the discretion with which it is formed and used. Like all the other faculties, the belief requires to be educated; as the feet are taught to walk, the lips and tongue to speak, so the capacity of belief must be taught how to build securely, yet not arrogantly, on the data of experience. Faith is not that belief of Saint

Augustine, whose merit increased with the absurdity of the proposition, nor that which attributed to the instigation of God the real or projected murder of an only son. An irrational faith grew out of the opposite extreme of incredulity,[10] when men refused to believe the truth, unless authenticated by sensuous evidence that confounded their understandings. True faith is a belief in things probable; it is the assigning to certain inferences a hypothetical objectivity, and upon the conscious acknowledgement of this hypothetical character alone depends its advantage over fanaticism; its moral value and dignity. Between the opposite risks of credulity and scepticism, it must be guided by those broad principles of reason which all the faculties require for their regulation. Reason alone can in each case determine where credulity begins, and fix the limit beyond which the mind should cease to assign even a qualified objectivity to its own imaginations. In its advanced stages faith is a legitimate result of the calculation of probabilities; it may transcend experience, but can never absolutely contradict it. Faith and knowledge tend mutually to the confirmation and enlargement of each other; faith by verification being often transformed into knowledge, and every increase of knowledge supplying a wider and firmer basis of belief. Faith, as an inference from knowledge, should be consistently inferred from the whole of knowledge; since, when estranged and isolated, it loses its vitality, and the estrangement is as effectual when it is hastily and unfairly inferred as where it is wholly gratuitous. The same experience which is the source of knowledge being, therefore, the only legitimate foundation of faith, a sound faith cannot be derived from the anomalous and exceptional. It is the avidity for the marvellous, and the morbid eagerness for a cheap and easy solution of the mysteries of existence – a solution supposed to be implied in the conception of an arbitrary and unintelligible rule, which has ever retarded philosophy and stultified religion. Faith naturally arises out of the regular and undeviating. The same unerring uniformity, which alone made experience possible, was also the first teacher of the invisible things of God. It is this

> Elder Scripture, writ by God's own hand,
> Scripture authentic, uncorrupt by man,[11]

which is set before every one, without note or comment, and which even Holy Writ points out as the most unquestionable authority by which, both in heaven and earth, the will of God is interpreted to mankind. If man is not permitted to solve the problem of existence, he is at least emboldened to hope, and to infer so much from its actual conditions as to feel confident as to its results. Faith takes up the problem exactly where knowledge leaves it, and, as from confounding the objects of the two have arisen the discords of sects and the puzzles of philosophy, so the discovery of their true relations and limits enables the mind to reconcile and account for the controversies of the past, and in some measure to penetrate the mysteries that occasioned them (*Vol. I*, p. 35).

Having thus indicated the ground on which he takes his stand, Mr Mackay commences his survey and delineation of religious development, selecting that of the Hebrews and Greeks as the most typical and complete, and tracing it up to the period when the combination of the two modes of thought in the Alexandrian theosophy formed that web of metaphysical and religious dogma, which constitutes speculative Christianity. While the Hebrew and Greek religions are his main subject, he has not neglected the copious illustration to be drawn from the Persian, the Hindoo and the Northern mythologies, by indicating instances of analogy and of possible derivation, and thus the *Progress of the Intellect*, is, perhaps, the nearest approach in our language to a satisfactory natural history of religion. The third chapter on the 'Metaphysical Idea of God' is a rich mine of associated facts and ideas; but while admiring the range of learning which it exhibits, it is here that we begin to perceive the author's defects, or rather his redundances. Some of his pages read like extracts from his common-place book, which must be, as Southey said of his own, an urn under the arm of a river-god, rather than like a digested result of study, intended to inform the general reader. Only a devotedness of research such as his own, can give interest and significance to the mass of allusions and particulars with which Mr Mackay overlays, rather than illustrates, his more general passages, which are usually at once profound and lucid. The popular lecturer on science comes before his audience with a selection of striking and apt experiments in readiness, and is silent as to the morning's preparation in the laboratory; and so the scholar, who would produce a work of general utility, must not drag his readers through the whole region of his own researches, but simply present them with an impressive *coup d'œil*. The occasional absence of this artistic working up of materials diminishes the effectiveness of Mr Mackay's admirable work.

The introduction of a truly philosophic spirit into the study of mythology – an introduction for which we are chiefly indebted to the Germans – is a great step in advance of the superficial Lucian-like tone of ridicule adopted by many authors of the eighteenth century, or the orthodox prepossessions of writers such as Bryant,[12] who saw in the Greek legends simply misrepresentations of the authentic history given in the book of Genesis. The enlarged acquaintance with Hindoo literature, and with the monumental records of other ancient nations, which the last half century has brought us, has rendered more possible that wide comparison which is a requisite for all true, scientific generalization. O. Müller[13] says, obviously enough, that if we possessed no other access to Grecian antiquity than its mythology, a systematic and philosophic explanation of the latter would be impossible; and so while the mythology of one nation is studied apart from that of others, or while what is really mythology in the records of any one nation is not recognized as such, but, though it presents the ordinary mythical elements, is accounted for by a special theory; we shall never arrive at a just and full estimate of this phase of man's religious tendencies.

Mr Mackay holds, with Creuzer,[14] that the basis of all mythology was a nature-worship; that 'those interpreters are in the main right, who held that the heathen Pantheon, in its infinite diversity of names and personifications, was but a multitudinous, though in its origin, unconscious allegory, of which physical phenomena, and principally the heavenly bodies, were the fundamental types'. This primitive period of the myth, in which sacerdotal influence was in the ascendant, he thinks may be designated the Orphic or Cabiric, in distinction from the Epic period, which was character-ized by a gradual merging of the mystic or religious feeling in the poetic. He says: – 'Between the life-like Epic and the sombre Orphic style, between the picturesque and eventful romance, in which the gods are the mere machinery of a human drama, and the mystical symbols of theological metaphysics, there must have been many varieties in the treatment of religious legend, tending to reduce its fragmentary materials to the consistent and positive forms in which they are found in Homer.' In this theory, mythical conception, instead of being a step in advance of fetishism, is a decadence of the religious sentiment from that monotheistic or pantheistic impression to which it leaps by its first impulse; general ideas in the process of transmission, or simply as a necessary result of the laws of expression in the early stages of thought, resolve themselves into the crystalline forms of the legend. We will quote the author's own presentation of his opinion. Under the head of 'Relation of Monotheism to Symbolism', he says: –

It is impossible to assume any period of time at which the vague sense of Deity ceased to be a mere feeling and assumed a specific form, or became an 'idea'. The notion of external power must have been almost instantaneously associated with some external object; and the diversified reflections of the Divine easily came to be looked on as substantive and distinct divinities. But however infinite the variety of objects which helped to develop the notion of Deity, and eventually usurped its place, the notion itself was essentially a concentrated or monotheistic one. A vague monotheism resided in the earliest exertions of thought, being nearly identical with that impression of unity and connexion in sensible phenomena, which in its simplest form appears to rise independently of any effort of philosophical comparison. The power of generalization, or of seeing the one in the many, that first element both of science and of religion, is so nearly innate or instinctive as to have been termed by Plato a divine or Promethean gift; and the philosophical conception of the oneness of the universe and of its author, usually regarded as the last acquisition of civilization and reflection, appears to have been anticipated by a natural revelation, an indefinite dread of the aggregate of supersensuous nature; which is said to be common even among savages. In this indefinite feeling must be sought, if anywhere, that conceptional monotheism of primitive ages, which like the virtues of the golden age, makes every successive epoch, unless it be the present, appear only as a stage in the progress of degeneracy and aberration. The genius of religion . . . does not wait for the co-operation of science in order to commence her task, the powers of combination are at work long before the maturity of the reason eventually found necessary to guide them; nay, the origin of religion, like that of civilization, may be said to be free from many of the corruptions attending its onward progress, which arise from the mind's inability to deal unembarrassed with the multitude of sensuous analogies. Generalization begins before a sufficient basis has been prepared to make it legitimate, and every successive step in the research into particulars seems to be in mysterious contradiction to the first hurried conclusion. Hence the universal blending of monotheism with polytheism, and the impossibility of discovering historically, which of the two is older or more original.

Mr Mackay's main proposition, that the substratum of religious symbolism was a worship or deification of the elements, is well sustained by the evidence; but he perhaps overstates the degree in which the monotheistic idea was originally co-existent with poly-theistic personification. To the uncultured intellect, a plurality of divine agencies, analogous to the human, would seem, by their conflicting wills and influences, a natural explanation of physical and moral vicissitudes. As the impression of unity in nature gained force, these agencies would gradually become subordinate to a higher power, but the impression would at first be hardly more than a shadowy presentiment – one of those

> High instincts, before which our mortal nature
> Doth shudder like a guilty thing surprised.[15]

That allegorical elements exist to a considerable extent, in the divine, if not in the heroic myths of Greece, there is strong evidence, both presumptive and internal; and the allegorical interpretation, on the lowest estimate of its soundness, is far superior to the pragmatical or semi-historical, which, in endeavouring to show a nucleus of fact in the myths, exhibits an utter blindness to the mental state in which they originated, and simply substitutes an unpoetical fable for a poetical one. But owing to the manysidedness of all symbols, there is a peculiarly seductive influence in allegorical interpretation; and we observe that all writers who adopt it, though they set out with the largest admissions as to the spontan-eous and unconscious character of mythical allegory, and the manifold modifications which have obscured it, acquire a sort of fanatical faith in their rule of interpretation, and fall into the mistake of supposing that the conscious allegorizing of a modern can be a correct reproduction of what they acknowledge to be unconscious allegorizing in the ancients. We do not see what unconscious allegory can mean, unless it be personification ac-companied with belief, and with the spontaneous, vivid conception of a symbol, as opposed to the premeditated use of a poetical figure; and this belief would lead to an elaboration of the myth, in harmony rather with the attributed personality than with the true physical characteristics of the object personified. As a painter, in treating an allegorical subject, is led on by his artistic feeling to add one detail after another, until the specific idea with which he began becomes subordinate to the general effect; so the exuberant religious imagination of the Greek, which set out with a personification of the sun or the ocean, would generate myths having relation rather to the human symbol than to the real phenomena of its cosmical prototype. Hence it appears to us, that any attempt extensively to trace consistent allegory in the myths must fail. Nor need we regret it, since our interest in the subject is of a different nature from that of the ancient philosophical interpreters, who, living at a period when the myths still constituted the popular religion, were under the necessity of bringing them into accordance with their own moral and religious views. It is enough for us if we have sufficient insight into the myths to form an approximate conception of the state of mind which produced them, and to assign them their true rank in the scale of religious development. Mr Mackay has not escaped the influence of the allegorizing mania; he does not despair of finding the true cosmical meaning of the most natural human incidents in the *Odyssey*, or of the tragic conceptions of the dramatists; but if, like the alchymists, he is sometimes in quest of things not in *rerum natura*,[16] he, like them, elicits much that is suggestive in his search. To criticize details would carry us beyond our limits, and we shall do a greater service to the reader by referring him to the work itself, which, open it where he may, will offer both food and stimulus to his thought.

While the poets of Greece were giving to its religious thought a more and more sensuous expression, its philosophers were working out an opposite result; and Mr Mackay traces this subtilizing process until it reaches the Aristotelian theosophy, of which he gives a comprehensive and clear account.

It is in his theory concerning the religious development of the Hebrews, and in his treatment of their records, that Mr Mackay departs the most widely from prevalent opinion. The idea that many parts of the Old Testament have a mythical character, an idea which was necessary to conciliate them, as well with the philosophic Hebrewism of Philo, as with the Christian morality of Origen,[17] and which has long been familiar to German critics, is still startling to the English theological mind. No thinker of ordinary intelligence can fail to perceive, not merely difference in degree of completeness, but contrast, between the religious conceptions which represented the Deity as sanctioning or prescribing the cunning trickery of Jacob,[18] or the savage cruelties of Joshua,[19] and those which preside over the sublime remonstrances of the prophets; but the explanation is still sought in the theory of accommodation, that is, the puerile and unworthy religious conceptions invariably accompanying an absence of intellectual culture, which in other nations are referred to the general principles of human development, are, in the case of the Hebrews, supposed to have been benevolent falsities on the part of the true God, whereby he allured a barbarous race to his recognition and worship. On this theory, because Abraham had but limited notions of honour and justice, God plagued Pharaoh and Abimelech[20] for being misled by the falsehoods of the father of the faithful, and made those falsehoods redound to the temporal advantage of his chosen servant; because the Israelites were surrounded by examples of idolatrous and sacrificial observance, and had a strong propensity to imitate them, Jehovah, in condescension to their weakness, prescribed for them a ritual analogous in spirit and in symbolism to that of their heathen neighbours: because they were a ferocious race, eager to 'eat of the prey and drink the blood of the slain',[21] a suitable vent for their destructive energies was found in such requirements as the slaughter of 3,000 in their own camp, and the war of extermination against the Canaanites, or in the especial injunction to Joshua to hough the enemy's horses. The only argument by which the theory of accommodation can be sustained is, that in conjunction with that divine countenance of human vice and weakness which it supposes, there were delivered and preserved certain elements of superhuman truth which attest the specifically divine origin of the religion – its distinctive character as a revelation. Now, while the mythical theory does not exclude that more enlarged idea of providential evolution, which sees in the peculiar religious and political history of the Hebrews, a preparation for ushering into the world a religion which anticipates and fulfils the yearnings of man's spiritual nature, it delivers the understanding from a heavy burthen of contradiction and absurdity, and the religious sentiment from the admission of painful anomalies. The fact, that the history of all other nations has a mythical period, urges a strong presumption, that the Hebrew records will not present an exception in this respect, and an unprejudiced examination confirms this presumption. We find there not only a generic similarity to the gentile myths, in a degrading conception of the divine attributes, with a corresponding crudeness and obliquity of moral views, in an ignorant interpretation of physical phenomena, a love of prodigy, and a lavish supposition of gratuitous miracle, but also a specific resemblance in symbolism. This is visible on a cursory glance, but a nearer investigation discloses overwhelming proof, that the Hebrew writings, far from meriting an exceptional confidence, require, from the evidence they exhibit that the Hebrew mind was peculiarly deficient in a true historical sense, special canons of caution in their interpretation. On applying the test of a critical analysis, the books of the Pentateuch resolve themselves into a compilation of distinct documents, differing in date and frequently in spirit and purpose, as may be seen from the variations and contradictions in their accounts of the same event; and the more ancient of these documents presents internal evidence, that it was not in existence earlier than the time of Samuel, about 400 years after Moses. The same artificial coherence, the same arbitrariness of classification and of titles, together with palpable inaccuracies and indications of partisanship, characterize large portions, not only of the remaining historical works, but also of the prophetic. Since these conclusions are denied by no competent critic uncommitted to the maintenance of certain tenets, it would be wise in our theological teachers, instead of struggling to retain a footing for themselves and their doctrine on the crumbling structure of dogmatic interpretation, to cherish those more liberal views of biblical criticism, which, admitting of a development of the Christian system corresponding to the wants and the culture of the age, would enable it to strike a firm root in man's moral nature, and to entwine itself with the growth of those new forms of social life to which we are tending. The spirit which doubts the ultimately beneficial tendency of inquiry, which thinks that morality and religion will not bear the broadest daylight our intellect can throw on them, though it may clothe itself in robes of sanctity and use pious phrases, is the worst form of atheism; while he who believes, whatever else he may deny, that the true and the good are synonymous, bears in his soul the essential element of religion. Viewed in this relation, the *Progress of the Intellect* is a valuable addition to recent examples of plain speaking – of that παρρησία[22] which Paul held to be the proper effect of confidence in the excellence of revelation, whose manifestation was in the spirit, and not in the letter.

Before stating Mr Mackay's theory concerning the Hebrew history and religion, we must express our regret that the force of his conclusions is weakened by his unduly insisting on details difficult of proof, by a frequently infelicitous citation, and by his not giving due value to a free poetical impulse in the figurative language of the Hebrews, a deficiency which sometimes leads him into an almost trivial literalness of interpretation. But notwithstanding these occasional defects, the chapters which treat principally of the Hebrews will repay a close study, both from their suggestiveness, and the soundness of their general views. Mr Mackay holds that the original God of the Israelites was no other than the Nature-God, El or Ilus, worshipped in Arabia, Palestine, and Phœnicia, with licentious and sanguinary rites, under the double aspect of Baal and Moloch; and that the purer worship of Jehovah, inculcated by the prophets, and established by Josiah, was a religious reformation among the Hebrews, generated by the growth in civilization consequent on an enlarged commercial intercourse with foreign nations, and contemporaneous with a movement of religious reform which took place throughout Asia, about 700 BC, 'connected in India with the name of Buddha, in Persia (or Media), with that of Zoroaster, and a century later extending itself by Xenophanes and Heraclitus into Greece'. According to this theory, the calf-worship in the wilderness and under the kings, the altars in the high places, and the atrocities of the valley of Hinnom, were not acts of apostasy, but of persistence in early barbarism. In Mr Mackay's opinion, the account of the Passover, as it now stands, is the veil which the purer conceptions of later Hebrews cast over the ancient custom of sacrificing firstborn children to the bloodthirsty El; the massacre of 3,000 Israelites, represented in Exodus as retributive, was probably sacrificial – a huge offering to the same demon, the rather that Aaron, the leader in the calf-worship, was not involved in the same destruction; the command by which God is said to have tempted Abraham, the vow of Jephthah, the slaughter of the seven descendants of Saul, whereby David sought to propitiate his God and avert a famine, are indications that human sacrifices were familiar to the Hebrews; above all, that 'passing of children through the fire', recorded of so many kings, and indignantly denounced by the prophets, as a practice habitual to the nation, is most probably to be interpreted as an actual immolation. The somewhat obscure passage, Amos 5:25, 26 – 'Have ye offered unto me sacrifices and offerings in the wilderness forty years, O house of Israel? But ye have borne the tabernacle of your Moloch and Chiun, your images, the star of your God which ye made to yourselves' – Mr Mackay thinks important as conveying a denial of the early existence of a pure, Jehovistic religion. A disputed passage is, of course, dubious ground for an inference; but there is ample evidence of a less questionable kind, that the early Hebrew God, whether identical or not with any heathen deity, was of a character widely different from the one proclaimed by Micah, as requiring nothing of man but to do justly, to love mercy, and to walk humbly with God.

The original presiding Deity of Israel was, in Mr Mackay's words, 'emphatically the terrific God'. The Old Testament abounds in pictures of Divine operations that cannot be regarded as true delineations of the real character of Deity; but only distortions of it, analogous to those exhibited in the mythologies of other countries. The judicious reader of the Hebrew Scriptures, however orthodox his faith, cannot fail to perceive that they exhibit a progress from degrading to enlightened views of Divine nature and government. The writings of the prophets are full of protests against the conceptions of popular ignorance, and by continually expanding and purifying the Jewish ideas of Deity, prepared the way for the reception of the teachings of Christ. This view of the progressive character of 'revelation' does not depend for its evidence on minute points of criticism; it rests rather upon broad facts which are open to the apprehension of the most unlearned: and the *Progress of the Intellect* abounds in statements which place them in the most forcible point of view. To a greater or less extent they are now recognized by Christians of all denominations, and it is impossible to take up the writings, or listen to the discourses of the leading men of any church or sect, without perceiving the influence which they have exerted upon their minds.

Mr Mackay's analysis and history of the theory of Mediation, from its earliest mythical embodiments, those 'flowers which fancy strewed before the youthful steps of Psyche, when she first set out in pursuit of the immortal object of her love', to its subtilization in philosophy – his delineation of the origin of Christianity as an expansion of the prophetic spiritualism, yet carrying within it certain elements of Jewish symbolism, which have arrested its true development and perverted its influence – his final sketch of the confluence of Greek Philosophy and Christianized Hebrewism – are admirable, both from their panoramic breadth and their richness in illustrative details. We can only recommend the reader to resort himself to this treasury of mingled thought and learning, and as a further inducement, we will quote the concluding passage from the section on the 'Mediation of Philosophy'.

The true religious philosophy of an imperfect being is not a system of creed, but, as Socrates thought, an infinite search or approximation. Finality is but another name for bewilderment or defeat, the common affectation of indolence and superstition, a temporary suspension of the mind's health arising from prejudice, and especially from the old error of clinging too closely to notions found instrumental in assisting it after they have ceased to be serviceable, and striving rather to defend and retain them, than to make them more correct. A remnant of the mythical lurks in the very sanctuary of science. Forms or theories ever fall short of nature, though they are ever tending to reach a position above nature, and may often be found really to include more than the maker of them at the time knew. To a certain extent they are reliable and complete; as a system of knowledge they are but intermediate and preparatory. As matter is the soul's necessary instrument, so ignorance, more or less mixed up with all its expressions and forms, may be said to be as it were the eyelid through which it gradually opens itself to the truth, admitting no more than it can for the time support, and, as through a veil, learning to support its lustre. The old religionists discovered a universal cause, personified it and prayed to it. The mere notion seemed not only to satisfy the religious feeling, but to solve all problems. Nations unanimously subscribed to the pious formula, which satisfied their imaginations, and pleased their vanity by cheating them into a belief that they were wise;

but which, at the same time, supplanted nature by tradition, the sources of truth by artificial disguises, and at last paralysed the sentiment which gave birth to it. Science, unlike the rude expedient which stupefied without nourishing the mind, gratifies the religious feeling without arresting it, and opening out the barren mystery of the one into more explicit and manageable 'forms' expressing, not indeed his essence, but his will, feeds an endless enthusiasm by accumulating for ever new objects of pursuit. We have long experienced that knowledge is profitable; we are beginning to find out that it is moral, and shall at last discover it to be religious. Aristotle declared the highest and truest science to be that which is most disinterested; Bacon, treating science as separate from religion, asserted knowledge to be power, and held that truth must be tested by its fruits, that is, its instrumentality in promoting the right and the useful. Both assertions may be justified and reconciled by the fact that, while no real knowledge is powerless or fruitless, the fruits differ in refinement and value, the highest being unquestionably those disinterested gratifications which minister to the highest wants of the highest faculties, and which earned for philosophy the title of a divine love, realizing the mysterious longing of the soul, and promoting the accomplishment of its destiny,

> To rise in science as in bliss,
> Initiate in the secrets of the skies.[23]

W. R. Greg's *The Creed of Christendom*

(*Leader*, 20 September 1851)

ENGLISH PROTESTANTISM, effete as it seems in its ecclesiastical and sectarian forms, is manifesting the vitality of its roots in the vigorous and rapid growth of free religious inquiry among earnest men. The writers who are heading the present movement against dogmatic theology, are not mere speculators enamoured of theory, and careless of its practical results. Still less are they anti-religious zealots, who identify all faith with superstition. They are men at once devout and practical, who have been driven into antagonism with the dominant belief by the force of their moral, no less than of their intellectual nature, and who have been led to the avowal of that antagonism, not simply by the impulse of candour, but by an interest in the spiritual well-being of society. They know that to call dogmatic Christianity the popular creed is a misnomer; that the doctrines taught in our pulpits neither have, nor can have, any hold on the masses; and that if our population is to be Christianized, religious teaching must be conducted in a new spirit and on new principles. They protest against the current faith, because they would substitute for it one purer and more influential; they lay the axe to the old, only that there may be freer play for the energies which are ever tending to the development of the new and more perfect.

Among these pioneers of the New Reformation, Mr Greg is likely to be one of the most effective. Without any pretension to striking originality or extensive learning, his work perhaps all the more exhibits that sound, practical judgement, which discerns at once the *hinge* of a question, and it bears throughout the impress of an honesty, geniality, and refinement which imply a moral nature of a very high order. The absence of any very profound critical erudition, far from disqualifying Mr Greg for the task he has undertaken, is essential to the aim of this book – namely, to show at what conclusions concerning the Bible and Christianity a sensible, educated layman is likely to arrive, with such an amount of critical attainment as is compatible with the work that lies before him in daily life. If such conclusions must necessarily be unsound because they are formed in ignorance of the last new edition of every biblical critic, orthodox or heterodox, the right of private judgement is a nullity, and the unclerical mind must either dismiss the subject altogether, or surrender itself to a more consistent spiritual despotism than that of Protestant divines. *The Creed of Christendom* claims the attention of the theologian, not that it may teach him biblical criticism, but that it may render him more familiar with the impression made by the vexed questions of his science on an earnest, cultivated mind, cut off by no barrier of caste or prejudice from full sympathy and acquaintance with the spirit and wants of the age. Another class of readers to whom it is adapted, are those struggling towards free religious thought amidst the impediments of critical ignorance and early artificial associations. To such, Mr Greg's book will be valuable, both as an introductory manual of biblical criticism and as a help in the consideration of certain moral questions.

In stating the reasons which urged him to publication, Mr Greg says: –

Much observation of the conversation and controversy of the religious world had wrought the conviction that the evil resulting from the received notions as to scriptural authority has been immensely underestimated. I was compelled to see that there is scarcely a low and dishonouring conception of God current among men, scarcely a narrow and malignant passion of the human heart, scarcely a moral obliquity, scarcely a political error or misdeed, which biblical texts are not, and may not be, without any violence to their obvious signification, adduced to countenance and justify. On the other hand I was compelled to see how many clear, honest, and aspiring minds have been hampered and baffled in their struggles after truth and light, how many tender, pure, and loving hearts have been hardened, perverted, and forced to a denial of their nobler nature and their better instincts, by the ruthless influence of some passages of Scripture which seemed in the clearest language to condemn the good and to denounce the true. No work contributed more than Mr Newman's *Phases of Faith*,[1] to force upon me the conviction that little progress can be hoped, either for religious science or charitable feeling, till the question of biblical authority shall have been placed upon a sounder footing, and viewed in a very different light.

Mr Greg sets out by examining the dogma of scriptural inspiration, which he justly regards as the keystone of Protestant orthodoxy. After considering separately each of the grounds on which it rests, he concludes that there is no valid foundation for believing the Hebrew and Christian canonical writings to be inspired, in the ordinary acceptation of the word – that is, dictated or suggested by God; that hence we must regard them '*as records, not revelations*; as histories, to be investigated like other histories; documents, of which the date, the authorship, the genuineness, the accuracy of the text, are to be ascertained by the same principles[2] as we apply to other documents'. Having thus cleared away the dazzling haze with which the inspiration dogma invests the biblical writings, he proceeds to investigate the genuineness and authenticity of the Old Testament canon, and traces briefly but forcibly the chief results of modern criticism in relation to this subject; indicating such of the reasons on which they are founded as are readily appreciable by the general reader. According to these results, no longer held debatable by critics of high standing, the Pentateuch, instead of being, as is popularly supposed, the production of Moses, is a compilation from separate documents, the earliest of which must have been written as late as the time of Saul; while the whole book of Deuteronomy, and many parts of the preceding books, are irrefragably proved by the subsequent history of the Hebrews to have had no existence prior to the reign of Josiah. Mr Greg instances some of the straits to which English divines have been driven, in the effort to maintain the authority of the Old Testament in the face of scientific discovery; and dwells on the advantage which would accrue, not only to the truthfulness of divines, but to the real instructiveness of the Hebrew writings, if the latter were regarded as merely human narratives, traditions, and speculations. He next discusses the prophecies, and adduces many considerations tending to prove how far we are from posses sing that clear knowledge concerning them which alone could warrant the conclusions of orthodoxy. In his opinion, –

The Hebrew prophets were wise, gifted, earnest men, deeply conversant with the Past – looking far into the Future – shocked with the unrighteousness around them – sagacious to see impending evil – bold to denounce wickedness in high places – imbued, above all, with an unfailing faith, peculiarly strong among their people, that national delinquency and national virtue would alike meet with a temporal and inevitable retribution – and gifted 'with the glorious faculty of poetic hope, exerted on human prospects, and presenting its results with the vividness of prophecy' – but prophets in no stricter sense than this.

The Theism of the Hebrews, Mr Greg maintains, was impure and progressive; they arrived at their monotheism by the same stages that characterize the development of the human race in general, the Old Testament exhibiting strong evidence that the Hebrew deity was originally a family god, elevated by Moses to the dignity of a national god, and ultimately, owing to the influence of prophets and sages, and yet more to the contact of the Hebrews with other Oriental nations, expanded into the God of the Universe.

The claims of the New Testament on our credence are next considered. The chapters on the 'Origin of the Gospels' and the 'Fidelity of the Gospel History' contain no fresh contributions to biblical criticism, nor anything new to persons conversant with this class of subjects; but they are a well-arranged summary of salient facts and arguments, gathered chiefly from Strauss, Hug, Schleiermacher, and Hennell.[3] The conclusions to which the writer is led are, that we have no certitude as to the Gospels conveying the testimony of eyewitnesses, while, on the other hand, there is the strongest evidence of their containing a large admixture of legend, and that we can trust them no further than as giving an outline of Christ's life and teaching. Hence Mr Greg holds that dogmas founded on sayings attributed to Jesus, but discordant with the impression of his character conveyed by the general tenor of the Gospels, must be rejected; for example, the dogmas of the necessity of belief to salvation, the proper Deity of Christ, and the Atonement. We quote some of his reflections on these results: –

In fine, then, we arrive at this irresistible conclusion, that, knowing many passages in the Evangelists to be unauthentic, and having reason to suspect the authenticity of many others, and not being able with absolute certainty to point to any which are perfectly and indubitably authentic – the probability *in favour* of the fidelity of any of the texts relied on to prove the peculiar and perplexing doctrines of modern orthodoxy, is far inferior to the probability *against* the truth of those doctrines. A doctrine perplexing to our reason, and painful to our feelings, *may* be from God; but in this case the proof of its being from God must be proportionately clear and irrefragable; the assertion of it in a narrative, which does not scruple to attribute to God's messenger words which he never uttered, is not only no proof, but does not even amount to a presumption. There is no text in the Evangelists, the Divine (or Christian) origin of which is sufficiently unquestionable to enable it to serve as the foundation of doctrines repugnant to natural feeling or to common sense.

But it will be objected, if these conclusions are sound, absolute uncertainty is thrown over the whole Gospel history, and over all Christ's teaching. To this we reply, *in limine*, in the language of Algernon Sydney, 'No consequence can destroy a truth';[4] the sole matter for consideration is, Are our arguments correct? – not, Do they lead to a result which is embarrassing and unwelcome?

But the inference is excessive; the premises do not reach so far. The uncertainty thrown is not over the main points of Christ's history, which, after all retrenchments, still stands out an intelligible, though a skeleton account – not over the grand features, the pervading tone of his doctrines or his character, which still present to us a clear, consistent, and splendid delineation; but over those individual statements, passages, and discourses which mar this delineation – which break its unity – which destroy its consistency – which cloud its clearness – which tarnish its beauty. The gain to us seems immense.

It is true we have no longer *absolute* certainty with regard to any one especial text or scene; such is neither necessary nor attainable; it is true that, instead of passively accepting the whole heterogeneous and indigestible mass, we must, by the careful and conscientious exercise of those faculties with which we are endowed, by ratiocination and moral tact, separate what Christ did, from what he did not teach, as best we may. But the task will be difficult to those only who look in the Gospels for a minute, dogmatic, and sententious creed; not to those who seek only to learn Christ's spirit that they may imbibe it, and to comprehend his views of virtue and of God, that they may draw strength and consolation from those fountains of living water.

In discussing the limits of apostolic wisdom and authority, Mr Greg's prepossessions, perhaps, lead him to heighten the difference between the spirit and teaching of the Apostles and those of their Master; but for much that he maintains under this head, he has strictly critical grounds. His observations on the misapprehension of the Apostles and the early Church concerning the 'gift of tongues', are especially just and pointed. In the chapter on miracles, he treats the subject chiefly on *a priori* grounds, and only cursorily touches on the question whether the miraculous narratives in the Gospels bear the marks of credibility. He argues for the position, long ago strenuously maintained by Locke,[5] and admitted by many even of our orthodox divines, that a miracle can never authenticate a doctrine; and he further shows, that miracles are not a safe foundation on which to rest the claims of Christianity, inasmuch as they are not susceptible of proof by *documentary* evidence. The crowning miracle of the Resurrection he considers separately, giving a condensed analysis of the evidence on which it rests. The conclusion that this evidence is insufficient is, he thinks, rendered needlessly painful by the undue doctrinal value assigned by theologians to the Resurrection of Christ, whether as a sanction of his doctrines, or as a type and pledge of our own resurrection; for, viewed in the one light it is superfluous, while in the other, it utterly fails of the supposed end, since a bodily resurrection after three days' interment, can bear no resemblance to anything that awaits ourselves.

Even after the renunciation of implicit credence in the Gospel narratives and apostolic writings, and the rejection of all miraculous evidence, the question remains – Is Christianity a revealed religion? Since, however, the lustre of Christ's life and teachings may have been obscured by the errors and limitations of his biographers and immediate disciples, it is still possible that he may have had a special divine mission. In seeking for an answer to this question, Mr Greg 'finds no adequate reason for believing Jesus to be the son of God, nor his doctrines to be a direct and special revelation'. The following is his conception of Jesus: –

We do not believe that Christianity contains anything which a genius like Christ's, brought up and nourished as his had been, might not have disentangled for itself. We hold that God has so arranged matters in this beautiful and well-ordered but mysteriously governed universe, that one great mind after another will arise from time to time, as such are needed, to discover and flash forth before the eyes of men the truths that are wanted, and the amount of truth that can be borne. We conceive that this is effected by endowing them – or (for we pretend to no scholastic nicety of expression) by having arranged that nature and the course of events shall send them into the world endowed with that superior mental and moral organization, in which grand truths, sublime gleams of spiritual light, will spontaneously and inevitably arise. Such a one we believe was Jesus of Nazareth – the most exalted genius whom God ever sent upon earth; in himself an embodied revelation; humanity in its divinest phase – 'God manifest in the flesh', according to Eastern hyperbole; an exemplar vouchsafed, in an early age of the world, of what man may and should become, in the course of ages, in his progress towards the realization of his destiny; an individual gifted with a glorious intellect, a noble soul, a fine organization, and a perfectly balanced moral being; and who, by virtue of these endowments, saw further than all other men –

> Beyond the verge of that blue sky,
> Where God's sublimest secrets lie;[6]

an earnest, not only of what humanity may be, but of what it will be, when the most perfected races shall bear the same relation to the finest minds of existing times, as these now bear to the Bushmen and the Esquimaux. He was, as Parker beautifully expresses it, 'the possibility of the race made real'.[7] He was a sublime poet, prophet, hero, and philosopher; and had the usual fate of such – misrepresented by his enemies, misconstrued by his friends; unhappy in this, that his nearest intimates and followers were not of a calibre to understand him; happy in this, that his words contained such undying seeds of truth as could survive even the media through which they passed. Like the wheat found in the Egyptian catacombs, they retain the power of germinating undiminished, whenever their appropriate soil is found. They have been preserved almost pure, notwithstanding the Judaic narrowness of Peter, the orthodox passions of John, and the metaphysical subtleties of Paul. Everything seems to us to confirm the conclusion that we have in the Christianity of Scripture a code of beautiful, simple, sublime, profound, *but not perfect* truth, obscured by having come down to us by the intervention of minds far inferior to that of its Author; narrowed by their uncultivation; marred by their misapprehensions; and tarnished by their foreign admixtures. It is a collection of grand truths transmitted to us by men who only half comprehended their grandeur, and imperfectly grasped their truth.

If Christianity be no longer regarded as a revelation, but as the conception of a fallible though transcendently gifted mind, it follows that only so much of it is to be accepted as harmonizes with the reason and conscience: Christianity becomes 'Christian Eclecticism'. Mr Greg unhesitatingly receives many of Christ's precepts as unsurpassable and unimprovable: for example, those which inculcate the worthlessness of ceremonial observance and the necessity of active virtue, purity of heart as the security for purity of life, universal philanthropy, forgiveness of injuries, self-sacrifice in the cause of duty, humility, and genuine sincerity. He regards as next in perfection the views which Christianity unfolds of God as a Father.

In the two great points essential to our practical life, viz., our feelings towards God and our conduct towards man, the Gospels contain little about which men can differ – little from which they can dissent. He is our Father, we are all brethren. This much lies open to the most ignorant and busy, as fully as to the most leisurely and learned. This needs no priest to teach it, no authority to endorse it. The rest is speculation; intensely interesting, indeed, but of no practical necessity.

Other tenets taught in the Christian Scriptures, however, Mr Greg thinks open to grave objections. He urges, for example, that the New Testament assigns an efficacy to prayer incompatible with any elevated conception of Deity; that it inculcates resignation, not as the result of a self-reasoning faith in the wisdom and justice of the supreme will, but on the narrow ground that sufferings are specially ordained for the benefit of the individual; and that it appeals to the selfish motives – the desire for recompense, rather than to the highest – the love of the good for its own sake. He holds that the conception of the pardon of sin, or repentance and conversion, tends to contravene the system on which man is trained and disciplined, and the entire scheme of God's government – the conviction that every breach of the Divine law is attended with inexorable consequences, being essential to a healthy condition of the conscience and a just theory of Providence: –

Let any one look back upon his past career, look inward on his daily life, and then say what effect would be produced upon him, were the conviction once fixedly embedded in his soul, that everything done is done irrevocably, that even the omnipotence of God cannot *uncommit* a deed, cannot make that undone which has been done; that every act of his *must* bear its allotted fruit according to the everlasting laws – must remain for ever ineffaceably inscribed on the tablets of universal Nature. And, then, let him consider what would have been the result upon the moral condition of our race, had all men ever held this conviction.

Perhaps you have led a youth of dissipation and excess which has undermined and enfeebled your constitution, and you have transmitted this injured and enfeebled constitution to your children. They suffer, in consequence, through life; suffering is entailed upon them; your repentance, were it in sackcloth and ashes, cannot help you or them. Your punishment is tremendous, but it is legitimate and inevitable. You have broken Nature's laws, or you have ignored them, and no one violates or neglects them with impunity. What a lesson for timely reflection and obedience is here!

Again – you have broken the seventh commandment. You grieve – you repent – you resolutely determine against any such weakness in future. It is well; but 'you know that God is merciful – you feel that he will forgive you'. You are comforted. But no – there is no forgiveness of sins – the injured party may forgive you – your accomplice or victim may forgive you, according to the meaning of human language; but *the deed is done*, and all the powers of Nature, were they to conspire in your behalf, could not make it undone; the consequences to the body – the consequences to the soul – though no man may perceive them, *are there* – are written in the annals of the past, and must reverberate through all time.

But all this, let it be understood, in no degree militates against the value or the necessity of repentance. Repentance, contrition of soul, bears, like every other act, its own fruit – the fruit of purifying the heart, of amending the future: not as man has hitherto conceived – of effacing the past. The commission of sin is an irrevocable act, but it does not incapacitate the soul for virtue. Its consequences cannot be expunged, but the course need not be pursued. Sin, though it is ineffaceable, calls for no despair, but for efforts more energetic than before. Repentance is still as valid as ever; but it is valid to secure the future, not to obliterate the past.

The moral to be drawn from these reflections is this: – God has placed the lot of man – not, perhaps, altogether of the individual, but certainly of the race – in his own hands, by surrounding him with *laws*, on knowledge of which, and on conformity to which, his well-being depends. The study of these, and the principle of obedience to them, forms, therefore, the great aim of education, both of men and nations. They must be taught: –

  1. The *physical laws*, on which God has made *health* to depend.

2. The *moral laws*, on which He has made *happiness* to depend.

3. The *intellectual laws*, on which He has made knowledge to depend.

4. The *social and political laws*, on which He has made *national prosperity* to depend.

5. The *economic laws*, on which He has made *wealth* to depend.

A true comprehension of all these, *and of their unexceptional and unalterable nature*, would ultimately rescue mankind from all their vice and nearly all their suffering, save casualties and sorrows.

Mr Greg also shows that Christianity teaches an ascetic and depreciating view of life, incompatible with that energetic devotion to the improvement of our races, and with that delight in the innocent adornment of our existence in this world, which are essential to a noble and well-balanced soul.

In the concluding chapter we have the author's reflections on 'the great enigma – the question of man's future existence'. He applies himself, evidently with his utmost strength, to prove the invalidity and even futility of a conclusion which, after all, he himself holds. He labours to make clear that the belief in a future state is not demanded by any process of our intellect or any tendency of our moral nature, in order that he may fall back with the greater confidence on the assertion of his belief in it as an intuition on a par with our belief in the reality of an external world.

We have endeavoured to give our readers a faithful idea of Mr Greg's work. Though far from setting our seal to all his opinions, we think that *The Creed of Christendom* sets forth very powerfully much truth of which society is in urgent need, while it opens to us an acquaintance with an individual mind possessing a strong moral and intellectual charm.

The deservedly respectful reception of Mr Greg's work by the periodical press, compared with that given twelve years ago to a work of kindred character – Hennell's *Inquiry Concerning the Origin of Christianity*[8] – is no slight indication of advancement, either in plain-speaking or in liberality of religious views. Though too distinct in their method, and to a considerable extent in their matter, for one to be regarded as superseding the other, both these works have the same object, to ascertain how far the popular idea of Christianity will sustain the test of impartial criticism; they are alike animated by a spirit of candour and reverence, and they have substantially the same result. Hennell, it is true, holds that Jesus shared the common theocratic hope of his nation, and thinks there is strong evidence that, at the commencement of his career, he expected the Divine attestation to his Messiahship to be given in such a general adhesion of the people to his cause as would enable him to free his nation from the Roman yoke by insurrection, and effect the political as well as the spiritual regeneration of Israel. He regards the character of Jesus as less exceptional than it appears under Mr Greg's view; but he estimates very highly the power and beauty of his nature and the value of his moral teaching. The *Inquiry Concerning the Origin of Christianity* is evidently the production of a mind which has brought to the independent study of the New Testament the rare combination of analytic acumen with breadth of conception. Its merit was at once recognized in Germany, where it was speedily translated. While in our own country it was welcomed by many distinguished minds, and has had an extensive, though latent, influence in promoting the intelligent study of the Christian Scriptures. That Mr Greg has found it a valuable aid is not only evidenced in his text, but avowed by frequent references in his notes, though, doubtless through a temporary forgetfulness, he speaks in his preface as if he had no predecessor among laymen in the path of free but reverent inquiry into the claims of Christianity.

Nevertheless, when Hennell's work first appeared, the Reviews dared not acknowledge the merit which it was privately admitted to possess, and four years after the appearance of the second edition, it received, from a periodical which has recently bestowed elaborate praise on *The Creed of Christendom*,[9] a rather contemptuous critique, the object of which was, obviously, to put down the book by no fairer means than that of presenting details, adduced by Hennell merely in the light of cumulative evidence, as if they formed the sole basis of his argument.

In this *annus mirabilis* of 1851, however, our reviewers have attained a higher standard of courage and fairness than could be ascribed to them in 1838, or even in 1845. 'La terre tourne,' says Pascal, 'malgré qu'on le nie; et vous aussi, mes révérends pères, vous tournez avec elle' – 'The earth turns in spite of all denials; and you also, my reverend fathers, turn with it.'[10]

Thomas Carlyle's *Life of John Sterling*

(*Westminster Review*, January 1852)

AS SOON as the closing of the Great Exhibition afforded a reasonable hope that there would once more be a reading public, *The Life of Sterling* appeared. A new work by Carlyle must always be among the literary births eagerly chronicled by the journals and greeted by the public. In a book of such parentage we care less about the subject than about its treatment, just as we think the *Portrait of a Lord* worth studying if it come from the pencil of a Vandyck. The life of John Sterling, however, has intrinsic interest, even if it be viewed simply as the struggle of a restless aspiring soul, yearning to leave a distinct impress of itself on the spiritual development of humanity, with that fell disease which, with a refinement of torture, heightens the susceptibility and activity of the faculties, while it undermines their creative force. Sterling, moreover, was a man thoroughly in earnest, to whom poetry and philosophy were not merely another form of paper currency or a ladder to fame, but an end in themselves – one of those finer spirits with whom, amidst the jar and hubbub of our daily life,

> The melodies abide
> Of the everlasting chime.[1]

But his intellect was active and rapid, rather than powerful, and in all his writings we feel the want of a stronger electric current to give that vigour of conception and felicity of expression, by which we distinguish the undefinable something called genius; while his moral nature, though refined and elevated, seems to have been subordinate to his intellectual tendencies and social qualities, and to have had itself little determining influence on his life. His career was less exceptional than his character: a youth marked by delicate health and studious tastes, a short-lived and not very successful

share in the management of the *Athenæum*, a fever of sympathy
with Spanish patriots, arrested before it reached a dangerous crisis
by an early love affair ending in marriage, a fifteen months'
residence in the West Indies, eight months of curate's duty at
Herstmonceux, relinquished on the ground of failing health, and
through his remaining years a succession of migrations to the
South in search of a friendly climate, with the occasional publication of an 'article', a tale, or a poem in *Blackwood* or elsewhere, –
this, on the prosaic background of an easy competence, was what
made up the outer tissue of Sterling's existence. The impression of
his intellectual power on his personal friends seems to have been
produced chiefly by the eloquence and brilliancy of his conversation; but the mere reader of his works and letters would augur
from them neither the wit, nor the *curiosa felicitas*[2] of epithet and
imagery, which would rank him with the men whose sayings are
thought worthy of perpetuation in books of table-talk and 'ana'.[3]
The public, then, since it is content to do without biographies of
much more remarkable men, cannot be supposed to have felt any
pressing demand even for a single life of Sterling; still less, it might
be thought, when so distinguished a writer as Archdeacon Hare
had furnished this, could there be any need for another. But, in
opposition to the majority of Mr Carlyle's critics, we agree with
him that the first life is properly the justification of the second.
Even among the readers personally unacquainted with Sterling,
those who sympathized with his ultimate alienation from the
Church, rather than with his transient conformity, were likely to
be dissatisfied with the entirely apologetic tone of Hare's life,
which, indeed, is confessedly an incomplete presentation of Sterling's mental course after his opinions diverged from those of his
clerical biographer; while those attached friends (and Sterling
possessed the happy magic that secures many such) who knew him
best during this latter part of his career, would naturally be
pained to have it represented, though only by implication, as a
sort of deepening declension ending in a virtual retractation. Of
such friends Carlyle was the most eminent, and perhaps the most
highly valued, and, as co-trustee with Archdeacon Hare of Sterling's literary character and writings, he felt a kind of responsibility
that no mistaken idea of his departed friend should remain before

the world without correction. Evidently, however, his *Life of Sterling* was not so much the conscientious discharge of a trust as a labour of love, and to this is owing its strong charm. Carlyle here shows us his 'sunny side'. We no longer see him breathing out threatenings and slaughter as in the *Latter-day Pamphlets*, but moving among the charities and amenities of life, loving and beloved – a Teufelsdröckh still, but humanized by a Blumine worthy of him.[4] We have often wished that genius would incline itself more frequently to the task of the biographer, – that when some great or good personage dies, instead of the dreary three or five volumed compilations of letter, and diary, and detail, little to the purpose, which two thirds of the reading public have not the chance, nor the other third the inclination, to read, we could have a real 'Life', setting forth briefly and vividly the man's inward and outward struggles, aims, and achievements, so as to make clear the meaning which his experience has for his fellows. A few such lives (chiefly, indeed, autobiographies) the world possesses, and they have, perhaps, been more influential on the formation of character than any other kind of reading. But the conditions required for the perfection of life writing, – personal intimacy, a loving and poetic nature which sees the beauty and the depth of familiar things, and the artistic power which seizes characteristic points and renders them with life-like effect, – are seldom found in combination. *The Life of Sterling* is an instance of this rare conjunction. Its comparatively tame scenes and incidents gather picturesqueness and interest under the rich lights of Carlyle's mind. We are told neither too little nor too much; the facts noted, the letters selected, are all such as serve to give the liveliest conception of what Sterling was and what he did; and though the book speaks much of other persons, this collateral matter is all a kind of scene-painting, and is accessory to the main purpose. The portrait of Coleridge, for example, is precisely adapted to bring before us the intellectual region in which Sterling lived for some time before entering the Church. Almost every review has extracted this admirable description, in which genial veneration and compassion struggle with irresistible satire; but the emphasis of quotation cannot be too often given to the following pregnant paragraph: –

The truth is, I now see Coleridge's talk and speculation was the emblem of himself. In it, as in him, a ray of heavenly inspiration struggled, in a tragically ineffectual degree, with the weakness of flesh and blood. He says once, he 'had skirted the howling deserts of infidelity'. This was evident enough; but he had not had the courage, in defiance of pain and terror, to press resolutely across said deserts to the new firm lands of faith beyond; he preferred to create logical *fata morganas*[5] for himself on this hither side, and laboriously solace himself with these.

The above-mentioned step of Sterling – his entering the Church – is the point on which Carlyle is most decidedly at issue with Archdeacon Hare.[6] The latter holds that had Sterling's health permitted him to remain in the Church, he would have escaped those aberrations from orthodoxy, which, in the clerical view, are to be regarded as the failure and shipwreck of his career, apparently thinking, like that friend of Arnold's[7] who recommended a curacy as the best means of clearing up Trinitarian difficulties, that 'orders' are a sort of spiritual backboard, which, by dint of obliging a man to look as if he were strait, end by making him so. According to Carlyle, on the contrary, the real 'aberration' of Sterling was his choice of the clerical profession, which was simply a mistake as to his true vocation: –

Sterling was not intrinsically, nor had ever been in the highest or chief degree, a devotional mind. Of course all excellence in man, and worship as the supreme excellence, was part of the inheritance of this gifted man; but if called to define him, I should say artist, not saint, was the real bent of his being.

Again: –

No man of Sterling's veracity, had he clearly consulted his own heart, or had his own heart been capable of clearly responding, and not been bewildered by transient fantasies and theosophic moonshine, could have undertaken this function. His heart would have answered, 'No, thou canst not. What is incredible to thee, thou shalt not, at thy soul's peril, attempt to believe! Elsewhither for a refuge, or die here. Go to perdition if thou must, but not with a lie in thy mouth; by the eternal Maker, no!'

From the period when Carlyle's own acquaintance with Sterling commenced, the *Life* has a double interest, from the glimpses it gives us of the writer, as well as of his hero. We are made present at their first introduction to each other; we get a lively idea of their colloquies and walks together, and in this easy way, without any heavy disquisition or narrative, we obtain a clear insight into Sterling's character and mental progress. Above all, we are gladdened with a perception of the affinity that exists between noble souls, in spite of diversity in ideas – in what Carlyle calls 'the logical outcome' of the faculties. This *Life of Sterling* is a touching monument of the capability human nature possesses of the highest love, the love of the good and beautiful in character, which is, after all, the essence of piety. The style of the work, too, is for the most part at once pure and rich; there are passages of deep pathos which come upon the reader like a strain of solemn music, and others which show that aptness of epithet, that masterly power of close delineation, in which, perhaps, no writer has excelled Carlyle.

We have said that we think this second *Life of Sterling* justified by the first; but were it not so, the book would justify itself.

Lord Brougham's Literature

(Leader, 7 July 1855)

IT IS matter of very common observation that members of the 'privileged classes', who, either from want of work or want of ability to do their proper work, find their time hang rather heavily on their hands, try to get rid of it by employments which, if not self-imposed, they would think rather pitiable. Kings and emperors have turned their hands to making locks and sealing-wax; ambassadresses have collected old stockings for the sake of darning them; and we knew a wealthy old gentleman who devoted himself to making pokers, which he presented to all the ladies of his acquaintance. It is generally presumed of such people that if they had brains to enable them to do anything better, they would prosecute this voluntary artisanship with less zeal; still, the case of these incapables is one to be charitably smiled at or sighed over, not gravely rebuked: we graciously accept the present of their lock or their poker and say no more about it. But it would be a different affair if these voluntary artisans were to set up shop – if, for example, Lord A., or Sir B. C., or any other of the tribe of wealthy Englishmen to whom foreigners give the generic title of *milord*, were not only to amuse himself with making boots, but were to hire a shop frontage, with plate glass, and exhibit his clumsy wares to the public with as much pomp and circumstance as if he were a very Hoby,[1] thereby inducing snobbish people to set the fashion of wearing and crying up Lord A.'s boots, to the depreciation of really well-made articles, and to the great detriment both of human candour and the human foot. Political economists and bootmakers, lady-loves and orthopædists, science and æsthetics, would vote the aristocratic Crispin[2] a nuisance.

A sufficiently close parallel to this hypothetic case is suggested by Lord Brougham's *Lives of Men of Letters*, the sight of which, re-published in a cheap form, has, we confess, roused our critical gall. Relieved from the labours of his chancellorship, Lord Brougham, we suppose, found a good deal of leisure on his hands; and how did he employ it? By taking to what we may call literary lock and poker-making – by writing third-rate biographies in the style of a literary hack! Biographies, too, of men whose lives had already been depicted in all sorts of ways, and presented to us in all sorts of lights – like Prince Albert's face and legs. If we had found these *Lives of Men of Letters* in a biographical dictionary, we should perhaps have thought them about up to the average of the piece-work usually to be met with in such compilations; finding them, as we did more than ten years ago, in an *édition de luxe* adorned with portraits, and with Lord Brougham's name on the title-page, we felt some simmering indignation at such gratuitous mediocrities in a pretentious garb; and now that we see them in a cheaper reissue – as if there were any demand for these clumsy superfluities, these amateur locks and pokers – our indignation fairly boils over. We have not the slightest wish to be disrespectful to Lord Brougham. His name is connected with some of the greatest movements in the last half century, and in general, is on the side of the liberal and the just. But he has been a successful man; his reputation is fully equal to his merit; society is unanimous in pronouncing that he has done many things well and wisely; and there is, therefore, no reason why we should be reticent of our criticism where, in our opinion, he has done some things less wisely and *not* well.

The first thing that strikes us in these *Lives* is the slovenliness of their style, which is thrown almost ludicrously into relief by the fact that many of Lord Brougham's pages are occupied with criticism of other men's style. The hard-run literary man, who is every moment expecting the knock of the printer's boy, has reason enough to renounce fastidiousness; but his lordship, in the elegant ease of his library, with no call impending but that of the lunch or dinner-bell, might at least atone for the lack of originality by finish – might, if he has no jewels to offer us, at least polish his pebbles. How far he has done this we will let the reader judge by giving some specimens of the manner in which Lord Brougham contrives

To blunt a moral and to spoil a tale.[3]

One of his reproaches against Gibbon's style is, that it is 'prone
to adopt false and mixed metaphors'; but we doubt whether the
Decline and Fall could furnish us with a more typical specimen of
that kind than one which he himself gives us in his life of Voltaire.
'Proofs also remain,' says Lord Brougham, 'which place beyond
all doubt his (Voltaire's) kindness to several worthless men, who
repaid it with the black ingratitude so commonly used as their
current coin by the base and spiteful, who thus repay their bene-
factors and *salve their own wounded pride by pouring venom on the hand
that saved or served them.*' Again, in the life of Johnson, we read:
'Assuredly, we may in vain search all the Mantuan *tracery of sweets*
for any to excel them in the beauty of numbers.' It may be our
ignorance of confectionery that prevents us from perceiving what
'tracery' can have to do with 'sweets'; as it is, however, we can
only explain his lordship's metaphor by supposing *tracery* to be a
misprint for *tea-tray*, since misprints abound in this volume. Lord
Brougham is very frequently quite as infelicitous in his phrases,
and in the structure of his sentences, as in his metaphors. For
example: 'It is none of the least absurd *parts* of Condorcet's work,
that he, being so well versed in physical and mathematical science,
passes without any particular observation the writings of Voltaire
on physical subjects, when he was so competent to pronounce an
opinion upon their merits.' 'Condorcet was a man of science, no
doubt, a good mathematician; but he was *in other respects* of a
middling understanding and *violent feelings.*' 'The lady treated him
with kindness, apparently as a child; his friend Saint Lambert did
not much relish the matter, being unable to adopt his singular
habit of *several lovers at one and the same time intimate* with one
mistress.' The style of Rousseau's *Confessions*, we are told, is 'so
exquisitely graphic without any effort, and so accommodated to its
subject without any baseness, *that there hardly exists another example of
the miracles which composition can perform.*' In the labour of turning his
heavy sentences, his lordship is sometimes oblivious of logic. Speaking of Johnson's Latin verses to Mrs Thrale, he says: 'Such offences
as "Littera Skaiæ" (*sic* – a misprint, of course, for *litora*) for an
Adonian in his Sapphics to "Thralia dulcis", would have called

down his severe censure on any luckless wight of Paris or Edinburgh who should peradventure have perpetrated them; nor would his being the countryman of Polignac or of by far the finest of modern Latinists, Buchanan, have operated except as an aggravation of the fault.' Why should it?

Remembering Sydney Smith's verdict on Scotch 'wut',[4] we are not very much surprised to find that Lord Broughman has some anticipation of a Millennium when men will cease to perpetrate witticisms – when not only will the lion eat straw like the ox, but latter-day Voltaires will be as heavy as Scotch lawyers. At least, this is the only way in which we can interpret his peroration to the 'Life of Voltaire'. After an allusion in the previous sentence to 'the graces of his style' and 'the spirit of his *immortal* wit', we read: 'But if ever the time shall arrive when men, intent solely on graver matters, and bending their whole minds to things of solid importance, shall be careless of such light accomplishments, and the writings which now have so great a relish more or less openly tasted, shall pass into oblivion, then,' etc., etc. We confess that we shudder at such a Millennium as much as at one predicted by Dr Cumming, or planned by Robert Owen.[5]

Another striking characteristic of these *Lives of Men of Letters* is the way in which the writer ignores what is not only notorious to all the educated world, but notoriously well known to Lord Brougham. The long-faced gravity with which he discourses on Voltaire's ridicule of religious dogmas, and on Hume's abstinence from such ridicule, might lead a very ignorant reader to suppose that Lord Broughman had led a retired life, chiefly in clerical and senile society, and could only with difficulty imagine a man passing a joke on the Trinity. He says of Hume that 'occasionally his opinions were perceivable' in his conversation, and that one day the inscription on the staircase of the college library, *Christo et Musis has ædes sacrarunt cives Edinenses*,[6] actually 'drew from the unbeliever an irreverent observation on the junction which the piety rather than the classical purity of the good town had made between the worship of the heathen and our own'. Astounding! Even this distant allusion to such irreverence might have had a pernicious effect by exciting in us an unhealthy desire to know what the irreverent observation was, had we not remembered that

Hume had no wit, but only 'wut', so that his joke was probably a feeble one . . . A still more surprising example of Lord Brougham's ignoring system as a writer is his comment on Voltaire's relation to Madame du Châtelet. He thinks that on the whole there is no sufficient reason for questioning that it was Platonic, and the chief grounds he alleges for this conclusion are: that the laws of French society at *that* time, as well as now, were exceedingly rigorous, that the relation was recognized by all their friends, that Voltaire mentions Madame du Châtelet in his letters, and that Frederick II sent his regards to her! One would think it did not require Lord Brougham's extensive acquaintance with the history of French society in the days of Voltaire and Rousseau to know that, whatever may be the truth of his conclusion, the grounds by which he supports it must sound like irony rather than like a grave statement of fact; and, indeed, he himself, – on another page, having laid aside his ignoring spectacles, talks of Grimm being the 'professed lover of Madame d'Epinay', and of Saint Lambert being 'the avowed lover' of Madame d'Houdetot.

We had marked several other points for notice, especially that very remarkable criticism of Lord Brougham's on the *Nouvelle Héloïse*, in which he implies, that for a lover to remind his mistress that she had allowed him to kiss her, is to tell her what a 'forward, abandoned wanton she proved', and his supposition, that because Johnson was sometimes wandering all night in the streets with Savage, he must necessarily have indulged in certain vices 'in their more crapulous form' (an unfortunate suggestion to come from the Brougham of Jeffrey's letters, who is described as 'roaming the streets with the sons of Belial'). But we must remember that when indignation makes reviews instead of Juvenalian verses, the result is not equally enjoyable by the reader. So we restrain our noble rage, and say good bye now and for ever to Lord Brougham's *Lives of Men of Letters*, hoping that the next time we meet with any production of his we may be able to express admiration as strongly as we have just now expressed the reverse.

The Morality of *Wilhelm Meister*

(*Leader*, 21 July 1855)

PERHAPS MR LEWES's *Life of Goethe*, which we now see advertised, may throw some new light on the structure and purpose of the much-debated novel – *Wilhelm Meister's Apprenticeship*. In the meantime, we are tempted by the appearance of a new translation to give the opinion which our present knowledge enables us to form on one or two aspects of this many-sided work.

Ask nineteen out of twenty moderately-educated persons what they think of *Wilhelm Meister*, and the answer will probably be – 'I think it an immoral book; and besides, it is awfully dull: I was not able to read it.' Whatever truth there may be in the first half of this judgement, the second half is a sufficient guarantee that the book is not likely to do any extensive injury in English society. Parents may let it lie on the drawing-room table without scruple, in the confidence that for youthful minds of the ordinary cast it will have no attractions, and that the exceptional youthful mind which is strongly arrested by it is of too powerful and peculiar a character to be trained according to educational dogmas.

But is *Wilhelm Meister* an immoral book? We think not: on the contrary, we think that it appears immoral to some minds because its morality has a grander orbit than any which can be measured by the calculations of the pulpit and of ordinary literature. Goethe, it is sometimes said, seems in this book to be almost destitute of moral bias: he shows no hatred of bad actions, no warm sympathy with good ones; he writes like a passionless Mejnour,[1] to whom all human things are interesting only as objects of intellectual contemplation. But we question whether the direct exhibition of a moral bias in the writer will make a book really moral in its influence. Try this on the first child that asks you to tell it a story.

As long as you keep to an apparently impartial narrative of facts you will have earnest eyes fixed on you in rapt attention, but no sooner do you begin to betray symptoms of an intention to moralize, or to turn the current of facts towards a personal application, than the interest of your hearer will slacken, his eyes will wander, and the moral dose will be doubly distasteful from the very sweetmeat in which you have attempted to insinuate it. One grand reason of this is, that the child is aware you are talking *for it* instead of *from yourself*, so that instead of carrying it along in a stream of sympathy with your own interest in the story, you give it the impression of contriving coldly and talking artificially. Now, the moralizing novelist produces the same effect on his mature readers; an effect often heightened by the perception that the moralizing is rather intended to make his book eligible for family reading than prompted by any profound conviction or enthusiasm. Just as far from being really moral is the so-called moral *dénouement*, in which rewards and punishments are distributed according to those notions of justice on which the novel-writer would have recommended that the world should be governed if he had been consulted at the creation. The emotion of satisfaction which a reader feels when the villain of the book dies of some hideous disease, or is crushed by a railway train, is no more essentially moral than the satisfaction which used to be felt in whipping culprits at the cart-tail. So we dismiss the charge of immorality against *Wilhelm Meister* on these two counts – the absence of moral bias in the mode of narration, and the comfortable issues allowed to questionable actions and questionable characters.

But there is another ground for the same accusation which involves deeper considerations. It is said that some of the scenes and incidents are such as the refined moral taste of these days will not admit to be proper subjects for art, that to depict irregular relations in all the charms they really have for human nature, and to associate lovely qualities with vices which society makes a brand of outlawry, implies a toleration which is at once a sign and a source of perverted moral sentiment. Wilhelm's relation to Mariana, and the charm which the reader is made to feel in the lawless Philina, many incidents that occur during Wilhelm's life with the players, and the stories of Lothario's loves in the present, preterite, and future, are shocking to the prevalent English. It is no answer to this objection to say – what is the fact – that Goethe's pictures are truthful, that the career of almost every young man brings him in contact with far more vitiating irregularities than any presented in the experience of Wilhelm Meister; for no one can maintain that *all* fact is a fit subject for art. The sphere of the artist has its limit somewhere, and the first question is, Has Goethe overstepped this limit, so that the mere fact of artistic representation is a mistake? The second: If his subjects are within the legitimate limits of art, is his mode of treatment such as to make his pictures pernicious? Surely the sphere of art extends wherever there is beauty either in form, or thought, or feeling. A ray of sunlight falling on the dreariest sandbank will often serve the painter for a fine picture; the tragedian may take for his subject the most hideous passions if they serve as the background for some divine deed of tenderness or heroism, and so the novelist may place before us every aspect of human life where there is some twist of love, or endurance, or helplessness to call forth our best sympathies. Balzac, perhaps the most wonderful writer of fiction the world has ever seen, has in many of his novels overstepped this limit. He drags us by his magic force through scene after scene of unmitigated vice, till the effect of walking among this human carrion is a moral nausea. But no one can say that Goethe has sinned in this way.

Everywhere he brings us into the presence of living, generous humanity – mixed and erring, and self-deluding, but saved from utter corruption by the salt of some noble impulse, some disinterested effort, some beam of good nature, even though grotesque or homely. And his mode of treatment seems to us precisely that which is really moral in its influence. It is without exaggeration; he is in no haste to alarm readers into virtue by melodramatic consequences; he quietly follows the stream of fact and of life; and waits patiently for the moral processes of nature as we all do for her material processes. The large tolerance of Goethe, which is markedly exhibited in *Wilhelm Meister*, is precisely that to which we point as the element of moral superiority. We all begin life by associating our passions with our moral prepossessions, by mistaking indignation for virtue, and many go through life without awaking from this illusion. These are the 'insupportables justes, qui du haut de leurs chaises d'or narguent les misères et les souffrances de l'humanité'.[2] But a few are taught by their own falls and their own struggles, by their experience of sympathy, and help and goodness in the 'publicans and sinners'[3] of these modern days, that the line between the virtuous and vicious, so far from being a necessary safeguard to morality, is itself an immoral fiction. Those who have been already taught this lesson will at once recognize the true morality of Goethe's works. Like *Wilhelm Meister*, they will be able to love the good in a Philina, and to reverence the far-seeing efforts of a Lothario.

Charles Kingsley's *Westward Ho!*

(Westminster Review, July 1855)

EVERY ONE who was so happy as to go mushrooming in his early days, remembers his delight when, after picking up and throwing away heaps of dubious fungi, dear to naturalists but abhorred of cooks, he pounces on an unmistakable mushroom, with its delicate fragrance and pink lining tempting him to devour it there and then, to the prejudice of the promised dish for breakfast. We speak in parables, after the fashion of the wise, amongst whom Reviewers are always to be reckoned. The plentiful dubious fungi are the ordinary quarter's crop of novels, not all poisonous, but generally not appetizing, and certainly not nourishing; and the unmistakable mushroom is a new novel by Charles Kingsley. It seemed too long since we had any of that genuine description of external nature, not done after the poet's or the novelist's recipe, but flowing from spontaneous observation and enjoyment; any of that close, vigorous painting of outdoor life, which serves as myrrh and rich spices to embalm much perishable theorizing and offensive objurgation – too long since we had a taste of that exquisite lyrical inspiration to which we owe –

> O, Mary! go and call the cattle home
> Along the sands of Dee.[1]

After courses of 'psychological' novels (very excellent things in their way), where life seems made up of talking and journalizing, and men are judged almost entirely on 'carpet consideration',[2] we are ready to welcome a stirring historical romance, by a writer who, poet and scholar and social reformer as he is, evidently knows the points of a horse and has followed the hounds, who betrays a fancy for pigs, and becomes dithyrambic on the virtues of tobacco. After a surfeit of Hebes and Psyches, or Madonnas and Magdalens, it is a refreshment to turn to Kiss's Amazon.[3] But this ruddy and, now and then, rather ferocious barbarism, which is singularly compounded in Mr Kingsley with the susceptibility of the poet and the warm sympathy of the philanthropist, while it gives his writings one of their principal charms, is also the source of their gravest fault. The battle and the chase seem necessary to his existence; and this Red Man's nature, planted in a pleasant rectory among corn fields and pastures, takes, in default of better game, to riding down capitalists and Jesuits, and fighting with that Protean personage – 'the devil'. If, however, Mother Nature has made Mr Kingsley very much of a poet and philanthropist, and a little of a savage, her dry-nurse Habit has made him superlatively a preacher: he drops into the homily as readily as if he had been 'to the manner born'; and while by his artistic faculty he can transplant you into whatever scene he will, he can never trust to the impression that scene itself will make on you, but, true to his cloth, must always 'improve the occasion'. In these two points – his fierce antagonism and his perpetual hortative tendency – lie, to our thinking, the grand mistakes which enfeeble the effect of all Mr Kingsley's works, and are too likely to impede his production of what his high powers would otherwise promise – a fiction which might be numbered among our classics. Poet and artist in a rare degree, his passionate impetuosity and theological prepossessions inexorably forbid that he should ever be a philosopher; he sees, feels, and paints vividly, but he theorizes illogically and moralizes absurdly. If he would confine himself to his true sphere, he might be a teacher in the sense in which every great artist is a teacher – namely, by giving us his higher sensibility as a medium, a delicate acoustic or optical instrument, bringing home to our coarser senses what would otherwise be unperceived by us. But Mr Kingsley, unhappily, like so many other gifted men, has two steeds – his Pegasus and his hobby: the one he rides with a graceful *abandon*, to the admiration of all beholders; but no sooner does he get astride the other, than he becomes a feeble imitator of Carlyle's *manège*, and attempts to put his wooden toy to all the wonderful paces of the great Scotchman's fiery Tartar horse. This imitation is probably not a conscious one, but arises simply from the fact, that Mr Kingsley's impetuosity and Boanerges'[4] vein give him an affinity for Carlyle's faults – his one-sided judgement of character and his undiscriminating fulminations against the men of the present as tried by some imaginary standard in the past. Carlyle's great merits Mr Kingsley's powers are not fitted to achieve; his genius lies in another direction. He has not that piercing insight which every now and then flashes to the depth of things, and alternating as it does with the most obstinate one-sidedness, makes Carlyle a wonderful paradox of wisdom and wilfulness; he has not that awful sense of the mystery of existence which continually checks and chastens the denunciations of the Teufelsdröckh;[5] still less has he the rich humour, the keen satire, and the tremendous word-missiles, which Carlyle hurls about as Milton's angels hurl the rocks. But Mr Kingsley *can* scold; he *can* select one character for unmixed eulogy and another for unmitigated vituperation; he *can* undertake to depict a past age and try to make out that it was the pattern of all heroisms now utterly extinct; he *can* sneer at actual doings which are only a new form of the sentiments he vaunts as the peculiar possession of his pet period; he *can* call his own opinion God, and the opposite opinion the Devil. Carlyle's love of the concrete makes him prefer any proper name rather than an abstraction, and we are accustomed to smile at this in him, knowing it to be mere Carlylian rhetoric; but with Mr Kingsley, who has publicly made a vehement disclaimer of all heterodoxy,[6] and wishes to be understood as believing 'all the doctrines of the Catholic Church', we must interpret such phraseology more literally. But enough of general remarks. Let us turn to the particular work before us, where we shall find all the writer's merits and faults in full blow. We abstain on principle from telling the story of novels, which seems to us something like stealing geraniums from your friend's flower-pot to stick in your own button-hole: you spoil the effect of his plant, and you secure only a questionable ornament for yourself. We shall therefore be careful to give the reader no hint of the domestic story around which Mr Kingsley has grouped the historical scenes and characters of *Westward Ho!*

Hardly any period could furnish a happier subject for an historical fiction than the one Mr Kingsley has here chosen. It is unhackneyed, and it is unsurpassed in the grandeur of its moral elements, and the picturesqueness and romance of its manners and events. Mr Kingsley has not brought only genius but much labour to its illustration. He has fed his strong imagination with all accessible material, and given care not only to the grand figures and incidents but to small details. One sees that he knows and loves his Devonshire at first hand, and he has evidently lingered over the description of the forests and savannahs and rivers of the New World, until they have become as vividly present to him as if they were part of his own experience. We dare not pronounce on the merit of his naval descriptions, but to us, landlubbers as we are, they seem wonderfully real, and not to smack at all of technicalities learned by rote over the desk. He has given a careful and loving study to the history and literature of the period, and whatever misrepresentation there is in the book, is clearly not due to ignorance but to prepossession: if he misrepresents, it is not because he has omitted to examine, but because he has examined through peculiar spectacles. In the construction of a story Mr Kingsley has never been felicitous; and the feebleness of his *dénouements* have been matter of amazement, even to his admirers. In this respect, *Westward Ho!* though by no means criticism-proof, is rather an advance on his former works, especially in the winding-up. It is true, this winding-up reminds us a little of *Jane Eyre*, but we prefer a partially borrowed beauty to an original bathos, which was what Mr Kingsley achieved in the later chapters of *Alton Locke* and *Yeast*. Neither is humour his forte. His Jack Brimblecombe is too much like a piece of fun *obbligato*, after the manner of Walter Scott, who remains the unequalled model of historical romancists, however they may criticize him. Mr Kingsley's necessity for strong loves and strong hatreds, and his determination to hold up certain persons as models, is an obstacle to his successful delineation of character, in which he might otherwise excel. As it is, we can no more believe in and love his men and women than we could believe in and love the pattern-boy at school, always cited as a rebuke to our aberrations. Amyas Leigh would be a real, lovable fellow enough if he were a little less exemplary, and if Mr Kingsley would not make him a text to preach from, as we suppose he is accustomed to do with Joshua, Gideon, and David.

Until he shakes off this parsonic habit he will not be able to create truly human characters, or to write a genuine historical romance. Where his prepossessions do not come into play, where he is not dealing with his model heroes, or where the drama turns on a single passion or motive, he can scarcely be rivalled in truthfulness and beauty of presentation; for in clothing passion with action and language, and in the conception of all that gives local colouring, he has his best gifts to aid him. Beautiful is that episode of Mr Oxenham's love, told by Salvation Yeo! Very admirable, too, is the felicity with which Mr Kingsley has seized the style and spirit of the Elizabethan writers, and reproduced them in the poetry and supposed quotations scattered through his story. But above all other charms in his writings, at least to us, is his scene-painting. Who does not remember the scene by the wood in *Alton Locke*, or that of the hunt at the beginning of *Yeast?* And *Westward Ho!* is wealthy in still greater beauties of the same kind. Here is a perfect gem. After a description of the old house at Stow, the residence of Sir Richard Grenvile, we read —

From the house on three sides, the hill sloped steeply down, and the garden where Sir Richard and Amyas were walking gave a truly English prospect. At one turn they could catch, over the western walls, a glimpse of the blue ocean flecked with passing sails; and at the next, spread far below them, range on range of fertile park, stately avenue, yellow autumn woodland, and purple heather moors, lapping over and over each other up the valley to the old British earthwork, which stood black and furze-grown on its conical peak; and standing out against the sky on the highest bank of hill which closed the valley to the east, the lofty tower of Kilkhampton church, rich with the monuments and offerings of five centuries of Grenviles. A yellow eastern haze hung soft over park, and wood, and moor; the red cattle lowed to each other as they stood brushing away the flies in the rivulet far below; the colts in the horse-park close on their right whinnied as they played together, and their sires from the Queen's park, on the opposite hill, answered them in fuller though fainter voices. A rutting stag made the still woodland rattle with his hoarse thunder, and rival far up the valley gave back a trumpet note of defiance, and was himself defied from heathery brows which quivered far away above, half seen through the veil of eastern mist. And close at home, upon the terrace before the house, amid romping spaniels and golden-haired children, sat Lady Grenvile herself, the beautiful Saint Leger of Annery, the central jewel of all that glorious place, and looked down at her noble children, and then up at her more noble husband, and round at that broad paradise of the west, till life seemed too full of happiness, and heaven of light.

It is pleasanter to linger over beauties such as these, than to point out faults; but unhappily, Mr Kingsley's faults are likely to do harm in other ways than in subtracting from the lustre of his fame, and a faithful reviewer must lift up his voice against them, whether men 'will hear, or whether they will forbear'.[7] Who that has any knowledge of our history and literature – that has felt his heart beat high at the idea of great crises and great deeds – that has any true recognition of the greatest poetry, and some of the greatest thoughts enshrined in our language, is not ready to pay the tribute of enthusiastic reverence to the Elizabethan age? In his glowing picture of that age, Mr Kingsley would have carried with him all minds in which there is a spark of nobleness, if he could have freed himself from the spirit of the partisan, and been content to admit that in the Elizabethan age, as in every other, human beings, human parties, and human deeds are made up of the most subtly intermixed good and evil. The battle of Armageddon in which all the saints are to fight on one side, has never yet come. It is perfectly true that, at certain epochs, the relations and tendencies of ideas and events are so clearly made out to minds of any superiority, that the best and ablest men are for the most part ranged under one banner: there was a point at which it must have become disgraceful to a cultivated mind not to accept the Copernican system, and in these days we are unable to draw any favourable inference concerning the intellect or morals of a man who advocates capital punishment for sheep-stealing or forgery. But things have never come to this pass with regard to Catholicism and Protestantism; and even supposing they had, Mr Kingsley's ethics seem to resemble too closely those of his bugbears the Dominicans, when he implies that it is a holy work for the 'Ayes' to hunt down the 'Noes' like so many beasts of prey. His view of history seems not essentially to differ from that we have all held in our childish days, when it seemed perfectly easy for us to divide mankind into the sheep and the goats, when we devoutly believed that our favourite heroes, Wallace and Bruce, and all who fought on their side, were 'good', while Edward and his soldiers were all 'wicked'; that all the champions of the Reformation were of unexceptionable private character, and all the adherents of Popery consciously vicious and base. Doubtless the Elizabethan age bore its peculiar fruit of excellence, as every age has done which forms a nodus, a ganglion, in the historical development of humanity – as the age of Pericles produced the divinest sculptures, or the age of the Roman Republic the severe grandeur of Roman law and Roman patriotism, or as the core of the Middle Ages held the germ of chivalrous honour and reverential love. Doubtless the conquest of the Spanish Armada was virtually the triumph of light and freedom over darkness and bondage. What then? Is this a reason why Mr Kingsley should seem almost angry with us for not believing with the men of that day in the golden city of Manoa and the Gulf-stream, or scold by anticipation any one who shall dare to congratulate himself on being undeceived in these matters? Doubtless Drake, Hawkins, Frobisher, and the rest,[8] were brave, energetic men – men of great will and in some sort of great faculty; but like all other human agents, they 'builded better than they knew'; and it would be as rational to suppose that the bee is an entomological Euclid, interested only in the solution of a problem, as to suppose that the motives of these mariners were as grand as the results of their work.

We had marked several passages as specimens of the small success which attends Mr Kingsley in his favourite exercise of deducing a moral, but our want of space obliges us to renounce the idea of quoting them, with the exception of one, which, we think, will in some degree justify our low estimate of Mr Kingsley's gifts as a philosophizer. Here is the passage –

Humboldt[9] has somewhere a curious passage; in which, looking on some wretched group of Indians, squatting stupidly round their fires, besmeared with grease and paint, and devouring ants and clay, he somewhat naïvely remarks, that were it not for science, which teaches us that such is the crude material of humanity, and this the state from which we have all risen, he should have been tempted rather to look upon those hapless beings as the last degraded remnants of some fallen and dying race. One wishes that the great traveller had been bold enough to yield to that temptation, which his own reason and common sense presented to him as the real explanation of the sad sight, instead of following the dogmas of a so-called science, which has not a fact whereon to base its wild notion, and must ignore a thousand facts in asserting it. His own good sense, it seems, coincided instinctively with the Bible doctrine, that man in a state of nature is a fallen being, doomed to death – a view which may be a sad one, but still one more honourable to poor humanity than the theory, that we all began as some sort of two-handed apes. It is surely more hopeful to believe that those poor Otomacs or Guahibas were not what they ought to be, than to believe that they were. It is certainly more complimentary to them, to think that they had been somewhat nobler and more prudent in centuries gone by, than that they were such block-heads as to have dragged on, the son after the father, for all the thousands of years which have elapsed since man was made, without having had wit enough to discover any better food than ants and clay.

Our voyagers, however, like those of their time, troubled their heads with no such questions. Taking the Bible story as they found it, they agreed with Humboldt's reason, and not with his science; or, to speak correctly, agreed with Humboldt's self, and not with the shallow anthropologic theories which happened to be in vogue fifty years ago; and their new hosts were in their eyes immortal souls like themselves, 'captived by the devil at his will', lost there in the pathless forests, likely to be lost hereafter.

Note the accuracy of Mr Kingsley's reasoning. Humboldt observes that, but for scientific data leading to an opposite conclusion, he could have imagined that a certain group of Indians were the remnants of a race which had sunk from a state of well-being to one of almost helpless barbarism. Hereupon, Mr Kingsley is sorry that Humboldt did not reject 'the dogmas of a so-called science', and rest in this conception which 'coincided with the Bible doctrine'; and he urges as one of his reasons for this regret, that it would be complimentary to the Otomacs and Guahibas to suppose that in centuries gone by, they had been nobler and more prudent. Now, so far as we are acquainted with the third chapter of Genesis, and with the copious exegeses of that chapter from Saint Paul downwards, the 'Bible doctrine' is *not* that man multiplied on the earth and formed communities and nations – amongst the rest, noble and prudent societies of Otomacs and Guahibas – in a state of innocence, and that *then* came the Fall. We have always understood that for the Fall 'we may thank Adam', and that consequently the very first Otomac or Guahiba was already 'captived by the devil', and 'likely to be lost hereafter'. Hence, what the question of the Otomacs and Guahibas having been nobler and more prudent in centuries gone by, can have to do with the doctrine of the Fall, we are at a loss to perceive. We will do no more than point to Mr Kingsley's cool arrogance in asserting that a man like Humboldt, the patriarch of scientific investigators, is 'misled by the dogmas of a so-called science, which has *not a fact* whereon to base its wild notions'. Indeed it is rather saddening to dwell on the occasional absurdities into which anomalous opinions can betray a man of real genius; and after all, the last word we have to say of *Westward Ho!* is to thank Mr Kingsley for the great and beautiful things we have found in it, as our dominant feeling towards his works in general is that of high admiration.

Geraldine Jewsbury's *Constance Herbert*

(Westminster Review, July 1855)

NEXT IN interest to *Westward Ho!* at least among the English novels of the quarter, is *Constance Herbert*. Miss Jewsbury has created precedents for herself which make critics exacting towards her. We measure her work by her own standard, and find it deficient; when if measured by the standard of ordinary feminine novelists, it would perhaps seem excellent. We meet with some beauties in it which, coming from the author of the *Half Sisters*, we take as a matter of course, but we miss other beauties which she has taught us to expect; we feel that she is not equal to herself; and it is a tribute to her well-attested powers if we dwell on what has disappointed us, rather than on what has gratified us. An easy, agreeable style of narrative, some noble sentiments expressed in the quiet, unexaggerated way that indicates their source to be a deep spring of conviction and experience, not a mere rain-torrent of hearsay enthusiasm, with here and there a trait of character or conduct painted with the truthfulness of close observation, are merits enough to raise a book far above the common run of circulating library fiction; but they are not enough to make a good novel, or one worthy of Miss Jewsbury's reputation. *Constance Herbert* is a *Tendenz-roman*; the characters and incidents are selected with a view to the enforcement of a principle. The general principle meant to be enforced is the unhesitating, uncompromising sacrifice of inclination to duty, and the special case to which this principle is applied in the novel, is the abstinence from marriage where there is an inheritance of insanity. So far, we have no difference of opinion with Miss Jewsbury. But the *mode* in which she enforces the principle, both theoretically in the *Envoi* and illustratively in the story of her novel, implies, we think, a false view of life, and virtually nullifies the very magnanimity she inculcates. 'If,' she says in the *Envoi*, 'we have succeeded in articulating any principle in this book, it is to entreat our readers to have boldness to act up to the sternest requirements that duty claims as right. Although it may at the time seem to slay them, it will in the end prove life. *Nothing they renounce for the sake of a higher principle, will prove to have been worth the keeping.*' The italics are ours, and we use them to indicate what we think false in Miss Jewsbury's moral. This moral is illustrated in the novel by the story of three ladies, who, after renouncing their lovers, or being renounced by them, have the satisfaction of feeling in the end that these lovers were extremely 'good-for-nothing', and that they (the ladies) have had an excellent riddance. In all this we can see neither the true doctrine of renunciation, nor a true representation of the realities of life; and we are sorry that a writer of Miss Jewsbury's insight and sincerity should have produced three volumes for the sake of teaching such copy-book morality. It is not the fact that what duty calls on us to renounce, will invariably prove 'not worth the keeping'; and if it *were* the fact, renunciation would cease to be moral heroism, and would be simply a calculation of prudence. Let us take the special case which Miss Jewsbury has chosen as her illustration. It might equally happen that a woman in the position of Constance Herbert, who renounces marriage because she will not entail on others the family heritage of insanity, had fixed her affections, not on an egotistic, shallow worldling like Philip Marchmont, but on a man who was fitted to make the happiness of a woman's life, and whose subsequent career would only impress on her more and more deeply the extent of the sacrifice she had made in refusing him. And it is this very perception that the thing we renounce is precious, is something never to be compensated to us, which constitutes the beauty and heroism of renunciation. The only motive that renders such a resolution as Constance Herbert's noble, is that keen sympathy with human misery which makes a woman prefer to suffer for the term of her own life, rather than run the risk of causing misery to an indefinite number of other human beings; and a mind influenced by such a motive will find no support in the very questionable satisfaction of discovering that objects once cherished were in fact worthless. The notion that duty looks stern, but all the while has her hand full of sugar-plums, with which she will reward us by and by, is the favourite cant of optimists, who try to make out that this tangled wilderness of life has a plan as easy to trace as that of a Dutch garden; but it really undermines all true moral development by perpetually substituting something extrinsic as a motive to action, instead of the immediate impulse of love or justice, which alone makes an action truly moral. This is a grave question to enter on *à propos* of a novel; but Miss Jewsbury is so emphatic in the enunciation of her moral, that she forces us to consider her book rather in the light of a homily than of a fiction – to criticize her doctrine rather than her story. On another point, too, we must remonstrate with her a little, chiefly because we value her influence, and should like to see it always in what seems to us the right scale. With the exception of Mr Harrop, who is simply a cipher awaiting a wife to give him any value, there is not a man in her book who is not either weak, perfidious, or rascally, while almost all the women are models of magnanimity and devotedness. The lions, i.e., the ladies, have got the brush in their hands with a vengeance now, and are retaliating for the calumnies of men from Adam downwards. Perhaps it is but fair to allow them a little exaggeration. Still we must meekly suggest that we cannot accept an *ex parte* statement, even from that paragon Aunt Margaret, as altogether decisive. Aunt Margaret tells us that in the bloom of youth and beauty, with virtues and accomplishments to correspond, she alienated her husband by pure devotion to him. 'No man,' she says, 'can bear entire devotion.' This reminds us of a certain toper, who after drinking a series of glasses of brandy-and-water one night, complained the next morning that the water did not agree with him. We are inclined to think that it is less frequently devotion which alienates men, than something infused in the devotion – a certain amount of silliness, or temper, or *exigeance*, for example, which, though given in small doses, will, if persevered in, have a strongly alterative effect. Men, in fact, are in rather a difficult position: in one ear a Miss Grace Lee,[1] or some such strong-minded woman, thunders that they demand to be worshipped, and abhor a woman who has any self-dependence; on the other, a melancholy Viola[2] complains that they never appreciate devotion, that they care only for a woman who treats them with indifference. A discouraging view of the case for both sexes! Seriously, we care too much for the attainment of a better understanding as to woman's true position, not to be sorry when a writer like Miss Jewsbury only adds her voice to swell the confusion on this subject.

Saint-Marc Girardin's *Love in the Drama*

(Leader, 25 August 1855)

M. SAINT-MARC GIRARDIN is a writer who makes the public not only desire his volumes, but wait for them. The reason of this, in the case of the *Cours de littérature dramatique,* is that it consists of lectures given by him at the Sorbonne, so that the volumes can only appear after their contents have been delivered in 'winged words'. The first volume was published in 1843, the second in 1849, and it is only now, after the lapse of another six years, that we obtain the welcome third. Nothing can be more charmingly easy and conversational than the style of these volumes. We have all experienced that 'who writes about amusing books must himself be amusing', is as far from being an axiom as Johnson's immortal parody, 'Who drives fat oxen must himself be fat';[1] and that a work on the *belles lettres* may be as drowsy as one on weights and measures. But M. Saint-Marc Girardin is one of those writers who make a graceful subject still more graceful; he enhances the beauty of the flowers he gathers by the tasteful way in which he weaves them together. Qualities which make him delightful as a critic are his ready appreciation of beauty, even when that beauty is mingled with much quaintness and absurdity, and his lively sensibility to every trait of genuine feeling. He has at once chastity and largeness of thought – not a common conjunction anywhere, and perhaps especially uncommon in France; he is liberal without being lax, and pure without the least *soupçon* of prudery.

In the latter part of his second volume he examined the three grand influences which have modified the character of Love, and made us differ so widely from the ancients in our conception and presentation of that passion, namely, Christianity, chivalry, and the doctrine of Platonic love. In the present volume he pursues the subject of Love and traces its modifications in the sixteenth and seventeenth centuries by analysing, or rather graphically sketching, the three typical romances. The *Amadis*,[2] which represents chivalrous love in its more softened and effeminate stage; the *Astrée*,[3] which mingles Platonic with chivalrous love, under the name of pastoral love; and the *Clélia*,[4] which is the code of *la galanterie honnête*,[5] and 'marks the apogee of woman's preponderance in the world and in literature'. We recommend readers who would like to be told, in the pleasantest way, something about those antediluvian romances, to turn to this volume of M. Saint-Marc Girardin's. He will show them matter for admiration, even in D'Urfé and Mademoiselle Scudéry, and it is always worth while to widen our circle of admiration. After thus surveying the general expression of Love under the varying conditions of society, from antiquity down to the seventeenth century, M. Girardin enters on an examination of the particular expressions given to this passion in the drama, the romance, and the pastoral, and it is this part of his work which is most attractive. He opens for us one book after another, perhaps lying dusty on our shelves, points out beautiful passages and significant traits, makes Theocritus appear the most tempting author in the world, and pastorals in general seem readable – which we humbly confess we have rarely found them – shows a fine appreciation of Shakspeare, and winds up by charming his reader's interest to Madame Deshoulières,[6] who ought to be held in grateful recollection, if for nothing else, at least for having written those incisive lines –

> Nul n'est content de sa fortune
> Ni mécontent de son esprit – [7]

an epigram to which La Rochefoucauld has given a new dress in his *Maximes*.

It is of course impossible for us to follow him through this lengthy survey, so, by way of selection, we turn to his observations on *Romeo and Juliet*, in which he compares Shakspeare's tragedy with the novel of Luigi da Porto.[8] In the novel it is Juliet who makes the first advance to Romeo; at the first glance they exchange, the young maiden feels that her heart is no longer her own, and when the progress of the dance brings Romeo near to her, she says,

'Welcome to my side, Messer Romeo'. M. Girardin observes that this treatment of the subject is entirely in the spirit of ancient poetry and proceeds:

Why, in ancient poetry and in the Italian novel, which is here in entire unison with ancient poetry, why do the women love before being loved? why do they feel the passion before inspiring it? and why, in modern poetry and romance, do we find the contrary? Dido loves Aeneas before we know whether she was loved in return, and we may even doubt whether she was ever loved. Medea loves Jason before being loved by him. Is it that the love-smitten heroines of antiquity had less modesty than the love-smitten heroines of modern times? or is it that the modern poets and romancers are more refined and reserved in the pictures they give of woman's sentiments? The manners of antiquity may explain why, in ancient poetry, woman wants that reserve in feeling, and yet more in words, which is her rule in modern times. Shut up in the gynaeceum,[9] and never mixing in the society of men, who themselves found objects of love elsewhere, women were compelled, when love took possession of their hearts, to proffer the avowal of their passion; they must themselves reveal their secret, or let it remain for ever unknown . . . The less free woman is made by laws and conventionalities, the freer does she become through passion when she yields herself up to it. Thus, the women whose passion made them famous in antiquity were compelled to forget at once the first and last proprieties of their sex. In order to be loved, they were forced to say that they loved; and hence ancient poetry was accustomed to represent its heroines as making the first avowals of love.

M. Girardin then goes on to say that Shakspeare, 'who is altogether a modern', differs in his treatment from the Italian novelist, in assigning the first movement and expression of love to Romeo; as if he meant to imply that Shakspeare is an example of the antithesis he has just been stating between ancient and modern love, or rather love-making. He could hardly have made a more unfortun-ate selection of a case in point, for – inconvenient as the fact may be for those whose creed includes at once the doctrine of Shak-speare's infallibility and doctrines of modern propriety – Shak-speare's women have no more decided characteristic than the frankness with which they avow their love, not only to themselves, but to the men they love. If Romeo opens the duet of love with a few notes *solo*, Juliet soon strikes in, and keeps it up in as impassioned a strain as he. Sweet Desdemona, 'a maiden never bold', encourages Othello, not only by a 'world of sighs',[10] but by the broadest possible hint that he has won her heart. Rosalind, in her first interview with Orlando, tells him he has 'overthrown more than his enemies'.[11] Portia is eloquent in assurances of her love before the casket is opened –

> One half of me is yours, the other half yours –
> Mine own, I would say; but if mine, then yours,
> And so all yours![12]

And this frankness towards the lover is generally followed up by the most impassioned soliloquies or confessions to confidants. Then there are the women who love without being loved in return, and some of whom even sue for love. Helena in *All's Well that Ends Well*, the Helena in the *Midsummer Night's Dream*, the shepherdess Sylvia, Viola, and Olivia, who woos so prettily that the action justifies itself. Curious it is to contrast these Shakspearean heroines with some of Walter Scott's painfully-discreet young ladies – the Edith Bellendens, Alice Bridgworths, and Miss Wardours.[13] Whatever may be the respectability of these modern heroines, it is clear that little could be made of them dramatically; they are like trees trained in right lines by dint of wall and hammer. But we are wandering from the point we had undertaken to prove, namely, that Shakspeare cannot properly be contrasted with the ancients in the expression he gives to woman's love. If so – if this feminine frankness is not peculiar to the ancients, the cause of it in them must lie deeper than the restraints of the gynaeceum, to which M. Girardin attributes it: it must be simply a natural manifestation which has only been gradually and partially repressed by the complex influences of modern civilization.

In his criticism of Shakspeare, M. Girardin sometimes reminds us of the Germans by his discovery of profound philosophical intentions where Shakspeare had probably nothing more than poetical and dramatic intentions. For example, Caliban, he tells us, is meant in the first instance to typify the inevitable brutality of human nature in the savage state, in opposition to the marvellous stories of voyagers in Shakspeare's days; and in the second instance, when he 'tastes of civilization' – that is, of Trinculo's wine –

Caliban is meant as a caveat to the hasty panegyrists of civilized life. But, unlike the Germans, M. Girardin touches lightly on such subjects – just dips his wings in the *mare magnum*[14] of philosophical interpretation, but generally floats along in the lighter medium of tasteful criticism and quotation. He promises us, at some future time, a fourth volume on the dramatic treatment of religious enthusiasm, a volume which will come to us recommended by the memory of much pleasure due to its predecessors.

Ashford Owen's *A Lost Love*
and C. W. S Brooks's *Aspen Court*

(Westminster Review, October 1855)

WE ARE inclined to think that when all the beasts of the field and fowls of the air were brought to Adam, 'to see what he would call them', this large demand on his 'organ of language' must have been rather embarrassing to him, and he would have found it much more convenient if the naming had been deferred until he could have the help of Eve, who doubtless was as ready as most of her daughters at telling her husband what to say. Something like this embarrassing position of Adam's is the case of that unfortunate son of Adam, a reviewer who sits surrounded with books on which he is required there and then to render an opinion, –for is not all opinion, nay, all science, simply a *naming*? Of the genus *belles lettres*, novels are usually the most numerous species, for assuredly they are fruitful, and multiply, and replenish the earth; but it so happens that this quarter they form no large proportion of the books before us. We give the precedence to a very unpretending one in a single volume of anything but close print. We mean *A Lost Love* by Ashford Owen. Take up this volume, not of course in the grave morning hours, when you want something strong and substantial, but when you come in agreeably tired with your walk, or, for want of conversation, between dinner and tea. You will find a real picture of a woman's life; not a remarkable woman, not one of those heroines who have such amazing moral strength that they despise happiness and like to be disappointed, or who are so wonderfully intellectual as to give even serious views of 'female competition'; yet not a commonplace woman, but one who, while loving and thirsting to be loved, can give up her one hope in life when sympathy and good sense demand it, without having any fine theories about her deed, or any consciousness that she is doing something out of the common,– one with no great culture and no great powers, but with that true freshness and simplicity which makes any mind original and interesting. Such is Georgy, the heroine of *A Lost Love*; a parasitic plant, but a vigorous one, with a strong preference of the particular tree to which it will cling. The story is a melancholy one, but without any exaggerated sorrows; the tragic notes in it belong to that 'still, sad music of humanity', which seems to make hardly a perceptible element in the great world-symphony. But every tender and watchful nature has an ear for such notes; and Georgy's tale will remind most readers of something they have seen in life. The writing is not remarkable otherwise than for the excellent quality of simplicity: there are none of the fine sayings which often fall by the way from a superior writer, even when bent on merely telling a story; but in the absence of this merit, there is the scarcely inferior merit of not *aiming* to say fine things. The author is unquestionably a woman, and writes like one in the best sense, namely, by keeping to the delineation of what a woman's experience and observation bring within her special knowledge.

Quite an opposite kind of talent is exhibited in *Aspen Court*, which has been gathered into three volumes from the numbers of *Bentley's Miscellany*. Like all fiction written for periodical appearance, it bears the stamp of that demand for periodical effect, which opposes itself to a natural development of character and incident; and so far *Aspen Court* is under a disadvantage when read consecutively. It belongs to the class of cleverly-written novels which are as far as possible from boring us, but, having done their work of amusement, are laid down and forgotten. There is unusually smart writing and satirical sketching, but no grasp of character, no close, genuine presentation of life. It professes to be a story of our own day, and in one sense fulfils that profession, since its scenes are all selected as representative of various social aspects. We have a lawyer's office, a scene in the House of Commons, a club-house, high political society, a lock-up house, a fight, interviews with a manager, the reading of a play in the green-room and its subsequent production on the stage, a hunt, a chop-house, and the intrigues of a Catholic priest. But these scenes, one and all, are vitiated by the constant presence of unreality; often amusing, they are always fantastic; and while locality and costume imply that we are making acquaintance with the things and people of actual life, we are in fact among beings little less unreal than my Lord Marquis of Carabas. The great merit of the book is lively writing; witty sayings and humorous touches abound. For example: among the clerks in a lawyer's office is Mr Maunder, who 'wrote a beautiful hand, borrowed money from every new clerk, and was rather supposed to be an atheist, *because he never swore, and because he had been detected reading Voltaire's Charles XII.*' – 'Mrs Basnet, the monthly nurse, had annexed an embroidered pocket handkerchief from the drawers of a lady, who, at the time, was not nearly so well as could be expected.' – 'The Countess of Rookbury, having presented the Earl with an heir, became dissatisfied with the Court physician, and called in a homœopathist. *Being thus left a widower*, Lord Rookbury announced, to prevent trouble to the mothers of families – for he was a very gentlemanly man – that little Viscount Dawton was not to have a step-mamma.' – 'He found not ... the meretricious cross-breed in art by which the modern French school contrives to depict the Magdalene with the *united attractions of Palestine and the Palais-Royal.*'

The great defect of *Aspen Court* is a want of earnestness as a background to the liveliness; the author is never thoroughly serious even in the most serious situations. But the power of the writing and the change of scene carry one over the ground, and the book everywhere titillates the palate, though it satisfies no craving.

Margaret Fuller and Mary Wollstonecraft

(*Leader*, 13 October 1855)

THE DEARTH of new books just now gives us time to recur to less recent ones which we have hitherto noticed but slightly; and among these we choose the late edition of Margaret Fuller's *Woman in the Nineteenth Century*, because we think it has been unduly thrust into the background by less comprehensive and candid productions on the same subject. Notwithstanding certain defects of taste and a sort of vague spiritualism and grandiloquence which belong to all but the very best American writers, the book is a valuable one: it has the enthusiasm of a noble and sympathetic nature, with the moderation and breadth and large allowance of a vigorous and cultivated understanding. There is no exaggeration of woman's moral excellence or intellectual capabilities; no injudicious insistence on her fitness for this or that function hitherto engrossed by men; but a calm plea for the removal of unjust laws and artificial restrictions, so that the possibilities of her nature may have room for full development, a wisely stated demand to disencumber her of the

> Parasitic forms
> That seem to keep her up, but drag her down –
> And leave her field to burgeon and to bloom
> From all within her, make herself her own
> To give or keep, to live and learn and be
> All that not harms distinctive womanhood.[1]

It is interesting to compare this essay of Margaret Fuller's, published in its earliest form in 1843, with a work on the position of woman, written between sixty and seventy years ago – we mean Mary Wollstonecraft's *Rights of Woman*.[2] The latter work was not continued beyond the first volume; but so far as this carries the subject, the comparison, at least in relation to strong sense and loftiness of moral tone, is not at all disadvantageous to the woman of the last century. There is in some quarters a vague prejudice against the *Rights of Woman* as in some way or other a reprehensible book, but readers who go to it with this impression will be surprised to find it eminently serious, severely moral, and withal rather heavy – the true reason, perhaps, that no edition has been published since 1796, and that it is now rather scarce. There are several points of resemblance, as well as of striking difference, between the two books. A strong understanding is present in both; but Margaret Fuller's mind was like some regions of her own American continent, where you are constantly stepping from the sunny 'clearings' into the mysterious twilight of the tangled forest – she often passes in one breath from forcible reasoning to dreamy vagueness; moreover, her unusually varied culture gives her great command of illustration. Mary Wollstonecraft, on the other hand, is nothing if not rational; she has no erudition, and her grave pages are lit up by no ray of fancy. In both writers we discern, under the brave bearing of a strong and truthful nature, the beating of a loving woman's heart, which teaches them not to undervalue the smallest offices of domestic care or kindliness. But Margaret Fuller, with all her passionate sensibility, is more of the literary woman, who would not have been satisfied without intellectual production; Mary Wollstonecraft, we imagine, wrote not at all for writing's sake, but from the pressure of other motives. So far as the difference of date allows, there is a striking coincidence in their trains of thought; indeed, every important idea in the *Rights of Woman*, except the combination of home education with a common day-school for boys and girls, reappears in Margaret Fuller's essay.

One point on which they both write forcibly is the fact that, while men have a horror of such faculty or culture in the other sex as tends to place it on a level with their own, they are really in a state of subjection to ignorant and feeble-minded women. Margaret Fuller says: –

Wherever man is sufficiently raised above extreme poverty or brutal stupidity, to care for the comforts of the fireside, or the bloom and ornament of life, woman has always power enough, if she choose to exert it, and is usually disposed to do so, in proportion to her ignorance and childish vanity. Unacquainted with the importance of life and its purposes, trained to a selfish coquetry and love of petty power, she does not look beyond the pleasure of making herself felt at the moment, and governments are shaken and commerce broken up to gratify the pique of a female favourite. The English shopkeeper's wife does not vote, but it is for her interest that the politician canvasses by the coarsest flattery.

Again: –

All wives, bad or good, loved or unloved, inevitably influence their husbands from the power their position not merely gives, but necessitates of colouring evidence and infusing feelings in hours when the – patient, shall I call him? – is off his guard.

Hear now what Mary Wollstonecraft says on the same subject: –

Women have been allowed to remain in ignorance and slavish dependence many, very many years, and still we hear of nothing but their fondness of pleasure and sway, their preference of rakes and soldiers, their childish attachment to toys, and the vanity that makes them value accomplishments more than virtues. History brings forward a fearful catalogue of the crimes which their cunning has produced, when the weak slaves have had sufficient address to overreach their masters . . . When, therefore, I call women slaves, I mean in a political and civil sense; for indirectly they obtain too much power, and are debased by their exertions to obtain illicit sway . . . The libertinism, and even the virtues of superior men, will always give women of some description great power over them; and these weak women, under the influence of childish passions and selfish vanity, *will throw a false light over the objects which the very men view with their eyes who ought to enlighten their judgement*. Men of fancy, and those sanguine characters who mostly hold the helm of human affairs in general, relax in the society of women; and surely I need not cite to the most superficial reader of history the numerous examples of vice and oppression which the private intrigues of female favourites have produced; not to dwell on the mischief that naturally arises from the blundering interposition of well-meaning folly. *For in the transactions of business it is much better to have to deal with a knave than a fool, because a knave adheres to some plan, and any plan of reason may be seen through sooner than a sudden flight of folly.* The power which vile and foolish women have had over wise men who possessed sensibility is notorious.

There is a notion commonly entertained among men that an instructed woman, capable of having opinions, is likely to prove an impracticable yoke-fellow, always pulling one way when her husband wants to go the other, oracular in tone, and prone to give curtain lectures on metaphysics. But surely, so far as obstinacy is concerned, your unreasoning animal is the most unmanageable of creatures, where you are not allowed to settle the question by a cudgel, a whip and bridle, or even a string to the leg. For our own parts, we see no consistent or commodious medium between the old plan of corporal discipline and that thorough education of women which will make them rational beings in the highest sense of the word. Wherever weakness is not harshly controlled it must *govern*, as you may see when a strong man holds a little child by the hand, how he is pulled hither and thither, and wearied in his walk by his submission to the whims and feeble movements of his companion. A really cultured woman, like a really cultured man, will be ready to yield in trifles. So far as we see, there is no indissoluble connexion between infirmity of logic and infirmity of will, and a woman quite innocent of an opinion in philosophy, is as likely as not to have an indomitable opinion about the kitchen. As to airs of superiority, no woman ever had them in consequence of true culture, but only because her culture was shallow or unreal, only as a result of what Mrs Malaprop[3] well calls 'the ineffectual qualities in a woman' – mere acquisitions carried about, and not knowledge thoroughly assimilated so as to enter into the growth of the character.

To return to Margaret Fuller, some of the best things she says are on the folly of absolute definitions of woman's nature and absolute demarcations of woman's mission. 'Nature,' she says, 'seems to delight in varying the arrangements, as if to show that she will be fettered by no rule; and we must admit the same varieties that she admits.' Again: 'If nature is never bound down, nor the voice of inspiration stifled, that is enough. We are pleased that women should write and speak, if they feel need of it, from having something to tell; but silence for ages would be no misfortune, if that silence be from divine command, and not from man's tradition.' And here is a passage, the beginning of which has been often quoted: –

If you ask me what offices they (women) may fill, I reply – any. I do not care what case you put; let them be sea-captains if you will. I do not doubt there are women well fitted for such an office, and, if so, I should be as glad as to welcome the Maid of Saragossa, or the Maid of Missolonghi, or the Suliote heroine, or Emily Plater. I think women need, especially at this juncture, a much greater range of occupation than they have, to rouse their latent powers . . . In families that I know, some little girls like to saw wood, others to use carpenter's tools. Where these tastes are indulged, cheerfulness and good-humour are promoted. Where they are forbidden, because 'such things are not proper for girls', they grow sullen and mischievous. Fourier[4] had observed these wants of women, as no one can fail to do who watches the desires of little girls, or knows the *ennui* that haunts grown women, except where they make to themselves a serene little world by art of some kind. He, therefore, in proposing a great variety of employments, in manufactures or the care of plants and animals, allows for one third of women as likely to have a taste for masculine pursuits, one third of men for feminine . . . I have no doubt, however, that a large proportion of women would give themselves to the same employ-ments as now, because there are circumstances that must lead them. Mothers will delight to make the nest soft and warm. Nature would take care of that; no need to clip the wings of any bird that wants to soar and sing, or finds in itself the strength of pinion for a migratory flight unusual to its kind. The difference would be that *all* need not be constrained to employments for which *some* are unfit.

A propos of the same subject, we find Mary Wollstonecraft offering a suggestion which the women of the United States have already begun to carry out. She says: –

Women, in particular, all want to be ladies. Which is simply to have nothing to do, but listlessly to go they scarcely care where, for they cannot tell what. But what have women to do in society? I may be asked, but to loiter with easy grace; surely you would not condemn them all to suckle fools and chronicle small beer. No. *Women might certainly study the art of healing, and be physicians as well as nurses* . . . Business of various kinds they might likewise pursue, if they were educated in a more orderly manner . . . Women would not then marry for a support, as men accept of places under government, and neglect the implied duties.

Men pay a heavy price for their reluctance to encourage self-help and independent resources in women. The precious meridian years of many a man of genius have to be spent in the toil of routine, that an 'establishment' may be kept up for a woman who can understand none of his secret yearnings, who is fit for nothing but to sit in her drawing-room like a doll-Madonna in her shrine. No matter. Anything is more endurable than to change our established formulæ about women, or to run the risk of looking up to our wives instead of looking down on them. *Sit divus, dummodo non sit vivus* (let him be a god, provided he be not living), said the Roman magnates of Romulus; and so men say of women, let them be idols, useless absorbents of precious things, provided we are not obliged to admit them to be strictly fellow-beings, to be treated, one and all, with justice and sober reverence.

On one side we hear that woman's position can never be improved until women themselves are better; and, on the other, that women can never become better until their position is improved – until the laws are made more just, and a wider field opened to feminine activity. But we constantly hear the same difficulty stated about the human race in general. There is a perpetual action and reaction between individuals and institutions; we must try and mend both by little and little – the only way in which human things can be mended. Unfortunately, many over-zealous champions of women assert their actual equality with men – nay, even their moral superiority to men – as a ground for their release from oppressive laws and restrictions. They lose strength immensely by this false position. If it were true, then there would be a case in which slavery and ignorance nourished virtue, and so far we should have an argument for the continuance of bondage. But we want freedom and culture for woman, because subjection and ignorance have debased her, and with her, Man; for —

> If she be small, slight-natured, miserable,
> How shall men grow?[5]

Both Margaret Fuller and Mary Wollstonecraft have too much sagacity to fall into this sentimental exaggeration. Their ardent hopes of what women may become do not prevent them from seeing and painting women as they are. On the relative moral excellence of men and women Mary Wollstonecraft speaks with the most decision: –

Women are supposed to possess more sensibility, and even humanity, than men, and their strong attachments and instantaneous emotions of compassion are given as proofs; but the clinging affection of ignorance has seldom anything noble in it, and may mostly be resolved into selfishness, as well as the affection of children and brutes. I have known many weak women whose sensibility was entirely engrossed by their husbands; and as for their humanity, it was very faint indeed, or rather it was only a transient emotion of compassion. Humanity does not consist 'in a squeamish ear', says an eminent orator. 'It belongs to the mind as well as to the nerves.' But this kind of exclusive affection, though it degrades the individual, should not be brought forward as a proof of the inferiority of the sex, because it is the natural consequence of confined views; for even women of superior sense, having their attention turned to little employments and private plans, rarely rise to heroism, unless when spurred on by love! and love, as an heroic passion, like genius, appears but once in an age. I therefore agree with the moralist who asserts 'that women have seldom so much generosity as men'; and that their narrow affections, to which justice and humanity are often sacrificed, render the sex apparently inferior, especially as they are commonly inspired by men; but I contend that the heart would expand as the understanding gained strength, if women were not depressed from their cradles.

We had marked several other passages of Margaret Fuller's for extract, but as we do not aim at an exhaustive treatment of our subject, and are only touching a few of its points, we have, perhaps, already claimed as much of the reader's attention as he will be willing to give to such desultory material.

Translations and Translators

(*Leader*, 20 October 1855)

A CLERGYMAN (of the Charles Honeyman species)[1] once told us that he never set about preparing his sermons till Saturday evening, for he 'trusted to Providence'. A similar kind of trust, we suppose, must be prevalent among translators, for many of them are evidently relying on some power which

> Can teach all people to translate,
> Though out of languages in which
> They understand no part of speech —[2]

a *Nachklang*, or resonance, perhaps, of the famous legend about those early translators, the Seventy who turned the Old Testament into Greek, which legend tells how Ptolemy shut them up in separate cells to do their work, and how, when they came to compare their renderings, there was perfect agreement! We are convinced, however, that the translators of the Septuagint had some understanding of their business to begin with, or this supernatural aid would not have been given, for in the matter of translation, at least, we have observed, that 'God helps them who help themselves.' A view of the case, which we commend to all young ladies and some middle-aged gentlemen, who consider a very imperfect acquaintance with their own language, and an anticipatory acquaintance with the foreign language, quite a sufficient equipment for the office of translator.

It is perfectly true that, though geniuses have often undertaken translation, translation does not often demand genius. The power required in the translation varies with the power exhibited in the original work: very modest qualifications will suffice to enable a person to translate a book of ordinary travels, or a slight novel, while a work of reasoning or science can be adequately rendered only by means of what is at present exceptional faculty and exceptional knowledge. Among books of this latter kind, Kant's *Critique of Pure Reason* is perhaps the very hardest nut – the peach-stone – for a translator to crack so as to lay open the entire uninjured kernel of meaning, and we are glad at last to believe that a translator of adequate power has been employed upon it. For so far as we have examined the version placed at the head of our article, it appears to us very different indeed from the many renderings of German metaphysical works, in which the translator, having ventured into deep waters without learning to swim, clings to the dictionary, and commends himself to Providence. Mr Meiklejohn's translation – so far, we must again observe, as we have examined it – indicates a real mastery of his author, and, for the first time, makes Kant's *Critik der reinen Vernunft* accessible to English readers.

It may seem odd that we should associate with this mighty book – this terrible ninety-gun ship – such a little painted pleasure-boat as Miss (or Mrs) Burt's miscellaneous collection of translations from German lyric poets. But we are concerning ourselves here simply with translation – not at all with Kant's philosophy or with German lyrics considered in themselves, and these two volumes happen to be the specimens of translation most recently presented to our notice. With regard to prose, we may very generally use Goldsmith's critical recipe, and say that the translation would have been better if the translator had taken more pains; but of poetical attempts we are often sure that no amount of pains would produce a satisfactory result. And so it is with Miss Burt's *Specimens of the German Poets*. She appears to have the knowledge and the industry which many translators want, but she has not the poetic power which makes poetical trans-lations endurable to those acquainted with the originals. Amongst others, however, who have no such acquaintance, Miss Burt's translations seem to have been in some demand, since they have reached a second edition. She has been bold enough to attempt a version of Goethe's exquisite *Zueignung* (*Dedication*), and here is a specimen of her rendering. Goethe sings with divine feeling and music –

Für andre wächst in mir das edle Gut,
Ich kann und will das Pfund nicht mehr vergraben,
Warum sucht' ich den Weg so sehnsuchtsvoll,
Wenn ich ihn nicht den Brüdern zeigen soll?[3]

Miss Burt follows him much as a Jew's harp would follow a piano –

Entombed no longer shall my *talent* be,
That treasure I amass, shall others share?
To find the road – oh, why such zeal display,
If I guide not my brethren on their way?

A version like this bears about the same relation to the original as the portraits in an illustrated newspaper bear to the living face of the distinguished gentlemen they misrepresent; and considering how often we hear opinions delivered on foreign poets by people who only know those poets at second hand, it becomes the reviewer's duty to insist again and again on the inadequacy of poetic translations.

The Germans render our poetry better than we render theirs, for their language, as slow and unwieldy as their own post-horses in prose, becomes in poetry graceful and strong and flexible as an Arabian war-horse. Besides, translation among them is more often undertaken by men of genius. We remember, for example, some translations of Burns, by Freiligrath,[4] which would have arrested us by their beauty if we had seen the poems for the first time, in this language. It is true the Germans think a little too highly of their translations, and especially are under the illusion, encouraged by some silly English people, that Shakspeare according to Schlegel is better than Shakspeare himself – not simply better to a German as being easier for him to understand, but absolutely better as poetry. A very close and admirable rendering Schlegel's assuredly is, and it is a high pleasure to track it in its faithful adherence to the original, just as it is to examine a fine engraving of a favourite picture. Sometimes the German is as good as the English – the same music played on another but as good an instrument. But more frequently the German is a feeble echo, and here and there it breaks down in a supremely fine passage. An instance of this kind occurs in the famous speech of Lorenzo to Jessica.[5] Shakspeare says –

> Soft stillness and the night
> Become the touches of sweet harmony.

This Schlegel renders –

> Sanfte Still und Nacht
> Sie werden *Tasten* süsser Harmonie.

That is to say, 'Soft stillness and the night *are* the *finger-board* of sweet harmony.' A still worse blunder is made by Tieck (whose translation is the rival of Schlegel's) in the monologue of Macbeth. In the lines –

> That but this blow
> Might be the be-all and the end-all here –
> But here upon this bank and shoal of time,
> I'd jump the life to come –

Tieck renders, 'Upon this bank and shoal of time', 'Auf dieser *Schülerbank* der Gegenwart', that is, 'On this *school-bench* of the present!' These are cases of gross inaccuracy arising from an imperfect understanding of the original. Here is an instance of feebleness. Coriolanus says –

> And like an eagle in the dovecote, I
> Flutter'd the Volscians in Corioli.

For the admirably descriptive word 'fluttered', Schlegel gives *schlug*, which simply means 'slew'. Weak renderings of this kind are abundant.

Such examples of translators' fallibility in men like Schlegel and Tieck might well make less accomplished persons more backward in undertaking the translation of great poems, and by showing the difficulty of the translator's task, might make it an object of ambition to real ability. Though a good translator is infinitely below the man who produces *good* original works, he is infinitely above the man who produces *feeble* original works. We had meant to say something of the moral qualities especially demanded in the translator – the patience, the rigid fidelity, and the sense of responsibility in interpreting another man's mind. But we have gossiped on this subject long enough.

Thomas Carlyle

(*Leader*, 27 October 1855)

IT HAS been well said that the highest aim in education is analogous to the highest aim in mathematics, namely, to obtain not *results* but *powers*, not particular solutions, but the means by which endless solutions may be wrought. He is the most effective educator who aims less at perfecting specific acquirements than at producing that mental condition which renders acquirements easy, and leads to their useful application; who does not seek to make his pupils moral by enjoining particular courses of action, but by bringing into activity the feelings and sympathies that must issue in noble action. On the same ground it may be said that the most effective writer is not he who announces a particular discovery, who convinces men of a particular conclusion, who demonstrates that this measure is right and that measure is wrong; but he who rouses in others the activities that must issue in discovery, who awakes men from their indifference to the right and the wrong, who nerves their energies to seek for the truth and live up to it at whatever cost. The influence of such a writer is dynamic. He does not teach men how to use sword and musket, but he inspires their souls with courage and sends a strong will into their muscles. He does not, perhaps, enrich your stock of data, but he clears away the film from your eyes that you may search for data to some purpose. He does not, perhaps, convince you, but he strikes you, undeceives you, animates you. You are not directly fed by his books, but you are braced as by a walk up to an alpine summit, and yet subdued to calm and reverence as by the sublime things to be seen from that summit.

Such a writer is Thomas Carlyle. It is an idle question to ask whether his books will be read a century hence: if they were all burnt as the grandest of Suttees on his funeral pile, it would be only like cutting down an oak after its acorns have sown a forest. For there is hardly a superior or active mind of this generation that has not been modified by Carlyle's writings; there has hardly been an English book written for the last ten or twelve years that would not have been different if Carlyle had not lived. The character of his influence is best seen in the fact that many of the men who have the least agreement with his opinions are those to whom the reading of *Sartor Resartus* was an epoch in the history of their minds.[1] The extent of his influence may be best seen in the fact that ideas which were startling novelties when he first wrote them are now become common-places. And we think few men will be found to say that this influence on the whole has not been for good. There are plenty who question the justice of Carlyle's estimates of past men and past times, plenty who quarrel with the exaggerations of the *Latter-day Pamphlets*, and who are as far as possible from looking for an amendment of things from a Carlylian theocracy with the 'greatest man', as a Joshua who is to smite the wicked (and the stupid) till the going down of the sun.[2] But for any large nature, those points of difference are quite incidental. It is not as a theorist, but as a great and beautiful human nature, that Carlyle influences us. You may meet a man whose wisdom seems unimpeachable, since you find him entirely in agreement with yourself; but this oracular man of unexceptionable opinions has a green eye, a wiry hand, and altogether a *Wesen*, or demeanour, that makes the world look blank to you, and whose unexceptionable opinions become a bore; while another man who deals in what you cannot but think 'dangerous paradoxes', warms your heart by the pressure of his hand, and looks out on the world with so clear and loving an eye, that nature seems to reflect the light of his glance upon your own feeling. So it is with Carlyle. When he is saying the very opposite of what we think, he says it so finely, with such hearty conviction – he makes the object about which we differ stand out in such grand relief under the clear light of his strong and honest intellect – he appeals so constantly to our sense of the manly and the truthful – that we are obliged to say 'Hear! hear!' to the writer before we can give the decorous 'Oh! oh!' to his opinions.

Much twaddling criticism has been spent on Carlyle's style.

Unquestionably there are some genuine minds, not at all given to twaddle, to whom his style is antipathetic, who find it as unendurable as an English lady finds peppermint. Against antipathies there is no arguing; they are misfortunes. But instinctive repulsion apart, surely there is no one who can read and relish Carlyle without feeling that they could no more wish him to have written in another style than they could wish gothic architecture not to be gothic, or Raffaelle not to be Raffaellesque. It is the fashion to speak of Carlyle almost exclusively as a philosopher; but, to our thinking, he is yet more of an artist than a philosopher. He glances deep down into human nature, and shows the causes of human actions; he seizes grand generalizations, and traces them in the particular with wonderful acumen; and in all this he is a philosopher. But, perhaps, his greatest power lies in concrete presentation. No novelist has made his creations live for us more thoroughly than Carlyle has made Mirabeau and the men of the French Revolution, Cromwell and the Puritans. What humour in his pictures! Yet what depth of appreciation, what reverence for the great and god-like under every sort of earthly mummery!

It is several years now since we read a work of Carlyle's *seriatim*, but this our long-standing impression of him as a writer we find confirmed by looking over Mr Ballantyne's selection. Such a volume as this is surely a benefit to the public, for alas! Carlyle's works are still dear, and many who would like to have them are obliged to forgo the possession of more than a volume or two. Through this good service of Mr Ballantyne's, however, they may now obtain for a moderate sum a large collection of extracts – if not the best that could have been made, still very precious ones.

To make extracts from a book of extracts may at first seem easy, and to make extracts from a writer so well known may seem superfluous. The *embarras de richesses* and the length of the passages make the first not easy; and as to the second, why, we have reread these passages so often in the volumes, and now again in Mr Ballantyne's selection, that we cannot suppose any amount of repetition otherwise than agreeable. We will, however, be sparing. Here is

David, the Hebrew King

On the whole, we make too much of faults: the details of the business hide the real centre of it. Faults? The greatest of faults, I should say, is to be conscious of none. Readers of the Bible above all, one would think, might know better. Who is called there 'the man according to God's own heart'? David, the Hebrew King, had fallen into sins enough; blackest crimes; there was no want of sins. And thereupon the unbelievers sneer and ask, Is this your man according to God's heart? The sneer, I must say, seems to me but a shallow one. What are faults, what are the outward details of a life, if the inner secret of it, the remorse, temptations, true, often-baffled, never-ended struggle of it, be forgotten? 'It is not in man that walketh to direct his steps.' Of all acts is not, for a man, *repentance* the most divine? The deadliest sin, I say, were that same supercilious consciousness of no sin; – that is death; the heart so conscious is divorced from sincerity, humility, and fact; is dead: it is 'pure' as dead dry sand is pure. David's life and history, as written for us in those Psalms of his, I consider to be the truest emblem ever given of a man's moral progress and warfare here below. All earnest souls will ever discern in it the faithful struggle of an earnest human soul towards what is good and best. Struggle often baffled, sore baffled, down as into entire wreck; yet a struggle never ended; ever, with tears, repentance, true unconquerable purpose, begun anew. Poor human nature! Is not a man's walking, in truth, always that: 'a succession of falls'? Man can do no other. In this wild element of a Life, he has to struggle onwards; now fallen, deep-abased; and ever, with tears, repentance, with bleeding heart, he has to rise again, struggle again still onwards. That his struggle *be* a faithful unconquerable one: that is the question of questions.[3]

In another way how excellent is this on

The Worth of Formulas

What we call 'Formulas' are not in their origin bad; they are indispensably good. Formula is *method*, habitude, found wherever man is found. Formulas fashion themselves as Paths do, as beaten Highways, leading towards some sacred or high object, whither many men are bent. Consider it. One man, full of heartfelt earnest impulse, finds out a way of doing somewhat – were it of uttering his soul's reverence for the Highest, were it but of fitly saluting his fellow-man. An inventor was needed to do that, a *poet*; he has articulated the dim-struggling thought that dwelt in his own and many hearts. This is his way of doing that; these are his footsteps, the beginning of a 'Path'. And now see: the second man travels naturally in the footsteps of his foregoer: it is the *easiest* method. In the footsteps of his foregoer; yet with improvements, changes where such seem good; at all events with enlargements, the Path ever *widening* itself as more travel it; – till at last there is a broad Highway whereon the whole world may travel and drive. While there remains a City or Shrine, or any Reality to drive to, at the farther end, the Highway shall be right welcome! When the City is gone, we will forsake the Highway. In this manner all Institutions, Practices, Regulated Things in the world have come into existence, and gone out of existence. Formulas all begin by being *full* of substance; you may call them the *skin*, the articulation into shape, into limbs and skin, of a substance that is already there: *they* had not been there otherwise. Idols, as we said, are not idolatrous till they become doubtful, empty for the worshipper's heart. Much as we talk against Formulas, I hope no one of us is ignorant withal of the high significance or *true* Formulas; that they were, and will ever be, the indispensablest furniture of our habitation in this world.[4]

Finally, this characteristic passage tempts us: –

The Apes of the Dead Sea

Perhaps few narratives in History or Mythology are more significant than that Moslem one, of Moses and the Dwellers by the Dead Sea. A tribe of men dwelt on the shores of that same Asphaltic Lake; and having forgotten, as we are all prone to do, the inner facts of Nature, and taken up with the falsities and outer semblances of it, were fallen into sad conditions – verging indeed towards a certain far deeper Lake. Whereupon it pleased kind Heaven to send them the Prophet Moses, with an instructive word of warning, out of which might have sprung 'remedial measures' not a few. But no: the men of the Dead Sea discovered, as the valet-species always does in heroes or prophets, no comeliness in Moses; listened with real tedium to Moses, with light grinning, or with splenetic sniffs and sneers, affecting even to yawn; and signified, in short, that they found him a humbug, and even a bore. Such was the candid theory these men of the Asphalt Lake formed to themselves of Moses, That probably he was a humbug, that certainly he was a bore. Moses withdrew; but Nature and her rigorous veracities did not withdraw. The Men of the Dead Sea, when we next went to visit them, were all 'changed into Apes'; sitting on the trees there, grinning now in the most *un*affected manner; gibbering and chattering *complete* nonsense; finding the whole Universe now a most undisputable Humbug! The Universe has *become* a Humbug to the Apes who thought it one! There they sit and chatter, to this hour; only I think, every Sabbath there returns to them a bewildered half-consciousness, half-reminiscence; and they sit, with their wizened smoke-dried visages, and such an air of supreme tragicality as Apes may; looking out, through those blinking smoke-bleared eyes of theirs, into the wonderfulest universal smoky Twilight and undecipherable disordered Dusk of Things; wholly an Uncertainty, Unintelligibility, they and it; and for commentary thereon, here and there an unmusical chatter or mew: – truest, tragicalest Humbug conceivable by the mind of man or ape! They made no use of their souls; and *so* have lost them. Their worship on the Sabbath now is to roost there, with unmusical screeches, and half remember that they had souls. Didst thou never, O Traveller, fall in with parties of this tribe? Meseems they are grown somewhat numerous in our day.[5]

Robert Browning's *Men and Women*

(Westminster Review, January 1856)

WE NEVER read Heinsius[1] – a great admission for a reviewer – but we learn from M. Arago[2] that that formidably erudite writer pronounces Aristotle's works to be characterized by a *majestic obscurity which repels the ignorant*. We borrow these words to indicate what is likely to be the first impression of a reader who, without any previous familiarity with Browning, glances through his two new volumes of poems. The less acute he is, the more easily will he arrive at the undeniable criticism, that these poems have a 'majestic obscurity', which repels not only the ignorant but the idle. To read poems is often a substitute for thought: fine-sounding conventional phrases and the sing-song of verse demand no co-operation in the reader; they glide over his mind with the agreeable unmeaningness of 'the compliments of the season', or a speaker's exordium on 'feelings too deep for expression'. But let him expect no such drowsy passivity in reading Browning. Here he will find no conventionality, no melodious commonplace, but freshness, originality, sometimes eccentricity of expression; no didactic laying-out of a subject, but dramatic indication, which requires the reader to trace by his own mental activity the underground stream of thought that jets out in elliptical and pithy verse. To read Browning he must exert himself, but he will exert himself to some purpose. If he finds the meaning difficult of access, it is always worth his effort – if he has to dive deep, 'he rises with his pearl'. Indeed, in Browning's best poems he makes us feel that what we took for obscurity in him was superficiality in ourselves. We are far from meaning that all his obscurity is like the obscurity of the stars, dependent simply on the feebleness of men's vision. On the contrary, our admiration for his genius only makes us feel the more acutely that its inspirations are too often straitened by the garb of whimsical mannerism with which he clothes them. This mannerism is even irritating sometimes, and should at least be kept under restraint in *printed* poems, where the writer is not merely indulging his own vein, but is avowedly appealing to the mind of his reader.

Turning from the ordinary literature of the day to such a writer as Browning, is like turning from Flotow's[3] music, made up of well-pieced shreds and patches, to the distinct individuality of Chopin's Studies or Schubert's Songs. Here, at least, is a man who has something of his own to tell us, and who can tell it impressively, if not with faultless art. There is nothing sickly or dreamy in him: he has a clear eye, a vigorous grasp, and courage to utter what he sees and handles. His robust energy is informed by a subtle, penetrating spirit, and this blending of opposite qualities gives his mind a rough piquancy that reminds one of a russet apple. His keen glance pierces into all the secrets of human character, but, being as thoroughly alive to the outward as to the inward, he reveals those secrets, not by a process of dissection, but by dramatic painting. We fancy his own description of a poet applies to himself: –

> He stood and watched the cobbler at his trade,
> The man who slices lemons into drink,
> The coffee-roaster's brazier, and the boys
> That volunteer to help him at the winch.
> He glanced o'er books on stalls with half an eye,
> And fly-leaf ballads on the vendor's string,
> And broad-edge bold-print posters by the wall.
> *He took such cognizance of men and things,*
> *If any beat a horse, you felt he saw;*
> *If any cursed a woman, he took note;*
> *Yet stared at nobody, – they stared at him,*
> *And found, less to their pleasure than surprise,*
> *He seemed to know them and expect as much.*[4]

Browning has no soothing strains, no chants, no lullabys; he rarely gives voice to our melancholy, still less to our gaiety; he sets our thoughts at work rather than our emotions. But though eminently a thinker, he is as far as possible from prosaic; his mode of presentation is always concrete, artistic, and, where it is most felicitous, dramatic. Take, for example, 'Fra Lippo Lippi', a poem at once original and perfect in its kind. The artist-monk, Fra Lippo, is supposed to be detected by the night-watch roaming the streets of Florence, and while sharing the wine with which he makes amends to the Dogberrys[5] for the roughness of his tongue, he pours forth the story of his life and his art with the racy conversational vigour of a brawny genius under the influence of the Care-dispeller.

> I was a baby when my mother died
> And father died and left me in the street.
> I starved there, God knows how, a year or two
> On fig-skins, melon-parings, rinds and shucks,
> Refuse and rubbish. One fine frosty day
> My stomach being empty as your hat,
> The wind doubled me up and down I went.
> Old aunt Lapaccia trussed me with one hand,
> (Its fellow was a stinger as I knew)
> And so along the wall, over the bridge,
> By the straight cut to the convent. Six words, there,
> While I stood munching my first bread that month:
> 'So, boy, you're minded,' quoth the good fat father
> Wiping his own mouth, 'twas refection time, –
> 'To quit this very miserable world?
> Will you renounce' . . . The mouthful of bread? thought I;
> By no means! Brief, they made a monk of me.
>
> *
>
> 'Let's see what the urchin's fit for' – that came next.
> Not overmuch their way, I must confess.
> Such a to-do! they tried me with their books.
> Lord, they'd have taught me Latin in pure waste!
> *Flower o' the clove,*
> *All the Latin I construe is, 'amo' I love!*
> But, mind you, when a boy starves in the streets
> Eight years together as my fortune was,
> Watching folk's faces to know who will fling
> The bit of half-stripped grape-bunch he desires,
> And who will curse or kick him for his pains –
> Which gentleman processional and fine,
> Holding a candle to the Sacrament,

Will wink and let him lift a plate and catch
The droppings of the wax to sell again,
Or holla for the Eight and have him whipped, –
How say I? – nay, which dog bites, which lets drop
His bone from the heap of offal in the street!
– The soul and sense of him grow sharp alike,
He learns the look of things, and none the less
For admonitions from the hunger-pinch.
I had a store of such remarks, be sure,
Which, after I found leisure, turned to use:
I drew men's faces on my copy-books,
Scrawled them within the antiphonary's marge,
Joined legs and arms to the long music-notes,
Found nose and eyes and chin for A's and B's,
And made a string of pictures of the world
Betwixt the ins and outs of verb and noun,
On the wall, the bench, the door. The monks looked black.
'Nay,' quoth the Prior, 'turn him out, d'ye say?
In no wise. Lose a crow and catch a lark.
What if at last we get our man of parts,
We Carmelites, like those Camaldolese
And Preaching Friars, to do our church up fine
And put the front on it that ought to be!'
And hereupon they bade me daub away.
Thank you! my head being crammed, their walls a blank,
Never was such prompt disemburdening.
First, every sort of monk, the black and white,
I drew them fat and lean: then, folks at church,
From good old gossips waiting to confess
Their cribs of barrel-droppings, candle-ends, –
To the breathless fellow at the altar-foot,
Fresh from his murder, safe and sitting there
With the little children round him in a row
Of admiration, half for his beard and half
For that white anger of his victim's son
Shaking a fist at him with one fierce arm,
Signing himself with the other because of Christ,
(*Whose sad face on the cross sees only this*
After the passion of a thousand years)
Till some poor girl, her apron o'er her head
Which the intense eyes looked through, came at eve

On tip-toe, said a word, dropped in a loaf,
Her pair of ear-rings and a bunch of flowers
The brute took growling, prayed, and then was gone.
I painted all, then cried ''tis ask and have –
Choose, for more's ready!' – laid the ladder flat,
And showed my covered bit of cloister-wall.
The monks closed in a circle and praised loud
Till checked (taught what to see and not to see,
Being simple bodies), 'that's the very man!
Look at the boy who stoops to pat the dog!
That woman's like the Prior's niece who comes
To care about his asthma: it's the life!'
But there my triumph's straw-fire flared and funked –
Their betters took their turn to see and say:
The Prior and the learned pulled a face
And stopped all that in no time. 'How? what's here?
Quite from the mark of painting, bless us all!
Faces, arms, legs and bodies like the true
As much as pea and pea! it's devil's-game!
Your business is not to catch men with show,
With homage to the perishable clay,
But lift them over it, ignore it all,
Make them forget there's such a thing as flesh.
Your business is to paint the souls of men –
Man's soul, and it's a fire, smoke . . . no it's not . . .
It's vapour done up like a new-born babe –
(In that shape when you die it leaves your mouth)
It's . . . well, what matters talking, it's the soul!
Give us no more of body than shows soul.

*

Have it all out!' Now, is this sense, I ask?
A fine way to paint soul, by painting body
So ill, the eye can't stop there, must go further
And can't fare worse! Thus, yellow does for white
When what you put for yellow's simply black,
And *any sort of meaning looks intense*
When all beside itself means and looks nought.
Why can't a painter lift each foot in turn,
Left foot and right foot, go a double step,
Make his flesh liker and his soul more like,
Both in their order? Take the prettiest face,

The Prior's niece . . . patron-saint – is it so pretty
You can't discover if it means hope, fear,
Sorrow or joy? won't beauty go with these?
Suppose I've made her eyes all right and blue,
Can't I take breath and try to add life's flash,
And then add soul and heighten them threefold?
Or say there's beauty with no soul at all –
(I never saw it – put the case the same –)
If you get simple beauty and nought else,
You get about the best thing God invents, –
That's somewhat. And you'll find the soul you have missed,
Within yourself when you return Him thanks!

*

    You be judge!
You speak no Latin more than I, belike –
However, you're my man, you've seen the world
– The beauty and the wonder and the power,
The shapes of things, their colours, lights and shades,
Changes, surprises, – and God made it all!
– For what? do you feel thankful, ay or no,
For this fair town's face, yonder river's line,
The mountain round it and the sky above,
Much more the figures of man, woman, child,
These are the frame to? What's it all about?
To be passed o'er, despised? or dwelt upon,
Wondered at? oh, this last of course, you say.
But why not do as well as say, – paint these
Just as they are, careless what comes of it?
God's works – paint anyone, and count it crime
To let a truth slip. Don't object, 'His works
Are here already – nature is complete:
Suppose you reproduce her – (which you can't)
There's no advantage! you must beat her, then.'
For, don't you mark, we're made so that we love
First when we see them painted, things we have passed
Perhaps a hundred times nor cared to see;
And so they are better, painted – better to us,
Which is the same thing. *Art was given for that –*
God uses us to help each other so,
Lending our minds out.

Extracts cannot do justice to the fine dramatic touches by which Fra Lippo is made present to us, while he throws out this instinctive Art-criticism. And extracts from 'Bishop Blougram's Apology', an equally remarkable poem of what we may call the dramatic-psychological kind, would be still more ineffective. 'Sylvester Blougram, styled *in partibus Episcopus*', is talking

> Over the glass's edge when dinner's done,
> And body gets its sop and holds its noise
> And leaves soul free a little,

with 'Gigadibs the literary man', to whom he is bent on proving by the most exasperatingly ingenious sophistry, that the theory of life on which he grounds his choice of being a bishop, though a doubting one, is wiser in the moderation of its ideal, with the certainty of attainment, than the Gigadibs theory, which aspires after the highest and attains nothing. The way in which Blougram's motives are dug up from below the roots, and laid bare to the very last fibre, not by a process of hostile exposure, not by invective or sarcasm, but by making himself exhibit them with a self-complacent sense of supreme acuteness, and even with a crushing force of worldly common sense, has the effect of masterly satire. But the poem is too strictly consecutive for any fragments of it to be a fair specimen. Belonging to the same order of subtle yet vigorous writing are the 'Epistle of Karshish, the Arab Physician', 'Cleon', and 'How it Strikes a Contemporary'. 'In a Balcony' is so fine, that we regret it is not a complete drama instead of being merely the suggestion of a drama. One passage especially tempts us to extract.

> All women love great men
> If young or old – it is in all the tales –
> Young beauties love old poets who can love –
> Why should not he the poems in my soul,
> The love, the passionate faith, the sacrifice,
> The constancy? I throw them at his feet.
> Who cares to see the fountain's very shape
> And whether it be a Triton's or a Nymph's
> That pours the foam, makes rainbows all around?
> You could not praise indeed the empty conch;
> *But I'll pour floods of love and hide myself.*

These lines are less rugged than is usual with Browning's blank verse; but generally, the greatest deficiency we feel in his poetry is its want of music. The worst poems in his new volumes are, in our opinion, his lyrical efforts; for in these, where he engrosses us less by his thought, we are more sensible of his obscurity and his want of melody. His lyrics, instead of tripping along with easy grace, or rolling with a torrent-like grandeur, seem to be struggling painfully under a burthen too heavy for them; and many of them have the disagreeable puzzling effect of a charade, rather than the touching or animating influence of song. We have said that he is never prosaic; and it is remarkable that in his blank verse, though it is often colloquial, we are never shocked by the sense of a sudden lapse into prose. Wordsworth is, on the whole, a far more musical poet than Browning, yet we remember no line in Browning so prosaic as many of Wordsworth's, which in some of his finest poems have the effect of bricks built into a rock. But we must also say that though Browning never flounders helplessly on the plain, he rarely soars above a certain table-land – a footing between the level of prose and the topmost heights of poetry. He does not take possession of our souls and set them aglow, as the greatest poets – the greatest artists do. We admire his power, we are not subdued by it. Language with him does not seem spontaneously to link itself into song, as sounds link themselves into melody in the mind of the creative musician; he rather seems by his commanding powers to compel language into verse. He has *chosen* verse as his medium; but of our greatest poets we feel that they had no choice: Verse chose them. Still we are grateful that Browning chose this medium: we would rather have 'Fra Lippo Lippi' than an essay on Realism in Art; we would rather have 'The Statue and the Bust' than a three-volumed novel with the same moral; we would rather have 'Holy Cross-Day' than 'Strictures on the Society for the Emancipation of the Jews'.

By way of counterbalancing our judgement, we will give a parting quotation from one of the most musical of the rhymed poems.

> My perfect wife, my Leonor,
>   Oh, heart my own, oh, eyes, mine too,
> Whom else could I dare look backward for,

With whom beside should I dare pursue
　The path grey heads abhor?

For it leads to a crag's sheer edge with them;
　Youth, flowery all the way, there stops –
Not they; age threatens and they contemn,
　Till they reach the gulf wherein youth drops,
One inch from our life's safe hem!

*

My own, confirm me! If I tread
　This path back, is it not in pride
To think how little I dreamed it led
　To an age so blest that by its side
Youth seems the waste instead!

My own, see where the years conduct!
　At first, *'twas something our two souls*
Should mix as mists do: each is sucked
　Into each now; on, the new stream rolls,
Whatever rocks obstruct.[6]

Peter von Bohlen's *Introduction to the Book of Genesis*

(*Leader*, 12 January 1856)

WHAT IS the office of the biblical critic in relation to the Old Testament? There are various answers to this question.

Extreme orthodoxy says, that since there is irrefragable external evidence for the divine origin and direct verbal inspiration of the Hebrew Scriptures, the critic has simply to interpret the meaning of the text: any record which is in contradiction with the text, if not reconcilable by hypothesis, is to be pronounced false; but if an undeniable fact turns out to be in contradiction with the text, the received interpretation is to be reconsidered and altered so as to agree with the undeniable fact. According to this theory the critic has not to examine the Hebrew writings in order to ascertain their origin, but having beforehand settled their origin, he has to explain everything so as to make it accord with this premiss. He is not an inquirer, but an advocate. He has not to weigh evidence in order to arrive at a conclusion, but having arrived at a conclusion, he has to make it the standard by which he accepts or rejects evidence. His criticism is a deductive process, which has for its axiom, The Hebrew writings are from beginning to end revealed truth. And it is only while orthodoxy strictly adheres to this point of view that it is on safe and consistent ground; for if we are to examine a book for proof – though it be only confirmatory proof – of its origin, we must have some criteria to judge it by, and we can only obtain such criteria by borrowing them from pure historical criticism, an ally that must be ultimately incompatible with rigid orthodoxy. As long as we rely implicitly on testimony as evidence of a man's health, we have no need to examine the indications of health in his person; but the moment we feel the testimony insufficient, we must have recourse to physiological criteria, which are common to every human organism.

The first symptom that orthodoxy begins to feel the pressure of historical criticism is shown in an extension of the 'accommodation' theory. As the Deity, it is said, in speaking to human beings, must use human language, and consequently anthropomorphic expressions, such as the 'eye of God', the 'arm of God', the 'laughter and jealousy of God', which we have no difficulty in understanding figuratively, so he must adapt the form of His revelations to the degree of culture, which belongs to men at the period in which His revelations are made. He teaches them as a father teaches his children, by adapting the information he gives to their narrow stock of ideas. It was in this way that the candid Dr Pye Smith[1] explained the narratives of the Creation and the Deluge, to the great scandal of his Evangelical brethren. It is easy to see that this system of interpretation is very elastic, and that it may soon amount to little more than a theological formula for the history of human development. The relation between the theory of *accommodation* and that of *development* is analogous to the relation between the doctrine that the brain is the organ of mind, and the doctrine that mind is the function of the brain; in both cases the manifestation of mind is determined by the conditions of the body. And thus the 'accommodation' theory necessarily leads to what may be called a mitigated orthodoxy or a mild heterodoxy, which allows the presence of mythical and legendary elements in the Hebrew records, and renounces the idea that they are from beginning to end infallible, but still regards them as the medium of a special revelation, as the shell that held a kernel of peculiarly divine truth, by which a monotheistic faith was preserved, and the way prepared for the Christian dispensation. They who hold this theory believe that the Hebrew nation was the grandest instrument of Providence – the Hebrew writings, the vehicle of superhuman truth; but they do not believe in talking serpents and talking asses, or in divine commands to butcher men wholesale; and they hold that, to identify a belief in such fables with the faith of a Christian, is as dangerous to reverence as it would be to fix an absurd popinjay on the divine symbol of the Cross. The laws of Moses are something more to them than the laws of Menu[2] – a Hebrew prophet something more than a religious and patriotic poet; a chapter of Isaiah something more than the Hymn of Cleanthes.[3] They do not feel about the Hebrew temple and the Hebrew worship as they feel about a temple of Isis or the Eleusinian mysteries:[4] the history of Israel is a sacred precinct to them – they take their shoes from off their feet, for it is holy ground. To them, therefore, the Old Testament is still an exceptional book; they only use historical criticism as a winnowing fan to carry away all demands on their belief, which are not strictly involved in their acceptance of Christianity as a special revelation.

Extreme heterodoxy, on the contrary, holds no conviction that removes the Hebrew Scriptures from the common category of early national records, which are a combination of myth and legend, gradually clarifying at their later stages into genuine history. It enters on the examination of the Old Testament with as perfect a freedom from presuppositions, as unreserved a submission to the guidance of historical criticism, as if it were examining the Vedas or the Zendavesta, or the fragments of Manetho and Sanchoniathon.[5] On thus looking at the Hebrew records by the 'light of common day', without the lamp of faith, heterodoxy finds in them no evidence of anything exceptionally divine, but sees in them simply the history and literature of a barbarous tribe that gradually rose from fetichism to a ferocious polytheism, offering human sacrifices, and ultimately, through the guidance of their best men, and contact with more civilized nations, to Jehovistic monotheism. It finds in them, as in other early records, a mythical cosmogony, an impossible chronology, and extravagant marvels tending to flatter national vanity, or to aggrandize a priesthood; it finds discrepant conceptions of Deity in documents attributed to one and the same source; it finds legislative enactments, springing from an advanced period, stamped with the sanction of primæval names, or of mythical crises in the national history; in short, it not only finds in the Hebrew writings nothing which cannot be accounted for on grounds purely human, but it finds them of a character which it would be monstrous to attribute to any other than a human origin.

These are results arrived at in the present day by very grave and competent scholars, and whatever opinion may be held concerning them, no educated person can dispense with some knowledge of the evidence on which they are based. There are few books, at least in English, better adapted to give such knowledge in a concise form than the *Introduction to Genesis* by Von Bohlen, named at the head of our article. Von Bohlen's was a thoroughly earnest and reverent mind, and orthodox believers need never be shocked by his manner, if they are inevitably pained by his matter. To this admirable qualification he added that of immense learning, especially in the department of Hindoo literature, his fame having been first won by a work on ancient India. We have only to regret that Mr Heywood did not heighten the value of his disinterested labour in editing the *Introduction to Genesis*, by publishing it in a cheaper and more portable form.

The first volume is chiefly occupied with considerations on the origin and character of the Pentateuch, or five books of Moses, generally, considerations which embrace the course of Hebrew history until after the Captivity, or transplantation to Babylon. Every important particular is discussed clearly and briefly, but not scantily, and the reader, though he may not accept Von Bohlen's conclusions, is placed in an excellent position for pursuing the investigation by a closer study of the Scriptures themselves. Mr Heywood has added in an appendix to this volume the valuable remarks of Von Bohlen on the Week, extracted from his *Ancient India*.

The second volume contains a commentary on the opening portion of Genesis. Von Bohlen wrote a commentary on the whole book, but the translation is limited to the first ten chapters which comprise the important narratives of the Creation, the Fall, the Flood, and the Dispersion of mankind. Mr Heywood has enriched this volume by notes and by additional remarks on the flood; he has also inserted some interesting extracts on this subject and on the Paradisaic myth from Professor Tuck's Commentary on Genesis.[6]

Instead of quoting from the more argumentative and critical portion of the volumes, which would not be effective in the cursory reading usually given to newspapers, we will borrow from them an admirable Hebrew myth which has arisen since the Christian era. We cannot agree with Von Bohlen that it is 'true to the spirit of antiquity'. The tolerance it breathes is unknown to the Books of the Law: –

Pococke[7] is said to have actually found this chapter in a manuscript at Cairo. The Talmud, too, is supposed to have been acquainted with it. Saadi alludes to it in his 'Bustan' (*Asiatic Journal*, vol. 3, p. 315). Taylor cites it in the middle of the seventeenth century, and it has now become generally known through the means of Franklin [by whom it was communicated to Lord Kames], who quotes it in his 'Sketches' as a parable against intolerance. It runs as follows: –

1. Now it came to pass that Abraham sat at the door of his tent in the heat of the day. 2. And behold a man drew nigh from the wilderness, and he was bowed down with age, and his white beard hung down even to his girdle, and he leant upon his staff. 3. And when Abraham saw him he stood up, and ran to meet him from the door of his tent, and said, 4. Friend, come in; water shall be brought thee to wash thy feet, and thou shalt eat and tarry the night, and on the morrow thou mayest go on thy way. 5. But the wayfaring man answered and said, Let me, I pray thee, remain under the tree. 6. And Abraham pressed him sore; then he turned and went into the tent. 7. And Abraham set before him cream and milk and cake, and they ate and were satisfied. 8. And when Abraham saw that the man blessed not God, he said to him, Wherefore dost thou not honour the Almighty, the Creator of the heavens and the earth? 9. And the man answered, I worship not thy God, neither do I call upon his name; for I have made gods for myself that dwell in my house, and hear me when I call upon them. 10. Then the wrath of Abraham was kindled against the man, and he stood up and fell upon him, and drove him forth into the wilderness. 11. And God cried, Abraham! Abraham! and Abraham answered, Here am I. 12. And God said, where is the stranger that was with thee? 13. Then answered Abraham and said, Lord, he would not reverence thee nor call upon thy name, and therefore have I driven him from before my face into the wilderness. 14. And the Lord said unto Abraham, Have I borne with the man these hundred and ninety-eight years, and given him food and raiment although he has rebelled against me, and canst thou not bear with him one night? 15. And Abraham said, Let not the wrath of my Lord be kindled against his servant, behold I have sinned! forgive me. 16. And Abraham stood up and went forth into the wilderness, and cried and sought the man, and found him and led him back into his tent, and dealt kindly by him, and the next morning he let him go in peace.

The *Antigone* and Its Moral

(Leader, 29 March 1856)

'LO! HERE a little volume but great Book' – a volume small enough to slip into your breast pocket, but containing in fine print one of the finest tragedies of the single dramatic poet who can be said to stand on a level with Shakspeare. Sophocles is the crown and flower of the classic tragedy as Shakspeare is of the romantic: to borrow Schlegel's comparison, which cannot be improved upon, they are related to each other as the Parthenon to Strasburg Cathedral.

The opinion which decries all enthusiasm for Greek literature as 'humbug', was put to an excellent test some years ago by the production of the *Antigone* at Drury Lane.[1] The translation then adopted was among the feeblest by which a great poet has ever been misrepresented; yet so completely did the poet triumph over the disadvantages of his medium and of a dramatic motive foreign to modern sympathies, that the Pit was electrified, and Sophocles, over a chasm of 2,000 years, once more swayed the emotions of a popular audience. And no wonder. The *Antigone* has every quality of a fine tragedy, and fine tragedies can never become mere mummies for Hermanns and Böckhs[2] to dispute about: they must appeal to perennial human nature, and even the ingenious dullness of translators cannot exhaust them of their passion and their poetry.

E'en in their ashes live their wonted fires.[3]

We said that the dramatic motive of the *Antigone* was foreign to modern sympathies, but it is only superficially so. It is true we no longer believe that a brother, if left unburied, is condemned to wander a hundred years without repose on the banks of the Styx;

363

we no longer believe that to neglect funeral rites is to violate the claims of the infernal deities. But these beliefs are the accidents and not the substance of the poet's conception. The turning point of the tragedy is not, as it is stated to be in the argument prefixed to this edition, 'reverence for the dead and the importance of the sacred rites of burial', but the *conflict* between these and obedience to the State. Here lies the dramatic collision: the impulse of sisterly piety which allies itself with reverence for the Gods, clashes with the duties of citizenship; two principles, both having their validity, are at war with each. Let us glance for a moment at the plot.

Eteocles and Polynices, the brothers of Antigone, have slain each other in battle before the gates of Thebes, the one defending his country, the other invading it in conjunction with foreign allies. Hence Creon becomes, by the death of these two sons of Œdipus, the legitimate ruler of Thebes, grants funeral honours to Eteocles, but denies them to Polynices, whose body is cast out to be the prey of beasts and birds, a decree being issued that death will be the penalty of an attempt to bury him. In the second scene of the play Creon expounds the motive of his decree to the Theban elders, insisting in weighty words on the duty of making all personal affection subordinate to the well-being of the State. The impulses of affection and religion which urge Antigone to disobey this proclamation are strengthened by the fact that in her last interview with her brother he had besought her not to leave his corpse unburied. She determines to brave the penalty, buries Polynices, is taken in the act and brought before Creon, to whom she does not attempt to deny that she knew of the proclamation, but declares that she deliberately disobeyed it, and is ready to accept death as its consequence. It was not Zeus, she tells him – it was not eternal Justice that issued that decree. The proclamation of Creon is not so authoritative as the unwritten law of the Gods, which is neither of today nor of yesterday, but lives eternally, and none knows its beginning.

> Οὐ γάρ τι νῦν γε κἀχθές, ἀλλ' ἀεί ποτε
> Ζῆ ταῦτα, κοὐδεὶς οἶδεν ἐξότου 'φάνη.[4]

Creon, on his side, insists on the necessity to the welfare of the State that he should be obeyed as legitimate ruler, and becomes exasperated by the calm defiance of Antigone. She is condemned to death. Hæmon, the son of Creon, to whom Antigone is betrothed, remonstrates against this judgement in vain. Teiresias also, the blind old soothsayer, alarmed by unfavourable omens, comes to warn Creon against persistence in a course displeasing to the Gods. It is not until he has departed, leaving behind him the denunciation of coming woes, that Creon's confidence begins to falter, and at length, persuaded by the Theban elders, he reverses his decree, and proceeds with his followers to the rocky tomb in which Antigone has been buried alive, that he may deliver her. It is too late. Antigone is already dead; Hæmon commits suicide in the madness of despair, and the death of his mother Eurydice on hearing the fatal tidings, completes the ruin of Creon's house.

It is a very superficial criticism which interprets the character of Creon as that of a hypocritical tyrant, and regards Antigone as a blameless victim. Coarse contrasts like this are not the materials handled by great dramatists. The exquisite art of Sophocles is shown in the touches by which he makes us feel that Creon, as well as Antigone, is contending for what he believes to be the right, while both are also conscious that, in following out one principle, they are laying themselves open to just blame for transgressing another; and it is this consciousness which secretly heightens the exasperation of Creon and the defiant hardness of Antigone. The best critics have agreed with Böckh in recognizing this balance of principles, this antagonism between valid claims; they generally regard it, however, as dependent entirely on the Greek point of view, as springing simply from the polytheistic conception, according to which the requirements of the Gods often clashed with the duties of man to man.

But, is it the fact that this antagonism of valid principles is peculiar to polytheism? Is it not rather that the struggle between Antigone and Creon represents that struggle between elemental tendencies and established laws by which the outer life of man is gradually and painfully being brought into harmony with his inward needs? Until this harmony is perfected, we shall never be able to attain a great right without also doing a wrong. Reformers, martyrs, revolutionists, are never fighting against evil only; they are also placing themselves in opposition to a good — to a valid principle which cannot be infringed without harm. Resist the payment of ship-money, you bring on civil war; preach against false doctrines, you disturb feeble minds and send them adrift on a sea of doubt; make a new road, and you annihilate vested interests; cultivate a new region of the earth, and you exterminate a race of men. Wherever the strength of a man's intellect, or moral sense, or affection brings him into opposition with the rules which society has sanctioned, *there* is renewed the conflict between Antigone and Creon; such a man must not only dare to be right, he must also dare to be wrong – to shake faith, to wound friendship, perhaps, to hem in his own powers. Like Antigone, he may fall a victim to the struggle, and yet he can never earn the name of a blameless martyr any more than the society – the Creon he has defied, can be branded as a hypocritical tyrant.

Perhaps the best moral we can draw is that to which the Chorus points – that our protest for the right should be seasoned with moderation and reverence, and that lofty words – μεγάλοι λόγοι[5] – are not becoming to mortals.

John Ruskin's *Modern Painters, Vol. III*

(Westminster Review, April 1856)

OUR TABLE this time does not, according to the favourite metaphor, 'groan' under the light literature of the quarter, for the quarter has not been very productive; but, in compensation, we ourselves groan under it rather more than usual, for the harvest is principally of straw, and few grains of precious corn remain after the winnowing. We except one book, however, which is a rich sheaf in itself, and will serve as bread, and seed-corn too, for many days. We mean the new volume of Mr Ruskin's *Modern Painters*, to which he appropriately gives the subordinate title, 'Of Many Things'. It may be taken up with equal pleasure whether the reader be acquainted or not with the previous volumes, and no special artistic culture is necessary in order to enjoy its excellences or profit by its suggestions. Every one who cares about nature, or poetry, or the story of human development – every one who has a tinge of literature, or philosophy, will find something that is for him and that will 'gravitate to him' in this volume. Since its predecessors appeared, Mr Ruskin has devoted ten years to the loving study of his great subject – the principles of art; which, like all other great subjects, carries the student into many fields. The critic of art, as he tells us, 'has to take *some* note of optics, geometry, geology, botany, and anatomy; he must acquaint himself with the works of all great artists, and with the temper and history of the times in which they lived; he must be a fair metaphysician, and a careful observer of the phenomena of natural scenery'. And when a writer like Mr Ruskin brings these varied studies to bear on one great purpose, when he has to trace their common relation to a grand phase of human activity, it is obvious that he will have a great deal to say which is of interest and importance to others besides painters. The fundamental principles of all just thought and beautiful action or creation are the same, and in making clear to ourselves what is best and noblest in art, we are making clear to ourselves what is best and noblest in morals; in learning how to estimate the artistic products of a particular age according to the mental attitude and external life of that age, we are widening our sympathy and deepening the basis of our tolerance and charity.

Of course, this treatise 'Of Many Things' presents certain old characteristics and new paradoxes which will furnish a fresh text to antagonistic critics; but, happily for us, and happily for our readers, who probably care more to know what Mr Ruskin says than what other people think he *ought* to say, we are not among those who are more irritated by his faults than charmed and subdued by his merits. When he announces to the world in his Preface, that he is incapable of falling into an illogical deduction – that, whatever other mistakes he may commit, he cannot possibly draw an inconsequent conclusion, we are not indignant, but amused, and do not in the least feel ourselves under the necessity of picking holes in his arguments in order to prove that he is not a logical Pope. We value a writer not in proportion to his freedom from faults, but in proportion to his positive excellences – to the variety of thought he contributes and suggests, to the amount of gladdening and energizing emotions he excites. Of what comparative importance is it that Mr Ruskin undervalues this painter, or overvalues the other, that he sometimes glides from a just argument into a fallacious one, that he is a little absurd here, and not a little arrogant there, if, with all these collateral mistakes, he teaches truth of infinite value, and *so* teaches it that men will listen? The truth of infinite value that he teaches is *realism* – the doctrine that all truth and beauty are to be attained by a humble and faithful study of nature, and not by substituting vague forms, bred by imagination on the mists of feeling, in place of definite, substantial reality. The thorough acceptance of this doctrine would remould our life; and he who teaches its application to any one department of human activity with such power as Mr Ruskin's, is a prophet for his generation. It is not enough simply to teach truth; that may be done, as we all know, to empty walls, and within the covers of unsaleable books; we want it to be so taught as to compel men's attention and sympathy. Very correct singing of very fine music will avail little without a *voice* that can thrill the audience and take possession of their souls. Now, Mr Ruskin has a voice, and one of such power, that whatever error he may mix with his truth, he will make more converts to that truth than less erring advocates who are hoarse and feeble. Considered merely as a writer, he is in the very highest rank of English stylists. The vigour and splendour of his eloquence are not more remarkable than its precision, and the delicate truthfulness of his epithets. The fine *largo* of his sentences reminds us more of De Quincy[1] than of any other writer, and his tendency to digressiveness is another and less admirable point of resemblance to the English Opium-eater. Yet we are not surprised to find that he does not mention De Quincy among the favourite writers who have influenced him, for Mr Ruskin's style is evidently due far more to innate faculty than to modifying influences; and though he himself thinks that his constant study of Carlyle must have impressed itself on his language as well as his thought, we rarely detect this. In the point of view from which he looks at a subject, in the correctness of his descriptions, and in a certain rough flavour of humour, he constantly reminds us of Carlyle, but in the mere tissue of his style, scarcely ever. But while we are dilating on Mr Ruskin's general characteristics, we are robbing ourselves of the room we want for what is just now more important – namely, telling the reader something about the contents of the particular volume before us.

It opens with a discussion of the 'Grand Style', which, after an analysis and dismissal of Sir Joshua Reynolds's opinion, that it consists in attending to what is invariable, 'the great and general ideas only inherent in universal nature',[2] Mr Ruskin concludes to be 'the suggestion by the imagination of noble grounds for noble emotions'. The conditions on which this result depends are, first, *the choice of noble subjects*, i.e., subjects which involve wide interests and profound passions, as opposed to those which involve narrow interests and slight passions. And the choice which characterizes the school of high art, is seen as much in the treatment of the subject as the selection. 'For the artist who sincerely chooses the noblest subject, will also choose chiefly to represent what makes that subject noble, namely, the various heroism or other noble emotions of the persons represented.'[3] But here two dangers present themselves: that of superseding expression by technical excellence, as when Paul Veronese makes the Supper at Emmaus a background to the portraits of two children playing with a dog; and that of superseding technical excellence by expression.

This is usually done under the influence of another kind of vanity. The artist desires that men should think he has an elevated soul, affects to despise the ordinary excellence of art, contemplates with separated egotism the course of his own imaginations or sensations, and refuses to look at the real facts around about him, in order that he may adore at leisure the shadow of himself. He lives in an element of what he calls tender emotions and lofty aspirations; which are, in fact, nothing more than very ordinary weaknesses or instincts, contemplated through a mist of pride.[4]

The second condition of greatness of style is *love of beauty* – the tendency to introduce into the conception of the subject as much beauty as is possible, consistently with truth.

The corruption of the schools of high art, so far as this particular quality is concerned, consists in the sacrifice of truth to beauty. Great art dwells on all that is beautiful; but false art omits or changes all that is ugly. Great art accepts Nature as she is, but directs the eyes and thoughts to what is most perfect in her; false art saves itself the trouble of direction, by removing or altering whatever it thinks objectionable. The evil results of which proceeding are twofold.

First. That beauty deprived of its proper foils and adjuncts ceases to be enjoyed as beauty, just as light deprived of all shadow ceases to be enjoyed as light. A white canvas cannot produce an effect of sunshine; the painter must darken it in some places before he can make it luminous in others; nor can an uninterrupted succession of beauty produce the true effect of beauty: it must be foiled by inferiority before its own power can be developed. Nature has for the most part mingled her inferior and nobler elements as she mingles sunshine with shade, giving due use and influence to both; and the painter who chooses to remove the shadow, perishes in the burning desert he has created. The truly high and beautiful art of Angelico is continually refreshed and strengthened by his frank portraiture of the most ordinary features of his brother monks, and of the recorded peculiarities of ungainly sanctity; but the modern German and Raphaelesque schools lose all honour and nobleness in barber-like admiration of handsome faces, and have, in fact, no real faith except in straight noses and curled hair. Paul Veronese opposes the dwarf to the soldier, and the negress to the queen; Shakespeare places Caliban beside Miranda, and Autolycus beside Perdita; but the vulgar idealist withdraws his beauty to the safety of the saloon, and his innocence to the seclusion of the cloister; he pretends that he does this in delicacy of choice and purity of sentiment, while in truth he has neither courage to front the monster, nor wit enough to furnish the knave.

It is only by the habit of representing faithfully all things, that we can truly learn what is beautiful, and what is not. The ugliest objects contain some element of beauty; and in all, it is an element peculiar to themselves, which cannot be separated from their ugliness, but must either be enjoyed together with it, or not at all. The more a painter accepts nature as he finds it, the more unexpected beauty he discovers in what he at first despised; but once let him arrogate the right of rejection, and he will gradually contract his circle of enjoyment, until what he supposed to be nobleness of selection ends in narrowness of perception. Dwelling perpetually upon one class of ideas, his art becomes at once monstrous and morbid; until at last he cannot faithfully represent even what he chooses to retain; his discrimination contracts into darkness, and his fastidiousness fades into fatuity.[5]

The third characteristic of great art is *sincerity*. The artist should include the largest possible quantity of truth in the most perfect possible harmony. *All* the truths of nature cannot be given; hence a choice must be made of some facts which can be represented from amongst others which must be passed by in silence. 'The inferior artist chooses unimportant and scattered truths; the great artist chooses the most necessary first, and afterwards the most consistent with these, so as to obtain the greatest possible and most harmonious scene.' Thus, Rembrandt sacrifices all other effects to the representation of the exact force with which the light on the most illumined part of an object is opposed to its obscurer portions. Paul Veronese, on the contrary, endeavours to embrace all the great relations of visible objects; and this difference between him and Rembrandt as to light and shade is typical of the difference between great and inferior artists throughout the entire field of art. He is the greatest who conveys the largest sum of truth. And as the sum of truth can always be increased by delicacy of handling, it follows

that all great art must have this delicacy to the utmost possible degree.

This rule is infallible and inflexible. All coarse work is the sign of low art. Only, it is to be remembered, that coarseness must be estimated by the distance from the eye; it being necessary to consult this distance, when great, by laying on touches which appear coarse when seen near; but which, so far from being coarse, are, in reality, more delicate in a master's work than the finest close handling, for they involve a calculation of result, and are laid on with a subtlety of sense precisely correspondent to that with which a good archer draws his bow; the spectator seeing in the action nothing but the strain of the strong arm, while there is, in reality, in the finger and eye, an *ineffably delicate estimate of distance, and touch on the arrow plume.*[6]

The last characteristic of great art is *invention.* It must not only present grounds for noble emotion, but must furnish these grounds by imaginative power, i.e., by an inventive combination of distinctly known objects. Thus imaginative art includes the historical faculties, which simply represent observed facts, but renders these faculties subservient to a poetic purpose.

And now, finally, since this poetical power includes the historical, if we glance back to the other qualities required in great art, and put all together, we find that the sum of them is simply the sum of all the powers of man. For as (1) the choice of the high subject involves all conditions of right moral choice, and as (2) the love of beauty involves all conditions of right admiration, and as (3) the grasp of truth involves all strength of sense, evenness of judgement, and honesty of purpose, and as (4) the poetical power involves all swiftness of invention, and accuracy of historical memory, the sum of all these powers is the sum of the human soul. Hence we see why the word 'Great' is used of this art. It is literally great. It compasses and calls forth the entire human spirit, whereas any other kind of art, being more or less small or narrow, compasses and calls forth only *part* of the human spirit. Hence the idea of its magnitude is a literal and just one, the art being simply less or greater in proportion to the number of faculties it exercises and addresses. And this is the ultimate meaning of the definition I gave of it long ago, as containing the 'greatest number of the greatest ideas'.[7]

We have next a discussion of the False Ideal, and first of all, in Religious Art. The want of realization in the early religious painters prevented their pictures from being more than suggestions to the feelings. They attempted to express, not the actual fact, but their own enthusiasm about the fact; they covered the Virgin's dress with gold, not with any idea of representing her as she ever was or will be seen, but with a burning desire to show their love for her. As art advanced in technical power and became more realistic, there arose a more pernicious falsity in the treatment of religious subjects; more pernicious, because it was more likely to be accepted as a representation of fact.

Take a very important instance. I suppose there is no event in the whole life of Christ to which, in hours of doubt or fear, men turn with more anxious thirst to know the close facts of it, or with more earnest and passionate dwelling upon every syllable of its recorded narrative, than Christ showing Himself to his disciples at the lake of Galilee. There is something pre-eminently open, natural, full fronting our disbelief in this manifestation. The others, recorded after the resurrection, were sudden, phantom-like, occurring to men in profound sorrow and wearied agitation of heart; not, it might seem, safe judges of what they saw. But the agitation was now over. They had gone back to their daily work, thinking still their business lay net-wards, unmeshed from the literal rope and drag. Simon Peter saith unto them, 'I go a fishing.' They say unto him, 'We also go with thee.' True words enough, and having far echo beyond those Galilean hills. That night they caught nothing; but when the morning came, in the clear light of it, behold, a figure stood on the shore. They were not thinking of anything but their fruitless hauls. They had no guess who it was. It asked them simply if they had caught anything. They said no. And it tells them to cast yet again. And John shades his eyes from the morning sun with his hand, to look who it is; and though the glinting of the sea, too, dazzles him, he makes out who it is, at last; and poor Simon, not to be outrun this time, tightens his fisher's coat about him, and dashes in, over the nets. One would have liked to see him swim those hundred yards, and stagger to his knees on the beach.

Well, the others get to the beach, too, in time, in such slow way as men in general do get, in this world, to its true shore, much impeded by that wonderful 'dragging the net with fishes'; but they get there – seven of them in all; – first the Denier, and then the slowest believer, and then the quickest believer, and then the two throne-seekers, and two more, we know not who.

They sit down on the shore face to face with Him, and eat their broiled fish as He bids. And then, to Peter, all dripping still, shivering, and amazed, staring at Christ in the sun, on the other side of the coal fire, – thinking a little, perhaps, of what happened by another coal fire, when it was colder, and having had no word once changed with him by his Master since that look of His, – to him, so amazed, comes the question, 'Simon, lovest thou me?' Try to feel that a little, and think of it till it is true to you; and then, take up that infinite monstrosity and hypocrisy – Raphael's cartoon of the *Charge to Peter*. Note, first, the bold fallacy – the putting *all* the Apostles there, a mere lie to serve the papal heresy of the Petric supremacy, by putting them all in the background while Peter receives the charge, and making them all witnesses to it. Note the handsomely curled hair and neatly tied sandals of the men who had been out all night in the sea-mists and on the slimy decks. Note their convenient dresses for going a-fishing, with trains that lie a yard along the ground, and goodly fringes, – all made to match, an apostolic fishing costume. Note how Peter especially (whose chief glory was in his wet coat *girt* about him and naked limbs) is enveloped in folds and fringes, so as to kneel and hold his keys with grace. No fire of coals at all, nor lonely mountain shore, but a pleasant Italian landscape, full of villas and churches, and a flock of sheep to be pointed at; and the whole group of Apostles, not round Christ, as they would have been naturally, but straggling away in a line, that they may all be shown.

The simple truth is, that the moment we look at the picture we feel our belief of the whole thing taken away. There is, visibly, no possibility of that group ever having existed, in any place, or on any occasion. It is all a mere mythic absurdity, and faded concoction of fringes, muscular arms, and curly heads of Greek philosophers.[8]

Mr Ruskin glances rapidly at the False Ideal in profane art – the pursuit of mere physical beauty as a gratification to the idle senses; and then enters into an extended consideration of the True Ideal, distinguished by him into three branches. 1. Purist Idealism, which results from the unwillingness of pure and tender minds to contemplate evil, of which Angelico is the great example, among the early painters; and among the moderns, Stothard exhibits the same tendency in the treatment of worldly subjects. 2. Naturalist Idealism, which accepts the weaknesses, faults, and wrongnesses in all things that it sees, but so places them that they form a noble whole, in which the imperfection of each several part is not only harmless, but absolutely essential, and yet in which whatever is good in each several part shall be completely displayed. 3. The Grotesque Ideal, which is either playful, terrible, or symbolical. The essence of an admirable chapter on 'Finish' is, that all real finish is not mere polish, but *added truth*. Great artists finish not to show their skill, nor to produce a smooth piece of work, but to *render clearer the expression of knowledge*.

We resist the temptation to quote any of the very fine things Mr Ruskin says about the 'Use of Pictures', and pass on to the succeeding chapter, in which he enters on his special subject, namely, landscape painting. With that intense interest in landscape which is a peculiar characteristic of modern times, is associated the 'Pathetic Fallacy' – the transference to external objects of the spectator's own emotions, as when Kingsley says of the drowned maiden, –

> They rowed her in across the rolling foam –
> The *cruel, crawling foam*.[9]

The pleasure we derive from this fallacy is legitimate when the passion in which it originates is strong, and has an adequate cause. But the mental condition which admits of this fallacy is of a lower order than that in which, while the emotions are strong, the intellect is yet strong enough to assert its rule against them; and 'the whole man stands in an iron glow, white hot, perhaps, but still strong, and in nowise evaporating; even if he melts, losing none of his weight'. Thus the poets who delight in this fallacy are chiefly of the second order – the reflective and perceptive – such as Wordsworth, Keats, and Tennyson; while the creative poets, for example, Shakspeare, Homer, and Dante, use it sparingly.

Next follows one of the most delightful and suggestive chapters in the volume, on 'Classical Landscape', or the way in which the Greeks looked at external nature. Take a specimen on the details of the Homeric landscape: –

As far as I recollect, without a single exception, every Homeric landscape, intended to be beautiful, is composed of a fountain, a meadow, and a shady grove. This ideal is very interestingly marked, as intended for a perfect one, in the fifth book of the *Odyssey*; when Mercury himself stops for a moment, though on a message, to look at a landscape, 'which even an immortal might be gladdened to behold'. This landscape consists of a cave covered with a running vine, all blooming into grapes, and surrounded by a grove of alder, poplar, and sweet-smelling cypress. Four fountains of white (foaming) water, springing *in succession* (mark the orderliness), and close to one another, flow away in different directions, through a meadow full of violets and parsley (parsley, to mark its moisture, being elsewhere called 'marsh-nourished', and associated with the lotus); the air is perfumed not only by these violets and by the sweet cypress, but by Calypso's fire of finely chopped cedar wood, which sends a smoke, as of incense, through the island; Calypso herself is singing; and finally, upon the trees are resting, or roosting, owls, hawks, and 'long-tongued sea-crows'. Whether these last are considered as a part of the ideal landscape, as marine singing-birds, I know not; but the approval of Mercury appears to be elicited chiefly by the fountains and violet meadow.

Now the notable things in this description are, first, the evident subservience of the whole landscape to human comfort, to the foot, the taste, or the smell; and secondly, that throughout the passage there is not a single figurative word expressive of the things being in any wise other than plain grass, fruit, or flower. I have used the term 'spring' of the fountains, because, without doubt, Homer means that they sprang forth brightly, having their source at the foot of the rocks (as copious fountains nearly always have); but Homer does not say 'spring', he says simply flow, and uses only one word for 'growing softly', or 'richly', of the tall trees, the vine, and the violets. There is, however, some expression of sympathy with the sea-birds; he speaks of them in precisely the same terms, as in other places of naval nations, saying they 'have care of the works of the sea'.

If we glance through the references to pleasant landscape which occur in other parts of the *Odyssey*, we shall always be struck by this quiet subjection of their every feature to human service, and by the excessive similarity in the scenes. Perhaps the spot intended, after this, to be most perfect, may be the garden of Alcinous, where the principal ideas are, still more definitely, order, symmetry, and fruitfulness; the beds being duly ranged between rows of vines, which, as well as the pear, apple, and fig-trees, bear fruit continually, some grapes being yet sour, while others are getting black; there are plenty of '*orderly* square beds of herbs', chiefly leeks, and two fountains, one running through the garden, and one under the pavement of the palace to a reservoir for the citizens. Ulysses, pausing to contemplate this scene, is described nearly in the same terms as Mercury, pausing to contemplate the wilder meadow; and it is interesting to observe, that, in spite of all Homer's love of symmetry, the god's admiration is excited by the free fountains, wild violets, and wandering vine; but the mortal's, by the vines in rows, the leeks in beds, and the fountains in pipes.[10]

The mediæval feeling for landscape is less utilitarian than the Greek. Everything is pleasurable and horticultural – the knights and ladies sing and make love in pleasaunces and rose-gardens. There is a more sentimental enjoyment in external nature; but, added to this, there is a new respect for mountains, as places where a solemn presence is to be felt, and spiritual good obtained. As Homer is the grand authority for Greek landscape, so is Dante for the mediæval; and Mr Ruskin gives an elaborate study of the landscape in the *Divina Commedia*. To the love of brilliancy shown in mediæval landscape, is contrasted the love of clouds in the modern, 'so that if a general and characteristic name were needed for modern landscape art, none better could be found than "the service of clouds"'. But here again Mr Ruskin seeks for the spirit of landscape first of all in literature; and he expects to surprise his readers by selecting Scott as the typical poet, and greatest literary man of his age. He, very justly, we think, places Creative literature such as Scott's, above Sentimental literature, even when this is of as high a character as in some passages of Byron or Tennyson.

To invent a story, or admirably and thoroughly tell any part of a story, it is necessary to grasp the entire mind of every personage concerned in it, and know precisely how they would be affected by what happens; which to do requires a colossal intellect; but to describe a separate emotion delicately, it is only needed that one should feel it oneself; and thousands of people are capable of feeling this or that noble emotion for one who is able to enter into all the feelings of somebody sitting on the other side of the table ... I unhesitatingly receive as a greater manifestation of power the right invention of a few sentences spoken by Pleydell and Mannering across their supper-table, than the most tender and passionate melodies of the self-examining verse.[11]

This appreciation of Scott's power puts us in such excellent humour, that we are not inclined to quarrel with Mr Ruskin about another judgement of his, to which we cannot see our way, in spite of the arguments he adduces. According to him Scott was eminently *sad*, sadder than Byron. On the other hand, he shows that this sadness did not lead Scott into the pathetic fallacy: the bird, the brook, the flower, and the cornfield, kept their gladsomeness for him, not withstanding his own melancholy. But the more we look into Mr Ruskin's volume, the more we want to quote or to question; so, remembering that we have other books to tell the reader about, we must shut this very seductive one, and content ourselves with merely mentioning the chapters on the 'Moral of Landscape', and on the 'Teachers of Turner', which occupy the remaining pages; the latter preparing the way for the special consideration of Turner, which is to follow in the fourth volume. If the matter of this book had arrested us less, we should, perhaps, have laid more stress on the illustrations, some of which are very beautiful: for example, a view of the Apennines by sunset, and a group of leaves and grasses, from the author's own pencil.

Harriet Beecher Stowe's *Dred*,
Charles Reade's *It is Never Too Late to Mend*
and Frederika Bremer's *Hertha*

(*Westminster Review*, October 1856)

AT LENGTH we have Mrs Stowe's new novel, and for the last
three weeks there have been men, women, and children reading it
with rapt attention – laughing and sobbing over it – lingering with
delight over its exquisite landscapes, its scenes of humour, and
tenderness, and rude heroism – and glowing with indignation at
its terrible representation of chartered barbarities. Such a book is
an uncontrollable power, and critics who follow it with their
objections and reservations – who complain that Mrs Stowe's plot
is defective, that she has repeated herself, that her book is too long
and too full of hymns and religious dialogue, and that it creates an
unfair bias – are something like men pursuing a prairie fire with
desultory watering-cans. In the meantime, *Dred* will be devoured
by the million, who carry no critical talisman against the enchant-
ments of genius. We confess ourselves to be among the million, and
quite unfit to rank with the sage minority of Fadladeens.[1] We
have been too much moved by *Dred* to determine with precision
how far it is inferior to *Uncle Tom*,[2] too much impressed by what
Mrs Stowe *has* done to be quite sure that we can tell her what she
ought to have done. Our admiration of the book is quite distinct
from any opinions or hesitations we may have as to the terribly
difficult problems of Slavery and Abolition – problems which
belong to quite other than 'polite literature'. Even admitting Mrs
Stowe to be mistaken in her views, and partial or exaggerated in
her representations, *Dred* remains not the less a novel inspired by a
rare genius – rare both in intensity and in range of power.

Looking at the matter simply from an artistic point of view, we
see no reason to regret that Mrs Stowe should keep to her original
ground of negro and planter life, any more than that Scott should

have introduced Highland life into *Rob Roy* and *The Fair Maid of Perth*, when he had already written *Waverley*. Mrs Stowe has *invented* the Negro novel, and it is a novel not only fresh in its scenery and its manners, but possessing that *conflict of races* which Augustin Thierry[3] has pointed out as the great source of romantic interest – witness *Ivanhoe*. Inventions in literature are not as plentiful as inventions in the paletot and waterproof department, and it is rather amusing that we reviewers, who have, for the most part, to read nothing but imitations of imitations, should put on airs of tolerance towards Mrs Stowe because she has written a second Negro novel, and make excuses for her on the ground that she perhaps would not succeed in any other kind of fiction. Probably she would not; for her genius seems to be of a very special character: her *Sunny Memories* were as feeble as her novels are powerful. But whatever else she may write, or may not write, *Uncle Tom* and *Dred* will assure her a place in that highest rank of novelists who can give us a national life in all its phases – popular and aristocratic, humorous and tragic, political and religious.

But Mrs Stowe's novels have not only that grand element – conflict of races; they have another element equally grand, which she also shares with Scott, and in which she has, in some respects, surpassed him. This is the exhibition of a people to whom what we may call Hebraic Christianity is still a reality, still an animating belief, and by whom the theocratic conceptions of the Old Testament are literally applied to their daily life. Where has Scott done anything finer than the character of Balfour of Burley, the battles of Drumclog and Bothwell Brigg, and the trial of Ephraim Mac-Briar? And the character of Dred, the death scenes in the Swamp, and the Camp Meeting of Presbyterians and Methodists, will bear comparison – if we except the fighting – with the best parts of *Old Mortality*. The strength of Mrs Stowe's own religious feeling is a great artistic advantage to her here; she never makes you feel that she is coldly calculating an effect, but you see that she is all a-glow for the moment with the wild enthusiasm, the unreasoning faith, and the steady martyr-spirit of Dred, of Tiff, or of Father Dickson. But with this, she has the keen sense of humour which preserves her from extravagance and monotony; and though she paints her religious negroes *en beau*, they are always specifically negroes – she never loses hold of her characters, and lets dramatic dialogue merge into vague oratory. Indeed, here is her strongest point: her dramatic instinct is always awake; and whether it is the grotesque Old Tiff or the aërial Nina, the bluff sophist Father Bonim or the gentlemanly sophist Frank Russell, her characters are always like themselves; a quality which is all the more remarkable in novels animated by a vehement polemical purpose.

The objection which is patent to every one who looks at Mrs Stowe's novels in an argumentative light, is also, we think, one of their artistic defects; namely, the absence of any proportionate exhibition of the negro character in its less amiable phases. Judging from her pictures, one would conclude that the negro race was vastly superior to the mass of whites, even in other than slave countries – a state of the case which would singularly defeat Mrs Stowe's sarcasms on the cant of those who call slavery a 'Christianizing Institution'. If the negroes are really so very good, slavery has answered as moral discipline. But apart from the argumentative suicide involved in this one-sidedness, Mrs Stowe loses by it the most terribly tragic element in the relation of the two races – the Nemesis lurking in the vices of the oppressed. She alludes to demoralization among the slaves, but she does not depict it; and yet why should she shrink from this, since she does not shrink from giving us a full-length portrait of a Legree or a Tom Gordon?

It would be idle to tell anything about the story of a work which is, or soon will be, in all our readers' hands; we only render our tribute to it as a great novel, leaving to others the task of weighing it in the political balance.

Close upon *Dred* we have read Mr Charles Reade's novel – *It is Never Too Late to Mend*; also a remarkable fiction, and one that sets vibrating very deep chords in our nature, yet presenting a singular contrast with *Dred*, both in manner and in the essential qualities it indicates in the writer. Mr Reade's novel opens with some of the true pathos to be found in English country life: the honest young farmer, George Fielding, unable to struggle against 'bad times' and an exhausted farm, is driven to Australia to seek the fortune that will enable him to marry Susan Merton, the woman he loves. It then carries us, with a certain Robinson, a clever thief, who has been rusticating as George Fielding's lodger, to the gaol, and makes us shudder at the horrors of the separate and silent system, administered by an ignorant and brutal gaoler, while we follow with keen interest the struggle of the heroic chaplain against this stupid iniquity – thus bringing home the tragedy of Birmingham gaol to people whose sympathies are more easily roused by fiction than by bare fact. Then it takes us to Australia, and traces George Fielding's fortunes and misfortunes – first through the vicissitudes of the Australian 'sheep-run', and then through the fierce drama of gold-digging – bringing him home at last with £4,000 in his pocket, in time to prevent his Susan from marrying his worst enemy.

In all the three 'acts' of this novel, so to speak, there are fine situations, fine touches of feeling, and much forcible writing; especially while the scene is in the gaol, the best companion who drops in you will probably regard as a bore, and will become earnest in inviting to remain only when you perceive he is determined to go. Again, honest George Fielding's struggles, renewed at the antipodes, and lightened by the friendship of Carlo the dog – of the reformed thief, Robinson – and of the delightful 'Jacky', the Australian native – are a thread of interest which you pursue with eagerness to the *dénouement*. 'Jacky' is a thoroughly fresh character, entirely unlike any other savage *frotté de civilisation*,⁴ and drawn with exquisite yet sober humour. In the English scenes every one who has seen anything of life amongst our farmers will recognize many truthful, well-observed touches: the little 'tiff' between the brothers George and William Fielding, old Merton's way of thinking, and many traits of manner in the heroine, Susan Merton. In short, *It is Never Too Late to Mend* is one of the exceptional novels to be read not merely by the idle and the half-educated, but by the busy and the thoroughly informed.

Nevertheless, Mr Reade's novel does not rise above the level of cleverness: we feel throughout the presence of remarkable talent, which makes effective use of materials, but nowhere of the genius which absorbs material, and reproduces it as a living whole, in which you do not admire the ingenuity of the workman, but the vital energy of the producer. Doubtless there is a great deal of nonsense talked about genius and inspiration, as if genius did not and must not labour; but, after all, there remains the difference between the writer who thoroughly possesses you by his creation, and the writer who only awakens your curiosity and makes you recognize his ability; and this difference may as well be called 'genius' as anything else. Perhaps a truer statement of the difference is, that the one writer is himself thoroughly possessed by his creation – he lives *in* his characters; while the other remains outside them, and dresses them up. Here lies the fundamental contrast between Mrs Stowe's novel and Mr Reade's. Mrs Stowe seems for the moment to glow with all the passion, to quiver with all the fun, and to be inspired with all the trust that belongs to her different characters; she attains her finest dramatic effects by means of her energetic sympathy, and not by conscious artifice. Mr Reade, on the contrary, seems always self-conscious, always elaborating a character, after a certain type, and carrying his elaboration a little too far – always working up to situations, and over-doing them. The habit of writing for the stage misleads him into seeking after those exaggerated contrasts and effects which are accepted as a sort of rapid symbolism by a theatrical audience, but are utterly out of place in a fiction, where the time and means for attaining a result are less limited, and an impression of character or purpose may be given more nearly as it is in real life – by a sum of less concentrated particulars. In Mr Reade's dialogue we are constantly imagining that we see a theatrical gentleman, well 'made up', delivering a repartee in an emphatic voice, with his eye fixed on the pit. To mention one brief example: – Hawes, the gaoler, tells Fry, the turnkey, after Mr Eden's morning sermon on *theft*, that he approves of preaching *at* people. The same day there is an afternoon sermon on *cruelty*; whereupon Hawes remarks again to Fry, 'I'll teach him to preach at people from the pulpit.' 'Well,' answers Fry, 'that is what I say, Sir: but you said you liked him to preach at folk?' 'So I do,' replied Hawes, angrily, 'but not at me, ye fool!' This would produce a roar on the stage, and would seem a real bit of human nature; but in a novel one has time to be sceptical as to this extreme *naïveté* which allows a man to make palpable epigrams on himself.

In everything, Mr Reade seems to distrust the effect of moderation and simplicity. His picture of gaol life errs by excess, and he wearies our emotion by taxing it too repeatedly; the admirable inspiration which led him to find his hero and heroine among Berkshire homesteads, is counteracted by such puerile and incongruous efforts at the romantic and diabolical, as the introduction of the Jew, Isaac Levi, who is a mosaic character in more senses than one, and the far-seeing Machiavelianism of the top-booted Mr Meadows; and even when he is speaking in his own person, he lashes himself into fury at human wrongs, and calls on God and man to witness his indignation, apparently confounding the importance of the effect with the importance of the cause. But the most amazing foible in a writer of so much power as Mr Reade, is his reliance on the magic of typography. We had imagined that the notion of establishing a relation between magnitude of ideas and magnitude of type was confined to the literature of placards, but we find Mr Reade endeavouring to impress us with the Titanic character of modern events by suddenly bursting into capitals at the mention of 'THIS GIGANTIC AGE!' It seems ungrateful in us to notice these minor blemishes in a work which has given us so much pleasure, and roused in us so much healthy feeling as *It is Never Too Late to Mend*; but it is our very admiration of Mr Reade's talent which makes these blemishes vexatious to us, and which induces us to appeal against their introduction in the many other books we hope to have from his pen.

The appearance of a new novel by Miss Bremer, revives the impressions of ten years ago, when all the novel-reading world was discussing the merits of *The Neighbours*, *The President's Daughters*, *The H— Family*, and the rest of the 'Swedish novels', which about that time were creating a strong current in the literary and bookselling world. The discussion soon died out; and perhaps there is hardly another instance of fictions so eagerly read in England which have left so little trace in English literature as Miss Bremer's. No one quotes them, no one alludes to them: and grave people who have entered on their fourth decade, remember their enthusiasm for the Swedish novels among those intellectual 'wild oats' to which their mature wisdom can afford to give a pitying smile. And yet, how is this? For Miss Bremer had not only the advantage of describing manners which were fresh to the English public; she also brought to the description unusual gifts – lively imagination, poetic feeling, wealth of language, a quick eye for details, and considerable humour, of that easy, domestic kind which throws a pleasant light on every-day things. The perusal of *Hertha* has confirmed in our minds the answer we should have previously given to our own question. One reason, we think, why Miss Bremer's novels have not kept a high position among us is, that her luxuriant faculties are all over-run by a rank growth of sentimentality, which, like some faint-smelling creeper on the boughs of an American forest, oppresses us with the sense that the air is unhealthy. Nothing can be more curious than the combination in her novels of the vapourishly affected and unreal with the most solid Dutch sort of realism. In one page we have copious sausage sandwiches and beer posset, and on another rhapsodies or wildly improbable incidents that seem rather to belong to sylphs and salamanders, than to a race of creatures who are nourished by the very excellent provisions just mentioned. Another reason why Miss Bremer's novels are not likely to take rank among the permanent creations of art, is the too confident tone of the religious philosophy which runs through them. When a novelist is quite sure that she has a theory which suffices to illustrate all the difficulties of our earthly existence, her novels are too likely to illustrate little else than her own theory.

These two characteristics of sentimentality and dogmatic confidence are very strongly marked in *Hertha*, while it has less of the attention to detail, less of the humorous realism, which was the ballast of Miss Bremer's earlier novels. It has been written not simply from an artistic impulse, but with the object of advocating the liberation of women from those legal and educational restrictions which limit her opportunities of a position and a sphere of usefulness to the chance of matrimony; and we think there are few well-judging persons who will not admire the generous energy with which Miss Bremer, having long ago won fame and independence for herself, devotes the activity of her latter years to the cause of women who are less capable of mastering circumstance. Many wise and noble things she says in *Hertha*, but we cannot help regretting that she has not presented her views on a difficult and practical question in the 'light of common day', rather than in the pink haze of visions and romance. The story is very briefly this: –

Hertha, who has lost her mother in childhood, is, at the age of seven-and-twenty, becoming more and more embittered by her inactive bondage to a narrow-minded, avaricious father, who demands obedience to the pettiest exactions. Her elder sister, Alma, is slowly dying in consequence of the same tyranny, which has prevented her from marrying the man she loves. We meet our heroine, with her gloomy and bitter expression of face, first of all, at the rehearsal of a fancy ball, which is to take place in a few days in the good town of Kungsköping; and after being introduced to the various *dramatis personæ* – among the rest, to a young man named Yngve Nordin, who interests Hertha by his agreement in her opinions about women, we accompany her to her cheerless home, where she is roughly chid by her father, the rigid old Director, for being later than the regulation-hour of eight; and where, by the bedside of her sister Alma, she pours out all the bitterness of her soul, all her hatred and smothered rebellion towards her father for his injustice towards them. She and Alma have inherited a share in their mother's fortune, but according to the Swedish law they are still minors, and unable to claim their property. This very night, however, a fire breaks out, and lays waste a large district of the town. The Director's house is consumed, and he himself is only saved by the heroic exertions of Hertha, who rushes to his room, and carries his meagre, feeble body through the flames. This act of piety, and the death of Alma, who, in her last moments, extracts from her father a promise to give Hertha independence, win some ungracious concessions from the crabbed Director towards his daughter. He still withholds her property and a declaration of her majority; but she has power in the household, and greater freedom of action out of doors. A Ladies' Society has been organized for relieving the sufferers from the fire, and Hertha is one of those whose department is the care of the sick and wounded. The patient who falls to her share is no other than Yngve Nordin, who has been severely hurt in his benevolent efforts on the fatal night, and is now lodged in the house of the good pastor, who is at the head of the Society. Here is an excellent opportunity for discovering that Yngve is just the friend she needs to soothe and invigorate her mind, by his sympathy and riper experience; and the feeling which is at first called friendship, is at last confessed to be love. After certain jealousies and suspicions, which are satisfactorily cleared up, Yngve asks the Director for Hertha's hand, but is only accepted prospectively, on condition of his attaining an assured position. Yngve goes abroad, and for seven years Hertha submits to the procrastination of her marriage, rather than rebel against her father in his last years. It is only when Yngve is hopelessly ill that she sacrifices her scruples and marries him. In the mean time she has made her seven years of separation rich in active usefulness, by founding and superintending two schools – one in which girls are instructed in the ordinary elements of education, forming a sort of nursery-garden for the other, in which voluntary pupils are to be led to a higher order of thought and purpose by Hertha's readings, conversation, and personal influence. Her schools are successful; but after Yngve's death she begins to sink under her long trial, and follows him rapidly to the grave.

This bare outline of the story can only suggest and not fully explain the grounds of our objection to *Hertha*. Our objection is, that it surrounds questions, which can only be satisfactorily solved by the application of very definite ideas to specific facts, with a cloudy kind of eloquence and flighty romance. Take, for example, the question whether it will not be well for women to study and practise medicine. It can only tend to retard the admission that women may pursue such a career with success, for a distinguished authoress to imply that they may be suitably prepared for effective activity by lectures on such a very nebulous thesis as this – 'The consciousness of thought ought to be a living observation and will', or to associate the attendance of women by the sick-bed, not with the hard drudgery of real practice, but with the vicissitudes of a love-story. Women have not to prove that they can be emotional, and rhapsodic, and spiritualistic; every one believes that already. They have to prove that they are capable of accurate thought, severe study, and continuous self-command. But we say all this with reluctance, and should prefer noticing the many just and pathetic observations that Miss Bremer puts into the mouth of her heroine. We can only mention, and have not space to quote, a passage where Hertha complains of the ignorance in which women are left of Natural Science. 'In my youth,' she concludes, 'I used to look at the rocks, the trees, the grass, and all objects of nature, with unspeakable longing, wishing to know something about their kinds, their life, and their purpose. But the want of knowledge, the want of opportunity to acquire it, has caused nature to be to me a sealed book, and still to this moment it is to me a tantalizing, enticing, and ever-retreating wave, rather than a life-giving fountain which I can enjoy, and enjoying, thank the Creator.'

William Lecky's *The Influence of Rationalism*

(*Fortnightly Review*, 15 May 1865)

THERE IS a valuable class of books on great subjects which have something of the character and functions of good popular lecturing. They are not original, not subtle, not of close logical texture, not exquisite either in thought or style; but by virtue of these negatives they are all the more fit to act on the average intelligence. They have enough of organizing purpose in them to make their facts illustrative, and to leave a distinct result in the mind even when most of the facts are forgotten; and they have enough of vagueness and vacillation in their theory to win them ready acceptance from a mixed audience. The vagueness and vacillation are not devices of timidity; they are the honest result of the writer's own mental character, which adapts him to be the instructor and the favourite of 'the general reader'. For the most part, the general reader of the present day does not exactly know what distance he goes; he only knows that he does not go 'too far'. Of any remarkable thinker, whose writings have excited controversy, he likes to have it said that 'his errors are to be deplored', leaving it not too certain what those errors are; he is fond of what may be called disembodied opinions, that float in vapoury phrases above all systems of thought or action; he likes an undefined Christianity which opposes itself to nothing in particular, an undefined education of the people, an undefined amelioration of all things: in fact, he likes sound views – nothing extreme, but something between the excesses of the past and the excesses of the present. This modern type of the general reader may be known in conversation by the cordiality with which he assents to indistinct, blurred statements: say that black is black, he will shake his head and hardly think it; say that black is not so very black, he will reply, 'Exactly.' He has no hesitation, if you wish it, even to get up at a public meeting and express his conviction that at times, and within certain limits, the radii of a circle have a tendency to be equal; but, on the other hand, he would urge that the spirit of geometry may be carried a little too far. His only bigotry is a bigotry against any clearly-defined opinion; not in the least based on a scientific scepticism, but belonging to a lack of coherent thought – a spongy texture of mind, that gravitates strongly to nothing. The one thing he is staunch for is, the utmost liberty of private haziness.

But precisely these characteristics of the general reader, rendering him incapable of assimilating ideas unless they are administered in a highly diluted form, make it a matter of rejoicing that there are clever, fair-minded men, who will write books for him – men very much above him in knowledge and ability, but not too remote from him in their habits of thinking, and who can thus prepare for him infusions of history and science, that will leave some solidifying deposit, and save him from a fatal softening of the intellectual skeleton. Among such serviceable writers, Mr Lecky's *History of the Rise and Influence of the Spirit of Rationalism in Europe* entitles him to a high place. He has prepared himself for its production by an unusual amount of well-directed reading; he has chosen his facts and quotations with much judgement; and he gives proof of those important moral qualifications, impartiality, seriousness, and modesty. This praise is chiefly applicable to the long chapter on the history of Magic and Witchcraft, which opens the work, and to the two chapters on the antecedents and history of Persecution, which occur, the one at the end of the first volume, the other at the beginning of the second. In these chapters Mr Lecky has a narrower and better-traced path before him than in other portions of his work; he is more occupied with presenting a particular class of facts in their historical sequence, and in their relation to certain grand tide-marks of opinion, than with disquisition; and his writing is freer than elsewhere from an apparent confusedness of thought and an exuberance of approximative phrases, which can be serviceable in no other way than as diluents needful for the sort of reader we have just described.

The history of magic and witchcraft has been judiciously chosen by Mr Lecky as the subject of his first section on the Declining Sense of the Miraculous, because it is strikingly illustrative of a position with the truth of which he is strongly impressed, though he does not always treat of it with desirable clearness and precision, namely, that certain beliefs become obsolete, not in consequence of direct arguments against them, but because of their incongruity with prevalent habits of thought. Here is his statement of the two 'classes of influences', by which the mass of men, in what is called civilized society, get their beliefs gradually modified: –

If we ask why it is that the world has rejected what was once so universally and so intensely believed, why a narrative of an old woman who had been seen riding on a broomstick, or who was proved to have transformed herself into a wolf, and to have devoured the flocks of her neighbours, is deemed so entirely incredible, most persons would probably be unable to give a very definite answer to the question. It is not because we have examined the evidence and found it insufficient, for the disbelief always precedes, when it does not prevent, examination. It is rather because the idea of absurdity is so strongly attached to such narratives, that it is difficult even to consider them with gravity. Yet at one time no such improbability was felt, and hundreds of persons have been burnt simply on the two grounds I have mentioned.

When so complete a change takes place in public opinion, it may be ascribed to one or other of two causes. It may be the result of a controversy which has conclusively settled the question, establishing to the satisfaction of all parties a clear preponderance of argument or fact in favour of one opinion, and making that opinion a truism which is accepted by all enlightened men, even though they have not themselves examined the evidence on which it rests. Thus, if any one in a company of ordinarily educated persons were to deny the motion of the earth, or the circulation of the blood, his statement would be received with derision, though it is probable that some of his audience would be unable to demonstrate the first truth, and that very few of them could give sufficient reasons for the second. They may not themselves be able to defend their position; but they are aware that, at certain known periods of history, controversies on those subjects took place, and that known writers then brought forward some definite arguments or experiments, which were ultimately accepted by the whole learned world as rigid and conclusive demonstrations. It is possible, also, for as complete a change to be effected by what is called the spirit of the age. The general intellectual tendencies pervading the literature of a century profoundly modify the character of the public mind. They form a new tone and habit of thought. They alter the measure of probability. They create new attractions and new antipathies, and they eventually cause as absolute a rejection of certain old opinions as could be produced by the most cogent and definite arguments.

Mr Lecky proceeds to some questionable views concerning the evidences of witchcraft, which seem to be irreconcilable even with his own remarks later on; but they lead him to the statement, thoroughly made out by his historical survey, that 'the movement was mainly silent, unargumentative, and insensible; that men came gradually to disbelieve in witchcraft, because they came gradually to look upon it as absurd; and that this new tone of thought appeared, first of all, in those who were least subject to theological influences, and soon spread through the educated laity, and, last of all, took possession of the clergy'.

We have rather painful proof that this 'second class of influences' with a vast number go hardly deeper than Fashion, and that witchcraft to many of us is absurd only on the same ground that our grandfathers' gigs are absurd. It is felt preposterous to think of spiritual agencies in connexion with ragged beldames soaring on broomsticks, in an age when it is known that mediums of communication with the invisible world are usually unctuous personages dressed in excellent broadcloth, who soar above the curtain-poles without any broomstick, and who are not given to unprofitable intrigues. The enlightened imagination rejects the figure of a witch with her profile in dark relief against the moon and her broomstick cutting a constellation. No undiscovered natural laws, no names of 'respectable' witnesses, are invoked to make us feel our presumption in questioning the diabolic intimacies of that obsolete old woman, for it is known now that the undiscovered laws, and the witnesses qualified by the payment of income-tax, are all in favour of a different conception – the image of a heavy gentleman in boots and black coat-tails foreshortened against the cornice. Yet no less a person than Sir Thomas Browne[1] once wrote that those who denied there were witches, inasmuch as they thereby denied spirits also, were 'obliquely and upon consequence a sort, not of infidels, but of atheists'. At present, doubtless, in certain circles, unbelievers in heavy gentlemen who float in the air by means of undiscovered laws are also taxed with atheism; illiberal as it is not to admit that mere weakness of understanding may prevent one from seeing how that phenomenon is necessarily involved in the Divine origin of things. With still more remarkable parallelism, Sir Thomas Browne goes on: 'Those that, to refute their incredulity, desire to see apparitions, shall questionless never behold any, nor have the power to be so much as witches. The devil hath made them already in a heresy as capital as witchcraft, *and to appear to them were but to convert them.*'[2] It would be difficult to see what has been changed here but the mere drapery of circumstance, if it were not for this prominent difference between our own days and the days of witchcraft, that instead of torturing, drowning, or burning the innocent, we give hospitality and large pay to – the highly-distinguished medium. At least we are safely rid of certain horrors; but if the multitude – that 'farraginous concurrence of all conditions, tempers, sexes, and ages' – do not roll back even to a superstition that carries cruelty in its train, it is not because they possess a cultivated Reason, but because they are pressed upon and held up by what we may call an external Reason – the sum of conditions resulting from the laws of material growth, from changes produced by great historical collisions shattering the structures of ages and making new highways for events and ideas, and from the activities of higher minds no longer existing merely as opinions and teaching, but as institutions and organizations with which the interests, the affections, and the habits of the multitude are inextricably interwoven. No undiscovered laws accounting for small phenomena going forward under drawing-room tables are likely to affect the tremendous facts of the increase of population, the rejection of convicts by our colonies, the exhaustion of the soil by cotton plantations, which urge even upon the foolish certain questions, certain claims, certain views concerning the scheme of the world, that can never again be silenced. If right reason is a right representation of the co-existences and sequences of things, here are co-existences and sequences that do not wait to be discovered, but press themselves upon us like bars of iron. No seances at a guinea a head for the sake of being pinched by 'Mary Jane' can annihilate railways, steam-ships, and electric telegraphs, which are demonstrating the interdependence of all human interests, and making self-interest a duct for sympathy. These things are part of the external Reason to which internal silliness has inevitably to accommodate itself.

Three points in the history of magic and witchcraft are well brought out by Mr Lecky. First, that the cruelties connected with it did not begin until men's minds had ceased to repose implicitly in a sacramental system which made them feel well armed against evil spirits; that is, until the eleventh century, when there came a sort of morning dream of doubt and heresy, bringing on the one side the terror of timid consciences, and on the other the terrorism of authority or zeal bent on checking the rising struggle. In that time of comparative mental repose, says Mr Lecky –

All those conceptions of diabolical presence; all that predisposition towards the miraculous, which acted so fearfully upon the imaginations of the fifteenth and sixteenth centuries, existed; but the implicit faith, the boundless and triumphant credulity with which the virtue of ecclesiastical rites was accepted, rendered them comparatively innocuous. If men had been a little less superstitious, the effects of their superstition would have been much more terrible. It was firmly believed that any one who deviated from the strict line of orthodoxy must soon succumb beneath the power of Satan; but as there was no spirit of rebellion or doubt, this persuasion did not produce any extraordinary terrorism.

The Church was disposed to confound heretical opinion with sorcery; false doctrine was especially the devil's work, and it was a ready conclusion that a denier or innovator had held consultation with the father of lies. It is a saying of a zealous Catholic in the sixteenth century, quoted by Maury in his excellent work, *De la Magie* – 'Crescit cum magia hæresis, cum hæresi magia.'[3] Even those who doubted were terrified at their doubts, for trust is more easily undermined than terror. Fear is earlier born than hope, lays a stronger grasp on man's system than any other passion, and remains master of a larger group of involuntary actions. A chief aspect of man's moral development is the slow subduing of fear by the gradual growth of intelligence, and its suppression as a motive by the presence of impulses less animally selfish; so that in relation to invisible Power, fear at last ceases to exist, save in that interfusion with higher faculties which we call awe.

Secondly, Mr Lecky shows clearly that dogmatic Protestantism, holding the vivid belief in Satanic agency to be an essential of piety, would have felt it shame to be a whit behind Catholicism in severity against the devil's servants. Luther's sentiment was that he would not suffer a witch to live (he was not much more merciful to Jews); and, in spite of his fondness for children, believing a certain child to have been begotten by the devil, he recommended the parents to throw it into the river. The torch must be turned on the worst errors of heroic minds – not in irreverent ingratitude, but for the sake of measuring our vast and various debt to all the influences which have concurred, in the intervening ages, to make us recognize as detestable errors the honest convictions of men who, in mere individual capacity and moral force, were very much above us. Again, the Scotch Puritans, during the comparatively short period of their ascendancy, surpassed all Christians before them in the elaborate ingenuity of the tortures they applied for the discovery of witchcraft and sorcery, and did their utmost to prove that if Scotch Calvinism was the true religion, the chief 'note' of the true religion was cruelty. It is hardly an endurable task to read the story of their doings; thoroughly to imagine them as a past reality is already a sort of torture. One detail is enough, and it is a comparatively mild one. It was the regular profession of men called 'prickers' to thrust long pins into the body of a suspected witch in order to detect the insensible spot which was the infallible sign of her guilt. On a superficial view one would be in danger of saying that the main difference between the teachers who sanctioned these things and the much-despised ancestors who offered human victims inside a huge wicker idol, was that they arrived at a more elaborate barbarity by a longer series of dependent propositions. We do not share Mr Buckle's opinion that a Scotch minister's groans were a part of his deliberate plan for keeping the people in a state of terrified subjection;[4] the ministers themselves held the belief they taught, and might well groan over it. What a blessing has a little false logic been to the world! Seeing that men are so slow to question their premises, they must have made each other much more miserable, if pity had not sometimes drawn tender conclusions not warranted by Major and Minor; if there had not been people with an amiable imbecility of reasoning which enabled them at once to cling to hideous beliefs, and to be conscientiously inconsistent with them in their conduct. There is nothing like acute deductive reasoning for keeping a man in the dark: it might be called the *technique* of the intellect, and the concentration of the mind upon it corresponds to that predominance of technical skill in art which ends in degradation of the artist's function, unless new inspiration and invention come to guide it.

And of this there is some good illustration furnished by that third node in the history of witchcraft, the beginning of its end, which is treated in an interesting manner by Mr Lecky. It is worth noticing, that the most important defences of the belief in witchcraft, against the growing scepticism in the latter part of the sixteenth century and in the seventeenth, were the productions of men who in some departments were among the foremost thinkers of their time. One of them was Jean Bodin,[5] the famous writer on government and jurisprudence, whose *Republic*, Hallam thinks, had an important influence in England, and furnished 'a store of arguments and examples that were not lost on the thoughtful minds of our countrymen'.[6] In some of his views he was original and bold; for example, he anticipated Montesquieu in attempting to appreciate the relations of government and climate. Hallam inclines to the opinion that he was a Jew, and attached Divine authority only to the Old Testament. But this was enough to furnish him with his chief data for the existence of witches and for their capital punishment; and in the account of his *Republic* given by Hallam, there is enough evidence that the sagacity which often enabled him to make fine use of his learning was also often entangled in it, to temper our surprise at finding a writer on political science of whom it could be said that, along with Montesquieu, he was 'the most philosophical of those who had read so deeply, the most learned of those who had thought so much', in the van of the forlorn hope to maintain the reality of witchcraft. It should be said that he was equally confident of the unreality of the Copernican hypothesis, on the ground that it was contrary to the tenets of the theologians and philosophers and to common sense, and therefore subversive of the foundations of every science. Of his work on witchcraft, Mr Lecky says: –

The *Démonomanie des sorciers* is chiefly an appeal to authority, which the author deemed on this subject so unanimous and so conclusive, that it was scarcely possible for any sane man to resist it. He appealed to the popular belief in all countries, in all ages, and in all religions. He cited the

opinions of an immense multitude of the greatest writers of pagan antiquity, and of the most illustrious of the Fathers. He showed how the laws
of all nations recognized the existence of witchcraft; and he collected
hundreds of cases which had been investigated before the tribunals of his
own or of other countries. He relates with the most minute and circumstantial detail, and with the most unfaltering confidence, all the proceedings at the witches' Sabbath, the methods which the witches employed in
transporting themselves through the air, their transformations, their
carnal intercourse with the Devil, their various means of injuring their
enemies, the signs that lead to their detection, their confessions when
condemned, and their demeanour at the stake.

Something must be allowed for a lawyer's affection towards a
belief which had furnished so many 'cases'. Bodin's work had been
immediately prompted by the treatise *De Prestigiis Dæmonum*, written by John Wier, a German physician, a treatise which is worth
notice as an example of a transitional form of opinion for which
many analogies may be found in the history both of religion and
science. Wier believed in demons, and in possession by demons,
but his practice as a physician had convinced him that the so-
called witches were patients and victims, that the devil took
advantage of their diseased condition to delude them, and that
there was no consent of an evil will on the part of the women. He
argued that the word in Leviticus translated 'witch' meant 'pois-
oner', and besought the princes of Europe to hinder the further
spilling of innocent blood. These heresies of Wier threw Bodin
into such a state of amazed indignation that if he had been
an ancient Jew instead of a modern economical one, he would
have rent his garments. 'No one had ever heard of pardon being
accorded to sorcerers'; and probably the reason why Charles
IX died young was because he had pardoned the sorcerer, Trois
Echelles! We must remember that this was in 1581, when the
great scientific movement of the Renaissance had hardly begun –
when Galileo was a youth of seventeen, and Kepler a boy of
ten.

But directly afterwards, on the other side, came Montaigne,
whose sceptical acuteness could arrive at negatives without any
apparatus of method. A certain keen narrowness of nature will
secure a man from many absurd beliefs which the larger soul,

vibrating to more manifold influences, would have a long struggle to part with. And so we find the charming, chatty Montaigne – in one of the brightest of his essays, 'Des Boiteux', where he declares that, from his own observation of witches and sorcerers, he should have recommended them to be treated with curative hellebore – stating in his own way a pregnant doctrine, since taught more gravely. It seems to him much less of a prodigy that men should lie, or that their imaginations should deceive them, than that a human body should be carried through the air on a broomstick, or up a chimney by some unknown spirit. He thinks it a sad business to persuade oneself that the test of truth lies in the multitude of believers – 'en une presse où les fols surpassent de tant les sages en nombre'.[7] Ordinarily, he has observed, when men have something stated to them as a fact, they are more ready to explain it than to inquire whether it is real: 'Ils passent par dessus les propositions, mais ils examinent les conséquences; *ils laissent les choses, et courent aux causes.*'[8] There is a sort of strong and generous ignorance which is as honourable and courageous as science – 'ignorance pour laquelle concevoir il n'y a pas moins de science qu'à concevoir la science'. And *à propos* of the immense traditional evidence which weighed with such men as Bodin, he says – 'As for the proofs and arguments founded on experience and facts, I do not pretend to unravel these. What end of a thread is there to lay hold of? I often cut them as Alexander did his knot. *Après tout, c'est mettre ses conjectures à bien haut prix, que d'en faire cuire un homme tout vif.*'[9]

Writing like this, when it finds eager readers, is a sign that the weather is changing; yet much later, namely, after 1665, when the Royal Society had been founded, our own Glanvil,[10] the author of the *Scepsis Scientifica*, a work that was a remarkable advance towards a true definition of the limits of inquiry, and that won him his election as fellow of the society, published in energetic vindication of the belief in witchcraft, of which Mr Lecky gives the following sketch: –

The *Sadducismus Triumphatus*, which is probably the ablest book ever published in defence of the superstition, opens with a striking picture of the rapid progress of the scepticism in England. Everywhere, a disbelief in witchcraft was becoming fashionable in the upper classes; but it was a disbelief that arose entirely from a strong sense of its antecedent improbability. All who were opposed to the orthodox faith united in discrediting witchcraft. They laughed at it, as palpably absurd, as involving the most grotesque and ludicrous conceptions, as so essentially incredible that it would be a waste of time to examine it. This spirit had arisen since the Restoration, although the laws were still in force, and although little or no direct reasoning had been brought to bear upon the subject. In order to combat it, Glanvil proceeded to examine the general question of the credibility of the miraculous. He saw that the reason why witchcraft was ridiculed was, because it was a phase of the miraculous and the work of the devil; that the scepticism was chiefly due to those who disbelieved in miracles and the devil; and that the instances of witchcraft or possession in the Bible were invariably placed on a level with those that were tried in the law courts of England. That the evidence of the belief was overwhelming, he firmly believed; and this, indeed, was scarcely disputed; but, until the sense of *a priori* improbability was removed, no possible accumulation of facts would cause men to believe it. To that task he accordingly addressed himself. Anticipating the idea and almost the words of modern controversialists, he urged that there was such a thing as a credulity of unbelief; and that those who believed so strange a concurrence of delusions, as was necessary on the supposition of the unreality of witchcraft, were far more credulous than those who accepted the belief. He made his very scepticism his principal weapon; and, analysing with much acuteness the *a priori* objections, he showed that they rested upon an unwarrantable confidence in our knowledge of the laws of the spirit world; that they implied the existence of some strict analogy between the faculties of men and of spirits; and that, as such analogy most probably did not exist, no reasoning based on the supposition could dispense men from examining the evidence. He concluded with a large collection of cases, the evidence of which was, as he thought, incontestable.

We have quoted this sketch because Glanvil's argument against the *a priori* objection of absurdity is fatiguingly urged in relation to other alleged marvels which, to busy people seriously occupied with the difficulties of affairs, of science, or of art, seem as little worthy of examination as aëronautic broomsticks. And also because we here see Glanvil, in combating an incredulity that does not happen to be his own, wielding that very argument of traditional evidence which he had made the subject of vigorous attack in his *Scepsis Scientifica*. But perhaps large minds have been peculiarly liable to this fluctuation concerning the sphere of tradition, because, while they have attacked its misapplications, they have been the more solicited by the vague sense that tradition is really the basis of our best life. Our sentiments may be called organized traditions; and a large part of our actions gather all their justification, all their attraction and aroma, from the memory of the life lived, of the actions done, before we were born. In the absence of any profound research into psychological functions or into the mysteries of inheritance, in the absence of any comprehensive view of man's historical development and the dependence of one age on another, a mind at all rich in sensibilities must always have had an indefinite uneasiness in an undistinguishing attack on the coercive influence of tradition. And this may be the apology for the apparent inconsistency of Glanvil's acute criticism on the one side, and his indignation at the 'looser gentry', who laughed at the evidences for witchcraft, on the other. We have already taken up too much space with this subject of witchcraft, else we should be tempted to dwell on Sir Thomas Browne, who far surpassed Glanvil in magnificent incongruity of opinion, and whose works are the most remarkable combination existing, of witty sarcasm against ancient nonsense and modern obsequiousness, with indications of a capacious credulity. After all, we may be sharing what seems to us the hardness of these men, who sat in their studies and argued at their ease about a belief that would be reckoned to have caused more misery and bloodshed than any other superstition, if there had been no such thing as persecution on the ground of religious opinion.

On this subject of Persecution, Mr Lecky writes his best: with clearness of conception, with calm justice, bent on appreciating the necessary tendency of ideas, and with an appropriateness of illustration that could be supplied only by extensive and intelligent reading. Persecution, he shows, is not in any sense peculiar to the Catholic Church; it is a direct sequence of the doctrines that salvation is to be had only within the Church, and that erroneous belief is damnatory – doctrines held as fully by Protestant sects as by the Catholics; and in proportion to its power, Protestantism has been as persecuting as Catholicism. He maintains, in opposition to the favourite modern notion of persecution defeating its own object, that the Church, holding the dogma of exclusive salvation, was perfectly consequent, and really achieved its end of spreading one belief and quenching another, by calling in the aid of the civil arm. Who will say that governments, by their power over institutions and patronage, as well as over punishment, have not power also over the interests and inclinations of men, and over most of those external conditions into which subjects are born, and which make them adopt the prevalent belief as a second nature? Hence, to a sincere believer in the doctrine of exclusive salvation, governments had it in their power to save men from perdition; and wherever the clergy were at the elbow of the civil arm, no matter whether they were Catholic or Protestant, persecution was the result. 'Compel them to come in' was a rule that seemed sanctioned by mercy, and the horrible sufferings it led men to inflict seemed small to minds accustomed to contemplate, as a perpetual source of motive, the eternal unmitigated miseries of a hell that was the inevitable destination of a majority amongst mankind.

It is a significant fact, noted by Mr Lecky, that the only two leaders of the Reformation who advocated tolerance were Zuinglius and Socinus, both of them disbelievers in exclusive salvation. And in corroboration of other evidence that the chief triumphs of the Reformation were due to coercion, he commends to the special attention of his readers the following quotation from a work attributed without question to the famous Protestant theologian, Jurieu, who had himself been hindered, as a Protestant, from exercising his professional functions in France, and was settled as pastor at Rotterdam. It should be remembered that Jurieu's labours fell in the latter part of the seventeenth century and in the beginning of the eighteenth, and that he was the contemporary of Bayle, with whom he was in bitter controversial hostility. He wrote, then, at a time when there was warm debate on the question of Toleration; and it was his great object to vindicate himself and his French fellow-Protestants from all laxity on this point.

Peut on nier que le paganisme est tombé dans le monde par l'autorité des empereurs Romains? On peut assurer sans temerité que le paganisme seroit encore debout, et que les trois quarts de l'Europe seroient encore payens si Constantin et ses successeurs n'avaient employé leur autorité pour l'abolir. Mais, je vous prie, de quelles voies Dieu s'est il servi dans ces derniers siècles pour rétablir la veritable religion dans l'Occident? *Les rois de Suède, ceux de Danemarck, ceux d'Angleterre, les magistrats souverains de Suisse, des Païs Bas, des villes libres d'Allemagne, les princes électeurs, et autres princes souverains de l'empire, n'ont ils pas emploié leur autorité pour abbattre le Papisme?*[11]

Indeed, wherever the tremendous alternative of everlasting torments is believed in – believe in so that it becomes a motive determining the life – not only persecution, but every other form of severity and gloom are the legitimate consequences. There is much ready declamation in these days against the spirit of asceticism and against zeal for doctrinal conversion; but surely the macerated form of a Saint Francis, the fierce denunciations of a Saint Dominic, the groans and prayerful wrestlings of the Puritan who seasoned his bread with tears and made all pleasurable sensation sin, are more in keeping with the contemplation of unending anguish as the destiny of a vast multitude whose nature we share, than the rubicund cheerfulness of some modern divines, who profess to unite a smiling liberalism with a well-bred and tacit but unshaken confidence in the reality of the bottomless pit. But, in fact, as Mr Lecky maintains, that awful image, with its group of associated dogmas concerning the inherited curse, and the damnation of unbaptized infants, of heathens, and of heretics, has passed away from what he is fond of calling 'the realizations' of Christendom. These things are no longer the objects of practical belief. They may be mourned for in encyclical letters; bishops may regret them; doctors of divinity may sign testimonials to the excellent character of these decayed beliefs; but for the mass of Christians they are no more influential than unrepealed but forgotten statutes. And with these dogmas has melted away the strong basis for the defence of persecution. No man now writes eager vindications for himself and his colleagues from the suspicion of adhering to the principle of toleration. And this momentous change, it is Mr Lecky's object to show, is due to that concurrence of conditions which he has chosen to call 'the advance of the Spirit of Rationalism'.

In other parts of his work, where he attempts to trace the action of the same conditions on the acceptance of miracles and on other chief phases of our historical development, Mr Lecky has laid himself open to considerable criticism. The chapters on the Miracles of the Church, the æsthetic, scientific, and moral Development of Rationalism, the Secularization of Politics, and the Industrial history of Rationalism, embrace a wide range of diligently gathered facts; but they are nowhere illuminated by a sufficiently clear conception and statement of the agencies at work, or the mode of their action, in the gradual modification of opinion and of life. The writer frequently impresses us as being in a state of hesitation concerning his own standing-point, which may form a desirable stage in private meditation but not in published exposition. Certain epochs in theoretic conception, certain considerations, which should be fundamental to his survey, are introduced quite incidentally in a sentence or two, or in a note which seems to be an afterthought. Great writers and their ideas are touched upon too slightly and with too little discrimination, and important theories are sometimes characterized with a rashness which conscientious revision will correct. There is a fatiguing use of vague or shifting phrases, such as 'modern civilization', 'spirit of the age', 'tone of thought', 'intellectual type of the age', 'bias of the imagination', 'habits of religious thought', unbalanced by any precise definition; and the spirit of rationalism is sometimes treated of as if it lay outside the specific mental activities of which it is a generalized expression. Mr Curdle's famous definition of the dramatic unities as 'a sort of a general oneness',[12] is not totally false; but such luminousness as it has could only be perceived by those who already knew what the unities were. Mr Lecky has the advantage of being strongly impressed with the great part played by the emotions in the formation of opinion, and with the high complexity of the causes at work in social evolution; but he frequently writes as if he had never yet distinguished between the complexity of the conditions that produce prevalent states of mind, and the inability of particular minds to give distinct reasons for the preferences or persuasions produced by those states. In brief, he does not discriminate, or does not help his reader to discriminate, between objective complexity and subjective confusion. But the most muddle-headed gentleman who represents the spirit of the age by observing, as he settles his collar, that the development-theory is quite 'the thing' is a result of definite processes, if we could only trace them. 'Mental attitudes', and 'predispositions', however vague in consciousness, have not vague causes, any more than the 'blind motions of the spring' in plants and animals.

The word 'Rationalism' has the misfortune, shared by most words in this grey world, of being somewhat equivocal. This evil may be nearly overcome by careful preliminary definition; but Mr Lecky does not supply this, and the original specific application of the word to a particular phase of biblical interpretation seems to have clung about his use of it with a misleading effect. Through some parts of his book he appears to regard the grand characteristic of modern thought and civilization, compared with ancient, as a radiation in the first instance from a change in religious conceptions. The supremely important fact, that the gradual reduction of all phenomena within the sphere of established law, which carries as a consequence the rejection of the miraculous, has its determining current in the development of physical science, seems to have engaged comparatively little of his attention; at least, he gives it no prominence. The great conception of universal regular sequence, without partiality and without caprice – the conception which is the most potent force at work in the modification of our faith, and of the practical form given to our sentiments – could only grow out of that patient watching of external fact, and that silencing of preconceived notions, which are urged upon the mind by the problems of physical science.

There is not room here to explain and justify the impressions of dissatisfaction which have been briefly indicated, but a serious writer like Mr Lecky will not find such suggestions altogether useless. The objections, even the misunderstandings, of a reader who is not careless or ill-disposed, may serve to stimulate an author's vigilance over his thoughts as well as his style. It would be gratifying to see some future proof that Mr Lecky has acquired juster views than are implied in the assertion that philosophers of the sensational school 'can never rise to the conception of the disinterested'; and that he has freed himself from all temptation to that mingled laxity of statement, and ill-pitched elevation of tone, which are painfully present in the closing pages of his second volume.[13]

POEMS

From *Armgart*

(*Macmillan's Magazine*, July 1871)

Armgart was written in 1870, just before Eliot embarked on *Middlemarch*. It is a dramatic poem about a woman singer who first refuses marriage for her art and then loses her voice, and with it her art. It opens with Armgart flushed with triumph after singing Gluck's *Orpheus*; the leading character is a male artist (though the part is written for a female voice) who defies death in search of his dead wife, is destroyed and sings in death. We print the scene in which Armgart refuses the Graf, whom she loves, for her art. When she despairs at the loss of her voice, her old teacher Leo and her maid Walpurga teach her that there is still a life of devotion to others.

The singer is one type of the woman artist in early female fiction, as Ellen Moers shows in her studies of Madame de Staël's *Corinne* and George Sand's *Consuelo*, an early favourite of Eliot's (*Literary Women: The Great Writers*, 1977). The figure recurs in *Daniel Deronda*, divided between the delicate-voiced Mirah, who becomes Daniel's wife and shares his mission, and Daniel's mother, the Alchirisi, a great singer who destroys her affections and abandons her son in order to exercise her genius.

SCENE 2

The same Salon, morning. ARMGART *seated, in her bonnet and walking dress. The* GRAF *standing near her against the piano.*

GRAF: Armgart, to many minds the first success

Is reason for desisting. I have known
A man so various, he tried all arts,
But when in each by turns he had achieved
Just so much mastery as made men say,
'He could be king here if he would,' he threw
The lauded skill aside. He hates, said one,
The level of achieved pre-eminence,
He must be conquering still; but others said –

ARMGART: The truth, I hope: he had a meagre soul,
Holding no depth where love could root itself.
'Could if he would?' True greatness ever wills –
It breathes in wholeness like an unborn child,
And all its strength is knit with constancy.

GRAF: He used to say himself he was too sane
To give his life away for excellence
Which yet must stand, an ivory statuette
Wrought to perfection through long lonely years,
Huddled in the mart of mediocrities.
He said, the very finest doing wins
The admiring only; but to leave undone,
Promise and not fulfil, like buried youth,
Wins all the envious, makes them sigh your name
As that fair Absent, blameless Possible,
Which could alone impassion them; and thus,
Serene negation has free gift of all,
Panting achievement struggles, is denied,
Or wins to lose again. What say you, Armgart?
Truth has rough flavours if we bite it through;
I think this sarcasm came from out its core
Of bitter irony.

ARMGART: It is the truth
Mean souls select to feed upon. What then?
Their meanness is a truth, which I will spurn.
The praise I seek lives not in envious breath
Using my name to blight another's deed.
I sing for love of song and that renown
Which is the spreading act, the world-wide share,
Of good that I was born with. Had I failed–

Well, that had been a truth most pitiable.
I cannot bear to think what life would be
With high hope shrunk to endurance, stunted aims,
Like broken lances ground to eating-knives,
A self sunk down to look with level eyes
At low achievement, doomed from day to day
To distaste of its consciousness. But I —
GRAF: Have won, not lost, in your decisive throw.
  And I too glory in this issue; yet,
  The public verdict has no potency
  To sway my judgement of what Armgart is:
  My pure delight in her would be but sullied,
  If it o'erflowed with mixture of men's praise.
  And had she failed, I should have said, 'The pearl
  Remains a pearl for me, reflects the light
  With the same fitness that first charmed my gaze —
  Is worth as fine a setting now as then.'
ARMGART (*rising*): O you are good! But why will you
    rehearse
  The talk of cynics, who with insect eyes
  Explore the secrets of the rubbish heap?
  I hate your epigrams and pointed saws
  Whose narrow truth is but broad falsity.
  Confess, your friend was shallow.
GRAF: I confess
  Life is not rounded in an epigram,
  And saying aught, we leave a world unsaid.
  I quoted, merely to shape forth my thought
  That high success has terrors when achieved—
  Like preternatural spouses whose dire love
  Hangs perilous on slight observances:
  Whence it were possible that Armgart crowned
  Might turn and listen to a pleading voice,
  Though Armgart striving in the race was deaf.
  You said you dared not think what life had been
  Without the stamp of eminence; have you thought
  How you will bear the poise of eminence
  With dread of sliding? Paint the future out

As an unchecked and glorious career,
'Twill grow more strenuous by the very love
You bear to excellence, the very fate
Of human powers, which tread at every step
On possible verges.

ARMGART: I accept the peril.
I choose to walk high with sublimer dread
Rather than crawl in safety. And, besides,
I am an artist as you are a noble:
I ought to bear the burthen of my rank.

GRAF: Such parallels, dear Armgart, are but snares
To catch the mind with seeming argument –
Small baits of likeness 'mid disparity.
Men rise the higher as their task is high,
The task being well achieved. A woman's rank
Lies in the fullness of her womanhood:
Therein alone she is royal.

ARMGART: Yes, I know
The oft-taught Gospel: 'Woman, thy desire
Shall be that all superlatives on earth
Belong to men, save the one highest kind –
To be a mother. Thou shalt not desire
To do aught best save pure subservience:
Nature has willed it so!' O blessed Nature!
Let her be arbitress; she gave me voice
Such as she only gives a woman child,
Best of its kind, gave me ambition too,
That sense transcendent which can taste the joy
Of swaying multitudes, of being adored
For such achievement, needed excellence,
As man's best art must wait for, or be dumb.
Men did not say, when I had sung last night,
''Twas good, nay, wonderful, considering
She is a woman' – and then turn to add,
'Tenor or baritone had sung her songs
Better, of course: she's but a woman spoiled.'
I beg your pardon, Graf, you said it.

GRAF: No!

How should I say it, Armgart? I who own
The magic of your nature-given art
As sweetest effluence of your womanhood
Which, being to my choice the best, must find
The best of utterance. But this I say:
Your fervid youth beguiles you; you mistake
A strain of lyric passion for a life
Which in the spending is a chronicle
With ugly pages. Trust me, Armgart, trust me:
Ambition exquisite as yours which soars
Toward something quintessential you call fame,
Is not robust enough for this gross world
Whose fame is dense with false and foolish breath.
Ardour, atwin with nice refining thought,
Prepares a double pain. Pain had been saved,
Nay, purer glory reached, had you been throned
As woman only, holding all your art
As attribute to that dear sovereignty –
Concentering your power in home delights
Which penetrate and purify the world.

ARMGART: What, leave the opera with my part ill-sung
While I was warbling in a drawing-room?
Sing in the chimney-corner to inspire
My husband reading news? Let the world hear
My music only in his morning speech
Less stammering than most honourable men's?
No! tell me that my song is poor, my art
The piteous feat of weakness aping strength –
That were fit proem to your argument.
Till then, I am an artist by my birth –
By the same warrant that I am a woman:
Nay, in the added rarer gift I see
Supreme vocation: if a conflict comes,
Perish – no, not the woman, but the joys
Which men make narrow by their narrowness.
O I am happy! The great masters write
For women's voices, and great Music wants me!
I need not crush myself within a mould

Of theory called Nature: I have room
To breathe and grow unstunted.

GRAF: Armgart, hear me.
I meant not that our talk should hurry on
To such collision. Foresight of the ills
Thick shadowing your path, drew on my speech
Beyond intention. True, I came to ask
A great renunciation, but not this
Towards which my words at first perversely strayed,
As if in memory of their earlier suit,
Forgetful . . .
Armgart, do you remember too? the suit
Had but postponement, was not quite disdained –
Was told to wait and learn – what it has learned –
A more submissive speech.

ARMGART (*with some agitation*): Then it forgot
Its lesson cruelly. As I remember,
'Twas not to speak save to the artist crowned,
Nor speak to her of casting off her crown.

GRAF: Nor will it, Armgart. I come not to seek
Other renunciation than the wife's,
Which turns away from other possible love
Future and worthier, to take his love
Who asks the name of husband. He who sought
Armgart obscure, and heard her answer, 'Wait' –
May come without suspicion now to seek
Armgart applauded.

ARMGART (*turning towards him*): Yes, without suspicion
Of aught save what consists with faithfulness
In all expressed intent. Forgive me, Graf –
I am ungrateful to no soul that loves me –
To you most grateful. Yet the best intent
Grasps but a living present which may grow
Like any unfledged bird. You are a noble,
And have a high career; but now you said
'Twas higher far than aught a woman seeks
Beyond mere womanhood. You claim to be
More than a husband, but could not rejoice

That I were more than wife. What follows, then?
You choosing me with such persistency
As is but stretched-out rashness, soon must find
Our marriage asks concessions, asks resolve
To share renunciation or demand it.
Either we both renounce a mutual ease,
As in a nation's need both man and wife
Do public services, or one of us
Must yield that something else for which each lives
Besides the other. Men are reasoners:
That premiss of superior claims perforce
Urges conclusion – 'Armgart, it is you.'

GRAF: But if I say I have considered this
With strict prevision, counted all the cost
Which that great good of loving you demands –
Questioned my stores of patience, half-resolved
To live resigned without a bliss whose threat
Touched you as well as me – then finally,
With impetus of undivided will
Returned to say, 'You shall be free as now;
Only accept the refuge, shelter, guard,
My love will give your freedom' – then your words
Are hard accusal.

ARMGART: Well, I accuse myself.
My love would be accomplice of your will.

GRAF: Again – my will?

ARMGART: O your unspoken will.
Your silent tolerance would torture me,
And on that rack I should deny the good
I yet believed in.

GRAF: Then I am the man
Whom you would love?

ARMGART: Whom I refuse to love!
No, I will live alone and pour my pain
With passion into music, where it turns
To what is best within my better self.
I will not take for husband one who deems
The thing my soul acknowledges as good –

The thing I hold worth striving, suffering for,
To be a thing dispensed with easily,
Or else the idol of a mind infirm.

GRAF: Armgart, you are ungenerous; you strain
My thought beyond its mark. Our difference
Lies not so deep as love – as union
Through a mysterious fitness that transcends
Formal agreement

ARMGART: It lies deep enough
To chafe the union. If many a man
Refrains, degraded, from the utmost right,
Because the pleadings of his wife's small fears
Are little serpents biting at his heel, –
How shall a woman keep her steadfastness
Beneath a frost within her husband's eyes
Where coldness scorches? Graf, it is your sorrow
That you love Armgart. Nay, it is her sorrow
That she may not love you.

GRAF: Woman, it seems,
Has enviable power to love or not
According to her will.

ARMGART: She has the will –
I have – who am one woman – not to take
Disloyal pledges that divide her will.
The man who marries me must wed my art –
Honour and cherish it, not tolerate.

GRAF: The man is yet to come whose theory
Will weigh as nought with you against his love.

ARMGART: Whose theory will plead beside his love.

GRAF: Himself a singer, then? who knows no life
Out of the opera books, where tenor parts
Are found to suit him?

ARMGART: You are bitter, Graf.
Forgive me; seek the woman you deserve,
All grace, all goodness, who has not yet found
A meaning in her life, or any end
Beyond fulfilling yours. The type abounds.

GRAF: And happily, for the world.

ARMGART: Yes, happily.
  Let it excuse me that my kind is rare:
  Commonness is its own security.
GRAF: Armgart, I would with all my soul I knew
  The man so rare that he could make your life
  As woman sweet to you, as artist safe.
ARMGART: O I can live unmated, but not live
  Without the bliss of singing to the world,
  And feeling all my world respond to me.
GRAF: May it be lasting. Then, we two must part?
ARMGART: I thank you from my heart for all. Farewell!

※

From *The Spanish Gypsy*

(1868)

The Spanish Gypsy was written in 1867 and published in 1868.
It had been conceived and largely written, in dramatic form,
in 1864, when it caused its author so much distress that
Lewes had to take it away from her. Eliot told William
Blackwood, 'It is not historic, but has merely historic con-
nexions. The plot was wrought out entirely as an incorpora-
tion of my own ideas' (*Letters, Vol. IV*, pp. 354–5).

It is set in Spain at the time when 'the struggle with the
Moors was attaining its climax'. Its heroine, Fedalma, is to
marry Duke Silva, when she discovers that she is the daughter and heir of the captive gypsy chieftain, Zarca, who
imposes on her the duty of leaving her love and leading her
people. Silva, when he cannot move her resolve, attempts to
become a Zincalo, but his own conflict of loyalties tears him
apart, and he kills Zarca in a quarrel. Fedalma is left to lead
the Zincali in her search for a national home in Africa,
prefiguring Deronda's search for a Jewish national home.

Eliot wrote that the poem was inspired by a

small picture of Titian's [*An Annunciation*]. It occurred to me that
here was a great dramatic motive of the same class as those used by
the Greek dramatists, yet specifically differing from them. A young
maiden, believing herself to be on the eve of the chief event of her
life – marriage – about to share in the ordinary lot of womanhood,
full of young hope, has suddenly announced to her that she is
chosen to fulfil a great destiny, entailing a terribly different experience from that of ordinary womanhood. She is chosen, not by any
arbitrariness, but as a result of foregoing hereditary conditions: she
obeys. 'Behold the handmaid of the Lord.' Here, I thought, is a

subject grander than that of Iphigeneia, and it has never been used [Cross, pp. 42–3].

'I required the opposition of race to give the need for renouncing the expectation of marriage,' she wrote.

There is an excellent review of the poem by Henry James that is worth studying in full. It was published in the *North American Review* in October 1868. James admires the poem, with caveats, of which the most important are to do with the abstract nature of the characters and their problem. He wrote, 'It is very possible that the author's primary intention may have had a breadth which has been curtailed in the execution of the work, – that it was her wish to present a struggle between nature and culture, between education and the instinct of race.' James points out that the poem is a *romance*, which might exonerate it from the hard-headed attention to realism of character or action. But he is pushed to be generous.

Fedalma is not a real Gypsy maiden. The conviction is strong in the reader's mind that a genuine Spanish Zincala would have somehow contrived to follow her tribe and to keep her lover. If Fedalma is not real, Zarca is even less so. He is interesting, imposing, picturesque; but he is very far, I take it, from being a genuine *Gypsy* chieftain. They are both ideal figures, – the offspring of a strong mental desire for creatures well-rounded in their elevation and heroism, – creatures who should illustrate the nobleness of human nature divorced from its smallness ... I have said enough to lead the reader to perceive that the poem should not be regarded as a rigid transcript of actual or possible fact, – that the action goes on in an artificial world, and that properly to comprehend it he must regard it with a generous mind.

We have printed the opening of the poem because it gives a good idea of Eliot's rhetoric, whose faults, again according to James, 'arise from an excess of rhetorical energy, from a desire to attain to perfect fulness and roundness of utterance; they are faults of overstatement'. The opening is a vigorous picture of a whirling clash and conflict of dead and living beliefs, cultures and ideas, and is interesting for that reason. The other passage we print is Fedalma's acceptance of her renunciation from Book III. It contains four excellent lines:

No good is certain, but the steadfast mind,
The undivided will to seek the good:
'Tis that compels the elements, and wrings
A human music from the indifferent air.

From Book I

'TIS THE warm South, where Europe spreads her lands
Like fretted leaflets, breathing on the deep:
Broad-breasted Spain, leaning with equal love
(A calm earth-goddess crowned with corn and vines)[1]
On the Mid Sea that moans with memories,
And on the untravelled Ocean, whose vast tides
Pant dumbly passionate with dreams of youth.[2]
This river, shadowed by the battlements
And gleaming silvery towards the northern sky,
Feeds the famed stream that waters Andalus
And loiters, amorous of the fragrant air,
By Córdova and Seville to the bay
Fronting Algarva and the wandering flood
Of Guadiana. This deep mountain gorge
Slopes widening on the olive-plumèd plains
Of fair Granáda: one far-stretching arm
Points to Elvira, one to eastward heights
Of Alpujarras where the new-bathed Day
With oriflamme uplifted o'er the peaks
Saddens the breasts of northward-looking snows
That loved the night, and soared with soaring stars;
Flashing the signals of his nearing swiftness
From Almería's purple-shadowed bay
On to the far-off rocks that gaze and glow –
On to Alhambra, strong and ruddy heart
Of glorious Morisma, gasping now,
A maimèd giant in his agony.
This town that dips its feet within the stream,
And seems to sit a tower-crowned Cybele,[3]
Spreading her ample robe adown the rocks,
Is rich Bedmár: 'twas Moorish long ago,
But now the Cross is sparkling on the Mosque,

And bells make Catholic the trembling air.
The fortress gleams in Spanish sunshine now
('Tis south a mile before the rays are Moorish) –
Hereditary jewel, agraffe bright
On all the many-titled privilege
Of young Duke Silva. No Castilian knight
That serves Queen Isabel has higher charge;
For near this frontier sits the Moorish king,
Not Boabdil the waverer, who usurps
A throne he trembles in, and fawning licks
The feet of conquerors, but that fierce lion
Grisly El Zagal, who has made his lair
In Guadix' fort, and rushing thence with strength,
Half his own fierceness, half the untainted heart
Of mountain bands that fight for holiday,
Wastes the fair lands that lie by Alcalá,
Wreathing his horse's neck with Christian heads.

To keep the Christian frontier – such high trust
Is young Duke Silva's; and the time is great.
(What times are little? To the sentinel
That hour is regal when he mounts on guard.)
The fifteenth century since the Man Divine
Taught and was hated in Capernaum
Is near its end – is falling as a husk
Away from all the fruit its years have ripened.
The Moslem faith, now flickering like a torch
In a night struggle on this shore of Spain,
Glares, a broad column of advancing flame,
Along the Danube and the Illyrian shore
Far into Italy, where eager monks,
Who watch in dreams and dream the while they watch,
See Christ grow paler in the baleful light,
Crying again the cry of the forsaken.
But faith, the stronger for extremity,
Becomes prophetic, hears the far-off tread
Of western chivalry, sees downward sweep
The archangel Michael with the gleaming sword,

And listens for the shriek of hurrying fiends
Chased from their revels in God's sanctuary.
So trusts the monk, and lifts appealing eyes
To the high dome, the Church's firmament,
Where the blue light-pierced curtain, rolled away,
Reveals the throne and Him who sits thereon.
So trust the men whose best hope for the world
Is ever that the world is near its end:
Impatient of the stars that keep their course
And make no pathway for the coming Judge.

But other futures stir the world's great heart.
Europe is come to her majority,
And enters on the vast inheritance
Won from the tombs of mighty ancestors,
The seeds, the gold, the gems, the silent harps
That lay deep buried with the memories
Of old renown.
No more, as once in sunny Avignon,
The poet-scholar spreads the Homeric page,
And gazes sadly, like the deaf at song;
For now the old epic voices ring again
And vibrate with the beat and melody
Stirred by the warmth of old Ionian days.
The martyred sage, the Attic orator,[4]
Immortally incarnate, like the gods,
In spiritual bodies, wingèd words
Holding a universe impalpable,
Find a new audience. For evermore,
With grander resurrection than was feigned
Of Attila's fierce Huns, the soul of Greece
Conquers the bulk of Persia. The maimed form
Of calmly-joyous beauty, marble-limbed,
Yet breathing with the thought that shaped its lips,
Looks mild reproach from out its opened grave
At creeds of terror; and the vine-wreathed god[5]
Rising, a stifled question from the silence,[6]
Fronts the pierced Image with the crown of thorns.

The soul of man is widening towards the past:
No longer hanging at the breast of life
Feeding in blindness to his parentage –
Quenching all wonder with Omnipotence,
Praising a name with indolent piety –
He spells the record of his long descent,
More largely conscious of the life that was.
And from the height that shows where morning shone
On far-off summits pale and gloomy now,
The horizon widens round him, and the west
Looks vast with untracked waves whereon his gaze
Follows the flight of the swift-vanished bird
That like the sunken sun is mirrored still
Upon the yearning soul within the eye.
And so in Córdova through patient nights
Columbus watches, or he sails in dreams
Between the setting stars and finds new day;
Then wakes again to the old weary days,
Girds on the cord and frock of pale Saint Francis,
And like him zealous pleads with foolish men.
'I ask but for a million maravedis:
Give me three caravels to find a world,
New shores, new realms, new soldiers for the Cross.
Son cosas grandes!' Thus he pleads in vain;
Yet faints not utterly, but pleads anew,
Thinking, 'God means it, and has chosen me.'
For this man is the pulse of all mankind
Feeding an embryo future, offspring strange
Of the fond Present, that with mother-prayers
And mother-fancies looks for championship
Of all her loved beliefs and old-world way
From that young Time she bears within her womb.
The sacred places shall be purged again,
The Turk converted, and the Holy Church,
Like the mild Virgin with the outspread robe,
Shall fold all tongues and nations lovingly.

But since God works by armies, who shall be

The modern Cyrus? Is it France most Christian,
Who with his lilies and brocaded knights,
French oaths, French vices, and the newest style
Of out-puffed sleeve, shall pass from west to east,
A winnowing fan to purify the seed
For fair millennial harvests soon to come?
Or is not Spain the land of chosen warriors? –
Crusaders consecrated from the womb,
Carrying the sword-cross stamped upon their souls
By the long yearnings of a nation's life,
Through all the seven patient centuries
Since first Pelayo and his resolute band
Trusted the God within their Gothic hearts
At Covadunga, and defied Mahound;
Beginning so the Holy War of Spain
That now is panting with the eagerness
Of labour near its end. The silver cross
Glitters o'er Malaga and streams dread light
On Moslem galleys, turning all their stores
From threats to gifts. What Spanish knight is he
Who, living now, holds it not shame to live
Apart from that hereditary battle
Which needs his sword? Castilian gentlemen
Choose not their task – they choose to do it well.

From Book III

ZARCA: Will then to stay!
    Say you will take your better, painted such
    By blind desire, and choose the hideous worse
    For thousands who were happier but for you.
    My thirty followers are assembled now
    Without this terrace: I your father wait
    That you may lead us forth to liberty –
    Restore me to my tribe – five hundred men
    Whom I alone can save, alone can rule,
    And plant them as a mighty nation's seed.
    Why, vagabonds who clustered round one man,
    Their voice of God, their prophet and their king,

Twice grew to empire on the teeming shores
Of Africa, and sent new royalties
To feed afresh the Arab sway in Spain,
My vagabonds are a seed more generous,
Quick as the serpent, loving as the hound,
And beautiful as disinherited gods.
They have a promised land beyond the sea:
There I may lead them, raise my standard, call
All wandering Zincali to that home,
And make a nation – bring light, order, law,
Instead of chaos. You, my only heir,
Are called to reign for me when I am gone.
Now choose your deed: to save or to destroy.
You, woman and Zincala, fortunate
Above your fellows – you who hold a curse
Or blessing in the hollow of your hand –
Say you will loose that hand from fellowship,
Let go the rescuing rope, hurl all the tribes,
Children and countless beings yet to come,
Down from the upward path of light and joy,
Back to the dark and marshy wilderness
Where life is nought but blind tenacity
Of that which is. Say you will curse your race!

FEDALMA (*rising and stretching out her arms in deprecation*):
No, no – I will not say it – I will go!
Father, I choose! I will not take a heaven
Haunted by shrieks of far-off misery.
This deed and I have ripened with the hours:
It is a part of me – a wakened thought
That, rising like a giant, masters me,
And grows into a doom. O mother life,
That seemed to nourish me so tenderly,
Even in the womb you vowed me to the fire,
Hung on my soul the burden of men's hopes,
And pledged me to redeem! – I'll pay the debt.
You gave me strength that I should pour it all
Into this anguish. I can never shrink

Back into bliss – my heart has grown too big
With things that might be. Father, I will go.
I will strip off these gems. Some happier bride
Shall wear them, since I should be dowered
With nought but curses, dowered with misery
Of men – of women, who have hearts to bleed
As mine is bleeding.

   (*She sinks on a seat, and begins to take off her jewels.*)
   Now, good gems, we part.
Speak of me always tenderly to Silva.

   (*She pauses, turning to* ZARCA.)
O father, will the women of our tribe
Suffer as I do, in the years to come
When you have made them great in Africa?
Redeemed from ignorant ills only to feel
A conscious woe? Then – is it worth the pains?
Were it not better when we reach that shore
To raise a funeral-pile and perish all?
So closing up a myriad avenues
To misery yet unwrought? My soul is faint –
Will these sharp pangs buy any certain good?

ZARCA: Nay, never falter: no great deed is done
By falterers who ask for certainty.
No good is certain, but the steadfast mind,
The undivided will to seek the good:
'Tis that compels the elements, and wrings
A human music from the indifferent air.
The greatest gift the hero leaves his race
Is to have been a hero. Say we fail! –
We feed the high tradition of the world,
And leave our spirit in Zincalo breasts.

FEDALMA (*unclasping her jewelled belt, and throwing it down*):
Yes, I will say that we shall fail! I will not count
On aught but being faithful. I will take
This yearning self of mine and strangle it.
I will not be half-hearted: never yet

Fedalma did aught with a wavering soul.
Die, my young joy – die, all my hungry hopes –
The milk you cry for from the breast of life
Is thick with curses. Oh, all fatness here
Snatches its meat from leanness – feeds on graves
I will seek nothing but to shun base joy.
The saints were cowards who stood by to see
Christ crucified: they should have flung themselves
Upon the Roman spears, and died in vain –
The grandest death, to die in vain – for love
Greater than sways the forces of the world!
That death shall be my bridegroom. I will wed
The curse of the Zincali. Father, come!

Brother and Sister Sonnets

(from *Jubal and Other Poems*, 1874)

This sequence of Shakespearean sonnets was written in 1869 though not published until 1874. The material that Eliot draws on is her childhood relationship with her estranged brother, Isaac, which is also at the centre of *The Mill on the Floss* (1860). She wrote to William Blackwood about it in April 1874, in answer to his account of a children's picnic.

I hope that the brother and sister love each other very dearly: life might be so enriched if that relation were made the most of, as one of the highest forms of friendship. A good while ago I made a poem, in the form of sonnets after the Shakspeare type, on the childhood of a brother and sister ... little descriptive bits on the mutual influences in their small lives. This was always one of my best-loved subjects. And I was proportionately enraged about that execrable discussion raised in relation to Byron. The deliberate insistence on the subject was a worse crime against society than the reputed fact (*Letters, Vol. V*, pp. 402–3).

The poems very successfully embody ideas that recur in the novels: the childhood relationship as 'My present Past, my root of piety' and the learning of love in the recognition of the limitations on the self imposed by the recognition of others:

> Widening its life with separate life discerned,
> A Like unlike, a Self that self restrains.
>
> (Sonnet 9)

1

I CANNOT choose but think upon the time
When our two lives grew like two buds that kiss
At lightest thrill from the bee's swinging chime,
Because the one so near the other is.

He was the elder and a little man
Of forty inches, bound to show no dread,
And I the girl that puppy-like now ran,
Now lagged behind my brother's larger tread.

I held him wise, and when he talked to me
Of snakes and birds, and which God loved the best,
I thought his knowledge marked the boundary
Where men grew blind, though angels knew the rest.

   If he said 'Hush!' I tried to hold my breath
   Wherever he said 'Come!' I stepped in faith.

2

Long years have left their writing on my brow,
But yet the freshness and the dew-fed beam
Of those young mornings are about me now,
When we two wandered toward the far-off stream

With rod and line. Our basket held a store
Baked for us only, and I thought with joy
That I should have my share, though he had more,
Because he was the elder and a boy.

The firmaments of daisies since to me
Have had those mornings in their opening eyes,
The bunchèd cowslip's pale transparency
Carries that sunshine of sweet memories,

   And wild-rose branches take their finest scent
   From those blest hours of infantine content.

3

Our mother bade us keep the trodden ways,
Stroked down my tippet, set my brother's frill,
Then with the benediction of her gaze
Clung to us lessening, and pursued us still

Across the homestead to the rookery elms,
Whose tall old trunks had each a grassy mound,
So rich for us, we counted them as realms
With varied products: here were earth-nuts found,

And here the Lady-fingers in deep shade;
Here sloping toward the Moat the rushes grew,
The large to split for pith, the small to braid;
While over all the dark rooks cawing flew,

And made a happy strange solemnity,
A deep-toned chant from life unknown to me.

4

Our meadow-path had memorable spots:
One where it bridged a tiny rivulet,
Deep hid by tangled blue Forget-me-nots;
And all along the waving grasses met

My little palm, or nodded to my cheek,
When flowers with upturned faces gazing drew
My wonder downward, seeming all to speak
With eyes of souls that dumbly heard and knew.

Then came the copse, where wild things rushed unseen,
And black-scathed grass betrayed the past abode
Of mystic gypsies, who still lurked between
Me and each hidden distance of the road.

A gypsy once had startled me at play,
Blotting with her dark smile my sunny day.

5

Thus rambling we were schooled in deepest lore,
And learned the meanings that give words a soul,
The fear, the love, the primal passionate store,
Whose shaping impulses make manhood whole.

Those hours were seed to all my after good;
My infant gladness, through eye, ear, and touch,
Took easily as warmth a various food
To nourish the sweet skill of loving much.

For who in age shall roam the earth and find
Reason for loving that will strike out love
With sudden rod from the hard year-pressed mind?
Were reasons sown as thick as stars above,

   'Tis love must see them, as the eye sees light:
   Day is but Number to the darkened sight.

6

Our brown canal was endless to my thought;
And on its banks I sat in dreamy peace,
Unknowing how the good I loved was wrought,
Untroubled by the fear that it would cease.

Slowly the barges floated into view
Rounding a grassy hill to me sublime
With some Unknown beyond it, whither flew
The parting cuckoo toward a fresh spring time.

The wide-arched bridge, the scented elder-flowers,
The wondrous watery rings that died too soon,
The echoes of the quarry, the still hours
With white robe sweeping-on the shadeless noon,

   Were but my growing self, are part of me,
   My present Past, my root of piety.

7

Those long days measured by my little feet
Had chronicles which yield me many a text;
Where irony still finds an image meet
Of full-grown judgements in this world perplext.

One day my brother left me in high charge,
To mind the rod, while he went seeking bait,
And bade me, when I saw a nearing barge,
Snatch out the line, lest he should come too late.

Proud of the task, I watched with all my might
For one whole minute, till my eyes grew wide,
Till sky and earth took on a strange new light
And seemed a dream-world floating on some tide –

    A fair pavilioned boat for me alone
    Bearing me onward through the vast unknown.

8

But sudden came the barge's pitch-black prow,
Nearer and angrier came my brother's cry,
And all my soul was quivering fear, when lo!
Upon the imperilled line, suspended high,

A silver perch! My guilt that won the prey,
Now turned to merit, had a guerdon rich
Of hugs and praises, and made merry play,
Until my triumph reached its highest pitch

When all at home were told the wondrous feat,
And how the little sister had fished well.
In secret, though my fortune tasted sweet,
I wondered why this happiness befell.

    'The little lass had luck,' the gardener said:
    And so I learned, luck was with glory wed.

9

We had the self-same world enlarged for each
By loving difference of girl and boy:
The fruit that hung on high beyond my reach
He plucked for me, and oft he must employ

A measuring glance to guide my tiny shoe
Where lay firm stepping-stones, or call to mind
'This thing I like my sister may not do,
For she is little, and I must be kind.'

Thus boyish Will the nobler mastery learned
Where inward vision over impulse reigns,
Widening its life with separate life discerned,
A Like unlike, a Self that self restrains.

His years with others must the sweeter be
For those brief days he spent in loving me.

10

His sorrow was my sorrow, and his joy
Sent little leaps and laughs through all my frame;
My doll seemed lifeless and no girlish toy
Had any reason when my brother came.

I knelt with him at marbles, marked his fling
Cut the ringed stem and make the apple drop,
Or watched him winding close the spiral string
That looped the orbits of the humming top.

Grasped by such fellowship my vagrant thought
Ceased with dream-fruit dream-wishes to fulfil;
My aëry-picturing fantasy was taught
Subjection to the harder, truer skill

That seeks with deeds to grave a thought-tracked line,
And by 'What is,' 'What will be' to define.

II

School parted us; we never found again
That childish world where our two spirits mingled
Like scents from varying roses that remain
One sweetness, nor can evermore be singled.

Yet the twin habit of that early time
Lingered for long about the heart and tongue:
We had been natives of one happy clime,
And its dear accent to our utterance clung.

Till the dire years whose awful name is Change
Had grasped our souls still yearning in divorce,
And pitiless shaped them in two forms that range
Two elements which sever their life's course.

But were another childhood-world my share,
I would be born a little sister there.

FROM *IMPRESSIONS*
OF THEOPHRASTUS SUCH
(1879)

ELIOT INTENDED to call this collection of eighteen essays *Characters and Characteristics, or Impressions of Theophrastus Such* and name herself as its editor. The essays were written during Lewes's last illness, and the first edition has a publisher's note: 'The manuscript of this Work was put into our hands towards the close of last year, but the publication has been delayed owing to the domestic affliction of the author.'

The essays are sometimes heavily witty. The first, 'Looking Inward', describes the character of the narrator, a bachelor, who has been an 'attentive companion' to himself all his life and now chooses to be garrulous on paper. The character has things in common with the narrative persona of 'The Sad Fortunes of the Rev. Amos Barton' and the choice of the Theophrastian form shows an abiding interest in the collections of 'Characters' discussed in Eliot's essay on Madame de Sablé.

Theophrastus (c. 371–c. 287 BC) was a pupil and friend of Aristotle, a scientific inquirer and philosopher best remembered for his *Characters*. La Bruyère (1645–96), who is cited in this essay, translated Theophrastus and wrote his own *Characters* in imitation.

In his *Characters of Theophrastus*, La Bruyère divides men into three kinds: those who desire precise methodical definitions of virtue and vice; those who reduce morals to a matter of physically caused passions; and a third kind who like to read books about the mixture of the good and the bad, the wise and the silly, by applying their own moral principles to the study of particular men and manners, 'correcting each by comparison with the others, through these images of things so familiar to them, from which they have nevertheless not taken thought to draw instruction'. These principles bear an obvious close relation to Eliot's earliest thoughts about both characterization and instruction.

Debasing the Moral Currency

'IL NE faut pas mettre un ridicule où il n'y en a point: c'est gâter le goût, c'est corrompre son jugement et celui des autres. Mais le ridicule qui est quelque part, il faut l'y voir, l'en tirer avec grâce et d'une manière qui plaise et qui instruise.'[1]

I am fond of quoting this passage from La Bruyère, because the subject is one where I like to show a Frenchman on my side, to save my sentiments from being set down to my peculiar dulness and deficient sense of the ludicrous, and also that they may profit by that enhancement of ideas when presented in a foreign tongue, that glamour of unfamiliarity conferring a dignity on the foreign names of very common things, of which even a philosopher like Dugald Stewart[2] confesses the influence. I remember hearing a fervid woman attempt to recite in English the narrative of a begging Frenchman who described the violent death of his father in the July days. The narrative had impressed her, through the mists of her flushed anxiety to understand it, as something quite grandly pathetic; but finding the facts turn out meagre, and her audience cold, she broke off, saying, 'It sounded so much finer in French – j'ai vu le sang de mon père, and so on – I wish I could repeat it in French.' This was a pardonable illusion in an old-fashioned lady who had not received the polyglot education of the present day; but I observe that even now much nonsense and bad taste win admiring acceptance solely by virtue of the French language, and one may fairly desire that what seems a just discrimination should profit by the fashionable prejudice in favour of La Bruyère's idiom. But I wish he had added that the habit of dragging the ludicrous into topics where the chief interest is of a different or even opposite kind is a sign not of endowment, but of deficiency. The art of spoiling is within reach of the dullest faculty: the coarsest clown with a hammer in his hand might chip the nose off every statue and bust in the Vatican, and stand grinning at the effect of his work. Because wit is an exquisite product of high powers, we are not therefore forced to admit the sadly confused inference of the monotonous jester that he is establishing his superiority over every less facetious person, and over every topic on which he is ignorant or insensible, by being uneasy until he has distorted it in the small cracked mirror which he carries about with him as a joking apparatus. Some high authority is needed to give many worthy and timid persons the freedom of muscular repose under the growing demand on them to laugh when they have no other reason than the peril of being taken for dullards; still more to inspire them with the courage to say that they object to the theatrical spoiling for themselves and their children of all affecting themes, all the grander deeds and aims of men, by burlesque associations adapted to the taste of rich fishmongers in the stalls and their assistants in the gallery. The English people in the present generation are falsely reputed to know Shakspeare (as, by some innocent persons, the Florentine mule-drivers are believed to have known the *Divina Commedia*, not, perhaps, excluding all the subtle discourses in the *Purgatorio* and *Paradiso*); but there seems a clear prospect that in the coming generation he will be known to them through burlesques, and that his plays will find a new life as pantomimes. A bottle-nosed Lear will come on with a monstrous corpulence from which he will frantically dance himself free during the midnight storm; Rosalind and Celia will join in a grotesque ballet with shepherds and shepherdesses; Ophelia in fleshings and a voluminous brevity of grenadine will dance through the mad scene, finishing with the famous 'attitude of the scissors' in the arms of Laertes; and all the speeches in *Hamlet* will be so ingeniously parodied that the originals will be reduced to a mere *memoria technica* of the improver's puns – premonitory signs of a hideous millennium, in which the lion will have to lie down with the lascivious monkeys whom (if we may trust Pliny)[3] his soul naturally abhors.

I have been amazed to find that some artists whose own works have the ideal stamp, are quite insensible to the damaging tendency of the burlesquing spirit which ranges to and fro and up and down on the earth, seeing no reason (except a precarious censorship) why it should not appropriate every sacred, heroic, and pathetic theme which serves to make up the treasure of human admiration, hope, and love.[4] One would have thought that their own half-despairing efforts to invest in worthy outward shape the vague inward impressions of sublimity, and the consciousness of an implicit ideal in the commonest scenes, might have made them susceptible of some disgust or alarm at a species of burlesque which is likely to render their compositions no better than a dissolving view, where every noble form is seen melting into its preposterous caricature. It used to be imagined of the unhappy mediæval Jews that they parodied Calvary by crucifying dogs; if they had been guilty they would at least have had the excuse of the hatred and rage begotten by persecution. Are we on the way to a parody which shall have no other excuse than the reckless search after fodder for degraded appetites – after the pay to be earned by pasturing Circe's herd[5] where they may defile every monument of that growing life which should have kept them human?

The world seems to me well supplied with what is genuinely ridiculous: wit and humour may play as harmlessly or beneficently round the changing facets of egoism, absurdity, and vice, as the sunshine over the rippling sea or the dewy meadows. Why should we make our delicious sense of the ludicrous, with its invigorating shocks of laughter and its irrepressible smiles which are the outglow of an inward radiation as gentle and cheering as the warmth of morning, flourish like a brigand on the robbery of our mental wealth? – or let it take its exercise as a madman might, if allowed a free nightly promenade, by drawing the populace with bonfires which leave some venerable structure a blackened ruin or send a scorching smoke across the portraits of the past, at which we once looked with a loving recognition of fellowship, and disfigure them into butts of mockery? – nay, worse – use it to degrade the healthy appetites and affections of our nature as they are seen to be degraded in insane patients whose system, all out of joint, finds matter for screaming laughter in mere topsy-turvy, makes every passion preposterous or obscene, and turns the hard-won order of life into a second chaos hideous enough to make one wail that the first was ever thrilled with light?

This is what I call debasing the moral currency: lowering the value of every inspiring fact and tradition so that it will command less and less of the spiritual products, the generous motives which sustain the charm and elevation of our social existence – the something besides bread by which man saves his soul alive. The bread-winner of the family may demand more and more coppery shillings, or assignats, or greenbacks[6] for his day's work, and so get the needful quantum of food; but let that moral currency be emptied of its value – let a greedy buffoonery debase all historic beauty, majesty, and pathos, and the more you heap up the desecrated symbols the greater will be the lack of the ennobling emotions which subdue the tyranny of suffering, and make ambition one with social virtue.

And yet, it seems, parents will put into the hands of their children ridiculous parodies (perhaps with more ridiculous 'illustrations') of the poems which stirred their own tenderness or filial piety, and carry them to make their first acquaintance with great men, great works, or solemn crises through the medium of some miscellaneous burlesque which, with its idiotic puns and farcical attitudes, will remain among their primary associations, and reduce them throughout their time of studious preparation for life to the moral imbecility of an inward giggle at what might have stimulated their high emulation or fed the fountains of compassion, trust, and constancy. One wonders where these parents have deposited that stock of morally educating stimuli which is to be independent of poetic tradition, and to subsist in spite of the finest images being degraded and the finest words of genius being poisoned as with some befooling drug.

Will fine wit, will exquisite humour prosper the more through this turning of all things indiscriminately into food for a gluttonous laughter, an idle craving without sense of flavours? On the contrary. That delightful power which La Bruyère points to – 'le ridicule qui est quelque part, il faut l'y voir, l'en tirer avec grâce et d'une manière qui plaise et qui instruise' – depends on a discrimination only compatible with the varied sensibilities which give sympathetic insight, and with the justice of perception which is another name for grave knowledge. Such a result is no more to be expected from faculties on the strain to find some small hook by which they may attach the lowest incongruity to the most momentous subject, than it is to be expected of a sharper, watching for gulls in a great political assemblage, that he will notice the blundering logic of partisan speakers, or season his observation with the salt of historical parallels. But after all our psychological teaching, and in the midst of our zeal for education, we are still, most of us, at the stage of believing that mental powers and habits have somehow, not perhaps in the general statement, but in any particular case, a kind of spiritual glaze against conditions which we are continually applying to them. We soak our children in habits of contempt and exultant gibing, and yet are confident that – as Clarissa one day said to me – 'We can always teach them to be reverent in the right place, you know.' And doubtless if she were to take her boys to see a burlesque Socrates, with swollen legs, dying in the utterance of cockney puns, and were to hang up a sketch of this comic scene among their bedroom prints, she would think this preparation not at all to the prejudice of their emotions on hearing their tutor read that narrative of the *Apology*[7] which has been consecrated by the reverent gratitude of ages. This is the impoverishment that threatens our posterity: – a new Famine, a meagre fiend with lewd grin and clumsy hoof, is breathing a moral mildew over the harvest of our human sentiments. These are the most delicate elements of our too easily perishable civilization. And here again I like to quote a French testimony. Sainte-Beuve, referring to a time of insurrectionary disturbance, says: 'Rien de plus prompt à baisser que la civilisation dans des crises comme celle-ci; on perd en trois semaines le résultat de plusieurs siècles. La civilisation, la *vie* est une chose apprise et inventée, qu'on le sache bien: "*Inventas aut qui vitam excoluere per artes.*" Les hommes après quelques années de paix oublient trop cette vérité: ils arrivent à croire que la *culture* est chose innée, qu'elle est la même chose que la *nature*. La sauvagerie est toujours là à deux pas, et, dès qu'on lâche pied, elle recommence.'[8] We have been severely enough taught (if we were willing to learn) that our civilization, considered as a splendid material fabric, is helplessly in peril without the spiritual police of sentiments or ideal feelings. And it is this invisible police which we had need, as a community, strive to maintain in efficient force. How if a dangerous 'Swing'[9] were sometimes disguised in a versatile entertainer devoted to the amusement of mixed audiences? And I confess that sometimes when I see a certain style of young lady, who checks our tender admiration with rouge and henna and all the blazonry of an extravagant expenditure, with slang and bold *brusquerie* intended to signify her emancipated view of things, and with cynical mockery which she mistakes for penetration, I am sorely tempted to hiss out '*Pétroleuse!*' It is a small matter to have our palaces set aflame compared with the misery of having our sense of a noble womanhood, which is the inspiration of a purifying shame, the promise of life-penetrating affection, stained and blotted out by images of repulsiveness. These things come – not of higher education, but – of dull ignorance fostered into pertness by the greedy vulgarity which reverses Peter's visionary lesson[10] and learns to call all things common and unclean. It comes of debasing the moral currency.

The Tirynthians, according to an ancient story reported by Athenæus,[11] becoming conscious that their trick of laughter at everything and nothing was making them unfit for the conduct of serious affairs, appealed to the Delphic oracle for some means of cure. The god prescribed a peculiar form of sacrifice, which would be effective if they could carry it through without laughing. They did their best; but the flimsy joke of a boy upset their unaccustomed gravity, and in this way the oracle taught them that even the gods could not prescribe a quick cure for a long vitiation, or give power and dignity to a people who in a crisis of the public well-being were at the mercy of a poor jest.

TRANSLATIONS

David Friedrich Strauss's
The Life of Jesus

(1846)

STRAUSS'S *Das Leben Jesu* appeared in 1835; Eliot's translation appeared in 1846, entitled *The Life of Jesus, Critically
Examined*. It was Eliot's first major work, undertaken after
Rufa Brabant had found the task too difficult. Sarah Hennell,
sister of Charles Christian Hennell, author of the *Inquiry into
the Origins of Christianity*, had also turned it down, but she
was consulted extensively by Eliot, of whom she was a
lifelong friend. The work took Eliot two years (there are
1,500 pages of German); she was paid £20 and her name did
not appear on the title-page.

The translation was done whilst Eliot was looking after her
father, whose health was failing. Haight records her distress
during this work. She 'had a cast about twenty inches high
of Thorwaldsen's "Risen Christ" standing in her study, and
on the wall an engraving of Delaroche's *Christ*, which she had
once thought of using for a frontispiece. She told the Brays
that "she was Strauss-sick – it made her ill dissecting the
beautiful story of the crucifixion, and only the sight of her
Christ-image and picture made her endure it"' (*Life*, p. 58).

Strauss's book was one of the most influential in the
changing attitudes to Christian belief and interpretation. He
used new mythological and historical methods to examine
the texts of the accounts of Christ's sayings and doings,
pointing out how often New Testament stories and statements were apparently written in order to 'confirm' Old
Testament prophecies, and relating the 'mythi' of biblical
narrative to analogous stories from other cultures.

Ernest Renan, whose own highly and deliberately imagi-

native *Life of Jesus* (1863) was also very influential, said
of Strauss's *Leben Jesu*, 'The historian finds it too devoid of
facts; the critic, too uniform in its processes; the theologian,
founded upon a hypothesis subversive of Christianity.'
Robert Browning used the work of both Renan and Strauss[1]
in his extraordinary poem on the death of Saint John, *A
Death in the Desert*, and presented Strauss and his arguments
in *Christmas-Eve and Easter-Day*. Strauss's work is presumably
among the German thought with which the unfortunate
Casaubon is discovered to be unacquainted in *Middlemarch*.

The passages from Strauss that we have selected are from
his 'Introduction: Development of the Mythical Point of View
in Relation to the Gospel Histories' and his 'Concluding Dissertation: The Dogmatic Import of the Life of Jesus', in which
he discusses the Christology of F. E. D. Schleiermacher,
Immanuel Kant, W. M. L. de Wette, E. H. Schelling and
others, and ends by discussing the problem for a theologian
who reached these conclusions in relation to his work in the
Church. The speculative theologian, Strauss says, 'in his
discourses to the Church, will indeed adhere to the forms of
the popular conception, but on every opportunity he will
exhibit their spiritual significance, which to him constitutes
their sole truth, and thus prepare – though such a result is
only to be thought of as an unending progress – the resolution
of those forms into their original ideas in the consciousness of
the Church also'. The theologian will teach Easter as a
symbol of spiritual death and resurrection with Christ. The
danger is, Strauss admits, that the community will discover
the difference between the beliefs of the theologian and the
cultural forms in which he still sets them out, and the
preacher will appear to the community 'and consequently to
himself, a hypocrite. In this difficulty, the theologian may
find himself driven, either directly to state his opinions and
attempt to elevate the people to his ideas; or, since this
attempt must necessarily fail, carefully to adapt himself to
the conception of the community; or, lastly, since, even on
this plan, he may easily betray himself, in the end to leave
the ministerial profession' (*The Life of Jesus*, pp. 444–5).

From 'Introduction: Development of the
Mythical Point of View in Relation
to the Gospel Histories'

ADMITTING THAT the biblical history does not equally with the heathen mythology offend our idea of Deity, and that consequently it is not in like manner characterized by this mark of the un-historical, however far it be from bearing any guarantee of being historical, – we are met by the further question whether it be not less accordant with our idea of the world, and whether such discordancy may not furnish a test of its unhistorical nature.

In the ancient world, that is, in the east, the religious tendency was so preponderating, and the knowledge of nature so limited, that the law of connexion between earthly finite beings was very loosely regarded. At every link there was a disposition to spring into the Infinite, and to see God as the immediate cause of every change in nature or the human mind. In this mental condition the biblical history was written. Not that God is here represented as doing all and every thing himself: – a notion which, from the manifold direct evidence of the fundamental connexion between finite things, would be impossible to any reasonable mind: – but there prevails in the biblical writers a ready disposition to derive all things down to the minutest details, as soon as they appear particularly important, immediately from God. He it is who gives the rain and sunshine; he sends the east wind and the storm; he dispenses war, famine, pestilence; he hardens hearts and softens them, suggests thoughts and resolutions. And this is particularly the case with regard to his chosen instruments and beloved people. In the history of the Israelites we find traces of his immediate agency at every step: through Moses, Elias, Jesus, he performs things which never would have happened in the ordinary course of nature.

447

Our modern world, on the contrary, after many centuries of tedious research, has attained a conviction, that all things are linked together by a chain of causes and effects, which suffers no interruption. It is true that single facts and groups of facts, with their conditions and processes of change, are not so circumscribed as to be unsusceptible of external influence; for the action of one existence or kingdom in nature intrenches on that of another: human freedom controls natural development, and material laws react on human freedom. Nevertheless the totality of finite things forms a vast circle, which, except that it owes its existence and laws to a superior power, suffers no intrusion from without. This conviction is so much a habit of thought with the modern world, that in actual life, the belief in a supernatural manifestation, an immediate divine agency, is at once attributed to ignorance or imposture. It has been carried to the extreme in that modern explanation, which, in a spirit exactly opposed to that of the Bible, has either totally removed the divine causation, or has so far restricted it that it is immediate in the act of creation alone, but mediate from that point onwards; – i.e., God operates on the world only in so far as he gave to it this fixed direction at the creation. From this point of view, at which nature and history appear as a compact tissue of finite causes and effects, it was impossible to regard the narratives of the Bible, in which this tissue is broken by innumerable instances of divine interference, as historical.

It must be confessed on nearer investigation, that this modern explanation, although it does not exactly deny the existence of God, yet puts aside the idea of him, as the ancient view did the idea of the world. For this is, as it has been often and well remarked, no longer a God and Creator, but a mere finite Artist, who acts immediately upon his work only during its first production, and then leaves it to itself; who becomes excluded with his full energy from one particular sphere of existence. It has therefore been attempted to unite the two views so as to maintain for the world its law of sequence, and for God his unlimited action, and by this means to preserve the truth of the biblical history. According to this view, the world is supposed to move in obedience to the law of consecutive causes and effects bound up with its constitution, and God to act upon it only mediately: but in single instances, where he finds it necessary for particular objects, he is not held to be restricted from entering into the course of human changes immediately. This is the view of modern Supranaturalism, evidently a vain attempt to reconcile two opposite views, since it contains the faults of both, and adds a new one in the contradiction between the two ill-assorted principles. For here the consecutiveness of nature and history is broken through as in the ancient biblical view; and the action of God limited as in the contrary system. The proposition that God works sometimes mediately, sometimes immediately, upon the world, introduces a changeableness, and therefore a temporal element, into the nature of his action, which brings it under the same condemnation as both the other systems; that, namely, of distinguishing the maintaining power, in the one case from individual instances of the divine agency, and in the other from the act of creation.

Since then our idea of God requires an immediate, and our idea of the world a mediate, divine operation; and since the idea of combination of the two species of action is inadmissible: – nothing remains for us but to regard them both as so permanently and immovably united, that the operation of God on the world continues for ever and every where twofold, both immediate and mediate; which comes just to this, that it is neither of the two, or this distinction loses its value. To explain more closely: if we proceed from the idea of God, from which arose the demand for his immediate operation, then the world is to be regarded in relation to him as a Whole: on the contrary, if we proceed from the idea of the finite, the world is a congeries of separate parts, and hence has arisen the demand for a merely mediate agency of God: – so that we must say – God acts upon the world as a Whole immediately, but on each part only by means of his action on every other part, that is to say, by the laws of nature.

This view brings us to the same conclusion with regard to the historical value of the Bible as the one above considered. The miracles which God wrought for and by Moses and Jesus, do not proceed from his immediate operation on the Whole, but presuppose an immediate action in particular cases, which is a contradiction to the type of the divine agency we have just given. The supranaturalists indeed claim an exception from this type on behalf of the biblical history; a presupposition which is inadmissible from our point of view, according to which the same laws, although varied by various circumstances, are supreme in every sphere of being and action, and therefore every narrative which offends against these laws, is to be recognized as so far unhistorical.

The result, then, however surprising, of a general examination of the biblical history, is that the Hebrew and Christian religions, like all others, have their mythi. And this result is confirmed, if we consider the inherent nature of religion, what essentially belongs to it and therefore must be common to all religions, and what on the other hand is peculiar and may differ in each. If religion be defined as the perception of truth, not in the form of an idea, which is the philosophic perception, but invested with imagery; it is easy to see that the mythical element can be wanting only when religion either falls short of, or goes beyond, its peculiar province, and that in the proper religious sphere it must necessarily exist.

It is only amongst the lowest and most barbarous people, such as the Esquimaux, that we find religion not yet fashioned into an objective form, but still confined to a subjective feeling. They know nothing of gods, of superior spirits and powers, and their whole piety consists in an undefined sentiment excited by the hurricane, the eclipse, or the magician. As it progresses however, the religious principle loses more and more of this indefiniteness, and ceasing to be subjective, becomes objective. In the sun, moon, mountains, animals, and other objects of the sensible world, higher powers are discovered and revered; and in proportion as the significance given to these objects is remote from their actual nature, a new world of mere imagination is created, a sphere of divine existences whose relations to one another, actions, and influences, can be represented only after human analogy, and therefore as temporal and historical. Even when the mind has raised itself to the conception of the Divine unity, still the energy and activity of God are considered only under the form of a series of acts: and on the other hand, natural events and human actions can be raised to a religious significance only by the admission of divine interpositions and miracles. It is only from the philosophic point of view that the world of imagination is seen again to

coincide with the actual, because the thought of God is comprehended to be his essence, and in the regular course itself of
nature and of history, the revelation of the divine idea is acknowledged.

It is certainly difficult to conceive, how narratives which thus
speak of imagination as reality can have been formed without
intentional deceit, and believed without unexampled credulity;
and this difficulty has been held an invincible objection to the
mythical interpretation of many of the narratives of the Old and
New Testament. If this were the case, it would apply equally to
the Heathen legends; and on the other hand, if profane Mythology
have steered clear of the difficulty, neither will that of the Bible
founder upon it. I shall here quote at length the words of an
experienced inquirer into Grecian mythology and primitive history, Otfried Müller,[2] since it is evident that this preliminary
knowledge of the subject which must be derived from general
mythology, and which is necessary for the understanding of the
following examination of the evangelic mythus, is not yet familiar
to all theologians.

How shall we reconcile this combination of the true and the false, the real
and ideal, in mythi, with the fact of their being believed and received as
truth? The ideal, it may be said, is nothing else than poetry and fiction
clothed in the form of a narration. But a fiction of this kind cannot be
invented at the same time by many different persons without a miracle,
requiring, as it does, a peculiar coincidence of intention, imagination, and
expression. It is therefore the work of one person: – but how did he
convince all the others that his fiction had an actual truth? Shall we
suppose him to have been one who contrived to delude by all kinds of
trickery and deception, and perhaps allied himself with similar deceivers,
whose part it was to afford attestation to the people of his inventions as
having been witnessed by themselves? Or shall we think of him as a man
of higher endowments than others, who believed him upon his word; and
received the mythical tales under whose veil he sought to impart wholesome truths, as a sacred revelation? But it is impossible to prove that such a
caste of deceivers existed in ancient Greece (or Palestine); on the contrary,
this skilful system of deception, be it gross or refined, selfish or philanthropic, if we are not misled by the impression we have received from
the earliest productions of the Grecian (or Christian) mind, is little suited
to the noble simplicity of those times. Hence an inventer of the mythus in

the proper sense of the word is inconceivable. This reasoning brings us to the conclusion, that the idea of a deliberate and intentional fabrication, in which the author clothes that which he knows to be false in the appearance of truth, must be entirely set aside as insufficient to account for the origin of the mythus. Or in other words, that there is a certain necessity in this connexion between the ideal and the real, which constitutes the mythus; that the mythical images were formed by the influence of sentiments common to all mankind; and that the different elements grew together without the author's being himself conscious of their incongruity. It is this notion of a certain necessity and unconsciousness in the formation of the ancient mythi, on which we insist. If this be once understood, it will also be perceived that the contention whether the mythus proceed from one person or many, from the poet or the people, though it may be started on other grounds, does not go to the root of the matter. For if the one who invents the mythus is only obeying the impulse which acts also upon the minds of his hearers, he is but the mouth through which all speak, the skilful interpreter who has the address first to give form and expression to the thoughts of all. It is however very possible that this notion of necessity and unconsciousness, might appear itself obscure and mystical to our antiquarians (and theologians), from no other reason than that this mythicizing tendency has no analogy in the present mode of thinking. But is not history to acknowledge even what is strange, when led to it by unprejudiced research?

From 'Concluding Dissertation: The Dogmatic Import of the Life of Jesus'

THOUGH I may conceive that the divine spirit in a state of renunciation and abasement becomes the human, and that the human nature in its return into and above itself becomes the divine; this does not help me to conceive more easily, how the divine and human natures can have constituted the distinct and yet united portions of an historical person. Though I may see the human mind in its unity with the divine, in the course of the world's history, more and more completely establish itself as the power which subdues nature; this is quite another thing, than to conceive a single man endowed with such power, for individual, voluntary acts. Lastly, from the truth, that the suppression of the natural existence is the resurrection of the spirit, can never be deduced the bodily resurrection of an individual.

We should thus have fallen back again to Kant's point of view,[1] which we have ourselves found unsatisfactory; for if the idea have no corresponding reality, it is an empty obligation and ideal. But do we then deprive the idea of all reality? By no means: we reject only that which does not follow from the premises. If reality is ascribed to the idea of the unity of the divine and human natures, is this equivalent to the admission that this unity must actually have been once manifested, as it never had been, and never more will be, in one individual? This is indeed not the mode in which Idea realizes itself; it is not wont to lavish all its fullness on one exemplar, and be niggardly towards all others – to express itself perfectly in that one individual, and imperfectly in all the rest: it rather loves to distribute its riches among a multiplicity of exemplars which reciprocally complete each other – in the alternate appearance and suppression of a series of individuals. And is this no true realization of the Idea? is not the idea of the unity of the divine and human natures a real one in a far higher sense, when I regard the whole race of mankind as its realization, than when I single out one man as such a realization? is not an incarnation of God from eternity, a truer one than an incarnation limited to a particular point of time?

This is the key to the whole of Christology, that, as subject of the predicate which the Church assigns to Christ, we place, instead of an individual, an idea; but an idea which has an existence in reality, not in the mind only, like that of Kant. In an individual, a God-man, the properties and functions which the Church ascribes to Christ contradict themselves; in the idea of the race, they perfectly agree. Humanity is the union of the two natures – God become man, the infinite manifesting itself in the finite, and the finite spirit remembering its infinitude; it is the child of the visible Mother and the invisible Father, Nature and Spirit; it is the worker of miracles, in so far as in the course of human history the spirit more and more completely subjugates nature, both within and around man, until it lies before him as the inert matter on which he exercises his active power; it is the sinless existence, for the course of its development is a blameless one, pollution cleaves to the individual only, and does not touch the race or its history. It is Humanity that dies, rises, and ascends to heaven, for from the negation of its phenomenal life there ever proceeds a higher spiritual life; from the suppression of its mortality as a personal, national, and terrestrial spirit, arises its union with the infinite spirit of the heavens. By faith in this Christ, especially in his death and resurrection, man is justified before God: that is, by the kindling within him of the idea of Humanity, the individual man participates in the divinely human life of the species. Now the main element of that idea is, that the negation of the merely natural and sensual life, which is itself the negation of the spirit (the negation of negation, therefore), is the sole way to true spiritual life.

This alone is the absolute sense of Christology: that it is annexed to the person and history of one individual, is a necessary result of the historical form which Christology has taken. Schleiermacher was quite right when he foreboded, that the speculative view would not leave much more of the historical person of the Saviour than was retained by the Ebionites.[2] The phenomenal history of the individual, says Hegel, is only a starting point for the mind. Faith, in her early stages, is governed by the senses, and therefore contemplates a temporal history; what she holds to be true is the external, ordinary event, the evidence for which is of the historical, forensic kind – a fact to be proved by the testimony of the senses, and the moral confidence inspired by the witnesses. But mind having once taken occasion by this external fact, to bring under its consciousness the idea of humanity as one with God, sees in the history only the presentation of that idea; the object of faith is completely changed; instead of a sensible, empirical fact, it has become a spiritual and divine idea, which has its confirmation no longer in history but in philosophy. When the mind has thus gone beyond the sensible history, and entered into the domain of the absolute, the former ceases to be essential; it takes a subordinate place, above which the spiritual truths suggested by the history stand self-supported; it becomes as the faint image of a dream which belongs only to the past, and does not, like the idea, share the permanence of the spirit which is absolutely present to itself. Even Luther subordinated the physical miracles to the spiritual, as the truly great miracles. And shall we interest ourselves more in the cure of some sick people in Galilee, than in the miracles of intellectual and moral life belonging to the history of the world – in the increasing, the almost incredible dominion of man over nature – in the irresistible force of ideas, to which no unintelligent matter, whatever its magnitude, can oppose any enduring resistance? Shall isolated incidents, in themselves trivial, be more to us than the universal order of events, simply because in the latter we presuppose, if we do not perceive, a natural cause, in the former the contrary? This would be a direct contravention of the more enlightened sentiments of our own day, justly and conclusively expressed by Schleiermacher.[3] The interests of piety, says this theologian, can no longer require us so to conceive a fact, that by its dependence on God it is divested of the conditions which would belong to it as a link in the chain of nature; for we have outgrown the notion, that the divine omnipotence is more completely manifested in the interruption of the order of nature, than in its

preservation. Thus if we know the incarnation, death and resurrection, the *duplex negatio affirmat*,[4] as the eternal circulation, the
infinitely repeated pulsation of the divine life; what special importance can attach to a single fact, which is but a mere sensible
image of this unending process? Our age demands to be led in
Christology to the idea in the fact, to the race in the individual:
a theology which, in its doctrines on the Christ, stops short at
him as an individual, is not properly a theology, but a homily.

Ludwig Feuerbach's
The Essence of Christianity

(1854)

LUDWIG FEUERBACH was born in 1804 and died in 1872. He was a student of Hegel in Berlin from 1824 to 1828 and taught philosophy at Erlangen, but retired to a life of scholarship. His philosophical works have had a wide and powerful influence on Western culture: his materialism was crucially important for Marx, his theories of sexuality for Freud and D. H. Lawrence. Among his important writings are *Das Wesen des Christentums* (*The Essence of Christianity*, 1841), *Die Philosophe der Zukunft* (*The Philosophy of the Future*, 1843) and *Des Wesen der Religion* (*The Essence of Religion*, 1851).

Eliot translated *Das Wesen des Christentums* in 1854, and inserted her own name, Marian Evans, on the final proof of the title-page; this was the only time it appeared in print. I have said something of how much the book meant to her in my Introduction (p. xxvii). She wrote to Sarah Hennell that Feuerbach's work was 'considered *the* book of the age there [in Germany]; but Germany and England are *two* countries' (*Letters, Vol. II*, p. 137). Her translation reads powerfully and is still considered definitive. It was reissued in a Harper Torchbook in 1957, with an introductory essay by Karl Barth; I am indebted to this edition for the quotations from Feuerbach that follow.

Barth said that Feuerbach summarized his teaching at the beginning of his third Heidelberg lecture, which became *The Essence of Religion*. 'Theology is anthropology, that is, in the object of religion which we call *Theos* in Greek and *Gott* in German, nothing but the essence of man is expressed' (*The Essence of Religion*, p. 10). But he also said, 'While I do reduce

457

theology to anthropology, I exalt anthropology to theology; very much as Christianity, while lowering God into man, made man into God' (*The Essence of Christianity*, p. 40).

Feuerbach's philosophy, Barth wrote, begins with the sentence, 'I am a real, a sensuous, a material being; yes, the body in its totality is my Ego, my being itself.' His teaching aimed to be 'a frankly sensuous philosophy'. For 'only where sensuousness begins do all doubt and conflict cease. The secret of immediate knowledge is sensuousness' (*The Philosophy of the Future*, pp. 43, 72–3). And man, the essential being of man, exists 'only in community, it is found only in the unity of man with man – a unity that is supported only by the reality of the difference between I and Thou'. 'Man with man – the unity of I and Thou – is God' (*The Philosophy of the Future*, p. 41).

The passages we have selected from Feuerbach are from Chapter 8, 'The Mystery of the Cosmogonical Principle in God', Chapter 9, 'The Mystery of Mysticism, or of Nature in God' and Chapter 16, 'The Distinction between Christianity and Heathenism'. The first illustrates Feuerbach's idea of Christ as the Imagination, the second his discussion of sexual difference, and the third his idea of the species as the perfect being. The phrase 'my fellow-man is my objective conscience' from the last of these sections is central to Eliot's thought.

The Mystery of the
Cosmogonical Principle in God

THE SECOND PERSON, as God revealing, manifesting, declaring himself (*Deus se dicit*), is the world-creating principle in God. But this means nothing else than that the second Person is intermediate between the noumenal nature of God and the phenomenal nature of the world, that he is the divine principle of the finite, of that which is distinguished from God. The second Person as begotten, as not *a se*, not existing of himself, has the fundamental condition of the finite in himself. But at the same time, he is not yet a real finite Being, posited out of God; on the contrary, he is still identical with God, – as identical as the son is with the father, the son being indeed another person, but still of like nature with the father. The second Person, therefore, does not represent to us the pure idea of the Godhead, but neither does he represent the pure idea of humanity, or of reality in general: he is an intermediate Being between the two opposites. The opposition of the noumenal or invisible divine nature and the phenomenal or visible nature of the world, is however nothing else than the opposition between the nature of abstraction and the nature of perception; but that which connects abstraction with perception is the imagination: consequently, the transition from God to the world by means of the second Person, is only the form in which religion makes objective the transition from abstraction to perception by means of the imagination. It is the imagination alone by which man neutralizes the opposition between God and the world. All religious cosmogonies are products of the imagination. Every being, intermediate between God and the world, let it be defined how it may, is a being of the imagination. The psychological truth and necessity which lies at the foundation of all these theogonies and cosmogonies, is the truth and necessity of the imagination as a middle term between the abstract and concrete. And the task of philosophy, in investigating this subject, is to comprehend the relation of the imagination to the reason, – the genesis of the image by means of which an object of thought becomes an object of sense, of feeling.

But the nature of the imagination is the complete, exhaustive truth of the cosmogonic principle, only where the antithesis of God and the world expresses nothing but the indefinite antithesis of the noumenal, invisible, incomprehensible Being, God, and the visible, tangible, existence of the world. If, on the other hand, the cosmogonic being is conceived and expressed abstractly, as is the case in religious speculation, we have also to recognize a more abstract psychological truth as its foundation.

The world is not God; it is other than God, the opposite of God, or at least that which is different from God. But that which is different from God, cannot have come immediately from God, but only from a distinction of God in God. The second Person is God distinguishing himself from himself in himself, setting himself opposite to himself, hence being an object to himself. The self-distinguishing of God from himself is the ground of that which is different from himself, and thus self-consciousness is the origin of the world. God first thinks the world in thinking himself: to think oneself is to beget oneself, to think the world is to create the world. Begetting precedes creating. The idea of the production of the world, of another being who is *not* God, is attained through the idea of the production of another being who is *like* God.

This cosmogonical process is nothing else than the mystic paraphrase of a psychological process, nothing else than the unity of consciousness and self-consciousness, made objective. God thinks himself: – thus he is self-conscious. God is self-consciousness posited as an object, as a being; but inasmuch as he knows himself, thinks himself, he also thinks another than himself; for to know oneself is to distinguish oneself from another, whether this be a possible, merely conceptional, or a real being. Thus the world – at least the possibility, the idea of the world – is posited with consciousness, or rather conveyed in it. The Son, i.e., God thought by himself, objective to himself, the original reflection of God, the other God, is the principle of Creation. The truth which lies at the foundation of this is the nature of man: the identity of his self-consciousness with his consciousness of another who is identical with himself, and of another who is not identical with himself. And the second, the other who is of like nature, is necessarily the middle term between the first and third. The idea of another in general, of one who is essentially different from me arises to me first through the idea of one who is essentially like me.

Consciousness of the world is the consciousness of my limitation; if I knew nothing of a world, I should know nothing of limits: but the consciousness of my limitation stands in contradiction with the impulse of my egoism towards unlimitedness. Thus from egoism conceived as absolute (God is the absolute Self) I cannot pass immediately to its opposite; I must introduce, prelude, moderate this contradiction by the consciousness of a being who is indeed another, and in so far gives me the perception of my limitation, but in such a way as at the same time to affirm my own nature, make my nature objective to me. The consciousness of the world is a humiliating consciousness; the Creation was an 'act of humility'; but the first stone against which the pride of egoism stumbles, is the *thou*, the *alter ego*. The *ego* first steels its glance in the eye of a *thou*, before it endures the contemplation of a being which does not reflect its own image. My fellow-man is the bond between me and the world. I am, and I feel myself, dependent on the world, because I first feel myself dependent on other men. If I did not need man, I should not need the world. I reconcile myself with the world only through my fellow-man. Without other men, the world would be for me not only dead and empty, but meaningless. Only through his fellow does man become clear to himself and self-conscious; but only when I am clear to myself, does the world become clear to me. A man existing absolutely alone, would lose himself without any sense of his individuality in the ocean of Nature; he would neither comprehend himself as man, nor Nature as Nature. The first object of man is man. The sense of Nature, which opens to us the consciousness of the world as a world, is a later product; for it first arises through the distinction of man from himself. The natural philosophers of Greece were preceded by the so-called seven Sages,[1] whose wisdom had immediate reference to human life only.

The *ego*, then, attains to consciousness of the world through consciousness of the *thou*. Thus man is the God of man. That he is, he has to thank Nature; that he is man, he has to thank man; spiritually as well as physically, he can achieve nothing without his fellow-man. Four hands can do more than two; but also, four eyes can see more than two. And this combined power is distinguished not only in quantity but also in quality from that which is solitary. In isolation human power is limited, in combination it is infinite. The knowledge of a single man is limited, but reason, science, is unlimited, for it is a common act of mankind; and it is so, not only because innumerable men co-operate in the construction of science, but also in the more profound sense, that the scientific genius of a particular age comprehends in itself the thinking powers of the preceding age, though it modifies them in accordance with its own special character. Wit, acumen, imagination, feeling as distinguished from sensation, reason as a subjective faculty, – all these so-called powers of the soul, are powers of humanity, not of man as an individual; they are products of culture, products of human society. Only where man has contact and friction with his fellow-man are wit and sagacity kindled; hence there is more wit in the town than in the country, more in great towns than in small ones. Only where man suns and warms himself in the proximity of man, arise feeling and imagination. Love, which requires mutuality, is the spring of poetry; and only where man communicates with man, only in speech, a social act, awakes reason. To ask a question and to answer, are the first acts of thought. Thought originally demands two. It is not until man has reached an advanced stage of culture that he can double himself, so as to play the part of another within himself. To think and to speak are therefore with all ancient and sensuous nations, identical; they think only in speaking; their thought is only conversation. The common people, i.e., people in whom the power of abstraction has not been developed, are still incapable of understanding what is written if they do not read it audibly, if they do not pronounce what they read. In this point of view Hobbes[2] correctly enough derives the understanding of man from his ears!

Reduced to abstract logical categories, the creative principle in God expresses nothing further than the tautological proposition:

the different can only proceed from a principle of difference, not from a simple being. However the Christian philosophers and theologians insisted on the creation of the world out of nothing, they were unable altogether to evade the old axiom – 'nothing comes from nothing', because it expresses a law of thought. It is true that they supposed no real matter as the principle of the diversity of material things, but they made the Divine understanding (and the Son is the wisdom, the science, the understanding of the Father) – as that which comprehends within itself all things, as *spiritual matter* – the principle of real matter. The distinction between the heathen eternity of matter and the Christian creation in this respect, is only that the heathens ascribed to the world a real, objective eternity, whereas the Christians gave it an invisible, immaterial eternity. Things were, before they existed positively, – not, indeed, as an object of sense, but of the subjective understanding. The Christians, whose principle is that of absolute subjectivity, conceive all things as effected only through this principle. The matter posited by their subjective thought, conceptional, subjective matter, is therefore to them the first matter, – far more excellent than real, objective matter. Nevertheless, this distinction is only a distinction in the mode of existence. The world is eternal in God. Or did it spring up in him as a sudden idea, a caprice? Certainly man can conceive this too; but, in doing so, he deifies nothing but his own irrationality. If, on the contrary, I abide by reason, I can only derive the world from its essence, its idea, i.e., one mode of its existence from another mode; in other words, I can derive the world only from itself. The world has its basis in itself, as has everything in the world which has a claim to the name of species. The *differentia specifica*, the peculiar character, that by which a given being is what it is, is always in the ordinary sense inexplicable, undeducible, is through itself, has its cause in itself.

The distinction between the world and God as the creator of the world, is therefore only a formal one. The nature of God – for the divine understanding, that which comprehends within itself all things, is the divine nature itself; hence God, inasmuch as he thinks and knows himself, thinks and knows at the same time the world and all things – the nature of God is nothing else than the abstract, *thought* nature of the world; the nature of the world nothing else than the real, concrete, perceptible nature of God. Hence, creation is nothing more than a formal act; for that which, before the creation, was an object of thought, of the understanding, is by creation simply made an object of sense, its ideal contents continuing the same; although it remains absolutely inexplicable how a real material thing can spring out of a pure thought.*

So it is with plurality and difference – if we reduce the world to these abstract categories – in opposition to the unity and identity of the Divine nature. Real difference can be derived only from a being which has a principle of difference in itself. But I posit difference in the original being, because I have originally found difference as a positive reality. Wherever difference is in itself nothing, there also no difference is conceived in the principle of things. I posit difference as an essential category, as a truth, where I derive it from the original being, and *vice versa*: the two propositions are identical. The rational expression is this: difference lies as necessarily in the reason as identity.

But as difference is a positive condition of the reason, I cannot deduce it without presupposing it; I cannot explain it except by itself, because it is an original, self-luminous, self-attesting reality. Through what means arises the world, that which is distinguished from God? through the distinguishing of God from himself in himself. God thinks himself, he is an object to himself; he distinguishes himself from himself. Hence this distinction, the world, arises only from a distinction of another kind, the external distinction from an internal one, the static distinction from a dynamic one, – from an *act* of distinction: thus I establish difference only through itself; i.e., it is an original concept, a *ne plus ultra* of my thought, a law, a necessity, a truth. The last distinction that I can think, is the distinction of a being from and in itself. The distinction of one being from another is self-evident, is already implied in their existence, is a palpable truth: they are two. But I first establish difference for thought when I discern it in one and the same being, when I unite it with the law of identity. Herein lies

---

* It is therefore mere self-delusion to suppose that the hypothesis of a Creation explains the existence of the world.

the ultimate truth of difference. The cosmogonic principle in God, reduced to its last elements, is nothing else than the act of thought in its simplest forms, made objective. If I remove difference from God, he gives me no material for thought; he ceases to be an object of thought; for difference is an essential principle of thought. And if I consequently place difference in God, what else do I establish, what else do I make an object, than the truth and necessity of this principle of thought?

From 'The Mystery of Mysticism,
or of Nature in God'

NATURE IN distinction from personality can signify nothing else than difference of sex. A personal being apart from Nature is nothing else than a being without sex, and conversely. Nature is said to be predicated of God, 'in the sense in which it is said of a man, that he is of a strong, healthy nature'. But what is more feeble, what more insupportable, what more contrary to Nature than a person without sex, or a person, who in character, manners, or feelings, denies sex? What is virtue, the excellence of man as man? Manhood. Of man as woman? Womanhood. But man exists only as man and woman. The strength, the healthiness of man, consists therefore in this: that as a woman, he be truly woman; as man, truly man. Thou repudiatest 'the horror of all that is real, which supposes the spiritual to be polluted by contact with the real'. Repudiate then before all, thy own horror for the distinction of sex. If God is not polluted by Nature, neither is he polluted by being associated with the idea of sex. In renouncing sex, thou renouncest thy whole principle. A moral God apart from Nature is without basis; but the basis of morality is the distinction of sex. Even the brute is capable of self-sacrificing love in virtue of the sexual distinction. All the glory of Nature, all its power, all its wisdom and profundity, concentrates and individualizes itself in distinction of sex. Why then dost thou shrink from naming the nature of God by its true name? Evidently, only because thou hast a general horror of things in their truth and reality; because thou lookest at all things through the deceptive vapours of mysticism. For this very reason then, because Nature in God is only a delusive, unsubstantial appearance, a fantastic ghost of Nature, – for it is based, as we have said, not on flesh and blood, not on a real ground, – this attempt to establish a personal God is once more a failure, and I, too, conclude with the words, 'the denial of a personal God will be scientific honesty': – and, I add, scientific truth, so long as it is not declared and shown in unequivocal terms, first *a priori*, on speculative grounds, that form, place, corporeality, and sex, do not contradict the idea of the Godhead; and secondly, *a posteriori*, – for the reality of a personal being, is sustained only on empirical grounds, – what sort of form God has, where he exists, – in heaven, – and lastly, of what sex he is.

Let the profound, speculative religious philosophers of Germany courageously shake off the embarrassing remnant of rationalism which yet clings to them, in flagrant contradiction with their true character; and let them complete their system, by converting the mystical 'potence' of Nature in God into a really powerful, generating God.

From 'The Distinction between Christianity and Heathenism'

THE TOTAL absence of the idea of the species in Christianity is especially observable in its characteristic doctrine of the universal sinfulness of men. For there lies at the foundation of this doctrine the demand that the individual shall not be an individual, a demand which again is based on the presupposition that the individual by himself is a perfect being, is by himself the adequate presentation or existence of the species.* Here is entirely wanting the objective perception, the consciousness, that the *thou* belongs to the perfection of the *I*, that *men* are required to constitute humanity, that only men taken together are what man should and can be. All men are sinners. Granted: but they are not all sinners in the same way; on the contrary, there exists a great and essential difference between them. One man is inclined to falsehood, another is not; he would rather give up his life than break his word or tell a lie; the third has a propensity to intoxication, the fourth to licentiousness; while the fifth, whether by favour of Nature, or from the energy of his character, exhibits none of these vices. Thus, in the moral as well as the physical and intellectual elements, men compensate for each other, so that taken as a whole they are as they should be, they present the perfect man.

Hence intercourse ameliorates and elevates; involuntarily and

---

* It is true that in one sense the individual is the absolute – in the phraseology of Leibnitz, the mirror of the universe, of the infinite. But in so far as there are many individuals, each is only a single and, as such, a finite mirror of the infinite. It is true also, in opposition to the abstraction of a sinless man, that each individual regarded in himself is perfect, and only by comparison imperfect, for each is what alone he can be.

without disguise, man is different in intercourse from what he is when alone. Love especially works wonders, and the love of the sexes most of all. Man and woman are the complement of each other, and thus united they first present the species, the perfect man.* Without species, love is inconceivable. Love is nothing else than the self-consciousness of the species as evolved within the difference of sex. In love, the reality of the species, which otherwise is only a thing of reason, an object of mere thought, becomes a matter of feeling, a truth of feeling; for in love, man declares himself unsatisfied in his individuality taken by itself, he postulates the existence of another as a need of the heart; he reckons another as part of his own being; he declares the life which he has through love to be the truly human life, corresponding to the idea of man, i.e., of the species. The individual is defective, imperfect, weak, needy; but love is strong, perfect, contented, free from wants, self-sufficing, infinite; because in it the self-consciousness of the individuality is the mysterious self-consciousness of the perfection of the race. But this result of love is produced by friendship also, at least where it is intense, where it is a religion, as it was with the ancients. Friends compensate for each other; friendship is a means of virtue, and more: it is itself virtue, dependent however on participation. Friendship can only exist between the virtuous, as the ancients said. But it cannot be based on perfect similarity; on the contrary, it requires diversity, for friendship rests on a desire for self-completion. One friend obtains through the other what he does not himself possess. The virtues of the one atone for the failings of the other. Friend justifies friend before God. However faulty a man may be, it is a proof that there is a germ of good in him if he has worthy men for his friends. If I cannot be myself perfect, I yet at least love virtue, perfection in others. If therefore I am called to account for any sins, weaknesses and faults, I interpose

* With the Hindoos (Inst. of Menu) he alone is 'a perfect man who consists of three united persons, his wife, himself, and his son. For man and wife, and father and son, are one.' The Adam of the Old Testament also is incomplete without woman; he feels his need of her. But the Adam of the New Testament, the Christian, heavenly Adam, the Adam who is constituted with a view to the destruction of this world, has no longer any sexual impulses or functions.

as advocates, as mediators, the virtues of my friend. How barbarous, how unreasonable would it be to condemn me for sins which I doubtless have committed, but which I have myself condemned, in loving my friends, who are free from these sins!

But if friendship and love, which themselves are only subjective realizations of the species, make out of singly imperfect beings an at least relatively perfect whole, how much more do the sins and failings of individuals vanish in the species itself, which has its adequate existence only in the sum total of mankind, and is therefore only an object of reason! Hence the lamentation over sin is found only where the human individual regards himself in his individuality as a perfect, complete being, not needing others for the realization of the species, of the perfect man; where instead of the consciousness of the species has been substituted the exclusive self-consciousness of the individual; where the individual does not recognize himself as a part of mankind, but identifies himself with the species, and for this reason makes his own sins, limits and weaknesses, the sins, limits and weaknesses of mankind in general. Nevertheless man cannot lose the consciousness of the species, for his self-consciousness is essentially united to his consciousness of another than himself. Where therefore the species is not an object to him as a species, it will be an object to him as God. He supplies the absence of the idea of the species by the idea of God, as the being who is free from the limits and wants which oppress the individual, and, in his opinion (since he identifies the species with the individual), the species itself. But this perfect being, free from the limits of the individual, is nothing else than the species, which reveals the infinitude of its nature in this, that it is realized in infinitely numerous and various individuals. If all men were absolutely alike, there would then certainly be no distinction between the race and the individual. But in that case the existence of many men would be a pure superfluity; a single man would have achieved the ends of the species. In the one who enjoyed the happiness of existence, all would have had their complete substitute.

Doubtless the essence of man is *one*; but this essence is infinite; its real existence is therefore an infinite, reciprocally compensating variety, which reveals the riches of this essence. Unity in essence is multiplicity in existence. Between me and another human being – and this other is the representative of the species, even though he is only one, for he supplies to me the want of many others, has for me a universal significance, is the deputy of mankind, in whose name he speaks to me, an isolated individual, so that, when united only with one, I have a participated, a human life; – between me and another human being there is an essential, qualitative distinction. The other is my *thou*, – the relation being reciprocal, – my *alter ego*, man objective to me, the revelation of my own nature, the eye seeing itself. In another I first have the consciousness of humanity; through him I first learn, I first feel, that I am a man: in my love for him it is first clear to me that he belongs to me and I to him, that we two cannot be without each other, that only community constitutes humanity. But morally, also, there is a qualitative, critical distinction between the *I* and *thou*. My fellow-man is my objective conscience; he makes my failings a reproach to me, even when he does not expressly mention them, he is my personified feeling of shame. The consciousness of the moral law, of right, of propriety, of truth itself, is indissolubly united with my consciousness of another than myself. That is true in which another agrees with me, – agreement is the first criterion of truth; but only because the species is the ultimate measure of truth. That which I think only according to the standard of my individuality, is not binding on another, it can be conceived otherwise, it is an accidental, merely subjective view. But that which I think according to the standard of the species, I think as man in general only can think, and consequently as every individual must think if he thinks normally, in accordance with law, and therefore truly. That is true which agrees with the nature of the species, that is false which contradicts it. There is no other rule of truth. But my fellow-man is to me the representative of the species, the substitute of the rest, nay his judgement may be of more authority with me than the judgement of the innumerable multitude. Let the fanatic make disciples as the sand on the sea-shore; the sand is still sand; mine be the pearl – a judicious friend. The agreement of others is therefore my criterion of the normalness, the universality, the truth of my thoughts. I cannot so abstract myself from myself as to judge myself with perfect freedom and disinterestedness; but another has an impartial judgement; through him I correct, complete, extend my own judgement, my own taste, my own knowledge. In short, there is a qualitative, critical difference between men. But Christianity extinguishes this qualitative distinction; it sets the same stamp on all men alike, and regards them as one and the same individual, because it knows no distinction between the species and the individual: it has one and the same means of salvation for all men, it sees one and the same original sin in all.

Because Christianity thus, for exaggerated subjectivity, knows nothing of the species, in which alone lies the redemption, the justification, the reconciliation and cure of the sins and deficiencies of the individual, it needed a supernatural and peculiar, nay a personal, subjective aid in order to overcome sin. If I alone am the species, if no other, that is, no qualitatively different men exist, or, which is the same thing, if there is no distinction between me and others, if we are all perfectly alike, if my sins are not neutralized by the opposite qualities of other men: then assuredly my sin is a blot of shame which cries up to heaven; a revolting horror which can be exterminated only by extraordinary, superhuman, miraculous means. Happily, however, there *is* a natural reconciliation. My fellow-man is *per se*, the mediator between me and the sacred idea of the species. *Homo homini Deus est.* My sin is made to shrink within its limits, is thrust back into its nothingness, by the fact that it is only mine, and not that of my fellows.

Notes

ESSAYS

Woman in France: Madame de Sablé
(Westminster Review, October 1854, pp. 448–73)

Eliot was with Lewes in Weimar when, on 5 August 1854, she received a letter from Chapman, suggesting that either she or Lewes should review Victor Cousin's *Madame de Sablé* for the *Westminster.* She replied, 'On reading your letter we determined to get Cousin's book and to unite it with several others as a subject for an article *by me* on "French Writers on Women" . . . I happen to have the material at hand to make such an article piquant and fresh, which are perhaps the qualities likely to be most welcome to you' *(Life,* p. 158). The article was finished by the end of the month, but it seemed in need of revision. On 30 August she wrote to Chapman, 'I had made up my mind to send you my article – that is, to dispatch it from this place – on Monday next, but I think I can make it more satisfactory by rendering the introductory part fuller . . . I have just read the part to which I refer to Mr Lewes, and he thinks the ideas are crowded and would impress the reader more if they were diluted a little' *(Letters, Vol. II,* p. 172). The article was dispatched to London on 8 September.

Victor Cousin (1792–1867), French philosopher and writer. Here Eliot is reviewing his *Madame de Sablé: Études sur les femmes illustres et la société du dix-septième siècle,* as well as *Portraits de femme* by Charles Augustin Sainte-Beuve (1804–69) and *Les Femmes de la révolution* by Jules Michelet (1798–1874). Madame de Sablé, whose full name was Magdeleine de Laval-Montmorency, Marquise de Sablé (*c.* 1599–1678), was hostess of a famous literary salon. Apart from Cousin's book, the main source of information about her life is Nicolas Ivanoff's *La Marquise de Sablé et son salon* (Paris, 1927).

1. *the priest in Don Quixote.* The Señor Licentiate Pero Pérez, who burnt Don Quixote's books 'that they may not lead some other who reads them to follow the example of my good friend' *(Don Quixote,* Part 1, Chapter 5).
2. *Richardson's Lady G.* Charlotte, Lady Grandison, in Samuel Richardson's *Sir Charles Grandison* (1753–4).
3. *Madame de Sévigné.* Marie de Rabutin-Chantal, Marquise de Sévigné (1626–

96), best known for her *Letters* to her daughter (published 1725 and later) concerning the daily life of the French nobility.

4. *Madame Dacier*. Anne Dacier (*c.*1654–1720), Hellenist and Latinist. She was the translator of Aristophanes, Plautus and Terence, and also translated the *Iliad* and the *Odyssey*.

5. *Madame de Staël*. Anne-Louise-Germaine Necker, Madame de Staël (1766–1817), novelist and miscellaneous writer. Her novels *Delphine* (1802) and *Corinne* (1807) deal with the isolation of the intellectual woman.

6. *Madame Roland*. Marie-Jeanne Philipon, Madame Roland (1754–93). Her salon was a meeting place for the Girondins.

7. *George Sand*. Pseudonym of Lucile-Aurore Dupin (1804–76), novelist. In 1846 Eliot read her novel *Jacques* and wrote to Sarah Hennell, 'I should never dream of going to her writings as a moral code or text-book. I don't care whether I agree with her about a marriage or not – whether I think the design of her plot correct or that she had no precise design at all but began to write as the spirit moved her and trusted to Providence for the catastrophe, which I think the more probable case – it is sufficient for me as a reason for bowing before her in eternal gratitude to that "great power of God" manifested in her – that I cannot read six pages of hers without feeling that it is given to her to delineate human passion and its results – (and I must say in spite of your judgement) some of the moral instincts and their tendencies – with such truthfulness such nicety of discrimination such tragic power and withal such loving gentle humour that one might live a century with nothing but one's own dull faculties and not know so much as those six pages suggest' (*Letters, Vol. I*, pp. 277–8).

8. *Jean Jacques*. Jean-Jacques Rousseau (1712–78), philosopher. In the same 1846 letter to Sarah Hennell she wrote, 'Rousseau's genius has sent that electric thrill through my intellectual and moral frame which has awakened me to new perceptions, which has made man and nature a fresh world of thought and feeling to me – and this not by teaching me any new belief. It is simply that this rushing mighty wind of his inspiration has so quickened my faculties that I have been able to shape more definitely for myself ideas which had previously dwelt as dim *Ahnungen* in my soul.'

9. *Richelieu*. Armand-Jean du Plessis, Cardinal et Duc de Richelieu (1585–1642), Chief Minister to Louis XIII.

10. *Marquise de Rambouillet*. Catherine de Vivonne (1588–1665), Marquise de Rambouillet. Her salon at the Hôtel de Rambouillet, active from 1618 to 1650, was the meeting place of many influential thinkers and writers, and the model for those that followed.

11. *Précieuses ridicules and Les Femmes savantes*. Topical and satirical comedies by Molière. They were produced in 1659 and 1672 respectively, not 1660 and 1673 as Eliot claimed.

12. *Madelon and Cathos*. Daughters of Gorgibus in Molière's *Précieuses ridicules* who are infatuated with the affected speech and manners of French society. Cathos is misprinted as 'Caltros' in the *Westminster*.

13. *Mademoiselle Scudéry.* Madeleine de Scudéry (1607–1701). Her *Le Grand Cyrus* (1649–53) and *Clélie* (1654–60) offer satirical portraits of her contemporaries.

14. *bouts rimés.* Set rhymes.

15. *Mademoiselle d'Orleans.* Louise d'Orléans, Duchesse de Montpensier (1627–93), known as 'La Grande Mademoiselle' because of her height.

16. *Madame de la Fayette and La Rochefoucauld.* Marie-Madeleine, Comtesse de La Fayette (1634–93), novelist, and François, Duc de La Rochefoucauld (1699–1777), moralist.

17. *La Bruyère.* Jean de La Bruyère (1645–96), author of *Caractères de Théophraste traduits du grec, avec les Caractères ou les Mœurs de ce siècle* (1688).

18. *Wednesday dinner at Madame Geoffrin's, with d'Alembert, Mademoiselle de l'Espinasse Grimm, and the rest.* Marie-Thérèse Rodet, Madame Geoffrin (1699–1777), had a literary salon that met on Wednesdays. Jean le Rond d'Alembert (1717–83), mathematician and *philosophe.* Julie-Jeanne-Éléonore de Lespinasse (1732–76). Her salon was a meeting place for the *encyclopédistes.* Frédéric-Melchior, Baron de Grimm (1723–1807), writer and literary critic.

19. *Condorcet and his lovely young wife.* Marie-Jean-Antoine-Nicolas de Caritat, Marquis de Condorcet (1743–94), mathematician, philosopher, politician and revolutionary. His wife, Sophie de Grouchy (1764–1822), was said to have been one of the most beautiful women of her time.

20. *Madame d'Epinay.* Louise-Florence, Madame d'Épinay (1726–83), protectress of Rousseau. In his *Confessions* he wrote, 'She was very thin, very pale, her breast was as flat as my hand. This defect alone would have been sufficient to freeze me' (Book 9, 1756).

21. *Bossuet and Massillon.* Jacques-Bénigne Bossuet (1627–1704), priest and theologian. Jean-Baptiste Massillon (1663–1742), Bishop of Clermont-Ferrand and preacher at the Court of Versailles.

22. *a volume on the youth of the Duchesse de Longueville.* His *La Jeunesse de Madame de Longueville* (1853).

23. *Conrart.* Valentin Conrart (1603–75), man of letters and a founder of the Académie Française.

24. *'un heureux mélange de raison, d'esprit, d'agrément, et de bonté'.* The line translates as 'a happy mixture of reason, wit, charm and kindness'.

25. *Mademoiselle de Bourbon.* Anne-Geneviève de Bourbon (1619–79), afterwards Duchesse de Longueville.

26. *Madame de Motteville.* Françoise Bertaut, Madame de Motteville (1621–89), lady-in-waiting to Anne of Austria and author of *Mémoires pour servir à l'histoire d'Anne d'Autriche* (1643–66).

27. *Tallemant de Réaux.* Gédéon Tallemant des Réaux (1619–92) wrote 376 *Historiettes* (1834), anecdotal and often scandalous memoirs of his contemporaries.

28. *lèse-amitié.* Injured friendship.

29. *galimatias.* Nonsense, or confused language.

30. *Malheureuse . . . le savoir.* 'Ignorance is unfortunate:/More unfortunate is knowledge.' Jean Bertaut (1552–1611), Court poet to Henri III and Henri IV.

31. *Princesse de Paphlagonia.* That is, the Princesse de Paphlagonie. For 'Reine de

Mionie' read 'Reine de Misne'.

32. *Port-Royalists*. A community of scholars and intellectuals established in 1633 at the abandoned convent of Port-Royal des Champs near Versailles. It was dispersed in 1660 by Louis XIV in a wave of anti-Jansenism (see also note 48).

33. *'En vérité . . . me saigner?'* 'In sooth, I believe I could do no better than to leave everything, and to go and live there. But what would become of those fears of not having physicians to choose from, nor any surgeon to bleed me?'

34. *friandise.* Delicacies.

35. *bonnes bouches.* The best bits.

36. *'Je vous demande . . . j'en ai scrupule'.* 'I beg you in the name of God not to prepare any dainty dish of food especially for me. Above all, do not give me a feast. In the name of God, let there be nothing but what one can eat, for you know it is of no use to me; moreover, I have qualms of conscience about that.'

37. *La non . . . très fine.* 'The peerless Bois-Dauphine./Among ladies the most real pearl.' Paul Scarron (1610–60), burlesque writer and a rebel against the preciosity of his literary contemporaries.

38. *frondeurs.* Members of the Fronde, that is, the party opposed to Mazarin and the Court of France during the minority of Louis XIV. A general term for malcontents.

39. *'vaquer enfin à son aise aux soins de son salut et à ceux de sa santé'.* She could 'at last attend to her heart's content, to the duties of her salvation and the cares of her health'.

40. *'Vous savez . . . les replis du cœur.'* The French here is somewhat garbled. The correct version is to be found in the *Œuvres Complètes* of La Rochefoucauld (Martin-Chauffier and Marchand, eds., Paris, 1964, p. 634). It translates as 'You know that I believe that only you are to be trusted on certain chapters, and above all about the secret places of the heart.'

41. *Je crois . . . inviolablement, madame, votre, etc.* 'I believe I am the only person capable of doing so well the exact opposite of what I mean to do, for it is true that there is not anybody I honour more than you. And I have acted in such a way as to make it impossible for you to believe it. To have failed for so long to write to you was not enough to persuade you of my being unworthy of your favour and remembrance: I still had to delay for another fortnight the allowing myself the honour of answering your letter. In sooth, madam, it makes me look such a culprit that were not my offence against you I would rather be actually guilty than attempt such a hard task as the vindication of my conduct. But I feel so innocent in my heart and I profess so much regard, respect and affection for you, that it seems to me that it must be obvious to you a hundred miles off, although I do not say a word about it to you. That is what gives me the courage to write to you at the present hour, but it is not that which has prevented me from doing it so long. I first had no alternative but to fail you under the pressure of many troubles, and since then it has been through shame, and I confess that if I now were without the confidence you gave me by your reassurance and that which I draw from my own feelings for you, I would never presume to try and have you remember me. But I trust in your

forgetting my faults on my assuring you that I shall never allow myself to be hardened in them again, but I shall remain inviolably, madam, yours etc.'

42. *Nicole and Domat*. Pierre Nicole (1625–95), moralist and theologian. Jean Domat (1625–96), jurist.

43. *Rohault*. Jacques Rohault (1620–75), French physicist and leading advocate of French Cartesianism. His major work is the *Traité de physique* (1671). He was the first to observe capillary action in narrow glass tubes.

44. '*L'envie de faire des maximes se gagne comme le rhume.*' 'The desire to make maxims is caught like a cold in the head.'

45. '*Voilà tout . . . un ragoût de mouton.*' 'Here are all the maxims I have, but since I give nothing for nothing, I ask you for a soup of carrots and a mutton stew.'

46. '*On ne pourroit faire . . . mon libérateur*'. 'No instructions more proper to a catechumen might be written to win over to God both his mind and his will. Even though there were only this piece of writing in existence in the world, and the Gospel, I would still want to be a Christian. The one would teach me how to obtain knowledge of my afflictions, and the other how to beseech my saviour for release.'

47. *Je vous envoie . . . Mandez-moi ce qu'il vous semble de ce dictum*. 'I am sending you what I succeeded in wringing from my brains to put them in the *Journal des savants*. I have put in that part you feel so much about, with a view to overcoming the embarrassment which made you put in [Eliot has *mettre*; the original reads *donner au public*] the preface without striking anything out – nor did I scruple to do so, as I am confident that you will not have it printed even though everything else in it proved agreeable to you. I can assure you that I shall be more grateful if you treat it as something belonging to you, and correct it or throw it in the fire, than if you do to it an honour it does not deserve. We great authors are too rich to fear the loss of anything of our own making. Let me know how you like this dictum.' Eliot abridged the French somewhat in this case. The original can be found in the *Maximes* of La Rochefoucauld (J. Truchet, ed., Paris, 1967, pp. 580–81).

48. *Jansenism*. A reforming (or heretical) movement within the Roman Catholic Church, in France associated with the struggle against Richelieu and Louis XIV. They took their name from Cornelius Otto Jansen (1585–1638).

49. *I one day asked M. Nicole . . . count them*. From Sainte-Beuve's *Portraits de femmes*.

Evangelical Teaching: Dr Cumming
(*Westminster Review*, October 1855, pp. 436–62)

Dr John Cumming (1807–81) was the Minister of the evangelical Scottish National Church, London, from 1832 to 1879, and a prolific author on the subject of biblical prophecy.

Eliot had begun preparing this article in June of 1855. Cumming's work, as Haight remarked, 'offered Marian ample ammunition for an annihilating account of the beliefs she had held so earnestly in girlhood' (*Life*, p. 186). According to Cross's biography, it was this article that convinced Lewes of 'true genius in her writing' (*Cross*, p. 384). Shortly after its publication, she wrote to Charles Bray, who had guessed that she was the author: 'Since you have found out the "Cumming", I write by today's post just to say, that it *is* mine, but also to beg that you will not mention it as such to anyone likely to transmit the information to London, as we are keeping the authorship a secret. The article appears to have produced a strong impression, and that impression would be a little counteracted if the author were known to be a *woman*. I have had a letter addressed to "the author of article No. 4", begging me to print it separately for "the good of mankind in general"' (*Letters, Vol. II*, p. 218).

The books by Cumming reviewed here are: *The Church before the Flood*; *Occasional Discourses*; *Signs of the Times; or, Present, Past, and Future*; *The Finger of God*; *Is Christianity from God? or, a Manual of Christian Evidence, for Scripture-readers, City Missionaries, Sunday-school Teachers, etc.*; *Apocalyptic Sketches; or, Lectures on the Book of Revelation*, first and second series; and *Prophetic Studies; or, Lectures on the Book of Daniel.*

1. *Goshen.* Ironic reference to the region of Egypt occupied by the Israelites before the Exodus. A place of plenty.
2. *predestination . . . latitudinarian . . . pre-millennial Advent.* Belief in predestination is a cornerstone of Calvinism. It is the action of God by which certain persons are assured of salvation. For its biblical source see Romans 8:28–30. Latitudinarian is a term of seventeenth-century origin that was used to describe a group of Anglicans who attached little importance to dogma. Its more general meaning refers to toleration in religious matters. The pre-millennial Advent is the Second Coming of Christ.
3. *Moore's Almanack.* An annual publication, begun in 1700 by Francis Moore, containing predictions of events.
4. '*horn that had eyes*', '*the lying prophet*', and the '*unclean spirits*'. Respectively Daniel 7:8, Revelation 16:13 and Revelation 9:10.
5. *Amphitryon.* A host, or entertainer to dinner, from Plautus's comedy of the same name.
6. *Puseyites.* After Edward Bouverie Pusey (1800–1882), High Anglican and leading member of the Oxford Movement.
7. *Dr Chalmers and Mr Wilberforce.* Thomas Chalmers (1780–1847), Scottish Presbyterian preacher and theologian. From 1843 he was the first Moderator of the Free Church of Scotland, having been influenced towards evangelicalism by reading *A Practical View of the Prevailing Religious System* (1797) by William Wilberforce (1759–1833), evangelical and abolitionist.
8. *Robert Hall, Foster the Essayist, or Isaac Taylor.* Robert Hall (1764–1831) and John Foster (1770–1843), Baptist preachers. Isaac Taylor (1787–1846), evangelical Anglican.
9. '*clouts o' cauld parritch*'. Andrew Fairservice's description of degenerate preaching in Walter Scott's *Rob Roy*.
10. *little horn, the river Euphrates, or the seven vials.* The 'little horn' is referred to in Daniel 7:8. The Euphrates was one of the rivers of Eden. The 'seven vials' are mentioned in Revelation 21:9.

11. *Christianitatem, quocunque modo, Christianitatem.* 'Christianity, by any means, Christianity.'

12. *Amiable impulses . . . rank of laws.* Omitted in the 1884 edition.

13. *that professor of Padua.* Francesco Sizi (or Sizzi) attacked Galileo with this argument in his *Dianoia Astronomia* (1610).

14. *Though gay . . . I quit the scene.* From 'On this day I Complete My Thirty-sixth Year' (1824).

15. *Leland.* More probably Charles Leslie (1650–1722), author of *A Short and Easie Method with the Deists* (1698). Eliot may have been thinking of a work by John Leland (1691–1766), *A View of the Principal Deistical Writers That Have Appeared in England during the Past and Present Centuries* (1754–6).

16. *the bachelors of Salamanca. Don Quixote*, Part 2, Chapter 33.

17. *sunt quibus non credidisse honor est, et fidei futuræ pignus.* 'There are some for whom it is an honour not to have believed, and their unbelief is a guarantee of future faith.'

18. *'perplext in faith . . . deeds'.* Alfred, Lord Tennyson, *In Memoriam*, 96.

19. *David Hume* (1711–76), Scottish philosopher. His views on religion are expressed in his *Dialogues Concerning Natural Religion* (1779) and in his essay 'Of Miracles' in *Inquiry Concerning Human Understanding* (1748).

20. *Si Dieu n'existait pas, il faudrait l'inventer.* 'If God did not exist, it would be necessary to invent him.' Voltaire (François Marie Arouet, 1694–1778) in his *À L'Auteur du livre des trois imposteurs.*

21. *the vulgar fables about Voltaire's death.* That he died in a state of terror and despair.

22. *in majorem gloriam Dei.* 'For the greater glory of God.'

23. *the author of the Vestiges.* Robert Chambers (1802–71), author of *Vestiges of the Natural History of Creation* (1844). The book contains an early statement of the theory of evolution.

24. *of the whole Bible . . . criterion of its meaning.* Omitted in the 1884 edition.

25. *Boanerges.* A name given to James and John, the sons of Zebedee, because they threatened to call down 'fire from Heaven' to consume the Samaritans for not receiving Jesus Christ. It translates as 'sons of thunder' or better as 'sons of tumult' (Luke 9:54 and Mark 3:17).

26. *Cardinal Wiseman.* Nicholas Patrick Stephen Wiseman (1802–65), a leading figure in the Catholic revival in England, became a cardinal in 1850.

27. *'Whether we live . . . unto the Lord.'* Romans 14:8.

28. *A closer walk . . . heavenly frame.* From William Cowper (1731–1800), 'Walking with God', in the collection known as the *Olney Hymns* (1779).

29. *the prophecy concerning the Man of Sin.* Second Epistle to the Thessalonians 2:4.

30. *'cathedrize here . . . pray yonder'.* Matthew 26:37. The Revised Version reads 'Sit ye here while I go yonder and pray.'

31. *Grace Darling.* Grace Darling (1815–42), joint keeper, with her father, of the Longstone Lighthouse. She achieved considerable fame when, in 1838, she rowed a mile in a small boat in stormy conditions to rescue the occupants of a wrecked ship.

32. *Let knowledge grow . . . But vaster.* From Tennyson's Prologue to *In Memoriam*.

German Wit: Heinrich Heine
(*Westminster Review*, January 1856, pp. 1–33)

Heinrich Heine (1797–1856), German poet and writer. Eliot had probably become interested in him during her trip to Germany with Lewes in 1854. While in Berlin they had read aloud the *Geständnisse*. 'The wit burns low after the first fifty pages,' she wrote, 'and the want of principle and purpose make it wearisome' (*Life*, p. 193). Pinney noted that S. L. Wormley, in his *Heine in England* (1943), claimed that this essay 'probably did more than any other single work in introducing to English-speaking peoples the genius that was Heine's.'

Here Eliot is reviewing *Vermischte Schriften von Heinrich Heine* (1854) and *Heinrich Heine's Sammtliche Werke* (1855). She had previously reviewed his *Reisebilder* in the *Leader* of 1 September 1855, and subsequently reviewed his *Buch der Lieder* in the *Saturday Review* of 26 April 1856, and *Recollections of Heine* in the *Leader* of 23 August 1856.

1. '*Nothing,*' says Goethe, '*is more significant . . . laughable.*' In *Die Wahlverwandtschaften* (1808–9).
2. *The history and literature . . . wit in others.* Omitted in the 1884 edition.
3. *a Chamfort or a Sheridan.* Sebastian Roch Nicolas Chamfort (1741–94), French man of letters.
4. *In fact they . . . subsequent races.* 'It was their lot to live seriously through stages which to later generations . . .' 1884 edition.
5. *amiable looking pre-Adamite amphibia . . . their kindred.* Richard Owen (1840–92), naturalist, had supervised in 1854 the construction (from brick, iron and stucco) of twenty-nine prehistoric creatures at Crystal Palace Park in London. They are still there.
6. *lex talionis, as in Reineke Fuchs.* Lex talionis is the law of retaliation: 'an eye for an eye and a tooth for a tooth'. *Reineke Fuchs* (1794) is Goethe's redaction of *Reynard the Fox*.
7. *the old Mysteries.* The biblical dramas of the English medieval period.
8. *good and beautiful on this earth.* In the 1884 edition, 'better and more beautiful'.
9. *Charles Lamb's.* Charles Lamb (1775–1834), English man of letters.
10. *Micromégas.* Voltaire's imitation of *Gulliver's Travels*, published in 1792. Its eponymous hero is the gigantic inhabitant of a planet revolving around Sirius.
11. *Chanticleer.* Chanticleer is a traditional name for a cockerel. The reference here is probably to the cockerel in *Reynard the Fox*.
12. *Jean Paul.* Pseudonym of Johann Paul Friedrich Richter (1763–1825), German satirist.
13. *Identität.* Identity.
14. *Empirismus.* Empiricism.
15. *Vetter Michel.* Eliot probably meant *Deutscher Michel*, a proverbially easy-going, good-natured and simple-minded stock figure. The archetypal German peasant.

16. *Barclay's treble X.* A particularly strong beer brewed by the London firm of Barclay, Perkins & Co.

17. *Proteus's joke ... Shakspearian wit.* The Two Gentlemen of Verona, Act I, Scene 1. The section from 'and one of these ...' to 'his facial muscles' was omitted in the 1884 edition.

18. *Lessing.* Gotthold Ephraim Lessing (1729–81), German dramatist credited with introducing modern dramatic techniques to the German theatre.

19. *Hamburgische Dramaturgie.* A collection of Lessing's commentaries on theatrical problems and dramatic techniques, published 1767–8.

20. *Phidian statue.* Phidias (*c.* 500–*c.* 430 BC), Greek sculptor who worked in various metals, including gold.

21. *Talents.* See Matthew 25:14–30.

22. *1799.* Heine was born in 1797. This error was not corrected in the 1884 edition.

23. *Wie mächtig auch mein stolzer ... Liebe.* The first extract is from the sonnet 'An Meine Mutter B. Heine, Geborne van Geldern' and translates as 'However strongly my mind puffs itself up,/in your blessedly sweet, familiar presence/A humble timidity often seizes me.' The second extract translates as 'And ever I wandered after Love, ever/After Love, but Love found I never,/And came back home, sick and sad./But then you came towards me/And ah! what was swimming in your eye/That was the sweet, the long-sought Love.'

24. *Elise von Hohenhausen ... Chamisso, Varnhagen, and Rahel (Varnhagen's wife).* Adelbert von Chamisso (1781–1838), German poet and botanist. Karl August Varhagen von Ense (1785–1858), German writer, diplomat and a leading figure in the Berlin salon that became a centre of intellectual debate. Eliot and Lewes had met them during their visit to Germany in 1854. Rahel Varnhagen (1771–1833) was a Jewess who led a most remarkable life. Hannah Arendt wrote a biography of her, *Rahel Varnhagen: The Life of a Jewess* (1957).

25. *'Paris vaut bien une messe' ... 'Berlin vaut bien une prêche.'* 'Paris is certainly worth a mass' ... 'Berlin is certainly worth a sermon.'

26. *Hegel.* Georg Wilhelm Friedrich Hegel (1770–1831), German philosopher.

27. *Meyerbeer.* Giacomo Meyerbeer (orig. Jakob Liebmann Beer; 1791–1864), German operatic composer.

28. *Johnson's advice to Hannah More.* In *Anecdotes of Samuel Johnson* (S. C. Roberts, ed., 1932).

29. *Börne.* Ludwig Börne (orig. Löb Baruch; 1786–1837), German writer who believed that the function of literature was to further political causes. Heine's biography was published in 1840 and caused such offence that he was slightly injured in a resulting duel.

30. *Spontini, or Kalkbrenner.* Gaspare Spontini (1774–1851), Italian operatic composer. Frédéric Kalkbrenner (1785–1849), French musician of German extraction.

31. *Short swallow ... skim away.* Alfred, Lord Tennyson, *In Memoriam*, 48.

32. *She dwelt alone ... to me.* Eliot is misquoting again. William Wordsworth wrote 'She lived unknown'.

33. *Kennst du die Hölle des Dante nicht ... Zu solcher Hölle verdammen.* This translates as 'Knowest thou not Dante's Hell/ The terrible *terza rima*?/ He whom the Poet

cast therein/No God can redeem again./No God, no Saviour, frees him ever/
From out these singing flames!/Take care for yourself, that we do not/Condemn
you to such a hell.

34. *One more quotation . . . only one eye.* Omitted in 1884 edition.

The Natural History of German Life
(Westminster Review, July 1856, pp. 51–79)

This essay was written during Eliot's stay at Ilfracombe in May and June of 1856,
and is, in part, a review of *Die bürgerliche Gesellschaft* (1851) and *Land und Leute*
(1853) by Wilhelm Heinrich von Riehl (1823–97), German journalist, folklorist
and cultural historian. The essay is a crucial statement of her views on society, and
of her doctrine of 'sympathy', and thus foreshadows her subsequent fictional
concerns. For a useful discussion of its relation to her novels, see Simon Dentith's
George Eliot (1986), Chapter 2.

1. *a 'Bradshaw'.* George Bradshaw began issuing his *Monthly Railway Guide* in 1841.
2. *Teniers or the ragged boys of Murillo.* David Teniers the Younger (1610–90),
   Flemish painter, chiefly of genre scenes of peasant life. Bartolomé Esteban
   Murillo (1617–82), Spanish painter, chiefly of religious subjects.
3. *Even one of the greatest painters . . . ornaments.* William Holman Hunt (1827–1910)
   exhibited this painting at the Royal Academy in 1852. It is now in the
   Manchester City Art Gallery.
4. *L.E.L.* Letitia Elizabeth Landon (1802–38), poet and novelist. She was a
   favourite of Rosamond Vincy in *Middlemarch* (see Chapter 27). The painting
   'Cross Purposes' remains unidentified.
5. *Opera peasants, whose unreality excites Mr Ruskin's indignation.* In *Modern Painters
   Vol. IV*, published in April 1856, John Ruskin wrote, 'If all the gold that has
   gone to paint the simulacra of the cottages, and to put new songs in the mouths
   of the simulacra of the peasants, had gone to brighten the existent cottages,
   and to put new songs in the mouths of the existent peasants, it might in the
   end, have turned out better so, not only for the peasant, but even for the
   audience' (Part 5, Chapter 19).
6. *Luckie Mucklebackit's cottage.* Luckie Mucklebackit is a character in *The Antiquary*
   (1816).
7. *Alton Locke gazing yearningly . . . ever saw.* In *Alton Locke* (1850), Chapter 11.
8. *Hornung.* Joseph Hornung (1792–1870), Swiss painter.
9. *Mrs Plornish's colloquial style.* In Charles Dickens's *Little Dorrit*, then being
   published in monthly parts (December 1855–June 1857).
10. *'Boots'.* A generic name for the servant in hotels responsible for cleaning boots
    and shoes. Probably a reference to Cobbs, the boots in Dickens's 'The Holly-
    tree Inn' (1855).
11. *Eugène Sue's idealized proletaires.* Marie Joseph (Eugène) Sue (1804–57), French
    novelist and journalist, whose reputation was built on his tales of Parisian low
    life, particularly *Les Mystères de Paris* (1842–3).

12. *altruism*. A term coined by Auguste Comte. It was introduced into English usage by Lewes in his *Comte's Philosophy of the Sciences* (1853).

13. *the relations of men to their neighbours ... artificial system of culture.* References to Jeremy Bentham's 'felicific calculus' and to the Young England movement outlined in Benjamin Disraeli's *Coningsby* (1844).

14. *Lusatia.* A region of Germany around Dresden.

15. *Dandie Dinmont's importunate application to Lawyer Pleydell ... worse hands.* In Walter Scott's *Guy Mannering* (1815). Eliot's reference to 'the peasant's inveterate habit of litigation' recalls Mr Tulliver's behaviour in *The Mill on the Floss*.

16. *Mr Saddletree.* In Scott's *Heart of Midlothian* (1818).

17. *Triptolemus Yellowley's application of the agricultural directions in Virgil's Georgics to his farm in the Shetland Isles.* In Scott's *The Pirate* (1822).

18. *Ihr mögt mir immer ungescheut ... Ich von Philister-netzen.* Translates as 'You may, without shame, still put up a monument to me,/Similar to Blücher's!/He freed you from the French,/I from the nets of the Philistines.'

Silly Novels by Lady Novelists
(*Westminster Review*, October 1856, pp. 442–61)

In July 1856 Eliot wrote to John Chapman, 'I wonder what the story called "Compensation" is. I have long wanted to fire away at the doctrine of Compensation, which I detest, considered as a theory of life' (*Letters, Vol. II*, p. 258). Two weeks later she wrote to him again: 'I think an article on "Silly Women's Novels" might be made the vehicle of some wholesome truth as well as of some amusement. I mentioned this to Mr Lewes last night and he thought the idea a good one' (*Letters, Vol. II*, p. 258).

The writing of the article was made more difficult by persistent and severe toothache. She wrote to Charles Bray that she had written to Chapman, 'begging him to let me off and get a substitute, but he cruelly wrote back that he *must* have the article. So here I am on this blessed first of September with this odious article to write in a hurry and with Mr Lewes coming home to reduce my writing time to the minimum' (*Letters, Vol. II*, p. 261). It was finished by 12 September. Eleven days later she noted in her journal, 'Began to write "The Sad Fortunes of the Rev. Amos Barton", which I hope to make one of a series called *Scenes of Clerical Life*' (*Life*, p. 210).

1. *Compensation. Compensation: A Story of Real Life Thirty Years Ago* (1856) by Henrietta Georgiana Marcia Lascelles, Lady Chatterton (1806–76).

2. *Ossianic.* Bombastic or magniloquent, after Ossian (or Oisin), legendary Gaelic bard.

3. *'Agape'.* Brotherly love.

4. *Creuzer.* Friedrich Creuzer (1771–1858), German philologist and archaeologist.

5. *Laura Gay.* Anonymous (1856).

6. *Miss Wyndhams and Mr Redfords abound.* Characters in *Laura Gay.*

7. *Almack's, Scotch second-sight, Mr Rogers's breakfasts.* Almack's was a suite of

fashionable assembly rooms in Saint James's, London. Scotch second-sight is a reference to the alleged prophetic abilities of the Scots. Mr Rogers's breakfasts were breakfasts hosted by Samuel Rogers (1763–1855) and attended by leading social and literary figures.

8. *Rank and Beauty*. *Rank and Beauty; or, the Young Baroness*, anonymous (1856).

9. *Puseyites*. After Edward Bouverie Pusey (1800–1882), High Anglican and leading member of the Oxford Movement.

10. *The Enigma*. *The Enigma: A Leaf from the Archives of Wolchorley House*, anonymous (1856).

11. *Dr Cumming to Robert Owen ... Spirit-rappers*. For Dr Cumming and Robert Owen, see Eliot's essay on Cumming and her review, 'Lord Brougham's Literature', note 5. Spiritualism had enjoyed a great deal of attention in England following the visit in 1855 of the American Spiritualist Daniel Dunglas Home. In 1869 Eliot wrote to Harriet Beecher Stowe, 'so far as "spiritualism" (by which I mean, of course, spirit communications by rapping, guidance of the pencil, etc.) has come within reach of my judgement on our side of the water, it has appeared to me either as degrading folly, imbecile in the estimate of evidence, or else as impudent imposture' (*Letters, Vol. V*, pp. 48–9).

12. *Pleaceman X*. We have been unable to identify this allusion.

13. *May Meetings*. The Church of England Missionary Society's annual meetings at Exeter Hall, London.

14. *Church of the United Brethren*. The Moravian Brethren, a Protestant sect characterized by their strict discipline.

15. *Orlando*. Rosalind's lover in *As You Like It*.

16. *The Old Grey Church*. By Caroline Lucy Scott, Lady Scott (1856).

17. *Mrs Stowe's pictures of religious life among the negroes?* Eliot reviewed Harriet Beecher Stowe's *Dred* in the same issue of the *Westminster*. It is reprinted here on pp. 379 ff.

18. *Jannes and Jambres ... Sennacherib ... Demetrius the silversmith*. For Jannes and Jambres, see 2 Timothy 3:8. Sennacherib was King of Assyria, 705–681 BC. For Demetrius the silversmith, see Acts 19:24ff.

19. *Was ihr den Geist der Zeiten heisst*. From Goethe's *Faust*, Part 1, 'Nacht', 577–9. The lines translate as 'What you call the spirit of the age/Is but the Critic's spirit, in whose page/The age itself is darkly glassed.'

20. *Adonijah: A Tale of the Jewish Dispersion*. By Jane Margaret Strickland (1856).

21. *Miss Sinclair*. Catherine Sinclair (1800–1864), Scottish popular novelist.

22. *Dr Daubeny, Mr Mill, or Mr Maurice*. Charles Giles Daubeny (1795–1867), chemist. John Stuart Mill (1800–1873), philosopher and economic theorist. Frederick Denison Maurice (1805–72), Professor of Theology at King's College, London.

23. *Harriet Martineau, Currer Bell, and Mrs Gaskell*. Harriet Martineau (1802–76), novelist and miscellaneous writer. Currer Bell, pseudonym of Charlotte Brontë (1816–55), novelist. Elizabeth Cleghorn Gaskell (1810–65), novelist.

24. *La Fontaine's ass*. This reference remains unidentified.

Worldliness and Other-Worldliness: The Poet Young
(*Westminster Review*, January 1857, pp. 1–42)

Edward Young (1683–1765), cleric, poet and dramatist, became Rector of Welwyn in 1730. Eliot had been a great admirer of his poetry when young. According to Haight (*Life*, pp. 216–17), she had greatly admired his *Night Thoughts* and committed long passages of it to memory. In August 1838 she wrote to Maria Lewis, 'I know you do not love quotations so I will not give you one but if you do not distinctly remember it, do turn to the passage in Young's "Infidel Reclaimed" beginning O vain vain vain all else, Eternity! and do love the lines for my sake' (*Letters, Vol. I*, p. 7). Under review here are *Young's Works* (1767); *Johnson's Lives of the Poets* (ed. Peter Cunningham, 1854); *Life of Edward Young, LL D* by John Doran, prefixed to *Night Thoughts*; the *Gentleman's Magazine* of 1782; *Nichols's Literary Anecdotes, Vol. I*; and *Spence's Anecdotes*.

Eliot made extensive revisions to this essay before it was reprinted in 1884.

1. *a creation of peers*. A reference to Young's relentless seeking after preferment.
2. *the profligate Duke of Wharton*. Philip, Duke of Wharton (1698–1731), President of the Hell Fire Club, gambler, and, according to the *DNB*, indirectly responsible for the death of Earl Stanhope (from a burst blood vessel) after a particularly lively parliamentary exchange.
3. *And no man . . . spiritualities*. Omitted in 1884 edition.
4. *'an ornament of religion and virtue'*. From Herbert Croft's biography in Samuel Johnson's *Lives of the English Poets, Vol. III* (Peter Cunningham, ed., 1854, p. 310).
5. *'Oui, mais faîtes comme si je ne le savais pas.'* From Molière's *Le Bourgeois Gentilhomme* (1670), Act II, Scene 4. The line translates as 'Yes, but proceed as though I didn't know it.' This whole paragraph was omitted in the 1884 edition.
6. *1681*. 1683.
7. *'kissed, with dignified emotion . . . namesake'*. In the *Life of Edward Young, Vol. I* (1854), p. xiii, by John Doran (1807–78), miscellaneous writer. Eliot's italics. The words 'We may confidently assume . . . gown and band' were omitted in the 1884 edition.
8. *chyme and chyle*. Chyme and chyle are food at different stages of digestion.
9. *Tindal, the atheist*. Matthew Tindal (1653–1733), described as a theist in the *DNB*.
10. *'a foolish youth . . . poet's'*. Quoted in Johnson's *Lives*, 'Croft'.
11. *'he gives her Majesty praise . . . to earth'*. In Johnson's *Lives*, 'Croft'.
12. Here, as throughout this article, Eliot's quotation from Young is peppered with inaccuracies. The lines should read, 'While other Bourbons rule in other lands,/And if man's sin forbids not, other Annes.'
13. *BCL*. Bachelor of Civil Law.
14. *a dedication attributing to the Duke all virtues*. The Duke reciprocated with a gift of £2,000.
15. *each gift of Nature and of Art . . . an honest heart*. In the 'Epistle to Cobham', lines 192–3.

16. *Christopher Pitt.* Christopher Pitt (1699–1748), poet and translator.

17. *'far superior to the French poet . . . repartees'.* Doran, *Life*, p. xxxiii.

18. *1725 and 1726.* In fact, they span the period 1725–8 so that, as Pinney noted, the coincidence mentioned in the next paragraph 'is of Eliot's manufacture'.

19. *that royal hog's.* 'that monarch's' in the 1884 edition.

20. *MADAM, – I know . . . more than any.* From Johnson's *Lives*, 'Croft'.

21. *1741 and 1745.* 1742–6.

22. *'I have great joy . . . declared his surprise.'* In Doran, *Life*, pp. lxiii–lxv.

23. *Colley Cibber.* Colley Cibber (1671–1757), actor and dramatist.

24. *'I had some talk with him . . . I should have done it.'* In Johnson's *Lives*, 'Croft'. Eliot's comment in the last sentence of the paragraph was omitted in 1884.

25. *'Mrs Hallows . . . improved by reading'.* *Gentleman's Magazine* (1782).

26. *'She was a very coarse woman,' says Dr Johnson.* *Journal of a Tour to the Hebrides* (1785).

27. The letters that follow are from John Nichols's *Literary Anecdotes of the Eighteenth Century.*

28. *Dr Birch.* Thomas Birch (1705–76), historian and biographer.

29. *Clearly . . . forwarded poultry too.* Omitted in the 1884 edition.

30. *seven years later, namely, in 1782.* Eliot means 'seventeen'.

31. *'the interests of religion . . . Dr Young'.* In Johnson's *Lives*, 'Croft'.

32. *Good Dr Young, . . . THO CANT.* In Johnson's *Lives*, 'Croft'.

33. *The impertinence . . . and reserve.* In Doran, *Life*, p. lxxii.

34. *That there was an air of benevolence . . . his expectations.* In James Boswell's *Life of Johnson* (1791).

35. *Pope said of Young . . . common sense.* In Johnson's *Lives*, 'Croft'.

36. *embonpoint.* In good condition or, in its secondary sense, plump and well-nourished.

37. *that 'Gothic demon' . . . thunder in rhyme.* From Young's 'Conjectures on Original Composition' in *The Complete Works, Vol. II* (1854), p. 566.

38. *Pope's characters of Sporus and Atticus.* In Pope's 'Epistle to Dr Arbuthnot', Sporus is a satirical representation of Lord John Hervey, and Atticus is a satirical representation of Joseph Addison.

39. *'have but few books . . . live in the country'.* In 'The Man of Ton: A Satire' by John Wilson under the pseudonym of 'Christopher North' (1785–1854).

40. *'the hand of God hath touched'.* Job 19:21.

41. *Again . . . towards the stars.* Omitted in the 1884 edition.

42. *Wherever abstractions appear . . . deficient feeling.* Omitted in the 1884 edition.

43. *And I should say . . . enthusiasm for music.* Omitted in the 1884 edition.

44. *Thus far . . . 'virtue with immortality expires'.* This was rewritten to read, 'Thus far the man who "denies himself immortal" might give a warrantable reply to Young's assumption of peculiar loftiness in maintaining that "virtue with immortality expires."'

45. *the extension and intensification . . . plurality of worlds.* Amended in 1884 to read, 'the widening and strengthening of our sympathetic nature, – it is surely of some moment to contend, that they have no more direct dependence on the

belief in a future state than the interchange of gases in the lungs on the plurality of worlds'.

46. *Do writers of sermons ... honesty and good-will?* Omitted in the 1884 edition.

47. *We can imagine ... evolution is ensured.* This was changed in the 1884 edition to read, 'We can imagine that the proprietors of a patent water-supply may have a dread of common springs; but for those who only share the general need there cannot be too great a security against a lack of fresh water – or of pure morality. It should be a matter of unmixed rejoicing if this latter necessary of healthful life has its evolution ensured.'

48. *Dr Whewell.* William Whewell (1794–1866), Master of Trinity College, Cambridge, and prolific author. The remark is made in his *Lectures on the History of Moral Philosophy* (1852).

49. *excludes.* 'supersedes' in the 1884 edition.

50. *has affinity with Art.* Omitted in the 1884 edition.

51. *pre-eminently didactic.* 'predominantly didactic' in the 1884 edition.

52. *Dr Watts, or James Montgomery.* Isaac Watts (1674–1748), hymn writer. James Montgomery (1771–1854), minor Scottish poet.

53. *Waller.* Edmund Waller (1606–87), reported in Joseph Spence's *Anecdotes*. The whole section from 'A certain poet ... in himself' was omitted in 1884.

54. *'pathetic fallacy'.* In John Ruskin's *Modern Painters, Vol. III*, reviewed in the *Westminster*, April 1856.

55. *Cowper.* William Cowper (1731–1800), poet, in *The Task* (1785).

The Ilfracombe Journal
(8 May–26 June 1856)

1. *It stands the maestrie ... western land.* From 'On the Same' (i.e., the church of Saint Mary Redcliffe) by Thomas Chatterton (1752–70), poet, who wrote *Felix Farley's Bristol Journal* (1768), but claimed to have discovered it in the church of Saint Mary Redcliffe. The lines quoted begin, 'Thou seest this maestrie'.

2. *Gosse recommends in his Devonshire Coast.* Philip Henry Gosse (1810–88), naturalist. His *A Naturalist's Rambles on the Devonshire Coast* was published in 1853.

3. Two and a half lines were deleted here.

4. *an article on Riehl's books.* 'The Natural History of German Life', which was published in the *Westminster* in July 1856.

5. *the Curate Mr Tugwell.* George Tugwell (1830–1910), curate of Ilfracombe from 1853 to 1869. Lewes reviewed his *Manual of the Sea Anemones of the English Coast* (1856) in the *Leader* of 25 October 1856.

6. *Lloyd.* W. Alford Lloyd was a naturalists' supplier.

7. *Landsborough's book.* David Landsborough the Elder (1779–1854), author of *A Popular History of British Seaweeds* (1849).

8. *Corporal Nym's philosophy.* In *Henry V*, Act II, Scene 1, line 19.

9. *Gosse's Rambles on the Devonshire Coast* (see note 2 above).

10. *Trench's Calderon.* Richard Chenevix Trench (1807–86), Irish poet, theologian

and philologist. His translation of Pedro Calderón de la Barca's *Life's a Dream: The Great Theatre of the World* was published in 1856.

11. *the ratification of the Peace.* The Peace with Russia was declared at the end of April 1856.

12. *Rosinantes.* After Don Quixote's horse.

13. *'the race is not to the swift'.* Ecclesiastes 9:11.

14. *a 'Hunt' picture.* William Holman Hunt (1827–1910), Pre-Raphaelite painter.

Notes on Form in Art

1. *Harvey and Bichat.* William Harvey (1578–1657), English physician, the first to demonstrate the function of the heart and the circulation of the blood. Marie François Xavier Bichat (1771–1802), French anatomist. Auguste Comte saw Bichat as the pioneer of positive biology, with his theory that 'referred the properties of organs to the general laws of component tissues' (J. S. Mill, *Auguste Comte and Positivism* [n.d.], p. 51). Bichat was Lydgate's ideal in *Middlemarch*.

2. ἀναγνώρισις (*anagnorisis*) and περιπέτεια (*peripeteia*). Eliot misspelt this in the MS, *peripateia*. 'Recognition' and 'irony of events' or 'dramatic irony', terms from Aristotle's *Poetics*, Chapter 11, lines 2 and 4. 'The best form of Recognition is coincident with a Reversal of Intention, as in the *Oedipus* ... This recognition [of persons] combined with Reversal [*peripeteia*] will produce either pity or fear; and actions producing these effects are those which, by our definition, Tragedy represents' (Butcher's translation).

THE GEORGE ELIOT–FREDERIC HARRISON
CORRESPONDENCE

1. *Lord Cranbourne.* Sir Robert Arthur Talbot Gascoyne Cecil (1830–1903) became Viscount Cranborne in 1865.

2. *Bekker's Charicles. Charikles, oder Bilder altgriechischer Sitte* (1840) by Wilhelm Adolf Becker (1796–1846).

3. *At present I am going to take up again a work which I laid down before writing Felix.* Eliot was referring to *The Spanish Gypsy*.

4. *International Essays.* Harrison had edited and contributed to *International Policy* (1866).

5. *fifty pages of a bluebook, and finally left the printer only yesterday.* Harrison was a member of the Royal Commission on Trades Unions. The 'blue book' referred to was an appendix to a minority report on legislation.

6. ἦθος. Ethos.

7. *'The Positivist Problem'.* Harrison's article in the *Fortnightly Review* (1 November 1869, pp. 469–93) was both explanatory and defensive in tone. At the end of the article (p. 491) Harrison twice alluded to his schism with Congreve concerning Positivism's religious pretensions. He then went on to urge its claims as a social and political panacea.

Brothers in Opinion; Edgar Quinet and Jules Michelet
(*Coventry Herald and Observer*, 30 October 1846, p. 2)

This is the earliest review definitely attributed to Eliot, although Haight (*Life*, p. 61) referred to 'a number of anonymous articles for the *Herald*'. The *Coventry Herald* had been purchased by her friend Charles Bray in June of 1846 to counter the conservative influence of its rival, the *Coventry Standard*. Her translation of *Das Leben Jesu* had been published on 15 June in the same year.

Edgar Quinet (1803–75), French historian and political philosopher and apostate from Protestantism. He was appointed Professor of Literature at the Collège de France in Paris in 1842 but was hounded from his Chair after four years because of his antagonism to Catholic authoritarianism in general, and to the Jesuits in particular, and for his vocal support of republicanism. *Christianity in Its Various Aspects, from the Birth of Christ to the French Revolution* is the translation of his 1846 work under review.

Jules Michelet (1798–1874), historian, was, like Quinet, a republican who incurred the disapproval of the Catholic Church. *Priests, Women and Families*, the translation of his 1816 work reviewed here, was placed on the *Index* of prohibited books shortly after its publication.

1. *Loyola.* Saint Ignatius Loyola (1491–1556), founder of the Society of Jesus, the Jesuits.
2. *ut cadaver . . . senis baculus.* 'As a dead body' and 'old man's staff'.
3. From Michelet's *Priests, Women and Families*, pp. 190–91.

J. A. Froude's *The Nemesis of Faith*
(*Coventry Herald and Observer*, 16 March 1849, p. 2)

James Anthony Froude (1818–94), historian and man of letters, and younger brother of the Tractarian R. H. Froude, was a student of Oriel College, Oxford, during the late 1830s, where he fell briefly under John Henry Newman's influence, contributing a biography to his series 'Lives of the English Saints'. But Froude subsequently underwent a religious change of heart, and the furore surrounding the publication of the partly autobiographical *The Nemesis of Faith* in 1849 (the book was publicly burned in Oxford) prompted his resignation from his Fellowship of Exeter College.

Eliot was so enthusiastic about the book, a copy of which had been sent to her by John Chapman, that she sent Froude a note of thanks, signing herself 'The Translator of Strauss'. Froude replied via Chapman, and subsequently Caroline Bray wrote to Sarah Hennell in March of 1849, reporting Eliot's excitement at his reply, and adding that, 'He says he recognized her hand in the review in the *Coventry Herald*, and if she thinks him a fallen star, she might help him to rise, "but he believes he has only been dipped in the Styx, and is not so much the worse for the bathing". Poor girl! I am so pleased she should have this little episode in her dull life, but I suppose she won't continue the correspondence' (*Letters, Vol. I*, p. 279n). For subsequent events, see Haight's *Life* (pp. 68–9).

1. *bright particular star. All's Well that Ends Well*, Act I, Scene 1, line 97.
2. *'son of the morning'*. Isaiah 14:12, 'How art thou fallen from heaven, O day star, son of the morning.'
3. From *The Nemesis of Faith* (with slight inaccuracies), pp. 6–34 *passim*.
4. ibid., p. 43.

R. W. Mackay's *The Progress of the Intellect*
(*Westminster Review*, January 1851, pp. 353–68)

Robert William Mackay (1803–82) trained as a lawyer before turning his attention to the study of philosophy and theology. *The Progress of the Intellect, as Exemplified in the Religious Development of Greeks and Hebrews* was his first book. Frances Power Cobbe claimed (*Life of Frances Power Cobbe*, 1894) that Mackay was the model for the character of Casaubon in *Middlemarch*. He is not the only possible model, but there is certainly a touch of the Casaubon in Mackay's work.

The Progress of the Intellect was published by John Chapman in 1850 and presented to Eliot for review in October of that year. This was to be her first contribution to the *Westminster*, the journal of which she became editor in the following year.

1. *Auguste Comte*. Auguste Comte (1798–1857), French social theorist and founder of Positivism. According to Pinney (*Essays*, p. 28n) this is Eliot's first recorded allusion to Comte's influential work.
2. *'awful eye'*. Milton, *On the Morning of Christ's Nativity*, 'The Hymn', line 59.
3. *idola theatri*. From Francis Bacon's *The Advancement of Learning* (1605). The 'Idols of the Theatre' are habits of mind to do with received systems of thought.
4. *Cudworth*. Ralph Cudworth (1617–68), Anglican divine and leading member of the Cambridge Platonists. His book *The True Intellectual System of the Universe* (1678) had been republished in 1845.
5. *theory of practice and duty*. Mackay reads 'theory and practice of duty'.
6. *sensibility*. Mackay reads 'insensibility'.
7. *natural*. Mackay reads 'notional'.
8. *ascensio mentis in Deum per scalas creatarum rerum*. This translates as 'the ascent of the mind towards God on the ladder of created things'.
9. *external*. Mackay reads 'substantial'.
10. *opposite extreme of incredulity*. Mackay reads 'opposite irrational extremes'.
11. *Elder Scripture . . . uncorrupt by man*. We have been unable to identify this quotation.
12. *Bryant*. Jacob Bryant (1715–1804). Among his works is *A New System; or an Analysis of Ancient Mythology* (1774–6).
13. *O. Müller*. Karl Otfried Müller (1797–1840), author of the *Prolegomena zu einer Wissenschaftlichen Mythologie* (1825).
14. *Creuzer*. Friedrich Creuzer (1771–1858), historian of religion and author of *Symbolik und Mythologie der alten Völker, besonders bei den Griechen* (1810–12). Another possible model for Casaubon.
15. *High instincts . . . guilty thing surprised*. William Wordsworth, 'Ode: Intimations of Immortality from Recollections of Early Childhood', lines 150–51.

16. *rerum natura.* In the natural order.

17. *Philo . . . Origen.* Philo (*c.* 20 BC–AD 40), philosopher. Origen (*c.* 185–*c.* 235), theologian.

18. *the cunning trickery of Jacob.* Genesis 27:18ff.

19. *the savage cruelties of Joshua.* Joshua 8:1–29.

20. *God plagued Pharaoh and Abimelech.* Genesis 12:10–20 and Genesis 20 respectively.

21. '*eat of the prey . . . of the slain'.* Numbers 23:24.

22. παρρησία. Plain-speaking.

23. *To rise in science . . . of the skies.* We have been unable to identify this quotation.

W. R. Greg's *The Creed of Christendom*
(*Leader*, 20 September 1851, pp. 897–9)

William Rathbone Greg (1809–81), essayist, made a living contributing articles on political and economic subjects to various quarterlies. Eliot wrote to John Chapman in February 1851, offering to review Greg's *The Creed of Christendom: Its Foundation and Superstructure*, which he had just published, 'not for money, but for love – of the subject as connected with the *Inquiry* [Charles Christian Hennell's *Inquiry Concerning the Origins of Christianity* (1838)]'. However, the editor of the *Westminster Review* did not want to take the review, claiming that there would not be room for it, and that the subject was not suitable. When Chapman bought the *Westminster* later that year, it was on condition that William Hickson, the outgoing editor, publish Eliot's review, but it was James Martineau's notice that appeared instead (*Westminster Review*, vol. 55, July 1851). This review thus became her first contribution to the *Leader*, a weekly paper founded by Lewes and Thornton Leigh Hunt in 1850 in offices just around the corner from Chapman.

In his Preface, Greg wrote, 'The three conclusions which I have chiefly endeavoured to make clear, are these: – that the tenet of the Inspiration of the Scriptures is baseless and untenable under any form or modifications which leaves to it a dogmatic value; – that the Gospels are not textually faithful records of the sayings and actions of Jesus, but ascribe to him words which he never uttered, and deeds which he never did; – and that the Apostles only partially comprehended, and imperfectly transmitted, the teaching of their great master' (pp. viii–ix).

Eliot wrote to Sarah Hennell in October 1851 that 'Mr Greg thought the Review "well done and in a kindly spirit", – but thought there was not much in it – dreadful true, since there was only all his book. I think he did not like the apology for his want of theological learning – which, however, was just the thing most needed, for the *Eclectic* [vol. 94, 1851, p. 410] trips him up on that score' (*Letters, Vol. I*, p. 369).

1. *Mr Newman's Phases of Faith.* Francis Newman (1805–97) (brother of John Henry Newman) had published his autobiographical *Phases of Faith; or, Passages from the History of My Creed* the previous year.

2. *principles.* Greg reads 'principles of investigation'.

3. *Strauss, Hug, Schleiermacher, and Hennell.* David Friedrich Strauss (1808–74),

German theologian and New Testament critic. Eliot's translation of his *Life of Jesus* had been published in 1846. Johann Leonhard Hug (1765–1846), Catholic biblical scholar who held firmly to the historicity of the New Testament. His *Introduction to the New Testament* was translated into English in 1827. Friedrich Daniel Schleiermacher (1768–1834), German Protestant theologian with a Romantic hostility to the rational and deistic Christianity of the eighteenth century. Charles Christian Hennell (1809–50) undertook a study of the New Testament in order to confirm his own Christian beliefs and found that the process undermined them instead. His *Inquiry Concerning the Origin of Christianity* was instrumental in shaking the foundations of Eliot's Christian belief (see *Life*, p. 39ff) and was translated into German at the instigation of Strauss.

4. *in limine, in the language of Algernon Sydney, 'No consequence ... a truth'. In limine* means 'on the threshold'. Algernon Sidney (1622–83) was the author of *Discourses Concerning Government* (1698).

5. *Locke.* John Locke (1632–1704), philosopher. Author of the *Essay Concerning Human Understanding* (1619) and the *Reasonableness of Christianity* (1695).

6. *Beyond the verge ... secrets lie.* We have been unable to identify this quotation.

7. *'the possibility of the rare made real'.* Matthew Parker (1504–75), Archbishop of Canterbury. 'Race' is misprinted as 'rare' in the *Leader*.

8. This mention of Hennell allows Eliot to pay tribute to the book that had helped precipitate her break with Christianity. Greg wrote to Eliot about her criticism of his unacknowledged indebtedness to Hennell. She, in turn, wrote to Caroline Bray (*Letters, Vol. I*, p. 363) to 'tell Sara especially that Greg wishes the writer of the notice in the *Leader* to know that he did not intend to omit Hennell for whose work he has a high esteem'.

9. *a periodical which has recently bestowed elaborate praise on The Creed of Christendom.* A reference to James Martineau's review in the *Westminster* of July 1851 (vol. 55, pp. 429–53).

10. *'La terre tourne ... tournez avec elle'.* From Blaise Pascal (1623–62), mathematician and philosopher.

Thomas Carlyle's *Life of John Sterling*
(*Westminster Review*, January 1852, pp. 247–51)

Thomas Carlyle (1795–1881), Scottish historian and social critic.

John Sterling (1806–44), Scottish poet, novelist and essayist. His memory survives mainly through Carlyle's *Life*, in which Carlyle wrote, 'a more perfectly transparent soul I have never seen'. In October 1851 Eliot wrote to the Brays that 'I have been reading Carlyle's *Life of Sterling* with great pleasure – not for its presentation of Sterling but of Carlyle. There are racy bits of description in his best manner and exquisite touches of feeling' (*Letters, Vol. I*, p. 370).

This review appeared in the first number of the *Westminster* to be edited by Eliot.

1. *The melodies abide/ Of the everlasting chime.* From John Keble, *The Christian Year* (1827), 'Saint Matthew', lines 27–8.
2. *curiosa felicitas.* 'Careful facility' or 'beauty of phrase'.
3. *'ana'.* A collection of table-talk, gossip or anecdotes.
4. *a Teufelsdröckh still, but humanized by a Blumine worthy of him.* A reference to the subject of Carlyle's *Sartor Resartus* and his Beatrice.
5. *fata morganas.* Mirages or illusions.
6. *Archdeacon Hare.* A reference to Julius Hare's earlier biographical essay on Sterling (1848), which treated him principally as a cleric and passed over more controversial issues, including the correspondence between Sterling and Hare on the subject of David Friedrich Strauss.
7. *that friend of Arnold's.* John Keble. The Arnold in question is Thomas, father of Matthew. The incident is recounted in Dean Stanley's *Life of Arnold, Vol. I* (1844), pp. 21–2.

Lord Brougham's Literature
(*Leader,* 7 July 1855, pp. 652–3)

Lord Henry Peter Brougham (1778–1868), Scottish statesman, lawyer and historian. He became a Member of Parliament in 1810 and achieved fame in 1825 as defender of Queen Caroline when she was accused of adultery by George IV. He later became one of the founders of London University. His *Lives of Men of Letters and Science Who Flourished in the Time of George III* was published in six volumes in 1845. For Eliot's defence of this review, see the Introduction to this edition.

1. *Hoby.* An expensive shoe shop in Saint James's Street, London.
2. *Crispin.* Patron saint of shoemakers.
3. *To blunt a moral and to spoil a tale.* From Samuel Johnson's *The Vanity of Human Wishes* (1749). The quotation is actually 'To point a moral, or adorn a tale'.
4. *Sydney Smith's verdict on Scotch 'wut'.* 'Their only idea of wit, or rather that inferior variety of this electric talent which prevails occasionally in the North, and which, under the name of WUT, is so infinitely distressing to people of good taste, is laughing immoderately at stated intervals' (in *A Memoir of the Rev. Sydney Smith, Vol. I,* by Elizabeth Vassall Fox, Lady Holland, 1855, p. 25).
5. *Dr Cumming, or planned by Robert Owen.* For Eliot's opinion of Dr Cumming, see her essay in this volume. Robert Owen (1771–1858) was a socialist thinker of whom she also had a low opinion. In 1843 she wrote to Sarah Hennell, 'I saw Robert Owen yesterday . . . and I think if his system prosper it will be in *spite* of its founder, and not because of his advocacy' (*Letters, Vol. I,* p. 161).
6. *Christo et Musis . . . Edinenses.* This translates as 'The Citizens of Edinburgh have dedicated this temple to Christ and the Muses'.

The Morality of *Wilhelm Meister*
(*Leader*, 21 July 1855, p. 703)

Eliot had spent the late summer and autumn of 1854 with Lewes in Weimar, where he had been collecting material for the biography of Goethe that she was later to review in the *Leader*.

Rosemary Ashton remarked of this article that it was 'an important one, both as being unmistakably by the tolerant observer who later provided the guiding consciousness in the novels, and as indicating how public attitudes to Goethe had and had not changed over thirty or forty years . . . [It showed] how George Eliot, in criticizing *Wilhelm Meister*, which still needed explaining to English readers, found expression for those basic beliefs about realism, observation, imagination, and sympathy which informed her writings from then till her death' (*The German Idea*, 1980, pp. 169–71).

The translation of *Wilhelm Meister's Apprenticeship* reviewed here is by R. Dillon Boylan.

1. *passionless Mejnour*. A character in Edward Bulwer-Lytton's *Zanoni* (1842). At one point he says, 'If happiness exists it must be centred in a SELF to which all passion is unknown.'
2. '*insupportables justes, qui du haut de leurs chaises d'or narguent les misères et les souffrances de l'humanité*'. This translates as 'the intolerable just ones, who from the height of their golden seats, look dismissively down on the miseries and sufferings of mankind'. We have not found the source for this quotation.
3. '*publicans and sinners*'. Mark 2:16.

Charles Kingsley's *Westward Ho!*
(*Westminster Review*, July 1855, pp. 288–94)

Charles Kingsley (1819–75), novelist, poet, Anglican clergyman, later Professor of Modern History at Cambridge. Kingsley used his writing as a didactic vehicle for the religious views of his friend F. D. Maurice, and for the social gospel of Thomas Carlyle. His *Westward Ho! or The Voyages and Adventures of Sir Amyas Leigh, Knight . . .* appeared in 1855.

Eliot reviewed *Westward Ho!* twice, the first time in the *Leader* in May of 1855. The *Westminster* review is rather more hostile than that in the *Leader*, in which she wrote, 'When we say that the "art of the book suffers" we mean that the preacher overcomes the painter often, which, though creditable to the writer's earnestness and honesty, injures his work as a mere work of art. It is as if a painter in colour were to write, "Oh you villain!" under his Jesuits or murderers; or to have a strip flowing from the hero's mouth, with "imitate me, my man!" on it. No doubt the villain is to be hated, and the hero loved, but we ought to see that sufficiently in the figures of them. We don't want a man with a wand, going about the gallery and haranguing us. Art is art, and tells its own story' (*Leader*, 19 May 1855, pp. 474–5).

Two years later Kingsley wrote to Maurice after a book of his had been savaged in the *Westminster*, advising him, 'I do hope you will not bother your soul about what the *Westminster* says. The woman who used to insult you therein – and who I suppose does so now – is none other than Miss Evans, the infidel esprit fort, who is now G. H. Lewes's concubine – I met him yesterday, and lucky for me that I had not had your letter when I did so; or I certainly should have given him (he probably being the co-sinner for he pretends to know all about the philosophers, and don't) a queer piece of my mind to carry home to his lady. Let them be' (see R. B. Martin, *The Dust of Combat*, London, 1959, p. 181). In fact, the review in question was written by H. B. Wilson.

1. *O, Mary! . . . the sands of Dee*. Misquoted from Walter Scott's 'The Sands of Dee'. The lines should read, 'O Mary, go and call the cattle home,/ And call the cattle home,/ And call the cattle home,/ Across the sands of Dee.'

2. *'carpet consideration'*. In *Twelfth Night*, Act III, Scene 4, line 258, Sir Toby Belch describes Sir Andrew Aguecheek as a 'knight, dubbed with unhatched rapier, and on carpet consideration', i.e., knighted at court and not on the battlefield.

3. *Kiss's Amazon*. August Kiss (1802–65), German sculptor, exhibited his 'Mounted Amazon Attacked by a Tiger' at the Great Exhibition of 1851.

4. *Boanerges*. A name given to James and John, the sons of Zebedee, because they threatened to call down 'fire from Heaven' to consume the Samaritans for not receiving Jesus Christ. It translates as 'sons of thunder' or better as 'sons of tumult' (Luke 9:54 and Mark 3:17).

5. *the denunciations of the Teufelsdröckh*. In Carlyle's *Sartor Resartus* (1838).

6. *a vehement disclaimer of all heterodoxy*. A reference to Kingsley's letter to the *Guardian* in 1851 in which he defended himself against an attack on the morality of his novel *Yeast*. He wrote, 'whosoever henceforth, either explicitly or by insinuation, says that I do not hold and believe *ex animo*, and in the simple and literal sense, all the doctrines of the Catholic and Apostolic Church of England, as embodied in her Liturgy or Articles, shall have no answer from me but Father Valerian's *Mentiris impudentissime* [a reference to a Capuchin in the fifteenth of Pascal's *Provincial Letters*]'.

7. *'will hear, or whether they will forbear'*. Ezekiel 2:5, 2:7 and 3:11.

8. *Drake, Hawkins, Frobisher, and the rest*. Sir Francis Drake (*c.* 1540–96), circumnavigated the world 1577–80. Sir John Hawkins (1532–95), naval commander and slave-trader. Sir Martin Frobisher (*c.* 1535–94), explorer of Canada's north-east coast.

9. *Humboldt*. Alexander von Humboldt (1769–1859), German scientist and explorer.

Geraldine Jewsbury's *Constance Herbert*
(*Westminster Review*, July 1855, pp. 294–6)

This review was written only a few weeks after Eliot had come to London to live with Lewes, having established that there was no possibility of a reconciliation between him and his wife. Haight suggested (*Life*, p. 182) that Eliot's personal interest in Jewsbury's theme led her to give the novel more space than it merited.

Geraldine Jewsbury (1812–80), novelist and reviewer, with a lifelong interest in 'the woman question'. She reviewed *Adam Bede* for the *Athenæum* in 1859, describing it as 'a work of true genius . . . a novel of the highest class'.

1. *Miss Grace Lee*. Eponymous heroine of a novel by Julia Kavanagh (1855).
2. *a melancholy Viola*. In *Twelfth Night*.

Saint-Marc Girardin's *Love in the Drama*
(*Leader*, 25 August 1855, pp. 820–21)

Saint-Marc Girardin (1801–73), French writer and sometime Professor of French Poetry at the Sorbonne. His principal work, the first three volumes of which are reviewed here, was the *Cours de littérature dramatique, ou l'usage des passions dans le drame* (fifteen volumes, 1843–68).

1. '*Who drives fat oxen must himself be fat*'. Attributed to Samuel Johnson in James Boswell's *Life of Johnson*, entry for June 1784.
2. *Amadis*. The *Amadis de Gaule*, a massive (24-volume) chivalric romance of mixed Portuguese and Spanish ancestry, translated into French prose between 1540 and 1615.
3. *Astrée*. A prose romance by Honoré d'Urfé (1567–1625), published between 1610 and 1627. Its prose form and thinly disguised portraits of real people make it a putative 'realist' text.
4. *Clélia*. *Clélie*, a romantic *roman-à-clef* in ten volumes by Madeleine de Scudéry (1607–1701), French novelist, published between 1654 and 1660.
5. *la galanterie honnête*. Honourable gallantry.
6. *Madame Deshoulières*. Antoinette Deshoulières (1638–94), French lyric poet.
7. *Nul n'est content/de son esprit*. 'No man is satisfied with his fortune or discontented with his wit.'
8. *Luigi da Porto*. Italian novelist (1485–1529). His story of *Giulietta e Romeo* is one of the source texts for Shakespeare's *Romeo and Juliet*.
9. *gynaeceum*. A building set aside for women, or the women's quarters in a household.
10. '*world of sighs*'. *Othello*, Act I, Scene 3, line 159.
11. '*overthrown more than his enemies*'. *As You Like It*, Act I, Scene 2, line 266.
12. *One half of me is yours . . . And so all yours! The Merchant of Venice*, Act III, Scene 2.

13. *the Edith Bellendens, Alice Bridgworths, and Miss Wardours.* Characters from, respectively, *Old Mortality, Peveril of the Peak* and *The Antiquary.*

14. *mare magnum.* Great sea.

Ashford Owen's *A Lost Love* and C. W. S. Brooks's *Aspen Court*
(*Westminster Review,* October 1855, pp. 610–11 and pp. 611–12)

Ashford Owen was the pseudonym of Anna C. Ogle (1832–1918), novelist.

(Charles William) Shirley Brooks (1816–74), editor of *Punch* (from 1870), playwright and novelist. As Eliot pointed out, *Aspen Court: A Story of Our Own Time* had originally been published in parts in *Bentley's Miscellany,* a monthly magazine that ran from 1837 to 1868.

Margaret Fuller and Mary Wollstonecraft
(*Leader,* 13 October 1855, pp. 988–9)

Margaret Fuller Ossoli (1810–50), feminist author and critic, Transcendentalist and revolutionary. The extracts from her *Women in the Nineteenth Century, and Kindred Papers Relating to the Sphere, Condition and Duties of Woman* in this review have a close bearing on the character of Rosamond Vincy in *Middlemarch.* It is also probable that Margaret Fuller was a model for Dorothea Brooke (see 'Margaret Fuller and Dorothea Brooke' by Patricia Derry in *Review of English Studies,* vol. 36, 1985, pp. 379–85).

Eliot had reviewed the *Memoirs of Margaret Fuller Ossoli* in the *Westminster* in April 1852. There she wrote, 'In conversation she was as copious and oracular as Coleridge, brilliant as Sterling, pungent and paradoxical as Carlyle; gifted with the inspired powers of a Pythoness, she saw into the hearts and over the heads of all who came near her; and, but for a sympathy as boundless as her self-esteem, she would have despised the whole human race! Her frailty, in this respect, was no secret either to herself or her friends. She quizzed them and boasted of herself to such an excess as to turn disgust into laughter – yea, so right royally did she carry herself that her arrogance became a virtue, worshipful as the majesty of the gods' (*Westminster,* April 1852, p. 665).

1. *Parasitic forms . . . distinctive womanhood.* From Alfred, Lord Tennyson, *The Princess* (1847), 7, lines 253–8.

2. *Rights of Woman.* Mary Wollstonecraft (1759–97), English radical and feminist, published her *Vindication of the Rights of Woman* in 1792.

3. *Mrs Malaprop.* In Richard Sheridan's *The Rivals* (1775), hence 'malapropism'.

4. *Fourier.* Charles Fourier (1772–1837), French social theorist, whose ideal of co-operative communities was actually implemented in neo-Utopian agricultural communities in France and America. He was regarded as insane by some.

5. *If she be small . . . shall men grow?* Tennyson, *The Princess,* 7, lines 249–50.

Translations and Translators
(*Leader*, 20 October 1855, pp. 1014–15)

Here Eliot is reviewing Immanuel Kant's *Kritik der reinen Vernunft*, translated by J. M. D. Meiklejohn, and *Specimens of the Choicest Lyrical Productions of the Most Celebrated German Poets*, translated into English verse by Mary Anne Burt.

1. *Charles Honeyman.* Foolish incumbent of Lady Whittlesea's Chapel, Mayfair, in William Makepeace Thackeray's *The Newcomes* (1853–5).
2. *Can teach all people . . . no part of speech.* From *Hudibras*, Part 1, Canto 1, lines 660–62 by Samuel Butler (1612–80).
3. *Für andre wächst . . . zeigen soll?* An alternative translation is, 'For others shall your glorious light shine brightly/I neither can nor will my talent hide/I should not for your revelations long/If they were not to all men to belong' (from *Goethe's Poems*, trs. Dyrsen, 1878).
4. *Freiligrath.* Ferdinand Freiligrath (1810–76), German lyric poet and translator of, among other things, *Hiawatha*.
5. *the famous speech of Lorenzo to Jessica. The Merchant of Venice*, Act V, Scene 1. Eliot's concern about August Wilhelm von Schlegel's choice of the word *Tasten* may be partly misplaced, as the 'touches' of the original relates to the playing or fingering of a musical instrument.

Thomas Carlyle
(*Leader*, 27 October 1855, pp. 1034–5)

Thomas Carlyle (1795–1881), Scottish historian and social critic. Eliot is reviewing *Passages Selected from the Writings of Thomas Carlyle* by Thomas Ballantyne.

1. *the reading of Sartor Resartus was an epic in the history of their minds.* Eliot had first read Carlyle in 1841. At the time she wrote to Martha Jackson, 'Have you, dear Patty, read any of Thomas Carlyle's books? He is a grand favourite of mine, and I venture to recommend to you his *Sartor Resartus* . . . His soul is a shrine of the brightest and purest philanthropy, kindled by the live coal of gratitude and devotion to the Author of all things. I should observe that he is not "orthodox"' (*Letters, Vol. I*, pp. 122–3).
2. *a Joshua who is to smite the wicked . . . going down of the sun.* See Joshua, *passim*.
3. *On the whole . . . question of questions.* From *On Heroes, Hero-Worship and the Heroic in History* (1841).
4. *What we call 'Formulas' . . . habitation in this world.* Also from *Lectures on Heroes*.
5. *Perhaps few narratives . . . numerous in our day.* From *Past and Present* (1843).

Robert Browning's *Men and Women*
(*Westminster Review*, January 1856, pp. 290–96)

Robert Browning (1812–89). Eleven years after writing this review, Eliot wrote to Frederic Harrison, 'My conscience made me a little unhappy after I had been speaking of Browning on Sunday. I ought to have spoken more of the veneration I feel for him, and to have said that in his best poems – and by these I mean a large number – I do not find him unintelligible, but only peculiar and original' (*Letters, Vol. IV*, pp. 395–6).

1. *Heinsius*. Daniel Heinsius (1586–1655), Dutch classical scholar and editor of Aristotle's *Poetics*.
2. *M. Arago*. A particularly obscure reference. There are several possible candidates. The two most likely are Étienne Arago (1802–92) and Jacques-Étienne-Victor Arago (1790–1855), but we have been unable to locate any reference to Daniel Heinsius by either of them.
3. *Flotow*. Friedrich Flotow (1812–83), German composer.
4. *He stood and watched . . . expect as much*. 'How It Strikes a Contemporary' (1855), lines 23–35 (Eliot's italics).
5. *Dogberrys*. An ignorant and inconsequential official (from the foolish constable in Shakespeare's *Much Ado about Nothing*).
6. *My perfect wife, my Leonor . . . Whatever rocks obstruct*. From 'By the Fireside', 21.

Peter von Bohlen's *Introduction to the Book of Genesis*
(*Leader*, 12 January 1856, pp. 41–2)

Peter von Bohlen (1796–1840), sometime Professor of Oriental Languages and Literature at Königsberg. His *Die Genesis historisch-kritisch erläutert* (1835) was translated into English in 1855 and edited by James Heywood.

1. *Dr Pye Smith*. Nonconformist divine and tutor at Homerton College, Cambridge. Eliot had read his *Relation between the Holy Scripture and Some Points of Geological Science* (1839) in 1841. At the time she wrote to Martha Jackson, 'there is very much that is valuable in it, and the main subject of the work, the interpretation of the Mosaic records, is fully satisfactory to me'.
2. *Menu*. Author of the Laws in Hindu mythology.
3. *the Hymn of Cleanthes*. Cleanthes (*c*. 331–*c*. 232 BC), Stoic philosopher. His 'Hymn to Zeus' is one of his few surviving works.
4. *Eleusinian mysteries*. Religious rites of ancient Greece, focusing on the goddess Demeter.
5. *Vedas or the Zendavesta, or the fragments of Manetho and Sanchoniathon*. The Vedas are the sacred scriptures of the Hindus. The Zend-Avesta is the sacred book of the Parsees, the collected writings of Zoroaster or Zarathustra. Manetho was an

ancient historian of Egypt (*c.* third century BC). Sanchoniathon was an ancient historian of Phoenicia.

6. *Professor Tuck's Commentary on Genesis.* Johann Christian Friedrich Tuch (1806–67), author of the *Kommentar Über die Genesis* (1838).

7. *Pococke.* Edward Pococke (1604–91), traveller and orientalist.

The *Antigone* and Its Moral
(*Leader*, 29 March 1856, p. 306)

Eliot is reviewing the Oxford Pocket Classics edition of *The Antigone of Sophocles.*

1. *the production of the Antigone at Drury Lane.* Pinney noted that this occurred on 1 May 1850. Eliot was not in London at the time.

2. *Hermanns and Böckhs.* Johann Gottfried Jacob Hermann (1772–1848), classical scholar and philologist. August Böckh (1785–1867), archaeologist and philologist.

3. *E'en in their ashes live their wonted fires.* Slightly misquoted from Thomas Gray's 'Elegy Written in a Country Church-Yard' (1750).

4. Οὐ γάρ τι νῦν γε καχθές ... ἐξοτου φάνη. From Sophocles' *Antigone*, lines 456–7. The lines translate as 'not now, nor yesterday's, they always live, and no one knows their origin in time' (from the translation of Elizabeth Wyckoff in David Grene and Richmond Lattimore's *The Complete Greek Tragedies*, Chicago, 1954).

5. μεγάλοι λόγοι. Lofty words.

John Ruskin's *Modern Painters, Vol. III*
(*Westminster Review*, April 1856, pp. 625–33)

Eliot was a great admirer of John Ruskin (1819–1900). In February of 1856 she wrote to Sarah Hennell, 'We are delighting ourselves with Ruskin's third volume, which contains some of the finest writing I have read for a long time (among recent books)' (*Letters, Vol. II*, p. 228). In June of the same year she wrote to Barbara Leigh Smith, 'What books his two last are! I think he is the finest writer living.' This review is a crucial statement of her views on realism.

In July 1856 she reviewed *Modern Painters, Vol. IV* in the *Westminster* (pp. 274–8). She wrote, 'It has all the transcendent merits and all the defects of its predecessor; it contains an abundance of eloquent wisdom and some eloquent absurdity; it shows a profound love and admiration for the noble and the beautiful, with a somewhat excessive contempt or hatred for what the writer holds to be the reverse of noble and beautiful.' She then goes on to quote extensively from Ruskin's passages on mountain scenery (*Modern Painters, Vol. IV* in the *Works of John Ruskin*, E. T. Cook and Alexander Wedderburn, eds., 1903–9, p. 441) on the influence of the Warwickshire topography on Shakespeare's genius: 'He seems to have been sent essentially to take universal and equal grasp of the *human* nature; and to have been removed, therefore, from all influences which could in the least warp or bias his thoughts. It was necessary that he should lean *no* way; that he should contemplate, with absolute equality of judgement, the life of the court, cloister, and tavern, and be able to sympathize so completely with all creatures as to deprive himself, together with his personal identity, even of his conscience, as he casts himself into their hearts'.

1. *De Quincy.* Thomas De Quincey (1785–1859), English essayist, critic and opium addict.

2. *'the great and general ideas only inherent in universal nature'.* From Chapter 1 of *Modern Painters, Vol. III.* The line reads 'the great and general ideas fixed and inherent in universal nature'.

3. *'For the artist . . . persons represented.'* Chapter 3, Section 9.

4. *This is usually done . . . mist of pride.* Chapter 3, Section 11.

5. *The corruption of the schools . . . fades into fatuity.* Chapter 3, Sections 13–15.

6. *that all great art . . . arrow plume.* Chapter 3, Section 20 (Eliot's italics).

7. *And now, finally . . . greatest ideas.* Chapter 3, Section 24.

8. *Take a very important instance . . . Greek philosophers.* Chapter 4, Section 16.

9. *They rowed her in . . . crawling foam.* Chapter 12, Section 5. The lines from Charles Kingsley are from *Alton Locke* (1850).

10. *As far as I recollect . . . fountains in pipes.* Chapter 13, Section 16.

11. *To invent a story . . . self-examining verse.* Chapter 16, Section 29.

Harriet Beecher Stowe's *Dred*, Charles Reade's *It is Never Too Late to Mend* and Frederika Bremer's *Hertha*
(*Westminster Review*, October 1856, pp. 570–73, pp. 573–5 and pp. 575–8)

Harriet Beecher Stowe (1811–96), American writer and philanthropist. *Dred: A Tale of the Great Dismal Swamp* was published in 1856. Eliot greatly admired Stowe, and they corresponded in the 1860s.

Charles Reade (1814–84), novelist and dramatist. *It is Never Too Late to Mend: A Matter of Fact Romance* was published in 1856.

Frederika Bremer (1801–65), Swedish novelist. The English translation of *Hertha* appeared in 1856. Eliot had met Bremer when she visited England in 1851. At the time she wrote to Charles Bray, 'I don't advise you to come to see Frederika Bremer – she is old – extremely ugly, and deformed – I should think she is nearly sixty. Her eyes are sore – her teeth horrid' (*Letters, Vol. I*, p. 365). But three days later she wrote to Sarah Hennell, 'Altogether I am beginning to repent of my repugnance' (*Letters, Vol. I*, p. 367).

1. *Fadladeens.* Fadladeen is a character in Thomas Moore's *Lallah Rookh* (1817), an infallible judge of everything.

2. *Uncle Tom.* Stowe's *Uncle Tom's Cabin* (1852).

3. *Augustin Thierry*, Jacques Nicholas Augustin Thierry (1795–1856), French historian.

4. *frotté de civilisation.* On whom civilization has rubbed off.

William Lecky's *The Influence of Rationalism*
(*Fortnightly Review*, 15 May 1865, pp. 43–55)

In December 1864 Frederic Chapman (of Chapman & Hall) and Anthony Trollope came to dinner to discuss the editorship of a new periodical to be called the *Fortnightly Review*, which would 'remove all those restrictions of party and editorial "consistency" which in other journals hamper the full and free expression of opinion' (*Saturday Review*, 25 March 1865). Lewes agreed to become its editor. One revolutionary feature of the new journal was to be the abandonment of anonymity by its contributors. As Anthony Trollope later wrote, 'Much of the literary criticism which we have now is very bad indeed; so bad as to be open to the charge both of dishonesty and incapacity. Books are criticized without being read ... If the names of the critics were demanded, editors would be more careful' (*Autobiography*, Oxford, 1980, p. 192).

To the first issue Eliot contributed her (signed) review of *History of the Rise and Influence of the Spirit of Rationalism in Europe*, along with a brief notice of *The Grammar of Ornament* on pp. 124–5. On 18 May she wrote to Sarah Hennell, 'We have nothing to do with the *Fortnightly* as a money speculation. Mr Lewes has simply accepted the post of editor, and it was seemly that I should write a little in it. But do not suppose that I am going into periodical writing' (*Letters, Vol. IV*, p. 193). In fact, it was her last piece of work as a reviewer.

1. *Yet no less a person than Sir Thomas Browne.* Thomas Browne (1605–82), English physician and writer, in *Religio Medici* (1643), Part 1, Section 30.

2. *'Those that, to refute their incredulity ... to convert them.'* From Thomas Browne's *Religio Medici* (1643), Part 1, Section 30 (Eliot's italics). The original reads 'confute'.

3. *'Crescit cum magia hæresis, cum hæresi magia.'* Translates as 'Heresy increases with magic, and magic with heresy.' In Louis Ferdinand Maury (1817–92) *La Magie et l'astrologie dans l'antiquité at au moyen âge* (Paris, 1860).

4. *We do not share Mr Buckle's opinion ... terrified subjection.* In Chapter 4 of *History of Civilization in England, Vol. III* (1861) by Henry Thomas Buckle (1821–62).

5. *Jean Bodin.* Jean Bodin (1530–96), French political economist, author of *Six livres de la République* (1576).

6. *'a store of arguments ... countrymen.'* From *Introduction to the Literature of Europe in the Fifteenth, Sixteenth and Seventeenth Centuries* (1837–9), Part 2, Chapter 4, Sections 47–75, by Henry Hallam (1777–1859), barrister and (later) historian.

7. *'en une presse où les fols surpassent de tant les sages en nombre'.* From Montaigne's *Essais, Vol. III*, 11. The line translates as 'in a crowd in which fools so largely outnumber wise men'.

8. *'Ils passent par dessus les propositions ... courent aux causes.'* Montaigne's *Essais, Vol. III*, 11. Montaigne reads 'Ils examinent curieusement les conséquences'. The lines translate as 'They disregard the antecedents, but carefully examine the consequences' (Eliot's italics).